The fiery brilliance of the Zebra Hologram Heart which you see on the cover is created by "laser holography." This is the revolutionary process in which a powerful laser beam records light waves in diamond-like facets so tiny that 9,000,000 fit in a square inch. No print or photograph can match the vibrant colors and radiant glow of a hologram.

So look for the Zebra Hologram Heart whenever you buy a historical romance. It is a shimmering reflection of our guarantee that you'll find consistent quality between the covers!

MASTER OF DESIRE

One moment she was springing for his throat like a she lynx, the dagger bravely brandished aloft, and the next she was pinned beneath him on the rushes, stunned by the speed with which he had moved.

He twisted the weapon from her grip before she could use it on herself and hurled it across the bower. She screamed a string of curses and managed to wrench free of him, squirming this way and that, scrabbling to escape him, desperation in her eyes and in her heart.

"It's no use, wench," he rasped, jerking back his head to avoid her talons as she struck out blindly for his face. "Curses will not help you now—you'll never escape me!"

Sick with defeat, she closed her eyes and pleaded with her gods to make him kill her.

"'Tis my turn now, is it not?" he breathed, imprisoning her wrists against her sides in his unbreakable grip.

Her eyes flew open, wide and dilated with panic, to find him gazing down at her, a mocking smile curving his hard mouth, his smoky eyes dark with lust.

The next moment he had flung her easily over his shoulder and bore her to the bed.

"Aye, Lady Freya," he said softly, "I am master here, none other. What I wish to do with you and your lovely body, I will do!"

SEA JEWEL

PENELOPE NERI

ZEBRA BOOKS
KENSINGTON PUBLISHING CORP.

ZEBRA BOOKS

are published by

Kensington Publishing Corp.
475 Park Avenue South
New York, NY 10016

First printing: September 1986

Printed in the United States of America

Prologue

Kolina, the midwife, carried the infant away from the curtained chamber and the covered body of her dead mother to where Thorfast, Lord of Danehof, sat brooding upon his high carved chair.

Her heart was thudding with apprehension in her plump bosom as she approached him, for his foul expression boded ill. Of a sudden, she was aware that all eyes were upon her, that all conversation had abruptly ceased in the crowded long-house, the only sounds now the measured tread of her feet upon the rushes as she plodded steadily toward the central hearth with her unwelcome burden. It was as if all present were holding their breath and waiting, waiting for the storm that hung in the air to break—as well they might, Kolina thought grimly, for no doubt the fur would fly when she made her announcement! After the custom of their people, she gently laid the newborn babe upon the rush-strewn floor at her lord's feet.

"Your daughter, if it please you, sir," she murmured, touching the small talisman of blessed Frey that hung about her neck as she did so, and praying against all odds to the contrary that Thorfast would accept his child and sprinkle her with water after their pagan rites.

As if she understood, the infant squirmed in her swaddling upon the rushes, flung out both chubby fists, and began to bawl lustily, her fair pink-and-white complexion turning a furious crimson as she did so.

"Please me? Nay, it does *not* please me, old woman!"

5

Thorfast thundered, turning a bloodshot, malevolent eye upon the quaking midwife and not so much as glancing at the infant squirming on the ground at his feet. "'Twas a son I wanted, as well you know—a fine, brave lad to follow me in battle and become lord of this hall in his turn—not this puling, puny girl-brat!" he sneered. "Take it away!"

"But my lord, the child needs to be suckled," Kolina protested bravely. "If not put to the breast, she will soon die! What shall I do? Look! The poor little mite is hungry, sir!"

Thorfast's bloodshot eyes gleamed cruelly. The *jarl* took a long draught from the silver-banded drinking horn in his hand, wiped his mouth on his hairy knuckles, and glowered at her, not deigning to cast so much as a glance at his daughter before answering.

"Do? I told thee once, woman—I care not what happens to it!" he said harshly. "Throw it in the fjord! Or leave it out for the weather or the wolves to deal with like any thrall's brat, and be gone with you! You dice with death when you eye me thus!" He brought his fist down upon the trestle table before him with such a crash that the wine flagon placed there jumped, and so did the midwife.

"Aye, my lord," Kolina whispered, her lips frostily pursed, disapproval in her eyes despite her lord's threat. Hel the Hag take him! She should have known she wasted her breath in appealing to the *jarl's* kinder instincts. The evil old brute had none! Cooing to the infant, she snatched her up and carried her away toward the curtained kitchens at the rear of the hall muttering, "Spiteful old goat!" under her breath as she did so.

"Wine! Meats! Women! I must drown my sorrows in drink, and forget this dark day!" Thorfast bellowed after her, and the house thralls—easily recognized by their white kirtles—began to fly hither and thither to do his bidding, tripping over each other in terror of their master's black mood.

In minutes the hall was abuzz with the news that their lord had not only rejected his newborn daughter, but seemed not a whit grief-stricken by the death of his lady, Verdandi. Furthermore, the humming said, he had demanded a feast, to drown his bitter sorrow at the child being born female. Thorfast's men joined him about the central hearth with their

6

own drinking horns to commiserate with their lord in his disappointment, while in the kitchens the women's tongues clacked their disapproval like nervous hens, interspersed with oohs and aahs over the pretty newborn.

"Ah, your sire's a cruel one, he is. Let you die, indeed!" Kolina muttered indignantly to the infant when they had all left off admiring her to busy themselves preparing the feast. She jiggled the babe in the manner of one well accustomed to babes—*ja*, and why shouldn't she be accustomed to them? Seven of her own she'd borne and raised, not to mention countless others brought safe into the world at her hands. "Ah, and 'tis a cruel, cruel world for an unwanted girl-babe such as yourself, my lovie," she crooned sadly, looking down at the tiny, puckered face.

What a good, wee babe she was, Kolina thought, aye, and a beauty too! She'd stopped crying and was now endeavoring to nurse upon a little clenched fist thrust into her rosebud mouth. Seconds later she drifted off to sleep in Kolina's capable arms, the surprisingly dark lashes trembling against plump, rosy cheeks. Men! Why, it was a sin not to want a child as healthy and beautiful as this perfect little scrap in her arms, simply because she had been born female! Babes were too often born dead or in some way imperfect for Kolina to condone the rejection of this whole, vigorous infant. She hoped Thorfast lived to rue the day he'd cast her off, aye, that she did!

Thorfast was deep in his cups, his bearded chin buried in the fur of his jerkin, his body lolling drunkenly in his chair, when Sven the Skald strode into the hall sometime later, snowflakes clinging to his woolen mantle, his fair cheeks ruddy with cold.

All about the *jarl* his rough-and-ready company of men sang bawdy songs or roared with raucous merriment at coarse jests, and greedily slopped drink from horns overflowing with mead and ale. Between times they gorged themselves on great slabs of roasted beef or morsels of duck, gnawed on joints of savory venison and delicious smoked salmon, on salted herring and gulls' eggs, on barley bread and oatcakes and more. Others, grown lusty with strong drink, tumbled the terrified female thralls to the rushes, flung their kirtles up over their heads, and energetically mounted them then and there before all like

7

mating dogs, with no thought for privacy. Sven picked his way through the rabble to his lord's side. As he approached, Thorfast jerked awake and opened one bleary eye.

"Ah, 'tis our good Sven, is it!" the *jarl* jeered drunkenly, lurching forward with his elbows propped upon the trestle table. His golden beard was matted with food drippings and wine, his once ruggedly handsome face mottled with red veins and grossly bloated with overindulgence. "Have you come to gloat, eh?"

"Why would I wish to gloat, sir?"

Thorfast snorted. "You knew full well my Verdandi would die, did you not? You knew the child would be female?"

"Aye, sir, I did," Sven admitted.

"And yet you said nothing?" Thorfast roared, lumbering to his feet and swaying drunkenly there.

Sven flushed. "Nay, my lord. Knowing could change nothing. The threads of our destinies are woven on the looms of Fate even before the moment of our birth, are they not?"

"Bah!" Thorfast snarled. "Destiny! Be gone from my sight, before I forget myself and have your throat cut, you cursed milksop! A woman!" he roared. "By Thor's Beard, bring me a woman! The dark slut with the tumbling black hair!" He waggled a finger at Sven. "Mayhap I'll breed a fine son upon another wench this day, think you not, my friend?" He grinned wolfishly and slumped to his chair, taking up the flagon at his elbow and pouring the mead straight from it into his eager, open mouth.

"All things are possible, my lord," Sven murmured. He bowed and left, undisturbed by his lord's threat.

It was not that Sven was possessed of greater courage than other men. Nay! Merely that he had known Thorfast would do nothing, despite his anger, even as he had known Verdandi would die in delivering her infant daughter. How had he known? He had *seen* this day years before, when they were newly returned from Britain, by virtue of the eerie power of the "sight" that had come down to him through his mother's bloodline. Over the years he had gradually come to accept the gift—or curse—the gods had given him.

For as far back as he could remember, even as a lad, he had

been different from the others. While the lads of his uncle's hall had chased the wenches and played at battle, he had been of a quieter nature, much preferring knowledge to warfare. To this end he had sought out the company of one of his uncle's thralls, an enslaved and learned monk brought from the misty green isle of Eire named Brother Timothy.

He'd listened enchanted to Timothy's tales of the Christian White Christ, Jesus, who had been filled with love and a radiant light that showered blessings on all about Him. Brother Timothy's stories had excited the young Sven beyond their adventurous content. With his keen intelligence, he had realized that this Jesus greatly resembled his own Norse god, Balder the Beautiful, son of Odin. And with this realization had come a stunning insight. If the gods worshipped by the enemies of the Danes were so similar in attributes to their own gods, could then the people themselves be so very different? This insight was to change him forever, for he could not stomach the thought of waging bloodshed and rapine on people so like himself and his own.

This reluctance to spill blood might have proved disastrous were it not for his strange gift, for the men of his uncle's hall had neither patience nor pity for a quiet shy lad such as he, and baited and cuffed him mercilessly. Then one night as he lay upon his mantle, drifting in the moments between wakefulness and slumber, a vision had flashed before his eyes, like reflections seen clearly in a rectangle of polished tin.

He had seen his uncle's hall overrun by the neighboring clan of Thorfast Jorgensen, with whom they had had a blood feud for many decades, and witnessed with wide, horror-filled eyes the bloody destruction of his kin; had seen himself snatched up and carried off to become a slave to the mighty Lord of Danehof, who, upon hearing of his strange gift, had elevated him above the status of a lowly house thrall, to become Thorfast's personal seer and advisor. Not many days hence, it had all happened as he had foreseen. His skill with the harp and *lur* horn and his facility for storytelling had also proved valuable beyond Sven's humble expectations, and his position at Danehof over the years had become something betwixt that of an advisor, a *skald* or minstrel, a composer of sagas, and

9

a prophet.

Since that fateful day, his visions had been many. Not once had they failed him! Though the "sight" gave him no inkling of when the things he saw might come to pass, as surely as day followed night, in due course they would occur just as he had envisioned. In this manner he had seen the birth of Thorfast's daughter, and also the death of his wife, Verdandi, in childbed. So too the Saxon Queen Wilone's lovely face often swam up from the depths of memory to taunt him, mouthing words he could not hear, while behind her reared a great black bear, the ruff of its hackles up, its massive jaws fiercely agape. The vision of her was as real as the others, and one day, some day, it would come to pass, he knew it! Guilt, he wondered? Was it but guilt that caused her to haunt his visions? Perhaps—for he had not slain her as his lord Thorfast had commanded . . .

He saw other things too—strange things he did not as yet understand. He saw Thorfast as an old man; alone and unloved, robbed of his sight by white membranes that clouded his eyes. In his visions, the old sea-wolf nodded by the hearth while another *jarl* led the men of the hall of Danehof on their raids over the western seas; a young warrior with red-gold hair whom Sven did not recognize. The memories tumbled through his brain like unleashed pups as he made his way to the kitchens.

He found the infant girl wrapped snugly in a lamb's fleece and a covering of rabbit's fur, her cradle only a willow basket set beside the bread-baking stones of the cooking fire, where it was warm. Kolina nodded at him from across the spit, hope flaring in her heart. All knew Sven the *skald* for a gentle, kind-hearted man. If anyone could do aught for the poor wee girl, he could, Kolina knew.

"A fine, healthy babe, sir," she told him eagerly. "Look!" Her eyes dared him to deny it.

And look he did. The infant was tiny, to Sven's bachelor eyes, yet perfect in every way. Waves of dark gold hair molded to her well-shaped head. Tawny lashes—dark for such a fresh complexion—trembled on the rosy curves of her little cheeks. The rosebud mouth held a slightly downward droop, as if pouting, and the lips quivered as she suckled in her dreams.

Sven, a stranger to babes and, if the truth were known, a little afraid of them, was fascinated. He tentatively reached out to where a small fist lay, having escaped the swaddling. The tiny fingers with their delicate nails reminded him of rose petals clasped tight in a bud. He reached out a rough-textured finger and hesitantly stroked the soft, soft skin. At once the little hand unfurled, then fastened tightly about his finger, and Sven was lost.

For it seemed, in that moment when love flooded through him, that she held in her little hand not his finger, but his heart!

That Thorfast could summarily reject such a healthy, lovely child as this, and give orders that she was to be exposed to the elements and left to die like the child of a lowly thrall, filled him with outrage. Sons were indeed a man's pride, but surely his daughters were his joy?

Clumsily he lifted the babe into his arms, nodded to Kolina, who now had tears of relief streaming down her seamed cheeks, and wrapped his mantle warmly about the child before carrying her outside the hall and to his horse. Not a league's distant, he knew of a young slave woman taken from Britain the year before—Nissa by name—who had recently birthed a stillborn babe, much to her fisherman master's disappointment and her own grief. She had ample milk—and love—for the unwanted little girl, Sven knew, and with her kind and generous heart and skill with herbs would prove a good nurse and mother to the child. He sprinkled the babe with drops of icy water from the Limsfjord after the Viking manner of a father accepting a child, and named her Freya, for to him her infant prettiness promised greater beauty yet to come—and surely the goddess of love and beauty would lend her name to such as she?

And so it began.

Nissa and Sven between them raised the child, becoming both her mother and the father she never knew. When at the age of eighteen months she was weaned, Nissa was brought by Sven to the hall of Danehof as little Freya's nurse, for Sven believed firmly that the child should be raised to the position she had been born to.

The babe grew from crawling infant to pretty, toddling child,

11

and her merry smile and infectious baby chuckles captured many a heart—though never her father's heart. When she learned to walk, his arms were never there to catch her when she fell. When she progressed from walking to running, he never once delighted in her swiftness and grace. When the baby chatter was replaced by a little girl's lively prattle and revealed a quick and clever mind to match her prettiness, not once did he bask in fatherly pride. Indeed, it was doubtful whether Thorfast remarked his daughter's existence at all, for his attention was completely taken now by a demanding wench named Dagmar, a sulky black-haired beauty stolen in a blood feud, on whose lusty body he swore he'd sire a son.

As little Freya grew, so did her awareness that all was not as it should be. She knew that Thorfast was her sire and wondered why, unlike the other fathers, he showed no awareness that she was his daughter; no pride in her looks or feminine accomplishments, as did they with their young daughters. That she was different was strongly brought home by the other children of the hall, who began to tease her cruelly and pick on her with vicious pinches and slaps until someone—perhaps Nissa or Sven or a tender-hearted thrall—would pull them off her.

"Girl-brat! Girl-brat! Your father doesn't want you!" came the cruel, singsong taunts. "Good-for-nothing girl-brat!"

Freya flung about, golden curls flying, to see Olaf Olafson standing before her, his fists on his hips, his sky-blue eyes mocking her as he grinned broadly. It was the final straw in a week of hurtful, relentless teasing.

"I'm not! He does!" she cried furiously, tears of rage brimming in her dark blue eyes. She flew at him like a cornered she-lynx, small fists pummeling at his head, his chest, his arms, everywhere.

For all that he was four years older and over two heads taller than she, the unexpectedness of her attack knocked him off balance. Olaf sprawled backward to the rushes, with the little wildcat flailing furiously atop him. Blood was streaming from his nose when he begged for mercy.

"Quarter! Quarter!" he gasped.

"Nay! Nay!" she cried furiously, "Take it back! Take back

what you said, Olaf Olafson, or you'll be sorry!"

He had a black eye, a split lip, and a hank or two of hair missing, clutched in Freya's furious fist, when Thorfast's steward at last pulled them apart, cuffing their ears soundly and bidding them cease their scrapping.

For all his throbbing face, there was a glimmer of admiration in young Olaf's eyes when he struggled to his feet and faced the red-cheeked little girl. By Loki, she was little more than a babe, less than half his size, he realized belatedly, thoroughly ashamed of himself. But for all that, she was no coward! Her tears were tears of anger, not hurt, he sensed. "I'm sorry," he mumbled, eyes downcast. "I—I take it back."

Fists on hips, Freya glowered at him. "*Ja*, you big bully, and so you should!" she retorted hotly, fjord-blue eyes tempestuous.

"Friends, then?" Olaf suggested casually, extending his hand to clasp hers in offer of friendship.

"Never!" Freya hotly refused, and flew away, gold curls bouncing, skirts flying, leaving Olaf gaping after her and feeling surprisingly crushed by her refusal.

Nevertheless, her fierce defense of herself had, unknown to her, engendered a grudging but sincere admiration in Olaf for the brave little maid. As the months went by, he managed—though with only the greatest difficulty—to become not only her friend but her defender, self-appointed protector, and partner in mischief too. The days henceforth were happier ones; Freya clambering up to the low mountain meadows in the *Shieling* month to cut the sweet grass for fodder, with Olaf dogging her heels like a faithful russet hound. Or the two of them haunting the kitchens and stealing treats from the cook, Fat Hilda, or the stables, the smokehouse or the *sauna*, the bath house, in search of adventure and pranks. Olaf was always willing to take part in her naughty schemes, despite the whippings that inevitably resulted for himself, for all presumed that as the older of the pair and the male, he was the ringleader—though Olaf knew better!

But despite her outward happiness, inside Freya was confused, puzzled by her father's coldness. Though she tried and tried, she could remember no naughty deed, however distant and buried in the past, that might have caused him to ignore her so utterly. She ached, yearned with all her little heart, for him to notice her, to say he was pleased with some small thing she had done. But though she constantly sought small ways to show a daughterly affection to the Lord of Danehof, if Thorfast noticed them he gave no sign that he had done so. At last, in desperation, she determined to ask Sven what grave sin she had committed to turn Thorfast against her. Uncle Sven would tell her the truth. He never lied to her!

"It is simply because you are a girl, Freya, and not a boy," Sven told her with great gentleness. "Your lord father dearly wanted a son when you were born, and he is bitter that he has none."

"Are boys better than girls, then, Uncle Sven?" she had demanded with childlike innocence and trust in her jewel-blue eyes.

"Better, no," Sven answered her solemnly, wondering how to soften the new hurt and the bitterness that the truth must instill in her. "But different—yes, they are different." He drew her onto his knees and fondly tousled her untidy curls. "A boy child grows up to be a warrior, like his father. He can become *jarl* when his father goes to Valhalla, and lead his men on raids."

"Then what worth have girl-children?"

"Why, a girl-child marries, and that is a very worthy thing to do, for she may bring her father allies by the joining of two enemy households and thus put an end to the bloodshed and feuding of many years. She must also bear children for her lord husband—and remember, *min yndling*, it is the woman who bears those new lives, not the man; she who nurtures the child in her body and brings it forth into the world. That is the great gift a woman—and only a woman—can give. The gift of Life!"

Freya wrinkled her little nose in distaste. "Pah! Cows give life to little cows, and bitches to their whelps, do they not? It does not seem so very special to me, Uncle Sven, if even the animals can do it! Is that all girls were intended for—to drop babes, one after the other?" she asked, obviously disgusted.

Sven laughed. "Nay, not all. But for most women—your mother, for one—it is ample."

Freya snorted and tossed her head. "Perhaps it is enough for most girls, but never for me! Why, I can fight as well as any boy! Olaf says so. He and I fought Eric yester even, and he is older by three winters than Olaf—but 'twas us who won, not he!"

He laughed at the fiercely stubborn, indignant light in her eyes. "You are more like your lord father than he would ever believe," he said softly, for her expression was Thorfast's. "But little fierce one, you must learn to accept your lot in life, if you are ever to be happy."

"Accept?" She shook her head stubbornly. "No, uncle, I will not. You taught me that the path to knowledge or any worthy prize is paved with questions and striving, not blind acceptance. I am as brave as any lad in this hall—or any hall, anywhere! You tell me that my lord father wanted a son? Well, I, Freya, shall be that son! Just watch me, Sven! I'll learn to hunt and to fight with the broadsword and the battleaxe, you'll see! In a few winters Thorfast will have quite forgotten that the Lady Verdandi bore him a lowly daughter, and take pride in me, his little Freya! I'll make it so!"

Her jewel eyes shone with such fierce determination, Sven's heart ached. How could he find the words to tell her that it would never succeed? How could he break her tender little heart in two by saying that no warrior's skills on her part could ever soften Thorfast's cold heart? Instead, he sidestepped. "We'll talk more on this anon," he promised vaguely. "For now, my pretty, Nissa awaits you at your loom." His eyes twinkled. "Concentrate on your tablet-braiding for now, Lady Freya, and put aside all thoughts of swordplay."

She again wrinkled her nose in distaste. "Tablet-braiding, Uncle Sven? *Nej!* If I must do something, I suppose I'll practice my scrivening. The script with its pretty pictures is much more fun than such women's work!" she said with obvious scorn.

She dropped a kiss upon his cheek and skipped from the room, curls flying, her shift and overpinnings hitched up about her slim, bare legs.

It was the last time he was to see her in skirts for many, many years.

Chapter 1

After the little girl had skipped away, Sven remained where he was, staring into the small, steady flame of a single oil lamp as if mesmerized by its golden radiance. There was a peculiar heaviness in his heart now, such as he experienced when one of his visions unfolded before his eyes; the heaviness of dread at the inevitable, mingled with a sense of helplessness, for no mortal man could control destiny.

So he had felt as his little Freya made her brave vow. Something had been unleashed by her words—some power was even now stirring in the air like a primeval dragon awakening from the depths of sleep, and he, Sven, could do naught to stop it. He could only be there to help her in whatever small ways his gift of sight had armed him with. He sighed heavily. It had all begun so long, long ago, years before the maid had been born. His head nodded slightly and his eyes closed as the memories came flooding back, as vivid as if they had occurred only yesterday . . .

Danehof, hall of Thorfast, had slumbered. The whale-oil lamps with the floating wicks had long since burned down, and all had been mantled by darkness that wintry night save for where the last, lazily curling flames from the central hearth pit illumined a shaggily bearded face or a plumply rounded cheek, or caught the dull silver wink of a mantle brooch, before relinquishing all once more to heavy shadow.

Yet it was not a silent darkness in Thorfast's vast, smoky hall, for many Norsemen slept there—some who snored, some who muttered in their sleep, and some who belched even in the depths of slumber, and grimaced at the taste of soured wine and mead coating the backs of their throats. Nor were the massive hunting hounds silent, but snuffled and yelped softly as they hunted their dream-prey, limbs twitching, tails awag. Nor, for that matter, was Thorfast himself, chieftain of them all, lost in the depths of slumber, for he tossed and turned and grunted on the bench strewn with furs that was his bed, as if he wrestled mighty Midgard, the great serpent monster that coiled about the world. Across the hall, Sven had also lain awake. He had noted his lord's restlessness and shrewdly guessed its cause, for many times since they had left Britain Thorfast had told the *skald* of his sleeplessness, in the hope that he could give him wise counsel and offer some solution. So it had been that winter's night.

"Sven!" Thorfast had called, his voice sounding strangled. "Sven, curse thee! In Odin's name, where are you?"

Sven had rolled himself into his mantle and padded to his lord's side. "Here, sir."

"Can you, with all your mewling wisdom in all things, do nothing for me? My body craves sleep, and yet it evades me each night as a clever buck avoids the hunter's arrow!" He groaned and shifted heavily upon his sleeping couch. "In truth, I am weary beyond belief!"

"Perhaps a soothing draught—?"

"Nay, no draughts! Sleeping draughts are for weaklings and women," he muttered scornfully. "Nay, a draught will not cure what plagues me. 'Tis magic, I tell thee, Sven. It has come to my mind that the Saxon queen set a curse on me before you slew her—that dark-haired witch! A curse to rob me ever after of my rest!"

"A curse?" Sven echoed, swallowing. "Nay, I think not, sir. The—the woman was a Christian, was she not?"

Thorfast grunted grudging agreement. "Then what other reason do you offer for my wakefulness, eh, wise one?"

Sven shrugged. "It is said that—that when a man's actions are at odds with all that he knows to be right and true, he may

17

suffer doubts which will prevent him from—from sleeping, sir."

"Ah! So it is said, is it?" Thorfast sneered, levering himself up onto his elbow. "Then I should of a certainty have little difficulty in finding sleep, should I, good Sven, for all that I have done in my life has been right and true, as befits Viking honor, has it not?"

It was a loaded question, and Sven knew it. Accordingly, he answered with the utmost care and in soothing tones. "Your life has been an example to all good Vikings, my lord. I am certain that this sleeplessness is but a passing phase. Meanwhile I will play my harp softly to lull you to sleep . . ."

Yet neither Sven's reassurances nor his playing had helped, for the *jarl* Thorfast had awakened yet again the following night with that now-familiar sense of something deeply awry, something indefinable that he could not at once put his finger upon. So he had lain each and every night since he had raided the Kentish hamlet, whether aboard his sturdy longship on the return voyage to Jutland, or here at Danehof, Thorfast thought sourly, staring up at the high rafters in his gloomy hall, and that cursed *skald* had been able to offer him no ease . . .

Enmeshed still in a cobwebby dream state halfway betwixt waking and sleep, Thorfast lay there, going over in his mind first the day's feasting, in celebration of their victorious return from Britain, and then further back, to the very day they had attacked the eastern coastal hamlet of Kenley that had been their target.

He had grinned broadly as he and his men loped stealthily up the shingled riverbanks and crept silently on through the mist-drenched woods. The cluster of thatched wattle-and-daub dwellings had been unguarded, vulnerable beyond the belief of the ever-wary Norseman, plumes of woodsmoke rising through the smoke holes to mingle with the pearl-gray dawn light. Not a single guard had stepped forward to bar their path, nor a solitary hound given voice to warn the Saxons of their coming!

He had given the war cry even as they approached the first hut, he recalled, coupling the blood-curdling imprecation to mighty Odin and the Valkyries with a ferocious brandishing of the blood-axe in his fist. Like wolves they had fallen upon the simple hut; the stout door of timber was battered down in short order by well-placed boots and massive shoulders, weighty as hams. The unsuspecting family had been rudely jolted from sleep screaming and wild-eyed, to find themselves looking into the bearded face of Death!

Thorfast, as chieftain, had slain the father himself, scorning the man's pitiful pleas to spare his woman and little ones. He had cleaved the slow-moving cooper in two with a single, powerful downward stroke of his axe that had sliced through brains and bone and gut as if through warmed butter, and splattered great gouts of crimson across the earthen floor. As he moved to a second man, who sprang at him from a corner with a stout club raised to attack, Thorfast glimpsed a wealth of tumbling red hair, caught a fleeting eyeful of bared female flesh, before the first of the women was flung to the floor and eagerly and roughly mounted by his men in turn. Soon her screams had joined those of the others who had been felled by the axes and broadswords and daggers of Thorfast's raiding party as they overran the village and the chieftain's hall, sparing no man nor child—save a pitiful handful who managed to flee them—and precious few of the women.

Before dawn had fully broken, or the bright morning star paled into the charcoal of the sky, or the birds had begun their singing to herald the new day, the village had been put to the torch and swiftly consumed by hungry flames. The dead and the near-dead still within its walls had added the stench of burning human flesh to the acrid odor of crackling thatch and wattle.

The captured women had huddled together beneath a spreading oak where they had been dragged, weeping softly for the children torn from their breasts and ruthlessly killed, for the husbands who would never hold them again. Others had remained stonily silent, their eyes glazed with the horrors they had seen or experienced, their minds unhinged.

Off to one side Thorfast's men had amused themselves with some of the terrified maids, or loaded what booty the village had yielded into skins, which were then lashed securely and carried to the waiting longships, concealed by brush and morning mist a half league downriver.

Thorfast, his mantle and *leistabraekr* spattered with fresh blood, his blood-axe still dripping gore, looked about him hungrily, filled with the heady lust that always followed hot on the heels of bloodshed and victory. A woman! By Odin, he needed a woman!

His gaze came to rest on one who stood apart from the other bawling cows, a woman with the proud, regal bearing of an Anglo-Saxon princess. Her braided hair had at some point been wrested from its tidy confines and now spilled in a thick black cascade to her hips, which were full and invitingly rounded. A plump, rose-crested white breast jutted from the torn bodice of her woolen shift, yet she made no modest move to cover herself. Rather, she seemed to sense Thorfast's burning eyes upon her and turned to look at him directly, meeting the blazing blue of his leer with a level brown gaze of her own that was, to the chieftain's mind, peculiarly disconcerting.

"You, wench!" he growled, aware that the thick, viscous breathing of lust slurred his speech. "Here!"

It was clear she understood the intent of his command if not the words themselves, for with only a second's hesitation she moved gracefully, proudly, toward him across the greensward. Tall for a woman, she yet reached only to the shoulders of the towering, golden-bearded Thorfast, who was a giant amongst a race of giants. Looking up into his cruelly handsome, bearded face, she had calmly awaited his next words.

Her serenity irked Thorfast, and with somewhat greater force than he might otherwise have used upon a captured female, he knotted his warrior's gnarled hand in her shining black hair and wrenched her brutally to him.

"Hold!" she cried loudly.

Despite himself, her imperious tone gave Thorfast pause. With a curse, he abruptly released her. "Sven!" he bellowed. "What says the black-haired witch?"

Sven hurried forward, glancing from the woman and back to his chieftain. "The—the woman bade you 'Hold' in her tongue, my lord," he translated.

Thorfast's red-gold brows arched in disbelief. He let out a great roar of scornful laughter. "Did she indeed, good Sven?

And ask her, by Loki, who is she, that she dares give commands to Thorfast Jorgensen, *jarl* of Danehof!"

The men around him stopped what they were about and turned to watch the exchange with keen interest now.

Sven did as bidden. The woman answered him softly, yet her manner was as aloof and controlled as before, and her composure filled the *skald* with respect, for few women behaved so when faced by a rutting Norseman such as his lord. "She says that she is Wilone, the Desired One, lady wife to the high chieftain Aeldred, descendant of the kings of Kent, whom you and your men butchered along with their two sons this morn," Sven translated, his encouraging smile fled now.

"And what of it?" Thorfast snarled, a suspicious glint in his eyes. "She is but a woman to be used, like all the rest."

"She asks that you spare her, my lord! And in return, she swears she will please you in any manner you might ask of her."

Thorfast's eyes glittered hotly. She was a bold bitch, if ever he'd seen one! Against his volition, she fired his blood with her cool composure and her witch's dark comeliness. He yearned to break her spirit, to see her grovel before him and beg his mercy . . .

"Asks, does she now? Why does she not beg me, eh, Sven, like the other bawling cows of her village? Ask her, *skald*, why I should bargain like a Rhenish wine merchant for her body, when I can take it at my pleasure?" he scoffed arrogantly, fists planted on his hips, his legs, shod in hairy boots and gaitered leggings, braced apart. There was a sly, lustful glitter to his eyes now, the hooded wink of an old wolf who knows he has the upper hand, yet sports at playing with his prey. It was an expression Sven knew all too well—and one that made the blood run cold in his veins with dread.

He had haltingly repeated his chieftain's words, turning to Thorfast with eyes downcast and fair-skinned cheeks a deep crimson with embarrassment. "The Lady Wilone acknowledges that you can indeed take her by force, if that is what you will, my lord. However, she bade me tell you that she is very skilled in the mating arts, and would willingly demonstrate her—talents—if you would spare her life. And—and she bade

21

me also remind you again that her very name means 'The Desired One' in the Anglo-Saxon tongue."

Thorfast rubbed his flaxen beard, nonplussed. He sorely doubted the black-haired witch could teach him aught that was new. He was no stranger to women nor their bodies, either willing and hot, or reluctant and struggling vainly to flee him; had not been since he had reached manhood at the age of twelve winters and taken his first thrall wench. Yet—her quiet confidence intrigued him. He wetted his lips and eyed her covertly, feeling the tumescence in his groin engorge as he feasted his gaze on her full, ripe body. Could this Anglo-Saxon bitch mayhap know some trick he did not . . . ? The Saxon women were lusty bitches, hot and eager to the last, he had heard in coarse conversations with traders in Hedeby. And it was rumored that the Saxon maids were instructed from youth in the varied ways to pleasure men. "Why?" he demanded, wetting his lips. "Why does this Kentish—queen—not place her honor above her life, as befits the woman of a chieftain? Why does she offer herself like a camp follower to the slayer of her menfolk and children?"

Again Sven and the woman conversed. "The Lady Wilone says that her lord had no brothers, sir. That his two little sons killed this morn were the last of his line—save for the child she now carries in her womb. She says that sons are a man's immortality, sir, his link with the—the gods. If you will accept the bargain she offers, then Aeldred will thus live on in his son or daughter."

Thorfast grunted and hid a cruel smile. For all her loveliness, the woman was a fool! Why would he, Thorfast, allow even one of Aeldred's cubs to grow to manhood? Did the farmer permit weeds to flourish unhampered in his fields? Nay, not a one! A wise farmer knew that a single weed left to flourish could become many, many weeds, and choke the life-giving stalks of grain. So it was with cubs . . . But his stony features revealed none of his thoughts. Instead, he nodded.

"So be it." A cruel grin creased his lips. "But tell the 'lady' she must please me mightily if she wishes to save her unborn whelp's life—and I am not a man easily pleasured by a woman. If she fails, it will go ill with her—I swear it by Mjolnir, the mighty Hammer of Thor!" So saying, he touched the hammer-shaped talisman of bronze that hung on a cord about his bull neck, and leered at her.

To his satisfaction, the woman named Wilone paled.

It was dusk before Thorfast struggled up from the flattened bed of bracken and furs where he had lain with the woman all the day long. He laboriously donned his leggings and trousers, his linen tunic and chain-mail coat, cursing his weakness. For all that he was a man grown, his knees trembled like a callow lad's after his first night of wenching! He buckled on his broad belt and made to stride away, back toward the river and his men. But before he went, he could not resist one last, backward glance at the bewitching woman sprawled at his feet. She had inflamed him, drained him, yea, pleasured him more than any woman had ever done, this summer's day long!

By Thor, she was a sorceress, he thought regretfully. He had enjoyed her many times since the dawning. Yet after each coupling she had fondled him, stirred him, until yet again he hungered for her. And each time his manhood had reared to the challenge as lustily and vigorously as any young stallion's, despite his middle years! If it weren't for the child she carried within her, he would have borne her away to Jutland and his hall and kept her for his pleasure alone, for beside her, the lush beauty of his plump, placid, golden-haired Verdandi paled. The woman Wilone's bare body was the golden hue of mead, honey-sweet and mellow and as ripely full as any man could desire. Her shining hair, damp now with her sweat as was the deep cleft between her full breasts, was a tangled blue-black river, streaming down over the gold. In passion she was as the she-lynx, fierce and fiery. Even now, her woman's musk and the pungent, spicy scent of yellow gorse filled his nostrils and left him dizzy. He was almost swayed from leaving, so potent was the spell she had woven about him.

At his feet, Wilone panted shallowly, her eyes dark with fear and dark-ringed with exhaustion as she looked up at cunning Thorfast and saw that the coarse Norseman was bent on rejoining his men. Mistrust was evident in her tired features.

She reached out and stayed him, grasping at his hairy boot as a drowning man clutches desperately for a passing branch. She cried something in a cracked, husky voice that was wracked with terror and uncertainty.

Her tone was enough for him to know that she asked if she had pleased him; if their bargain would be kept, and he would leave her and her unborn babe unharmed.

"*Ja*, witch, *ja*," he growled, and nodded for her benefit before shrugging off her hand and striding quickly away, afraid that if he tarried he would weaken. As he went, he swung his mantle about his shoulders, his fingers trembling on the round silver brooch that served to pin it at the right shoulder so that he pricked himself. He growled an oath as the blood ran crimson down the sleeve of his axe arm, to mingle with the rusty stains of old gore before dripping to the golden gorse.

Wilone saw this, and despite her exhaustion a tiny smile of triumph curved her lips. "Blood of my blood, blood of your blood, I curse thee, mighty Thorfast!" she whispered, a distant, dreaming light in her dilated sloe-black eyes that hinted at madness. "They will mingle, yea, mingle ere long— and mine will, at the last, vanquish yours. I, Wilone, swear it . . . !"

Thorfast had found Sven and his men on the river banks, awaiting him.

"The booty has been stowed aboard ship, sir," the translator informed the chieftain. "Your spies spoke truly. Aeldred's settlement was far more prosperous than it appeared from without. We found many golden torcs, both silver and bronze cups and ornaments, finely woven cloth, and—"

"And the Christian convent?" Thorfast barked, avarice in his blue eyes.

"The holy sisters had fled into the hills, sir, save for their lady prioress, who sought to protect her God's riches with her life, and was slain for her trouble," Sven told him. He looked uncomfortable. "But we looted the convent nonetheless. It yielded crucifixes, crucibles of gold studded with jewels, silver candlesticks and chains—"

24

"Silver, eh? Ah, 'tis good!" his lord cut in sharply, strangely eager to be far from this place with night imminent. "The moon's rising, Sven. The winds and currents favor us. Let's be gone from here!"

"As you will, my lord," Sven agreed eagerly, heading toward the serpentine silhouettes of the three gloriously painted *karfis*, longships, that waited in the purple dusk, rocking gently on the tide in the mouth of the river Thames.

"Sven!" Thorfast called after him, and Sven's heart sank.

"My lord chieftain?" Sven asked, turning reluctant feet back toward his lord.

"Aeldred's woman. She lies back there, in the bracken. Deal with her, Sven." He made to go on his way.

Gentle Sven was aghast. He called after the *jarl*, "But—did she not please you, my lord?"

"Aye, she did," Thorfast murmured softly. "She is well named." He scowled. "But I'll permit none of Aeldred's cubs to survive this day. Sons of murdered fathers have a way of rising up and seeking revenge, Sven. I shall pass no sleepless nights on Aeldred's account!"

Sven's face paled in the gathering dusk and the gorge rose in his throat. "As—as you command, sir," he stammered, and turned back the way his chieftain had come, drawing his dagger as he went.

They had returned to Jutland soon after, Sven recalled, but Thorfast had never been the same from that day forth. Hitherto he had been a man to be reckoned with, bold and fearless, confident in his abilities as a warrior and a leader, and as a man. But little by little doubt had nibbled away at his self-confidence, as an ant slowly but surely will carry off each crumb of a loaf of bread. *Ja*, Thorfast soon came to wonder if he had been cursed by the Saxon queen before her death, for though he felt neither remorse nor guilt for the fate of Aeldred's bewitching Wilone, nor for the unborn child that had died with her, something of her lingered yet, nagging in his mind as a wolf worries a wounded deer, and would not be exiled:

Sons are a man's immortality, Thorfast Jorgensen, she had said, *his link with the gods* . . .

And there was the rub, Sven decided. For although Thorfast was a mighty chieftain amongst his people, at that time he had yet to sire a child—male or female—on either his wife or one of the many female slaves he mated at whim. And he was no longer a young man . . . !

Ja, surely it was this that troubled his sleep and made him lie restless and uneasy in his hall each night, while all about him slept on, Thorfast had also decided. He'd been a fool to think his sleeplessness was the result of a curse. Such superstitious fears were for old women . . . and *skalds.*

Offerings to Frey, god of fertility, had been many over the next seven years, Sven recalled, as had been the sleepless nights of Thorfast, spent in uneasy wakefulness as he pondered the gnawing possibility that he was no true man, since he failed to father a child—either in frequent and lusty coupling with his woman, Verdandi, or with female thralls—to prove his fears groundless.

Icy Jutland winters had passed into flowering springs, and with each spring Thorfast had again left Danehof and gone a-Viking; springs had thawed into idyllic summers, and Thorfast and his men had returned to harvest their crops before raiding again throughout the late autumn until the onset of the frigid winters.

The raids of the Danish sea-wolves on the isle of Britain had been many in those years, and the name of Thorfast Jorgensen and his household had grown in stature and wealth, until Thorfast the Cunning and his deeds took their place in the sagas of the poets and *skalds,* the minstrels, alongside those of the gods.

Yet Thorfast had found no pleasure in either booty or renown, becoming more morose and still shorter tempered as he grew older. His woman, Verdandi, far younger than her lord, knew full well the cause of his melancholy, and that Thorfast, in his desperation to sire a child, had grown to hold her accountable for his fatherless state. She yearned for the better days when the chieftain had first taken her as his woman, and cared for naught but her golden loveliness and her eagerness to please him. She had come close to resolving to risk taking a lover, in the hope that a younger man might mayhap prove successful where her husband had failed, when the miracle happened. Verdandi was at long last with child!

Never had a rooster strutted nor a stallion pranced as arrogantly in its maleness as did Thorfast when he learned his dearest wish was to be granted. He had clasped Verdandi about the waist and swung her high into the air as if she were but a child herself, causing heads to turn in the smoky hall and chatter to cease as if severed by a blade.

"Praise be to the gods, woman!" he roared, wicked blue eyes dancing with merriment, "and to blessed Frey—though Odin knows he took his merry time to answer Thorfast's prayers! A son! At last I, Thorfast the Cunning, will have my link with the gods!"

Verdandi had nodded happily. She knew nothing—and cared less—of "links with the gods," for she was a simple creature, much like the placid cows that grazed the sweet mountain meadows all summer long beyond the *shielings,* the summer dwellings, with no thought for anything but that they should be content. Nor was she as convinced as her husband that the child would be male. Yet she was proud and pleased that she had been able to conceive at last and bring her lord such obvious joy. With a relieved sigh, she happily confided to Sven her hopes that perhaps now Thorfast's temper would be improved and their hall a place of peace and harmony. In this she was proved correct.

Human sacrifice had been offered up in thanks for Verdandi's happy state, a virgin female thrall delivered up to bountiful Frey upon a stone altar in a sacred grove strewn with flowers. Ah, *ja,* it seemed the gods had smiled upon them, for the following months were indeed good ones, with Thorfast exhibiting a jovial and generous humour to all and an affectionate indulgence to Verdandi, the bearer of his son who—if the chieftain's boasts were to be believed—would be a combination of mighty Odin, greatest of the Norse gods and lord of war, and Balder the Beautiful One, Odin's own son.

Such a happy state of affairs might well have continued, Sven mused, had Verdandi not gone into a long and difficult childbirth in the dark depths of the endless northern winter, and relinquished her own life to bring into the world her lord and husband's firstborn, the tiny daughter whom Sven had now grown to love more than life itself—and whom he knew Thorfast would never accept, whatever she might try to do. Nay, not if he lived to be a hundred!

He stood and moved wearily to the lamp, spat upon his fingers, and pinched out the tiny flame. It died with a hiss, and to Sven it was as if all the goodness and light that had filled his empty life in the years since Freya's birth died with it.

The dragon of destiny had stirred, and would soon thrust them into the uncertain future he had envisioned. No mortal hand could hold back the beast and alter what was to come. What would the future bring for his little Freya, the blessed daughter of his heart, if not his loins? He could only wait and wonder—and pray.

Chapter 2

Far away, west over sea on the eastern coast of the isle of Britain, a black-haired lad lay flat upon his belly on the crest of a gentle rise, gazing eagerly down toward the barley field below. The fallen leaves beneath him crunched as he wriggled forward to get closer, and his companion hissed at him to be still.

"Oaf! Do you want them to run before we get a good look at them?" the older lad demanded.

"Of course not. Sorry, Cullen," the boy, chagrined to have behaved so childishly, mumbled in a contrite tone.

Below, in a field bathed by the pumpkin-gold of a harvest moon, a family of hares cavorted amongst the stubble, leaping and bounding about. Large as hounds and long of ear and foot, they seemed strangely human in the ethereal light, resembling dancers celebrating some pagan rite. The rare sight of the Hares' Dance had been one the boy had heard talked of for many years by the Old Ones, but had thought never to witness himself—or at least not before he left for Wessex the following day, to begin his training as a warrior. Excitement made him wriggle a second time with the sheer pleasure of it all, and when Cullen cursed him again the sharp sound carried on the night wind to the field below. The hares pricked their ears, lifted their noses and caught the man-scent, and vanished.

"They're gone," Cullen muttered unnecessarily. He sighed and sat up. "I should have known better than to bring a young pup like you along." Though only three years the other boy's senior, that seniority weighed heavily upon Cullen's shoulders, and he rarely missed an opportunity to remind Alaric that he was older, wiser, more skilled in fighting, better at hunting, and so on. It irked him that despite this, Alaric rarely responded with more than a careless shrug or a casual apology. Cullen supposed that was all part of being the dead chieftain's eldest son. You need feel bettered by no one, knowing all the while that you would one day be chieftain in your father's stead. He scowled. "We should go home. Mayhap your 'nurse' has wakened and is looking for you? Lona will want her precious charge to get a good night's rest before he leaves on the morrow."

Alaric hid a smile at this none-too-subtle barb. "Mayhap," he agreed easily, refusing to be baited. "It's a pity about the hares, is it not, Cullen? If you hadn't cursed me, they wouldn't have disappeared."

"And if you hadn't wriggled like a hound nipping fleas, I would have had no reason to curse you!" Cullen retorted crossly, knowing from Alaric's tone that he was grinning. He stood, shouldering his bow. "Come on!"

Together they made their way through the skeletal woods, the only sounds the crunch of fallen leaves beneath their boots and the occasional hooting of a hunting owl, gliding pale and ghostlike amongst the bare trees. The air was cold and frosty, carrying the scents of autumn to their nostrils: damp leaves and berries, loam, hazels and chestnuts, and the faintly acrid odor of wood smoke from the hearths of their settlement a quarter league's distance to the north. The full moon touched the branches and the ground underfoot with silvery dapplings, making their path easy to follow in the gentle radiance of its light and the light of myriad icy stars that twinkled like silver rowels far above.

"So," Cullen began, "has my father said his farewells to you and Farant yet?"

"Nay. But he left word that he wished to speak with us in the morning, before we leave."

"Ah!" Cullen grinned. "No doubt he intends to warn the three of us of the dangers of strong drink and the tents of the camp followers, eh, cousin? I for one will let all that he says enter by one ear—and go out by the other!"

Alaric laughed. "'Twill not be too difficult, cousin, seeing as how there is naught to halt his words' passage between the two!"

Cullen cursed and cuffed his younger cousin. "Make jests if you will, boy," he said importantly. "But we'll see who jests in Aethelred's camp! It is said the soldiers of the high king's *fyrd* care little for raw newcomers, and sport at making life hard for them!" In truth the thought made his own belly churn, but he allowed no hint of this to show in either his tone or his expression.

Alaric shrugged. "If we wish to become seasoned warriors, what better place to learn than amongst men already hardened by warfare?" he offered, and Cullen fell silent, knowing the younger lad was right.

The acrid odor of smoke grew stronger as they left the woods, and the two youths exchanged quick, uneasy glances. In the moonlight Cullen saw the sudden flaring of the younger Alaric's gray eyes, and felt the blood drain from his own face. Surely it couldn't be—?

Wordlessly, they started running, their breath condensing in great clouds on the frosty air and rasping from their lungs in choking sobs. The ground flew beneath their boots as each ran wordlessly toward the settlement that was their home, neither daring to put his fears into words. Alaric was first to reach the wooden palisade that surrounded the huts of Kenley and the great hall that housed the dead chieftain's sons.

He leaned against the palisade and wept—wept with tears of relief. There was but one hut ablaze, and in the dancing light of the flames he saw a chain of men and women rapidly passing wooden buckets of water from hand to hand to douse it. No helmeted flaxen-haired giants wielding battle-axes. No screams and war cries as invaders committed pillage and rape upon the womenfolk. Only a small family, their faces pale and sad in the ruddy firelight and billowing clouds of smoke as they huddled together and wept over the loss of their dwelling and their meager belongings.

"'Tis but a hut, Cullen, fear not," Alaric whispered when he was able. "A spark from the hearth must have caught the wattle. See? The smithy's family is safe, the blaze almost

31

under control."

"I wasn't afraid!" Cullen insisted indignantly, yet there was a tremor to his voice.

"Then you are indeed braver than I," Alaric confessed ruefully, "for my legs feel as if I have run five leagues without stopping, they quiver so!"

His frank admission immediately chastened Cullen. "In truth," he mumbled, "aye, I was afraid. Only a fool would not have been, smelling the smoke from afar and not knowing . . ."

Weak-kneed, they both sank down to the hard, dark earth to catch their breath and recover their composure. There was no need to exchange the thoughts that had teemed in their heads as they raced toward the settlement, for their thoughts and fears had been one: Danes! They'd feared the Danes had again raided Kenley and razed it in their wake, hence the acrid odor of smoke on the chill wind.

It was no idle fear, for the East Angles, neighbors to the northeast of Kent, had all been conquered by the Danes in past years, and their lands forfeited to become part of the vast Viking kingdom known as the Danelaw. The conquered Angles had been forced to pay yearly tribute—bribes—to their new masters henceforth in the form of silver, the danegeld. So it was with much of the lands that had once been eastern or northern Britain. Far to the north, in the new Northumbrian Viking capital of Jorvik, the Danes had established vigorous trade and commerce and used the thriving port-stronghold as a center from which they erupted from time to time to wage war on neighboring chieftains and their peoples and add their wealth and lands to their growing empire. Only Aethelred, King of Wessex, had been able to withstand their attacks, and had successfully repelled the invaders.

Kent, a small kingdom on the eastern borders of Wessex, stood perilously alone against the coast, uneasily straddling the Danelaw on its northernmost tip and bordered by the freemen of the west on the other. It was forgotten by the Danes for more than a decade after they, led by the Danish *jarl* Thorfast the Treacherous, had butchered and pillaged and raped all within its confines as part of an invasion of the eastern and southeastern coasts of Britain led by Ivar the

32

Boneless, finally burning the old settlement of Kenley to the ground after the Viking manner. Stripped of her wealth and inhabitants, Kenley had offered no prizes in the form of booty or thralls, slaves, for the Viking raiders, and she had been left in peace.

That had been fourteen years ago. But there was again reason to fear, for people had returned to Kenley. The farms were now well tilled and yielded plentiful harvests. Jewel-smiths and workers in common and precious metals, coopers and millers and tanners, hunters and traders had returned to do business within her walls. With renewed prosperity, Kenley was once again an inviting challenge—certainly rich prize enough for any glory-seeking Dane. Alaric, well schooled by his maternal uncle, Ordway, in the subtle strategies of attack and defense by virtue of his noble birth, knew that this threat was no hollow one, but terrifyingly real. It was in preparing to defend his ealdorman's kingdom against future raids at the hands of the Danish sea-wolves that he and his brother, Farant, and his cousin, Cullen, rode west on the morrow.

His head swam in the aftermath of relief as he recalled all that he had been told of that fateful summer day fourteen years before; of how his mother had been forced to watch helpless while the Danes raped and carried off the screaming womenfolk of the settlement to become slaves and concubines in a foreign land, torching the cluster of huts before they left, and with them, the bodies of the slain menfolk and young ones. At that time his mother, the young Lady Wilone, had seen her husband cloven in two by a Norseman's blade, her two little sons' heads lopped off like chickens'. Mindless with shock and grief, her only thought had been to save herself and in so doing, her lord's only remaining child, still carried in her womb.

She had given herself willingly to that bloody, rapacious sea-wolf many times, his Uncle Ordway had told him and Farant, begging him as she did so to spare her and her unborn babe in return for the pleasures of her body. But the Norseman, God curse him, had meant from the first to renege on his oath, and had sent one of his men, Sven by name, after him to slit her throat. The man had been that rarity amongst Norsemen, a man of compassion. He had let the woman live. Wilone had fled into the woods and dwelt there, alone in her shame, like a wild creature. A few months later she had been delivered of not one son but two, twin boys she had named Alaric and Farant, he and his brother.

Without food and shelter, the winter had been bitterly cold, seemingly endless. Weakened by the shock of Thorfast's rape, by exposure and the birth of the children, their lady mother had lost her reason. But against all odds the babes had survived for three days, until their mother's brother, Ordway, who had newly returned from the land of the Franks and learned of the raid on his sister's settlement, found them, still clasped in Wilone's rigid arms. He had taken the babes to his gentle wife, Valonia, to raise along with their only son, Cullen. The Lady Wilone had been carried to a convent, there to pass her remaining days in the dream world of the mad, and in crazed mutterings. So went the sad tale of the birth of Alaric and Farant.

Alaric's jaw tightened. One day, when he—the firstborn of the two—was made chieftain, he would repay the Dane Thorfast tenfold for the butchery committed on his kin, and for what had been done to his mother that day, he vowed hotly. It was a vow he had made countless times since he had been old enough to understand the horror of the murder of his father and older brothers, and the tragedy of Wilone's wasted life, and one which by now had been burned deep and bitter into his soul. Others might forget and grow unwary and complacent with the passing of the seasons, but never he, Alaric, son of Aeldred, ealdorman of Kent and the burh of Kenley! Never . . .

"Come, we should go on in," Cullen suggested, his voice still a little shaky and lacking its normal cocksure tone. "What with all the uproar, they may not have noticed our absence. Let's hope so. There'll be Lucifer himself to pay if they have!"

With a curt shake of his head, Alaric turned aside, unaccountably feeling as if he had aged ten years in the past few minutes. "You go on, Cullen. I'll join you shortly." So saying, he flung away from the burning hut and plunged into the shadowed woods in search of solitude. Finding a friendly oak, he crouched down and leaned against its broad, rough trunk, deep in thought.

"Alaric? It is you there in the dark, isn't it?"

His head jerked up at the sound of the husky female voice intruding upon his musings, and he saw her, standing not more than two tailors' lengths away, the harvest moon lighting her from above. Her tumbling black curls were immodestly neither covered with a kerchief nor braided. Even in the pale moonlight, the glistening red of her lips and the bright sparkle in her tawny eyes would not be dimmed, and a familiar but unrequited aching began in his groin.

"Yea, 'tis I, Kendra. What do you here?" Even to his own ears his voice sounded quavering and false, and he inwardly cursed himself for his childishness.

"I—I came looking for you, Lord Alaric. I heard talk that you are to leave on the morrow?"

"Yea. 'Tis so," he admitted gruffly.

"And yet you said nothing to me?" There was accusation in her tone.

"I—had no wish to upset you, Kendra."

"Ah—then you knew I would be upset?"

"I thought perhaps you would be, yes," he mumbled. Her low, mocking laughter trilled on the autumn hush, and again the yearning, the aching, bittersweet and fiery, swept over him. Cold sweat prickled down his spine despite the chill of the night. Sweet Jesu, what was it about her that caused him to tremble so?

She stepped across the frost-rimmed grass to stand before him. "You were right, Alaric. I was indeed upset! I would not have had you leave here without a word to send you on your way, without so much as a Godspeed and fare thee well from my lips!" She stepped closer, so close her breath came hot and sweet against his cheeks. The heady warmth of her body rose about him like a miasma, surrounding them both. He swayed, dizzied by her closeness. Her lips, her moist cherry-red lips, almost brushed his as she repeated in a smoky voice, "Godspeed and fare thee well, my lord Alaric."

He was drowning in her eyes, those tawny eyes that were strangely at odds with her youthful face: old eyes, filled with all knowledge, both of good and of great evil. Eyes that, despite the youth of their setting, had seen everything, and for whom the world no longer held secrets and mysteries to be explored. A thrill ran through him. He shivered, then all at once grew hot, his cheeks flaming. Of a sudden he had fastened his arms clumsily about her, was kissing her with a rough exuberance that only youth and innocence can impart, dizzied by the feel of her hard young breasts crushed against his chest, of her rounded female body squirming in his trembling arms, the tantalizing scent of her musk sharp in his nostrils.

Laughing throatily, she broke away, her eyes twin topazes glowing in the moonlight, her lips glistening wetly. "Is it but innocent kisses that you hunger for, my lord, my dark, handsome young lord? Or—that which *men* hunger for?"

His gray eyes blazed in answer like cinders ignited by the wind, and reaching out, she silently clasped his hand in her own and led him away, behind the huts of the settlement to a byre where horses and milk-cows were stabled, and fresh straw was theirs aplenty.

Pulling him down beside her in the scented gloom, she again offered him her lips, strange mewling whimpers breaking against his mouth as he kissed her hungrily again. She brought her hips snugly against his flanks until they were pressed against each other their entire length, mouth to mouth, chest to bosom, hard belly to rounded hip, legs entwined. The breath came rasping from him now, as if torn from his lungs in great, fiery bursts. When Kendra at length untangled her arms from about him, she lifted her kirtle over her head, flung it carelessly aside, and shook free her ebony curls in a single, lithe move that stunned him.

Gasping, he saw for the first, the very first time an unclothed maid, for she had worn no linen undergarment beneath her kirtle. For endless moments she did not move, nor did she speak. She simply curled there, catlike, upon the straw, in all her bewitching beauty, mantled only by her ebony curls and by the moonlight streaming its silver through the wind-eye to dapple her bare, nut-brown flesh and reflect silver fire in the amulet that hung between her breasts. Her eyes burned seductively into his from beneath their fringe of thick, sooty lashes, and reddening with shame and deeply thankful of the shadows, he felt his manhood stir and grow, becoming huge and alien and filled with a sweet fire, an aching throb that would not be stilled.

Kendra lay back upon the straw and held out her arms to him. Her breasts were golden as apples in the gloom, dark rose nubbins rising at their center. In their dark valley, he again glimpsed as she moved a silvery flash from the heart-shaped amulet that hung there on a slim silver chain. A pagan charm, surely, his mind registered dimly, but then the thought was quickly gone as his gaze dropped down over the lush, inviting lines of her hips and belly and to the joining of her pale thighs, where her maidenhair showed as a small, dark shield, defending the secrets within.

All the whispers he had heard of women and their delights, the secrets of their sweet and tempting flesh shared by lads scarce less innocent than he in the dark of night, came back to niggle in his ear: "A virgin, once taken, can never be pleasured fully by any save him who claimed her maidenhead." "A virgin's untouched body is the sweetest pleasure a man can ever know." Sweat poured from him. Was she virgin? Aye, surely she was. Then how was he to breach her maidenhead? He did not know, and aye, he feared her teasing laughter if he failed!

His heartbeat throbbed in his ears, a hammer beating in time with the pulsing throb in his loins. The blood sizzled through his veins like burning tallow, sending its fire throughout him, centering its heat in his groin. *I will! I must! I shall!* The beat, the words repeated like a litany in his brain . . .

Then, through it all, came *her* voice, low and purring, fanning the fire that raged throughout him: "Come, my dark lord Alaric! Let me teach you what it means to be a man!"

And Kendra, bastard daughter of the Abbess Aethelfreda, she of but sixteen summers, she of the gypsy-black tresses and the red, red lips, taught him well.

His gray eyes filled with silent pleas as she stroked and fondled his lithe young body, learning what pleased him and what did not; where it was he would be stroked and pressed and squeezed and tasted, where her touch and her maddening lips gave him greatest pleasure, until he quivered all over like a single reed in the wind; until he trembled at the certainty that

37

soon, before it had scarce begun, he would be done!

He, in his turn, stroked her with trembling fingers, guided by the light but urgent pressure of her hands to cup her firm young breasts and tweak her swollen nipples, to fondle her slender thighs and explore the delightful mystery between them, burnishing her fiery softness with fumbling, wondering hands until he could bear it no longer. Sweat streamed from his brow when Kendra, sensing his need, at last peeled his tunic and leggings from him and pulled him roughly down upon her, her thighs flung wide, her small, grasping hands ready and eager to guide him to his release.

The shock of their bared flesh meeting was as searing as the pierce of a blade. The smell of her musk and her sweat, the wild-grass scent of her hair, the elusive herbal fragrance that rose from the amulet that nestled in the valley between her breasts were powerful conquerors of innocence. With an anguished cry he fell upon her and let instinct rule, burying himself to the hilt in her dark, wet warmth. Her body seemed to beckon him deeper, deeper into the honeyed well at its center, driving harder and faster into that velvet sheath until he feared that to go further into the beguiling depths would be to surrender his very soul—!

Too soon it was done. Too soon the moment came, then passed, then was lost forever, as always is the first time, as are all first times. Too soon his exultant cry was borne away on the night wind. He fell back to the straw, spent and panting heavily, close to weeping and to laughing at once, both ashamed of his haste and fiercely arrogant at the taking of his first woman.

Kendra's throaty laughter rippled through the shadows. "Have no shame, my lusty young lord. 'Tis often so quickly ended for lads the first time. Next time 'twill be better for you, you'll see. Rest awhile, and I'll show you. Aye, my handsome lord, Kendra will show you! The moon's scarce up. We've time and plenty of it, till day breaks . . ."

"We have," he murmured huskily, covering a firm breast with his hand and rousing the pert nipple with the ball of his thumb. His gray eyes glittered with an almost feverish heat. "Show me, Kendra. *Show me!*"

And there was a rough, masculine edge of command to his lad's voice that she had never heard before; an edge that excited her. The amulet winked slyly silver in the moonlight that streamed through the wind-eye, and she shivered with pleasure as she felt its dark powers go coursing through her, to him.

Alaric had watched the Hares' Dance as a lad. But he rode forth from Kenley the next dawning as a man.

Chapter 3

The pagan goddess Eostre garlanded the meadows and the lees, and in every bush and sweetbriar the birds sang ballads to the sun. The rolling meadows were dotted with ewes and lambs, like reflections of the fluffy clouds that sailed above, and beyond, upon the hill, set atop a sturdy ring of earthworks and bowered by verdant forests, the square wood and stone walls of the new Kenley Hall rose dark and powerful before the vivid blue sky. Little less blue were the standards, emblazoned with a black bear, that snapped and furled above the gate towers.

"We are home, my lord!" Cullen bellowed.

The massive dark man who rode the curvetting black stallion beside him laughed deeply.

"'My lord' is it now, Cullen?" he bantered, his cinder-dark eyes alive with merriment. "What happened to 'Alaric, my monkish cousin' of last night?"

Cullen grinned. "Last night, sir, I was drowning in my cups, as well you know, and overly—er—draped with comely camp followers!"

"Indeed you were," his lord and cousin agreed, "and greedy to the last!" He turned in the saddle, rising in the stirrups to see better ahead. "Ah, 'tis good to be home!"

"Aye, it is, Alaric. I warrant little has changed in the past nine years since we joined King Aethelred's court, save for the building of the new hall."

"Indeed it has, cousin." Alaric, solemn now, disagreed. "We have changed. We left here as innocent lads, knowing little of life beyond Kenley, with naught but hope and stars in our eyes. We are returning as men, wiser, by the grace of God, and far stronger than when we left. Both wisdom and strength will save our lands from the onslaught of the pillaging Danes."

Both men fell silent, quietly sitting their horses and gazing down at the gently rolling valley below. A lone gnarled oak rose from the green carpet, and Alaric wondered if Cullen, like himself, was remembering Ashdown and their first battle in what had come to be known as the Year of Battles, fought about a lone thorn tree, shortly after joining Aethelred's ranks.

The king, he recalled, had been receiving Mass in his tent, even as the rowdy, jeering Danes had amassed on the hill above Aethelred's encampment, ready to attack. Despite his advisors' urgings, Aethelred had refused to cut short his devotions, insisting sternly that he would not disrupt the service of his God for the service of man. Alfred, his younger brother, had paled. Even now, the Danes were readying themselves to attack. To hesitate even a moment would mean relinquishing the advantage of drawing first blood to the enemy!

Ordering the royal standard of the House of Wessex raised aloft, the golden dragon furling proudly in the breeze, shield bosses, swords, and helmets flashing brightly in the harsh winter sunlight against the sparse grass of the chalky downs, Alfred himself had given the order to attack in his brother's stead, and led the army of Wessex up the hillside in a sweeping charge that some had likened afterward to the ferocious rush of a maddened boar. After many hours the Danes had fled to Reading, defeated, leaving the broken bodies of Wessex men and Danes, a Viking king and several of his *jarls*, strewn about the twisted thorn tree. Their victory, if such it could be termed, had been short lived. Many such bloody battles had followed in succeeding years, but though Alfred's triumphs were many, the Danes still sought to add the kingdom of Wessex to the Danelaw.

Alfred had been made king at twenty-two years, following Aethelred's death the spring after the battle of Ashdown, and had swiftly proved himself an able leader, despite the doubts of many who had feared a young man so studious as he would prove faint-hearted in battling the Danes. Yet the blood of his warring grandsire, Egbert, flowed fierce and hot in his veins, and he had surprised them all, becoming to his armies and people not simply 'Alfred, the King' but 'Alfred, the Great' by virtue of his wisdom, his brilliant ability to lead, and his refusal to accept defeat no matter what odds.

Nine years, nine long and arduous years, he and Cullen had spent in Alfred's service! They had known the triumphs and the heartaches of battle, and Alaric, the friendship of the king himself, a friendship he did not take lightly, for he found much to admire in Alfred as a man. He was returning to Kenley with the title of Viceroy, Ealdorman Alaric of Kent, and with the promise of at least a brief respite from war, since the new Treaty of Chippenham.

Alaric had no illusions that the treaty would last overlong. The Danes were notorious for agreeing to treaties, and then breaking them when the fancy struck them, or when the promise of danegeld or other riches beckoned. Nor was Alaric convinced that the Viking leader, Guthrum, having bowed to a victorious Alfred's wishes and accepted baptism into the Christian faith for himself and several of his followers, would make this treaty any more inviolable than those in the past. He was simply wearied of battle after endless, bloody battle, and eager for any promise of peace, however brief, in which to rekindle ties of blood with his family, see that his lands had prospered under his uncle Ordway's stewardship, and mayhap take a bride and begin a family. He was no longer a young lad, but a grown man. He needed sons to follow him.

He grinned as he recalled a night in camp perhaps a year after they had joined Alfred. The day had been long and grueling for him and Cullen, and by the camp fire their thoughts had turned nostalgically—and if the truth were known, a little drunkenly—to home. Alaric had thought with great fondness—and no little youthful lust—of the young woman, Kendra. Made maudlin by homesickness, mead, and battle, he had confessed to Cullen that he had taken the maid's virginity, and added dreamily, gazing into the fire, "I mean to return to her ere long, cousin, and make her my bride."

Cullen had gaped, then snorted in disgust, his snorts swiftly becoming great raucous guffaws of merriment. "Kendra? *Kendra?* She of the golden eyes?" he'd echoed in disbelief. "Nay, cousin, tell me it is not so—that my cousin Alaric *cannot* be such an innocent!"

"How so?" Alaric had demanded, bristling with indignation and reddening with embarrassment.

"Kendra was no more a maiden when you had her than she was when *I* first enjoyed her charms, you great dolt! For all your prowess with the sword, you are truly an innocent, cousin! I warrant your 'chaste' maid has been ridden more times than the spavined mounts they've given us to ride here in camp—aye, and relished each and every rider, if I know lusty Kendra! I had her myself more than once—and I know of several others before me. She's certainly a toothsome sweetmeat for any man's bed, but hardly fitting for your bride!"

With Cullen's revelations and scorn, the loss of Alaric's innocence had been complete. From that night, he had given no further thought to Kendra until some three years had passed, when he received a summons to return to Kenley for the celebration of his twin brother Farant's wedding. The bride in question had proved to be golden-eyed, black-haired Kendra!

He, Farant, and their cousin Cullen had left for Wessex together that long-ago dawn to learn the soldiering arts in Aethelred's camp, but Farant had lasted only six months before returning to Kenley. He had loathed the coarse army life, and had been the butt of the soldiers' cruel jests and taunts that he was soft and womanly, unfit to join their numbers. Alaric had known that this was not so; that Farant had courage and manliness aplenty, but of a nature different from that which Aethelred's men prized. He did not flaunt the strength of his muscles, nor his prowess with the sword, for his was an inner strength. Nor did he pay only lip service to his Christian teachings—he lived them, no matter what the cost. If a man struck him, he offered the other cheek in humility and extended his hand to the assailant in brotherhood. If he learned that a man lacked something he possessed, he gave it freely and gladly without thought of recompense. To Alaric's mind, Farant and Kendra were ill matched, but despite his first subtle attempts to dissuade him, gentle Farant had been adamant about marrying her.

"She is loving and warm, brother, all that is woman, aye, and a beauty! Indeed, she is all I have ever wanted in a wife," he'd said with gruff obstinacy.

"She is no innocent maid, Farant. You know this?" Alaric had at last said bluntly, subtlety having failed to dissuade him.

Farant's face, so like his own, had darkened. "I know full well that Kendra has been badly used by more than one man, aye." There was accusation in Farant's tone, causing Alaric to wonder what it was Kendra had told Farant about her relationship to himself. "Her mother, the Lady Abbess, has adjusted her bride price accordingly. All is proper, as it should be, believe me." His tone had brooked no argument. His fist had closed over the hilt of his sword, and Alaric—who had never before seen his quiet, bookish brother so stirred—had determined to hold his peace. He had seen the way Farant's eyes followed the black-haired vixen, seen the love and tender worship in their depths, and known then that his words would fall only on deaf ears.

But not seventy-two hours after their marriage, upon retiring he'd found the blushing bride, his new sister-in-law, in his own bed, as bare as on the day of her birth, offering herself to him, Alaric, in no uncertain terms! Had she changed in the six years since then, he pondered? He doubted it, but for Farant's sake he sorely hoped so!

"Ride on, Cullen," he ordered soberly.

Onward they rode, down into the shallow valley below, their weary, battle-scarred horses catching the scent of their excitement and prancing now like frisky colts, the black and the gray straining side by side up the hill toward Kenley Hall and the promise of water, oats, and rest.

Fists on her slim hips, Freya turned away from the slitted wind-eye through which she had been gazing broodingly out at the dense green forests and faced Sven, defiance stamped on

44

her finely molded features.

"I'm sorry, Uncle Sven, but it has already been decided. The *Althing* agreed that I should lead the clan in my father's stead, and there is naught you can do to change that! The Cuckoo month is all but past. The snows have melted, the cattle will soon be taken to the upland pastures near the *shielings*. The fields are all ploughed and sown, the peat dug and the wood cut. There is nothing to detain me longer here at Danehof!"

Watching her, seeing the determination in her proud, lovely face, Sven was momentarily reminded of that day, some eighteen years before, when the infant girl had grasped his finger in her baby hand, and in so doing, taken his heart in her fierce little grip. 'Twas not so very different now, he mused, even after all this time! He still found it difficult to refuse her anything. "I could ask you not to go—out of love for me, who has raised you like a father?" he suggested, stroking his beard, knowing what her answer would be.

"You could, uncle," she admitted, a smile curving her lips and deepening the dimples in her cheeks, "but you will not! You are a man of great honor, and your love for me far too deep and true to bind me to you against my will. You once said that true love should be gladly given, the heart a wild bird free to soar or light where it will, not bound about by cords and conditions, did you not?"

He smiled, for she was as clever as she was lovely. She knew full well he could not—would not—argue against his own words! "I did," he admitted. "But what of you, Lady Freya? What of the small girl who vowed she'd always do as her uncle wished, without questioning his wisdom?" There was mild reproof in his tone.

Unabashed, she laughed merrily, showing white, even teeth between pretty pink lips. Her golden hair, now in her womanhood darkened to a stunning red-gold, stirred about her slim shoulders, a lively complement to her fresh complexion, which was vibrant with good health. Her fjord-blue eyes twinkled, the dark reddish-brown brows—seeming darker by contrast against her fair complexion—arching slightly as she laughed to give her the appearance of a startled fawn. "I was a child then, Uncle Sven, as well you know! I believed you a god.

45

I thought each word you said was a priceless gem spilled from your lips!"

"And now?"

She smiled, but there was sadness behind the merriment. "I still believe it, Uncle Sven, but—I must test my wings and fly!"

He nodded. "Aye. And so you must! Forgive me. I have a father's fears for you, my child . . . and an old man's misgivings."

"And a vision," she reminded him.

"Aye, and a vision," he admitted, reluctant to dwell on the matter. Had he not told her, warned her countless times of the things his gift of the "sight" had revealed to him, of seeing her taken in a raid by a great bear and carried off to its cave-lair? Had not his every vision thus far come to pass as he had foretold? As would the rest . . .

Thorfast's eyes were dimmed now, their sky-blue lost under a cloudy white membrane that had robbed him of his sight. He sat by the hearth, an embittered old man, neglected by his young wife, the barren, black-haired Dagmar, who amused herself with younger, lustier men—the sons of those who had once gone a-Viking with her husband in his youth—and openly mocked her feeble lord. And had not Freya, from the day she had sworn at his knees she would do so, become in every way but one the son Thorfast had longed for? A warrior with red-gold hair in truth led Thorfast's men a-Viking, as his visions had foretold—albeit that warrior was a woman! So would the remainder of his vision come to be, he knew. And he was afraid for her, aye, so very much afraid! Though not the child of his loins, she was the child of his heart, and he loved her dearly.

"Whether I gainsay you or nay, you will go," he said heavily at length, "The *Althing* has agreed to your chieftaincy, and who am I to question the judgment of a committee of wise ones? But I have a compromise that will, I hope, please us both."

"Tell it!"

He drew a breath, knowing well her fiery temper and the reaction his words would engender. "I shall go a-Viking with you."

"You, Uncle Sven?" The deep blue eyes widened in

disbelief, then anger. "You mean to go west over sea to Britain? Nay! I, as the new chieftain of this clan, forbid it! You're an old man, uncle. I—I would not see any harm befall you. Stay here. Rule the hall for me while I am gone, and wait on my return in the Corncutting month." There was a plea in her tone and in her eyes.

He shook his head, his gray beard and his long gray hair stirring about his shoulders as he crossed the chamber toward her. "No. There are others who are better fitted to the overseeing of the hall, as well you know. Ulf, for one. Or Brann? And I am not so old as you, in your youth, believe! If you want my blessing, then I must go with you. Otherwise I will not give it."

She scowled and angrily tossed her red-gold hair. "Sometimes you are as stubborn as my father, good Sven!" she gritted, giving him a darkling glance.

His eyes twinkled. "And sometimes, my lady chieftain, *you* sound very much as your sire used to sound—as stubborn as a goat! Is it settled?" he pressed.

"Do I have a choice?" she retorted, flouncing angrily across the chamber, away from him, her arms crossed over her breasts.

"There is always a choice, if one searches for it. Stay here, in Danehof."

"I cannot! The clan needs to learn that I am a worthy leader, one who will lead them to the new, fertile lands we so desperately need. If you will have it no other way, then you must go with us," she agreed reluctantly.

The waters of the Limsfjord were a deep, vivid sapphire that spring morn in the Lambs' Folding month when they set sail from the Hall of Danehof. The sky was a paler but no less vivid reflection of its hue. Gulls cut white swaths in the azure, wheeling and dipping over the lime cliffs and the *naust,* the boat house, and screaming threats like Valkyries on their winged horses at the fishermen mending nets or butchering whale blubber before it.

Beyond, at the head of the fjord, Thorfast's hall rose dark before the green of the dense pine and birch forests beyond. The massive, steeply pitched, sloping roof, thatched with sod, with spirals of blue peat smoke rising through the smoke holes to the powdery blue sky, and the walls of sturdy turf and stone were so dear and familiar this morn, that pain wrenched at Freya's heart, coupled with a sense of foreboding. Would she ever see Danehof again?

The hall had been her home now for eighteen years, and it was with an unexpected pang that she left it this morn—she had not felt so much as a twinge when they had gone raiding the Franks last year and the year before. Had Uncle Sven's strange visions instilled this feeling of doom inside her, she wondered? 'Twas probable. Or—was it simply that the hall represented the old life she knew and felt safe within, while her new position as leader of the thirty-two men aboard the *Wild Bird of the Wind* was a responsibility that frightened her somewhat, even as it filled her with pride and determination? A little of each, she decided, flinging back her red-gold hair to squint seaward against the brilliant light reflected off the sparkling water, at their sister ship, the *Sea Raven*, captained by Eric the Tall.

The *Wild Bird of the Wind* was an ocean-going vessel, a trim dragon-ship designed for speed on the open seas. Her prow rose high above the sapphire waters, carved cleverly into the shape of a screaming hawk, its beak agape, its red eyes filled with fury. It faced now toward the open sea, scaring the evil spirits of the waters away with the ferocity of its carving. The heavy rectangular sail, of *wadmal* dyed in crimson bands to contrast with the natural wool, bellied with the wind, fighting the restraint of the "old woman," the mainmast. The sides, painted smartly in crimson, black, and gold, gleamed against the sparkling water. Within them, in racks below the gunwales, stood over sixty round, wooden shields, the metal bosses flashing in the sunlight. Once they had left the fjord the shields would be taken down and stored so that the *Wild Bird* could maneuver in heavy swells, but for now they stayed where they were, a show of grandeur for the people of Danehof, who ran down to the cliffs to wave farewell and wish them good luck. The *Bird* was indeed a vessel to be proud of, Freya acknowledged, her heart swelling with pride.

All about their lady captain, the crew labored to stow the

48

provisions and weapons. The men, a few of them flaxen or red-headed like their fair Norwegian cousins, but for the greater part dark-haired, and all shaggily bearded, were dressed as was Freya in leggings with colored cross-gaiters and thigh-length, form-fitting linen shifts, belted at the waist. Short trousers clad their hips and thighs, and upon their feet they wore lightweight boots of soft, comfortable leather, for they had no need of the hairy winter boots with the skins turned outward that were the customary Viking garb, not in this warm spring weather. Each man wore a great broadsword slung over his shoulder and clanking against his back, and a dagger thrust into the leather belt at his waist. Some wore simple cone-shaped bronze helmets with a long piece extending in front to protect the nose in battle. Freya was no exception. Like her men, she was heavily armed and comfortably clad for action, though as leader she wore a helmet of silver, beautifully chased with designs of Thor's hammer and other talismans, and sporting as its crest a screaming hawk's head wrought in bronze. In her man's garb and with her helmet's nosepiece and her shoulder-length hair concealing her features, there was little about her to betray her sex—though she did not attempt to conceal it—other than the sure, graceful manner in which she moved and the womanly curves that filled her tunic.

"Look at her!" one of the crew, Karl by name, muttered to his fellow. "She should be wearing skirts and nursing babes and weaving, instead of strutting about this ship! The other clans must take us for fools, to have a stripling wench as our leader! 'Tis bad luck to have a woman aboard a longship—let alone as her captain!" He spat over the side, his expression dark and angry. Luck was everything to a Viking, and Karl was a man of his time.

"I did not see you protest her appointment as chieftain at the *Wapentake*, friend," the other man, steady Ragnar, countered. "Nay! You clashed your sword in agreement along with the rest of us when the vote was taken."

"Pah! The *Althing* grows weak and old-womanish," Karl argued sourly. "Too many of the council leaders have taken the soft Christian White Christ as their own, and forgotten our powerful warrior gods, else they would never have condoned a

49

woman as *jarl*. I am one amongst many. Who would hear but one voice in the clamor?"

"Think what you will, Karl," Ragnar said mildly, "but I for one can find no fault with the Lady Freya. She is as fierce in battle as was her father in his youth, and as cunning and fearless. Last year proved as much. Did she falter when we attacked that rich hamlet on the Seine? Nay! She moved forward in the van, sword raised, ahead of us all! The blood channel of her sword ran crimson with their gore . . . I say she earns our loyalty until she is proved in some way wanting! Until that time comes—if it should come—I'll follow her west over sea—or north or south or east, come to that!"

"Then you'll die a fool's and a coward's death, and end up with old Hel the Hag in the Underworld, instead of in the blessed feasting halls of Valhalla!" Karl jeered. His dark eyes grew sly. "What is it that makes ye so hot in her defense, eh, Ragnar? Have you a mind to tumble a wench that wears leggings in place of skirts, is that it?" He grinned. "If it's leggings yer after, I know of a pretty thrall lad that—"

Ragnar's fist came out and caught Karl square under the jaw, reeling him backward to the deck. The barrel of salted herring he'd been lashing in place rolled away, burst open and spilled its briny contents across the deck and across Karl.

"Why, you bastard son of Loki! I'll see your blood for that!" Karl roared, rubbing his jaw and struggling to standing.

"Come on, then!" Ragnar hissed, fists raised. "By Odin, you'll eat your words ere long—*ja*, and your mutinous tongue with them!"

But Karl raised no fists. Rather, he drew his heavy sword, *Wound-Dew Drinker*, the scrape of metal sharp on the air. Two-fisted, he swung the heavy weapon high above his head and was in the very act of bringing it down upon the unarmed Ragnar's bare head when a slender shadow fell across the pair; a second blade came out and crashed against the first as he brought it down, blocking the blow.

"Cease!" an imperious voice rang out, "or you'll want for a head, Karl, son of Ivar!"

Both men looked up to see the Lady Freya standing over them, legs braced apart, her sword in hand. Her eyes were as glacial as a fjord in winter now, ice and steel in their depths. For a second something reckless flickered in Karl's dark eyes, but was as swiftly frozen by the smile of the young woman, a mirthless, deadly smile. "Try it," she cajoled softly, "and the Valkyries will set another platter at supper in Valhalla this even!"

Karl wetted his lips, cursed under his breath, and dropped his sword with a clatter.

"Olaf!" Freya shouted, her eyes never once flickering from the glowering soldier before her.

Her second-in-command and friend since childhood, Olaf Olafson, the Oaken One, came at a run. At two-and-twenty winters, he now stood far taller than she, a massive, red-headed, red-bearded young giant nigh as broad as he was tall. His ruddy locks, worn shoulder length and raggedly trimmed, furled in the wind as he crossed the decks toward her.

"Trouble, my lady?" he demanded in a deep, resonant voice, eyes narrowing angrily as he took in the little tableau: Karl's murderous glare, Ragnar's indignant expression, the Lady Freya's tightly controlled features.

"Trouble indeed, Olaf," she agreed, jerking her head toward the two. "Despite my commands, these two worthless oafs saw fit to pick a fight on board. Bind them to the mast! Fifteen lashes each—no more, no less," she commanded curtly.

Silently, without question, Olaf nodded. He gestured to two others of the crew, who assisted him in binding the two men ready for the flogging, then took up a long-lashed whip, offering it first to Freya, then readying the whip himself to administer the punishment when she, tight-lipped, shook her head and coolly bade him see it done.

"You see!" Karl spat, fighting his bonds as a grim-faced Olaf brought the whip up over his head in one massive fist. "Do you see your wondrous lady chieftain now, and where your loyalty has brought you, you fool!"

"Thorfast himself would have done no less, and you know it!" Ragnar muttered, steeling himself for the first blow. "We knew full well what the consequences of fighting aboard ship would be, did we not?"

Their words were abruptly silenced then, swiftly replaced by

muffled, anguished groans as the fifteen lashes were adminis-
tered, for Viking pride forbade that they should screech like
beaten curs, and both men stoically smothered their pain.
After, they were cut loose and sent back to the duties assigned
them, the coarse cloth of their linen tunics stained with
ribbons of blood. But while Ragnar seemed to have accepted
the harsh punishment as his due, Karl muttered and cast
murderous side glances at the Lady Freya until he caught the
piercing attention of Olaf and hurriedly looked away.

"Would you have me lay a dozen more stripes across
Ivarson's back?" Olaf asked Freya, his eyes growing tender as
always as they lingered upon her proud, lovely face. "He yet
mutters against you."

"Nay," she denied firmly. "'Twas discipline enough to
serve as a warning, both for the two of them and the rest of the
crew. If they think to find me some milksop captain and leader,
they'll be sorely mistaken, Olaf, my friend, I promise you!"

He nodded, his bright blue eyes hooded. She was right.
Discipline was everything on a raid. But—how stern she
looked, he thought. How he longed to see her eyes grow misty
with tenderness for him, to find her soft and womanly at his
side, pleading for his kisses and caresses! Though he admired
the incredibly strong woman she had become, the valiant she-
lynx she had proven herself in battle, he dreamed of one day
having her respond to him as a woman rather than a comrade
or friend, to lie with her in a bed of warm furs and teach her the
woman's part in life. But, he had learned to his chagrin, Freya
had but one goal in life, one aim: to prove to her father—and
herself—that she was as good as any son sired from his
warrior's loins could ever have proven. Until she found the
approval she sought, he knew his cause was nigh hopeless. Nor
was he the only man who had tried to win the beautiful Freya's
heart. Nay! Many had. And as many had failed! Her rejection of
them all had earned her the name of Freya the Frozen Heart,
and it seemed a name justly given to those who knew her less
well than her friend Olaf.

Only he knew that buried deep beneath her outwardly cold
and warlike demeanor beat the tender heart of a young woman,
a wounded, closed heart, to which Thorfast alone held the key.

52

Would the day ever come when he would speak the words of love and pride his daughter ached to hear, and unlock the warmth, the tenderness and caring, so jealously guarded within? Thorfast had withdrawn into himself, was now a pitiful, blind old man who dribbled his porridge down his chin when he ate, and snapped and whined at everyone who came near him to leave him be. It was even doubtful if he knew he was no longer *jarl* of his hall, and that his daughter—the daughter he had scorned and ignored and spurned for eighteen long years—now ruled in his stead. How then could she hope to gain his approval? Like the wolves of the forest, she pined for the moon!

"Why so glum, friend Olaf?" came her low voice at his side. "The winds favor us. Thor smiles upon us. 'Twill be a good raid—I feel it in my bones! Speed on, *Wild Bird of the Wind!* Carry us swiftly to the isle of Britain!"

Olaf looked over her shoulder to where Sven, looking a little green about the gills, leaned against the gunwales. The old *skald's* expression was bleak, filled with foreboding, and uneasily Olaf wondered if, as everyone said, he could truly see into the future, and if so, what dire destiny his troubled expression might presage . . . ?

Chapter 4

To Sven, this day was a nightmare revisited. He had argued with Freya heatedly and at length until he was hoarse, but she would not listen to his pleas.

"The other raids went well this past month, did they not, girl? Our ships are filled with rich plunder, slaves and horses. 'Tis enough, Freya! Don't be foolhardy with yet another attack, and tempt the gods to desert us!"

"Hush, Uncle Sven, I know what I'm about," she had insisted stubbornly. "Look! These lands are good and sweet! See how prettily the wild flowers star the meadows and the riverbanks? See how fat the cattle and the sheep are in the fields, and how bowed are the fruit trees with their heavy blossom? We need new land for our growing people, Uncle Sven, more farms to feed and clothe them. Our own land is old and spent. Our crops are poor. Our cows sicken and die of the *vorsk*. This good new land and her bounty will be ours! I, Freya the Frozen Heart, will conquer it!"

And then, in a last, desperate attempt to dissuade her, Sven told her of that day long ago, and of how her father had once raided this same Kentish hamlet of Kenley.

"Your father, Thorfast, for all his cruelty, was a clever man in his youth. Rightly he feared the unborn cub of Aeldred who might rise up, if left to live, to slay him in retaliation for his father's death. He ordered me to kill the Lady Wilone, and thus put an end to such a threat—but I could not. My vision has warned of such a cub, as well you know. Raid farther down the coast if you must, but not here, not Kenley—!"

But ignoring his counsel, she had trod away from him across the decks and bade the longships lower their sails. Then she'd softly given the order for the men to row the vessels into the Thames river mouth and up between the green and fertile banks to the place known as Kenley, where Aeldred, ealdorman of Kent, descendant of the kings of Kent, had once been chieftain, and where Wilone, the Desired One, had bartered her body for her unborn child's life over a score of years before . . .

Trepidation filled the old *skald* as the events of that day flooded back. He remembered as clearly as if it had been but yesterday how he had gone back to the lovely, exhausted woman in the bracken, but had been unable to bring himself to kill her as Thorfast had commanded. Had Wilone perished that winter, he wondered? Or had she in truth survived to bear Aeldred's son, the cub Thorfast had so feared? If she had, it was none other's doing but his. He, Sven, was the one responsible! His bowels churned with misgivings, and damp, cold sweat broke out upon his brow and palms. His vision! It was all happening as he had foreseen—! His mind completely occupied with the turmoil of his thoughts and his fears for Freya, he did not notice when the one named Karl slipped over the longship's side at a narrow point in the river, and swam to shore.

Nor did any other man—or woman—mark his departure.

It had been a good spring since his and Cullen's return from the wars, Alaric reflected, reining in his stallion and rising in the stirrups to look out over his fertile lands. The crops of barley and oats were already sending up tender green shoots toward the sun, and the trees were weighted down with sea-foam blossom, pink and white, that gave promise of a fruitful harvest in the autumn. In the fields, newborn lambs and colts and calves frisked and gamboled with their mothers, and in the woods and along the riverbanks and the headlands, the wild flowers nodded serene pastel heads.

His lands had indeed prospered under his Uncle Ordway's

wise handling, and he was deeply grateful for his careful stewardship and wisdom. Indeed, his uncle had been all to him that a father could have been, his Aunt Valonia as loving as any mother . . .

His gray eyes darkened to slate under black, turbulent brows when he thought of his mother, for the very thought of her conjured visions that were deeply repugnant to him and caused his blood to boil with the lust for vengeance. His thoughts went back in time to that day long ago when he and his twin brother, Farant, had been summoned to his uncle's chambers.

"Alaric, Farant, my nephews, you are both grown men now," his uncle had begun, his face drawn and stern. "The time has come for you to learn the truth of what happened to your lady mother when Thorfast and his Danes last raided Kenley."

"The truth, uncle?" young Alaric had demanded, foreboding rearing its serpent's head in the pit of his gut.

"Aye," Ordway had acknowledged with a nod, his dark eyes filled with sorrow. He had turned from them, seeming unable to face them while he told the story. "You see, your lady mother is . . . not dead, as you were led to believe." Both young men had gasped, but he had continued, "The tale of her death was concocted by me to spare the two of you, in your youth and innocence, from the pain of knowing the truth."

And with these words, he had told them of Thorfast's raid upon Kenley, and all that had followed after.

His words had been like stones, dropped weightily into the deafening silence, ripples of unrest, anger, eddying throughout the room and the two youths in ever-widening circles as the import of his words registered through their stunned minds.

"You are telling us that our lady mother gave herself *willingly* to Thorfast, in exchange for her life, and thus ours?" Alaric, ever the more short-tempered of the pair, had exploded. His voice was loud yet strained, the words choked out. He saw his uncle nod, lines of pain carved into his cheeks like knife wounds, and his heart gave a great twist of guilt. For them, their mother had endured such shame. For his and Farant's lives, she had paid the greatest price a woman could pay . . .

"That two-faced Viking bastard! Is there no honor to be

56

found amongst these barbarians!" Alaric seethed, massive fists balled at his side. His gray eyes crackled with fury as he strode across the chamber, beating his fist against the palm of his other hand. "One day I'll tear his heart from his chest, aye, and his liar's tongue from his lips, I swear it on the Holy Cross!" he vowed. "The Viking blood-eagle will flap its wings against Thorfast's cursed back—or if not his, his son's—"

Farant echoed his furious words, though in lower tones, his gentle gray eyes bright and moist with unmanly tears.

"Does she yet live?" Alaric had then demanded hotly.

"She does," his uncle had confessed, his tone heavy. "She is somewhat better now, but will never again be the sister that I knew." There was deep sadness in his tone. "I escorted her to the convent northeast of here. The good sisters there have cared for her well these many years."

"I would see her," Alaric had ground out, feeling a great lump form in his throat that threatened to choke him. "I demand it!"

"And I," Farant had added, clasping his brother's shoulder to steady him, for Alaric appeared to be containing his violence only by exerting the strongest self-control.

"And so you shall," Ordway had agreed unhappily.

Some two days later they had ridden northeast to the convent, Alaric recalled, and at last, in a spartan cell, had met the woman who had given them life.

Her snow-white hair had fallen in long, thick braids over her shoulders. Her oval face had been beautiful indeed, though the burning dark eyes were sharply at odds with the ghostly pallor of her hair and milk-white complexion. They had greeted her in hushed tones, telling her with tears in their eyes that they were the sons she had borne, but she had stared at them blankly.

"Blood of my blood—stronger, far stronger than his! In the end he will see, yea, he will see!" she had muttered, her hands flying up before her face like strange, pale birds, swooping about to ward them off. "Hide them! Hsst! Make haste! The Northmen come! Hide them!"

Shocked, they had fallen back.

"Forgive me," Ordway had muttered, leading them from the spartan cell. "I should have prepared you better, but I'd thought—nay, hoped!—that seeing you, she would be different. 'Tis all my sister says now, muttering on about 'his blood' and 'her blood,' and making little of sense in her mutterings. Leave her the gifts you have brought, nephews, and we'll be gone. The good sisters will see that she receives them."

And so, stunned, they had ridden away from the convent, leaving the mantles and baskets of food they had brought.

Farant, always the quieter of the pair, had withdrawn still further into himself from that day forth. Glancing sideways, Alaric had seen how furiously his brother's jaw worked, how rapidly he blinked to control his emotions. Poor Farant, he'd thought, his own jaw clenched and jutting angrily, the shock of seeing our lady mother in her madness has been harder on him. He and I are like the two opposing sides of one coin: he tender and easily moved, his feelings worn like wounds upon his sleeve for all to see, and gentle, sensitive in every way. He will come to terms with this and find a measure of peace, while I—I can only seethe and rant with impotent rage, and yearn to sink my blade into Thorfast's foul throat!

The difference in their natures had stamped its mark upon their appearance, too, he reflected. Although he and Farant were indeed mirror images of each other in essence, both with black, curly hair, both gray-eyed, tall men, Farant was more slightly built, far less muscular and wiry than himself, and his face had a serenity that always put Alaric in mind of a saint or an apostle carved into the lid of a reliquary or upon a crucifix, while his own face, he knew, was more often than not fiercely scowling, angry at the injustices of life over which he strove to gain control; a hard, if handsome, face, some women had commented, with eyes that had seen much and knew full well that man was far, far from perfect.

Alaric's feelings for Farant had changed little with time. Aye, his brother was deserving of much—far, far more than life had given him thus far, Alaric brooded. A loving, gentle wife, for one!

What chink in Farant's character had driven him to take the Lady Kendra as his bride upon his return to Kenley, Alaric wondered, urging his stallion forward in a loose canter across the grassy meadows toward the convent? It was tantamount to mating a lamb with a she-wolf! And yet—Farant continued to love her well, to all appearances. Alaric had noted how his brother's eyes, with great tenderness in their depths, followed his lady wife; saw the little kindnesses and courtesies that Farant displayed toward her, and which she openly scorned. Nonetheless, Kendra, that panting bitch, had, as he'd half expected, attempted from the very first eve of his return from Wessex to seduce her husband's brother to her bed. She'd been incensed to learn that Alaric would have none of her!

"Nay, my Lady Kendra," he had coldly refused her blatant offer. "I'll not cuckold my own brother—albeit his lady wife has the morals of a she-cat!"

She had scowled, tawny eyes golden in the shadows of his chamber, reflecting the amber of the rush lights, and tossed back her glorious mane of black hair. "You did not refuse me before, my lord!" she'd breathed, a seductive smile curving her lips as she fingered the silver amulet at her throat. "Nay! You took me eagerly in the straw of the byre, if you recall."

"Aye. I remember well," he'd freely admitted. "But I was yet an innocent lad, and you were no man's wife then."

"And what if I am now?" she'd purred. "Farant is a good husband, a comely man—but he has not your fire nor your lustiness, my dark lord! Oh, how I hungered for you those long months after you left for Wessex, Alaric. I wanted you so! And then Farant returned, and he was so much like you, my lord . . . I wed him, when in truth 'twas thee I wanted!"

She'd sidled up against him and rubbed her woman's body against his own, until despite himself he'd felt the stirrings of lust—spurred on by memories—uncurl in his own body.

He'd turned her out of his bower with a curt dismissal, but her ploys to win him to her bed had not abated since that first night. Rather, they had gained in fervor as her desperation grew. Sooner or later the Lady Kendra would perforce have to be dealt with, once and for all, he knew, or brother would be turned against brother. Now, were she his wife—! Ah, but she was not, thanks be. And Farant would no more consider taking a whip to his wayward lady than he would spit upon a holy shrine!

He rode up to the convent, the gifts he had brought for his lady mother tucked into leather pouches that hung from his saddle. He rose in the stirrups to ring the bell that hung in a small arch cut in the stone gateway. Glancing over his shoulder, he saw that his guard of six soldiers of his garrison was only now cresting the hill above the river. It appeared they had a seventh man with them, he noted frowning, someone he did not recognize at this distance, and were hastening toward him at some speed.

The frown disappeared and he grinned in satisfaction while he waited for them to catch up with him, leaning down to stroke his stallion's arched neck, feeling with pleasure the powerful muscles rippling beneath the sleek ebony coat, full of strength and beauty, and fingering the rough black silk of its long mane. "Well done, my fleet Lucifer! Like the wolf, you have again outpaced them all!" he praised the beast, and the horse nickered in answer to his approval and gentle touch.

Just then, as he waited for his men, a young sister in a postulant's robes came to answer his summons, brown eyes widening, pale complexion turning rosy in a most unpious fashion as she saw that the handsome young ealdorman of Kent himself sat his mount outside the convent gates. She hurried to unbolt them and fling them wide, her head bowed, her fingers trembling upon locks and keys and bolts as she did so. The massive dark man upon his massive dark horse curvetted into the convent gardens.

"We did not expect you to answer our lady abbess's plea so swiftly, Your Grace, but we are indeed overjoyed that you have! According to Brother Vernon, who barely escaped with his life from the monastery at Mucking to come here and warn us, they are moving steadily down the coast, raiding and killing all in their wake!"

"And who are 'they,' Sister Ursula?" Alaric demanded, his gray eyes narrowed, his jaw tight.

From beyond the cloistered walls, the Abbess Aethelfreda's frightened voice rang out in supplication, sounding the Latin words he had prayed never to hear again:

"From the fury of the Northmen, God deliver us!"

And he knew. By God, he *knew!*

Chapter 5

The sun was high in the sky when Freya, at the head of a wedge of fierce fighting men, signaled for them to keep down, before crouching down in the cover of the bushes herself.

The *karfis* had been moored against the banks downriver, a third of her men—Uncle Sven among them—left to erect tents and guard both those and the slaves and booty taken in the past weeks, and scout the surrounding areas for horses. The others had donned *byrnies*, chain-mail tunics, and conical helmets, and taken up their bows, arrows, and other weapons and marched the last half league to the settlement. In the fore went the standard with the mighty Viking raven fluttering proudly upon it, an omen of their certain victory. As they marched, the *berserkers* had torn the shirts from their bodies and bared their chests, howling with their crazed lust for bloodshed and gnashing their teeth upon the blades of the *franciscas* and broadswords that they brandished like men driven mad.

The heady wine of danger and excitement flowed strongly through Freya's veins too, yet she frowned as she cocked her red-gold head to one side and listened. All was still. Not a hound barked warning of their coming. Not a single sentry gave voice to an alarm. She glanced across at the standard, and a lurch of apprehension suddenly twisted in her belly, for the raven no longer fluttered proudly upon it, but seemed strangely still and cowed, a portent that surely boded naught but ill fortune!

She wetted her lips. Like Heimdall, guardian of the rainbow

bridge that led from Asgard, home of the Norse gods, to the mortal world, she fancied she could even hear the grass growing, so absolute was the hush . . . Aye, that was it—it was *too* still! At this time of day there should have been people about; women drawing water, children playing, smoke rising up from the cooking fires—at least a sentry or two patrolling the earthworks and ramparts of the heavily fortified great hall that rose black against the sky. Instead, there was nothing. No one!

"I don't like it," she whispered to Olaf, who led the second wedge of men alongside her own.

"No more do I!" he agreed fervently, eyeing their ominously drooping banner askance.

"Signal your men to fall back," she hissed. "I'll do likewise. We'll send a man ahead to scout the settlement before we attack." She looked all about her, hackles rising and prickling at her nape as she realized that one of her men was missing. "Karl Ivarson—where is he?" she asked, cold chills of alarm suddenly sweeping through her like icy winds from the north.

Olaf shrugged. His bearded face grew grim. "I know not!"

"Ask of the other leaders if—!"

There was no further time for words, for even as she spoke she saw the Saxons ringing them behind, heard the clinking of their coats of mail, the snorts of their horses. They were surrounded! The settlement's deserted appearance had been nothing but a Saxon trick, her mind registered as she sprang to her feet, her double-edged broadsword, *Shining One,* brandished aloft in her two fists.

All at once there were Saxons everywhere in the woods, springing up like weeds, armed, like the Vikings, with axes and broadswords, slingshots and spears. Several of them were mounted, giving them the advantage. There was no time to nock arrows against bowstrings and pick off the farthest men, no choice but to engage the enemy immediately in fierce hand-to-hand combat! With great howls the *berserkers* charged, hacking to left and right. The rest of Freya's party surged after them, screaming curses and roaring their war cries. The crash and clash of steel against steel, of shield against spear tips, and the groans and screams of the wounded and dying soon echoed amongst the leafy tree tops. The bosses of shields and the spearheads, the jeweled hilts of their swords and helmets, flashed in the sunlight as they battled, and hoarse cries of "Odin!" and others of "God, deliver us!" were abruptly torn from lips soon to be silenced forever. The raven standard and its bearer toppled, and were trampled underfoot in the bloody skirmish.

"Jorgensen!" Freya screamed, eyes aflame, pride swirling like fire through her veins, and leaped to meet the Saxon swine who came at her with his sword held waist high and ready, nimbly dancing sideways and bringing up her small, round wooden shield to block the cruel sweep of his blade—for therein lay her warrior's skill: in her speed and agility.

His sword slammed against her shield. The ringing force of the blow ran up the length of her arm and numbed her fingers, which tingled painfully. She groaned, then bit her lip. Recovering swiftly, she danced out of reach. Her sidestep carried her across and forward, and with deadly grace she flung around and hacked him down from the side. He fell, blood spraying. She twisted back, turning immediately to the next man. Off to her left she glimpsed Olaf in the heat of battle, red hair and red beard flying out from beneath his bronze helmet as he swung his mighty battle-axe in great arcs that made the very air sing with its passage, and sent gore spattering in crimson gouts across the greensward and over the bodies of the fallen, Saxon and Viking alike. His opponent fell, and he whirled to take on another.

"Alaric, Bear of Kent!"

With this roared battle cry, a man sprang from the back of a snorting black war-stallion to take on Olaf the Oaken on foot, in hand-to-hand combat. He was easily as big as the Viking, and as magnificent, broad of shoulder and heavily muscled, yet for all his great size he moved with a warrior's virile grace. His curling hair furled like a standard in the wind, and was as ebony as the raven's wings. His grimly handsome face was stern and determined, the arms below his tunic bulging and knotted with cords as the first blows were struck, the strident ring of metal upon metal sounding sharp and clear on the air. His eyes flashed like the silver glint of a steel blade in the sunlight as he parried and swung.

The Saxon and Olaf were like the spirited wild stallions her father had been wont to match in combat for his sport, though it was sword or axe they flailed, not hooves, and it was axe and sword they gnashed, not fiercely bared teeth, Freya thought fleetingly, dispatching another of the Saxon number!

"Cullen of Kenley!" yet another attacker roared, and lunged at her, forcefully jerking her thoughts back to the battle at hand.

With naught but a hairbreadth saving her, she twisted sideways, feeling the rush of air disturbed by the heavy blade whistling past her cheek. She brought her sword across, yet found no target, for the stroke was expertly blocked by Cullen's broad blade, and metal rang against metal. Before she could recover he pressed his advantage, slamming her against the ribs with the flat of his weighty weapon in a blow that drove the breath from her body and sent stars of pain ricocheting through her. Like a felled wand, she sprawled backward to the grass. Cullen of Kenley fell heavily upon her and straddled her hips, raising his broadsword above his head to deliver the death stroke that would sever her head from her slender neck.

His heavy weight crushed her, robbed her of breath and strength. She couldn't move, could scarce breathe! *Blessed Frey, guardian of woman, help me, give me strength!* she screamed silently, straining until sweat bled from her brow to throw him off. Death was imminent. With awful certainty, she saw his arm begin its descent as if motion were slowed; dimly heard Olaf's bellow of rage nearby, followed by a strangled groan; saw the steel wink silver fire in the sunlight as the blade arced down—

"In God's Name, nay!" roared a voice, a dear, familiar voice, and a strangled cry escaped her as another body intruded itself between the blade and her own. Her nostrils were filled suddenly with the dear scent of her beloved Sven—and by the rank coppery stink of his blood as the Saxon blade cleaved into his shoulder and back. The one named Cullen flung the old man aside, disgust curling his lips as he clambered to his feet, looming over the fallen pair. He had raised his sword a second time to deal Freya the death blow, when the wounded man's eyes flickered open, filled with pleading.

"Pray, sir, nay!" he whispered in the Saxon tongue. "Spare her!"

Cullen's brows arched upward in grim amazement. "Her?" he growled, and extended the toe of his booted foot to roughly nudge the helmet from Freya's head, revealing her lovely woman's face and a tumble of red-gold hair. "Ah!" he roared, grinning. "A wench!"

"Spare her, I beg thee," the old man repeated, his voice quavering, "as I once spared Wilone of Kenley from Thorfast many years hence!"

"You were he, old man? The one named Sven?" Cullen, who knew full well the story, demanded incredulously.

The graybeard closed his eyes and nodded weakly, his hand fluttering to his shoulder to staunch the red flood that seeped through the cloth of his mantle and escaped in trickles between his fingers. "*Ja*, 'twas I," he acknowledged feebly. "She—she is the daughter—the only daughter—of the *jarl* Thorfast Jorgensen, he whom the—the Saxons once called 'The Treacherous.'"

Cullen was stunned, yet not so stunned he did not notice the warrior maid stealthily reaching for her fallen weapon. Like lightning his booted foot came out, clamping down heavily upon her wrist so that she cried out in sudden agony.

"Nay, wench, not so fast!" he growled. "If what the old one says is true, my lord will want you taken alive!"

"Never!" she seethed in the Saxon tongue—not unlike her own—that Sven had taught her long ago. "I am armed as a man, and I can fight like any man! Let me up and I will prove it to thee, Saxon dog—else I will also die like a man!" Her deep blue eyes glittered with hatred.

Cullen chuckled grimly at her fierceness, then shook his head. "Nay, wench." He glanced about him, then suddenly bent and swept her up into his arms, tossing her casually over his shoulder like a sack of grain. Despite her struggles to free herself and her outraged curses and screams, he bore her rapidly from the woods to where other Saxons waited, older men and boys for the most part, and at their feet he dropped her without ceremony. "Guard her well!" he growled. "If she escapes, 'twill be on your heads!" And with that, he returned to the bloody battle being waged in the woods.

By dusk, an eerie silence had settled over the still woods. The slick, red-soaked grass was churned and littered with bodies, twisted and broken in the obscene postures of death, and strewn with bloodied weapons. The greater number were Viking dead, recognizable by the green cross-gaiters they wore over their leggings, and by their beards and shaggy heads. The air reeked foully with the scent of blood and carnage as Alaric strode between the bodies. His tunic was torn and ringed with sweat, his dark hair sodden, yet his eyes were alive, lit inwardly with the victor's glow.

"We vanquished them, cousin, though they outnumbered us two to one!" he murmured.

"Aye, sir," Cullen agreed. "And our own losses were small. We've taught these Danish sea-wolves a lesson they'll never forget! They'll think twice before they invade our coasts again!"

"How many lost?"

"Twelve, sir. There are four more gravely wounded who might yet join them."

"Twelve good men! Twelve *charls* gone, good farmers who answered my summons to fight, and will never return to till their lands and feed their families again. Only twelve—but 'tis twelve too many, Cullen," Alaric growled.

"Indeed it is sir. But—" and he grinned, "—I have something to show you that I think will please you nonetheless."

"What?"

"Come with me, to where the horses are tethered."

"I am battle-weary, cousin, and in no mood for children's guessing games. What secret is this?" Alaric demanded impatiently as they strode from the woods.

"Look, sir, over there!"

Alaric looked, his brows lowering as he saw a slender wench, dressed in a man's leggings and tunic and byrnie, bound securely to a tree. Her hair made a bright splash of color against the dark greenery in the fading light. Her eyes, even from this distance, burned with rage at her capture.

66

"A captive woman who dresses like a man?" Alaric shook his head. "Take her as *your* prize, if you would have her, Cullen. Give me instead the warm and willing, comely wenches of Kent to warm my bed!" He winked. "With them, a man can at least be certain by their skirts that they are women!" With a weary grin he made to turn away toward the horses, but Cullen grasped him by the shoulder and stayed him.

"Nay, cousin, I took her captive for you," he insisted. "She is not just any woman, you see, sir. She is the daughter of one on whom you have long sworn to take vengeance."

"Not Thorfast's daughter?" Alaric asked, incredulous, glancing intently across at the wench.

"Aye," Cullen acknowledged, grinning at Alaric's sudden surge of interest. "None other!"

The first indication that Freya was not alone in the byre—where she had been roughly marched at spear point after the bloody battle—came when a massive shadow fell across the earthen floor before her, blocking out the light from the narrow wind-eye. She glanced up, eyes widening at what she saw.

A man loomed before her, legs braced apart like sturdy tree trunks. And what a man was this! Her gaze traveled up his great height to strong thighs encased in fitted leggings and a powerful torso emphasized by a tunic of darkest violet blue, on over a broad, bear-like chest across which a pair of well-muscled arms were folded above a light blue mantle, pinned by a large silver brooch at his right shoulder. The edges of the mantle were embroidered with bands of flowers worked in silver wire. His upper arms bulged under the fitted cloth of the tunic, while his lower arms were deeply tanned and corded with sinew, lightly forested with springy black hair. Farther up, Freya's fearful glance came upon a square, determined chin and jaws, clean shaven but with a marked swarthy blue shadow. A strong, straight nose jutted out above lips that were narrow without appearing thin, set now in a hard, straight slash against the tanned, weathered flesh. Eyes the hue of wood smoke burned into hers from beneath lowering black brows, which, contrasted against the tan of his broad, noble brow, were like the dark flirting of ravens' wings above each smoky orb. Curling black hair, so black it reflected captured blue lights in its ebony depths, capped his manly visage and fell in inky commas about his ears. A wide circlet of chased silver, set with rough-cut gemstones, banded his forehead and betrayed his ealdorman's rank, as did his silver wristbands. She recognized him as the one Olaf had battled, though she had not guessed his identity then.

"So," she breathed, "you are the great Alfred's viceroy, Alaric!" The bitterness and scorn in her tone was keener than a steel blade. "What do you here in my humble cell, Saxon lord? Is it time now to bring your enemy low? To avenge the murders of your father, your brothers, through me, Thorfast's daughter? How, great Lord of Kenley? In torture? Death? Ravishment? Do your damnedest! I am not afraid of you—and nor will I ever grovel at your feet and beg for mercy!"

With a great show of bravado that was at odds with the quiver that had darted through her belly at first sight of him, she tossed her tangled hair over her shoulders and defiantly dragged herself up from the cold earthen floor to stand before him, preferring to face him squarely, eye to eye. But that was not to be. She reached only to his shoulder, she realized, although she was a tall woman, and was forced, curse him, to look up at him. For all his great build, there was not an ounce of spare flesh on him that she could discern. His battle name— the Bear—was one well given . . .

"Death would be a welcome escape from me for the daughter of Thorfast, would it not?" he said, menace in his deep voice. "And I fancy for all your brave words, you would not long withstand torture." His eyes flickered calculatingly over her, but were without expression. "So it has been decided by my council that you shall live, Freya the Frozen Heart, to serve me as slave in any manner I might deem fitting."

"*Ja!*" she jeered, fists planted on her slender hips. "I have no illusions as to what manner you might 'deem fitting,' my lord!" A shudder ran through her, quickly covered. She lied! Oh, Blessed Odin, how she lied! Fearing no man in battle until now, she nonetheless feared rape at the hands of this one with

68

the burning gray eyes that seemed to see straight into her soul. "I'll die first!"

Suddenly she sprang across the byre with lithe, feline grace, her hand swooping to the dagger thrust into his belt. Her fingers had closed triumphantly about the jeweled hilt before his hand moved to close over her fist. With little effort he squeezed, his steely grip rendering her fingers numb in less than the twinkling of an eye. With a pained yelp and a curse, she released the weapon and felt it slide from her grip back into its short leather scabbard. She cursed again as with little effort he forced her onto her knees at his feet. He then leaned down and knotted his fingers in the silken mass of her red-gold hair, dragging her to her feet by its fiery reins alone. Her head jerked back as she glared into his eyes, her own jewel eyes spitting sapphire hatred, her lips peeled back from her even white teeth in a rictus of loathing that savagely marred her vivid beauty.

"Kill me!" she seethed. "Go on, Saxon, finish me! What are you waiting for?"

His hot breath came rasping against the pallid coolness of her cheek. "Nay, my Viking wildcat, you'll not die! Not by your own hand, nor any other's, I'll see to that. But—" and now his own cruel smile partnered hers, "—you'll come to wish you had!"

"Barbarian!" she seethed. "Saxon swine!" She spat full in his face and both hands clawed to rake his cheeks with her nails.

Alaric, naught but the twitch of a muscle at his temple betraying his amusement, reached out and gripped her by the wrists, easily wrenching her arms down to her sides.

"Man you might strive to become, Freya of the Frozen Heart—yet you are not man enough!" he mocked.

Faces scant inches apart now, their eyes met: his a smoldering, silvery gray beneath stormy black brows and impossibly long, ebony lashes; hers a fierce, glittering sapphire framed in tawny red-gold that seemed to blaze like blue fire in the gloom of the byre, and strike murderous sparks against the flint of his. With a growl he jerked her toward him, dragging her slender, rigid body against his length. The curse had scarce been torn from her enraged lips when he lowered his dark head

69

to the flame of hers and forced his mouth over her own, his muscled arms holding her fiercely against him, arching her body as it pleased him against his own hard frame.

With helpless rage she seethed under his kisses, hating the insolent intimacy of his cruel, masterful lips upon hers, his breath mingling with her own, the ungentle dominance of his lean fingers where they knotted in her hair. She twisted her head, trying to sink her teeth into his lips or tongue, but failed, infuriated to hear mocking laughter from him. She drew back her booted foot and kicked him hard in the shins time after time, frantically tossed her head from side to side to evade those hateful lips and kisses, squirmed her hips in an effort to slip free of his arms—yet it was all to no avail. She heard yet another low, triumphant laugh from deep in his throat as she finally surrendered, exhausted by her efforts, and remained still, though fury yet filled her. Her stillness relaxed his guard. Like a cornered vixen, she at once lashed out with her teeth, sinking them deep into the tender flesh of his lips as they moved over her mouth and joyfully tasted his warm, coppery blood on her tongue. Saxon blood . . .

"Vixen bitch!" he gasped, and added a pained, muffled oath, jerking away from her and lifting his fist to his mouth to gauge the damage. He drew it away, the knuckles crimson with blood.

Hands on hips, she glowered at him, a scornful smile curving her generous mouth. "Man enough to match you after all, 'twould seem, *ja*, Saxon?" she taunted, knowing she played with fire and courted certain burning, but unable to silence her incendiary tongue. Her long, shapely legs were braced arrogantly apart as she faced him, a profoundly masculine stance that, had she but known it, somehow only served to underscore her true gender, for it accented the thrust of her firm young breasts against the tight-fitting, blood-stained kirtle, and the sleek, rounded curves of her womanly hips, despite her attire. She tossed the red-gold mane away from her eyes, watching him warily. What would he do next? How would he react to her reckless resistance to him? Dared she hope for a quick and speedy end, she wondered, suddenly breathless.

To her surprise—and no little alarm—Alaric smiled.

70

"Man?" He chuckled, then the chuckle became a deep rumble of amused laughter. "A man? Nay, wench, you are of a certainty no man, for all your arrogant protests to the contrary! You may well have swung a sword on the battlefield a time or two, but you fight like a *woman* when cornered," he jeered, "with tooth and claw! Moreover, no *lad* was ever cursed with fine, full teats such as those that seek escape from your kirtle . . . and which I will fondle at my will, ere long!" His gray eyes feasted on those thrusting mounds with wolfish pleasure.

"Never!" she screeched. "I'll die first!" She lunged at him, cheeks flaming, eyes sparkling furiously with indignation at his taunts.

Instinctively Alaric raised his arms to shield his face from her claws. In so doing, his weighty elbow clipped her solidly beneath the chin, jerking her head sharply backward. With a peculiarly childlike sigh, she crumpled to the dirt and lay still.

Unconscious, she seemed far smaller and less worthy of his vengeance than awake, and for a fleeting second the iron gray of his eyes softened, lingering on the wealth of red-gold tresses that sprayed their fire across the straw and dung and drew the eye down to the rounded curve of her shoulder and the creamy swell of her breast where the rough woolen tunic gaped. His thirst for vengeance was tempered now by stirrings of lust.

"As your sire ravished my own lady mother, so will it be for you, Thorfast's daughter," he gritted. Then he spun about on his heel and left the byre.

Chapter 6

Freya awoke to the sensation of wetness and rubbing, of hands moving with little gentleness over her, to find that while she had lain dead to the world she had been taken somewhere else—to a bower within the towering fortress of Kenley, she surmised. There was a dull throbbing in her head and a less dull ache in her jaw where the Saxon's elbow had clipped her. Sitting up, she thrust away the hands and cloths that moved over her body, and rubbed her soreness.

"Let me be!" she hissed. "Don't touch me!"

An ancient serving wench leaned over where she lay upon a rough, unpillowed sleeping bench. "You'll do as I say, Viking wench! My lord has ordered that the filth be bathed from your body, and bathed you will be!" A pair of bright blue eyes gleamed determinedly from amidst a crab-apple face.

"Aye, *Lady* Freya," jeered a second voice. "And when you are clean and fit to be mounted, you will be taken to our lord, to serve his . . . pleasure."

Freya's head jerked about to see who the owner of this second, huskily mocking voice might be, and found herself staring into spiteful golden eyes framed by a mass of ebony hair. The voluptuously beautiful woman, richly robed in emerald and saffron, her hair, fingers, and throat ablaze with jewels, stood aloofly across the bower from her. "And who might you be?" she demanded. A wicked light kindled in her own eyes. "One of the ealdorman's Saxon whores?"

The woman's jaw tightened, and Freya knew by the sudden

firing in those golden orbs that her gibe had struck home. It was all the woman could do to control her emotions, to resist springing across the bower and scoring her talons down Freya's cheeks! The knowledge gave her perverse pleasure.

"I am the Lady Kendra, wife to our lord's brother, Farant. You would do well to curb your tongue, wench. Slaves who displease me are dealt with swiftly and harshly in this household."

"Aye, no doubt they are," Freya agreed, mocking the other woman with her sapphire eyes and a contemptuous curl to her lips. "All she-cats have claws!"

A dark flush rose up the beautiful older woman's face, and her hands balled into fists at her sides. She turned away, moving across the rushes with angry grace. "See that she is brought to Lord Alaric very soon, Lona." She turned back to face Freya. "I am certain he is most eager to begin her taming! We will see how bold she is on the morrow, will we not?"

The old serving woman cackled with obscene laughter.

Despite Freya's bravery, the woman Kendra's words struck icy tremors in the pit of her belly. Her taming! Her tongue dabbed nervously at her dry lips and she swallowed with effort, unable to still the sudden trembling to her limbs. By Odin's beard, how they quivered! Yet she would not be humbled, nay, no matter what the price. She was Viking, Viking to the core! She would give no quarter, not so long as there was life and breath left in her body!

She closed her eyes and lay back, letting the hideously wrinkled old crone clean the battle filth from her body while she tortured herself with visions of being impaled beneath that great bear of a brute's body. Oh, dear Uncle Sven, she cried silently, if only I had heeded the warning of your vision! If only I had listened to your words, instead of blindly following my will, you would not now be dead, and I would not be here! So many good, loyal men had followed her to their deaths—noble warriors' deaths with sword in hand that would bring them safe into Valhalla, 'twas true, but deaths nonetheless—and because of her obstinacy, and one man's enmity, because of the treacherous one named Karl's hatred of her—their deaths had all been for naught.

"You are ready, girl," the servant muttered, having raked a carved wooden comb through Freya's tangled hair. "Here, give me your wrists."

Freya returned from her gloomy musings with a start, to see that the woman held out a length of lightweight chain to which wristbands of iron were attached. She looked wildly about her, and the old woman smiled. "Let no thought of flight or refusal enter your head, my pretty. There are guards without these chambers. They have been instructed to prevent your escape from here in any manner, short of your death, that they deem fitting. I would advise you to yield, or it will be the worse for ye."

Freya turned her face from the old woman, unwilling to have her see the bleak despair she knew filled her eyes. "Very well," she murmured at length, tossing the red-gold curtain away from her face. Her chin came up defiantly. "Give me some garments to put on, and I will don these Saxon bracelets."

"No garments," the old woman said with finality, and grinned a toothy smile. "My lord left orders that you were to be brought to him stripped naked of all coverings—save for these bonds." Her heart gave a momentary stir of pity for the captive maid, but the stirring was quickly staunched. Had not this one's sire killed her charge Wilone's first two babes, the infants she'd wet-nursed at her own bosom, the dear little lads she'd loved as her own? Had Thorfast not brutally slain their father, Aeldred, the ealdorman, and driven his lovely Wilone to madness with his rape, forcing her to seek out the spartan comfort of a convent's cold walls? Whatever means Alaric might employ to break this one's spirit, to destroy that fierce Viking will and humble it to his bidding, he had old Lona's blessing! "Quickly, now," she urged, her tone colder than before, "my lord is not one who takes kindly to being kept waiting."

Freya felt dizziness overwhelm her. Heat flamed in her cheeks. The shame of it, to be brought naked and in chains to her enemy's bed! She could not do it. Nay, she would not!

She sprang to her feet, snatched up the pottery basin of bathing water, and hurled it into the old hag's face, then flung

74

about and flew to the curtained doorway, thrusting it aside. At once two rough guards stepped forward, spears in hand, to block her escape. Their eyes kindled eagerly at sight of her shapely bare body, and the lust raged beastlike there as they came toward her.

"Now, wench, there'll be no escaping us," one growled. "What has she done to ye, Lona?"

Old Lona tore the sodden coverchief from her bald head and tossed it aside, wiping her streaming face on her apron. "Naught much, to her disappointment, no doubt," she muttered irritably. "The chains! See them fastened, then take her to the hall."

Hands reached greedily for Freya's limbs, and though she struggled wildly she could not writhe free of the two burly men.

"Ah, 'tis a lucky man our lord will be tonight," one of the louts muttered, grinning wolfishly into her furious, flaming face as he clamped one of the iron bands about her wrist. "Mayhap he'll give us brave lads a taste o'this when he's had his fill . . ." As he drew his hand away, he let his rough fingers graze the curve of her breast, and tittered as the nipple puckered at his touch, eyeing his companion knowingly. "On yer feet, slave!"

He jerked her to standing. The chains bit cruelly into her wrists, but she gritted her teeth and muffled the gasp of pain that hissed from between her lips. "One day you'll pay for this!" she seethed. "On the Hammer of Thor, I swear it!"

"Nay, wench, 'tis *you* who'll be payin'—and on our lord's mighty 'hammer,' not your pagan Thor's!" The man tittered, and prodded her in the back with his spear. "Aye, Alaric the Bear will exact a goodly price from your comely flesh, slut! Get along with you!"

With countless crude insults and no little rough handling, she was taken, naked and in chains, from the bower and across the bailey, then inside to the hall proper and to the great chamber that was its heart.

To her growing horror, she saw that the vast aisled hall was filled with the members of Lord Alaric's court. Richly dressed men and women were seated at long benches spread with a sumptuous feast. Maids and menservants hovered at their elbows with ready flagons. But all turned with one accord to gaze upon her as she faltered in the wide entranceway.

Tapestries splashed their vivid color upon the smoke-blackened walls, and the wooden moldings were richly carved, she noted dully. Brilliant jewels winked and flashed in a blaze of light from the fingers and brows of the women and the sword hilts of the men. Goblets and bowls gleamed with golden light. Rushes, sweet-smelling herbs, and fragrant flower petals were strewn lavishly upon the earthen floor. Everything she saw, everywhere she chanced to look, boasted of the wealth and power of the man who was lord here, curse him!

Beyond, at the far end of the hall to the left of Alaric's high seat, heavily guarded and also chained, stood Olaf, dark blood staining his red hair. Beside him she recognized one other, this one free as a bird, the traitor Karl Ivarson, a brimming drinking horn in his fist, a leering smile spreading his lips wide!

The sight of the hated Karl, free to come and go as he pleased while her dear friend stood bound and humbled at his side, filled her with a courage she had not known she possessed until that moment. She straightened her shoulders, drawing herself erect and proud, shrugged off the marauding hands of her guards, and began the longest walk of her life, across the rushes and down the very center aisle of the vast hall, between the carved posts that towered like an avenue of straight trees on either side, to where the chieftain, Alaric, waited upon his high carved wooden chair.

The harpist ceased his playing, and the sudden silence trembled in the aftermath of his last note. A murmur grew in the hall, swelling as the lovely, naked Viking maid moved with grace and pride through their midst, seemingly oblivious of the hot eyes of the men feasting upon her nakedness and of the jealous spite in the eyes of the women, who—to their disappointment—found her beauty flawless in both face and form.

Despite himself, Alaric was moved to grudging admiration for the Viking wench. Though he had sought to humble her spirit by having her brought naked before him, she had, he realized, with her fierce pride and grace, neutralized in part his

76

intent by her regal bearing alone.

He watched her advance through hooded eyes, noting the way her lovely red-gold hair sprang away from her temples and brow with vigor, as if alive, before tumbling down past her shoulders in tempestuous waves. He found himself wondering how it would feel to twine those shining tendrils about his fingers, and a hot fire swept through him, centering its heat in his loins. His gaze dropped to the full curves of her breasts, drinking in their tempting creamy pallor, like fresh water pearls, and their inviting softness. His gray eyes smoldered like banked coals as he imagined how it would be to feast his mouth upon the pert, impudent buds that peeked rose pink from amidst the streamers of hair, or to part those slender, straight thighs and breach the womanhood that was crowned with red and gold curls as was her lovely head.

Slender-waisted yet womanly of hip, she came at last to a halt before him, flung back her glorious hair and faced him proudly, fists on hips despite her chains, her eyes hurling a challenge into his. *Take me*, they seemed to say, *yet you will never, never own me!*

And his smoky eyes darkened, accepting the challenge and flinging back an arrogant one of his own. *Aye, I shall take you, Freya of Danehof, and you will be tamed—by my hand and at my will!*

The color in her pale cheeks deepened furiously as she read that burning, masterful glance, and for a fleeting second her rigid composure was lost. She felt small and vulnerable and afraid—oh, so very afraid! She looked wildly about her, seeking and finding Olaf's sky-blue eyes boring into her own. Momentarily she was struck breathless by the helpless fury in their depths. "Forgive me!" she mouthed silently. A flicker of a change in his expression, and she knew that Olaf's anger was directed not at her but at Karl, who had betrayed them all, and to the Saxon lord who had sworn to dishonor her. Her heart went out to him, her dear, loyal Olaf, friend of her lonely childhood, and for a second she came perilously close to the foolish, feminine weakness of tears.

"My people!" rang out Alaric's deep, resonant voice. "You see before you the only child of Thorfast the Treacherous,

77

chieftain of the Viking sea-wolves who raided our lands nigh a score and seven years past. Some of us lost mothers and fathers, brothers or sisters, wives and little ones to the Norse attack. Thorfast showed them no mercy—as this day I have shown his men no mercy! Their dragon-ships have been burned, their slaves freed, their booty recaptured. Their broken pagan bodies lie unshriven in the woods, carrion for the crows, the ravens, and the wolves of the forest. All are dead or scattered, save for the three you see before you now: the redbeard, Olaf the Oaken One; Freya the Frozen Hearted, the *jarl* Thorfast's own daughter; and the traitor, Karl, son of Ivar.

"Thorfast himself has grown old and sickly now, and no longer goes a-Viking. Yet will I have our revenge on him! It is my decision to let the one named Olaf live. He will return to the Danish viper's nest from whence they came, and tell his *jarl* that his cherished warrior-daughter is now my slave—in all ways!"

He stepped down from the dais and strode across to Freya, cupping her chin in his large hand and squeezing cruelly as he jerked her head up so that he might look into her blazing sapphire eyes. "He will tell Thorfast that Alaric, ealdorman of Kent, viceroy to Alfred, *Bretwalda* of Wessex, takes his pleasure upon the body of Freya, his daughter! That the slave, Freya, his *own daughter*, Freya," he taunted mockingly, his hand sliding down her body to cup her bare breast, "will this very night surrender her maidenhead to me, her lord and master. Henceforth she will do my bidding, and will await my every pleasure with eagerness, as befits a bower slave."

"*No!*" A great roar came from Olaf, who would have flung himself upon the lord and throttled him barehanded, were he not chained. At once several guards came forward and dragged him, struggling, back. He was roaring curses in a mighty voice that shook the rafters and sent the hounds whining to the corners. "Your ploy will not work, Saxon! I will tell Thorfast nothing! Kill me and set her free, Alaric of Kent!"

A cruel smile curved Alaric's lips, and his hand continued its possessive, casual, insolent caresses of the girl's trembling body. "Ah! Your life for the maid's? Such love for your leader? Surely your loyalty goes beyond a Viking warrior's vow to serve his lord—or lady?"

"I deny nothing! I love the Lady Freya more than life itself!" Olaf gritted through clenched jaws. His fists were massively balled against his thighs. "Enslave me, torture me, if you would bring shame upon the house of Thorfast, for my own father was among Thorfast's men that day your father was killed. But Freya—she was not yet born! The faults of her father are not her faults. In Odin's name—in the name of your White Christ—free her!"

"Nay, Olaf. 'Twill be as I have said," Alaric said softly, releasing the furious, seething young woman and insolently thrusting her from him with a lingering smile that threatened more to come anon. He strode across to the red-bearded one and they exchanged hate-filled glances, eye to eye. "You will go free." Alaric turned to Karl. "As will you. You will leave my burh by dusk this very day. Or you will both suffer torture and death. Tell all whom you meet that Alaric, Bear of Kent, shows no mercy to Viking offal, be they male or female—even as the *jarl* Thorfast once showed the people of Kenley no mercy!" Behind Alaric, his Uncle Ordway, brother to the Lady Wilone, smiled and nodded with grim satisfaction.

A mighty roar of approval went up from the gathering, filling the hall to the rafters. Alaric waited until it had died away. "Release them!" he barked to the guards. "See them sent on their way!"

Karl eyed Olaf's murderous expression, and nervously wetted his lips, paling beneath his beard. "But—but sir, I was given to understand that I would receive reward and—and sanctuary here in return for the information I gave ye?" he spluttered.

"Indeed?" Alaric jeered, scorn curling his lips. "Do you take me for a fool, Karl Ivarson, to harbor a man who would turn traitor in our midst? Be gone! With the luck of your pagan gods on your side, you may escape your fellow Norseman—for a while." His gray eyes burned.

Turning to the leering guards at the captive maid's sides, he ordered, "Take her to my chamber!"

Farant came forward to stand at his brother's side as the captive maid was taken away amidst the hoots and jeers of the gathering. "You will use her cruelly," he said softly, a statement rather than a question, "in revenge for what befell our lady mother."

"I will," Alaric agreed, his expression cold and stern. "And in any manner I deem fitting. She will rue the day she led her sea-wolves upriver to Kenley!"

His brother frowned, the gray eyes—so like Alaric's own—darkening with sorrow. "Alaric, I urge you to think on this before you act in haste," Farant cautioned. "You intend to exact blood-vengeance for our father, our brothers, our lady mother. But—revenge cannot bring them back, cannot restore life to dead bodies, nor sanity to the insane! You have captured the maid, slain her followers, burned her ships. It is enough. Why not turn this moment into yet another small victory for Alfred? She is the daughter of a Viking *jarl*, a lady of the Viking nobility, is she not? Then offer her to Guthrum as hostage in exchange for ransom. Or demand *wergild* of him for our dead, and set her free. Use her capture for the good of the living—not to avenge the dead, who are gone beyond caring!"

A muscle in Alaric's jaw twitched. Give up the maid, untouched, in return for silver and gold? When their own mother had suffered repeated ravishment at her father Thorfast's hands, and would never again be as other women? When even now—aye, even now—he lusted hotly for her? His gray eyes were cold and gray as the North Sea when he turned to look back at Farant, and his brother shivered to think that they could be so chillingly different, and yet so uncannily similar.

"I am ealdorman here, brother, not you." Alaric spoke in low tones, yet each word carried weight. "'Tis for me to decide what will be done with the captive—and I say she shall not go free! If you have naught else to occupy your time save meddling in matters that do not concern you, see it better spent in diverting your lady wife—lest she find others to divert her in your stead."

Farant flushed darkly, eyes crackling, and in anger they were, for a fleeting second, more alike than they had ever been.

"You are wearied from the rigors of battle this morn, and not yourself, brother," Farant gritted. "I will forgive you your words, spoken in anger—this time. Should there be a next time, should you again force my hand, I can offer no guarantee that I will do so! Kendra is my lady wife. No man shall malign her in word or deed without answering to me—not even if that man be my own brother."

Alaric cursed inwardly, his anger dwindling as rapidly as it had surged through him. How had they come to this sad pass? Kendra would soon have them at each other's throats, one way or another, if he were not careful! He reached out and clamped a heavy hand over Farant's shoulder. "Forgive me, brother. I'm in truth more weary than I knew. Perhaps 'twould be better for all of us if you and your lady and certain of your household were to leave here for some few weeks—perhaps visit Alfred's court in Winchester? The journey would be a pleasant one at this time of year, and I'm certain your lady wife would take pleasure in meeting and conversing with Queen Ealhswith and her women, while you would enjoy the company of Alfred's learned teacher, Asser, with whom you have much in common. A change of scenery and company would benefit us all, I believe."

"Do you ask me, brother—or command me?" Farant demanded tensely.

"I ask," Alaric confirmed. "'Twill be for the best."

Slowly, Farant nodded. "Very well. 'Tis agreed then. I shall commence the necessary preparations for the journey on the morrow." Alaric grunted agreement and made to leave. "One thing more!" Farant called after him.

"Aye?"

"I—would not depart with discord between us, brother."

Alaric strode back to his side, and took his brother's shoulders in a fierce bear hug, which Farant wholeheartedly returned. "There is none in my heart, Farant," he disclosed, his voice husky with emotion.

"Nor in my own."

With that reassurance, Alaric left him and made his way to a small area at the rear of his fortress, formerly used as a storeroom, where the wounded from the morning's battle were being tended by his Aunt Valonia and her serving women. Assuring himself first that the brave men who had rallied to his

81

call to fight and had fallen were being well cared for, he then moved to the last straw pallet.

"So. How are your wounds, old man?" Alaric demanded, oak-sturdy legs spread, fists on hips as he looked down at the shrunken, waxy figure.

"'Old man' indeed!" his Aunt Valonia scolded from across the dimly lit chamber that smelled of grain and beer. "Do you forget that, but for this man, your lady mother might even now be dead? He has a name, as do you. Use it, pray."

Alaric smiled, the engaging, sheepish smile of a little boy, and Valonia wondered, not for the first time, at what a strange combination of great, playful lad and ruthless soldier he was. Ah, but it was a dangerous, deceptive combination, she thought as she bustled about the narrow chamber, as many had learned too late. She shook her head. Farant and he were so different in all but appearance, Farant by far the more gentle and quieter-natured of the two, much preferring to pore over texts and manuscripts than do battle. To be in his presence was like sitting beside a calmly flowing river, soothing to the spirit, while Alaric had only to enter a room and it crackled with his restless, virile energy. She shook her head, marveling that two born of the same womb and in the same hour could differ so greatly. Yet despite this, she loved them both as dearly as she loved her only son, Cullen. As she had tried, with little success, to love her sister's daughter, Kendra.

"You appear weary, my lady aunt," Alaric observed. "Why not let one of your ladies attend him," he nodded at the still figure sprawled on the straw of a bench in the corner, "and retire yourself?"

"I am quite well, Alaric, have no fear for me," Valonia insisted. "When I am weary, Lona will sit with him."

"Will he live?"

"I believe so. If his wound does not fester, that is. He had lost a great deal of blood before Cullen brought him to me, but for all his years he is strong, and has a great will to live."

The old man stirred, and at once Valonia was at his side. "Are you in pain, Master Sven?" she inquired kindly, her brown eyes concerned.

The old *skald's* eyes fluttered open. They were, Alaric saw, the blue of a summer's morn, and clear despite his great wound, though his face was haggard with pain.

"A—a little, good lady," Sven admitted, his voice strained. "I—I thank you for your care." Valonia nodded, raising his head so that he might sip from the silver goblet she raised to his lips. "Drink it all, if you can," she urged. "The wine will give you strength and a sound, healing sleep. The herbs within it will ease your pain. 'Tis naught but poppy flowers and such, as your own women might use, have no fear."

"I have none," Sven whispered, giving her a feeble smile. "You have been kind indeed, my lady, and I trust you with my worthless old life." Valonia patted his hand and wiped his dampened lips with a clean cloth, then rose and moved back to her nephew's side.

"You wished to speak with him?" she asked Alaric. He nodded. "Then do so now, and quickly. Soon the draught will make him sleep, and he will not awaken until dawn. And have a care that you do not upset him!" she chided.

"I would sooner risk a lion's wrath than yours, my lady aunt!" Alaric teased, and brushed past her to the cot, tweaking her plump cheek as he went. "Master Sven? Can you hear me?"

"*Ja, min jarl,*" came the old man's wavering voice.

"I am Alaric, Bear of Kent, son of the dead chieftain, Aeldred, the king's ealdorman. It is my hall at Kenley you have been taken to. The gracious lady who tends you is my lady aunt, Valonia."

"Ah. Then—then the cub Thorfast so feared has—has indeed grown to manhood! 'Tis all as I foresaw long ago—!" Sven mumbled. "What of—my lady Freya—? Is she—"

"Dead? Nay! Your timely words and deeds spared her at my cousin's hands, old man. The lady is very much alive—but my captive, of course."

"Of course," Sven echoed, and sighed heavily. "Captivity will not sit well upon my Freya's shoulders. I know her. She would prefer an honorable warrior's death in battle or by the sword a thousand times over imprisonment and thralldom in her enemy's household."

"The choice is not hers to make, old man, but mine, as

83

victor," Alaric said curtly. "The maid is as much a prize of the battle yesterday as are the gold plates and silver torcs we took from your dragon-ships. Furthermore, she is *my* prize, and I will not grant her freedom, nay, not even in death. She must pay for what her father did to my kinsmen! I intend to make her my slave. She will serve me in all ways, for as long as I will it. Thus will I bring shame and dishonor upon her father."

Sven saw the ruthless glitter in his gray eyes, and inwardly shivered. Aeldred's son. Thorfast had been right in that, after all. This bitter, vengeful man was indeed one to fear! But his little Freya was alive, and for that he was deeply grateful—for all that he knew she would feel no such gratitude to her captor! "I thank you for sparing her life, my lord Alaric," he murmured.

A cruel smile curled the lord's lips. "Do not thank me, old man. I granted her her life in return for what you did for my lady mother years ago. In sparing Thorfast's daughter, my debt to you is now paid. Perhaps your lady would not thank you for her life?" he added curiously, remembering the savage sapphire glitter of the girl's eyes.

"Nay, she would not," Sven agreed. "But I do." He closed his eyes, and for a moment Alaric thought the potion had brought him sleep. Then he opened them again and looked straight at Alaric. "You—you will bed her, of course, if you have not already done so, *ja?*" It was not a question, despite the questioning tone. Sven's voice had the ring of certainty about it.

For the first time, Alaric appeared caught off guard. "Aye," he said coldly, "though if she is well named Freya the Frozen Heart, I warrant she will not readily surrender herself. But—I will thaw your ice maiden, I swear it!"

"Then you will be the first," Sven told him, "for she has lain with no man before this. Indeed, no man has yet come close to capturing her heart, let alone her body, save for Olaf the Oaken, for whom she feels only a childhood affection. Since my *jarl* Thorfast cast her aside at birth for being born a daughter rather than the son he desired, she has closed her heart to all men, and denied and smothered all that is warm and womanly inside her. But have a care you do not break her spirit! If you do, you will break her will to live. She will then court death as a lovesick swain courts a comely maid, and you will not have the revenge you seek."

"Why do you tell me this, old man?" Alaric demanded. "Do you wish her tamed by me, her enemy?"

"Better tamed than dead, my lord," Sven said huskily, and there were tears in his eyes. "Though she has never acknowledged it, though she always pined for Thorfast's love and attention, I was a father to her in all but name, and she a daughter to me. I love her as my own flesh and blood. Need I tell thee more?"

Alaric's jaw tightened. There was pity in his eyes, and understanding of Sven's fears. "You need not, Sven of Danehof. I will remember all you have told me. Rest now, and grow strong!"

Sven's words stayed with him as he left the chamber. He knew that Sven was in all probability correct. Freya had been trained as a Viking warrior, taught to resist her enemies to the death. Force her, and she would turn on him like a wildcat, fight back with reckless courage as she had upon their first meeting in the byre, with tooth and talon, to the bitter end, if need be. She would never surrender, not if he took her savagely, as the vengeful lust within him urged. But there were other ways to tame a woman than by force. And he was well versed in all of them! She would melt, sooner or later . . .

The promise of the Viking beauty's surrender appealed to him. He smiled to himself as he returned to the vast banqueting hall and the rousing victory feast in progress.

Chapter 7

Dread coiled like a great sea serpent in the pit of her belly by the time Freya and her escort had reached Lord Alaric's bower, set like all the other sleeping bowers a little apart from the main hall. The guards, those coarse, snickering louts, removed her chains, flung her inside, loudly slammed the door in her wake, and took up positions outside it.

Despite her determination to ignore them, the guards' gleefully crude threats of what awaited her at *his* hands had struck home. In truth, the Saxon lord promised to be a monster of voracious appetites and perverse tastes, she thought, biting her lower lip, and a quiver of pure terror fluttered madly in the pit of her belly despite the steely facade of courage she had worn earlier.

The wide wristbands had chafed her slender wrists painfully when she attempted to squirm from the Saxon's foul touch. Rubbing them, she stumbled across the bower to the wide sleeping bench that dominated it. It was not unlike the carved beds of her father's hall, save that the four tall posts at its corners bore the simpering carved heads of Christian angels or saints, instead of four fierce dragons to scare away the evil night spirits, she noted in disgust. It appeared that even the demons of the White Christ's followers must be insipid creatures, to be so easily set to flight by such tame carvings!

A pallet—stuffed with eiderdown and not the usual straw, she surmised from its tempting softness—had been spread across the broad wooden slats. Fur pelts and fine blankets were

86

strewn on top of it. It was inviting, that softness, and she itched to stretch out upon it and rest her aching, battle-weary body. She had all but accepted the invitation when the foolhardiness of such a move struck her like a blow. She might as well spread herself across an altar in sacrifice as eagerly leap into the Saxon's bed! As if the sleeping couch were not feather-filled but made of red-hot iron, she sprang away, skittering across the bower like a nervous colt, her belly grumbling loudly from a mixture of apprehension and hunger.

The bower was large, half timbered, half gray stone, and illuminated by wavering rushlights, tiny flames writhing in the draft. Two narrow wind-eyes, their wooden shutters flung wide open to let in the bracing night air, also let in diffused showers of moonlight, patterning the rushes and herbs strewn on the stone floor with gray and silver coins and casting the shadowed corners into darker contrast, for there was neither horn nor oiled skins to pane them. A stone hearth, heaped with crackling logs, flanked one wall; a massive chest, bound in copper and bronze, in which, she discovered, many garments were folded, rested solidly behind a hanging curtain in an alcove set in another.

On a small table, intricately carved chess pieces of costly morse ivory, or walrus tusks, had been set and a game begun. *Viking* playing pieces, she realized, picking up the monstrous elephant with the howdah atop it. Whom had they once belonged to? How had their owner come to part with such treasures? Had he, perhaps, met his death? She shivered and tossed her head to rid it of such gruesome thoughts, instead inspecting the positions of the pieces and snorting in disgust, for the white player was obviously a fool where strategy was concerned, and lay dangerously open to defeat!

Involuntarily, Freya was forcefully reminded of cold winters' nights in Danehof, when the fjord had been frozen solid and snow furies had swirled about her father's hall. She and Uncle Sven had often whiled away the long hours in games of chess or draughts or dice close by the warmth of the hearth . . . Ah, poor, dear Uncle Sven! Even should she somehow escape this foul place, she was quite alone now that he was gone to Valhalla. A sad little sigh of despair hissed from between her lips, but was quickly cut short. She, Freya of Danehof, never cried, never gave in to weak, foolish tears; not since that day long ago when Sven had told her of her father's desire for a son rather than a weakling girl-child! She would not cry now! In a fit of grief and rage, she swept the chess pieces from the marble-topped board, scattering them in all directions, tears burning hotly behind her eyes despite her vow. *Nej, do not cry, Freya Jorgensen,* she told herself sternly when the rage had abated. *Do not dwell on your grief and pain! Instead, think how you will escape! Plot your revenge! Concentrate your energies on that, for it is all that matters now! Sven, poor, dear Sven, is beyond help.*

The Danelaw, under the Viking leader Guthrum, lay to the north and the east. Somehow she would flee this cursed place and make her way to Northumbria, and thence to Jorvic, its capital. With Guthrum's aid she would return with many, many longships and thirty times as many men, and raze the settlement of Kenley to the ground, aye, and her cursed lord with it!

And where was he? she wondered, sinking to the bed to rest her aching limbs and rubbing them. Feasting, no doubt, in celebration of his victory over her raiding party, she decided bitterly. She fell back against the pallet, groaning in pleasure at its welcoming softness. By Odin, every muscle in her body throbbed, clamored for rest! If she was to resist the Saxon to the last, she needed badly to recoup her strength. Aye, and she *would* resist his ravishment—to the death if need be, she vowed wearily, feeling her eyelids grow extraordinarily weighty. He would learn that, unlike the docile Saxon cows, a Viking woman was no easy victim . . .

Despite her vow to stay awake, she was deeply asleep when the scrape of a key in the Roman lock awoke her instantly. No shrill, winding blast blown from any horn could have roused her half as swiftly as that sound. At once she sat bolt upright, her heart thudding erratically. The time had come! Alaric had at last retired to his bower, curse him!

She sprang off the bed, snatched up the marble-inlaid

wooden chessboard from the table and flitted nimbly across the bower clutching it under her arm, taking up position behind the door. As she'd vowed earlier, she would not surrender to him without a fight! She smiled grimly. Her nerves were on edge and there were sickening flutters in her belly that were nigh impossible to still. Yet resolve swept through her nonetheless, changing the butterfly tremors of fear to a steely hawk of determination. The arrogant Bear of Kent might well find he had bitten off more than he could chew this time, *ja*, indeed he might! The door began to open, then stopped.

"... may go. Inform Ham that I will tend to myself tonight, and am not to be disturbed," she heard Alaric say, obviously to a servant, who answered with a sly chuckle in his tone, "Aye, indeed, my lord. None will disturb ye. A very good night to ye."

Alone! He would be alone! A tremendous elation swept through Freya as she raised the marble chessboard over her head two-handed, like a broadsword, drew a deep breath, and froze in place.

Alaric entered the bower with one stride, then another, his shadow gigantic as it leaped across the floor and shimmied up the wall. He bore a flaming torch aloft in his left hand, and a heavy golden sealing ring caught and reflected its dancing light. With his right hand he turned to close the door in his wake, and in that instant a bright red-gold flash caught his eye as Freya sprang after him. He turned—but too late! She whooped and brought her arms down with all her strength, crashing the board against the back of his head.

The chessboard was unwieldy, the shape wrong for the club she had intended—but it served admirably! There was a dull thud as wood and marble clipped skullbone. Alaric's raven-black brows rose in astonished, arched wings. His mouth opened silently, like a gasping fish. The light faded from his gray eyes like twin doused candles as he folded to the ground with a mighty thud, taking a heavily carved chair with him and losing the flaming torch as he fell. Sparks showered to the rushes, and Freya hurriedly stamped them out barefooted before retrieving the still-lighted torch and jamming it safely into a metal wall sconce.

Hands on hips, slender legs braced apart, she glowered down

at him in the shifting light as the torch smoked and wavered. He seemed far larger unconscious, she decided, and frowned. Now that she had him safely overpowered, how was she to keep him that way? She thought for a moment or two, and then a smile of wicked glee curved her lips and lent a naughty sparkle to her jewel eyes. And why should she not? she pondered, her chin resting thoughtfully on her knuckles, the idea taking firm root. He had done as much to her. Perhaps he would not be so arrogant, were the boot on the other foot . . . ! Besides, what had she to lose? she argued. She was his captive, aye; indeed, that much had not changed. Despite her momentary victory over Alaric, she was under no illusions that she'd be able to overpower the many stalwart guards beyond these doors. If he was angered enough by what she'd done, there was a good chance he might grant her the swift, honorable death by sword that she preferred to capture and shame, if escape were impossible.

She crouched down and firmly grasped him by the boots, hauling them off one by one and tossing them aside. It was no easy task. His legs were as solid and weighty as oak trunks, and she was panting when she was done. She scowled, at a loss as to how she should continue. By the gods! 'Twas a monumental task she'd set herself! An ant might as soon endeavor to move a great, hairy mountain! Yet she had seen her father to his bed on more occasions than one, though Thorfast never knew it. Could an unconscious Saxon be any more difficult to move than a snoring, drunken *jarl?* She doubted it. Somehow she'd manage.

Her face set in concentration, she stepped between his legs, gripped one knee under each arm, and hauled with all her might. By Odin, he was like a great bull walrus, so unwieldy and heavy! Yet, inch by agonizing inch at a time, she was able, with frequent respites to catch her breath, to haul and drag him across the rushes to the sleeping couch. So far, so good! Now to get him up and on it . . . She considered the problem, then went to crouch at his head. With little hesitation and no pity or care at all, she grasped a hefty hank of his midnight-black hair and raised his head by it, firmly jamming her knee against the back of his skull. He groaned as she shoved, for there it was she had struck him and a goose-egg-sized lump had erupted amidst the black curls, but she allowed not an inkling of pity to sway her from her intent as little by little, pushing with her knees as a wedge and leaning with all her weight against his shoulders, she raised him up.

Breathing heavily and gasping for breath, perspiration springing out upon her brow and palms, she at last had him sitting, after a fashion, his dark head lolling on his broad chest, his massive, corded arms dangling loosely like those of a fresh corpse. Another brief rest, and she shoved him hard so that he flopped forward across the bed. 'Twas as good as done now! A heave, a groan of immense effort from her, and his right leg was hooked awkwardly over the pallet alongside him. She grinned maliciously. Saxon dolt! He looked so foolish, as if he were trying to climb into bed while heavily in his cups, and unable to do so! Another push under his thigh and flanks, using her back this time as a brace, and his lean buttocks had at last risen off the ground. Now came the most strenuous part. She threw all her weight against him and heaved, and suddenly, when she least expected it, his own weight tipped him over onto the bed and took her with it. She lay sprawled across him, both of them atop the heap of blankets and the eiderdown pallet! Scrambling hurriedly off him and moving carefully now in her fear that he would soon come to, she hefted him over onto his back, rocked back on her heels, and inspected her considerable prize.

Good. He was still breathing—though why it should concern her that he be alive, that cursed ugly Saxon brute, she knew not! Belatedly remembering he was armed, she stood, leaned over him, and drew his jeweled dagger from its short leather scabbard, admiring it briefly before she used it to cut the belt from him. Still using his own blade, she deftly carved the leather of the belt into long, serviceable thongs, and raising first one arm, then the other over his head, and then each foot in turn, she knotted him securely to each of the four simpering-angel bedposts with intricate sailor's knots, knots that she knew from her experience aboard the *Wild Bird of the Wind* would not easily unfasten. Her grim smile now became a wide, delighted grin as she went a step further and cut her trussed captive's garments from him, nodding firmly once in satisfaction when she was done and he was quite naked. Ah, how honey-sweet was vengeance, however small! After all, he had done no less to her, forcing her to appear before him naked save for her chains!

"Look upon this, you simpering Christian angels!" she told the four carved bedposts with the angelic smiles, and grinned broadly, for she fancied they blushed in prudish dismay to see their lord thus—or was it but the wavering torchlight that caused her to think so?

By Odin, he was as naked as a newborn babe—and as fast asleep, she thought, unable to stifle a giggle as she dispassionately eyed his heavily muscled, hairy male body. But there all resemblance to babes ended. Mmm. He was a man *very* well endowed by nature, that much she could not deny: but then, no one possessed of eyesight could! And in his own swarthy, muscled, dark and virile way, he was not exactly uncomely, she supposed, with his glossy ebony hair and hard, dark features. Some maids might even find him attractive, though he did not appeal to her tastes, she told herself resolutely, nay, not at all—

He heaved a great sigh, and stirred. She checked the knots on his bonds, assuring herself that they would hold. How he would bellow when he awoke and found himself thus naked and bound! How he would struggle! How he would *roar!* So. Let him! 'Twas no more than he deserved, after all, after what he'd done to her—and her people—that day! A taste of his own bitter draught would do him good, and she would relish seeing him drink it down to the dregs!

Such thoughts of bitter draughts gave her an idea to hasten her revenge. She jumped up and crossed the bower to the curtained alcove where garments lay folded in the heavy chest, rummaging through them until she found one of Alaric's own tunics that seemed closer to her size than the others, and slipped it on. A cord belt followed, and she began to feel human again for the first time that day, albeit the garment's enormous size made it fit like a woman's kirtle upon her slender body, reaching clear to her ankles rather than her knees. Why hadn't she put on one of his garments earlier to cover herself, she wondered fleetingly, shrugging and deciding everything had happened too quickly; she had been too confused and upset to think clearly.

Clothed now, she went to where a silver flagon and a fine

amber-colored glass claw-beaker had been set upon a table. She sniffed the flagon's contents. Mead. She poured herself a full measure and drank it down as if it were but water, then returned to the bedside with the half-filled flagon. Without hesitation, she emptied the contents over Alaric's unsuspecting and immobile head!

He spluttered. He groaned. He shook the mead from his head, black hair spraying, and groaned again. He cursed foully, groaned a third time. At length he tried to move his arms, and she guessed he wanted to touch the burgeoning goose egg upon his head. He shifted his feet. Then his gray eyes flew open. They were smoldering with fury. The turbulent black brows came together in a murderous scowl. He caught sight of her hovering over him, and the smile he shot her was anything but pleasant as he strained at the thongs.

"So. 'Twas you who brained me, was it—then stayed to revel in your sport, eh, Viking?" he growled, aware suddenly, and to his horror, that he was quite naked. "'Twas your only mistake, wench—but a bad one! You should have fled whilst I was as yet helpless." He grinned thinly. "Or finished me."

"I know what I'm about, Saxon," she retorted, finding the foreign words hard to remember in her hatred of him and her nervousness, though they were very much like her own tongue. "You, you sought to shame me. You mocked me as I stood naked before everyone. It is not good, this shame I feel! Now you are naked for Freya. It is much better this way, I think, *ja?*" She grinned wickedly and strolled across to the bed, slapping the dagger's shining blade against her other palm.

Alaric watched her draw closer much as a mesmerized rabbit watches a weasel. "What are you about now?" he demanded, eyes wary.

She shrugged and smiled with enormous glee, for she saw the apprehension in his eyes. Let him squirm! she thought. Let him be plagued with the fears that had filled her earlier—which even now nudged in her mind! "Perhaps—nothing. Perhaps I will but pick my teeth—is sharp enough for this, yes?" she ran the ball of her thumb lightly down the blade, and instantly a tiny scarlet thread appeared. "Or—perhaps—?" The knife hovered over his middle, back and forth, left and right, closer then farther away, the blade catching the light and winking evilly, matching the bloodthirsty blue glitter in her eyes. "Perhaps I geld the Saxon stallion, *nej?*" she threatened softly. Alaric, despite himself, involuntarily shrank from the wicked blade, reluctant to lose those parts of his anatomy that he had grown fondest of over the years, wetting his dry lips on his tongue. "Viking bitch!" he gritted, furious at allowing himself to be laid low and trussed up like a slain boar by a stripling wench.

Freya laughed merrily and swaggered jauntily away, tossing the dagger to the far side of the bower. "I frighten you enough for now, Alaric of Kent. The time has come for something more, I think! What was it you plan for Freya tonight, my brave lord?" She smiled coyly, eyeing him through half-closed eyes as she ran her index finger down across his furry chest to his hard, flat belly and drew slow, lazy whorls across it with her cool, slender fingertip. "Ah. *Ja.* Now I remember!" she purred throatily. "You vowed to dishonor me, did you not? To ravish Thorfast's daughter?"

To Alaric's own undying shame, his treacherous manhood swelled hugely in response to her light, scornful caress, rising like an oaken staff. He saw her smile broaden, the dimples in her cheeks growing deeper. Apprehension flooded through his gut. Surely this Viking hellcat was a madwoman, he thought, feeling a trickle of cold sweat begin its slow sliding down his spine. And madwomen were capable of anything!

"Who named you Frozen Heart, witch?" he panted, writhing against the thongs as her slender, cool hands moved enflamingly over his body. "Of a certainty, they knew you not! You are a firebrand!"

In answer, she smiled and eyed him slyly, head cocked to one side, her dark lashes sweeping down to conceal whatever thoughts were betrayed in the sapphire depths of her eyes. "My touch stirs you, Saxon?" she asked, all innocence.

"It does," he agreed gruffly. "Untie me, and I will please thee likewise."

"You would?" she asked, tawny brows rising as if in astonished anticipation.

His guard was down now. She saw the taut cords in his muscled arms slacken. "Verily, I would," he answered in a husky, sensual voice.

She suddenly raised her fist and struck him with all her might in his hard belly. The breath rushed from him in a startled "whoosh!" and he cursed foully. "Never, Saxon cur!" she denied triumphantly. "No touch of your foul hand could ever pleasure me!"

The tip of her small pink tongue darted out to moisten her lips as she cocked her head to one side and glared at him. Their coral hue glistened in the torchlight, and through the gaping neck of her tunic—or rather, his tunic—he glimpsed the swell of her creamy white breasts, tipped with tiny dark-coral buds, as she leaned over him, coming closer, closer.

He forgot the sickening ache in his belly, the throbbing agony in his skull as her breasts rubbed teasingly against his flank, and he groaned, but not with pain—with longing to cup their soft, voluptuous weightiness in his hands, to savor the tempting raspberry nipples that he had glimpsed earlier on his tongue and between greedy lips and teeth. 'Twas madness to be so enflamed by the flame-headed Danish bitch, while helpless and bound and, moreover, yet suffering from her wiles! But the ache of lust in his loins had become fiery now, and to his chagrin, he could conceal none of his manly desire from her, for proof of it was rampant!

Suddenly her body inadvertently brushed against his throbbing shaft. His hips gave a great jerk, and there was a loud, cracking sound as one of the bedposts gave a little under his sudden movement. He grinned, heartened by the sound. For a second Freya's eyes were wide, horrified sapphire pools, fear mirrored in their depths. She darted quickly to each corner post to inspect her knots, relieved to find all had held.

"You frighten me, Saxon! For a moment I think you are free!" she said shakily.

"Believe me, vixen, you would know it full well were that so!" he threatened grimly.

"Indeed?" she mocked, fists on hips, chin at an arrogant angle.

"Aye, indeed! I would fling you down upon this bed, thrust up your skirts, and—"

"Enough!" she cried hotly, her heart skipping a beat. "You will do nothing to me, do you hear me! You are *my* prisoner now!"

"Ah, but for how long, Freya? How long before I am able to get free to do as I've promised? Sooner or later it will be dawn. Then my manservant will come to wake me. You can keep me here perhaps—but you cannot hold back the dawn! Think on that, Freya the Frozen Heart! How long have you left before I claim my battle prize, before I take my pleasure of thee—?"

His threat, delivered in a deep, taunting, yet husky voice with the ring of utter confidence, made her belly turn over in apprehension. Little quivers skittered through her loins like scalded cats. She wet her lips. By all the gods of Asgard, if he should get free now, after what she had done to him—! It was a thought that did not bear contemplating . . .

"Silence!" she snapped, swooping across the room and scrabbling to regain the fallen dagger. "You spoke truly, Saxon. I was a fool to linger and take my vengeance on you. I should be gone from here—!"

In that second, further sharp, cracking sounds rent the air as wood splintered and shattered. Each one was like the crack of doom! She flung about, red-gold tresses flying, to see Alaric, naked, rising from the bed, four splintered bedposts dangling from the thongs she had so carefully tied! With a flick of his powerful wrists he was free of them, the bedposts crashing heavily to the floor, though the thongs she had so carefully fastened were still firmly knotted about his wrists.

"What now, my lovely Delilah? Your Samson is free!" Alaric menaced, eyes narrowed to glittering silver slits.

She did not understand the meaning of the Biblical jest, but the threatening note was unmistakable. Eyes wide blue pools of horror, she shrank back against the wall as he tore the bonds from his ankles, swung off the bed, and rose to standing, a towering, black-haired giant whose eyes all but impaled her to the wall with their keenness. Summoning all her courage, she raised the jeweled dagger before her and tossed the hair from her eyes.

"Touch me and you die, Alaric!" she cried.

He grinned as, fist on hips, he strode menacingly toward her. "I shall do more than touch you, my Viking vixen, I promise thee. Far, far more . . ."

Chapter 8

All happened so swiftly after that. One moment she was springing for his throat like a she-lynx, the dagger bravely brandished aloft, and in the next she was pinned beneath him on the rushes, stunned by the speed with which he had moved. He twisted the weapon from her grip before she could use it on herself, and hurled it across the bower. She screamed a string of curses and managed to wrench free of him, squirming this way and that, scrabbling to escape him, desperation in her eyes and heart.

"Unhand me, you cursed offspring of a sea-cow!" she raged.

"It's no use, wench," he rasped, jerking back his head to avoid her talons as she struck out blindly for his face. "Curses will not help you now! You'll never escape this bower, should you perchance escape me—which I sorely doubt!" He grunted in surprise as a well-placed and surprisingly powerful knee slammed like a battering ram into his groin, and then she was out from under him, on her feet and flying for the door. With a roar he was up and after her, arms outstretched on either side to catch her. With a whimper she feinted a left, then ducked under his right arm, barely evading him, darting to the table where the silver flagon and goblet were set. She picked them up and hurled them at him one by one, yet her missiles were easily deflected by his raised arms or shoulders. A low, infuriating chuckle came from him. Laughter danced in his eyes.

"By Saint George! Ice maiden? You are a very firebrand, in truth!" he panted. "Well? What next, vixen?"

She looked desperately about her for further objects with which to bombard him, but there were none. Sick with dread, the agony of certain defeat uncurling in her belly, she made for the narrow wind-eye. Better death in an escape attempt than surrender, she decided desperately! But she had no sooner reached it than he sprang at her like a great dark panther. Steely fingers clamped over her shoulder and spun her about to face him.

"Nay, firebrand, nay!" he breathed, his hands now locked tight about her wrists. "I warned you, did I not? Death will not spare Thorfast's daughter my bed!"

Sick with defeat, she closed her eyes and pleaded with her gods to make him kill her. Exhausted from her struggles, she could put up only a feeble protest as he pulled the kirtle up over her head and tossed it aside, leaving her naked and squirming in his arms for the second time that day.

"'Tis my turn now, is it not?" he breathed, imprisoning her wrists against her sides in his unbreakable grip.

Her eyes flew open, dilated with panic, to find him gazing down at her, a mocking smile curving his hard mouth, his smoky eyes dark with lust. Her hands moved instinctively to shield her nakedness from his hungry gaze, yet she could not raise them, and he feasted his eyes upon her bared loveliness at will.

"Bastard Saxon!" she seethed, straining to free herself. "Unhand me!"

"Nay, Viking bitch!" Alaric retorted easily, releasing one hand and stroking her flat, velvety belly, grinning as her smooth flesh shivered away from the touch of his rough palm as earlier his own had done at her touch. "I will enjoy you thus—without your wildcat's talons clawing my face or scrabbling for some weapon or other to plunge into my back." As if to underline his mastery, he covered one of her pleasing breasts in his tanned, lean hand and fondled it, squeezing gently, pressing the firm curve lustfully with long, strong fingers, his smile broadening as her eyes widened still further and she strove desperately to escape her bonds. "Aye, Lady Freya," he added softly, "I am master here, none other. What I wish to do with you or with your lovely body, I will do . . . !"

So saying, he flung her easily over his shoulder and bore her

98

to the broken bed, kicking aside the shattered bedposts as he went. Once there, he dropped her like a sack of barley to the pelts and quickly followed her down before she could flee. With one wiry leg lightly furred with springy black hair planted heavily across her thighs to hold her still, he dipped his dark head and covered a rosy nipple with his mouth. Deaf to her wails and cries and curses, he drew the hot sweetmeat of swollen flesh deeply between his lips and teeth and sucked greedily, his tongue darting fire against the very tip until she bucked like a wild mare. Yet his grip held fast. When he was done with the first breast, he repeated his actions upon its twin, feeling her warm flesh swell and grow rigid, unfurling in the heat of his mouth like a taut rosebud opening its silken petals to the heat of the summer sun.

"Frey curse you!" she seethed, tossing her head wildly from side to side, her upper arms aching from the pressure of his fingers. "*Ja*, may he curse you, Alaric of Kenley—may he see you gelded!" she raged.

Softly he chuckled, his hot breath fanning her chilled flesh so that gooseflesh rose all over her, prickling down her spine. "Curse all you wish, my Viking mare. I am of a certainty no gelding, but a lusty stallion—as soon you will learn!"

His threats sent further chills prickling through her. She jabbed at him with her knees, trying to draw them up to batter his groin again, but she was unable to throw off his heavy weight to do so. A second time he dipped his ebony head and pressed his lips to her flat, almost concave belly, his tongue dancing down to her navel and lapping greedily there as if it were a tiny well at which he drank, until she screamed aloud at his ticklish torment. He shifted his weighty leg, but before she could flail at him, his hand had cupped the silken-curled triangle of her mons and pressed, then stroked and squeezed, then parted her thighs and delved within, thrusting a questing finger between the silken lips and alternately caressing the hidden, velvety well and the sensitive bud within.

She shrank from his hateful touch, loathing the way he touched her so intimately where no man had ever dared to touch her before, when she could do naught to prevent him. Oh the shame, the shame and frustrated rage that simmered within her! She writhed and squirmed to avoid his touch, but there was no slackening of his fierce grip upon her, and with a sinking heart she acknowledged that her fight was good as over.

Despite her struggles and protests, Alaric found a virginal barrier beneath his touch that had yet to be breeched by any man. Sven had spoken truly. He smiled down at her in satisfaction, hiding his astonishment as he saw that her face had grown ashen now, and that something naked and vulnerable and deathly afraid was, for a fleeting second, etched on her lovely, furious face and in her dilated eyes.

"So, a Saxon stallion will be the first to mount Thorfast's daughter!" he said softly, readying her for his throbbing manhood with maddening, thrusting fingers. "Lie still, wench, else I will summon my guards to share my battle prize," he warned her sternly, knowing his taking of her would be less painful if she lay still and ceased to resist him, but unwilling to admit to her that he wished to spare her pain. No doubt the firebrand would take any such admission as a sign of weakness!

"Summon your guards? *Nej!* You would not!" she cried, half imploring, half threatening, her dark blue eyes deep pools of shining dread.

"I am lord here. I do as I see fit," he insisted, his tone rough to cover the lie, for he had no intent of sharing her with any man. "And when I am done with you, I may yet give you to them, should you prove untameable to me. 'Twould be well, my wild one, that you strive to please me, and give me no cause to share you with others."

"Better I should die than give you or any Saxon pleasure, Kentish cur!" she hissed from between clamped jaws. "Freya of Danehof is no Saxon slut, to open her legs for any man that bids her! Do what you will, worm of Hel, but I will fight thee every step of the way!"

He hid an amused smile at her choice of words, which reeked of the raw male company she had grown accustomed to, leading the men of her father's hall. "As you will," he murmured. He shrugged and rose from the bed, and his manhood again sprang into view.

She quailed and looked away from the arrogant, throbbing shaft that rose from a curling ebony forest. Thor's thunderbolts, it was greater, more enormous than she had ever imagined any male's shaft could possibly be—in truth, 'twas

100

like a stallion's, grown ready to cover a mare! And he would impale her virgin body on its great length . . . would surely rend her in two! Blood pounded in her temples. Oh blessed Frey, surely she would die!

Hands on hips, he stood quite still, knowing full well the effect his nakedness created, for many far more eager women than this innocent maid had been amazed by the great size of his manhood.

A lazy smile tugged at the corners of his mouth, revealing a glimpse of white teeth. Disheveled blue-black curls fell in inky commas about his handsome brow and temples. His shoulders, brawny with muscle and damp with sweat, were silhouetted against the rushlight, gleaming here and there like bronze where touched by its glow. His broad chest was dark with curling hair, hair that was thick about the dark-rose male nipples but thinned out across his flat belly, only to reassert itself as a heavy black pelt at his loins. His thighs were long, corded beneath dark flesh and crisscrossed with old silvery scars; his calves were enormous, as powerfully muscled and hairy as the rest of him; his feet square and solid, a fitting, sturdy foundation for such as he. Everything about him was emphatically male, from his fiercely arrogant stance to his scent, a mixture of mead and salt sweat and wood smoke, she thought numbly, nostrils flaring. Her shocked silence became a frightened gasp as he leaned purposefully toward her, for she could look at nothing but that mighty rearing shaft, carried well to the fore like a battle lance . . .

This time he did not lie beside her, but knelt on the pallet at her feet. His smoky eyes holding hers captive, he grasped her slender ankles in his steely fists and parted her shapely, rigid legs, at the same time shifting his body to kneel between her thighs. She felt the fiery spearhead of his manhood butt eagerly against her vulnerable core like a miniature battering ram and she stiffened, every nerve and muscle strung taut and quivering like the strings of a harp. She struggled to bring her thighs together, but it was impossible with his body lodged snugly between them, and with a sinking heart she knew he had won.

"'Tis time, Viking," he breathed, not unkindly, his voice husky with lust, his gray eyes devouring her nakedness.

"What must be, must be. Accept me, and 'twill be easier for you."

"Never!" she moaned weakly, the moan becoming an anguished sob as she felt his strong hands slide beneath her buttocks, the better to raise her body to take his manhood.

"Submit, little fool!" he growled, and thrust his hips strongly forward.

He saw her face grow still paler in the meager light, the blood draining from it. For a second, he was filled with pity—and shame.

"Does your feeble Christian conscience prick you, Saxon?" she at once jeered, sensing his shift in mood and pressing the advantage. "You have yet to match my lord father in cruelty, so why do you falter? Press on, great lord! Thrust hard, drive deep, prove victor over this maid, as Thorfast once did over your mother! Ah, *ja*, 'twill be a proud victory, will it not? You will sleep well after, I wager, brave, noble lord!" Her voice broke at the latter words. She turned her head to look at him, startled to find his gray eyes wide open and staring down at her with a strange and unfathomable expression in their cinder depths.

For a moment he remained quite still, staring down at the distraught face beneath his, seeing now the single drop of blood upon her lower lip, where her teeth had clamped into the tender flesh to keep from crying out. Her eyes were shining, awash with tears ready to brim over.

Had her words swayed him, she wondered, hope springing into her breast? He seemed uncertain now . . .

Alaric had, for a moment, been taken aback by her cutting words. But then her pale face was replaced by an image of his mother's pale oval face, framed by a heavy curtain of ebony hair. In his mind's eye he saw suddenly, clearly his lady mother Wilone's body, round with child, covered by the Viking *jarl* Thorfast's hairy body, and pity was replaced by his lust for vengeance upon Freya's sire. He thrust savagely forward, and felt the silken barrier that had impeded him rend and give way beneath his onslaught, the sudden hot gush of her blood that eased his passage, and he was through. Clasping her upper body, he drove deep into the narrow sheath, then lay still to give her time to accept his penetration.

"Give up the fight! You are mine now, lovely Freya, and a maiden no more," he urged, fighting the heady lust that urged him to go on. "Let me give thee pleasure now, for the deed is done, the victory mine. There can be no advantage to you in fighting me further." He lowered his head to hers, covering her mouth with his own, hungry for his first taste of her tempting coral lips and suddenly eager to show her the many pleasures of coupling that could be theirs—quite forgetting in his own pleasure that she was no willing woman.

He yelped as teeth as sharp as knives clamped down hard upon his tongue and lips, once, twice, drawing blood, then recoiled as she spat full in his face for the second time that day. Pity and mercy were no more. Gripping her taut buttocks fiercely in his large hands, he drove into her again and again, as vigorously as if he rode an easy alehouse slattern, savoring her swollen breasts, stroking her smooth flanks until, with a great roar, he felt the great storm inside him break and fill him with throbbing spasms of pleasure.

It was soon over, though to Freya it seemed endless. Stunned, she moaned as he suddenly relaxed, full weight upon her, crushing her beneath him so heavily that she could neither breathe nor move, until she feared she would suffocate beneath the hateful, hairy brute! It seemed an eternity until he rolled off her, to lie at her side.

There was pain between her thighs, and a stickiness that was her virgin blood and his foul, hot seed commingled. His male scent clung to her body, filled her nostrils. His loathsome touch seemed branded into her flesh. He seemed everywhere, both within and without her, inescapable as the very air she breathed. Yet—yet she had survived his ravishment!

She turned her face away, willing the tears that welled behind her eyelids to vanish, but they would not. They spilled forth and trickled down her cheeks, and it was only by the greatest control she was able to muffle the noisy sobs that accompanied them. *I hate him!* she seethed. By Odin, how I loathe him for what he has done to me! Some day he will pay, *ja*, some day, when he is no longer wary of me, all here at Kenley will pay!

A great aching swelled in her breast. A boulder seemed to lodge in her throat, too large, too dry, too painful to swallow.

After all, she had proven naught but a weakling, a stupid, bawling woman, she thought angrily; had proven vulnerable, despite her wits and her skills, to the greater strength of men. Had she not trained as a warrior? Had the *Althing* not found her worthy and agreed to her position as *jarl* of Danehof? Then why did she lie here in the Saxon's bed, whimpering with hurt, humbled by his taking of her maidenhead? Where had her courage and pride flown? Aye, he could well take her virginity, as he had so ably proved, and who needed it anyway? But those qualities of pride and courage he could never take from her, never!

"Well done, Lord Alaric!" she said brokenly. "Your savagery was worthy of any Viking!"

His black brows drew together in an angry scowl. She saw his lips tighten in the rushlight and drew pleasure from the knowledge that her barb had drawn blood. Curse him she might, but in comparing him to his hated enemy she had struck a telling blow indeed.

Without words, he rose and dressed, then left her alone in the bower.

All were sleeping in the hall, he saw, the servants rolled into mantles upon the rushes beside the hearth, others sprawled upon the fixed wooden benches against the walls. The hunting hounds thumped their tails in greeting as he approached and picked his angry way between the bodies, crossing the hall and exiting by a side door leading out to the bailey and the stables beyond. In the open air he drew great, greedy gulps of its nighttime sweetness before carrying on. The sentries were sleeping, and with a livid curse he shook them awake, reminding them in harsh tones that just that morn the Viking raiders might well have attacked them unawares, had it not been for the treacherous Dane Karl having slipped away to warn them. Promising harsh discipline come daybreak, he continued on.

Lucifer greeted him with a welcoming whicker, battering the wood of his stall with eager hooves at the sound of his master's voice. Pausing only to find a rope halter, Alaric slipped it over his stallion's black head and led him out, past the grooms and the stable boys who slept in the straw, into the bailey, before mounting him bareback. The guards manning the gates in the walls were more alert than their fellows about the hall, and challenged him as he rode up, spears angled and ready. He stilled their challenges with a soft-spoken, "Tis I, your lord. Let me pass!" before galloping between the gates and on down the hill and into the moonlit countryside.

The night air was cool and as refreshing as a dive into a chill woodland pool might be in midsummer. It dispersed the cobwebby misgivings and regrets that had bound him about with Freya's mocking words.

His masculine pride, ever fierce, had always prevented him from forcing himself upon women, even when the foot soldiers of the *fyrd* had succumbed to their lust and tumbled Danish camp followers after a battle. He'd had neither the need nor the desire to take by force any woman who feared and hated him, for willing women were easily come by, yet—he had done so this night. He scowled blackly. Aye, and what of it? From the first moment he had set eyes upon her his intent had been to dishonor Thorfast's daughter, to take her by force in retaliation for her sire's bloody doings, and in this fashion at least partially redeem his family's honor, had he not? If he had not done so, some other—perhaps many others of his garrison—would have used the maid for their pleasure. Better he, who had, after a fashion, tried to be gentle with her, than they. He need feel no qualms, no guilt for exacting his family's revenge, he told himself; indeed, out here, in the moon-dappled meadows and starlit woods, he felt none, as he had in his bower. Setting his jaw, he determined that on the morrow things would go very differently. The pretty witch would learn then who was her master, aye, once and for all time.

A half-league's riding along the riverbanks, Lucifer shied and raised his forelegs in a half rear, dancing on his haunches and screaming shrilly with alarm. Alaric reined in the night-black beast and brought him around, speaking softly to calm him. He plumbed the shadows for some sign of what had alarmed the horse, but glimpsed no slinking, amber-eyed wolf, nor yet the gray and white markings of a roaming badger. Then, on the bridle path ahead, he saw a sprawled body.

Dismounting, he quickly tethered the snorting stallion to a

handy bush and went forward on foot to investigate, his fist clasped over the hilt of his dagger. The bile rose up in his throat as moonlight cast silver on the bloody horror before him. The Viking Karl Ivarson sprawled face down in the mud of the riverbank. His back had been torn open, the lungs and entrails pulled free to flap their final, desperate breaths across his shoulders in the form of the infamous "blood-eagle"—the Viking method of execution for cowards or traitors.

"So, Olaf the Oaken found his traitor," Alaric muttered grimly. He stood and looked about him, yet the massed shadows of the bushes and willows and his own soldier's instincts, finely honed, gave no suspicion of a threat nearby. Olaf, it appeared, had moved on.

Remounting, Alaric left the river's course and rode out onto the open heathlands of rough turf and pungent gorse and heather, kicking his mount into a brisk canter. Lucifer's hoofbeats were like the muffled throb of a drum upon the turf. In minutes they had reached the seashore. The salt-and-kelp tang and the pounding of the waves was like a bracing draught to his senses. Starlight rimmed the waves with sparkling white foam. The rhythm of the tide soothed him. He rode the silent, moonwashed beaches until the effects of the morning's battle—and the later battle in his bower—overwhelmed him with weariness. Only then did he swing the stallion's head about, to return to the hall.

The cavernous great hall was much as he, sweating and smelling of horses and leather now, had left it, save for one who, like him, was not asleep. As he left the main hall and started outside across the rough-hewn path to his bower, he sensed someone waiting in the shadows ahead, heard the shallow rise and fall of their breathing.

"Kendra?" he queried softly, knowing instinctively that it was she.

"Aye, my lord. Tell me, how did you know I was here?" she whispered, delighted laughter in her voice. "Do you have eyes like a cat, that see in the dark?"

He ignored her question, instead demanding, "What do you here at this hour? Be gone to your bower, and your lord's bed."

"Ah, but it *is* my lord's bed that I wish to go to!" she purred

106

seductively, coming down the path and standing there before him, rocking slightly, so that her full bosom pressed against his chest. As always, he could feel the heat rising from her, smell the earthy, spicy musk of her flesh that put him in mind of an animal in heat. "My lord *Alaric*'s bed," she added throatily. Her hand came out, warm and dry, and she ran the back of it down his stubbled cheek. "Did she please you, my lord?" she asked, jealousy curdling her creamy tone. "Was the Viking wench as pleasing to you as I once was?"

He shrugged off her hand. "My business is no business of yours, Lady Kendra," he growled.

"I choose to make it so, my Alaric!" she countered. "You went riding abroad in the middle of the night, did you not? And for what reason? To seek respite from your lust in a swift gallop, I would wager! If the Viking slut brought you no ease, then Kendra assuredly can." Her hand slid down his chest and flanks to his thigh, and she caressed him. The other curled about his neck, rumpling the damp curls that hugged his corded neck with eager, knowing fingers. Closer she came, until her lips barely brushed his, until her breasts thrust against his chest and he could feel the large, hardened nipples burning through the fabric of her garment. Angrily he untangled her cloying arms, thrusting her firmly away from him and continuing on down the path to his bower, Kendra's disappointed curse following him through the darkness like the spitting hiss of an angry she-cat.

The rushlights had burned down. The bower lay in heavy shadow. Freya slept, the deep rise and fall of her breathing filling the darkness. As he crossed the bower, she whimpered in her dreams like a frightened child. Belatedly recalling that she was unbound, he fumbled in the darkness for the leather thongs he yet had fastened to him, and lashed one of her wrists to his own. Satisfied she could not move without wakening him, and weary himself, he tumbled into the bed beside her and slept deeply. His last thoughts before doing so were of Kendra and his brother, Farant. Tomorrow, he must take the course of action he had decided upon, and see them sent away from Kenley to Winchester and Alfred's court. There Kendra could not endeavor to practise her seductive wiles on him . . .

107

Chapter 9

The girl was still deeply asleep when he awoke the next morning. He untied the thong from about their wrists. She sighed heavily and murmured in relief, but did not waken. Pale lavender shadows stained the unblemished flesh beneath her eyes. Faint lilac shadows traced the lids, which were fringed by a crescent of dark, tawny lashes. Her breath came even and sweet from between full lips still stained a deep coral by his ardent kisses of the night before. In slumber, the haughty beauty of her face was relaxed and breathtakingly lovely, he thought, and again guilt dug its tiny spurs into his conscience. "You seem little more than a child, Freya of Danehof," he murmured softly, toying with a wandering red-gold curl, then instantly cast such an unwelcome thought aside. The knot upon his head still ached with a dull yet insistent throb. He should be cursing her, not mooning over her beauty!

Rising from the bed, he quickly donned fresh garments and left the bower to summon a guard, ordering him to bring food for the girl. Then he went in search of his old nurse, Lona, bidding her find clothes for his slave wench. The old woman, her wimple-framed face as dark and wrinkled as a walnut, beamed at him and promised to do so. After Kendra, he was her favorite amongst her former charges, and she could deny him nothing.

"Tamed is she, my lord?" she inquired hopefully, cocking her head to one side and peering up at him. She had never forgiven the Vikings for killing her chieftain's two young sons

108

all those years ago, nor for the loss of her young daughter, whom they had carried away in their dragon-ships to become a slave in their heathen lands.

"Tamed? That Viking she-wolf?" Alaric snorted. "Nay, Lona, not tamed, not yet! But soon—!" he promised her.

She nodded sagely, and flashed him a smile that owed more to gums than teeth. "Good lad," she murmured, gazing adoringly up at the towering dark man before her, "Bless you! You were ever a fine lad, young Alaric, and ever mindful of your duty and your birth, and even your old nurse. Make the Viking wench pay! That's the way of it!"

"I will do what I have to," Alaric promised, knowing only too well the bitterness and grief that had scarred his old nurse's life. They were the same wounds that had scarred his own. "Look not to your simples and potions, old mother. I will deal with her myself, and in my own way—not in the ways of the Old Ones!"

Lona managed to look indignant. "By the Blessed Cross, whatever are ye thinking of, my young lord?" she sputtered, eyeing him craftily. "Was your old Lona not baptized Christian by a fat bishop himself? I practice no pagan magic nor spellbinding!" She spat, a thin stream of yellow liquid arching to the rushes.

"Indeed?" He grinned. "Then how is it you have not aged this score of years, and still have the face and figure of a beauteous young maid?"

Old Lona threw back her head and cackled with laughter. "Get along with you and your false flattery, you young rogue! Not aged indeed! Look at this face—this crooked body—this seamed and spotted skin! Not aged!" she clucked, shaking her head. But for all that, she was pleased, he knew.

Grinning, Alaric left old Lona and made his way to the great hall where his steward and uncle, Ordway, his Aunt Valonia, their son, Cullen, Farant, and Kendra were breaking the night's fast, seated at fixed benches against the wall along one side of a long trestle table placed before them, while the slaves and serving wenches attended them from the other side.

Many men lay about the hall, dead to the world, drunk and snoring after the victory feast of the day before. Alaric picked his way between them and took his seat. After he had washed his hands in the basin of water that a servant held out to him, he dried them, and helped himself from a heaped platter to oatcakes dipped in clover honey and some stewed eel and smoked herring. As he speared the succulent eel with his knife and ate, he was aware that Kendra was watching him covertly from hooded eyes.

"Good morrow, my lord! Have you heard the news, sir?" she asked sweetly, but there was an undercurrent of acid to the sweetness.

"What news, sister?" he inquired with equal sweetness and an innocent grin. He would warrant he already knew what it was that had caused that curdled smile!

"My lord husband has decided we are to journey to Winchester, and Alfred's court," she supplied, tight-lipped.

"Indeed? Well, I have no doubt you will find such a visit pleasing, madam. There is little to entertain one here, whereas in Alfred's court there are minstrels and harpists, jugglers and acrobats, scholars and foreign visitors aplenty. I wager after a fourteen-nights' time, 'twill be difficult to draw thee back to Kenley after such entertainments, sister."

"Think you so, my lord? I beg to disagree! I find much that is pleasing and entertaining here, and am most loath to go!" There was a lightness to her words, but Alaric was not deceived. "I have begged my lord Farant to go alone. Without myself and my ladies, he could make the journey in half the time. But he will not." A sulky droop tugged at the corners of her generous mouth, and her eyes were malicious as they rested upon her husband. "Won't you speak with him, and advise him of the wisdom of traveling alone?"

"Nay, sister, I will not. Nor can I fault him. He is your lord, and his great love for you is obvious to everyone. I warrant it would seem to my brother as if his sun—your lovely self, madam—had fled his sky, were he to be parted from you!" He smiled lazily and inclined his head, noting the dark, angry flush that rose up her golden throat to stain her cheeks and the dangerously brilliant glitter of her eyes. She was yet a stunning woman, her mature, sensual beauty as potent a force as her youthful gypsy comeliness had proven. But if one looked

110

closely, there were tiny lines winging out from eye and lip now, marring her golden complexion, which was of somewhat coarser texture than it once had been. Her raven-black tumble of hair, still worn loose about her face after the fashion of a far younger woman, was woven here and there with silver threads. Aye, he thought, quaffing his mead and regarding her dispassionately over the rim of his goblet, the bloom was off this dark rose. Involuntarily, he found his thoughts straying to another, one whose very flesh glowed with the inner radiant vigor of good health and youth, whose jewel eyes sparkled with energy and life, whose lissome body was taut and firm, with no sign of the excesses in which Kendra had indulged all her life, and which were now beginning to take their toll on her already voluptuous figure.

Something of his thoughts must have been revealed by his expression, for Kendra cast Farant a still more withering glance, which her husband studiously ignored save for a telltale tightening of his jaw that betrayed his displeasure. She slammed her drinking horn down and rose abruptly to her feet, muttering that she begged their forgiveness, but was feeling out of sorts and would retire to her bower. So saying, she flung about and sped from the hall.

"Do you think I should go after her?" Valonia wondered aloud. "Perhaps your lady wife is at long last with child, Farant? That would explain her sudden indisposition, would it not?"

"Pray be seated, my lady aunt, and finish your meal. What ails my lady wife is naught but her temper, which I have crossed, nothing more. She will recover before long," Farant insisted wryly. "I shall ask after her health myself, by your leave?" Receiving it, he also rose and stalked from the hall.

"All this talk of women has reminded me—what of your slave, Alaric? How was she?" Cullen demanded, wearing a lecherous grin and waving his knife, with a succulent piece of eel speared upon it, about in the air, nudging the young ealdorman as he did so.

"Later, cousin. Would you offend your lady mother with bawdy talk?" Alaric answered evasively, gray eyes amused.

Cullen sighed. "Confound it, I know you well, Alaric. You

111

were never one to kiss and tell! My lady mother or nay, you will tell me naught, I know it. Mayhap—mayhap you would be willing to share the wench, that I may satisfy my curiosity myself?" he ended hopefully.

"As willing as are you, cousin, to share *your* wenches with me!" Alaric said with a grin. He turned from his cousin to his uncle. Ordway's eyes were twinkling at the two young men's good-natured exchange. "Uncle, I would discuss the matter of the king's *feorm* with the reeve, unless you have already spoken with Master Winfield?"

"Nay, not yet. But the king's food-rent seems fair to me. A day's provender for himself and his retinue provided by the churls of Kenley each year is little enough price to pay for the protection of his *fyrd* in times of attack, think you not? But we will talk more of all this anon. First I would have you discuss a more pressing matter—concerning the Lady Meredyth, Alaric." Ordway shot his nephew a glance that was laden with meaning.

"Fair Meredyth of Powys? Then you believe her lord father would favor a union between our households?"

"I do. Kent is small but powerful, and favored by the high king himself. Moreover, you are Alfred's viceroy, and a very wealthy man in your own right. Lord Eamonn would be a fool not to jump eagerly at the chance to have a powerful man such as yourself for a son-in-law, with the Danes almost battering at his back door!"

Alaric nodded, but was markedly lacking in enthusiasm.

"What is it, nephew?" Ordway asked. "Do you think to find the Lady Meredyth displeasing as your bride and chatelaine of Kenley?"

"Nay, 'tis not that. I have heard she is slender and very fair of face, virtuous and possessed of all the womanly graces and talents. She would be a fitting mistress for my hall. But—"

"But what? If you hesitate in this, Alaric, there are many others who will not—petty Welsh princes and lords who would be only too willing, aye, *eager,* to take the Lady Meredyth as wife. I have learned that the damosel and her father are to take ship from Wales to visit London next month. Will you go there to offer her father for her hand, or nay? Only say the word, and

I will arrange a meeting with him. If Eamonn agrees, as I am certain he will, you may be betrothed within the week, and wed within the year. What say you?"

Still Alaric hesitated, unwilling to commit himself. He had returned from years of battling the Danes eager to wed and beget heirs for Kenley, but somehow the thought of marriage to the Lady Meredyth left him cold. Unaccountably, Freya's vibrant beauty filled his mind, and he scoffed at the direction his thoughts had continually led him since she had exploded into his life. She was naught but a lowly slave, and yet—it almost seemed as if she had bewitched him in some way! Nay. 'Twas infatuation, that was all . . . He scowled, his jaw tightened, and he nodded to his uncle. "See the arrangements made. If the lady is as pleasing to me as she sounds, I will wed and bed her within the year as you suggest, uncle, and Kenley will be assured of its heir."

Ordway nodded in satisfaction. "I will see it done. And now, you wished to discuss the food-rent?"

They fell to discussion of the *feorm* and the estates and King Alfred's shrewd new plan to divide the garrisons of his thanes into two relays, one-half of which was to go to war, the other half meanwhile to tend the fields and farms at home, and for the moment both Meredyth and Freya were forgotten.

Freya awoke with a throbbing headache, her eyes opening then quickly screwing tightly shut as the brilliant shafts of early summer sunlight pierced through the narrow wind-eyes to blind her.

By Odin, how her head ached! In truth, the Saxon mead was stronger than that of Danehof. She stretched stiffly, wincing at the smarting between her thighs and at the aching of her limbs where she had been chained. Remembering suddenly that she had also discovered during the night that Alaric had returned and tied her wrist to his, she glanced down to find the thong had gone. To all intents and purposes, she was free to move about the room as she wished.

She stood and picked her way across the bower to retrieve Alaric's tunic from the floor where it lay, roughly discarded

113

the night before, and slipped it on to cover her nakedness. Pale bruises mottled her upper arms, a legacy of the furious battle she had waged against him to defend her honor. All to no avail, she thought miserably, shuddering as she remembered. How was it that men seemed to find such pleasure in such a vile and ridiculous act? There had been nothing but pain and shame and overwhelming distaste in it for her. But she was alive—and so long as there was breath remaining in her body, she would concentrate all her energies on escaping this prison. What was done was done. She could change none of it, and moping and bewailing the irrevocable loss of her innocence was not in keeping with her character. To fight back, when the odds against her were at their greatest, was.

Dressed now, she was aware of other urgent needs as her belly growled loudly. Never had she been so hungry! She had not eaten since the morn before the attack, she realized. Was this how the Saxons dealt with their slaves, she wondered irritably—by starving them into submission? Moreover, she had a pressing need to relieve herself, and though her hunger could wait, this natural function could not. She padded to the door and hammered loudly upon it. There was a rattle of keys, and then the door opened inward. A beefy man-at-arms stood there, eyeing her with suspicion.

"Aye?" he asked sourly.

"Where is your lord master?" she demanded arrogantly.

"Breaking his fast in the hall, wench," the man retorted, "not that it is any concern of yours." His eyes roved over her insolently, and despite herself she felt heat rise up her face, knowing what he must be imagining.

She tossed her head, and planted her small fists arrogantly on her hips. "Then summon him here, to his bower," she demanded. "I have certain needs, for all that I am his 'slave,'" she snapped, "and would see them dealt with."

"Needs?"

"*Ja!*" she retorted, made impatient by the slow working of his mind. "Is there no place here for such things—or do Saxons have no bladders, as they of a certainty have no backbones?"

The seasoned soldier blinked, then blushed, more embarrassed than angered. For all that the wench was a slave and a hated Viking, she was of noble birth, to all accounts, and noble women, to his mind, did not voice such needs aloud!

"The—the privy?" he ventured.

"*Ja, ja,* the privy!" she acknowledged. "Where is it?"

"I will ask my lord A—"

"There is no time for the asking, I tell you, dolt!" she flared. "You escort me, if you must!"

Grumbling, he grasped her elbow and reluctantly led her down through the fortress.

Many people were about, busy at their tasks. Through the opened doorways of bowers that led off the great feasting hall, she saw groups of women spinning and chattering as they worked, distaffs and spindles flying; yet others worked at their looms, keddles and shuttles moving as rapidly as their tongues. The results of their industry—finely worked tapestries depicting all manner of scenes—draped the walls, and gave the smoke-darkened wood and stone an appearance of wealth and luxury befitting a king. The timber beams were richly carved, and all manner of cleverly wrought little folk and animals, birds, and flowers peeked out at her as she passed. She drew more than one curious eye as her reluctant escort chivvied her along, not least of these the lecherous, questioning eyes of the one named Cullen of Kenley, who had captured her the day before. He halted in his passage through the hall and gazed at her in frank and open admiration.

"Saxon swine!" she hissed at him as they passed, but to her dismay and no little irritation, he seemed to find her insult amusing, and threw back his head and roared with laughter.

"Still sharp-tongued, vixen?" he queried. "If my lusty cousin cannot tame thee, wench, mayhap the task will happily fall to me!" he taunted, and in shame she felt her cheeks fill with color.

Haughtily tossing her burnished tresses, she followed the guard out to the bailey.

Many dwellings were clustered within the timber palisades of Kenley, housing the families of the ealdorman's smith, cooper, fletcher, fowler, and so on. Hunting hounds came loping from Alaric's hound-keeper's kennels to yap at her heels, but were quickly scattered by the guard's well-placed boot and roared curses. In one larger building she glimpsed a shaggy pony circling around and around, drawing the massive querns, grinding stones, to make flour from barley grain. Small children stared at her mutely as she passed, as if she were some strange and wondrous creature they had never seen before— which indeed she was, she thought wryly, for she was a hated Viking, their enemy! No doubt their mothers had told them that the Vikings devoured babes and drank their blood for mead! Women paused in the sweeping of their huts, in their kneading of bread, or in the nursing of their babes to hurl a curse or two in her wake.

"Murderer of innocent babes!" they screeched. "Viking whore—a curse on thee!"

Freya closed her ears to their words, stoically ignoring them. Such behavior had been the lot of the thralls brought from their homelands of Britain to Danehof in years past. She could expect no better treatment now that her position was reversed from captor to captive. If their treatment of her proved no worse than shouted insults, she could bear it.

They reached the screen of woven reeds that concealed the privy, and the guard bade her make haste. With an irritable nod, Freya ducked behind it.

Oh, how sweet was relief, Freya thought as he led her back through the throng and inside the enormous, rectangular aisled hall again moments later. If only they would permit her to wash herself and rid her body of the Saxon's lusty scent and the sensation of his foul hands upon her, she might feel a thousand times improved—

"The *sauna*," she asked. "Where is it?" Seeing him frown, she added for his dull-wit's benefit, "the bathhouse!"

"Bath?" Alarm flared in his eyes, and he hurriedly crossed himself and made the horned, two-fingered sign with his hand that was intended to ward off the evil eye, directing it at her. "Bah! All they say about the Northmen is true! Do ye not know that bathing is an abomination, wench?" he growled. "Our holy church teaches that it is the root of excessive pride in oneself, and lays one open to all manner of foul humors that would take over the body."

"*Ja,*" she agreed apparently, but with a little sniff of distaste, "and lack of it to all manner of other small crawling creatures, no doubt, and a reek that brings tears to the eyes! The river will suffice. You will take me there?"

"Nay, I dare not! For this, ye must ask of my lord!"

With a disappointed sigh Freya allowed him to march her back inside, only too well aware of the curious stares she received once again from servants and slaves en route back to Alaric's bower. As they made their way down a long, well-trod path toward it, she heard voices coming from beyond another bower door left ajar, Alaric's voice and another's, the one who had called herself Kendra, she realized. She pretended she had wrenched her ankle and paused to lean down and rub it while the guard waited, but in truth she was curious and wanted to hear what it was the pair discussed so heatedly.

"Must you ever try my patience!" the woman snapped angrily. "I have no wish to go to court, nor anywhere else for that matter. You cannot buy my favor with jewels and baubles! Go if you must, but I will stay!"

"I love thee, Kendra," the man said heatedly, and Freya saw Alaric attempt to embrace the woman, and her furious rebuff. "Why must there be this coldness between us?"

Kendra's answer was lost as the guard growled at Freya, "Get along, wench!" and they moved down the path to the ealdorman of Kenley's large bower.

"Who is she—the black-haired one?" she demanded of the guard.

"My lord Farant's lady wife," the guard supplied.

"Farant?"

"Aye. Lord Alaric's own brother." With that, he flung open the door and shoved her inside the bower.

In her absence a platter of victuals had been brought for her: a wedge of hard, black bread, some chunks of what looked like grayish eel, and a small earthen crock of Saxon beer. She sipped the beer first, and found it very good—superior to the Danish ale she was used to. The bread, however hard, and the marsh eel, though not her favorite dish, tasted delicious after so long without food, and she devoured it to the last crumb, morsel, and drop. Her belly's loud protests for the moment

117

stilled, her headache dulled, she sat back down upon the sleeping couch and considered her situation.

Her visit to the privy had served two purposes, one the obvious one, the second more devious. Had the guard but known it, she had been assessing everything they passed on their way through the Saxon fortress with a view to escape, should the chance ever present itself! She had noted the formidable earthworks circling the demesne, topped with a wood and stone walk and gate towers, all heavily patrolled and guarded by the soldiers of Alaric's garrison; had even counted the number of guards. The information might well prove useful some day. She was still pondering her possible escape when the door was flung open and Alaric himself strode inside.

He tossed several small combs, carved from deer antlers, and a kirtle of undyed creamy wool onto the bed beside her, nodding at them and ordering her gruffly, "Here, wench, put this on. We leave shortly."

She stiffened as he approached her, the previous night's events flooding through her. She eyed the garment he had tossed at her with blatant disgust, making no move to pick it up. "I will not!" she refused adamantly. She edged away from the worn but freshly laundered garment as if it crawled with vermin, and haughtily tossed her head.

"I do not ask thee, Viking. I command thee!" he uttered sternly, his massive fists balled against his thighs.

"And I refuse! It is the undyed garment of a thrall, *nej?* Well, I am no thrall!" she said hotly, her eyes bright with fierce pride and scorn.

"In your native Jutland, nay, you are not. But here in my burh, you are indeed my slave, like it or nay! Dress, and quickly, before I lose temper with thee," Alaric gritted, minded to wring her by the neck for her obstinacy.

"*Nej!*"

"Then have it your way." He strode to the door, aware of her quizzical tawny brows drawing together at his sudden capitulation. "If you will not dress, you will attend me as you were yesterday. Naked. There are many of my garrison who would relish such a treat as they enjoyed then—!"

Her haughty expression dwindled. The shame of that

moment flooded back to her in unpleasantly sharp clarity, and she again felt all those pairs of hot little eyes riveted upon her body as she walked through the feasting hall, the women's like tiny, sharpened knives, itching to shred her; the men's like slimy, loathsome little worms, squirming all over her. She sprang to her feet as he made to fling open the door and leave. "Wait! You—you would not!" she cried after him, her lilting Danish accent giving the words added pathos; then she caught the stern gleam in his gray eyes and added faintly, with a heavy sigh, "*Ja*, you would!"

With exquisite slowness, a slowness that would have made a snail seem a speedy creature indeed, she turned from him and yanked off his tunic and the cord that had belted it. Afterward, she picked up between her index fingers and thumbs the hated coarse kirtle he had brought and slipped the shapeless garment over her head, distaste stamped upon every feature and line of her proud face, from the curl of her coral lips to the contemptuous flaring of her nostrils. Defiantly she retrieved the tasseled cord and knotted it about her waist. "So," she muttered at great length, smoothing the garments down over her waist and hips, "you are perhaps satisfied now, Saxon?"

"I am. 'Twas a wise decision, Freya," he acknowledged, again closing the door and adding wickedly, "though 'tis a sin to hide such loveliness beneath garments."

She blushed at his bold words and looked hurriedly away, the rosy blush that bloomed in her cheeks a comely contrast to the sapphire frost in her eyes. Why must he stare at her so, as though although she was dressed, he still saw her as she had been last night beneath him, completely bared to his eyes? She did not know how to deal with this situation, and the knowledge frightened her. Why did he not make a lunge for her, like a stag in full rut, if he lusted for her? At least then she could fight him off, do *something*. But the bandying of flirtatious words was territory she knew little about. When the men of Danehof had attempted to flirt with her and tease her, a single frigid glance had been sufficient to freeze the bawdy words on their lips. But—such glances would have no such effect on this great black-haired lout, she knew without a shadow of doubt.

"And now," he continued as if he had not observed her loss of composure, though she knew full well he must have, "your hair. You will braid it, wench, and use the combs that I brought you to fasten it in place."

"*Nej!* I will not! Hair is worn braided only by matrons where I come from. For women who are—who are no longer maidens!" she protested weakly, crimson color flooding her cheeks to discuss such a subject with *him*.

"'Tis the same as our custom here, in Britain. And since last night, you are no longer a maid," he reminded her with obvious relish. "Save for when we are alone here, in my bower, and you serve my pleasure, you will braid your hair in this manner each morning henceforth," he commanded. "Begin!"

"But—everyone will know that you—that last night I—that you and I—!"

"They will indeed," he agreed softly, amusement dancing in his smoky eyes. "And it is my wish that all here should know I have bedded Thorfast's icy daughter, and that she is no longer a maid! However," and his grin deepened, "if you should be reluctant to bind up your hair, my captive beauty, we will stay here, and find some means to divert ourselves other than riding abroad . . . ?" He glanced pointedly toward the bed, then back at her, his gray eyes narrowing sensually as he feasted his gaze upon the rounded mounds of her breasts, thrusting like firm ripe pears against the cloth of her kirtle, and upon the womanly curves of her hips and buttocks, no doubt remembering only too well what lay beneath the garment.

So piercing, so knowing and hungry was the expression in his smoky eyes that a strange little quiver darted through her loins, and of their own volition her nipples hardened, expanded, thrusting against the kirtle's scratchy wool with an eager will of their own, as if urging him to—to gaze upon them, she thought, mortified by her body's treason. With a muttered curse, she folded her arms over her breasts and showed him her back, taking up the horn combs—which she now saw he had tossed to the bed, along with the kirtle—and commencing the task of combing and braiding the shining red-gold mane that cascaded like a waterfall halfway down her back, as he had commanded.

Alaric took a seat upon his carved chair to watch her and poured himself a draught of mead to quench his thirst while he did so. He had always enjoyed the seductive picture created by a lovely maid combing out her long hair, and this Viking wench was no exception. With graceful, even strokes, she combed the tumbling red-gold tresses back from her temples and brow, the teeth of the comb marking tiny furrows in the heavy, shiny curtain. It fascinated him that she could create such a picture of feminine beauty and grace, when at heart she was as fierce as her male counterparts. How different she appeared now, in her woman's garb, from the slender, legging-clad sea-wolf she had appeared yesterday!

When her hair was freed of all tangles, loose and gleaming like a sheet of beaten copper and gold with curling ends, she divided it into two even hanks, ready for braiding. Her graceful fingers moved deftly to part each of the two hanks into strands of three and braid them in shining ropes behind each ear. Afterward she twisted the braids like a coronet across the crown of her head and secured it by the smaller, delicately carved combs. Alaric hid a smile. So, she had fashioned herself a regal crown, had she? It was clear he yet had his work cut out for him in taming this proud beauty! Yet he said nothing of her small but pointed act of defiance, for he found himself transfixed by the vulnerable, downy nape of her neck that was exposed by the braiding.

"In truth, you are a vision!" he muttered, moved to words despite all wishes to the contrary as she turned her head slowly to look at him, for she was even lovelier clothed than he had ever imagined, for all that it was the rough, undyed woolen kirtle of a servant that clung to her supple curves. He wondered how she would appear robed richly, like a Viking queen, envisioning her in a kirtle edged with luxuriant fox fur, a mantle of matching fur falling away from her shoulders. Her shining red-gold mane would be woven with glittering jewels, a golden fillet adorning her lovely brow, her slender waist encircled by a belt of hammered gold, studded with more sparkling gems . . . and then he cursed himself silently for his flights of fancy.

He went to her and held her by the upper arms, firmly

121

raising her to stand before him without turning her about. He lowered his ebony head and pressed his flaming mouth to the soft, downy flesh of her nape, aware of the sudden response that leaped firelike through her trembling body as he did so. Fear, he wondered distantly, his tongue tip dancing over her nape in fiery little assaults, his lips eagerly tasting the sweet, warm flesh that was like the sunkissed skin of a fresh golden peach—or had he kindled her woman's desire? Still kissing her lovely, swanlike neck, he slipped his hands down her arms and around to her breasts, cupping their fullness in each of his large palms.

The nipples were already swollen, he learned, grazing the sensitive little peaks with the balls of his thumbs. To his pleasure, he discovered that they swelled still further under his gentle touch, becoming like large, wild raspberries, warm on the cane in the heat of the summer sun. With a groan he pulled her back against his chest and nuzzled the tiny, curling tendrils of hair that had proved too short and escaped her braids. Her hair had the scent of fresh-mown hay about it. He greedily inhaled its scent, still fondling her breasts through the cloth of her kirtle, fully aware that the hard, manly length of him was molded firmly to her slender back and the sweetly rounded, dimpled curves of her bottom, and that she could not help being aware of his arousal.

A little sob caught in her throat as his long, strong fingers idly continued their enflaming conquest. Nay! He would not force that—that *abomination* upon her again this morn! She tried to shrug off his marauding hands and arched forward, seeking escape from his embraces, her eyes fixed on the amber glass shards strewn on the rushes where she had flung the claw beaker at him the night before. If only she could reach them, they would prove a weapon to be reckoned with, brandished dagger-like in her fists! Muttering furiously, she endeavored to unclamp his strong fingers from about her body, forcing them hard against the bone, kicking backward with her bare feet.

In answer, he only laughed deeply and locked his arms still tighter about her waist, leaned down and whispered hotly in her ear. The stream of words was barbarous, uncouth, a soldier's rough language of desire, of lust and of coupling, that made her redden furiously with embarrassment and outrage—she, Freya of Danehof, who had thought herself incapable of maidenly blushes! But despite her revulsion, for some strange reason his lusty threats sent gooseflesh rising and tingling all over her, coupled with spirals of apprehension. Closing her eyes, she willed herself to submit to his caresses as he had commanded, knowing he would not hesitate to carry out his foul threats if she resisted; sensing that he *wanted* her to resist him—so, by Loki, she would not!

His hands moved knowingly over her breasts. His lean fingers kneaded them sensuously, rolling and gently tweaking the aching nipples between the balls of his fingers in a manner that all but caused her to cry out—but with breathless pleasure, not pain, she realized, horrified by her treacherous body's responses.

"Still so cold and haughty, my ice maiden?" he queried huskily against her shell-like ear. "Does your frigid Nordic blood warm to Alaric's touch, or is it yet frozen as a glacier?"

"Still cold, my lord, still cold," she snapped, yet she knew full well she lied! It was plain her father's hot blood flowed also in her veins, yet no man—or no man till this Saxon cur!—had ever brought that fiercely passionate nature bubbling to the surface, not even her dear friend Olaf, though he had desired her, she knew.

She felt her womanhood contract and quiver like the flutter of a frightened bird's wings, deep in her loins. A warm blush seeped through her entire body as the hard, fiery ridge of Alaric's great manhood burned and nudged against the small of her back, growing harder and more fiery by the minute. Like pictures upon a tapestry, she could see him in her mind's eye as he had been the night before, coming toward her with his towering, muscled, unclothed body a gleaming bronze in the torchlight, his manhood great and ready . . . The memory made tiny beads of perspiration spring out upon her upper lip and palms. Oh, dear Frey, let him cease this! Make him stop his maddening strokes and squeezes and feathery little caresses, before she succumbed to the restless quivers stirring within her and surrendered . . . ! There was an insistent throbbing, a miniature pulsing deep in her belly that was like nothing she had ever experienced before. The strange sensation of heat and discomfort made her want to press her hips against his hard flanks, and *somehow* ease the bittersweet hunger within her; to twine her fingers in his glossy black curls and draw that handsome, raven-black, hated head down to hers; to taste his hard, salty mouth and his hateful hot kisses upon her own, and feel the roughness of his swarthy male cheeks against her soft, womanly ones . . . Nay, nay, it could not be so, she cried silently, she could not—*would* not—find pleasure in his touch! Nay, not when his caresses, however pleasurable, led to that other, hurtful, awful act—! When he suddenly thrust her away from him, it was all she could do to staunch the sharp cry of relief that welled inside her. Or—was it relief . . . ?

"We must be gone," he said huskily, his smoldering eyes sending her a message that was oh, so very different to the one uttered by his lips.

"As you will," she retorted coldly, the words spilling from her too fast, too eagerly, the relief that he had been diverted from his dangerous purpose betrayed by her darkened eyes.

There were horses awaiting them outside in the bailey, and a groom or two to see them safely mounted. The horse chosen for her was a dappled gray mare, and she scrambled easily astride it without assistance, hoisting her skirts up about her thighs and baring pale gold flesh and pretty knees in the process.

Alaric rode his own great, shaggy black war stallion with the huge, feathered hooves. It was several handspans taller than her own dainty beast, and horse and rider dwarfed her and her finely-boned mount. They seemed well matched, she thought grudgingly, eyeing the fine picture Alaric made in a deep saffron tunic with a black mantle thrown carelessly over it, pinned at one shoulder. The silver mantle brooch was of a style she had never seen before, the top fashioned in a semicircle of radiating bars, set with teardrops of amber like the rays of the sun. The Saxon jewelers were clever fellows, apparently, and gifted at their craft, as were the armorers—or could be construed so by the magnificent jeweled hilt of the broadsword Alaric wore, which was fine enough to have been crafted by the legendary armorer Weland himself. A full rod in length, heavy and double-bladed but tapered toward the tip after the Norse fashion, the hilt and crosspiece were spun about with what at first glance appeared to be randomly wound ornamental gold wires, but which in effect gave the weapon a rough, serviceable grip that would not easily let it be lost despite the slickness of sweat and blood in combat. She sighed, wondering what had become of her own weapon, *Shining One,* since her capture. Did some cloddish Saxon churl polish the garnet and blue-glass-studded hilt and proudly call it his own? *Ja,* no doubt he did, she thought gloomily, fidgeting with the unaccustomed bunching of her skirts riding up about her thighs as she rode, and longing for the comfort of the leggings she was used to. Oh, if only she had *Shining One* now, she could fight her way free and ride swiftly northeast for the Wessex border!

There was no chance of that, however, for with two guards riding vanguard ahead of her and Alaric, and two other guards bringing up in the rear behind them, the cavalcade set off, riding beneath the timbered palisades and through the tower gate of Kenley, down gently rolling green hills stubbled with pines and bushes, and out into the countryside beyond.

Chapter 10

They rode over winding tracks of rough dirt littered with stones, tracks carved by decades of hooves alongside or between neatly planted strips of barley, oats, or corn, the crops—some as tall as a woman—shivering in the breeze like a sea a-ripple with green or golden waves. The churls tugged at their forelocks and paused in their labors to watch the cavalcade as it passed, and Alaric greeted them all by name, and with a warmth and familiarity that surprised her. Across rolling emerald fields, beyond which the distant sea showed as a pale gray-green stripe beneath the hazy horizon, they rode, and Freya observed, with a seasoned seafarer's knowing eyes, an ominous, lowering dark cloud over the distant chalky cliffs that bore the angry promise of a summer storm yet to come inland. Scarlet poppies nodded serene heads in the wild grasses that bordered the fields, as did the shepherd's purse, the modest daisy, the buttercup and the dandelion, and the wild magenta clover abuzz with furry bees. Wild lupins and vetch added their colors of vivid blue, pink, and red, and the sweet fragrance of honeysuckle wafted on the sultry, expectant breeze, intoxicating the senses.

It was a fair land, this isle of Britain, Freya reflected as she had just yesterday, that fateful morn she had planned to attack Kenley; a fecund, verdant land that could feed many.

She thought of her own lands of Jutland, and of how the marshes and the peat bogs took up most of the northernmost tip, and were useless for planting. Of how the sand swept in from the dunes during a fierce gale to strangle the crops in a salty, rootless embrace; of how each year the cattle grew less sleek, the calves fewer and with more and worse deformities; and she knew without doubt that her ambition to bring her people here to Britain, to a better land and a fairer climate, had been a good one, with their welfare and survival at its heart. How would the people of Danehof survive now, she wondered? Who would rule as *jarl* now that she was gone? *I beg thee, mighty Odin, let Olaf return to Danehof—let him become jarl in my stead!* she prayed fervently but silently. Olaf would see what must be done, she was certain.

Sven had, with a poet's lack of practicality, urged her to give up the raids that had become her people's way of life. Despite his great wisdom and learning in other matters, the old *skald* had not seen that the raids he so despised (which had indeed once been naught but a particularly bloody form of piracy) had altered, become deadly serious; a desperate and determined quest for new lands to conquer and farm that would nourish the Danish people and offer a far richer prize than Christian goblets and crucifixes and golden plate: the prize of life.

"Do you sulk, Viking?" Alaric asked suddenly, noting her silence and looking down at her solemn little face with a quizzical frown as they rode.

"Nay, Saxon. Viking warriors do not sulk!" she retorted acidly. "I was but thinking. I shall leave weak, female nonsense such as sulking to *Saxon* women. Your Lady Kendra—she has mastered this very well, I think, *ja?*"

For all that Alaric had little fondness for Kendra, he had no intent of maligning his kinswoman before a captive Dane wench with a sharp tongue. He grunted noncommittally. "No doubt you will also leave femininity and sweetness of disposition to our Saxon women, too, since 'tis obvious *you* have mastered neither. In truth, I pity the Viking men, who must take such shrews as you to wife! 'Tis little wonder they are eager to go raiding to north, south, east, and west!"

She flushed hotly but said nothing, instead tossing her red-gold head in a defiant gesture and staring stoically at the road ahead of them, her stubborn little jaw jutting. 'Twas obviously a tender subject for him. His caustic response proved as much!

Her mention of Kendra, the woman she had overheard him vow he loved but who, it appeared, gave not a whit for him, had pricked his temper. After the little scene she had eavesdropped upon earlier after her visit to the privy, she did not wonder at his sensitivity.

Alaric, believing his pointed comment had stung her pride and content with this reprimand, rode on in silence.

Some half league farther they came upon a stone marker set up by the roadside that pointed the way to a convent of holy sisters. Freya glanced up at Alaric as they turned the horses seaward in that direction, hoping his expression would give her some clue to his intentions. Could it be that since she had found no pleasure in coupling with him, had insisted she felt nothing at his touch, he had determined to wall her up in a Christian convent? Nay! She'd sooner submit to him or die, than spend her days in a world without fresh air, laughter, and comradeship; without being able to ride and hunt or fish and practice her swordplay. Why, it would not be life at all without these things, but rather a living death! Even her lot as a slave would be preferable to that! Prickles of foreboding filled her belly, and she instinctively reached up to her throat to touch the bronze talismans of Frey and Odin that she'd always worn there, looped on a leather thong, for reassurance, forgetting for an instant that at the time of her capture they had been taken away from her.

"Do you so fear the wrath of the White Christ, my pagan princess?" Alaric, noting the apprehensive gesture, mocked. "Can it be the fierce Viking warrior is afraid to enter a convent? Perhaps you fear He will strike you with thunderbolts for your worship of false Norse gods? For your people's raids on His monasteries and churches?" he jeered.

"I'm afraid of nothing—not this weak Christ who knows so little of war, nor this strange place of women priests, nor you!" she lied scornfully. "Many of my people follow your White Christ, as well as our own fierce, true gods. They scratch his cross symbol on the rune stones for good measure—along with proper Norse symbols. They do not fear Him, and nor do I. There is nothing to fear!"

"So, you fear nothing? Not capture, nor my wrath? Nor the

wrath of your gods nor mine? 'Tis my belief you are one of two things, my Lady of the Frozen Heart. A woman of peerless courage—or a fool!" He grinned. "Which are you?"

"A fool," she answered candidly, and with a firmness of tone that surprised him.

"How so?"

"You talk too much, Saxon cur. When you slept last night, I should have cut out your tongue with the glass splinters from the goblet. Or stabbed you in your foul heart. I did neither. This is why I am a fool!" she hissed.

Angered, but unable to protest without seeming to bear out her insulting comment regarding his verbosity, Alaric was nonplussed. His mind tying itself in knots for a means to put her firmly in her place—other than the obvious—he clamped his jaws tightly closed and stared rigidly ahead. As did she.

The abbey was little more than a series of connecting cells built of quarried gray stone, some of the walls carved from the cliffs themselves that overlooked the pounding sea. Each cell looked out onto a large common quadrangle where herbs and medicinal plants were grown. Lichens softened the harsh gray of these walls, as did twining ivy and yew trees. A high rock wall secluded it, with a cow bell set in its face, close by the main gate. Sister Ursula—the same young postulant who had answered Alaric's summons the day previous—again answered his ring, and at his command led the visitors to the Lady Wilone's spartan chamber.

Alaric's mother sat crosslegged upon a hard wooden bench, rocking back and forth crooning a singsong lullaby to what, at first glance, appeared to be a babe cradled in her arms. On closer inspection, it was obvious the babe existed only in her mind. Her low, eerie singing sent shivers crawling up and down Freya's spine. The woman seemed strange, and Freya had never felt comfortable amongst those afflicted in the mind. In truth, she feared them. She wanted to bolt, but dared not! Besides, Alaric's steely fingers were clamped about her elbow, preventing her escape.

"'Tis I, Alaric!" he said to the woman. "My lady mother, Wilone!"

He had to repeat the greeting several times before the

woman's head jerked up, as if awakened from some deep reverie. She gaped, then frowned, her eyes darting first to one, then the other of them, and then terror flitted across her face like the dark wings of the night owl. She scooped the imaginary infant into her arms and quickly bundled it under the rough brown blanket that lay rumpled on the sleeping bench, smoothing the coverlet over her imagined treasure.

"Gone!" she cried triumphantly, dark eyes cunning, "all gone!" and twined her fingers about each other, twisting and writhing them together like small, seething white snakes in a pit, her strange manner guaranteed to draw Freya's horrified fascination. "Gone! Lost! All lost . . ."

She cowered upon the bed, crouched over and guarding her precious secret, fingers moving, always moving, in and out, in and out, back and forth, back and forth, until Freya feared she would scream.

"Who is she?" she gasped. "Why did you bring me here? Take me away, I beg you!" The woman's madness and the holiness of the place frightened her as even Alaric and his virility had not.

Alaric grinned, his lips merely peeling back from his teeth to give the grin a peculiarly wolfish quality. "Freya of Danehof, it gives me pleasure to introduce to thee my lady mother. She has been this way since your father's raid on Kenley. Since he ravished her that spring morn!" The cold fury she had glimpsed in him from time to time had returned full force now, glittering and dancing in his eyes, turning their smoke-gray to shining silver. "He made her this way, he, Thorfast, your own sire! She was a comely woman once, aye, and a gifted one. Look at her now, curse thee, look!" Freya had turned her head away from the strange woman, but now Alaric strode across the cell and gripped her chin fiercely in his hand, jerking her head sideways and forcing her to look.

The two women's eyes met, one so dark they were the black of a moonless, starless night, the other the lively jewel-blue of starry sapphires. Wilone's smooth white brow creased in a frown. Her mouth dropped open, lips working soundlessly. One hand came up, then the other, the pair swooping and hovering and darting like fluttering white birds before her face as she rose from the bench and advanced on Freya.

"My blood. His blood. But mine will prove stronger at the last . . . !" she muttered. "Blood! Blood! *Blood!*"

The last was emitted as a piercing, bloodcurdling shriek, and Freya flattened herself against the wall, covering her ears and cringing like a whipped cur as Wilone came nearer, nearer.

"Take her away, I beg thee, Saxon! Do not let her near me!" she cried, but Alaric made no move at all to aid her. He simply stood there, smiling grimly as she cringed in utter terror.

All at once the door of the cell burst open and Sister Ursula and another, older nun rushed in. They calmed the madwoman with the skill of long practice, soothing her with words and embraces and reassuring caresses. Then they bundled her warmly in her blanket and gently handed her the imaginary babe, and the older nun led her away. Alaric's anxious eyes followed them, a gesture the young nun observed. Her tender heart went out to the young lord who, for all his confidence and strength, could look with such pain upon his poor, blighted mother.

"Fear not, sir, your lady mother will be cared for. She will pass the day in the infirmary, with a draught to soothe her to sleep."

"She seems worse this morning, sister."

"Aye, my lord. The excitement yesterday worsened her condition, you understand. Our hurried flight into the hills— the fear of being slaughtered by the Danes—it disturbed many of our infirm ones. And besides, your serving woman has blue eyes, does she not? Our Lady Wilone always reacts violently to those who are blue-eyed. By the morrow she will be much improved, I promise you."

Alaric nodded, but appeared little reassured by her words.

"Would your servant care for a sip of well water?" Sister Ursula asked Alaric kindly. "She appears somewhat shaken, does she not? I would be happy to draw some for her."

"My slave needs no water, sister. She is herself a Dane—the leader of the raiding party that planned to raze and loot Kenley just yesterday—and at her own words, she fears and wants for nothing!" he jeered, eyeing Freya askance.

"Blessed Jesu!" the nun exclaimed, hurriedly making the

Sign of the Cross over her breast, herself eyeing Freya now as if she had suddenly begun to sprout horns and tail and snort sulphurous smoke from her nostrils. "A Viking woman!" She might well have said "a witch!" or "an imp of Satan!" judging by the incredulity in her tone.

"A Viking indeed," Alaric agreed, a faint smile curling his lips. He strode to the door. "There are gifts for my lady mother outside, sister, and for your lady abbess and your order. I brought them yesterday, but they were forgotten in the—moment."

"Our heartfelt gratitude for your charity, sir! I will see them taken to our Lady Abbess, Aethelfreda," Ursula promised, "and you and your household will be included in our prayers."

"My thanks. And now I must be on my way." He turned to Freya and snapped, "Attend me!" before striding from the cell.

Curiously chastened and cowed, she scuttled after him.

Mounted again, Alaric dismissed his escort, bidding his guards return to Kenley without him. He nodded to Freya and in silence the two turned their horses for the return journey.

"Why did you take me to that place?" Freya demanded hoarsely. Her tone sounded strained to his ears, the words torn from her with obvious reluctance.

"I wished you to see with your own eyes what your sire did to my mother," he said curtly. "Perhaps now you will understand my hatred of your people, and realize what your raids have wrought on innocents such as she. She saw her husband slain, her two little sons brutally murdered. And then, to save myself and my brother, as yet unborn, she gave herself to your father. He in his turn sent Sven after him to slit her throat."

"And Sven could not," she finished wearily. "*Ja*. I believe it. Sven was ever a gentle man, a misfit amongst my people, who place greatest value on those who are fierce in battle, and do not shrink from bloodshed."

"It was he who raised you, was it not, when Thorfast spurned you from birth?"

"How do you know this?" she demanded sharply, turning to look at him. There was, for a second, a look about him that caused her to think he had been intending to say something more, then thought better of it.

"Karl Ivarson told me much of you, and of your life," he lied.

"Karl! Curse him to Hel's dank kingdom!" Freya spat, a trace of her former spirit resurfacing. "Would I could sink my dagger into his foul traitor's breast!"

"He is already dead," Alaric divulged. "His body was found on the riverbank. Olaf slew him after I sent them both forth from Kenley."

"Ah. 'Tis well he did," she said heatedly, and by her cold tone he knew she would have killed Ivarson herself without hesitation, given the chance.

For a while they both fell silent again, the only sounds the blowing of the horses and the sound of their hooves thudding against the springy turf as they rode. She surprised him by speaking first again.

"I feel nothing but hatred for you, Alaric of Kent. And nor will my feelings ever change. But seeing your mother as she is—I understand now what drove you to take your vengeance upon me. I would have done no less, were our positions reversed. There is no honor without vengeance. And the life that lacks honor is not worth living! This is the creed by which my own people live."

His black brows rose in astonishment that she could feel so, and what was more, would admit it to him. Somehow her admission gave him pleasure, stilled some of the anger that had resurfaced in him earlier. "You amaze me, Freya," he admitted frankly in his turn. "'Tis little wonder your men followed you so fearlessly. It demands great wisdom and courage of any leader to speak with such honesty to any man, and especially to your enemy, as you have now displayed."

"*Takke*, but I only speak the truth as I see it, Saxon. Do not mistake my honesty for surrender or submission to your will, for I intend no such surrender!"

He inclined his head, a smile tugging at the corners of his mouth. "Fear not, firebrand! I am no fool, that I would believe you so easily cowed!"

She nodded firmly, but made no comment.

The brilliant summer sunlight had faded since they entered the abbey, she noted, and the wind had risen now, its eerie moaning mingling with the uneasy, shrill scolding and twittering of birds huddled in the lowest branches of the trees, their feathers fluffed out for protection, their heads tucked under their wings. Above, the plaintive scream of wheeling white and black gulls, headed inland in the face of the storm, vied with the moaning wind to be heard. The peculiar brightness of a lemon-colored sun veiled by ominously ash-colored cloud masses, pregnant with rain, added its strange, hazy beauty to a vista of meadows bearded with tossing trees and shivering hedgerows, and grasses bent almost flat before the sudden wind.

As they cantered their horses faster to outride the fleet summer storm to Kenley, a bolt of thunder crackled loudly in the dun and dark blue sky above, followed quickly by a jagged forked arrow of lightning that turned the sky momentarily bright white. The dappled mare that Freya was riding reared up in terror, screaming shrilly. Her eyes rolled, her nostrils flared, and the muscles beneath her smooth coat bunched and twitched as if given independent life. Freya scarcely had time to take a firm grip on her reins before the nervous beast began circling and dancing on her haunches, tossing her charcoal head and flowing mane and snorting her displeasure all the while.

Alaric leaned down from his saddle, reaching for the mare's bridle, but with an angry muttering Freya kneed her horse out of his reach and the showy, highly strung mare shied nervously away.

"I ride as well as any Saxon, my lord," Freya protested indignantly. "I'll thank you to leave the handling of my mount to me!"

"It's not a question of your horsemanship, wench," Alaric countered, "but a question of a skittish mount and an imminent storm. Hand me your reins! Another lightning flash, and the mare will bolt—!"

No sooner had he voiced the thought than another peal of

thunder clattered loudly overhead. An enormous flash of lightning illuminated the woods and fields and the canopied gray sky. The mare circled once, then suddenly took the bit between her teeth and bolted forward, ignoring her rider's signals to halt, or even to slow down.

It was only by exerting the strongest self-control that Freya did not give way to panic and lose her seat. The mare's dainty legs worked furiously beneath her as they galloped at suicidal speed over the meadow, outracing the swift-scudding storm clouds. Blurs of charcoal color became one never-ending stripe of sooty brown and gray banded with the rich green grass beneath, flying under them like a moving tapestry as the mare's hooves thrummed the turf. The wind and the wildness of the ride tore the combs from her hair, wresting it free of the braids, until red-gold tresses streamed over her shoulders like pennants and whipped hectic color into her cheeks. The swift tattoo of her horse's hooves was partnered now by the thunder of another's hooves as Alaric kicked his stallion into pursuit. Even as she strived to control her horse, thoughts of escape flitted tantalizingly through her head. She had several horses' lengths lead on the Saxon. Dare she hope she could outdistance him and leave him behind—perhaps somehow cross the borders of the Danelaw to the north? The thought was swiftly cast aside as she was forced to turn her complete attention to controlling the bolting horse.

They rapidly left the meadows behind and plunged on into the dense woods, where sly branches lay in ambush across the bridle path and conspired to wrest the unwary rider from the saddle, or to score the cheeks with vicious stripes, like whips. Still Freya was carried furiously on, twisting and ducking in the saddle to avoid the wicked obstacles as the mare careened blindly between the rowans and the alders. Ahead, a massive felled oak lay across their path, barring the horse's headlong flight. There was no time to avoid it, she realized; their only hope lay in jumping.

She wound the reins about her hands and hunched forward in the saddle over her mount's arched neck, gripping her fiercely with both knees as if gathering the mare up beneath her. They cleared the fallen oak with scant inches to spare. The mare swiftly recovered her stride and careened crazily on. Behind her, Alaric sailed effortlessly over the jump astride his massive Lucifer, and thundered after her down a narrow defile.

"The shore!" he roared. "Turn her head for the shore!"

She realized the wisdom of his command instantly and strove to do so, hauling hard on the mare's reins until she screamed in pain as the bit gauged her tender mouth and reluctantly veered left, toward the sea.

A rubbled track led downward from the grassy headlands to the pale shore. Soon the mare's hooves were striking the heavy wet sand, its dragging, sucking texture perceptibly slowing her wild flight and throwing up great wet clods of sand in her wake. Gulls, curlews, and terns screamed their alarm and rose in great wheeling clouds from their cliff nests, circling angrily overhead as the two horses and their riders thundered along the sand and shingle.

The sand served its purpose. Soon the mare had slowed her wild gallop, and Alaric easily outdistanced her and leaned down from Lucifer's back to capture the animal's bridle. Both beasts slithered abruptly to a halt. Freya lost the reins and tumbled head over heels from her mount's back, rolled once, then lay still, face down on the shore.

At once Alaric slid from his stallion's back and ran quickly to crouch beside her, fearing she had been knocked senseless by the fall. He reached out to roll her over. To his surprise, in that instant she turned by herself and quickly sat up unaided. Wet sand plastered her nose and chin, her cheeks, her hair, giving her a comical cast. She saw the concern in his eyes, and her sapphire eyes sparkled merrily.

"Fear not, Saxon!" she said dryly, grimacing. "Your slave is quite unharmed, your property intact, other than suffering a bruise or two to her—dignity!" And to his further astonishment, she suddenly tossed back her head and laughed, brushing the sand from her face as she did so.

It was a husky, delightful sound, one he had not heard before. It did strange things to his breathing—when he again remembered to take a breath. Suddenly he realized he wanted badly to hear her carefree laughter once more; to see again that enchanting, bewitching smile that caused two small dimples in

136

her cheeks to deepen ... Grinning himself, gray eyes twinkling, he reached out a strong hand to help her to her feet, and to his surprise she grasped it and gladly accepted his help with thanks.

When she was again upright, he did not release her hand but simply stood there, looking down into her uptilted face like one bedazzled. She, in her turn, stared up at him as if seeing him—really seeing him—for the first time. There was, in the air between them, a sudden, sweet stirring; some strange, powerful, magical force that held them spellbound as they were, immobile, their gazes transfixed. The scream of the gulls, the roar of the waves beating against the rocks, the crackle of the distant thunder seemed to recede in that moment out of time. The dour heavens above and the wet, dark sand beneath ceased to exist. Master and slave had no meaning here, for they were both slaves in that moment to a far more potent, ancient force ... There was Alaric, the man. There was Freya, the woman. There was that magical moment between them. Nothing more.

"It's raining, Saxon," she breathed throatily, at length breaking the spell as she felt the wet splash of raindrops against her cheeks. The threatened storm was at last unleashed. Her pink tongue darted forth to lick the moisture from her lips, a provocative gesture that strangely fascinated him.

"Aye," he murmured. "It is."

"We should seek shelter," she insisted, and even as she said the words, that peculiar little quiver was there again, in the pit of her belly, uncurling, unfolding, spreading out, its warmth stealing through her ...

"Aye," he murmured again, and dimly wondered at his inability to act.

Of a sudden the ashen heavens opened up in earnest, the rain pattering down in a heavy deluge that drenched them instantly. It served to bring Alaric back from whatever daydream he had fallen into. He flicked his streaming black head to clear it like one wakening from a deep sleep, and took her hand. Leading the horses with the other, he hurriedly headed toward the cliffs, and to the mouth of a small cave there.

"We'll be dry here, until the storm passes," he said softly, and the hungry, yearning expression in his eyes only served to deepen her confusion.

"*Ja*," she agreed, not trusting herself with further words, and turned away from him into the gloom of cave. Tethering the horses by their reins to a gnarled bush that grew from the chalky cliff face, he followed her inside.

It was gloomy within, and the iodine tang of kelp was strong there in the damp, briny shadows. The smell brought sharply back to Freya memories of Danehof; childhood days she and Olaf had spent exploring the sand dunes and kelp-strewn beaches of Jutland, with the fresh, salty tang in their nostrils and the bracing wind off the cold sea whipping color into their faces. Those days were long past, as distant from this time and place as the days when the gods had fought to create the world! She sighed heavily and perched upon a convenient rock, looking up to see Alaric's great height and breadth filling the cave mouth, framed by the dour, misty sky beyond.

"Such a sigh of yearning, lady?" he said huskily, moving toward her. "What is it you grieve so for?"

"A time never to return again, Saxon," she murmured reluctantly.

"Because I have made thee my prisoner?"

"Nay!" she scoffed, unwilling to share her innermost thoughts with him. Nonetheless she continued, "Because I am grown, and childhood is no more."

"Was your childhood such a happy time, then?"

"*Nej*. Despite the rare happy moments, it was more often a time of confusion for me. A time of trying to learn who she was, this Freya in whose skin I lived and breathed. I wanted to be— to be someone else, and yet—I could not!"

"Because you could not be the son Thorfast longed for?" She nodded mutely. "The fault lay in Thorfast, wench, not thee," he observed, his tone surprisingly gentle.

"Aye, as my Uncle Sven told me, countless times. He bade me accept my lot as a woman, and warned me of the unhappiness that dissatisfaction would bring me. But I would not heed him! The lot of women seemed so unfair, even to the child I was then, while all glory, all that was good in life, was

138

wrought by men. I believed that by becoming versed in the male arts of warfare and such, I could somehow pretend that I had not been born female, and so better my lot." Her chin came up defiantly. "'Tis true that women are ever the pawns of men, is it not? Were I a man, I would not be here with you!"

"Nay. You would be dead, with the rest of your raiding party. Would you prefer death to being here with me?"

"A thousand times over, Saxon!"

He laughed and went to sit at her feet on the damp sand, reaching up behind him to tug her down onto his lap. She struggled, but only briefly, and soon she was nestled across his thighs, his strong arms embracing her rigid body. He noted that her breathing had quickened. He felt the sudden racing of her heart beneath his touch, a slight flutter like wings beneath the smooth flesh of her breast.

"Perhaps—perhaps I can give you reason to change your mind, ice-maiden, and be glad you survived the battle?" he whispered huskily, and his tongue tip darted forth to outline her ear, tickling maddeningly, causing gooseflesh to prickle down her arms and spine, and warmth to flood through her.

"Short of freeing me, you could not," she said firmly. "Cease what you're about!"

He ignored her and continued planting teasing kisses upon her little ears and cheeks, against the enchanting dimples he had glimpsed there, knowing full well the effect his warm breath created, fanned as it was against her chill flesh. "You do not command me, my lady," he chided her. "Though a cave may be our shelter, I am yet your master. By Saint George! Your kirtle is soaked! I would not see my property sicken of an ague! You will remove it at once, wench, else I will."

"Not—again!" she whispered, and the meager light glinted in her eyes. "Nay, nay, I will not!"

"You will," he countered, his tone brooking no refusal. His grip tightened about her. "I will not hurt thee, never fear. There'll be no pain when I take you, not this time, I swear it. But I will have you, by your will or nay. Soften, Viking! Surrender to me, lovely Freya, surrender—!"

She stiffened as his hand slipped beneath the sodden hem of her kirtle to stroke her ankles. From her ankles the warm, caressing fingers moved steadily upward, molding her slender calves and then her knees, until after what seemed endless moments one large hand lay curled against her trembling thigh. She protested and tried to squirm from his embrace, but there was no escaping the iron grip of his other arm about her, and she moaned as his marauding hand slipped between her clamped thighs and caressed the silken inner flesh there.

"You are smoother, softer than the finest silks of Byzantium, Freya of the Frozen Heart," he murmured, pressing his heated lips to the rapid pulse at the hollow of her throat and raining kisses along its length. "Silken without, and sweet, wild honey within." So saying, he fondled the pelt of soft, curling hair at her thighs' juncture before delicately plundering the folds of her womanhood.

She gasped at his intimate caresses and strove once again to wriggle free of him. Yet, as he held her still, as he continued to ready her with enflaming, knowing fingers, the will to fight him steadily ebbed. Madness! Her desperation was replaced by a heady breathlessness and a sensation of sweet pleasure that she would rather have died than confess to. His stroking touch sent warmth swirling through her, not pain. In fact, there was no pain at all, not this time. She stayed quite still, letting the heady, excited sensation he was creating rule her momentarily. Oh, what was wrong with her? Why did she weaken so at his touch? She did not want him to cease doing what he was doing . . . nay, never . . . "Enough, I beg you, enough!" she gasped, seeking to tear his hands from her, frightened by the warring emotions that battled within her.

"Nay, not enough, sweet Viking. Not nearly enough!" he breathed against the valley of her breasts, yet her damp garment impeded his lips from kissing her breasts. He released her and lowered her to the damp sand that was the cave's floor, unpinning his mantle and spreading it beneath them.

In silence marked only by his labored breathing and her own rapid breaths, the distant crescendo of the sea and the patter of the rain, he lifted his saffron tunic over his head, and folded it to pillow her head. Bare-chested, he leaned over her, grasped the hem of her kirtle, and drew it from her, baring the pale, lissome body that had the radiant luster of pearls in the gloom.

A moment more to unfasten his trousers and leggings and draw off his kid boots, and he was as bare as she. He knelt at her side, a towering dark silhouette looming over her, and for a while he made no move to touch her in any fashion. "Would that I had a torch, to see your loveliness," he said, and his voice had a husky timbre.

"Lucky am I that you have none, Saxon, and cannot see my shame!" she retorted hotly, and was furious to hear a low chuckle from him in response.

"Beauty knows no shame, Viking," he breathed, and gathered her up into his strong arms, firmly capturing her mouth beneath his. A thrill ran through him as he kissed her, for never had a kiss been so sweet, the meeting of two mouths so charged with sensation, as if flesh were peeled away and feelings danced upon bared nerves!

Her lips parted at the tender assault of his tongue, and eagerly he tasted her mouth, his tongue tip stroking and exploring the velvet within, until she sought to repel him with her own tongue. Their mouths warred, yet his hand captured treasured territories of rounded hip and long, silken flanks, a slender waist no wider than the span of a man's two hands, twin ripe breasts with tiny hardened hillocks at their peaks, and a valley where his touch found a moist, nectared surrender now—and lingered. He felt the quality of her breathing change against his lips, and the hands that had been pressed so fiercely against his chest to hold him at bay relaxed, lay loosely curled against his bare flesh, then stirred to caress him even as he caressed her, exploring his muscled shoulders, his smooth back, his broad chest made rough with springy hair, his fine head capped with damp, dark curls that grew dry and crisp beneath the faltering touch of her restless hands . . .

Blessed Frey, she wondered, stunned by her reactions, what magic power is it the Saxon warlock possesses? His touch seemed everywhere—upon her belly, stroking, stroking, until she all but purred in cat-like pleasure at his touch. Then again upon her breasts, gently cupping their aching fullness, teasing the tingling nipples until they swelled like the taut, furled buds of a new rose under his fingertips—and then again between her thighs, stroking rhythmically again within that secret, guarded place until she could not bear that he should cease the sweet torture! She throbbed there. She burned there. She melted there. She felt an aching, a yearning, a pulsing there to which only the delicate invasion of his long fingers gave some small measure of ease. "Nay! Nay, do not!" she cried against the smooth angle of his shoulders and throat, and yet there was a perverse, treacherous clamor inside her that insisted, "Aye!"

He pressed her down to the mantle. She lay still and panting there, waiting, waiting, wondering—her apprehension mounting—if now the pleasure would cease, and that hurtful other thing, that man-pleasure thing, begin. Yet he made no attempt to mount her. Instead, he gathered both her breasts in his hands, cupping them, and buried his lips against the firm flesh, his tongue dancing, flicking, swirling about her nipples until they seemed afire—as was she. Down his lips traveled, trailing lightning where they wandered, igniting wildfire where they touched upon the curves of her shoulders, her abdomen, her flat belly, until it seemed she could no longer lie still and quiet, but must seek her own end to his torment. Her hips arched upward and he parted her thighs and pressed kisses to the silken inner flesh where moments before his hands had rested. As his mouth moved higher still, she arched upward again and again to meet it, dazzled and dizzied by the frenzy of her body's response to his lips, his tongue upon the quivering core of her being. The throbbing grew and grew, until it became a great heartbeat of wanting centered between her thighs. She gasped and cried out. Knotting her fingers in the heavy dark head nestled against the pit of her belly, she implored her pagan gods—and Alaric—to grant her some release.

It came—oh *ja*, indeed *it came!*

Wondrously.

First as a tiny flutter that made her cry out again, little bird cries of rapture that were lost in the darkness of the cave and the roar of the pounding surf beyond; then as a great, warm wave that rippled throughout her body and seemed to lift her on its compelling tide, to carry her momentarily skyward on a crest of glorious rapture, before returning her slowly, shuddering, to earth once more. Never had she known such ecstasy existed! Never had she dreamed of such rapture and utter contentment of her woman's body—she who had always been filled with a reckless energy, a questing for something more that it seemed must always be denied her. Till now. Till this glorious moment in time! Till this man had brought her from maid to woman . . .

"Alaric!" She moaned softly. "Oh Alaric!"

In the shadows he smiled, and slid his hard body up the length of hers, nudging her thighs apart with his knees and filling her honeyed valley with his hardness in a way that made her shiver with sheer pleasure. "Aye, my sweeting, aye," he murmured, and tenderly kissed her closed eyelids, her throat, as he began to move.

Still dazed, she wondered at the lack of pain his entry had caused, at the intensely wonderful feelings he was stirring yet again inside her. The night before his manhood had been an instrument of pain and shame, yet now—now she arched upward to meet its powerful thrusts, seeking to draw him still more deeply into her. His possession was sweet, oh so sweet! She reveled in the strength and virility of his beautiful male body, gloried in the play of rippling muscles and cords beneath his taut flesh as he claimed her anew. Her fingers twined in his ebony curls and drew his rough cheek down to be kissed by her own hungry lips, and the very scent of him, salty and warm and masculine, played havoc with her senses. She stroked the flexing arms that cradled her, and the driving strength of the lean, taut flanks that pleased her so; drew a new pleasure from the rough caress of his hairy, broad chest against the crushed weight of her tingling breasts as he moved upon her. She delved between their bodies to stroke the hard, flat plateau of his belly, suddenly eager to learn every inch of him who had shown her such delights. Were all men so? she wondered dazedly, fiercely embracing Alaric's hips with her slender legs and curling her arms tightly about his neck as they moved as one—or could only he—*he*—ignite the fiery rapture that had thawed the ice within her heart?

Their gasps of delight broke closer one to the other as their passion soared to its zenith. Words became soft sighs, melted into kisses. Again Freya knew the yearning, the throbbing ache of desire, but now she welcomed it, embraced it, for she

143

knew that what came after was infinitely sweeter still. As the wave lifted her on its crest a second time, she felt Alaric grow still and heavy upon her, and a muted groan broke from his parted lips and was lost in the tumble of her damp hair as they found their release simultaneously. They clung fiercely together in a tangle of limbs until the shuddering moment had passed beyond them, and all again grew still within.

She awoke with a sudden jolt some while later, forgetting for an instant where she was or with whom, and wondering what could have jolted her so soundly from sleep.

Frowning, she scrambled to standing, then all but froze in place where she stood, for gooseflesh had risen along her arms and icy chills trickled down her spine. Suddenly she knew what it was that had wakened her; that sixth sense that every warrior hones to a keen edge; that guardian sense that never slumbers. *They were not alone here!*

Her keen senses had rarely failed her in the past. She had no cause to fear they had done so now. Yet a quick glance about her revealed nothing more than rocks and shadow. Nonetheless, the sensation of eyes watching her was still strong, and the fine hairs at her nape rose in response to the uncomfortable feeling. Had they unwittingly invaded the sea cave of a water sprite or some other magical creature? she wondered, dry-mouthed. Did that explain the peculiar sensation that they were being spied upon? Breath bated, she dropped onto one knee and pressed her fingertips to the sand in an age-old gesture to Mother Earth for strength, murmuring as she did so the sacred runes that would avert misfortune. When she straightened up again, the feeling had vanished. She heaved a sigh of relief and went quickly to the cave mouth.

The rain had ceased. The sky was a misty pale blue, without threat or clouds. A brilliant, shimmering bow of pastel colors arched across it like the heavenly bridge to Asgard. The storm had blown inland, and the deserted beach appeared freshly laundered and sparkling clean in its aftermath.

She glanced back over her shoulder toward where Alaric was sleeping. Had she imagined the sweet pleasures he'd revealed to her? That strangely magical moment between them? Or—had it been only a wishful dream?

Tossing her head, she discarded such tender thoughts, denied the strange warmth she knew flooded through her when she looked down at him. Such weakness must not be encouraged! She must not forget, not for an instant, that he was her enemy, she his slave.

She slipped from the cave, still naked, and ran down the beach to the sea, plunging into the water with a soft gasp of pleasure. She swam, feeling the water's salty caress cleanse her of the Saxon's touch, his male scent, and her own woman's musk. When she waded back out through the shallows and to the shingle-and-sand beach some while later, her resolve had returned. The horses still cropped the grass. Alaric was yet asleep. *Now!* a little voice whispered urgently in her ear. *Flee now, before he awakens! Forget him! Any man can do what he did to you!*

Tiptoeing quickly back into the cave to retrieve her kirtle and belt, she slipped them on and ran from the cave to the charcoal mare. Hitching up her skirts, she grasped its sooty mane to mount up. Yet with only one foot in the stirrup, she stiffened as a weighty hand clamped over the back of her neck.

She spun about to see Alaric towering at her back, still quite naked himself. Yet despite his lack of clothes, he made an ominous figure, powerful and threatening. The hue of his eyes was no longer dark and smoldering warmly with desire, but cold and furious.

"Nay, slave, you'll not flee me!" he gritted, and cruelly grasped her wrist, wrenching her from the horse and hauling her after him back to the cave. Inside it, he pushed her roughly down to the sand and released her, moving to gather up his clothes and dress, while, frustrated and seething, she sat and watched.

"Do you know the price a slave pays in this kingdom for fleeing her master?" he demanded, his tone harsh and rasping.

"I care not, curse you!" she retorted hotly, sapphire sparks igniting blue fire in her eyes.

"Aye, I warrant you do not. But I will tell you nonetheless. The price is stoning, wench! Not an easy death, nor a swift one, even for such as you. And should you have proved lucky and escaped me to reach the Danelaw, you would not have found a ready welcome there. My king has sworn a pact with your Norse chieftains. He has vowed to refuse sanctuary to runaway slaves who flee their kingdom for his—and Guthrum has sworn likewise."

"You would have me believe I would be spurned by my own people? That in this isle of Britain there is no place where I might escape you?" She snorted her disgust. "Save your tall tales for nights about the hearth, Saxon! I would find ready sanctuary in the north. I am the daughter of Thorfast, *jarl* of Danehof. My rank amongst the Viking people equals your own amongst the Saxons—or did you forget so soon?"

He moved toward the light at the cave mouth, and she saw that his expression was stern and rigid, his jaw set, his gray eyes as hard as flint. "Aye. For a moment, in truth, I forgot who you were. But I will not forget again, I promise thee, Thorfast's daughter! On the morrow you will go to my lady aunt and begin your position as a slave at Kenley. On your feet!"

So saying, he left the cave to return to the fortress, and Freya, almost in tears with thwarted rage, followed him mutely.

What had been between them earlier—that magical *something* in the air—was quite exiled now. Nor did it seem likely to return.

Chapter 11

"So! At last we meet, Freya," Valonia said kindly, her gaze resting on the defiant face of the slave girl who stood before her the following morning, her red-gold head bowed. Alaric had sent the girl to her, with the instruction that she was to be set to work, as was "fitting for a slave," yet Valonia was not so easily convinced that this was the true reason he wished the girl parted from him. She knew him too well for that!

"Tell me, child, are you afraid of me?" she asked.

"Nay!" Freya protested, indignation in both her tone and every line of her body.

"Then look at me," Valonia urged, smiling. "Though I am mistress here, I have yet to turn to stone anyone who has gazed into my eyes!" The gently teasing quality to her tone pierced as surely as any arrow the armor of indifference and pride Freya had donned as a defense. She jerked her head up and glowered at the fair-haired Saxon lady, meeting her eyes boldly. "There! That is much better. Now tell me, Freya, what skills do you possess that we might have need of here at Kenley? What is it you enjoy doing? Weaving, perhaps—or spinning?"

"Neither, my lady, " Freya mumbled, the words dragged from her. "I—I am skilled at neither." Her face reddened furiously with embarrassment, and she squirmed uncomfortably where she stood, wringing her hands together.

"Your mother taught you nothing of spinning and weaving? How so, child?" Valonia inquired, her gentle face frowning. It appeared the Viking people were even more barbaric than she had at first imagined, to allow their daughters to remain ignorant of such women's work.

"My—my mother, the Lady Verdandi, died bringing me into the world," Freya reluctantly confessed, tossing back her hair and setting her chin defiantly. "And Nissa—my nurse, the slave woman who raised me—she doted upon me, and let me do much as I wished. I—I did not wish to learn to weave or spin— and so I did not!" Her defiant tone was derived more from embarrassment at being found wanting in this Saxon household than shame over her lack of womanly skills.

"I see. Then tell me, what *can* you do?"

"Well, I can care for the horses and their trappings. I am very knowledgeable in the training of hunting hawks and falcons, and in the care of weapons. Any work that a man can do, I can also do!" Pride laced her tone now.

"I see. But Lord Alaric already has a master of his horse, and grooms aplenty, as well as a falconer and an armorer to see to his hawks and weapons. Besides, child, my nephew has instructed me to see that you are given duties within his hall, and made certain I understood you were not to be permitted to venture beyond it into the burh amongst his garrison of rough soldiers." She frowned again, thoughtfully this time. "There must be *something* else that you can do?" She rose and paced across the rushes, her fine-spun yellow linen skirts rustling against them as she went, her slender, beringed fingers toying thoughtfully with her chatelaine's belt of delicate gold links.

"I can read. And write," Freya divulged, her expression doubtful that such talents would be found worthy here.

"In Norse?"

The girl nodded. "*Ja.* And in the Christian Latin, too."

"How is this?" Valonia's surprise was obvious in her arched brows. Few those days could read, let alone write! That the girl was schooled in both, and in two languages moreover, astounded her.

"My Uncle Sven was a learned man. 'Twas he who taught me the Norse runes, as well as the Latin script, having learned it himself from an Irish monk taken prisoner when he was a boy. And Nissa, my nurse, spoke her own Saxon tongue, which I learned easily as a child, and improved with Sven's teaching.

148

"Ah yes, Sven." A small smile curved her mouth. "He is a good man, is he not?"

"Was, my lady. He was slain in the battle, by your own son." The bitterness in Freya's tone was rampant, and for a fleeting second her eyes sparkled with a dangerous, rebellious light—or was it but the bright sheen of tears Valonia saw in their depths?

Valonia met that glare with a level, deeply thoughtful gaze of her own. "Attend me, Freya," she ordered softly at length, beckoning with her finger. "If you are to be content and serve your lord well here at Kenley, there is something you must know, I believe." So saying, she lifted her trailing skirts and crossed the bower, pausing in the doorway to turn back to the girl. "Well, child?"

Freya followed the Lady Valonia through the hall, wondering what it could be that the woman meant to show her. They made their way down a few steps cut into the hard-packed earthen floor to a large chamber that opened out at the rear of the hall, and was set half below-ground. It was obviously a cellar or storeroom of some kind, for the smell of grain and mead was strong there.

Valonia affixed the torch she had taken from the passageway inside a wrought-iron holder and crossed the chamber, making her way between several straw pellets where men—obviously wounded in the recent battle, since some had their limbs swathed in linen bandages—lay resting, greeting them each by name and asking after them as she went. Before one she halted, and gestured Freya to come to her side.

An old man lay upon the straw, his bare upper body crisscrossed with linen dressings, his clean-shaven face drawn. Freya frowned. Was this poor old fellow someone she was supposed to know?

"Good sir," Valonia called softly, bending close to his ear. "Waken, sir. I have a visitor for thee. I fancy she does not know thee since you were shaved this morn!"

The old man stirred and turned his head. His sky-blue eyes opened, filling with warmth and pleasure as he saw the Lady Valonia at his side. He looked then to see who his visitor might be, and in that moment Freya recognized him and flung

149

herself past Valonia to kneel at his side, her arms going fiercely about his shoulders.

"Uncle Sven!" She sobbed, tears of joy spilling down her cheeks and onto the rough brown blanket of homespun pulled snugly about him. "Dear, dear Uncle Sven—I thought—I believed you slain in the battle! Praise and thanks to Odin, you are alive!"

Sven raised his hand to weakly tousle the tumble of red-gold curls that spilled across his chest, smiling as tears filled his own eyes. *"Nej,* little one, *nej!* my Freya, I am yet amongst the living, though I would indeed be long gone to the feast halls of Valhalla were it not for this skilled and gentle lady's nursing."

Freya sniffed back her tears, drying her eyes on her knuckles. She turned and looked up into Valonia's face, her expression incredulous. "You? 'Twas you who nursed him?" Seeing the older woman nod, she whispered, *"Takke!* Thank you, my lady, thank you a thousand time o'er! His wounds—will they heal?" she demanded eagerly.

"Aye, I believe so," Valonia said. "There is no sign as yet of poisoning, and God willing, there will be none. To my eyes he grows stronger every day. The flesh has already begun to heal and close the wound. In time he will be well again, I am certain." She looked down into the girl's shining face, momentarily stunned by the beauty she saw there. In her great joy, the cold Nordic haughtiness of Freya's strong features was softened. With her rare, vibrant coloring, she was utterly breathtaking, Valonia realized! It was small wonder that Alaric had seemed so anxious to be rid of her! Doubtless her vivid beauty had affected him greatly, and he feared a softening of his heart toward the girl on whom he had sworn vengeance . . .

Suddenly Freya rose and turned to face the Saxon lady. "Lady Valonia, I—I must beg your forgiveness," she said softly.

"Forgiveness? Why, child? You have done no wrong since you came here, to my knowledge."

"Aye, lady, I have!" Freya insisted frankly. "In my heart there was only hatred for you, and for your family. I was of a mind to refuse to do your bidding, and planned at first chance to flee your household. I—I vowed I would sooner die than serve any Saxon noblewoman as her slave! But now—seeing how gently you have cared for my—my dear Uncle Sven, I am deeply ashamed of my thoughts!" She knelt at Valonia's feet, drew the hem of her kirtle to her lips, and kissed it. "Whatsoever you command me, mistress, I will do it!" she vowed humbly, her head bowed.

"Stand, Freya," Valonia urged. "You need not humble yourself so before me. I am indeed your mistress here at Kenley, but I have not forgotten that you were also nobly born despite this, and accordingly I would have you treated with some measure of respect." She turned to look down again at Sven. "I have given some thought to the matter of what your Freya is to do here at Kenley, good sir. Since she claims she is able to write, I have decided to see if she could copy some holy texts for me, for the abbess of the little convent near here. Unlike their brother monks, the good sisters are sorely lacking in manuscripts, and it would please me to see this lack remedied in some small part. Tell me, good Sven, is your Freya capable of doing this task?"

"Indeed she is, my lady," Sven acknowledged, pride in his tone. "She has a pretty, flowing hand and an artist's eye. She would serve you well in this."

"Then it is agreed!" Valonia said with finality. "We will see a desk readied for you in a corner of my sewing bower, and will supply you well with the finest pens and inks and vellum. Bid your uncle farewell for now, child. I will see that you are given time to visit with him anon."

"As you will, my lady," Freya agreed readily, and flashed her uncle a tender smile, which he returned, before she followed the lady from the storeroom.

The girl's step was light and eager now, Valonia remarked with pleasure, as much evidence of her delight at learning her Uncle Sven lived as was the sunny smile she now wore. There would be little trouble with her forthwith, Valonia decided, well satisfied.

The work set her, Freya soon discovered, was more pleasure

151

than work. Never had she been able to practice her talents at scrivening upon such fine vellum as the sheets now set before her, nor with such quality of nibs and ink, and she thrilled to the challenge. The Lady Valonia would see that her trust in setting her such an important task was not misplaced, she determined. Her red-gold head bent studiously over her work, the tip of her tongue jutting between her lips in her concentration, she watched with enormous satisfaction as beneath her clever hand the sweeping lines and forms of the letters flowed elegantly onto the vellum without a single blot or smear, the tale of the pagan Saul's conversion to Christianity unraveling as she copied the epistle. The unfamiliar story was as engrossing as the script itself, like the tales of bygone heroes sung by the bards, and she eagerly looked forward to each new line as the day wore on, the shaft of sunlight that fell through the narrow wind-eye to burnish her fiery head gradually fading as morning dimmed into afternoon.

By dusk, several completed pages lay drying to one side, the first letters of each page illuminated cunningly with scrolling vines painted with the brilliantly colored inks. Cleverly drawn animals that had a peculiarly pagan gripping-beast appearance peeped out from between the crosspiece of an *A* or the curve of an elegant *S*. So utterly absorbed was she in her labors that she was not aware someone had entered the bower until a shadow fell across the vellum. Startled, she looked up to see the Lady Kendra standing there, a spiteful smile curling her lush red lips.

"Are you deaf, Viking, or merely addled?" Kendra snapped. "I bade thee run to the kitchens and fetch me a flagon of mead!"

"I did not hear you, Lady Kendra," Freya stammered. "But in any case, the Lady Valonia has instructed me to copy these pages. She—she gave me strict orders to remain here, in her sewing bower. I regret I cannot fetch the flagon for you."

Kendra's dark brows winged upward. "Cannot? You refuse my command? You—a mere slave—have the temerity to disobey *me?* Ha! I warned you once what the price of refusing my bidding would be, did I not, you insolent little slut? Do not think that because you have shared Alaric's bed you are too

152

good to do my bidding. Be off about the task I have set you, before I box your ears!"

Freya bit her lip. "Your pardon, my lady, but I cannot. As I told thee, Lady Valonia ordered me to—Oh!"

Like quicksilver, Kendra's arm darted out. Her clenched fist landed with a ringing smack against Freya's cheek. The blow knocked the girl sideways where she sat, overturning the ink horns from their stand and spilling a thick black river from an unstoppered one across the finished manuscript pages.

"Look what you've done!" Freya cried, jumping to her feet and trying unsuccessfully to save some of the pages before the ink ran farther. "A full day's work, all wasted! Why, I—!" Without thought for her precarious position in the enemy household, she sprang at Kendra, knotting her fingers in the woman's ebony hair and yanking furiously.

Kendra squalled like a she-cat, clawing wildly for Freya's face with her talons. "Viking slut! I'll scratch that fair face to ribbons! See if Lord Alaric will look with such lust upon thee then!" she panted.

"Jealous, Saxon?" Freya jeered, breathing heavily as she writhed sideways to evade Kendra's wicked nails. "I would sooner—"

"Enough!" roared a deep voice.

The two women sprang apart as if scalded, standing facing each other glowering, fists planted on hips, bosoms heaving in their fury, their hair falling in tangled disarray about their furious, flushed faces, the one midnight black, the other red gold. Neither glanced to left nor to right to see who had spoken as Farant stepped into the bower.

"What is the meaning of this?" he demanded, his normally gentle tone stern, looking first at Kendra, his wife, and then at the slave girl. When neither spoke he added sharply, "Answer me!"

"This—slave—was foolishly entrusted to copy some texts for your lady aunt," Kendra muttered. "I came to the bower in the nick of time to spy her spilling ink upon them. Alas, they are quite ruined, my lord! Look!" So saying, she gestured to the stained sheets of vellum.

Farant strode across the bower and sifted the sheets through his hands. Ink had indeed ruined the beautifully illuminated script. The waste of precious hours and the obvious talent expended, not to mention the costly materials themselves, appalled him, for he had a great love for all manuscripts. "Whose work is this?" he demanded.

"Mine," Freya acknowledged reluctantly.

"Yours? And yet you chose to destroy it? Why, pray?" he asked in gentler tones, astonished that the Viking maid should be so gifted in such an exacting skill.

Freya said nothing, gritting her lips. She had learned on the ride to the convent the day before that Alaric would permit no maligning of the Lady Kendra. To tell him the truth could therefore benefit her little. Besides, Alaric would never believe her word against that of Kendra, his kinswoman, not in a thousand years . . .

"Speak up, girl! Why did you do this?"

"I'll tell you why, my lord," Kendra volunteered when Freya remained stonily silent. "Spite! That is why! Your lady aunt generously allowed the girl the easy task of copying some texts for her instead of setting her to harder labor in the kitchens, as is her due. This one, hating all Saxons, obviously determined to abuse Valonia's kindness by destroying the work set her!"

"Is that so?" Farant pressed, his gray eyes narrowed.

"Since your lady Kendra says it is so, it must be, must it not, my lord?" Freya muttered sullenly.

Farant sighed. "You must be punished then, girl. I cannot permit such wanton destruction to go unanswered. You will remain here, without food or water this even, until each one of these pages has been recopied—even should the task take until far into the night. I will see that candles are brought here to light your work. Do you understand?"

"I do," Freya said stiffly.

Farant nodded and made to leave. "Then begin. You have a long night ahead of you."

"Your punishment is far too lenient, my lord," Kendra hissed angrily. "Why, the little cat sprang at me when I tried— in vain, alas—to prevent her from destroying the pages! She attacked me! You should have her whipped, at the very least,

154

for what she did!"

"Whipping the girl could not repair the pages, my lady," Farant pointed out. "In replacing them she will learn that such actions will not go unanswered, and will hesitate before she attempts such destruction again. Attend me, my lady. Your serving women are all at odds in determining which gowns will go with you to Winchester. You will return to your bower and instruct them in this matter. I would not have our departure on the morrow delayed. Not on any account!" His stern tone brooked no refusal.

"Aye, my lord," Kendra answered him sweetly, fluttering the dark lashes that fringed her tawny eyes like exotic fans. Yet inwardly she was herself sullen now. Before, she had always been able to twist Farant about her little finger, to bend him easily to her will with a lingering smile, a caress, or the dangled promise of a rare night spent in passion in her bed. But of late he was becoming more and more difficult to handle, confound him . . .

"Rest assured you will not share Alaric's bed this night, slut!" Kendra flung over her shoulder as she followed Farant from the bower. There was a gloating smile on her red lips. "Nor have you heard the last of this, I promise you . . ."

Freya watched their departure from the bower with simmering rage. That vicious cat! That lying bitch-woman! she seethed silently, filled with impotent rage.

But at length she turned back to the task at hand with a heavy sigh. The ruined pages seemed to stare accusingly up at her, and she could see in her mind's eye the Lady Valonia's gentle face wreathed in an expression of dismay, disappointment, and aye, even betrayal, when she saw them. She had promised the lady on her bended knees she would do her bidding in return for her caring for Sven, had she not? Well then, there was little else for it but to do as Alaric had commanded! She must recopy the pages, no matter how long it took, no matter if her stiff and aching wrists screamed for rest. Flexing her back and shoulders, which were already cramped from the day's copying, she took her seat at the desk once more. She rubbed her stiffened fingers, drew a crisp sheet of fresh vellum from the brass-bound morse-ivory scrivener's

155

casket, dipped nib in ink, and laboriously began over.

It was in the sewing bower that Alaric found her in the chilly dark hours before dawn.

All day he had hunted wild boar with his men, riding far and wide through the deeply wooded chases and rolling meadows of his lands, not returning till late in the afternoon, when the sun lay low and ruddy upon the hills. Despite his wishes to the contrary, and his anger at Freya for attempting to escape him the day previous, he had not been long back at his hall before he had been filled with the nagging desire to see her again—an urge he had grimly determined to drown in mead and other strong drink.

Nonetheless, when the evening had passed and he had yet to look upon her vibrantly beautiful face, he had taken himself off to his bower feeling disgruntled and more than a little drunk. He chafed to ask his aunt where the slave girl was, but hesitated to display such an open interest in the girl, curse her. Waving his bower servant away, he had fallen deeply asleep across his pallet without undressing or even removing his kid boots. The cold chill of the wee hours had wakened him, and finding Freya neither beside him in the bed nor curled in a mantle on the rushes in his bower, he had set out to search his hall for her.

The kitchens at the rear of the hall where the slaves made their beds had not yielded his prize to him. Nor had any of the many sleeping, blanket-wrapped bodies strewn about the hall or curled on the benches there proved to be hers. It was only by systematically searching the several small bowers that were adjoined to the main hall by narrow passageways, and which were not in use as sleeping quarters for his family, that he had at last found her.

The flaming torch in his fist wavered in the draught from the wind-eye as he held it aloft. The brilliant embroidered tapestries that graced the timber walls shifted in the cool current. The torchlight reflected off the fiery gleam of her hair as she lay curled like a small child upon a carved wooden chair, her head cradled on her arms on the sloping desk lid. Beside her

156

was placed a sheaf of completed pages, painstakingly copied, an Epistle by St. Paul, ink horns in a stand, each one neatly stoppered, and several pens, every nib wiped clean. Her work? he wondered, leafing through the pages. He was unable to keep from smiling, seeing the delightfully elfin creatures that came alive about each illuminated letter. Aye, it was her work. It could be none other's! Nonetheless, he found it hard to accept that the fiercely defiant, vigorous little creature he knew Freya to be could also be capable of so delicate and exacting a task as scrivening, let alone have a working knowledge of Latin! It seemed he had underestimated her. What a fascinating, complex creature she was, each aspect of her character a mystery never quite wholly revealed! He bent down and shook her gently by the shoulder.

"Hsst! Wake up, wench!" he murmured. Yet so deeply asleep was she in her weariness, she did not so much as stir. Finally, after several moments, he set the torch in a wall holder and scooped her gently into his arms, like a child hoisted over his shoulder to be borne to its cot. Retrieving the torch as he went, he carried her effortlessly back to his bower.

The desire for her that had awakened him took second place to his concern as he looked down at her—a circumstance that surprised even him. What was it about her, he wondered, that so confused and disturbed him? She was daughter to his sworn enemy, and by rights he should hate her. Yet the feelings inside him—though confused—were certainly not those of hatred! Since he had determined the afternoon before when they had left the sea cave never again to forget who she was, and to treat her as he would treat any slave taken in battle, he still had great difficulty in thinking of her in those terms. All the day long he had ached for a glimpse of that red-gold mane, those flashing sapphire eyes, he recalled, winding an errant gleaming curl about his callused finger. He had found the rigorous and bloody hunt difficult to concentrate upon, his thoughts straying from chase and quarry to Freya, always to her of the red-gold hair and the vibrant, glowing complexion; Freya of the fierce heart and the exquisite body, who could go from icy hauteur and disdain in one moment to fiery passion in his arms, a woman such as he had always dreamed of possessing, in the next. Possess? Could any mortal man possess such as she? It was tantamount to trying to capture and tame a bright flame that refused to be quenched!

He glanced down at her, his gray eyes lingering hungrily upon her small form nestled there upon the white of the fine-spun linen pallet, like a sheaf of golden corn spilled across its pristine pallor, gleaming in the shadows. Viking slave girl, he mused—or Viking sorceress, a Valkyrie maid sent from the icy north to bewitch him, ensorcel him with her powers? Flicking his head to rid it of such fanciful notions, he leaned over her.

Violet shadows rimmed her closed eyes, the circles darkened by the dusky crescent shadows cast by her long lashes. Her utter exhaustion was marked by the deep rise and fall of her breathing, the lack of even a single protest as he carefully stripped the garments from her sleep-heavy body and pulled a homespun blanket up about them both as he lay down beside her. He coiled one heavy arm about her tiny waist, drawing her bare, slender loveliness nearer to fit the curve of his own hard male body. His face buried in the scented mass of her hair, her warm female form close, he felt strangely contented, and quickly fell asleep.

His contentment was destined to be short lived, however, lasting barely till dawn pinked the eastern skies. He awoke to find her glowering down at him, and fancied it was the undisguised loathing in her jewel eyes that had roused him even from the deep sleep into which he had fallen.

Christ's Wounds, how much bitter hatred and enmity she could bestow in a single glance—poison enough to shred the very flesh from a man's bones! Glad he was she held no weapon in her fist, for with that hatred to give fire and strength to her sword arm, he would be good as dead!

"Your eyes reveal your thoughts, wench," he growled, struggling up onto his elbows. "Sheath them!" Black hair tousled, smoke-gray eyes yet heavy lidded and sensual from sleep, he watched as she sprang up off the bed and flounced across the bower. Tearing the deer-horn combs from her tangled hair, she began to force it into some semblance of order, freeing it of knots with little patience this morn. He noticed that she winced as she worked the unruly red-gold tresses.

"What pains you?" he asked idly. The look she shot him would have shriveled the buds upon the trees, or scorched the green grass brown with its heat.

"You ask—when my hurt is your doing?" she demanded, rubbing her aching wrists. "Was it not by your command I was made thus?" She recalled again the long, lonely hours of the night she had spent laboriously recopying the Christian text at his command while the rest of the hall slept on, and uttered a stream of foul curses in her Viking tongue, which Alaric nonetheless had little hardship deciphering.

"Enough!" he barked. "I will permit no such profanity to pass a woman's lips, nay, not in my presence, even if that woman be but slave to me. You brought your pains upon yourself, did you not? Then suffer them in silence!" Aye, her pains were of her own doing, he thought irritably. Had she not struggled, the iron bonds his guards had locked about her wrists would not have chafed so. "And if you would be more kindly treated, then display a kinder disposition, wench. Few men—or women—are moved to deal gently with a shrew."

"Shrew? Pah!" she snorted, and jabbed the last comb into her hair, which all the while she had been furiously braiding. Smoothing down her skirts, which were rumpled by sleep, she stormed toward the bower door.

"And where might you be bound?" Alaric demanded, springing across the bower after her, clad only in his linen small clothes. Fists planted aggressively on his hips, his wiry, hairy legs akimbo, he stood there scowling blackly at her.

In answer, she swept him a mocking curtsey. "By your leave, *min jarl*, but was it not your own decision that I should serve your lady aunt by day, and yourself by night?" The knife-edged scorn to her voice made him flinch.

"Aye," he agreed with obvious reluctance. His jaw clamped tightly in irritation.

"Well, look you through the wind-eye, sir! The sun is up! The night has fled! 'Tis day—so, fare thee well! I'll return to this prison cell ere moonrise." And with that, she flew through

159

the door before he could give voice to a command to halt her.

Alaric, never a patient man, was one it was imprudent to cross on an empty belly. Her waspish temper—aye, and after he had shown her only kindness in carrying her from the cold comfort of the sewing bower to the warmth of his bed the night before—filled him with outrage. He paced back and forth, fists clenched, half minded to have her whipped for her insolence, or fettered. Aye, then the Danish witch would learn who was master here, right enough!.Her words were not all that had angered him, though. Last night he had fondly imagined her moved to gentleness this morn, on finding he had borne her to his bower even as she slept, and had hoped to find her, if not eager for his attentions, then at the very least grateful and yielding in his arms. After all, he was her master, and under no obligation to show her any kindness at all. But not only had she not yielded—she had fled him! A curse on women, all of them! he uttered silently, pounding his massive balled fist against his other palm. "Fool! Dolt!" he muttered, "Aye, 'tis fool you were indeed, to expect gratitude from a Viking hellion such as she!"

"Sir?"

He flung angrily about to see his bower servant, Ham, hovering at his elbow, a crock of steaming water in one hand, a short-bladed knife in the other. He muttered a curse under his breath for his servant's benefit. "'Twas nothing, Ham. A thought spoken aloud. Will you razor me?"

"Aye, sir, all is in readiness."

Sourly Alaric nodded, taking his seat in the carved chair as Ham sharpened his knife upon the strop. While Ham, mindful of his master's black mood, carefully scraped the bluish stubble from his cheeks, chin, and jaw, his lord stared straight ahead at the bower wall. And seethed.

Freya went swiftly from the bower and across the bailey to the hall proper. Servants and slaves alike were already up, yawning and scratching themselves as they moved, bleary-eyed, to their first duties of the day. The first cock was just stretching its neck to crow, the cows in the byre were lowing to be milked, and the sky was the color of ashes, gilded with pink and gold from the rising sun. The morning air was sweet and cool, invigorating. 'Twas the sort of day the gods had created for men to ride free over the meadows and glory in the summer, the wild flowers, the ripening wheat with its long stalks that bowed low under the weight of ears filled to bursting with grain. Not a day to be spent in labor and slavery, in the household of one's enemy! She shrugged, ignoring the curious and appreciative eyes of the garrison as she left the bailey and entered the hall. Like it or nay, she had little choice but to do the tasks they set her. Alaric's men were too vigilant to relax their guard and permit their lord's bower woman to flee, she thought bitterly.

She found the Lady Valonia in the great hall, and a smile lit up her face as she crossed the rushes toward the older woman. The lady had shown her naught but kindness, and a friendly face in this Saxon household was a welcome sight indeed. "My lady, I am risen, and sorry I am for the lateness of the hour. What would you have me do today?" she asked breathlessly, bobbing a sketchy curtsey that did not come easily to one more used to leggings than woman's skirts, and command rather than servitude.

"Lona, my bower servant, is sickened of a summer fever, Freya," Valonia told her. "'Twas my hope that you would see to her tasks for the while."

"And what tasks are they, my lady?"

"Attending to the needs of the wounded. Do you feel capable of this?"

"*Ja*, mistress, I do!" she agreed eagerly. She would be able to visit with Sven while she worked! "I have a deft touch in cleansing wounds and in changing dressings, and no little knowledge of healing herbs, learned from my Uncle Sven and Nissa, my nurse. It—it is a task I would find pleasing, my lady." She blushed to have spoken so readily, and lowered her eyes. Yet at once Valonia's warm laughter set her at ease.

"'Tis well, fear not. All men—and women too—labor more willingly and well at tasks they find pleasing, I learned long ago, and so it is my custom to set my servants tasks they find kinship with. To the kitchens with you, girl, and tell the cooks I bade them feed you well. And after, be about the task I've set you." Freya curtsied again, and Valonia smiled inwardly. As yet, the girl moved as one unaccustomed to skirts, yet the promise of considerable feminine grace was already there in her coltish movements. The bold swagger she had affected was already gone. Ah, she sighed. 'Twas a great pity the girl was Dane, for Valonia found herself peculiarly drawn to her, as she had never been drawn to Kendra, for all that she had raised the wild, tawny-eyed Kendra from birth, as she had Farant and Alaric, along with Cullen, her only son. Perhaps she saw in this fair and courageous young woman the daughter she had always yearned for? Lads grew, and studied war, and went away. They came back torn and bleeding, bruised and broken. And sometimes—oftentimes—came back not at all. While a daughter, by the grace of God, was a mother's joy, a treasure to love forever! Aye, sons were a woman's pride, but daughters could be cherished without fear of grief. With a mother's touch to guide her, instruct her—with a woman of her own station in life to teach her, one who could be firm when needed, yet gentle and understanding—how different the Lady Freya might have become! Valonia shook her head at the vagaries of life. While she had longed to find herself soon again with child after Cullen's birth, the Viking Thorfast had cast his precious little daughter aside. When the peasant women bred like rabbits and their children grew like weeds, though with scant food to feed the ever-increasing number of bellies, how was it she had been left barren after the one son? Aye. 'Twas unfair— but it was God's will, and who was she to question His plans for her life?

Freya, noting her silence and pensiveness and believing herself dismissed, turned to go as bidden. But at the last moment, Valonia called after her.

"The scribing, child—I would have you know I was most pleased with your work. Anon you shall finish it for me, when Lona is herself again."

"Thank you, my lady." She blushed and quickly left the hall, headed for the kitchens. Farant was on his way into the hall as she left it, but she scarce acknowledged him as she brushed past, thinking he was Alaric and wanting no further

162

stormy exchange with *him*, curse him, this fair and sunny morn.

In old Lona's cottage, a short distance from the main hall, Kendra paced its small confines like a caged she-wolf, hugging herself about the arms as she did so. Her shoulders were rigid and her golden eyes gleamed with a spiteful light.

"What is this I hear? You say you will not? But I say I *command* you!" she hissed at the old woman, who shrank away from her on the pile of old straw heaped by the hearth, her breath whistling on the gloom with the ague that fevered her.

"Nay, nay, Kendra—do not ask this of me again, I beg you!" the old hag implored, her wrinkled old face streaming with tears. "I am too old, far too old for such things. The risk—'tis too great!" She shuddered. "The church would have me burned, should it be learned!"

Kendra, infuriated by her whining tone, crouched at her side and grasped her by the upper arms, shaking her until the old woman's wimple fell off and revealed a head nigh as smooth and hairless as an egg. Beneath her rough garments the old crone was naught but a bundle of feverish dry skin and bones, like dried sticks rattling in a sack, Kendra thought with distaste as she did so, and she smelled musty, like moldy dead leaves. "Who will learn of it, you old fool?" she snarled. "I'll never tell—and nor will you, so who will be the wiser?" She released her. "One last time, I beg you," she wheedled now, her tone silky and caressing. She gently stroked Lona's wrinkled cheek, inwardly sickened by the heated dryness, the ugliness of it. "One last use of your powers for Kendra, who has been like a daughter to thee all these years, mmm, Mother Lona?"

It was obvious her changed attitude worked far better than force and threats, for the fear dwindled from Lona's rheumy eyes.

"Just once more? What is it you seek, Kendra? Another amulet of the love charms? To draw Alaric?" She suddenly cackled with laughter. "It will not work, my pretty! That one will prove immune to this love spell, as he was to the last!"

"Was he, Lona? Was he in truth immune?" Or—did you

163

think to trick me, by turning your powers upon Farant instead?" To Kendra's satisfaction, the crafty glee faded from Lona's eyes.

"Nay, nay, I did not!" she whined hoarsely. Yet she lied.

"Curse you, you old hag, I'm no fool! You played me false, and I know it! But this time you will do it—and do it right, else I will denounce you for your witchcraft! Aye, Lona, I will, I swear it! And do not think your word will carry weight against mine. It will not! Think of your old bones snapping as the flames lick at them, the agony as that dried old flesh is seared, the—"

"Stop! Enough!" Lona moaned helplessly, shaking her head from side to side. "Aye. You've won, as you always do. I'll do it! Who is it you would draw to you?"

"'Tis no love spell I'm after, Old Mother, not this time! I seek something more." The golden eyes gleamed in the shadowed cottage, and when she again spoke her tone was like the low hiss of a snake. "Something—deadly."

The rheumy old eyes widened. "For—who?" Lona asked, fearing her answer.

Kendra smiled, the lush red lips curving maliciously. "For her whose father's sea-wolves stole your own young daughter from thee. The slave, Freya."

"Ah. That one!" Lona hissed. Her reluctance left her. She pushed herself up to sitting and retrieved her fallen wimple, chewing thoughtfully on her toothless gums as she fastened it over her bald head. "It can be done, but there are things I'll need, my pretty, things of hers. I am too old, too feeble to get them. For the spell to work, I must have your help."

"You'll have it!" Kendra vowed. "What things will you need?"

"Lean closer, while I tell thee," Lona muttered.

Chapter 12

Uncle Sven was healing well, Freya thought, as she recovered him with the blanket. They had been held at Kenley a week now, and in that time the wound had closed cleanly, without poisoning. Though he would hereafter carry the terrible scar and a certain amount of stiffness in that arm, he had weathered the worst and would live, and for that she was deeply grateful.

"You see, little one! I am not so soft after all, eh?" the old Norseman murmured fondly, a smile quirking his lips. "Like Thorfast, you always underestimated this old *skald's* strength."

"*Ja,* she agreed with a rueful smile, "and I thank the gods that I did!" *And Lady Valonia's nursing,* she added silently.

"The gods, the gods, always the gods," Sven exclaimed, shaking his head. "I would lie if I told you it was to them that I prayed for our lives that day, Freya! Nay. It was the White Christ I called upon to spare us. And he answered my pagan prayers, did he not?"

Her eyebrows arched in surprise. "You think to take the White Christ as your god? *Nej!* Don't say such things, uncle!" she scolded. "You will stir our Norse gods to wrath and revenge!"

"Pah! Vengeance. Sacrifice. Bloodshed. Butchery. These are our people's gods, Freya, though we have given them different names! I am tired of their bloody demands for sacrifice upon our people! I have decided that henceforth I will follow the God of the Christians, who asks for brotherhood between all men and would have us love even those whom we've blood-feuded. When I am healed, I will make good the vow I made when the Saxons carried me from the field of battle, here to Kenley."

"What vow was that?" she demanded sharply, fists on hips.

"To receive a Christian baptism. And after, I will seek to enter a holy order here in this isle of Britain—if the church will accept an old pagan convert!"

Slowly she shook her head from side to side. So he would become a monk, Freya realized. She was aware the revelation did not really surprise her, although she was against it. Sven had spoken to her so many times, and with such burning enthusiasm, of the Irish monk, Brother Timothy, from whom he had learned much in his youth. On some level she supposed she had always expected this might happen, sooner or later.

"Then I will lose thee after all, dear uncle," she said softly, "though to the Christian faith, not the shadowy realms of the dead."

"*Nej*, little one," he denied, "as long as I have breath in my body, you will never lose me. But—" he hesitated, "—the closeness we have shared is for now a thing of the past. You have your own destiny awaiting you, a destiny that I am to play little part in, for the time being at least."

"You've seen something, haven't you? Tell me what it is!"

His hand fluttered in a dismissing gesture. "Perhaps. And then again, perhaps not. Perchance it was but a dream, brought about by the draughts of poppy juice the Lady Valonia prepared for me." Those eyes twinkled. "Yea, I fear it must have been, for I doubt the truth of what I saw!"

"Doubt or nay, tell it," she demanded, impatient now.

"Very well. I saw you, Freya. You wore the chrisom cloth upon your head in the manner of the newly baptized, and—you bore a Christian name, the name Marissa—Child of the Sea."

The chrisom was a white cloth worn for nine days by a convert to Christianity, after his anointment with holy baptismal oil, Freya knew. "Ha!" She laughed scornfully, showing even white teeth, her fears stilled. "Then it was in truth the poppy juice that caused your visions this time, uncle!

166

I would sooner suffer torture and death than forsake our Norse gods."

"As you swore, no doubt, you would sooner suffer torture and death than surrender yourself to the Saxon lord?" he countered pointedly, gentle reproof in his tone.

She colored furiously and appeared flustered. "I was given no choice in that, as well you know," she retorted through gritted teeth.

"Hush, girl," Sven scolded. "I was not accusing you. I simply meant to impress upon you that things do not always go the way we expect them to. We change as we go through life, and we are changed by others, and by circumstances. I learned long ago never to be certain things would occur as I wished them. Too often in the past I was proved wrong—as in this you may well be proved wrong!"

She snorted in disbelief. She'd become a Christian, he said? Never, said she! 'Twas more likely a—a cow should jump over the moon!

Sven did not belabor his point, though her expression mirrored her disbelief. Time would bear him out, as it always had in the past. It was but a question of waiting, and he was a patient man.

Freya patted his hand fondly and moved on to the next straw pallet to see to the needs of the other wounded, rebinding a healing sword cut here, raising a painkilling draught to another's lips there. In the past week that old Lona had been sick, the Saxon men had come, if not to trust her, then at least not to fear her as much. They rarely shrank from her touch now, nor made the horned-finger sign against the "Viking witch," as they called her.

Valonia had seemed well satisfied that her trust in Freya had not been misplaced, and now permitted her to tend the Kenley wounded without supervision, which had caused Freya to admire her even more. The Lady Valonia alone in this enemy household treated her as a human being, worthy of trust, deserving of kindness and consideration. But then, Valonia was gentle to all, slave, servant, and noble alike. She even felt affection for the old crone, Lona, whom Freya had doused with dirty washing water on the day of her capture!

Freya frowned. She suddenly felt guilty for wishing the old woman would remain ill, so that in Lona's stead she might continue to care for the wounded herself—and consequently her uncle along with them! Had she not given Valonia her word to serve her truly in all things, in return for Sven's life? Even in thought, her word must not be broken. Viking honor forbade it!

Deciding quickly, she ladled beef and barley broth into an earthenware bowl from the steaming black kettle over the hearth and set it upon a rough-hewn wooden tray. She added a hunk of dark, coarse bread and a small crock of cool, fresh milk to the soup, then called upon another serving woman to watch over the wounded momentarily while she went up the three steps and out into the bailey, headed for Lona's cottage, which huddled close to Kenley's wooden palisades.

In the past few days since Kendra's unsettling visit, Lona's ague had worsened. She wheezed on her pallet of moldy straw in the hut's gloom, her breath whistling and rattling between her slack lips. She had fallen into yet another fitful doze when Freya, receiving no permission to enter when she called out at the doorway, ducked inside unbidden.

The hut's interior was dark and musty, since little light fell through the narrow wind-eye. Cobwebs graced the corners, Freya saw, squinting in the gloom, and pegs bearing a string of pungent onions, a shawl, and several worn leather satchels hung from the walls. The old woman lay very still, yet Freya could hear the difficulty with which she drew each labored breath. She lightly touched her hand, and found Lona's dry old skin clammy against her fingertips. She turned her attention to the fire, which had all but died down and was a miserable excuse for comfort now. 'Twas little wonder the old crone shivered even in her sleep! Valonia had mentioned that the Lady Kendra saw fit to tend her old nurse herself. Well, what manner of care was this, to let the old woman go cold and hungry and sleep on dirty straw, in her sickness? The cottage was in dire need of sweeping, dusting, and airing, that much was abundantly clear. A few judicious swipes with a broom would work wonders for the old woman's comfort, and ridding

168

her cottage of dust would of a certainty ease her labored breathing.

"Mother Lona!" she called, and gently shook the sleeping woman by the shoulder.

Lona came to with a start and a horrified gasp, to find herself gaping up into the face of her who had filled her dreams—or rather, her nightmares!—along with visions of leaping flames that licked at her old bones even as thick, black smoke choked off her breath . . .

"What do you here, girl?" she demanded in a hoarse croak that erupted into a violent fit of coughing.

Freya raised her up by the shoulders and thumped her on the back to help her catch her breath. The woman weighed almost nothing, she noted. "Better?"

"Aye," Lona gasped at length, clawing at her heart with a gnarled, liver-spotted hand. There was a suspicious gleam in her bright black eyes. What was the girl doing here? What was it she wanted?

"I've brought you some broth," Freya said by way of explanation, seeing the wariness in her eyes. "Come, Old Mother, let me help you to drink it before it cools."

The broth was rich and savory. The steaming brew eased her breathing and little by little, Lona felt strength oozing back into her body. When the broth was gone, Freya smiled in satisfaction.

"There. Now, if you've a broom, I'll set your cottage to rights. The dust in here! Why, I could suffer a coughing fit myself!"

Frowning, Lona gestured to a dark corner, and there Freya found a sturdy broom of bound birch wands. Minutes later the dust—and the cobwebs—had been cast vigorously from the cottage, its contents neatly righted. She was about to set the broom back in its corner when something caught her eye. She picked it up and examined it curiously. It was a crude little doll, no bigger than her palm, fashioned from baked clay. In the head had been set several long, reddish-gold hairs—the same color as her own hair, and small breastlike mounds upon its chest suggested the figure was female. The hackles rose on the

169

back of her neck. What dark magic was this?

"What is this, Old Mother?" she asked in a casual tone that belied the uneasy throb of her heart.

Old Lona blinked and muffled an oath. Curse that foolish Kendra! Had she not warned her to return the mannikin to the leather pouch where it belonged, instead of leaving it on the floor of the hut for anyone to see! Her heart thudded violently against her bony breast. If the girl suspected—!

"'Tis naught but a little charm, to ensure good crops at Kenley this autumn, girl," she said smoothly. "A little mannikin of our Harvest Lady, nothing more."

"A pagan charm, is it not?" Freya asked, her sapphire eyes suddenly intent upon the old woman.

"Aye, aye, 'tis so," Lona admitted with great reluctance. "And there are those who would see poor old Lona burned at the stake, if they knew I sometimes followed the old ways," she added in a whining tone, yet her eyes gleamed craftily. Such boldness was risky, but she had a notion that this bold maid would admire it in others.

Freya smiled. A harmless little fertility charm, nothing more. What a skittish fool she was, to have feared otherwise! "Your secret is safe with me, Old Mother, never fear. You see, I too follow the old gods of my countrymen," Freya confessed, her anxiety banished.

Lona nodded happily, relieved, and gave her a gummy smile. "There's a good little wench. That's the way, aye, that's the way! My thanks to ye for the tasty broth, and for sweeping my cottage," she added grudgingly. In return Freya flashed her a smile that seemed to light up the hut's gloomy confines as if a brilliant ray of golden sunlight were trapped there. Ah! 'Twas little wonder Kendra feared this beauty's influence over Alaric, Lona realized. The Viking girl was like a summer day, vivid and glowing with the high color and vitality of vibrant youth, while Kendra's night-dark comeliness was already on the wane. The . . . matter . . . she and Kendra had discussed some days before brought an ugly twinge of guilt lancing through her raddled old body, a twinge she quickly dismissed.

"What are ye about now, girl?" she demanded suspiciously as Freya crouched by the dying fire, feeding the dull red glow of the embers from the sparse store of kindling set by the hearth.

"If you'll let me, I know of a way to loosen the tightness in your chest."

"No Viking potions!" the old woman cried hoarsely, alarmed.

Freya smiled. "I'm no brewer of potions, Old Mother, never you fear! Rest and wait on my return. You'll not be sorry, I promise you."

Lona watched in frank mistrust as she left the hut.

She returned a short while later bearing a basket piled with smooth stones. The sick woman had yet again lapsed into sleep while she was away. Humming softly, she set the stones upon the now glowing fire and moved to the narrow wind-eye, which she covered with a shawl taken from a peg on the wall.

"Have you any pine balsam, Lona?" Freya asked. The old woman's eyes fluttered open. She wakened, nodded when Freya repeated her request, and waved a bony hand toward one of the scarred leather pouches.

"Aye. You'll find it over there—in the second satchel."

Freya followed her directions, and when a manservant brought a wooden bucket of water into the hut soon after at her request, she crumbled one of the fragrant resin cakes into it. All was in readiness now. The stones atop the fire glowed redly. Dismissing the serving man, who eyed her with open lust, she drew closed the door of the hut and went to crouch by the fire. Using her hands for a ladle, she scooped cool water onto the hot stones, pausing after each scooping to allow the water to spit and sizzle on their hot surfaces and make steam, then reheat, before repeating her actions.

Soon the hut was filled with fragrant, moist steam, which Lona inhaled with greedy, eager breaths. The damp heat and the piny medicinal vapor seemed to unfasten the clutches of the choking ague upon her lungs and to loosen the foul, sticky humor that clogged them. When she coughed again, it was easier, less painful, to do so. For the first time in the week since she had fallen ill, she felt better and believed she might live after all.

Freya kept up the steam treatment for an hour, then

uncovered the wind-eye and opened the door, first patting the old woman dry where the sweat bathed her, then drawing a rough blanket over her so she would not become further chilled.

"Does your chest pain you less now, Old Mother?" she asked.

"Aye, aye, it does," the old woman agreed, nodding vigorously. "Where did ye learn this healing skill, girl?"

"From my own nurse. Nissa, the Elfin One, her name is. We Danes in Jutland have always enjoyed the *sauna*, but only my Nissa—a Briton!—had the foresight to realize the steam would ease a hacking cough and loosen the lungs. She made the steam bath with balsam for me each time I sickened of a lung ague as a little girl and—oww!" She gave a yelp of alarm and pain as the old woman's clawlike hand suddenly darted out and her bony fingers clamped with surprising force over her upper arm, the nails gouging like talons.

"Nissa, you say?" Lona hissed, rheumy eyes bulging forth from her head.

"Aye, Nissa is her name. What of it? She was a slave woman who belonged to a fisherman," Freya added, eyeing Lona askance. "You see, my own mother, the Lady Verdandi, died giving me birth. Nissa had just recently delivered a stillborn babe herself, and so Sven, who is like a father to me, took me to Nissa to be wet-nursed. In truth, she is the only mother I've ever known, or wanted, and I've always loved her dearly."

"And—and what has become of her now?" Lona demanded, with, Freya thought, far more intense curiosity on her part than the tale warranted.

"She birthed five strong young ones for her master, and he, in his gratitude and fondness, freed her and took her as his woman. When I left Danehof she was expecting another little one, though she must be nigh the end of her childbearing days. Why do you ask?"

"My Nissa!" the old woman muttered to herself. "My little Nissa! Could it be? Nay, surely not! But aye, there's a chance, just a chance—"

"Surely not what?" Freya demanded, growing vexed.

"Where was your Nissa taken from, girl?" old Lona rasped.

"She was stolen from—from Britain, she told me," she

supplied. "But not from Kenley."

"Was it from Gippeswyk, mayhap?"

"*Ja*, I believe it was!" Freya exclaimed, curiosity bright in her own eyes now.

To her surprise, the old woman gave a low moan and began rocking back and forth, hugging herself about the arms and muttering, "Nissa, my pretty Nissa," over and over again.

"What was she to you, Lona?" Freya asked, and when the old woman did not answer but continued her rocking, Freya grasped her by the shoulder and shook her. "What was she to you, Old Mother?" she repeated sternly.

"Daughter," Lona managed finally. "Nissa was my daughter. The only child of the seven I carried in my belly to survive beyond birth! At fourteen summers she took a man of Gippeswyk for her mate, and left Kenley. Not a year later I learned her husband had been killed and that she had been taken captive by the Northmen in a raid—the same summer that your sire, curse him, raided Kenley, and slaughtered our chieftain and his little ones."

"Then you need worry about her no longer, Old Mother, for your daughter is alive and happy, the beloved wife and mother to her man and her own little ones." Aghast, Freya saw the old woman's rheumy dark eyes glisten with tears. "Believe me, 'tis so," she insisted. "I loved her, as all who meet her come to love her, for her gentleness and wisdom."

Nodding, tears in her rheumy old eyes, Lona brushed a silky lock of hair from the girl's face and patted her cheek with a dry, feverish claw. "I believe thee, my pretty," she said, her lower lip trembling. "'Tis just that for so many years I have fretted and wondered what fate befell my pretty Nissa. To learn she lived and built a new life for herself, raised ye as a daughter, and birthed five more of her own—in truth, I can scarce believe it!"

And then came a nagging thought, quite unbidden, into Lona's head. How could she now plot to harm this girl whom her own Nissa had loved and raised like a daughter? Aye, 'twas a knotty problem, the knottiest, but not one without hope of a solution, Kendra or nay, curse her . . .

*   *   *

Golden-eyed Kendra was livid with rage when Lona, later that same day, calmly informed her she would not work a curse against Freya as they had planned . . .

"You'll be sorry, you old hag!" she hissed, high, angry color flaming in her cheeks. "Aye, you'll wish you'd heeded me before this is done, mark my words!"

"Be that as it may, I'll not aid you against the girl my Nissa raised," Lona repeated, a curious calm and courage settling over her. "I'm old and tired. I've lived my span of years. I'm ready to go, Kendra, aye, more than ready now that I've learned what befell my Nissa. Your threats no longer frighten me."

"A brave boast! Perhaps you'll go very soon, Old Mother," Kendra ground out between her gritted teeth, her fists clenched so that the knuckles were bled white. "Aye, sooner than you think . . ."

She unpinned the mantle from her shoulder and wadded it into a heavy bundle. Holding it in both hands, she advanced on the old woman. Lona's rheumy eyes gazed steadily up into hers without fear, and for a second Kendra wavered. This ugly old crone, who smelled already of death, had once suckled her at her breasts, had lavished her love and affection upon her! How could she end her old life, how? For endless seconds, she wavered. But then the rage burned through her again, and all the love she had once felt for old Lona was cast out in a fiery, jealous blast. Lona had always said she loved her best, that she, Kendra, was her favorite of all the children she had been nurse to. How could the old bitch fail her now, whatever the Viking girl had told her? How could she!

She noted dully that Lona was smiling as she lowered the bundle over her face and pressed down, down. Lona writhed briefly, a final, involuntary struggle to hang onto life. Her scrawny arms came up and threshed, clawing for Kendra's gown, windmilling for moments that seemed an eternity to Kendra, who was breathing heavily now. Her legs threshed, her heels drumming against the pallet. But it was naught but a brief fight against death. Lona's arms went slack and she lay very still, her long life snuffed out like a pinched candle. Kendra fell, exhausted and weeping, to the earthen floor.

174

Much later, she looked up and dried her eyes upon her knuckles, a smile curving her lush, red lips. The old woman was dead, killed for her refusal to aid Kendra in getting rid of the Viking girl. Kendra threw back her head and laughed. But she had an idea in which Lona would help her after all, even after her death, like it or nay . . . !

Freya was serving at table when Kendra, her face streaked with tears, her eyes red and swollen, all but exploded into the hall. Farant, praise be, was nowhere in sight, Kendra observed thankfully, though Alaric sat broodingly at table alongside the others, watching the slave girl through hooded eyes as she moved about the hall. With a wailing cry Kendra ran across the rushes between the company and flung herself down at Valonia's knees, clutching at her skirts and sobbing.

"She is dead, my aunt!" she wailed. "Dead!"

"Dead? Who, Kendra? Calm yourself, my dear, and tell me, what has happened?" Valonia cried in alarm.

"Mother Lona! I—I went to her cottage—to see if there was anything she needed, you see, in her sickness. And—and she was dead!"

"Sweet Jesu!" Valonia exclaimed, crossing herself. "Poor Lona! Are you certain she is gone? Perhaps—!" Seeing Kendra shake her head, Valonia's shoulders slumped. "Ah, then there is nothing we can do, God grant her soul peace. She was like a mother to all of us, and we will miss her sorely here at Kenley, aye, and her skill with herbs. The ague must have been far worse than I imagined."

Freya swung about on hearing this. Mother Lona—dead? Nay! It was not so! It could not be so! the denial screamed inside her head. The old woman had seemed much improved when she had left her earlier that day. Why, the news of her daughter Nissa seemed to have given her new-found strength to draw upon. "By your leave, my lady?" she said hesitantly, bobbing a curtsey before the Saxon noblewoman.

"Speak, child," Valonia said absently, gesturing with a limp hand. Tears glimmered in her blue eyes.

"I—I went myself to Lona's cottage this morn, to take her

some hot beef broth. I—I also made her a steaming vapor with balsam in it, to ease her lungs, you understand? I—she seemed much better when I left her. I was certain she would rec——"

"Better—or dead?" Kendra cried, springing to her feet. "Nay! You killed her, you! You killed her with Viking magic! Balsam vapor? Ha! 'Twas witchcraft, not herb-craft! Look! I found this in her hut, close by poor Lona's body! Tell me, is this not pagan magic?"

The company at table gasped and recoiled in horror at her words. They crossed themselves to the last man as Kendra flung about and brandished aloft in her hand the ugly little mannikin Freya had found in the dust of the cottage. From its heart protruded a sharp, black thorn. "Have you seen this before, slave?" she cried.

"*Ja*, I have. It was in Lona's cottage earlier today. She said— She said it was a charm, to bring bounty to the harvest," Freya attempted to explain.

"Liar! You fashioned it!" Kendra shrieked.

Alaric got to his feet and strode across the crowded hall toward the women, his footfalls loud and ominous in the hush. He towered over his sister-in-law. "You accuse my bower slave of witchcraft, Kendra," he said softly but with steel in his eyes. "'Tis a grave charge, and could end in her death at the stake if the Church finds her guilty. Grief has unhinged you, sister. You are not yourself. Will you not withdraw your accusation?"

Kendra tossed her river of black hair over her shoulders. Her amber eyes glowed savagely into his in the gloom of the hall, and there was the glitter of triumph in their golden depths. "Nay, I will not. It is no more than she deserves, Alaric!" She flung about to face Freya and hurled the mannikin at her feet. "The proof is here! Witch! Viking witch! You'll burn for what you did to Lona this day!" she shrieked, pointing a finger that trembled with rage at Freya.

"What proof do you offer, other than that—mannikin?" Alaric demanded, a heaviness coiling through his innards.

"I need no further proof. She's a cursed pagan, is she not, by her own admission? And she has vowed from the day her sea-wolves attacked Kenley to revenge herself on all who were

176

responsible for her capture. Rolf, the guard, has heard her curses himself, did you not, Rolf?"

The tall blond guard, unnoticed by all until this moment, stepped from the shadows by the doorway. "Aye, Lady Kendra, I have. With my own ears I heard the slave say, 'One day you'll pay for this. On the Hammer of Thor, I swear it!' That's what she said. She was angered that Lona had forced her to don chains, ye see."

Alaric's face was a stern, implacable mask as he heard the guard's condemnation, though inwardly the great knot of foreboding tightened in his gut. He sorely doubted the truth of Kendra's accusations, which he was certain stemmed from jealousy. Lona had been well advanced in years, and sickly of late. 'Twas more likely her span of years had been played out than that Freya had worked some kind of black curse against her. Her death soon after Freya had visited her was naught but a coincidence, common sense told him! But—and here was the problem—how could he prove it? How could he take the word of a common slave against the word of his noble kinswoman? Such a move would cause uproar and dissent throughout Kenley! And yet—and his heart gave a painful twist—how could he let his beautiful bower slave suffer? How could he look on as the trials for witchcraft were conducted; the pricking of her flawless, glowing flesh with pointed bodkins to seek out the insensitive Devil's mark; the laying of smoking red-hot irons upon her lovely limbs; the binding and lowering into water until her lungs were afire with agony? The very notion caused the gorge to rise sourly in his throat, made the sweat form in beads upon his brow. Why he felt so, he knew not, but he could not permit the girl to suffer from Kendra's jealousy, Viking or nay—

He glanced up, aware as he did so that every eye in the hall was upon him, awaiting his decision. And there were those who, since his recent return to Kenley, would take this moment and from it form lasting opinions of his worthiness as their lord . . . Whatever his wishes to the contrary, he must show them the strength they demanded, or dissension would run rife in his burh.

"Take her!" he commanded in strong, stern tones and with

177

an implacable expression that gave no inkling of the turmoil within him. "Take her to the empty byre and hold her under close guard there, until I have determined what will be done with her!"

Freya's frightened sapphire eyes went first to Alaric, who met them unrelentingly, and then to Valonia, who smothered the pity in her expression and quickly looked away, and her hope dwindled to naught.

"Nay!" she cried, slowly shaking her head and backing away. "I am innocent of this! I did nothing to harm Lona, my lord, I swear it! Please, my Lord Alaric, Lady Valonia—you cannot do this! I am innocent of any witchcraft, you must believe me—*nay!*"

Ignoring her pleas, Alaric nodded curtly. The guard, Rolf, stepped forward and grasped her by the arms, hauling her from the hall. Over her shoulder as he dragged her away Freya caught Kendra's gloating smile, and her blood turned to ice.

Chapter 13

Was it six days or seven since she had been brought here to the byre, Freya wondered, gazing disinterestedly at a small brown mouse as it made a foray about her feet in search of crumbs. Good fortune, poor Master Mouse, she wished the creature, for with the meager food she had been brought she doubted he would find himself a meal! Naught but crusts of black bread, hard enough to break the teeth upon, and a thin, greasy broth had she been given once each day in all that time.

She sighed and shifted her position to ease her stiffness, but remained sitting, her head resting on her bent knees. When they had first brought her here she had paced restlessly back and forth, back and forth across the straw, like a captured wild thing, but after the first few days she had given up on futile pacing and now sat staring at nothing, or slept away the endless hours. What else could she do? The narrow wind-eyes let in scant light, and she was in heavy gloom from dawn till dusk. Now that a seven-night had passed, she could not bear herself any more than she could bear her prison, without water with which to wash and no fresh garments or clean straw, and with only a crude bucket in which to relieve herself. In truth, her enslavement to Alaric seemed but the gentlest of restraints compared to this misery!

Oh, how she longed to feel the sprindrift spray upon her limbs, to drink in the sharp, salty tang of brine and revel in the freedom of riding a proud dragon-ship once more over the wild waves! But over the monotonous days and in the dark of the long and empty nights she had begun to fear she would never see the sea again, let alone sail upon it. What else had she to look forward to but slavery hereafter, however gentle, even should she by some miracle be found innocent of witchcraft? Nay, if there were naught but that alternative to cling to, she would sooner die now; would welcome death as a compassionate friend.

Her spirit was ebbing, she knew, but it seemed she could do little to restore it. It had been bent and subjugated to the will of others too often since her capture. There were moments of late in which she feared that when the time came, as it must, she would be unable to summon enough courage to prove to the Saxons that Vikings could die as proudly and fearlessly as they lived.

So steeped in melancholy and despair was she that she did not notice when Alaric, having dismissed the guard, stepped inside her byre prison. Sweet Madonna Mary! Shock lanced through him when he saw her, for she had changed in the past seven days since he had seen her last. Her hair was lank, its vixen brightness dulled, and her posture was that of one defeated, head bowed, shoulders slumped. Aye, her posture expressed her emotions more than anything else did. Gone was her jaunty, challenging air, the regal carriage of her lovely head, like a proud blossom upon the slender willow stalk of her throat and shoulders. Inwardly, he sighed. Over the past week he had considered her plight, exploring all avenues for a way out—a way in which he could release her from her prison and yet maintain the respect of his people. Already there were mutterings among them that the girl had bewitched him with her beauty and her wiles, and it was for this reason he had not come to see her, though God knew he had wanted to!

There had been moments too, during the past week, when his fervor to see her cleared of Kendra's accusations had surprised even himself. But his return to Kenley as the burh's rightful lord was yet too recent to risk the inevitable dissension any apparent softening on his part toward the girl might cause. Why was this so? he wondered. Would he have felt so strongly were another slave falsely accused in her place? Strongly, aye—but not so strongly as he felt about Freya's innocence.

180

She glanced up then, and saw him there, and something twisted in his vitals to see the changes wrought in her pinched face. Her sapphire eyes were dulled, and filled with—what? Resignation, he decided, acceptance of her imprisonment, and the knowledge cut him to the quick. There were fading bruises marring her cheeks, and the twisting sensation inside him deepened, like the twist of a blade. Whoever the man might be who had struck her would not go unpunished, he swore silently as he strode across the byre toward her.

"It would seem you have been badly used, Freya," he said softly, the words almost sticking in his craw. "I will see that you are made more comfortable henceforth."

"Why bother?" she retorted, but without true spirit. "I am well. Give no thought to me, Saxon. I am yet fit to serve as kindling upon your Christian fire!"

A muscle in his jaw twitched violently. "Fear not. You will not burn, I swear it!"

"Indeed? Tell me, how will you prevent it, my lord? You cannot set me free, for there are many who would take such an act as but further proof that I have bewitched you, used my witchcraft to sway you from seeing justice done, are there not?" she reasoned, and he marveled at her keen grasp. "And besides, no one will respect you as Lord of Kenley if you pervert the laws of your church for the sake of a lowly slave— and a bloody Viking slave, at that. Admit it, my lord! There is nothing you can do, even should you want to. Before the trial is ever begun, I am already guilty in the minds of your people."

"Let them think what they will," he growled. "As you said, I am lord here, my word the only law that carries weight. I think you capable of many things, woman—aye, even murder, mayhap, if provoked, and with sword in hand—but not by witchcraft, and not with a wrinkled old hag as your victim. I believe you innocent of Kendra's charges."

"Ah, then all is well," she muttered with heavy sarcasm. "I can go to my death with the comforting knowledge that Lord Alaric alone at Kenley believed in me! Ha! 'Tis cold comfort you offer, sir!"

"I will make others believe it, too," he vowed. "I will force Kendra to withdraw her accusations."

181

"And how will you do this?"

"I know not as yet, but I will do it," he muttered obstinately, scowling.

"Oh, do what you will, for I care not! Death comes to all of us, one way or another," she said sullenly, and turned away.

At once he grasped her by the shoulder and spun her about to face him. "Little fool! You say you care not? I do not believe you! Look me in the eyes, and tell me you would welcome death!"

Sapphire eyes, without sparkle or spirit in their depths, met his gray ones. "Aye, Saxon, I would, for only in death can I escape your enslavement. What have I to look forward to? Nothing but captivity, even should I be found innocent. Death, take me, I say! I am ready."

He released her abruptly, scorn in his eyes, mockery in the timbre of his voice. "Christ's Wounds! It is as I suspected from the first, is it not? Behind all the fine, valiant words and your cocksure strut, your male clothing, you are as weak and womanish as the next maid, for all that you may crow otherwise and boast that you are better than they. Your teachers failed thee, madam, when they called thee a warrior. They did not teach you the most fundamental lesson, did not help you to develop the most formidable weapon any warrior has at his disposal with which to do battle; reliance upon himself! When your sword is dashed from your hand and your companions are all fallen about you, what course is there left? It is then a true soldier learns what he is made of. He draws on his inner courage and taps its wellspring. He does not hang his head in shame and defeat, and meekly accept his lot, as do you! When all seems darkest, when despair sits upon his shoulder and casts covetous eyes upon his soul, then does the true warrior show his valor, and leaps into the heat of the foray! Without that inner strength he can be naught but a coward—a man who gives up and runs away when the going becomes difficult, or the enemy of the moment more subtle and harder to pin down. Are you a coward, Freya of the Frozen Heart?"

A small, solid fist came out of nowhere and slammed into his cheek. A second followed it, the knuckles ringing against taut

182

flesh, the force of the blow snapping his dark head sharply sideways.

"No man calls me a coward, not without answering for his insults. Give me a sword and I will prove my mettle, Saxon cur! We will see which one of us is coward then!" she hissed, her sapphire eyes blazing, hectic color rising swift and hot up her cheeks.

"Nay, Viking," he countered, breathing heavily, "prove it at your own expense, not mine—without sword, without weapons of any kind! Draw on the weapons *within* you—if you can!" So saying, he spun about on his heel and left her alone— and still seething—in the gloomy byre.

As he strode through the bailey toward the hall, a small smile of satisfaction curved his lips. If nothing else, his visit to the girl had served one purpose; to jolt her from the quagmire of despair into which she had fallen. His grin deepened. She wanted to live now, if only to see him eat his words and fall dead by her hand!

Ordway and Cullen, his son, sat at table over horns of mead when he strode into the hall. Ordway looked up as he crossed to their table and offered him a draught, which he politely refused.

"Well, nephew, does the Viking witch woman confess her sins?" he asked.

"Nay, uncle. And nor do I believe she is guilty of any sins to confess."

"What is this?" Ordway demanded, incredulous. "She is a pagan, is she not, a worshipper of the old Norse gods?"

Alaric shook his head. "She is not of our faith, nay, but I would stake my life that she worked no witchcraft upon Lona.

"Pah! You would sooner take the word of a Viking over that of your kinswoman? Have her denials, her protests of innocence, so blinded you to the truth?" Ordway exploded, his complexion darkening with anger.

"My slave girl has not sought in any way to deny the charges made against her, uncle," Alaric said. "And yet, aye, I would take her part! I know Kendra well, as should you by now. She is jealous of the maid, for reasons best known to herself. Her accusations are but an attempt to rid herself of the girl."

"Why do you appear so bent on vindicating this—this slave? Can it be true what I have heard muttered this past seven-night—that she has cast a spell on you too? That you are bewitched by her? Would you have her set free, then?"

"Such mutterings are but idle gossip, uncle, as well you know. She has worked no spells on me. Aye, I would see her set free!"

"You forget to whom you speak then, lad!" Ordway thundered. "Your bed-wench's father killed—"

"No, it is you who forget, sir, that I am now lord here," Alaric broke in quietly. "Not you. And I am well aware of her father's guilt. Wilone is also my mother, even as she is your sister, sir, if you recall. But it is for me to decide what will be done with the woman Freya, as with all here in my burh. I will not see her, nor anyone else, burned at the stake when falsely accused—you may call it Christian charity, if it please you," he added with a faintly mocking smile. "Our quarrel was with Thorfast, not her. She has been deflowered by me and forced to become my slave. Her shame is enough for a proud one such as she."

"You have grown weak, Alaric. She has unmanned thee!" Ordway stormed.

"Nay, uncle, not so, I am my own man—as you have ever taught me to be. As you also once taught me that all are deserving of justice, be they peasant or king, did you not? So will I dispense justice my way—and mercy to the innocent or guilty, when it is warranted."

There was a long, crackling silence as they glared at each other. Ordway could not outstare the unwavering, cool gaze of his nephew, and looked away first. "Forgive me," he said gruffly. "Aye, forgive me. You are lord here, nephew, and what you say is right and true. The tutor soon forgets the lessons he teaches, does he not?" he added, abashed, "Whatever you decide, I am certain you will do so with wisdom, and I will endeavor to support you in it. Now, enough of this discord between us. Let us talk instead on the matter of your betrothal."

Alaric clapped a warm hand across his uncle's shoulders. "As you will. Has word already been sent to Wales?"

"Aye, but a short while ago. I made a messenger of young Hanley, Shire Reeve Winfield's second son. He is a trustworthy lad, and will see the missive delivered and a reply brought in good time. He is to take ship from London, and thence sail for Wales. Within two months we will know if Lord Eamonn and his daughter would be willing to meet with us in London and discuss a betrothal between the two of you. And by the grace of God, within the year an heir for Kenley might be started, eh, Alaric?"

Alaric nodded, smiling now. "Aye, indeed it might."

Cullen grinned. "Fair Meredyth of Powys! How I envy thee, Alaric!"

"Speak not of envy, cousin, until I have seen the maid with my own eyes! I have never yet praised a horse's lines or its smooth gait without having first seen it for myself."

His wicked cousin nudged him in the ribs with ribald merriment. "Or without having ridden it, eh, Alaric?"

"Aye, that too!" Alaric agreed, grinning broadly himself. All three men laughed.

"And what of the slave girl today? Does she sit in her prison stirring a bubbling brew and casting dark spells upon us all?" Cullen inquired.

"Would that she did, but nay. Rather, she has grown pale as a wraith, and is but a shadow of her former self." Alaric's expression was bleak.

"Ah. 'Tis a pity. She was as fiery as she was comely," Cullen murmured with regret.

"If you will permit me, I have business I must attend to," Ordway said stiffly.

It was obvious to Alaric that his uncle was reluctant to hear further discussion of the Viking girl he so detested, and he nodded his assent.

"Do not think badly of him, cousin," Cullen said when his father had left them. "It is hard for him to fall back and take second place now you are returned. He is convinced none but he can know what is best for Kenley. If he has a fault, it is that he has cared for your burh too well!"

"I understand. And I think no ill of your father. Rather, I am grateful for the care he has given Kenley in my absence.

Few would have done so well, or with such little thought for their own reward."

Cullen nodded. "I fancy when you are wed and settled, he will return to live on our estates at Dover. It has been many years since we dwelt there."

"They are in good repair?"

"Knowing my father, could you doubt it?" Cullen asked with a smile.

"If he should desire to return there, I will see him well rewarded for all he has done for me here, despite his protests that he asks for no reward."

"Your generosity does you credit, cousin."

"'Tis no more than his due."

There was a brief silence between them, then Cullen asked, "What you said—about the Viking wench being innocent of witchcraft? Do you truly believe it?" Seeing Alaric nod firmly, he continued, "But how will you prove her innocence?"

"There is but one way, if I am to do it and yet retain the confidence of my people. Kendra must be made to withdraw her accusations. It is how I can force her to do this that must yet be determined."

"You might threaten to tell Farant she has sought you out and offered herself to you many times," Cullen suggested, pouring himself more mead.

"I might. Yet the lady is no fool. She knows I would never do aught to sever the bond between Farant and myself, and will believe my threat a hollow one."

"True. But—what of the lady's dalliances with other men? Would you hesitate to use those against her?"

"Dalliances? With whom?" Alaric demanded, dark brows rising in surprise.

Cullen chuckled. "You are ever the innocent in some ways, Alaric, for all your years and professed knowledge of the fair sex. With half your garrison, man! Only those who are old, weak, and feeble—or else impotent and beyond hope!—have been spared mistress Kendra's honeyed . . . trap!"

A dark scowl crossed Alaric's face. "Half my garrison! By the Cross, the bitch must be insatiable in her appetites!"

"Insatiable indeed. She is known by the men as M'Lady

Cracked Goblet, for like a cracked vessel she is never filled!"
He chuckled.

"Do all at Kenley know of this save me?"

"All save our family! Farant knows nothing, of that I am
certain. She chooses her times well, most often when he leaves
Kenley to visit the monastery, as he has done today. Did you
know that he took the old Viking, Sven, with him, since his
wounds are nigh completely healed? For all their differing
origins, he and the old fellow have much in common, it seems.
They will pass the day poring over the monks' musty
scribblings, while Farant's lady wife betrays him yet again.
Aye, I believe if she could be taken in the act with one of her
pretty men-at-arms, she could be easily brought to see the error
of her ways." Cullen cocked his brows slyly. "What say you?"

A grin started at the corners of Alaric's mouth, and the
burden of the past week lifted as it spread to glint in his wood-
smoke eyes. "I think you have it, cousin!" he agreed. "Will
you help me in this? Four eyes are better than two!"

"Wild horses could not stop me, Alaric," Cullen said
scornfully. "Since we returned from the wars, I find a growing
hunger in myself for action and intrigue of some kind! 'Twill be
like when we were lads, and spied upon the soldiers and the
serving maids at their sport, will it not?"

"Aye. But this time a life hangs in the balance, dependent on
the results of our spying," Alaric added grimly.

From that day forth, the Lady Kendra went nowhere
without their unobtrusive surveillance. They dogged her every
move like shadows, yet not once did the woman slip up and
commit an indiscretion. After another week had passed, and
the arrival of the witchfinder his uncle had summoned was
growing imminent, Alaric began to despair.

"It is as if she knows what we're about, eh, cousin?" he
muttered angrily as they sat at supper in the hall one evening,
watching the lady in question farther down the table.

She was lovely this night, her dark cloud of hair caught
prettily in a web of fine gold, her lush body robed in the deep
saffron gold that matched her eyes and so well became her. She
caught their eyes upon her and interrupted her flirtatious
conversation with a starry-eyed Farant to raise her horn to

them in salute. "Your good health, cousins!" she toasted sweetly, raising her thick dark lashes like seductive fans.

"And yours, sweet coz!" Cullen rejoined gallantly, raising his own horn. "Your loveliness outshines the very candles this night, beauteous Kendra!"

"As does your gallantry, dear Cullen," she smoothly countered.

"She knows," Cullen muttered darkly as he turned back to Alaric.

"Aye," Alaric said morosely, "but how?"

"Guilt. She knows her accusations are hollow, and no doubt is on guard against anyone who might seek to have her withdraw them. She sees a threat in everything and everyone, I would warrant, us included."

"Mmmm. Then we must seem to remove that threat, think you not? Stroll over to Farant, and invite him to go a-hawking with us on the morrow. Accept no refusal. And be certain the lady overhears your plans."

Cullen was already up and on his feet, heading toward the pair. "That goes without saying, Alaric. I am on my way! And," he added with a chuckle, "I can scarce wait for the hunt to commence!"

"You have pondered what troubles you long enough, my lady," grumbled a deep, coarse young voice. "If we do not make haste, your lord husband will return from hawking!"

Kendra looked up, startled to see the young guard still sprawled on her bed. In truth, she had forgotten him for the while, her thoughts wrestling with the knotty problem of Farant, and how best to rid herself of him. The Viking girl had been a serious threat to her plans, but she was already well on her way to being naught but an unpleasant memory, Kendra thought with satisfaction. Aye, only Farant stood between her and Alaric now.

She turned her attention to young Rolf. Curse that Cullen and Alaric, she had been certain they had had her watched of late, though for what possible reason she could not fathom. But, and she smiled delightedly, they had both conventionally

188

gone a-hawking early this morning, and better still, persuaded Farant to go with them, and so she was free at last to pursue her own—diversions! In truth, after so many days of celibacy she was hot and eager for a man, any man, for her body's appetites were vast. This one was a prize, she thought, idly inspecting the young soldier, and had quickly become her favorite. He was flaxen-haired and a very pretty young fellow, his golden-haired torso broad yet lean, his arms well muscled, his legs sturdy. In manhood he was well enough endowed to please even the most demanding of women—and she was *very* demanding!

She smiled seductively, the tip of her pointed tongue darting out to moisten her red lips, her golden eyes flaring as they feasted on his youthful male beauty. Hands on her ample hips, she sidled voluptuously toward him.

"Aye, my ready young buck, you are right as usual. Your poor lady has troubles enough, 'tis true, but they belong not here, with us."

Pouting, she slipped the fur-trimmed bed robe off her shoulders and, quite naked now, stood poised for a moment or two before him, permitting him unobstructed view of her body, for she prided herself on her form. Her breasts were still full and firm, without the slightest hint of sagging, the nipples large and ripe as berries. Her waist was yet trim, her buttocks and hips generous yet taut, she thought smugly. She gave a low gasp of pleasure as she saw that the young guard obviously found her pleasing to look upon, for he could not hide his arousal. Like an ivory tower, his manhood reared up from his groin. Unable to draw her eyes from his magnificent member, she stepped across the bower and lay carefully down beside him on the pallet.

At once the youth captured a voluptuous breast in his coarse, callused soldier's hands and fondled it roughly, watching his lady's face carefully for signs of pleasure and pain as he did so. She liked it rough, she did, and he intended to give the black-haired bitch just what it was she wanted, aye! She was a fair tumble, as the others had promised, for all that her full breasts were no longer firm, and had begun to sag a mite, and her white rump was fleshier than was to his taste. Rolf liked his women slim-hipped and smaller-breasted, like Lord Alaric's

189

slave, the one they called Freya, who was even now languishing in the byre. She was a beauty, that one, an' no mistake, Rolf mused. Just thinkin' of her had made his staff grow hard. Yet the Lady Kendra paid him well, like the goose that laid the golden eggs, and he was no fool, not him! He'd tumble this noble "goose" royally, and accept any of the "golden eggs" the abbess's bastard daughter might hand out to him for his trouble, without batting an eye . . . ! His hairy, spatulate fingers dug more cruelly into her soft flesh, and he smiled in triumph as he saw the lust flare in her eyes even as it mingled with the hurt.

"Ye like what it is Rolf does to ye, eh, my fine lady?" he rasped, his own breathing grown coarse and husky now. Roughly he caught her other breast in his free hand and kneaded the two as if they were not flesh and blood but senseless, unfeeling toys created for his spiteful pleasure.

"Ah! Ah! Aye, my young stag, aye!" she panted, her hand grasping the engorged root that sprang from his golden loins, and working it eagerly back and forth in her slippery palm. "Take me! Take me now, Rolf!" she implored him.

"Nay, you eager slut!" the youth growled, adopting the tone of cruel dominance his lady tutor had schooled him well in, "First you'll see to my pleasure, and only then your own. Here, bitch!"

She obediently scrabbled across the bed and ducked her dark head to his thighs. For many long minutes, only the sounds of Rolf's labored breathing, growing steadily more rapid, and the little contented moans from deep in Kendra's throat, were heard in the bower. When at length he thrust her away, he could scarce speak with the heady pressure of his lust.

"Down on your knees, my lady, and quickly now, else your Rolf will beat ye for your disobedience!" he panted.

Whimpering in pretended fear of him, the Lady Kendra complied, hiding a breathless smile as she bent double before him, her red lips moistly parted, her ebony hair with its threadings of silver sweeping the embroidered linen pallet. Truly, the lad had learned his lessons *most* adequately, she thought in eager anticipation, her long fingers clamped about a pillow. She must see him well rewarded for his—skills. She

190

cried out in savage joy as Rolf gripped her cruelly about the waist and plunged into her like a stag in full rut.

Eagerly Rolf rode her, and was yet in full gallop, wooden bed slats creaking their protest, when the bower door crashed open and thundered against the wall, its leather hinges severed!

Alaric towered upon the threshold, massive arms folded across his chest, strong legs braced arrogantly apart. He was grinning broadly. Beside him stood Cullen, likewise smiling. Kendra spied them first and let out a shriek, and poor Rolf, suddenly grown limp with surprise, so to speak, was suddenly unhorsed and flung to the floor by his flummoxed mount.

Kendra sprang off the bed and ran about the bower like a chicken with its head axed, too panic-stricken to think coherently what it was she might have done with her clothing. "Get out! Get out of here, curse you both!" she shrieked, tears of mortification spilling down her crimson cheeks.

Rolf had now managed to gather up his tunic and leggings and made a sudden desperate bolt for the door, in fear for his very life.

"Not so fast, lad," Alaric roared, grasping him by the shoulder and spinning him about. "You'll dress yourself before you leave this bower. And none shall learn of what has taken place here this day, or by God, I'll have your tongue— and more!" His eyes were murderous, steel in their depths. Beneath the vise of his fingers, the young guardsman began to tremble.

Eyes bulging, Rolf nodded like one demented, hopping about as he hauled on boots and tunic and trousers. "I—I'll say naught, my lord, nay, I swear it, I do! 'Twas her what enticed me, not me her, I—!"

"Enough! Be gone!" Alaric threatened, and booted the youth in the rump. Through the door Rolf went, flying like the shaft from a bow.

Alaric strode across the bower to Kendra, who had managed to recover her robe, if not her composure, and had thrown it over herself to cover her nudity. Her eyes were wild, golden orbs of shock and outrage, and her mouth worked soundlessly like a gasping fish. In this moment she was a far from comely sight.

"Well, dear sister," Alaric said with heavy sarcasm, "'twould seem our hunt has yielded surprising quarry! No doubt my brother would be most angered to hear what we have witnessed this day, eh, my lady? Perhaps he'd even order you confined to a convent for the remainder of your days?"

"He'll not believe you!" Kendra spat. "He'll not! He adores me! He knows we were once lovers, and he'll believe 'tis your—your desire for me that causes you to lie."

"But it will be me who tells Farant he has been playing the cuckold, cousin, not Alaric," Cullen cut in, smiling gleefully. "Would you tell him we were once lovers also? Tut tut, my lady, your wicked past has returned to haunt thee!"

For once, Kendra's confidence wavered. Her mouth dropped open to retort, but the words failed her. Farant had known she was no virgin maid when they were wed. She had told him tearfully that Alaric had seduced her, and that blinded by her youthful love for him, she had reluctantly surrendered to his desires. But should Cullen tell him he had also enjoyed her body! Alaric was right, she acknowledged, wetting her suddenly dry lips. Farant, pious fellow that he was, would without question confine her to a convent if he ever learned of this, with walls so high she would never be able to scale them! And all that she coveted, all chance of riches, power—and Alaric—would be lost . . . It could not end so. It would not! She went to a chest and drew a kerchief from its depths, dabbing it at her eyes and sniffing noisily.

"Pray, my good understanding cousins, say nothing of this to my dear Farant!" she beseeched them tearfully. "I am but a poor, misguided woman, and one of—of considerable appetites, as well you have both learned, to my shame," she confessed, bowing her head. "Appetites that alas, my poor Farant is quite unequal to—"

"Have a care for what you say, Kendra," Alaric gritted. "For I warn thee, I am but a hairbreadth from strangling you with my bare hands!"

"Forgive me," she added hurriedly. "I meant Farant no disrespect, for he is truly the kindest, most gentle of husbands, and I do not deserve him. Please, Alaric, keep your silence, I beg you! And you too, Cullen?"

"There is a price for our silence," Alaric said.

She nodded. "I knew it." She sighed. "That—that Viking creature, is it not?"

Alaric nodded. "Freya. Aye! Confess, Kendra. Lona's death was the result of old age and sickness, not witchcraft, was it not?"

With a deep sigh, Kendra nodded. "It was," she lied, contrition in every line of her face and body. "I—I was jealous of the attention you gave the Viking, my lord, and thought to lay the blame for Lona's death at her feet."

"Then you will withdraw your accusations against the girl this very day, or as God is my judge, I will tell Farant what I have witnessed here! And furthermore, madam, you will depart for Winchester on the morrow, with your husband, without any further delay—and I would strongly suggest you make your absence from my burh a long one. My temper is roused, and I fear it will be long before it cools."

Her shoulders sagged. "As you will, my lord," she said meekly—but within she seethed.

Alaric and Cullen exchanged grins.

"Dress yourself fittingly, sister," Alaric commanded sternly. "You have something to tell the people of Kenley straightway, do you not?"

Eyes bright, her jaw clenched, her knuckles white upon the loose girdle that encompassed her waist, Kendra forced herself to nod.

Chapter 14

Freya sat her horse upon the sandy shore and let the cooling wind from off the sea fan her damp face and riffle her unbound hair. It streamed away from her lovely profile like bright silken banners, exposing the fluid line of her throat and shoulders. Her smooth flesh glistened with a faint sheen since the swift gallop they had made from Kenley. Her eyes were closed, her nostrils flared to catch each nuance of the salty air. With her quickened breathing her breasts rose and fell provocatively against the rough cloth of her kirtle, the nipples outlined as tiny, firm hillocks beneath its thickness. Alaric, watching her as a hound watches an especially delectable bone, felt desire ripple through him, and his strong hands tensed upon the reins, his powerful thighs clamped tighter against his stallion's glossy sides, in involuntary response. Beneath him, Lucifer tossed his ebony head and pranced, catching the musk of his master's excitement on the air.

Kendra had withdrawn her accusations against Freya the evening before, while all of Kenley sat at supper in the aisled hall and listened. It had taken all of Alaric's forbearance to nod sternly following her faltering explanations and accept her withdrawal; then, with apparent nonchalance, to order the girl released the following morning. Christ's Wounds, it had cost him, that nonchalance! Everything within him had bade him run straightway to her byre cell and fling the doors wide, but such was impossible! Instead, he had returned to finish his meal in a leisurely manner, to drink deeply and converse wittily, and thus carefully conceal his impatience from the gathering.

Their ride along the shore following her release this morning had been his suggestion. The memory of the last time they had come here, on the day of the storm, and the highly pleasurable coupling they had enjoyed in the cave still loomed large in his memory. She had seemed different that day, wild and free and passionate as the sea itself, and he had nurtured the fond hope that today would be the same. Certainly she must feel gratitude toward him, after he had told her that she was to be spared the horrors of a witch trial, must she not? And women were often moved to express their gratitude in the form of favors, freely and eagerly given . . . In short, they repaid a man's kindness with their bodies. Though a part of him was ashamed of the calculating direction in which his thoughts were leading him, he stoutly smothered any twinges of guilt. He had wanted her for too many long, lonely nights to allow any foolish scruples to stand in his way, and it was with bated breath he had awaited her reaction. To his vast relief, she had quietly accepted his announcement that she was cleared of all charges of practicing witchcraft, as well as his invitation to go riding, and they had ridden from the burh side by side.

For several moments she yet sat quite still, the only movement that of her hair tossing in the sea breeze. At length she twisted in the saddle toward him and gave him a strangely wistful little smile. *"Takke,"* she murmured, and quickly turned away again, the dimples deepening in her cheeks, seeming reluctant—or unable—to look him in the eye.

"Takke?"

She nodded, and her sapphire eyes, fringed with lashes of dark gold, came up to meet his once again. *"Ja.* I said 'Thank you.'"

It was his turn to nod now. Here was the gratitude he had expected. So would the rest go as he had calculated! "You are welcome, Freya. I said you would not suffer for something you had no part in, and I meant it," he said gruffly.

"And if your Lady Kendra had kept silent?"

He ignored the slight emphasis she had placed upon "your" and replied, "Then I would have found some other way to spare you."

"You are a strange man, Saxon," she observed, her brow crinkling in puzzlement. "I confess I cannot fathom you."

To her surprise—and his!—he blushed beneath his swarthy complexion. "Then why do you try?" he suggested, almost curtly. "I am but a man, like any other. No more, no less."

She tossed back her head and laughed, the silvery ripple causing seabirds to rise from their rocky nests amongst the cliffs at their backs and wheel away over the sparkling gray-blue of the sea. "Nay, not so, Saxon! You are a man, *ja*, but very different from other men I have met, Alaric of Kent—in many ways, if not in all," she amended, with a rueful little twist of her lips. "How can I help wondering what it is that sets you apart?" she added softly. "You made a vow that I would be shamed and dishonored in your household in revenge for my father's acts, did you not, but now I find you have become my champion, of sorts." She shook her head. "And not only this, but when my spirits were at their lowest ebb you came to me and made me angry enough to want to live again—if only to make you eat your words! You have either great compassion or great cunning, my lord. You made me remember just how precious life is, *ja*, even life as your slave, though you did not have to do this. And you were right! I was lying to myself. Even when everything seemed darkest, I still wanted very badly to live. I—I suppose, *ja*, I was a coward, as you said, to accept defeat and give way to despair so readily."

"Perhaps. But to my mind, dying is the easy part. It is living that is hardest to do. You summoned the courage to fight back from within yourself, and for that you have yourself to thank, not I."

He dismounted, using action, any action, to divert his thoughts from his lust. When she looked at him so trustingly, it was all he could do to think straight, to keep from nibbling her tempting little pink ears or smothering her throat with greedy kisses, and yet she had said he was different from other men. In that moment he honestly and earnestly wished he was as admirable as she believed! His manhood had no such conscience, however. It strained against the cloth of his chausses like an eager hound straining at the end of a chain. Muttering an obscenity under his breath, he asked her, "Will you bathe in the sea?"

"*Ja,* if it please you, my lord. I—I've thought of little else since I was—locked up," she confessed eagerly, her jewel eyes lively now.

He strode to her horse and lifted her down from the saddle, stunned by how light she had grown in the past fourteen nights as he firmly clasped her waist. His fingers almost spanned it. Christ's Wounds, she weighed little more than a child now! he thought, and his guilt returned to plague him anew.

As he stood her safely upon the damp sand, he was aware of the warmth of her body, the undiminished sexual attraction she held for him, and knew he desired her not one whit less here and now than he had desired her each night they had been apart! A groan welled up from deep in his gut, but he covered it with a short, patently false fit of coughing.

Nonetheless, she had read the sudden darkening of his eyes, noted the almost involuntary movement of his body toward hers, and a little shudder ran through her. With this heady, reckless feeling of relief and sheer joy to be alive coursing through her veins, she was vulnerable, oh so vulnerable, to his nearness, she knew! He must never guess how dearly she wanted to be held, just held and comforted, by someone. She brought her palm up to lodge against his broad chest, the cloth of his tunic rough against her skin, the steady beat of his heart palpable. Her lips parted in silent admonition. Their eyes met, and unbidden he stepped back to let her pass unhampered, recognizing in her expression a plea for him to curb his desires, to give her time.

She moved past him, and as she did so he saw color fill her cheeks and wondered what thought had made the roses bloom in them. She headed away from him toward several large, craggy rocks that would afford her some privacy. His eyes lingered on the wet imprints her bare feet had left in the sand long after she had disappeared behind them, and he lost himself in lustful imaginings, wishing it were he who unclasped the coarse rope girdle from about her slender waist, he who raised the rough homespun kirtle over her head and bared her lovely body to the golden sun and the sea breezes and his eager, trembling hands. So lost was he in his daydreams

197

that their object had finished her disrobing and scampered into the sea before he raised his gaze from the sand. He was granted only the impudent twinkle of a pert derrière as she arched forward and dived beneath the sparkling surface.

Cursing his ill fortune, but grinning nonetheless, he found himself a comfortable spot to sit and sprawled on the sand to wait for her, leaning against a natural rocky breakwater, softened by hairy fronds of emerald seaweed and encrusted with small white limpets, to do so. For some reason, all things seemed new and fresh this morn, he noticed suddenly, as if he had never seen them before; the sand was more golden, the sky more cerulean, the air more fresh and laden with the scents of life, of sea and land. Happiness seemed to bubble within him like a small yet irrepressible spring, and as he looked offshore, to where limbs pale as marble crested the waves and a bright red-gold head contrasted sharply against the gray-blue water, he knew that out there, in the sea, was the cause of his happiness.

He sternly smothered the feelings of annoyance and guilt such admissions pricked in his conscience. It was only lust he felt for the slave wench, after all, nothing more. There was nothing wrong with a master finding pleasure in his bed slave, and taking pains to ensure that she continued to be available to ease him. The noblemen he knew thought nothing of using their female slaves to ease their lust, or even in purchasing pretty maids who caught their eye from their families for a few copper coins, even if those maids were scarce more than children of eleven or twelve years. That was her purpose, after all, was it not, to serve his needs with her body? If Ordway or Cullen or even his Aunt Valonia had more than once implied of late, by word or expression, that there was something more to it than lust alone, then let them. He knew better . . .

Freya, meanwhile, had all but forgotten the past miserable weeks and, if the truth were known, Alaric with them. The water cradled her like a lover's arms, caressing her, stroking every inch of her flesh with fluid embraces that tantalized her breasts and nipples and flowed silkily between her thighs, ticklish embraces and caresses that caused a restless little quiver to begin deep in her belly and remain there, pulsing like

198

the pulse of her blood through her veins.

She turned and floated on her back, her eyes closed, rocked in her sea cradle, the fears and doubts of the past two weeks evaporating, cleansed from body and soul by the water's embrace. Her slender arms rested limply upon the water, and her hair was twisting and flowing about her with the rhythm of the lapping tide, like exotic, fronded seaweed.

If only she could stay here, she mused, float away from Alaric and Kenley, back to Danehof and the people of her hall, and all she had left behind! Summer was half gone, and soon the harvest time would come. But the men of Danehof would never return to Jutland to cut the corn, to slaughter the beasts culled from their dwindling herds that would provide food for their families during the harsh months of the northern winter. Tears filled her eyes. She had failed them, *ja,* failed them all! Perhaps Karl Ivarson had been right. Perhaps the position of *jarl* of Danehof should never have been given to a woman, and especially not to one as headstrong and determined and—and reckless—as she had proved. She sighed heavily. Now she had been called to account, and was paying the price for her mistakes with the loss of her freedom. Surely that was enough, was it not? But her heart was heavy as the answer came back to her, for she knew the answer was right. For the many lives that had been lost, it would never be enough.

She opened her tear-filled eyes then and gazed up at the fluffy cloud drifts scudding eastward with the wind across the sky. They were like proud, white dragon-ships, *wadmal* sails bellying in the breeze as they crested the sky-waves. Take me with you, she implored them silently; take me home, and I will somehow make up for what I have done! But only the harsh scream of a wheeling white gull answered her as it dipped low over the water to snatch up a small silvery fish. It seemed to Freya that it mocked her with its cry. The pleasure she had found in the water was quite gone now. She turned onto her stomach and with easy strokes swam to shore, wading through the shallows until she stood once more upon the sand.

A movement upon the chalk cliffs that backed the tiny cove caught her eye, and she glanced up sharply, shading her eyes against the brilliant light. She caught a brief impression of a slender figure—long, white hair streaming out in the wind, and the flurry of a dark robe—before whoever it had been was gone as suddenly as she had appeared. Aye, Freya fancied the watcher had been a woman. The Lady Wilone? she wondered, frowning, then discarded such a thought. Alaric's mother had appeared well taken care of, and it was unlikely that the holy sisters would let her wander off unattended, lest she do harm to herself. If there had been anyone up there on the cliffs, it was more likely that that someone had been a salt gatherer, headed farther down the shore to inspect her tide pools.

Alaric had fallen asleep in the sunshine, she saw, leaning up against a breakwater. He had taken off his tunic to enjoy the warmth and bracing air, and was bare chested where he sprawled.

Quietly she padded across the wet sand toward him, her hair falling in seaweed strands about her face and shoulders, droplets of water clinging to her nude body like diamonds. A pace or two from him she halted and stood there, gazing down at him. The pulsing deep inside her was still there, but stronger now. She glanced down, and saw that her nipples had hardened to ruched little points, exquisitely sensitive even to the currents of fresh air upon them. Could it be she desired him, her hated Saxon, she wondered, amazed? Did her body simply yearn for a man, any man, responding to his overt maleness as a healthy young female animal responded to a male? Or was it that she longed to be held, and knew that in succumbing to his lust for her she would receive the comforting she sought? He expected to have her when he awoke, she knew. He had tried, albeit unsuccessfully, to hide his lust from her earlier, but it had been betrayed by his smoldering gray eyes! No doubt he expected her eager surrender as his due, in thanks for him having forced that bitch-woman, Kendra, to withdraw her accusations. She frowned. The thought that Alaric would take her as if he had every right to use her, as he would use a chair or a bed for his ease, angered her. Her body was her own, not his! Would he accept such a lot with grace and submission were their situations reversed, she his mistress and he her virile slave? The idea made her giggle despite her confusion, and she quickly staunched the sound, her mind made up. She wanted him! For whatever reason, and quite despite her vows to remain unmoved by him, he had awakened her body to the new and compelling desires of a woman. *Ja*, she wanted him! He would take her by force if she fought to refuse him, and the end result would still be the same. So—what did she have to lose by making her own desires known? she rationalized, winding a dripping curl about her finger?

With bated breath she dropped to her knees beside him on the sand, her gaze moving over him from head to toe, as he had so often raked her body with his smoldering gaze. His broad torso was tanned a pale gold, the dark mat of hair glinting blue-black against the paler flesh in the light. His masculine nipples were dark rose and quite flat. She followed the line of dark hair with her eyes, down across his abdomen and thence to his hard belly, where it dwindled to nothing just above his navel. Farther down, hidden by his clothing, the dark hair reasserted itself strongly as a thick ebony swath to adorn his manhood, she recalled, and her shallow breathing quickened.

Lips curved in a smile, she reached out and retraced the passage of her eyes with her fingertips, circling his nipples once, twice, a third time. To her delight, they stirred and grew as firm as her own, tiny morsels of flesh that begged to be thoroughly nibbled. She leaned across him and flicked her tongue tip over them, aroused by the salty tang of his skin and his clean, manly scent. He grunted in his sleep and shifted his position, and for a moment she froze, scarce breathing, until he had settled once again.

When he had, she again touched him, pressing the flat of her palm against his belly and rubbing gently. The sudden surge of something firm and aroused against the cloth of his garments and thence against her thigh sent a thrill running down her spine and lancing through her belly. Even in the depths of sleep, the swarthy brute had responded to her touch! She lowered herself to the sand beside him and leaned over him, tousling the inky commas of hair that molded to his heavy dark head, drawing strands of her own damp hair lightly across his body to tickle him. Perhaps he was not completely unattractive after all, she decided generously. She liked his eyes, which were changeable as the sea and thickly lashed, and the way his raven brows offset them with their stormy darkness. His nose was fitting too for a man such as he, strong and straight and, *ja*, a little arrogant! The manly dark rose lips that gave her such pleasure were soft and unguarded in sleep, slightly parted and very tempting. She ducked her damp head and sealed her own to them, darting the tip of her tongue between them as he was wont to do when kissing her. As she kissed him, she let her fingertips trail downward, following the muscular curves of his arms and then flickering across his chest, tugging playfully at the curls foresting it. Against her bare thigh she felt him respond again, his shaft burning through the cloth of his trousers like a heated iron. Emboldened as he slept on, she fitted her palm over the massive shape outlined by the cloth and pressed him there, feeling a rippling awareness shudder through his body even as she did so.

His response heightened her own excitement. Breathing shallowly now, she moved closer to him, gasping against his mouth as her nipples grazed his hairy chest and tongues of fire leaped simultaneously through her loins. Her kiss deepened. Now she explored his mouth with the same eagerness with which he had once explored hers, delving between his lips with her tongue's entire length, thrusting, stroking the velvety inner surfaces, until it struck her of a sudden how closely the kissing act resembled the mating act, and she tore her mouth from his in sudden shame—or rather, would have, given the chance, for as she made to pull back a powerful hand came out and clamped firmly across the back of her head, forcing her lips down upon his once more! Her cry of protest was abruptly silenced as he turned her roughly beneath him and pinned her to the sand beneath his weight. He kissed her long and hard, and with obvious enjoyment.

"Rogue!" she stormed, lips a-tingle when he at last broke the kiss. "I thought you sleeping!"

"The first lesson of a warrior, my lovely vixen—never trust things to be as they appear! Did your precious Olaf not teach you that?" he retorted, laughing as he looked down at her. His gray eyes danced with merriment.

Infuriated, her hand raised to strike him, but the blow was deflected off his muscular shoulder as he leaned across her and trapped a pert nipple between his teeth. Growling with pretended fierceness, he drew the rosy sweetmeat deep into the flaming heat of his mouth and feasted upon it with such greed and hunger, she feared she would swoon! Her loins turned molten. The pulsing between her trembling thighs became a roaring throb, unbearable and still more unbearable as he devoured her other breast, then the silken plateau of her belly, then the inner, sensitive columns of her legs, rising higher and higher to their juncture. Gasp after gasp sighed from her parted lips as his glossy raven-black head nestled between her thighs. His springy curls tickled her sensitive flesh, made her writhe like a wanton on the hard, wet sand, her excitement keener than a blade.

"Be still," he commanded sternly, nuzzling aside the damp golden curls that concealed his prize from his eager lips, yet how *could* she be still, she wondered, *how could she*, when he was doing what he was doing and driving her to a sweet madness she could not contain!

His mouth devoured her, his tongue possessed her, his ravishment eliciting little moans that broke upon the shores of her fading consciousness like foam-rimmed waves lapping at the seashore. She laced her fingers in his thick, springy curls, arching upward like a bow as a crescendo of desire built and built inside her until she feared, in the but dimly remembered realms of sanity, that she must explode!

"*Ja, min yndling, ja!*" she cried again and again, tossing her head from side to side on the sand as the flickering contractions started, surging from a pressure-filled flutter to a fluid, flooding, hot release that spread outward like molten gold from her loins to every part of her, even lancing to the very top of her head and the tips of her toes, and filled her being with dazzling sunbursts of delight.

He chuckled softly at the kittenish purr of content that followed her release, and slid up her body to lie between her trembling thighs. He flexed his hips, and in that single, practiced motion entered her with ease, yet if she was aware of it she gave no sign. Her face was that of a woman already sated by her man; rosily glowing, radiant, features a little blurred, eyes heavy-lidded, expression one of transported ecstasy.

She returned from the velvet void into which she had been hurled to feel the weight of him upon her, his powerful strokes filling her.

"Blessed Frey!" she cried, a delicious thrill running through her anew as his hardness expanded and plunged deeper into her, creating new, wondrous pressures more intense than those that had gone before. She wanted to give and go on giving, to take him ever deeper and deeper into herself and make his possession complete, she thought, dazed. Was she insatiable? Wanton? Mad? Could she never have enough of him? she wondered dizzily, and slid her arms up between them to clasp his dark head in her palms. "What a man you are, Saxon!" she murmured throatily, open admiration in her eyes.

Her words pleased him. He grinned down at her lovely face as he thrust deeper and deeper, and then kissed her lips, a wet, smacking kiss more lusty than tender. His eyes were lambent gray pools that drew her inexorably into their depths. "And what a woman are you, Viking!" he growled, and renewed his ardent thrusts two-fold, teasing her erect nipples between his fingers and the balls of his thumbs as he rode her until she cried out again and again in her pleasure.

Freya had thought that nothing could match the sweet delight he had given her with his mouth, but she was wrong—and happy to be proved wrong. Alaric had known many women, knew the varied ways in which they enjoyed being pleased by a man, and he brought all his skills in the love arts into play for her delight there on the seashore, in the secluded little cove backed by the chalky cliffs.

At his husky command she wrapped her slender legs about his waist and matched the rhythm of her undulating hips to the driving power of his flanks until they were as one being, fused, inseparable; or turned eagerly to lie on her belly that he might pleasure her from behind; or straddled his glistening manhood and took her ease in that fashion, herself now controlling their ardor and the tempo of their joining, until she was utterly drained, limp and sated in every limb, as wave after wave of rapture roiled through her. Only when she was exhausted, all wanting fulfilled, did he grow still upon her, his warm breath rasping unevenly against her flushed cheek. She waited, growing very still, knowing his own release was imminent, and then she cried out one last time as, with a wrenching groan, he spent gloriously, deeply inside her, his hot seed springing into her quivering womb.

For a brief moment they both lay still and stunned, senses reeling like planets on collision courses through the heavens. Then Freya sat up, groaning with a sweet exhaustion that made her limbs weigh heavy as lead. She made to pull herself up to standing, vaguely astonished at the effort it took to move at all, and by the not unpleasant dull aching between her thighs.

"Where are you going?" Alaric demanded drowsily, staying her with a steely hand coiled about her wrist.

"To swim, and to—to cleanse myself," she confessed, reddening with embarrassment.

"Later, my beauty, later . . ." he muttered, leaning over to press a lazy kiss to the warm, rounded swell of her hip, patterned now with damp sand. His arm coiling about her waist, he tugged her back down to sleep beside him, and sleep they did, limbs entangled under the vast blue sky, the sea birds wheeling in endless silver arcs above them and the lulling, rhythmic washing of the tides splashing against the shore.

He awoke expecting to find her yet deeply asleep, but she was instead sitting beside him, a pensive expression in her eyes. She was cupping a large, delicately pink shell to her ear and appeared to be listening intently to its song. Though she was still unclothed, she seemed quite unembarrassed by her nudity, and breathtakingly lovely, with the afternoon sunlight stroking her vivid hair and rosy flesh.

"Why so thoughtful?" he asked idly, rubbing her silky thigh with the back of his hand. "What secrets does the seashell whisper to you?"

"It tells me many things, my lord," she replied softly. "And bids me ask questions that—that I have been afraid to voice."

"And what are these questions?" he asked indulgently, still rubbing her thigh. Content flowed like honey through his veins. She could ask him anything, he thought, and be hard put to shatter the pleasant mood that was upon him now.

She shrugged. "I—I was but wondering, my lord, what

would happen if—if you were to get me with child?"

Her innocent question startled him despite his former certainty that nothing could, for, fool that he was, such a possibility had never occurred to him. "A child? Are you—?"

"Nay, I am not!" she retorted, upset and angered now by his amazed and indignant reaction. "But there is every chance, if we continue on as we have done this day, that I will get with child sooner or later, is there not?"

"Aye," he admitted grudgingly, eager to dismiss any such disquieting question. "There is. But we will concern ourselves about it when it happens, not before."

"I must insist that we discuss it now, my lord Alaric," she persisted, tossing aside the seashell and brushing the sand from her hands. "If—if I bear you a child, that child will also be a slave, born as it would be from the body of a slave, would it not? So it is in Denmark."

He nodded. "And here in Britain." The boldness of the wench, he thought, vaguely astonished by her gall. He had no intention of forgoing their coupling, not when she had the power to please him as no woman had ever pleased him before, if that was what lay behind her questions!

Apparently it was, for she sighed and continued, "'Tis as I feared, then. I cannot lie with you again, sir, for I will not willingly bring a child into this world who has no hope of freedom."

"Think you so?" he exploded, all languor vanished. "On the contrary, vixen, you will lie with me whensoever I wish it," he growled. "And *I* shall decide when and how often that will be, not you." The impudence of her! Just when he was feeling indulgent, basking in the rosy afterglow of the pleasure her body had afforded him, she had once again overstepped the limits of their relationship and acted as if all choices were hers to make—she, his bower wench! No doubt, since he had proved he would go to great lengths to prevent any harm coming to her, she felt she could now twist him around her little finger, the vixen! He frowned. Ah! Was this, then, the cause of her sudden wantonness . . . ? He should have realized at once that there was more to her unexpected capitulation and about-face than desire on her part. The way she had knelt beside him on

206

the sand and deliberately set out to arouse him no longer seemed an enchanting gesture of gratitude on her part, but something far more devious, something that smacked of intrigue. He rubbed his jaw, obviously vexed, for his wood-smoke eyes had changed to the color of a storm sky, flinty and hard. She had obviously set out to lull him into believing her tamed and eager for his attentions—but why? So that she could escape him, once his guard was down? Or was she trying to improve her lot, by forcing him to acknowledge any child she might bear him as his rightful heir? Aye, he thought it probable, that conniving little vixen . . . ! "Do you hear me, Freya?" he repeated sternly. "I am master here. The fate of any child you might have will be mine to decide. And if I wish to take you, I will, confound you!"

There was a lengthy silence as she absorbed his angry retort, and then her jaw tightened and the dreamy deep blue of her eyes darkened and flashed with angry glints of her own, becoming hard and brittle as glass.

"Then it will not be as pleasing for you as it was this day," she said with quiet conviction, "for I will have no choice but to fight you again, each and every time, and your efforts to subdue me will inevitably tarnish your pleasure, my lord! I had come to terms and accepted my captivity this past fourteen nights, deciding life in any fashion was preferable to burning at the stake. But though I could accept such a life for myself, I will fight tooth and nail to prevent any innocent babe of mine being born to such a fate. Mark me well, Saxon. I will have your sworn oath that you will acknowledge any child I might bear thee as free-born, or 'tis again war between us. Think on it!"

So saying, she flung about, sprang to her feet, her red-gold curls flying, and ran away down the shore, leaving him open-mouthed with shock and shaking with rage—and doubly determined never to give in to her outrageous demands.

Chapter 15

From that afternoon on, neither of them would relent or cry "quarter" to the other. Perversely, her obstinacy and her determination not to submit to him willingly only served to fuel the fires of Alaric's desire. He had wanted her before this with an ardor that amazed him, but now his ardor was quadrupled!

When he rode through his burh, he saw her everywhere; in the red-gold glint of a fox's brush as it disappeared through the woods; in the gentle curve of a hill that put him in mind of her lovely breasts; saw the glitter of her sea-sapphire eyes in the sparkling water. And each evening, when he returned to Kenley, there she was, waiting for him, fire in her eyes and an iron will in her veins that seemed not a whit diminished with passing time! What was she? he wondered, seething as he yet again lay sleepless in his bower one warm night in the month of July, after taming her to his hand once more—one of her Norse Valkyries, bent on dealing destruction? Or a lovely she-devil, sent straight from his Christian Hell to torment him?

It was quite unseemly that a mere woman should be possessed of such strong determination, and especially if that woman were a lowly slave! Such strength of will was more fitting in a man, but yet he had to admit he knew few men who could match her in obstinacy. How obstinate would she remain after a whipping or two? he wondered, almost tempted to order her so chastened. Almost . . .

He sighed heavily, scowling up at the rafters. To his mind,

something easily taken was scarce worthy of the battle, and so he had not had her whipped or otherwise chastised, as was his right. He grudgingly acknowledged in his heart of hearts that it was her very strength that drew him to her so powerfully, and there was the rub. A strong man such as he needed a strong woman like Freya, one who challenged him to tame her, and made every minute of every day spent with her a glittering prize to be fought for and won. Aye, Freya was just such a woman, for all that she was his captive, and he had no desire to see her fiery spirit humbled by the lash, nor her vibrant beauty marred in any way. He gave up all thoughts of having her whipped—yet gave up none of his attempts to tame her.

In truth—if he could only have admitted the truth and swallowed his pride!—she was in many ways the mate he had always craved, both in beauty and spirit, aye, and intelligence, and he would have been disappointed if she had meekly relented and bent her will to his. In his most secret thoughts he knew he had no wish to replace her in his bed with some milksop wench who hung upon his every word and tripped over herself to please him—and who lay beneath him like a log when they coupled, without fire or passion. Not a kiss nor an embrace did he get of the lovely Viking bitch that was given willingly, but by God, how sweet they were! What warrior sons a woman such as Freya would produce! A litter of courageous cubs worthy of the Bear of Kent, he thought, then hastily cast aside such dangerously attractive, yet weakening notions . . .

Arrogant, insufferable brute, Freya thought sourly, watching him the following day as he left the table without a glance in her direction and strode across his hall. She had as good as sworn she would come willingly to his bed if he would but promise any child she birthed would be born free, but even this one small boon he would not grant her! True, she was his slave, but her child would also be his child, were she to conceive. What manner of man would refuse his own offspring the right to freedom, were it in his power to grant it? An unfeeling Saxon swine known as Alaric, that was who!

Simmering still with rage, she flounced across the hall, her strides quick and impatient, her body rigid. So immersed was she in her anger that she did not notice the shaggy hunting hound lolling half under the table, and trod hard upon its tail. The hound let out a pained yelp, and at once turned on her, snarling with bared fangs and hackles up as it came menacingly toward her.

"Back where you belong, cur!" she hissed, raising her hand to cuff the creature soundly. But the tone in her voice alone was such that the dog retreated under the table without need for blows, instantly cowed and whining. Its ears drooped mournfully and it covered its muzzle with its huge paws.

With a click of satisfaction, Freya returned to gathering up the used platters and flagons left behind after the morning meal and continued on her way toward the kitchens. If only Alaric were as easily cowed as the hound, she thought as she went, but it was a hollow hope, for he showed no sign of weakening yet, she mused, shaking her head. And if he were cowed so readily, Freya, you would be sorely disappointed, would think less of him as a man, suggested a nagging little voice. *Ja,* she admitted to herself unhappily, she would, for his very persistence, his strength, his determination to tame her excited her as nothing else could, curse him!

It had become a point of honor with her now to refuse him, though she had begun to accept the possibility that he might never relent. Still, she stubbornly fought him off each time he laid eager hands upon her, willing herself to deny the pleasure she found once surrender was inevitable, and she could—at last!—pretend defeat and enjoy his lusty wooing. You are a hypocrite, Freya of Danehof, she scolded herself. Admit it, be honest, you have grown to enjoy the delights the Saxon makes you feel, and even to experience occasional twinges of regret that he is not a Viking and therefore unworthy of your—love. Love? Nay, not love, never that! she amended hurriedly. It was true they were well matched in temper and spirit, and there was a part of her—a part that had nothing to do with her request— that drew great pleasure from their war of wills, waged in Alaric's bed; but that had nothing at all to do with love . . .

Nevertheless, each passing day she found herself looking forward to nightfall with ever-increasing anticipation. On those nights when Alaric was away from Kenley about his ealdorman's business, or riding abroad over the countryside in search of brigands who had been terrorizing Kent with brutal, unprovoked attacks on innocent travelers for their gold, she missed him with a vengeance and fretted for his safety until he returned. She told herself she was afraid of what might befall her at Kenley should Alaric be slain and she were left to Ordway to dispose of, but there was more to it than that, and she knew it. She missed the brute, *ja*, and had terrible nightmares in which she saw him lying bleeding and sorely wounded in some dank ditch or other, nightmares that left her pale and drained and heartsick the following day, and caused an ever-perceptive Valonia to inquire gently after her health.

She wondered hopefully if Alaric missed her, or ever thought about her at all when he was gone, but pride forbade that she should put such a question to him, even when she lay sleek and sated in his arms after their loving. When he returned to the hall, did he steal side glances at her when he thought her unaware, she wondered? In truth, covert glances at *him* she had taken aplenty, and of late he seemed to have, well, grown a little—a *very* little—more pleasing to her eye, and to be far more agreeable in character than hitherto, or at least toward those other than herself.

Aye, he had appeared far more relaxed in many ways since Kendra and her husband and their retinue had suddenly left Kenley for Alfred's court at Winchester, she mused, as Kenley itself was more relaxed. It was as if a dark and malevolent cloud had been lifted to allow the sunshine into the burh since their hurried departure. She sincerely hoped that Kendra and her mysterious excuse for a husband would make their absence a long one, now that they had finally left! She had also observed on more than one occasion how gentle Alaric was with his gracious Aunt Valonia, according her the respect and teasing chivalry afforded a mother by a loving son, and which one day he would devote to his lady wife, whoever that unlucky maid might be. Though he had changed his manner and become gruff and aggressive whenever Freya was in earshot, he had not been able to deceive her. He could, when the fancy struck him, charm the very birds from the trees!

Likewise, with Ordway, his sour-tempered uncle, he was painstakingly respectful, but firm in his own wishes regarding the running of his hall, as befitted the lord. With Cullen, the bond of friendship he shared was obvious and sincere on both sides, born more of liking than blood ties. With the men of his garrison he was stern, if fair. He would accept no less than their best efforts on the drilling field, and since he asked no more of them than he asked of himself, and in effect often forced himself to greater effort than they to prove his worth as their leader, he had their admiration and respect and, Freya was equally certain, commanded their love and loyalty to follow him anywhere.

On several of those seemingly endless summer days when Alaric was about his business, Valonia set her to scrivening, and the Epistle of St. Paul, which she had begun so long ago, was at last completed. It was her first work of such an exacting nature or of such length, and it was with justifiable pride that she executed the final flourish at the bottom of the very last page.

Valonia had been generous with her praises, and gave her a fine new kirtle by way of gratitude, one that boasted the fashionable embroidered orphreys as borders, and which Valonia had stitched herself with fine golden wires.

Knowing that no such gesture had been required of the lady, Freya had been doubly delighted, and hurried to Alaric's bower to try on her gift at the first opportunity.

The kirtle was of finely spun linen, dyed the pale, tender green of the very first leaves of spring, and was as soft against her flesh as the brush of a bird's wing. It was a color that became her, she knew, and the richly worked borders showed off to advantage the bright gloss of her hair and the eye-catching high color of her complexion. The linen clung to her curves, covering all modestly but accentuating her rounded, feminine figure. For the first time in her life she was glad that she had been born a woman and not a man. It was a new sensation, this—this vanity! She twirled about, delighted by the sensual ripple of the cloth against her legs, the way the skirt swung gracefully from the wide belt—everything! Who would have thought that she, Freya Jorgensen, warrior maid of Danehof, confirmed wearer of leggings, could ever take such delight in a dainty and impractical kirtle? But she did!

As she angled this way and that, a rectangle of polished tin, framed by bronze set with jewels to form a mirror, she felt a sudden heady tingle of excitement in her veins. What would Alaric think, to see her robed in a garment worthy of her noble birth, and one that was not only feminine but flattered her besides? To date, he had seen her in ònly her slave's coarse, baggy garments of unbleached and undyed, scratchy wool. Surely—surely he would think her pretty? She felt a blush warm her cheeks at such an undeniably female notion, and shrugged irritably. By the gods, what on earth was wrong with her?

She glowered at the tin mirror, and her reflection made a hideous gargoyle scowl back, screwing up her features until she became a fearsome sight indeed. *Pretty?* Pah! 'Twas but a slip of the mind, nothing more, she amended hastily, for she cared not a jot if the Saxon cur found her pretty or nay! She carefully folded the garment and set it in Alaric's chest, hidden under his own clothing, wondering if the day would ever come when she would have occasion to wear it. Her duties about Kenley scarcely warranted the wearing of a gown more suited to a Saxon noblewoman than a slave!

But the opportunity came, as such opportunities often do, far sooner than she had anticipated.

Alaric had ridden out early that day, having received reports that a band of brigands was in the area of Kenley, razing cottages, killing livestock for sport, and òtherwise striking terror into the hearts of the countryfolk. Accordingly, he had summoned a number of his garrison and they had gone in search of the band, all armed to the teeth. Once again Freya had felt an unwelcome twinge of apprehension as she watched Alaric ride out, and had determined to throw herself into her work with a will, to put her niggling fears for his safety out of mind.

She was busily plucking a plump gray goose for the spit when another serving wench came looking for her.

"There ye are!" Edythe exclaimed, plump fists planted on plump hips. "The Lady Valonia would speak with ye, Freya."

"Did she tell you why?" Freya asked curiously.

The girl shook her head. "Nay, my lady. She said only for ye

213

to come to her in the sewing bower."

"You called me 'my lady' again, Edythe," Freya scolded gently. "I am not your lady, and you must not address me so. We are both servants here, and I am no better than you."

Edythe blushed. "Aye, I know it. Ye must forgive me again. But—but ye have an air about ye, Freya, that sets ye apart from me and—and t'others. When ye speak, why, 'tis as if ye were mistress of Kenley, it is, and 'tis hard put I am not to do yer bidding!" Edythe giggled.

"Then I must now ask your forgiveness," Freya said, frowning worriedly, "for I've never intended to act above my place, nor to set myself above all of you who've been here far longer than I."

"Oh, 'tis not that, Freya!" Edythe reassured her quickly. "'Tis just—well, that where ye came from, ye were used to giving orders to others, were ye not? It shows in your voice— like ye expect to be listened to an' obeyed, and will not take 'nay' for an answer! Ye cannot help it." Edythe grinned, and Freya returned her smile.

"Well, if that is so, I will try to behave differently in the future. Will you finish plucking this goose, while I see what it is our lady mistress wants of me?"

"Aye, my la—Freya!" Edythe hastily amended, shaking her head in self-reproach. Laughing, Freya wiped her hands on a damp rag and left the kitchens.

"Come," Valonia urged, as Freya entered the sewing bower and dropped the Saxon woman a deep curtsey, "I have something to show you that I believe will please you. Look there, on the table."

That "something" pleased Freya enormously, for it was the epistle she had copied for Lady Valonia, the beautifully written and cleverly illuminated pages now bound in costly calfskin, embossed with precious gems, to make a manuscript worthy of the most talented monk, and a gift fit for Queen Ealhswith herself. She stroked the elegant binding with a gentleness akin to reverence. "'Tis beautiful, Lady Valonia!" she said softly.

Valonia nodded, well pleased by her awe. "It is indeed. And since your hand was responsible for its creation, it seems only fitting that you should accompany me to the convent, and see

214

it presented to my sister the Abbess Aethelfreda. I had intended to ride there this morning. Would it please you to attend me?"

Freya's face lit up. "*Ja*, my lady, it would indeed!"

Valonia smiled at her eagerness. "Then make yourself ready. The green kirtle that I gave you would be fitting, and I have a mantle and a pretty belt of gold links that would look quite fetching with it . . ."

So it was that they had ridden to the convent upon the cliffs, Freya feeling as beautifully arrayed as any Saxon queen in her lovely new kirtle, a belt of wide golden links borrowed from Valonia clasping her waist, a veil of fine white linen covering her bright head, and a mantle of saffron wool falling gracefully from off her shoulders, where it was pinned with two circular bronze brooches studded with garnets and chips of green glass.

The abbess was delighted with Valonia's gift to her order, and even more astonished to learn that Freya, a pagan slave, had been mainly responsible for its creation. Over an enormous and eagerly eaten repast of roasted chickens, spiced with herbs from the convent gardens, fresh dark bread, and ripe fruits, washed down with watered wine, the buxom abbess had openly praised her talents, and afterward sternly admonished her to forsake her pagan gods in favor of the one true God, an admonition to which Freya had wisely not responded. Later Valonia had made a brief visit to the Lady Wilone's cell with a few gifts of garments and food, and then they had left, riding back toward Kenley.

They had only a brace of men-at-arms to accompany them, since Valonia had assured her husband their visit would be brief and their road both safe and well traveled. As they rode back, Valonia spoke to Freya with surprising freedom of her sister-in-law, Alaric's mother, and Freya was interested to hear more of the beautiful yet sadly unbalanced woman who had so frightened her on her first visit to the convent.

"Wilone was older than my lord Ordway, you see, and as such he looked up to his sister. He told me that after their mother died, she was mother and sister both to him, so 'tis little wonder he took her infirmity so hard, think you not?"

Freya nodded in understanding, but made no comment.

Although she was curious, the subject of Wilone's sickness was one she did not care to dwell upon, stirring as it did her guilt at her father's part in it. "And Alaric's father—what was he like?" she asked, hoping to change the subject.

"Aeldred? Well, let me see. He was comely, I suppose, very dark, very tall and well muscled. One much admired by other men as a warrior in his youth, I believe. 'Tis said that few could best him on the field of battle when he swung his axe or sword—not unlike Alaric. They both possessed the same quick temper, a trait of their Welsh forebears, I fancy, who also bequeathed them their dark coloring, which has quite overtaken the fair Saxon blood of Kenley. Aeldred also placed great value upon his honor and name, as does his eldest son, while Farant, on the other hand, is more like his mother Wilone—slower to enrage, possessed of a quieter demeanor, and far less obvious in his courage. He would have been better suited to joining the church rather than choosing marriage to Kendra, I do believe."

"Ah, the Lady Kendra!" Freya murmured, grimacing. "She has no liking for me!"

Valonia pursed her lips. "And for few others, selfish child! But she is my niece, and I promised Aethelfreda I would raise her as my own." The woman sighed.

"She is the abbess's daughter?" Freya's brows arched in surprise. Was it not rumored that the Christian priestesses were unwed virgins, every one?

"She is," Valonia confirmed. "Aethelfreda and her lord had been wed but a short while when the blood feud between her husband's hall and a neighboring clan erupted into violence. My sister's husband was slain in the skirmish, and she was brutally raped by one of the enemy clan before he left her for dead. Kendra was the result of that foul coupling, poor child. When she became aware of her condition Aethelfreda swore a sacred oath to give up the child upon its birth and to enter a convent, there to spend the remainder of her days in atonement for her sins. Kendra's birth did nothing to dissuade her from that vow. The child was scarce a week old when Aethelfreda had a wet-nurse—old Lona—deliver her to me."

"I see. And the Lady Wilone—is she never permitted to

leave the convent?"

Valonia looked at her sharply. There was in her expression, Freya fancied, something secretive, but she covered quickly and shrugged, gesturing with a heavily beringed hand to dismiss such a notion. "She has—left—the convent of her own accord once or twice, I believe. But she is not capable of fending for herself, and so of course the good sisters quickly found her and brought her back on each occasion. Why do you ask?"

It was Freya's turn to shrug now. "Once, when Lord Alaric and I were riding our horses along the shore, I thought I saw her on the headland. Perhaps I was mistaken."

"I am certain you must have been," Valonia agreed readily, and with a definite hint of relief in her voice.

They rode on for another half league, conversing amicably, and Freya found herself enjoying the older woman's company, for Valonia was not only one of the kindest, most gracious ladies she had ever known, Viking or otherwise, but she was also possessed of a keen intelligence and wit, and missed little that went on about the hall over which she reigned as chatelaine.

The two men-at-arms, one riding ahead and one at their backs, kept their horses at a slow trot, giving the two women ample opportunity to enjoy the countryside and the air and each other's company. Sunshine lanced down like showers of golden arrows between the trees. Pastel and gaudy wild flowers nodded sleepy heads in the tall grasses that bordered the bridle path. It was so quiet, so very peaceful, they could hear the drowsy, hypnotic hum of the bees in the clover and the soft whisper of the warm breeze as it tousled the grass.

But then the silence was abruptly torn asunder! From the dense hedgerows directly ahead of their path, there came a sudden burst of sound, a frenzied beating of desperate wings, and with one accord several birds took flight and soared into the air, their song of alarm loud and disturbing.

Without conscious thought, Freya at once raised her hand, her expression suddenly taut with apprehension. "Halt!" she cried, rising in the stirrups.

"What is it?" Valonia asked, reining in her palfrey and

217

looking about her.

"Up ahead. I—I have a feeling that something's awry. The birds! Why would they suddenly—!"

There was a strangled cry from farther down the path where it entered the dense green woods, a cry that ended on a groan and was abruptly cut short. The man who had been riding vanguard must have been attacked, Freya realized, looking all about her for signs of an ambush. Curse them! She was unarmed!

The second guard was now urging his mount up ahead, kneeing it to pass the two women.

"Hold!" Freya cried. "Only a coward would leave his lady unguarded! Your weapon, fool! Draw it, I say!"

Even as she snapped the command, several shaggy horses thundered from the woods; bare steel flashed in the sunlight and cudgels were brandished, as a band of brigands galloped from cover, screaming curses.

"Ride for Kenley, my lady!" Freya yelled, "and with all possible haste!"

She leaned low in her saddle to lash Valonia's gentle cream palfrey into a gallop with her reins, yet her frantic urging came too late, for they were surrounded by unkempt and grinning louts on horseback! The palfrey sank back on its haunches, screaming with fear as it pawed the air with its front hooves, eyes rolling and white in terror at the rank scent of coming death on the wind.

Freya saw Valonia's reins torn from her hand, and had little time to watch as the gentlewoman was dragged from her saddle by a husky ruffian, for coarse hands were scrabbling for her waist too.

She twisted and turned in the wooden saddle to evade them, lashing out with her only weapons, her hands and feet, and succeeded in landing a heavy—if random—kick in the groin of one fellow. With a gasp, he dropped her to nurse his throbbing privates, and the very second she thudded to the ground she was rolling away, clear of the wicked hooves of excited and terrified, milling horses, and clear of the melée.

The second man-at-arms lay dead on the grass, his chin severed and half his chest with it, drowned in his own blood.

218

His sword lay unbloodied at his side. Freya dived for it; her hand swooped and she caught the weighty blade up and brandished it single-handed in the Viking manner, whirling it over her head a time or two to test its weight, before swinging about to confront the first of the brigand band.

One man had noticed her twist free of his companion and now lumbered toward her, dagger in fist. Cursing her unwieldy skirts, she used the element of surprise against him, and instead of backing away as he expected, lunged lightly, powerfully, forward, her blade sliding in under his guard like a knife through butter.

He was not worthy of her swordsmanship, an insult to the good steel of her blade, she thought in disgust scant seconds later, giving him a contemptuous kick in the ribs where he lay dead in the ferns. She withdrew her blade and wiped the blood from it on the grass. Yet another came at her, and another, as she fought them single-handed. She employed every trick, every skill Olaf had ever taught her to fight them off, and some others she invented as she went along, yet even as her blade sang and whirred like a furious bee a-humming she was beginning to tire, her body having lost its endurance and stamina in the past weeks without the daily drilling she was accustomed to. With a sinking heart she saw how many of them there still were, circled all about the Lady Valonia; far more than she could ever hope to kill.

"Give us the rings yerself, my noble pigeon," one of the crude louts demanded, gripping the lady's chin in a vicious hairy paw, "else we'll cut off your fingers, one by one."

"I'll not, you thieving rogues!" Valonia retorted bravely, tossing her fair hair. She cried out in pain as the man dashed her hard across the mouth, drawing blood. She sprawled at his feet, and the brigand chieftain let out a great roar of evil laughter and made a move to drag her upright by her hair.

"Hold, fool!" Freya cried, turning her back on her bewildered opponent and racing across the grassy dell toward them, sword still in hand. "Have you taken leave of your senses?"

"Shut yer yap, lass, else Black Nevin will shut it fer ye— once and fer all time!" He grinned, showing a mouthful of

219

yellowed fangs. His black hair fell to his brawny shoulders in thick, matted ropes, and his beard was full and black and equally unkempt. He looked little more civilized than the beast from which the wolfskin jerkin he wore had been taken, and Freya's belly turned over with foreboding. "You!" he barked to one of his band, jerking his head toward her. "Take the firebrand's weapon, before she decides to use it again!"

A man moved toward her, and with a look of utter scorn Freya tossed the blade to the grass at his feet. "*Ja,* you'd best take it," she urged, contempt curling her lip, "for should I have been bent on keeping it, the likes of you would not have parted me from it, believe me!"

Fists on hips, she turned slowly to look each of the men circled about Valonia and herself full in the face. "What do you call yourselves?" she demanded.

"Us?" their chieftain jeered, eyeing her insolently. "Why, I am Black Nevin, and these are my men, good and true." He made her a mocking bow. "We are all—now how shall I put it?—lords of the highways, lass!"

The men chuckled and nudged each other, pleased by his romantic description.

Freya laughed too, doing nothing to disguise her scorn. "Lords of the highways?" She snorted. "Ha! You make my belly ache with laughter at your jests. 'Lords of the highways,' indeed! That's a merry one!"

The smile fled Black Nevin's face. He scowled, and his brown eyes became small, hot points of light in his hairy face. "Mock us again, lass, and I'll see ye do it on yer back, aye, and we'll take turns t'see who can make ye laugh the loudest, eh, lads?" The men nodded and muttered angry agreement.

"When you act like simpletons, what's a wench to believe?" Freya demanded. "A cunning man would have waited, let the lady and her party enter the woods proper before attacking. That way you could have spared the lives of your fellows there." She nodded at the three dead men, then forced a brilliant smile. "But even as it is, we can still see this made worth your while."

Black Nevin's eyes ignited with cunning. He rubbed his

black beard thoughtfully. "We can, can we, eh? And how's that?"

"With her!" Freya retorted, nodding at Valonia, who was standing now, though she appeared dazed.

"She carried no gold—nothing of value save the baubles she wears at her throat and hands. 'Tis poor pickings we've had this day," Black Nevin growled sourly.

"If you look only for the quick and easy road to riches, *ja*, I'll warrant you have. But with a little patience, a little cunning, you can yet turn this day into a victory, and have gold mancuses by the fistful to divide between you."

She smiled slyly, yet inwardly was far from as cocksure of herself as she appeared. Black Nevin's type was a dangerous one. He was wont to use his great size and not his brain to get his way in all things, she judged. And stupid men were apt to act rashly, or out of fear, and kill without thought of consequences. Indeed, their very stupidity gave them an edge! She must be wary and play her pieces with skill, else risk losing the game.

"How?" Nevin asked, greed oozing from his every pore.

"Ransom the woman," Freya said simply, as if such a course were the only sensible one. "Her husband and her nephew—who is himself ealdorman of Kent—dote upon her, the fools! They will pay, and pay well, to have her returned to them unharmed, I promise you."

Black Nevin's brown eyes raked her speculatively. "And who might you be, lass? The ealdorman's fair bride, mayhap? I'm thinking we can ask a pretty silver penny for your sweet self, too?"

"Bride? By Thor's Man-Staff, what innocents you are! Do I sound like a bride fit for a Saxon? *Nej!* I am the lady's serving woman—a Viking captive taken in battle some while ago. Aye, a Viking is what I said! They would sooner ransom a dog than ransom me! But—" she added thoughtfully, as if the idea had just crossed her mind, "those fools at Kenley have grown to trust me, and you will need someone whom they trust to go there, and deliver your ransom demands."

"She's no slave!" jeered one man. "Look at the gold on her

gown—the fine cloth—her manner! Tell me, Black Nevin, did ye ever before see a slave wench so free with words, or one who carries herself so?"

"'Twas no hard task to convince them of my worth, especially my master!" She grinned and rolled her eyes seductively. "And they have treated me far above my station. It pleases Alaric of Kent to see me prettily robed," she gestured to her kirtle, spattered with blood now, "as you can see." She shook her head. "Ah well, my friends, I tried to warn you. If you will not listen, then you will not. Content yourself with a few paltry baubles—and remember, you could have ridden away from this burh rich as kings!"

She turned and began walking away from them across the grass. As she had anticipated, Black Nevin lumbered after her and spun her about by the shoulder to face him.

"A minute more, lass," he snarled, spittle flying. "What is in this for ye?"

"Freedom!" she hissed, sapphire eyes blazing into his. "My freedom is all I ask!"

Chapter 16

Freya sat on her haunches across a crackling camp fire, staring between the writhing flames at Black Nevin, who was tearing into a dripping portion of venison as if it were his last meal on this earth.

Her impassioned plea for freedom had done the trick, touching as it did upon the heart's desire of all the brigands, for they were, to the last man, escaped slaves, and serfs knew full well the priceless value of being free.

After Black Nevin had agreed her suggestion to ransom the Lady Valonia was a good one, Freya and the brigand band had mounted up and ridden far from the site of the ambush, not stopping until they came at late afternoon to this place, a crumbling Roman villa nestled in a green dell. Trees and bushes grew about it in abundance and offered concealment for both men and horses.

To Freya's surprise, the cracked and lichened marble fountains still burbled water. She had looked apprehensively over her shoulder at every turn, expecting to see a centurion ghost or two flitting amongst the ruins, clacking armor and weapons as it made its eerie patrol. The sensation of the past pressing in close upon the present from all sides grew stronger after the golden moon had risen, and with the final falling of dusk. The colorful mosaics of birds and beasts that showed between thick vegetation, leafy vines grown rampant these past centuries, seemed to come alive in the flickering firelight and the shadows, and the creatures' eyes took on the greedy glitter of life. She shivered. It was misfortune enough that she found herself a virtual prisoner of Black Nevin and his rough band, without these other nameless, shadowy fears to spark her ever-superstitious imagination!

Black Nevin had denied her suggestion that they ride to Kenley and demand ransom for the Lady Valonia that very day.

"Nay," he'd said, shaking his shaggy black head and leering at her, "the morrow will be soon enough for that, lass. Let her lord husband and the ealdorman fret a while longer. They'll pay more eagerly fer the wait!"

Freya was reluctantly forced to admit that he made good sense, and accordingly stored away for possible future use this evidence that Nevin was not as dull-witted as he appeared.

There was another amongst the rough and ready brigands who seemed brighter than the rest, a fair-haired, lantern-jawed youth they called Oswald. He watched her as a fox watches a chicken—slyly. Though she suspected that he did so because he lusted after her, she was convinced lust was not his only reason. He mistrusted her story, and intended to keep an eye on her!

"Did you feed the hostage?" Freya asked casually, sinking her teeth into a chunk of savory venison Nevin had grudgingly tossed her, and eating with every appearance of a healthy appetite and a clear conscience.

"Feed her? Why waste good meat on the Saxon slut?" Nevin jeered, scratching his groin. Brown eyes glittered in the moonlight. "I've a mind to tumble her later, an' I fancy t'bitch will be all the more eager to please with an empty belly." He snickered.

"Nay! You'll feed her, then leave her be, unless you're a fool after all!" Freya snapped. "Did you not hear what I said, Nevin? Her husband will pay you well—but only if she's returned to him *unharmed*. Hurt her—touch her in any fashion—and he will hound you across Britain till your dying day. Mark my words! I know him."

"I think not," Nevin said craftily, "for there'll be no one left t'point him out our faces! No one. Let him bring the gold, and I'll tell your fine lord where to find his precious lady. Only she'll be dead, and so will you—and the likes o'us long gone!"

224

Freya wetted her lips, fighting the nausea that rose up her throat. She forced a smile. "You're a cunning fellow, Nevin," she said admiringly. "A man after my own style. Come, pass me the wineskin! We've the night to while away. Let's celebrate the riches that will be ours on the morrow."

"Ours?" Nevin echoed.

"Aye, ours," Freya said firmly. "You didn't mean what you said, and I know it. A fair man like you would not deny me my small portion of the ransom, would you now? I'll be no trouble to you afterward, no trouble at all. With my share of the gold I'll go north to Jorvic, and from there buy passage on a dragon-ship bound for Denmark, my home. Ah, this day was a day of good fortune, since I met up with Black Nevin and his band!" She smiled winningly, and Nevin was obviously entranced by the gesture—and by her. He scratched at his groin and grinned.

"Very well, ye'll have yer share, my bold lass. As I'll have mine!" He winked evilly, and tilted the wineskin to his foul mouth. Wine ran down into his beard and hung there in glistening drops. When he was done, he tossed the skin across to Freya, who pretended to take a long draught before handing it on to the next man.

"Go ahead, my friends," Oswald urged. "Drink! Make merry. I'll stand watch tonight."

His level blue gaze locked with Freya's over the fire. His eyes seemed to bore into her brain, to strip away the pretense and reveal the deceit in its depths. There would be little hope of escape with Oswald alert and armed, she decided, bowels churning, and a feeling of frustration and hopelessness swept through her.

Night fell. The crystal stars came out. A golden crescent moon arced like a Turkish scimitar across the black sky. The night wind moaned low about the ruins, and Freya, clad in only her kirtle, shivered with the chill. How much colder must the Lady Valonia be, used to the comforts of her bower, but now bound hand and foot and gagged, and tossed like a sack of grain in a corner of one of the cold, marble-floored rooms of the ruined villa. Freya's heart went out to the gentle lady. If only she could free her! There had to be a way, had to!

Her eyes narrowed as she glanced across the fire to where Black Nevin and his fellows lay, drunk and snoring. The first wineskin had been drained to the last drop. Others had followed. All slept now—all save the ever-watchful, ever-vigilant Oswald, curse his black soul! If she could only rid herself of him, then Valonia might be spirited away. The horses were tethered in a glade beyond the villa, and had been watered and were rested. If only Oswald—

She yawned and stretched, feigning a weariness she was far from feeling, for every nerve in her body tingled as if exposed; her blood sang with the thrill of danger; her muscles were coiled taut as bowstrings.

"By Odin, how my body plagues me!" she grumbled clearly and loudly. "One of you brutes must have caught me a fine wallop!" So saying, she pulled down the neck of her kirtle, exposing a rounded white shoulder and the topmost curve of a creamy breast. "There! 'Tis as I thought. Look at that bruise!"

Moonlight silvered her pearly flesh and burnished the red-gold of her tumbling hair, free of combs since the foray and falling loose and silken about her shoulders. Would Oswald find the sight of her arousing? she wondered, hope in her heart. She had never played the seductive siren before, had never once used her female body to sway a man, or for gain of any kind. The art of playing the temptress was strange territory to her, and one she knew little of. Would instinct serve? It must!

"I'm no fool like the others," Oswald said softly, yet his eyes glinted. "I'll not be taken in by a wench, and lulled by honeyed words and a shapely body. Cover yourself and go to sleep. I'll not fall for your tricks!"

"Is it pretty boys that please you, then?" She arched her brows. "For if it is, I can play the boy too, good Oswald, aye, and play it *very* well!"

"Curse you, I'm no heretic sodomist!" Oswald retorted, his tone tight and angry now, the lust that had slithered into his eyes quite dispelled. "Go to sleep, else I'll beat you for your impudence, wench!"

Her silvery laughter floated to him across the grass. "I but jested, good sir. 'Tis plain to see that you're a man—aye, and in every way! I was just—disappointed—that you don't find me pleasing, for I find you very pleasing indeed." Her voice was a seductive purr. "And a disappointed woman has a sharp and shrewish tongue."

She suddenly got to her feet and started across the ruin, away from him and toward the woods that pressed close all about, hips swinging beneath her kirtle with her loose-limbed gait.

"And where might you be after going?" Oswald demanded.

She grinned in the moonlight, and posed with fists planted challengingly on her hips. "Where else, but to find a convenient bush? Too much wine has filled me to bursting!"

"Make haste, then."

"I will, never fear."

She plunged into the woods and stood there in the shadows, waiting, watching to see what he would do, for in any battle one must first gauge the enemy and his actions, and use what one has learned against him. This was no exception. From where she stood she could see the top of Oswald's fair head, almost white-blond in the moonlight. She saw him fidget as the minutes passed, then stretch, then stand and pace. Just as he was about to go in search of her—having made no effort whatsoever to rouse his companions—she hurried from the woods and back toward the villa, almost colliding with him as she went.

"Shame on thee, Master Oswald! Did you think I'd run away?" she baited him, laughter in her tone as she tilted her face to teasingly look up into his. "Nay! I intend to have my share of the gold come the morrow, and have it I will. A good night to you, sir!"

She returned to her place alongside the fire and lay down. Oswald, his suspicions allayed with her return, again settled down to keep watch. Thinking her run away, he had not roused the others, she pondered, but had come after her himself. So. She had not misread the kindling in his eyes after all. He wanted her, right enough—but not here, where the others might know of it, or try to share her favors. There was every chance he would follow her away from the fire again, should she leave it—but this time she'd be ready for him.

An hour passed, then two. She had waited for what seemed an eternity when she rose yet again from her place by the fire. For a second time she headed for the woods.

"What now?" he barked.

"What else?" she retorted sharply, and flounced away from him, adding over her shoulder, "Can I help it if the wine was bitter and poor?"

Again she plunged into the black woods, too terrified for the success of her flimsy plan to fear the evil apparitions that were said to travel abroad by cover of darkness. Now she had only too many real and visible dangers to fret about, without worrying about those that were unseen!

Once a short distance from the villa, she rummaged about in the grass at her feet, searching for a rock. In minutes she had found one, and just in time too, for Oswald was coming after her! Her first absence to relieve herself had been a lengthy one, and so he moved without any real agitation, calling her softly as he came. His voice sounded irritable, but not unduly alarmed. Not yet. There was a husky undertone to his voice.

"Where are ye, wench?" he growled. "If ye still have that tumble in mind, I'm yer man fer it."

"Over here, good sir!" she called. "I'll not be a moment more."

No sooner had she said the words than she snatched up the rock and crept stealthily toward the sound of Oswald's voice. All of a sudden there he was, a lanky, blacker shadow looming up out of the blackness. He heard her in the final second before she struck out with the rock, but awareness came too late for Oswald. The rock slammed into the back of his skull, only marginally deflected by his upraised arm from crushing it like an eggshell. He groaned and dropped like a speared boar.

Hurriedly Freya picked up her skirts and twisted this way and that between the trees, headed in the direction of the moonlit villa.

Thank the gods, the brigands were yet deeply asleep! She circled them and the fire, then padded swiftly through the crumbling rooms of the villa, calling softly for Valonia. A muffled groan revealed her hiding place, and with shaking fingers Freya unknotted the bonds at her wrists and ankles, then wrenched the filthy gag from her mouth. The woman gasped, and drew in greedy gouts of air.

"Come on!" Freya urged. "We have no time to lose! Follow me!"

With Valonia moaning softly as the feeling flowed back into her numbed hands and feet, they made their way through the shadowed villa and out into the small glade behind it where the horses had been hobbled. They still wore their saddles, for their masters had wished to be ready to ride at a moment's notice, should any danger threaten them.

Finding her own gray mare easily in the moonlight, and the Lady Valonia's cream palfrey soon after, she all but tossed the noblewoman up into her saddle.

"If they catch you, they will kill you!" she whispered heatedly. "They will not honor any ransom agreement. You must ride as you have never ridden before, my lady!"

"But what—what of you?" Valonia demanded, her face a pale oval blur in the shadows. "I will not go without you!"

"I mean to scatter the other horses, then I'll follow you, I swear it. Be gone!"

"Very well. I shall find the river and let it lead me back to Kenley," Valonia whispered. "God be with you, child!" She leaned from her saddle to squeeze Freya's shoulder, then kicked her horse into a canter and was gone.

Immediately Freya flung about, and began tugging free the other horses' reins. The beasts milled about, then began edging away, heading for the woods and the meadows beyond, and their freedom. Only a few tethered beasts remained when Freya heard a shout from the villa. Oswald's voice! He had recovered from her blow, and was raising the alarm!

Hoisting up her skirts, she nimbly clambered astride the gray mare and wheeled its head about, headed after Valonia. But there stood Oswald, blocking her path, a dagger winking moonlight clenched in his fist. She lashed her steed and rode straight for him, bent on riding him underhoof. Let him leap aside, if he would! The horse screamed in fear. The blade flashed as it sang through the air, and a sharp, stinging pain pierced through her thigh. At once Oswald plunged forward, long arms groping for her stirrup, her bridle, seeking to wrest her from her horse. She lashed out with her foot and caught him full in the throat with a hefty kick that sent him sprawling to the grass. She wrenched the dagger from her thigh, dropping it in her agony and the resultant hot flood that coursed down her leg, but then all pain was gone and only the night lay ahead, and she was away, galloping her mount through the shadowed woods at reckless speed, while behind her the brigands wakened one by one from their drunken stupors, to give chase.

She caught up with Valonia half a league on, having, like her, followed the obsidian glint of the river toward Kenley. The woman cried out in relief to see her safe, but Freya bade her save her thanks. "They are up and after us," she told her breathlessly. "We must ride like the very wind, for there'll be no second chances, not now!"

They rode on, the thunder of their horses' hooves muffled by the thick carpet of greensward beneath. Behind them, coming up fast, was the dull drumming of many other hooves, growing louder and still louder by the minute as the brigand band raced in pursuit. Then, as they galloped across a rolling meadow, a party of horsemen loomed suddenly out of the darkness ahead. The scrape of steel as swords were drawn, and the jingling of bits and harness, sounded on the gloom.

"Hold! Who goes there?" rang out a voice, and Valonia responded, "My lord Ordway! 'Tis I, your lady wife! Blessed Jesu, you have found us!"

They reined in their horses, and at once Ordway and half of the garrison of Kenley surged forward to meet them.

"One of your men-at-arms was knocked senseless, but survived the ambush," Ordway grimly revealed, taking Valonia in his arms and lifting her gently down from her horse. "He let those cursed rogues think him dead, and heard the slave girl strike a bargain with the brigands to ransom thee, my dearest heart!"

"Nay!" Valonia protested.

"Yea," came Alaric's voice hard by Freya's horse. He sounded colder, angrier, than she had ever heard him before. "'Tis true! Is this how you repay my aunt's kindness, Dane—

230

with treachery? But then I should have expected no better of you—cursed Viking that you are!" he added bitterly. "Speak! Have you nothing to say in your defense?"

"I . . . I . . . !"

Freya's voice trailed away to silence, deep and profound, as she stared at him wide-eyed. He seemed to grow bigger and bigger, to loom up like some hateful giant from the shadows! Her head felt light and dizzy. She was suddenly aware of a warm trickle running down her thigh. She swayed, opened her mouth to moan, and then a thousand candles flared up inside her head and began spinning in crazy circles—

With a whimper she toppled from her horse's back and fell senseless to the dew-soaked grass.

Chapter 17

She seemed lost, whirling slowly in a void that was black and endless. No matter how she struggled, she could not find her way out of it, back to . . . back to . . . where? She did not know, could not remember, and the knowledge frightened her. At times there was a sensation of pain in her body, an intense pain that made her cry weakly for ease. A burning agony followed, and then there was only blackness once more, blessed and pain-free and still.

Sometimes she seemed close to finding her way from the void. She saw lights, heard murmurings, at first nearby and then farther away, and struggled to bring herself closer to them, swimming up through the blackness as if swimming through dragging water. Pale blurs—faces, perhaps?—looked down at her, but they were out of focus, fuzzy and indistinct. She tried to call out to them, but could not. Her throat seemed closed by a band of iron. Her head felt fuzzy, as if packed with down. Heat throbbed behind her eyes, "Nissa! Where are you?" she heard someone say. "Uncle Sven, don't leave me!" The voice reminded her of her own, but was cracked and hoarse. She tried to move, but it was as if her limbs bore leaden weights, and again she floated back down into the void.

She awoke to birdsong from somewhere nearby, and turning her head, she saw a wicker cage upon a small table. Within it, a pair of speckled thrushes warbled and trilled. *Pretty,* she thought, *Pretty song. Pretty birds.* She sensed someone bending over her, felt gentle hands turning her, bathing her fevered brow, tenderly soothing her aching body. Yet in her blurring vision and confusion she was uncertain who their owner might be. She sighed, and sank back down into a deep sleep.

When next she awoke the feverish sensation was gone, and the dawn chorus of the birds had ended. Turning her head slowly to one side, she saw in the rushlight that the pair of thrushes slept in their cage, heads tucked under their wings, feathers fluffed out for warmth. So she had not imagined them. They were real. Other than a gnawing throb in her leg and a bone-deep exhaustion, she felt quite well. She tested her arms and her head, and found she could move them normally, save for her wounded thigh. It seemed stiff and a little swollen. She licked her lips, which were parched and cracked, and opened her eyes.

Valonia sat at her bedside, her embroidery hoop in hand, her fair head bowed gracefully over her work, rushlight burnishing her hair. By the narrow wind-eye stood Alaric. He wore a brooding expression, his gray eyes hooded and moody. She swallowed, memories of his unfair accusations flooding through her like bile.

"My lady?" she whispered.

"Thank the Lord, you have awakened!" Valonia exclaimed, casting her embroidery aside and coming to take Freya's hand in her own. She squeezed it fondly, and a delighted smile lit up her grave face.

At once Alaric spun about and strode across the bower. He came to an abrupt halt a pace or two from the bed and stood there, glowering down at Freya. His hair was disheveled, unruly inky commas spilling over his broad brow. Fatigue haunted his eyes and made dark hollows beneath his cheekbones and furrows about his mouth. He looked exhausted and irritable, and all hopes she had fostered that he might be kind to her fled as she gazed mutely up at him. After a moment or two more he muttered an oath, turned on his heel, and strode from the bower.

To Freya's surprise, Valonia laughed softly, clapping her hands together.

"Men!" she exclaimed. "What little boys they all are! Alaric thinks naught of the perils of war, yet is afraid—and ashamed—to ask forgiveness of you!"

She had moved gracefully across the bower to a small table as she spoke, her skirts trailing over the rushes, her chatelaine's belt with its many attachments chinking softly as she went. She poured water from an ornate silver flagon into a glass claw-beaker, brought it to Freya, and raised her up as she tilted it to her lips. "Drink, my dear. You have lain in a fever for several days."

Freya drank thirstily. The water felt like sweet, rare wine coursing down her scratchy throat. When she had drunk her fill, she sank back on the downy softness of the pallet beneath her, exhausted by even so small an effort. "Afraid?" she echoed, referring to Valonia's startling comment about Alaric.

"Aye, afraid," Valonia confirmed, her lips pursed tight with irritation. "After you swooned from loss of blood the night we escaped from the brigands, Alaric lifted you up onto his horse and bore you back to Kenley himself. He was like a man possessed! No nurse would suffice for you but myself, though I reassured him a dozen times over I would permit none other to care for you, even should he ask it! Yet all the while he made arrangements for your care he muttered and raged, called thee names I cannot repeat, and swore he would call you to account for your treachery! I tried to explain what had really happened, that you had freed me and had never intended to aid those foul men, but he would have none of my protests. In this, I must confess, he was abetted by my lord husband, who is a dear man, but ofttimes quite unreasonable!" She grimaced. "I thought it best to see you cared for first, and meanwhile give Alaric time to vent his spleen a little. When he had recovered from his drinking—and he was deep in his cups for nigh two days and nights!—I was able to tell him what you had done, and now he is plagued by guilt for wrongly accusing you!" She shook her head. "I almost pity him his confusion, my poor, foolish nephew, but I fancy such self-reproach cannot help but enhance his character!"

So, Freya thought with relief, Valonia had cleared her. She need have no fear on that score. Alaric's brooding expression was his own doing, not hers. "I thank you for your care of me, my lady," she told her. "Once again I find I am in your debt. First Sven, and now myself. You must tell me how I can repay you."

"Not so, child! Why, if it were not for your bravery, the brigands would have murdered me and robbed my lord husband of his gold! They are no more, thanks to you, save for what the crows have left of their bodies, hanging still at the crossroads. Alaric saw to that. And do not thank only me, for the nursing of you was not mine alone. He sat with you too, bathed you at the height of your fever, though I doubt sorely that he will ever admit to having done so, now you are recovering." She eyed Freya thoughtfully. "In truth, I have never before seen the gruff Bear so tamed!" Nor so enamored of any maid, she added, but to herself.

Freya's eyes grew round with astonishment. Valonia's avowal that Alaric had tended her was hard to believe. But then a vague and confused memory of large hands, moving gently over her body and bringing ease where they touched, came to mind. Valonia spoke truly—she was certain of it, though no less puzzled.

She lay quite still while the Saxon lady unbound and cleansed her wound, then salved it with a cool unguent of soothing herbs and rebandaged it with soft strips of linen.

"There! 'Tis healing well now, though we feared to lose you from the poison a day or two hence. Your Uncle Sven was responsible for your healing. 'Twas he who told me of a certain moss that would help to draw the poisonous humors from the wound, and he who went in search of it and helped me to make the poultices from it. 'Tis clear he loves thee well, Freya. Now that you are awake and feeling much better, I will send him to you. I cannot tell thee how glad I am that you have recovered, child!"

Valonia was true to her word. Sven came to see her shortly after the Saxon lady left Alaric's bower to resume her chatelaine's duties for the evening. Though he walked with a slight stoop to one side now, and would always do so henceforth, he appeared fully recovered from his wound. Tears glinted in his eyes as he came across the bower to embrace her fondly.

"You are much improved this even, *ja*, my Freya?" he said.

"I am," she agreed, and smiled, looking him up and down. "Have you already donned the robes of a Christian monk then, uncle?"

He glanced down at the long, sober tunic he wore, belted with rope at the waist, and returned her smile. "If not of a monk, then of a man who has accepted his destiny, and will very soon embrace the Christian faith. It is all arranged. When you are recovered, I am to join the brotherhood at Mucking. Farant of Kenley kindly made the necessary arrangements before he left for Winchester. A good man, Farant."

"So. You will in truth desert me," she said a little petulantly. "I had hoped for a change of heart, uncle."

"Other hearts will indeed change, Freya," Sven retorted with a twinkle in his eye, "but mine will not be one of them, alas!"

She glanced up at him sharply, and the look she gave him was a piercing one. "What do you know that you have not told me, *skald?*" Her tone was imperious and laden with suspicion.

"Too much in some ways; not near enough in others. Another vision." He shrugged. "What else? Yet were I to tell it, you would laugh and deny it, as you did the last, so I will say naught more."

"Did it bode ill for me?" she could not resist asking.

"Would I leave thee alone here if it had?" he pointed out. "Sleep now, little one, and gather your strength. It will not be long in returning, I fancy, for your sharp tongue has already regained its former good health." He made as if to leave her to her rest.

"Uncle?"

"*Ja?*"

"Did I ever tell thee that—that I love thee?" she asked softly.

"Not for many, many years," Sven replied, turning to her once more and embracing her. "But it is never too late to make amends, little one."

"You have been a father to me, good Sven."

"Ah! Then you noticed after all, despite your vows to

impress Thorfast?" he teased.

"Of course! Forgive me, uncle. I was a selfish, wayward child, and did not think of the pain I must have caused you, trying to win my lord father's love and attention, when all the while I had all the love I could possibly ask for from you. I will miss you sorely when you leave here."

"As I will miss you," Sven said simply. "You have been my life these eighteen years." He leaned over and pressed his lips to her brow.

"And you mine. Without you and Nissa, I know not what would have become of me."

He nodded sagely. *"Takke.* I think I will come back to Kenley in a twelvemonth and ask of you if I am yet your life—or if another has usurped my place in your heart." His eyes, the untrammeled blue of a morning sky, twinkled.

"Usurped? By whom?" she demanded indignantly, certain no one could ever take his place in her affections.

But Sven would say no more. With a chuckle and a mysterious smile, he left the bower, leaving Freya staring after him and wondering what he had meant.

After supper that night, which consisted of a bowl of savory stew, thick with lamb, lentils, and onions, fresh white bread, and a horn of creamy milk laced with a pain-killing draught, she slept deeply again, and did not awaken until the following morning. She stretched and yawned, feeling well enough to get out of bed. But she did not, for she realized suddenly that Alaric stood across the bower from her.

"You are well enough to talk?" he asked gruffly, running a huge hand through his unruly black curls.

"Ja," she agreed, aware of a jittery flutter in her belly as he strode across the bower and took a seat beside her on the bed. How big he was, a giant almost, and how broad were his shoulders! The scent of him tantalized her nostrils. His body heat was almost palpable where she lay. Aye, his proximity was disturbing! It put her in mind of the deliciously wicked dreams that the poppy-induced sleep had brought her all the previous night long; dreams in which Alaric had figured prominently— and with a legendary virility!

"Valonia has told me that she owes you her life, and that I

237

was wrong. It would seem I accused you falsely," he began, obviously ill at ease.

"*Ja*. You did indeed." She would not make this any easier for him, by Loki she would not! Let him writhe a while longer on the lance point of his guilt! After all, he had not hesitated to believe her capable of harming Valonia, of casting her lot with that of Black Nevin and his louts. 'Twas no more than he deserved, that arrogant Bear.

He scowled down at her. "Freya, I would receive your acceptance of my apology!"

"Then offer it, and I will listen and see if I am moved to accept it or nay," she replied tartly, lying back comfortably on her soft pillows and returning his smoldering gaze with a cool stare.

He choked back an oath. "Christ's Wounds, have you no heart, vixen?"

"Have you no humility, Saxon?" she came back. Of a certainty, he had none now. His eyes were murderous, killing her inch by inch!

"Would it had been your vicious tongue wounded . . ." he muttered under his breath. Then he said stiffly, "I ask your forgiveness, Freya, for the wrong done you by my false accusations. There. Accept it, or the Devil take thee!"

"I will not accept it," she snapped back gleefully, and thought for a second he would take her by the throat and strangle her, wounded or nay.

"What more do you want of me?" he gritted. "Blood?"

"Nay, not blood!" she retorted with a grin. "A simple boon, no more, no less, is all I ask. Only in its granting will I be able to reassure Valonia—and myself—that you truly regret your vile and unwarranted accusations."

"Ask it then, wench, and let's have done with this nonsense!"

"You *will* grant it?"

Without hesitation, he nodded. "I will—with one exception."

"My freedom?"

"Aye."

"Fear not, I will not ask the impossible of you, only this:

Swear to me, upon your sword, my lord, that if I, Freya Jorgensen, slave to thee, Alaric of Kent, should ever give birth to your babe, you will acknowledge that child as freeborn."

Too late he realized that he had been gulled. He nodded curtly. Tight-lipped, he drew his sword and held it by the blade so that the hilt was uppermost, like a cross. He had given Valonia, soft-hearted, gentle, persistent Valonia, his word that he would do naught to upset the girl; indeed, would do all in his power to be kind to her in return for her having saved his aunt's life. And his word was inviolate—at least insofar as far as his aunt's wishes were concerned. He had no such concern for the Danish bitch, he told himself, smothering his annoyance.

"I give my vow, upon the sacred blade of this sword, that all shall be as you have asked."

She nodded, satisfied, and he jabbed the sword back into its scabbard, narrowly avoiding gelding himself in the process.

"Now 'tis done, I would have a boon from thee in return, firebrand. You will behave in a manner more befitting my slave henceforth. You will not seek to deny me your body, nor refuse my bidding in anything."

She considered this for a moment or so, saying at last, "To the former two, I agree, for such was the promise I made thee. But to the latter, I can say only that I will judge each request upon its own merit. More I cannot promise, lest I perjure myself." She smiled sweetly.

"If you were not wounded—!" he threatened, fists balled at his sides.

"Oh, I am recovered well enough. My thigh pains me a little, but 'tis of no great import, thank thee, sir. You were saying, 'If you were not wounded'—?"

She cocked her head to one side, waiting for him to continue, knowing full well what threats he had planned to make. When he remained silent, she stretched and yawned like a lazy tawny cat. She shook free her tousled red-gold curls, and was all rapt and innocent attentiveness as she gazed up at him, knowing very well as she did so that the coverlet had slipped and bared her to the waist. It was becoming a nuisance, the desire she had felt for him of late and that her dreams had only served to intensify, but what was she to do when her body clamored for him, and would not be placated by aught else . . . ?

His eyes were drawn to her lovely breasts as if by the magic drawing stone. Creamy of flesh, uptilted, full and crowned with impudent, rosy buds, they quite distracted him from the dire threats he had intended to make. In truth, he'd forgotten them! He licked his lips, and there was in his eyes now something else, something hot and lusty. "You are recovered, you say?" he echoed huskily.

"Quite well enough for what you have in mind, Saxon," Freya responded with a throaty purr, "should you handle me—gently." Her sapphire eyes glowed.

"And you will keep your part of our bargain?" he asked guardedly.

She spread her arms wide and looked up at him through half-closed eyelids, and he felt his manhood stir, like a sleeping dragon roused from its lair.

"I am yours to command, my lord," she murmured, and swept the coverlet aside. "Your will is mine."

As with alarming eagerness he made to disrobe, he was unable to take his eyes from her, fascinated by the sheen of her moist lips, the flutter of the pulse at the base of her throat, the heavy-lidded languor of her eyes. He had the peculiar, disturbing feeling that she *wanted* his attentions, that she desired him as a man, with or without the vow she had made to bind her, and that he had played into her hands . . . but just as suddenly he realized he no longer cared a whit if she had manipulated him or nay, for his desire for her was hot and sweet and all the fiercer for the knowledge that he had come close to losing her . . .

Soon there was only Freya. Freya, his Viking slave. Freya, his jewel from the sea . . . his blessing and his curse. And lying beside her, gently holding her, breathing her subtle, enflaming fragrance as he caressed her, all rational thought became impossible.

A FREE ZEBRA
HISTORICAL
ROMANCE
WORTH

$3.95

Chapter 18

Once Freya was up and about, Sven the Skald left Kenley
for the monastery at Mucking, there to seek the true God, and
perhaps himself in the process.

Though Freya was saddened to see him go, she was happy
for him too. He had never felt harmony within himself
following the old, savage Norse gods and the Norse way of life,
but had subjugated his true beliefs and desires for her sake. He
had the right to pursue his own way for the remainder of his
life, she decided.

Such selflessness did her credit. But if the truth were
known, her wish to see Sven made happy was not the only
reason she bade him a fond farewell without tears or remorse,
nor even the main one, she admitted ruefully. The truth was,
she had neither the time nor the inclination, sad to say, to
concern herself with her uncle, for since the moment Alaric
had come to her in the bower that day when she lay recovering
from her wounding, her life had been turned upside down. *Ja,*
it was as if a spell had been woven about them that day, for
nothing had been the same since. She felt different inside,
restless and giddy, brooding and moody all at once. She was
different on the outside too, Valonia had observed, and the
noblewoman had looked at her again in that strangely
contemplative way she had at times. Alaric looked different to
Freya too, but whether it was a true difference in his
appearance, or but a difference in her perception of him, she
could not fathom.

She had thought him not completely unattractive before, despite her hatred of him. Now she found him not only attractive but handsome, quite the comeliest man she had ever seen! She found herself drawn to watch the exact way his lips moved when he spoke, and dreamily imagined as she did so those same firm lips pressed against her flesh in passionate kisses. Each word he uttered seemed profound to her ears, however commonplace or trite it may have sounded to others. The most innocuous comment, and his deep voice seemed to reach out and enfold her like an embrace, the words meant for her and her alone. She could not look upon his hair without experiencing the urge to twine her fingers in those ebony curls and tug his dark head down to hers, nor watch the play of muscle, rippling through his arms and torso, without wanting to touch his body. She drowned in the depths of his wood-smoke eyes, quivered if they were dark and lambent with smoldering desire, went through agonies of trembling guilt and despair if they were pale and silvery with anger. Though she upbraided herself for a besotted, lovesick fool, though she cursed the fickle tides of her affections that bore her thither and yon and commanded herself to put such dangerous thoughts from her mind, she was helpless to do so, for her heart was now a hostage to his will!

When he bade her accompany him on hunts for wild boar, she rode beside him eagerly, and thrilled to every word he spoke, every gesture he made, recalling nothing of the chase or the kill afterward. When he bade her join him at the supper table, or don one of the lovely kirtles Valonia had caused to be made for her, she did so—and fretted that he would not find her lovely, all the while she dined on Odin knew what. Not that she ever told Alaric of this, or ever would. *Nej!* She hid her feelings well, and all the while feared that he'd suspect them and mock her.

She need have harbored no such fears, had she but known that Alaric's thoughts in many ways paralleled her own, though with equal reluctance.

For his part, he was convinced he was bewitched, and ofttimes wondered if the wench was more than she seemed—a notion that caused him more than once to cast darkling looks in her direction, which she returned with sweetly innocent smiles. Aye, too innocent, he fancied! No woman ever looked half so lacking in guile as did she. Besides, what else but witchery could explain the feelings that churned inside him of late? When Ordway spoke sharply to her and, with what seemed to him annoying frequency, set her to repeating some menial task, his blood boiled, and it was all he could do to bite his tongue and stay silent. When the men of his garrison cast lecherous eyes upon her and exchanged greedy glances among themselves, it took every ounce of his will to refrain from spitting them upon his sword like so many roasted quail. At times he could look at her and feel a giddy happiness well up inside him like a bubbling spring, and at others he plummeted into a quagmire of despondency. So was he one morning, early in the month of August. Oblivious to the brilliant sunlight outside, the cloudless cerulean skies, the heavy, scented air of a summer morn, he clung to the gloomy confines of his hall, finding there an atmosphere that partnered his mood.

"In truth, cousin, you appear morose this morn," Cullen observed idly, helping himself to an apple off the platter and slicing it into wedges with his dagger.

"I was but thinking," Alaric responded absently, gazing at his reflection in a silver flagon as if he hoped to find all the secrets of the universe therein.

"Aye, and I blame you not a whit," Cullen observed, a grin playing about the corners of his mouth. "I would think of her too, were she my bower slave—but with a smile, not a frown." He winked lecherously.

Alaric's great dark head came up and a muscle tightened in his jaw. "I was thinking not of her, cousin," he insisted with little conviction, "but of my estates."

"And I," Cullen retorted with a grin, "am Saint Cuthbert! Not thinking of her? Ha! 'Tis clear you think of little else of late. And you keep the wench closer to you than your own shadow."

"She must be watched. I am not convinced as yet that she does not mean to escape," Alaric protested lamely.

"Short of disappearing into thin air, she will not, under your watchful eye, cousin." Cullen chewed thoughtfully upon his apple for several moments, casually spitting the seeds to the rushes. "I was wondering—have you told her yet of the Lady Meredyth?"

Alaric rose and came around the table, imposing this morn in a tunic of dark blue that emphasized the breadth of his shoulders and his height. A light blue mantle was draped over his left shoulder, exposing the short jeweled dagger strapped to his right hip. "What is there to tell?" he snapped.

Cullen grinned and tossed his apple core aside. A hound rushed over to sniff at it, and turned away in disgust. "For a man who professes to know much of women, you are sadly ignorant, my lord! Any fool can see the Lady Freya has developed a fondness for you. What do you think her reaction will be when you tell her that it is very possible you will be betrothed ere long?"

Alaric scowled. "No doubt she will feel somewhat slighted."

"Somewhat slighted?" Cullen snorted. "Her? With that temper? Christ's Blessed Wounds, I know not if you speak seriously or in jest. Your Freya," he continued with great deliberation, "will be like a very tempest unleashed in her jealousy, and all that fury will be wreaked upon your head."

Alaric shook that same head. "Not so. Freya knows she is only a slave, and has accepted her place. Besides, she has a keen mind. I am certain she has already considered the possibility that I will take a bride, and has resigned herself to it as only right and fitting. You make too much of this, cousin."

Cullen made no comment on this, but instead continued, "After your betrothal—what of the slave girl then?"

"Everything will continue as before," Alaric said, obviously vexed, for he paced to and fro before the hearth.

"And at night—in whose bower will you sleep?"

"In whichever bower I choose, of course!" he retorted angrily. "Am I not master here?"

"Ah, then 'twill be as I thought. You will not only have to contend with your leman's fury, but with your lady wife's, for of a certainty neither will be reconciled to learning you have lain with the other!"

"You look for difficulties where there will be none, I tell you. Other men take a wife and also keep a bevy of other

244

women to please them without discord in their homes."

"Aye, they do. But their lemans are serfs, simple peasant wenches only too happy to have found favor with their lord, and eager for the baubles and trinkets which he brings, and which add comfort to their dreary existence. 'Tis not so with your Freya. She is as nobly born as we are, Alaric, used to the comforts of her station. How then will you placate her fury, soothe her jealousy? There are no jewels you can give her that she has not been given before. There are no pretty words you could ever say that can deny the truth: that you have made her your whore—aye, sir, your whore!—and will take another as your bride and lady."

Alaric's steely fingers closed over the hilt of his dagger. "Have a care, cousin! Do not force me to take action at your insults!"

"Insults? How so? 'Tis the truth, as I see it—and as others will see it. As the Lady Freya herself will see it," Cullen finished pointedly.

"You think so, do you? Then what would you have me do— wed the wench?"

Cullen appeared surprised that such a notion should ever have entered Alaric's mind. "Wed her? Perhaps so, cousin. Worse matches have been made, after all. As I said, she is of our rank, and a wedding between you and she would effect a small alliance between ourselves and the Danelaw, an alliance to help cement the uneasy peace we have now. As I see it, you have only three choices if you would keep harmony in your hall."

"And what are these three choices?" Alaric gritted sarcastically, his patience shredded.

Cullen grinned. "You may bed her, wed her, or shed her! First, you may carry on as you are now, and never think to take a bride or beget true heirs for Kenley. Or you may wed her, and accord her all the honors of your lady wife. Or you may shed her from your life and start afresh, give her her freedom and a little gold, set her on her way north, into the Danelaw, and marry the Lady Meredyth as my father wishes."

"Your strategies will not be necessary, Cullen. When I tell the girl I am to be betrothed, she will accept it."

"Then why wait? Tell her this very day! Fifty gold mancuses say she'll be consumed by jealousy!"

"Agreed," Alaric said firmly. "Count your coins for the last time, cousin. They'll be mine to count ere long!"

"You tricked me, Saxon!" Freya murmured accusingly. "There is no doe run to ground here!"

Hunting spear in hand, she spun about to find Alaric close behind her, but before she could duck past him he had his hands planted solidly on the rough tree trunk behind her, one on each side of her head, thus preventing her escape. He plucked the short spear from her hand and tossed it aside.

"Is there not, my little *deer?*" he teased, gray eyes alive with desire. "I, Alaric, the mighty hunter, have run you to ground, and will now close in for the—kill."

So saying, he hooked his finger under her chin and tilted her face up to his. Red-gold hair fell away from her lovely profile in heavy waves, unhampered by the slim golden fillet that bound her smooth brow. Her expression, off guard, was breathtakingly sweet and startled, and made the breath catch in his throat.

A smile tugged at the corners of his mouth as he lowered his lips slowly to hers, very slowly. He found he enjoyed her anticipation, enjoyed watching her face as she waited for his kiss. The tawny fringe of her lashes fluttered like dancing butterflies, hovering for breathless seconds upon her flushed cheeks before her eyes closed. Her nostrils flared. Her lips parted, and a breathless, shaky little sigh escaped her. One foot left the ground. Her hands twined behind her, seeking purchase on the rough tree trunk as if she feared to lose her balance. And then their lips met and parted, their tongues touched, played, warred, and her slender arms came up to curl about his neck.

Alaric invaded the velvet hollows of her mouth in a long and ardent kiss that melted her very bones—or so it seemed to Freyja. The fine hairs upon her nape rose as his hand swept down her body, molding its supple lines and curves. She shivered as the grip of his other hand about her tightened,

246

strong fingers burning through the cloth of her tunic to brand her with their mark. *I want him more and more each day*! she thought dazedly. *I desire him even as he desires me, with a hunger that drives me to madness!*

"Someone might happen upon us," she stammered, frightened by the sheer force of the emotions flooding through her.

"I care not," he growled against her ear, and gooseflesh rose along her arms. His virile scent filled her nostrils, and she swayed in the circle of his embrace. "Let them come!"

"You promised this morning would be spent in hunting—you swore you would not—!" she cried, the anger and resistance ebbing from her like an outpouring tide. Oh, why must the grass smell so fresh and green—so very sensual?

"Then curse me for a liar," he murmured, his hot breath tickling her ear.

"Liar! Oh, sweet, wicked liar!" she accused with little conviction, and melting against him noticed now the clear, sweet warble of the birds above them, the gurgling laughter of the brook as it played over the rocks—everything sharp, distinct, her senses heightened by desire.

"Lie also to me," he breathed hotly in her ear, "and let us be damned for a brace of liars! Lie, my sweeting, and tell me you do not desire me. Speak the word, and I will at once release you."

There was laughter in his voice as she cursed him in her anguish, for she could not speak the lie, *nej*, not when she quivered and trembled so; not when her breasts were tingling, the nipples tight, swollen nubbins of pleasure, as they were now. Even her veins were flowing with a throbbing current as hot and sweet as molten honey coursing through them! She could not deny it, not when between her thighs there was that sudden intense quiver, that pulse, that yearning for the exquisite pleasures she had come to expect from him! Curse him for his cunning touch, his clever kisses, his knowing, damnable ways! In truth she *was* his slave, her body a prisoner to his desire, to his caresses, even if her spirit yet soared free. And her heart, her closed and wounded heart—was that also slave to his will?

She felt as if she were drowning in the silvery sea of his eyes as he gently tugged her down to the springy carpet of curling young ferns beneath the trees, and thought, *Ja, perhaps that too! Perhaps . . . perhaps even my heart . . . !*

Gasping, she twined her fingers in his thick black curls, tugging his dark head away from where it rested heavily upon her belly. Impossible. She could not budge him, yet still he continued drawing lazy whorls upon the velvety plateau of her stomach with a rough-textured fingertip, tickling caresses that made her suck in gasp after shivery gasp. As he did so, his mouth, greedy and hot, nuzzled her smooth flesh. His hands slipped down, grazing the triangle of burnished curls that shielded her sex as he reached to stroke the slim, supple beauty of her legs.

"If Guthrum had an army of Nordic beauties such as you, Wessex would surrender in the twinkling of an eye," he murmured between kisses. "I should thank my Christian God he does not, hmm, pagan princess?"

"When I escape from Kenley, I will speak with Guthrum and tell him of your idea," Freya promised solemnly, no hint of teasing in her tone, although her sapphire eyes shone with a vivid light.

"Escape me?" He laughed. "Never!"

"Never? Do not be so arrogant, my lord," she warned. "Slaves escape their masters every day, do they not?"

"Aye, they do," he acknowledged, leaning up on one elbow to look at her keenly. "Yet 'tis a rare slave who would warn her master of her intent, think you not? 'Twould seem almost as if—she—wanted him to prevent her."

Freya blushed. "Such a slave would be a fool, I say!"

Alaric shook his head. "Perhaps no fool, but—someone too afraid to admit to what she feels. Someone who is ruled by pride, and deplores her change of heart as cowardly weakness."

"What else would it be but weakness?" Freya demanded. "To be taken slave is bad enough, but to *accept* it and make no effort to flee her master is an even greater sin. Such—such a woman as you speak of is no better than a camp follower, or a woman who sells herself for a silver penny by the wayside!"

"I disagree," Alaric murmured, uncomfortably recalling

Cullen's talk of whores even while rubbing a red-gold curl between his fingertips, and thinking how shiny it was in the sunlight that fell in golden-green shafts between the leafy boughs above. "The woman who sells her body feels nothing for the men who use her, neither lust nor love, but wants only the riches the act can bring her. The slave we speak of stands to gain nothing by her continued slavery, neither gold nor great riches. And yet, though she denies it even to herself, she wishes to stay with her master. Why?"

Freya shrugged irritably and sat up, thrusting his hands away. "She knows she cannot escape her master's guards. The burh is too well secured, her lord a watchful man, perhaps?"

"There are always ways, times, *if* she craves her freedom badly enough. I say she does not! I say her heart has melted, aye, her frozen, Nordic heart. I say it warms to the touch of her Saxon lord, and has felt the kindling of love within it! I say she would stay with her master whatever the future brings, even should her master decide to take a bride," he added hopefully.

"You're wrong!" she cried, jumping to her feet, and his hopes foundered. "It is not so, nay! I feel nothing for you but hatred, *ja*, and loathing, I swear it! 'The kindling of love'! Pah! You talk like an old woman, Saxon, with naught left her but dreams of love and lost youth." She made to run away, but took only a pace before his hand came out and clamped about her ankle, wrenching her off balance. She toppled and fell, landing across him, her face crimson with indignation, sapphire eyes glittering with ire.

"Did we speak of you?" he asked softly.

Their faces were a hairbreadth apart. He clamped his hand across the back of her head, knotted his fingers through her hair, and forced her mouth down upon his, kissing her hungrily. Her helpless moans of pleasure were muffled by his lips. Her rigid body relaxed, little by little, as the kiss lengthened. Deft fingers loosened her braided girdle. The same nimble fingers tugged down her tunic of soft, natural suede and bared her lovely shoulders and breasts to the waist. His mouth fastened over a breast and devoured it, even as his free hands roamed her body, roughly pressing the boyish curves of her buttocks to bring her hard against the length of his hips and his

throbbing shaft, which burned like a brand through hi
clothing and through hers, to her flesh beneath.

With a little sob of utter defeat, she impatiently shrugge
the tunic away and tossed it aside, then peeled away he
leggings and cast them after it, coming into his outstretche
arms like a ship to safe harbor. Her long hair swept his ches
and fell in silken strands about his cheeks as she dipped he
head to his. She kissed his broad brow, his nose. She trailed he
moist lips across the rough-textured angles of his jaw and chin
which were swarthy and rough with a bluish shadow, and the
at last pressed her mouth over his. He groaned and knotted hi
fingers tighter in her shining mane, returning her kisses with
hunger that set her heart to thudding madly and excitemen
spiraling through her.

He eased away his leggings and breeches and lifted he
astride his lean flanks. With yet another little sob, she lowere
herself slowly onto his great length, her nails gouging the tau
flesh of his shoulder as she took him deep within her. Sh
began to move upon him slowly and sensuously at first, bu
then with greater urgency as the fire leaped through her
raging out of control.

Sweat streamed in glistening runnels down the valle
between her breasts, which were swollen and exquisitel
sensitive to his fondlings. Each breath came rasping. Alari
grasped her hips and arched upward to meet her downwar
thrusts, his own pleasure heightened by the little cries an
gasps of ecstasy that broke from her parted lips, by th
transported delight in her expression. Clasping her tightly t
him, he rolled her beneath him without parting their bodies fo
so much as an instant. He thrust into her again and again
riding her with a savage urgency that rendered though
impossible.

In that moment she was a creature of sensation alone, a
woman-creature who existed only to feel what it was hi
mastery made her feel. Logic and reason, pride and shame
ceased to exist. There was only the rising, blissful pressure tha
filled her, the glory of his powerful thrusts hurtling he
skyward, the dazzling beauty of his body, oiled by sweat, th
cords dancing under taut, glistening flesh as he took her t

he heights.

Birds took noisy flight from the treetops when he roared out
his fulfillment. As he did so, she stiffened beneath him, and the
only movements between them were the spasms of rapture that
rippled through her body and held him fast. The honeyed
sheath of her womanhood tightened about him as wave after
wave of ecstasy flooded through her, and he knew that what he
was experiencing, she experienced too.

When the moment had passed for them both, he pressed his
lips to the glistening column of her throat, then to each eyelid
in turn. "We are all slaves to the desires within us, my lovely
Freya," he whispered, "I as much as you. I've sought to deny
what it is I feel for thee, and yet with every passing day it grows
harder to do so. Seek to flee me, and I will pursue you to the
very ends of the earth. You are mine, mine alone! I will never
let thee go!"

She lay there very still, with her eyes closed, yet she was
feigning sleep, for she did not trust herself to answer him, not
now, with such content within her. Better to say nothing, she
decided, than to bare her soul and regret it later.

After minutes had passed without further words from him
she risked opening one eye, and saw that he had fallen deeply
asleep, one arm flung possessively across her belly, his dark
head lodged intimately against the swell of her hip. *There are
always ways, times, if she wants her freedom badly enough,* Alaric
had said when speaking of the "hypothetical" slave. Now was
such a time. The deep rise and fall of his breathing promised he
would sleep for some time to come. The short spear lay
carelessly amongst the ferns. The horses were tethered within
a minute's walk of this place. She had everything she needed to
escape him: the opportunity, swift mounts, and a weapon with
which to hurt and protect herself—everything but the will to
do so. She made no motion to escape him. Why not? Because
she enjoyed his body, their lusty coupling? *Ja,* that was part of
it. To deny it was to lie to herself. But—if the pleasures of
coupling were all she sought, there were other men she might
find to please her.

Nay, it was this man and this man alone who, like the
magical stone with powers to draw metal, kept her by his side!

251

Odin's Beard, the thought of losing him to another, of another woman kissing his lips, holding him, touching him filled her with a murderous, jealous rage she'd never felt before. He had made mention of taking a bride, she recalled. Had he been serious, or but jesting? Of a sudden, she had to know. She shook him by the shoulder to wake him, and wake he did, grumbling as he struggled up onto his elbows.

"It had best be a worthy reason you have for waking me, Freya!" he threatened.

"Worthy enough, I believe, Saxon. You—you mentioned a bride, sir. Did you jest, or is a betrothal in the wind that I know naught of?"

"Are you my mother or my sister, that I must tell thee every little thing?" he came back curtly. "If I am to be betrothed, 'tis my business, not yours."

"So it is true!" she cried, wounded to the core, feeling betrayed, used, as she had never felt before. "When? Who?"

Alaric had the grace to look momentarily ashamed, but only momentarily. Her indignation roused in him a righteous anger. How dare she question his actions? "Aye, I am to be betrothed," he admitted, tight-jawed. "In ten days I travel to London, and there and then will we exchange our vows, if we find each other pleasing. Within the year we will be wed. The maiden's name is Meredyth, and she hails from distant Powys, in the lands of Wales, far east of here. 'Tis said—"

"I care not what is said!" she spat, a look of utter hatred in her eyes. "Why did you say nothing of this to me before? Why?"

"It does not concern you, woman. Why should I speak of it?"

"Not concern me? It should not *concern* me that you have but used me as your—your whore—until such time as your bride could fill my place in your bed? You arrogant, heartless, lecherous—foul *Saxon!*"

He looked at her long and hard, mentally handing Cullen a purse of fifty gold mancuses, for of a certainty the expression on her face was a jealous one, and a betrayed one. And a deeply wounded one.

"Nothing need change between us," he coaxed. "We may go

252

on as we have before."

"Fool!" she retorted, the tears spilling freely down her cheeks. "Everything will be changed!" *Ja*, it would, it had to, for she could not share him with another, nay, would not. Why? *Because you love him, fool!* came the harsh, accusatory voice of her conscience. *You love him!* And despite all her fantasies, her wishes that it be so, he did not love her in return.

She lay back, shrugging off his hands, staring fixedly up above her and gulping painfully time and time again to swallow the knot that lodged in her throat. Between two leafy boughs silvery threads had been spun, a miniature causeway that winked in the sunlight. Busily weaving at its heart was the spider herself, a large, long-legged brown horror that nimbly juggled warp and weft to build her trap. *Kendra*, Freya thought, looking at it, unkind in her new hurt. She smiled grimly as she blinked away fresh, jealous tears.

Freya would not have smiled, even grimly, had she but known that her malicious fantasies regarding Kendra were not far wrong. While Alaric and she lay side by side in stony silence in the curling, tender green ferns of the chase, or later raced their fleet horses homeward along the beach and ignored, as it washed over their mounts' hooves, the creamy froth of the inrunning tide that they usually took such pleasure in, the woman Kendra was already about her web-weaving, although in distant Winchester, and in time they would all become entangled in its sticky—and deadly—trap.

Kendra spun her hateful web with strands as black and bitter as her heart. She silently railed at Aethelfreda, her mother, who had foolishly fallen victim to a common peasant's lust and survived his rape of her; the woman who had given her a bastard's birth, then left her infant daughter to her sister Valonia's care, while she had gone herself to seek the cold and pious comfort of the cloisters of Our Lady of the Sea, there to hide her shame.

She railed at her own hot blood, at the fool's impulse that had driven her to wed Farant. Oh, what an impatient idiot she had been! Why had she not bided her time, why? But then, she amended, perhaps it had not been such a rash move after all. Who would ever have thought that Alaric would survive those long, grueling years spent battling the Danes through marshes and fens, living off his wits? Yet survive he had, and returned to Kenley to claim his inheritance, and in so doing, Farant's chances of becoming ealdorman in his stead, as second son, had dwindled to naught. Consequently Kendra had also been reduced to nothing yet again, the wife of a lowly second son with neither title nor wealth nor rank, save that which his brother lord would, from time to time, generously endow him.

Seeing Alaric now as a man grown, strong and comely in both face and form, and with a smoldering, smoky glance that turned the blood to molten honey in her veins, had convinced her still further that it had been folly indeed to wed Farant. Ah, such a man was Alaric, a lusty, masterful man who'd take a woman to his bed and give her endless pleasure of his virile body, aye, and in diverse ways, no doubt! So must the slave, Freya, that little sharp-clawed cat, have learned, though it had appeared the girl as yet had little liking for the bed sport, and still less for her master himself. But—and here the ebony-haired Kendra pursed her cherry-red lips in displeasure—Alaric did not appear to feel the same about her. Oh no! Any fool could see that he panted after the Viking slut like a dog sniffing after a bitch in heat, and that was the real reason he had wanted her to withdraw her accusations of witchcraft; he lusted after the girl! Curse her—her youth, her beauty, everything about her. Something must be done about the Lady Freya, and soon. Something irrevocable, for which she, Kendra, could not be blamed. And if that something should perchance include her spineless Farant—well, who was she to complain . . . ?

Chapter 19

While Kendra plotted and spun her webs of intrigue, Freya continued to simmer in a broth of jealous fury, a fury no little enhanced by the Lady Valonia's insistence, some ten days later, that Freya should accompany her to the town of London, with others of her ladies.

"By your leave, mistress, I would rather stay here at Kenley," she had insisted sulkily. She had no wish to be there when Alaric took vows to bind himself to another.

But Valonia would have none of her protests, and for reasons of her own insisted the girl should go. "Would you deny me your company, child?" she coaxed and scolded. "In truth, there is not one among my ladies whose companionship I prefer to your own. And besides, a visit to a large and bustling township such as London will afford you an opportunity to show off those new kirtles that I gave you. 'Twill be an adventure, Freya, I promise thee!"

Eventually Freya gave in, though with less grace than Valonia might have wished, and now, ten days later, as she disembarked from Alaric's river barge into the town itself, looked about her with an avid curiosity that temporarily made her forget her recent sulky demeanor.

London was larger and more densely inhabited than any town or village that Freya had ever seen. There seemed to be people everywhere, from richly dressed chieftains and their retinue upon horseback to humble folk scurrying up and down the dirt streets about their labors, with perhaps heavy faggots of wood bowing their backs, or else produce in wicker baskets that they were taking to sell at some market or other, for there were markets aplenty.

Along the wharves themselves Freya spied stout merchant ships from over a dozen different continental ports, Saxony and Francia among them, ample proof to her mind that although it was not the capital city of the Saxon lands of Wessex (an honor that went to Winchester, where King Alfred kept court), London was indeed its center of trade, as its reputation boasted. The serpentine Thames was the artery of that trade, bringing the ships and their cargoes that were its lifeblood to its throbbing heart.

Horses were hired to carry them to Alaric's town residence, a hall far smaller than Kenley but equally well appointed, with colorful tapestries and fine platters and goblets. As they rode to it, Freya was round-eyed at the number of dwellings that lined the streets, which, although but simple cottages, boasted doors of sturdy planks with, by Loki, locks! There were literally hundreds of such dwellings, and for every score or so huts, or so it seemed to her eyes, there was a Christian church. She smiled secretly to herself. The people of London must indeed be a wicked lot, to require so many holy temples to their White Christ!

If there was one thing that did not please her about London, it was the foul smell everywhere, for middens and refuse piles abounded on every side, overflowing and with their complements of swine and mangy dogs and swarming flies. Still, with so many people in such proximity, such drawbacks did not surprise her. It would have been a miracle if it were not so! Nonetheless, she made a mental note to herself never, ever to live in such a thriving town, whatever other attractions it might have to offer. She much preferred the sweet, grassy perfume of rural air, or the sharp, clean, briny tang from off the sea, to this stink.

She assisted the Lady Valonia to unpack her robes and such, surprised to see that it was close to dusk by the time they were settled and finally done.

"You may retire after supper," Valonia informed her as Freya brushed out her mistress's fair braids, "and rest yourself well for what comes on the morrow. There will be many of our Wessex noblemen and women at the Ealdorman of London's hall, as well as Lord Eamonn and his retinue from Wales, and I would have you show yourself to advantage before them."

"Advantage, my lady?" Freya asked with a puzzled frown. She and Valonia had become friends over the past weeks, and she knew that her best interests were always uppermost in the gracious Saxon lady's mind, but she was at a loss to know why her appearance on the morrow should concern the woman. "Why?"

Valonia smiled one of her increasingly frequent mysterious smiles. "If there must be a reason, then let it be said that I would not have one of my ladies-in-waiting outshone by those of a lady of Wales."

"I see," Freya murmured, though in truth she did not see at all.

As she left Valonia's bower for Alaric's, she all but collided with Ordway, about to retire himself. His eyes narrowed as he saw who it was, and stern faced, he crooked his finger and bade her draw aside into a private alcove to speak with him.

"On the morrow, you will do naught to draw attention to yourself, wench, do you hear me? One word out of place, a single gesture on your part to ruin all that I have done to bring about this betrothal, and you will be punished!"

"I understand quite well, my lord," she retorted with scant civility, livid that he should think her capable of such a thing. "Will that be all, sir?"

"For now, aye," he growled, and strode away.

Alaric's bower was empty, and she learned from Ham, his body servant, that the ealdorman had gone out to seek entertainment at the bear pits and cockfights that were plentiful in London. Ham did not expect him to return before dawn. This news pleased Freya, for since the day she had learned Alaric was to be betrothed she had found it hard to be close to him without suffering agonies of jealousy. She ate a light supper, bathed and washed her hair, mindful of Valonia's advice and heedless of superstition, and retired. Her last thoughts before she quickly fell asleep, drained by the exciting

257

upriver journey on Alaric's barge and all the other events of the day, were of the Welsh maid. What would she look like? Would Alaric find her pleasing to the eye? Oh, how she prayed the maid would be ugly as sin itself! Frey make it so!

Fair Meredyth of Powys! Better they had named her the Wilting Lily of Wales, that simpering milksop, that faint-heart of a wench, Freya thought the next morning, glowering across the hall at the company of Saxon nobles.

Oh, but she was fair, that part of it was no lie—more was the pity, she thought miserably. Compared to the fragile Meredyth, Freya felt large and ungainly, like a gaudy parrot shown to disadvantage by a dainty black-feathered merle. Aye, Meredyth's hair was as black as Kendra's, yet straight and shining as a dark waterfall. Her complexion was pale alabaster, tinted a delicate rose that owed more to art, Freya decided spitefully, than health or vigor. Her eyes were a clear, pure blue—even if they were somewhat vacant and set a little too close together in her heart-shaped face to be beautiful—and her body was as small and finely boned as a child's. And nigh as *flat!* Her voice, too, reminded Freya of a little girl's, thin and lisping, her phrases the faintly complaining outpourings of a spoiled brat. How Freya would have loved to pinch her, to tear out hanks of that shining dark hair and hear her caterwaul in distress!

Yet none of Freya's feelings showed in her face as the Welsh maid, robed in lavender bordered with hems of purple, delicate chains of silver crisscrossed between her impoverished breasts, passed by her on her father's arm, and swept Alaric a deep and graceful curtsey. She fluttered her lashes at him coyly as he bent low to kiss her hand.

"Lord Alaric of Kent, my lord father, Eamonn of Powys, and myself, his daughter Meredyth, bid you fond welcome to London!" she lisped, and Freya all but choked on the sickening simper in her tone.

"Word of your beauty has reached us in Kent from distant Powys, Lady Meredyth," Alaric responded, equally sickening to Freya's ears. He was smiling as he raised the girl to her feet and offered her his arm. "Yet meager words fall far short when employed to describe thee! Lord Eamonn, your lovely daughter outshines the brightest jewel."

Now Freya was certain she would retch . . .

Lord Eamonn, a burly, bearded thane with a bulging belly, threw back his silvered dark head and laughed. "I would be a liar if I said I disagreed with you, Lord Alaric! Come, come, daughter, see the ealdorman served with wine to refresh himself, while his uncle and I discuss—certain matters!" He winked broadly at his blushing daughter and motioned her away, turning to Ordway of Kenley who, smiling himself, awaited him nearby.

"At last we meet, Eamonn of Powys," Freya heard the Kentish seneschal say, "and not before time. Tell me, how was the sea voyage from Wales . . . ?"

They moved away, Ordway's arm slung familiarly about Eamonn's broad back. Yet as they went, Alaric's uncle gave her a piercing glance over his shoulder that was loaded with warning. *Stay out of this. Be silent, or you will regret it!* the look he gave her seemed to say, and she was reminded sharply yet again of the enmity he bore her for his sister's sake. Freya flushed angrily. What had stuffy Ordway expected her to do—cause some scene that might destroy Alaric's chances of betrothal with that milksop heifer, with whom he now sat so companionably, sipping wine from a brimming horn that Meredyth, curse her, had herself filled for him? Ha! Why should she care if he chose to wed, gift, and bed such a—a *ninny!* Like as not, on their wedding night the bride would faint clear away at first sight of her lord husband's eager staff, and swoon senseless to their bridal bed! The image gave her enormous relish. She let loose a merry chuckle—a chuckle that was abruptly silenced by yet another stern glance, this from Alaric. Imperiously he beckoned to her, unsmiling. Gritting her teeth, she made her way gracefully across the rushes to his side.

"My lord?"

He looked up from his seat at table, his expression bland, no inkling of his emotions revealed in his gray eyes. They might have been strangers. "Bring me another flagon from the kitchens, wench. This one is nigh empty," he commanded.

"At once, sir," Freya ground out, and turned smartly on her heel to do his bidding. If he thought to make her jealous, he would fail, she determined. Let him dally with his simpering Meredyth! In truth, they deserved each other!

A fresh flagon was soon filled, and despite her mood she bore it from the dish-thane's hand in the kitchens and back to Alaric without losing a drop, and set it carefully upon the trestle table before the cooing pair.

"Is there anything else you require, sir?" she asked sweetly, the very picture of the most dutiful of serving women.

"Meredyth?" he asked the Welsh maid.

"A dish of sweetmeats would be most welcome, dear Alaric," Meredyth suggested with a coy little smile and a disclaiming shrill titter that put Freya in mind of a horse's whinny. "I confess, sir, I have a sweet tooth!"

"As sweet as your lovely self, Meredyth," Alaric rejoined gallantly, and blinked at the fierce blast of heat that seemed to smolder of a sudden from Freya's eyes and singe him. He hid a grin. "Sweetmeats for the lady, girl, and make haste!" he commanded in lordly fashion.

"I will fly like the very wind, Lord Alaric," Freya vowed caustically, and once again disappeared.

Meredyth's narrow eyes narrowed still further. "Her accent is strange to me, sir," she said. "From where does your slave girl come? Francia? Or Saxony, mayhap?"

"She is a Dane," Alaric supplied sourly.

"Ah, I thought as much," Meredyth murmured with satisfaction. "'Tis said that Norsewomen are all as tall and ugly as giantesses." While Alaric choked on his wine, she covered her small mouth to hide a delicate yawn. "My lord father says they have the constitution of plough horses—and the same claim to beauty. I see he was not far wrong."

Freya had returned by now, and had caught the latter half of the Lady Meredyth's conversation. Rage filled her so, the platter of berry tarts and little almond cakes trembled in her fist. Plough horses indeed! she fumed. Why, that spiteful little ninny, she'd be sor——

"That will be all, girl," Alaric warned, jerking the platter from her hand and offering it to Meredyth as he saw Freya's mouth drop open and the brilliant sapphire flash that sparked suddenly in her eyes.

"My lord, I wished only to say that—" she began, thoroughly incensed.

"I told thee that would be all, wench!" he thundered. "Be gone from here, and await me in my apartments!"

Livid, she swung about and stormed from the hall, ignoring the Lady Valonia's questioning expression as she brushed past her. I should have said it anyway, she seethed as she left, her anger in full spate, I should have told that—that lickspittle Meredyth that I had heard the women of Wales also resembled plough horses—but plough horses viewed from the rear! It would have been well worth risking a whipping to have retaliated in kind!

Back in Alaric's bower, she flung herself sulkily upon his bed and lay there staring up at the smoke-blackened rafters. What was this war her emotions waged within her? She'd vowed many times that she'd belong to no man, least of all to him. She'd thought she yearned once again to be as free as the very winds that blew over the sea, and yet—and yet the thought of Alaric wedding the Welsh woman made her yearn to take Meredyth's place! Was this love, then? That wanting always to be with, if not belong to, one man and no other? And feeling as she did, could she ever hope to be free, truly free, ever again, she wondered sadly? Truly, we are all slaves of one fashion or another, she decided; some to greed, others to lust and the other vices, others, such as I, to their fickle hearts.

She was almost asleep, having exhausted herself with plotting ingenious and bloodthirsty means by which to bring about the Lady Meredyth's sudden—and exquisitely painful—demise, when the bells from what sounded like a thousand Christian churches let loose a deafening carillon that reverberated in her ears and set her head to clanging with them.

Bong! Dong! Dang! Bing! Dong!

Enough! She covered her ears with her hands and stuck her head under a feather-filled cushion. Why had Valonia insisted she should accompany her here, to this hateful, stinking, noisy city that closely resembled the lowliest Viking cesspit? And why had Alaric eagerly agreed she should do so? To make her jealous of his Meredyth? To force an admission from her? To make her say she loved him? Odin's Toenails, she'd sooner kiss the soles of Meredyth's tight slippers than admit to any such thing. If Alaric expected her to do so, he'd have a long, l-o-n-g wait!

She tossed the cushion aside and sat up, heedless of the untidy disarray of her braided coronet, from which red-gold tendrils had escaped to give her a wanton look, or the wrinkling of the lovely pale green kirtle with the orphreys of gold that she had donned so becomingly—and with such fierce pride—at Valonia's command that same morn. Why should she stay here, and meekly wait on Alaric's return? Why give that—that Saxon popinjay the satisfaction of finding her idly twiddling her thumbs when he did so, with naught to occupy her thoughts or restless hands but jealous visions of him and his lily-livered Meredyth together? She'd show him. When he returned, she'd be gone! She'd not escape, would not attempt that here in London, where her foreignness would be remarked and she'd be easily recaptured. But she'd show him nonetheless. She'd go exploring, and be gone long enough to cause him to wonder when—or if—she'd ever come back.

But when, several hours later, she sneaked past the men-at-arms and back into Alaric's bower, her face dropped in disappointment. Despite the lateness of the hour, he had yet to return!

A sulky pout dragged down the corners of her mouth, and what felt suspiciously akin to tears prickled behind her eyes. Had Meredyth, Frey forbid it, enticed him to her bed? Mayhap, though it seemed unlikely Meredyth would have possessed sufficient cunning. Freya cursed under her breath. She had not wanted to consider the idea of Alaric wedding another, and so she had not even deigned to ask him what a Christian marriage might entail. Perhaps this wedding part of it included the consummation, the ritual sharing of the marriage bed? Oh, the thought of him touching that—that mealymouthed flounder with desire in his eyes, of him bedding her, of Meredyth's lily-white fingers caressing his hard, manly body, made her blood boil with rage!

She was still a-simmer when Alaric at last returned. He noted the impatient, hostile way in which she drummed her fingers upon the scrivener's desk, and grimaced. She seemed in a high spate of temper, and after having smiled all day until he feared his face would crack, and listened to Meredyth's inane chatter and her father's fawning praises until he feared his ears would deafen in defense, he was ill-pleased to return to find a jealous shrew awaiting him in his bower.

"Idle yet again, woman? I should have known better than to expect to find my goblet filled, and my bath drawn. No doubt the Lady Merry will teach you your place and your duties in good time, however." He smiled mockingly. "We exchanged our wedding vows this afternoon. Next year at Easter we will be gifted, and Merry will be my lady wife. I will wait with bated breath for that golden day!" he lied.

To his fury, and yes, his disappointment, she eyed him calmly and then spat, with great deliberation and no little expertise, into the fire on the hearth. There was a loud sizzle. "Your Lady Meredyth—*that* is what I think of her, my lord!"

He faced her with his fists planted solidly on his hips, his booted feet braced aggressively apart. Ire crackled in the smoke-hue of his eyes and knotted his dark brow. His swarthy jaws were even darker in his rage, and his lips were thin and hard, with no hint of softness now. In his dark blue tunic and dark trousers, his huge, towering frame etched against the firelight, he made a threatening figure indeed. Not one, however, that intimidated Freya!

If his stance was rigid, then hers was more so. Tangled bright hair tossed over her shoulders, her own small fists lodged on her hips, she had determined to draw the first blood—a rigorous attack being the surest form of defense. She'd not relinquish him to his Meredyth without a fight! "And how *dare* you compare me, a Viking noblewoman, unfavorably to that— that whey-faced Welsh peasant, curse thee, Saxon!" she railed. "'Merry' is it now? Ha! I would sooner be compared badly to a—a mushroom, than that spiritless creature! In truth, a mushroom has more spine."

"Aye, I believe you have much in common," he agreed

acidly, "you and a mushroom being alike in cunning. But enough of my affairs. They need not concern you, hellion! Tell me, are your wits addled that you would leave this bower and my protection, and wander the city streets alone? Answer me!"

So. Some mealymouthed guardsman had noted her departure and reported it to him, had he? For a fleeting moment surprise robbed her of words, but she recovered well. "Your *protection*, my lord?" she retorted scathingly. "Thor's Toenails! 'Tis unlikely you even noticed my absence in the hall, sir, let alone took steps to ensure I was protected in this city, so closely did you cling to that vapid lily flower, may she sleep on stinging nettles!"

He did not reveal that, on being informed of her leaving the bower, he had sent a man on foot after her, to rescue her if she ran afoul of trouble. Nay, he would not grant her the satisfaction of learning that! "I will do as I wish, wench. I need no permission for my acts, not from you, nor anyone else. And you will do as I say. You too readily forget that I am your lord and master—as the Lady Merry will soon be your mistress." The latter comment gave him vicious pleasure, touching as it must upon an especially raw nerve—aye, a raw and jealous one.

"'Twill never be! If I must answer to her for the very food that touches my lips, I'll starve first," she flared. "If you must endure her company, then you have only yourself to blame, for 'twas you who agreed to wed the ninny. I made no such vow. And I will not abide in your household with that—that—ooohh!" Words sufficiently lurid to describe the hated Meredyth quite failed her. With an exasperated snarl she flung about and paced the bower, arms crossed over her heaving bosom.

For a second or two Alaric was dumbfounded by her audacity. Was there no manner in which he might tame this Viking vixen? When he finally found his voice, it was like thunder. "What is this you say? You will not *abide* in the same household as the Lady Meredyth? Ha! On the contrary, *slave,* you will not only abide with her, you will serve and honor her as your lady mistress, as will all members of my household!"

"Huh! I would sooner serve a—a smelly goat's cheese, than

serve her!"

"A *goat's cheese?*" he sputtered. "Hold your tongue, girl, before you push me too far!" His expression turbulent as a dark stormcloud, he paced back and forth, back and forth.

"Aye, a goat's cheese—all sickly curds and whey! My Lady Goat-Cheese, I shall address her—*ja*, I like it! It has a moldy, sour ring to it, does it not, my lord, and suits her well!" she continued in reckless glee, her sapphire eyes bluer than the bluest of cornflowers. She flung her unbound hair over her shoulders and thrust out her breasts, a challenge in her stance and expression. Look what I have to offer, fire and spirit and hot blood, her manner seemed silently to declare, while she has nothing! Oh, how his gray eyes smoldered with rage and dark desire, however unwillingly felt: how brooding was his expression, how clenched his fists! She would not be at all surprised should smoke suddenly stream from his nostrils, or his eyes glow demon red! Her jealousy was quite dispersed to see him thus! Despite his anger, he wanted her, wanted her badly, she knew . . .

He lunged for her. She sprang out of his reach and sped across the bower to take refuge behind the writing desk.

"Nay, my lord, you must touch me not!" she taunted. "Your betrothed will be most displeased—aye, even curdled!—should she hear you've lain with your plough-horse slave wench!"

"I mean to thrash thee, wench, not bed thee," he stormed, stalking her with all his hunter's virile grace. The light in his gray eyes was murderous.

"Liar!" she countered, breathless with excitement now. "You desire me, and I know it. By Odin's loins, you cannot think to hide your lust from me, Alaric! I know thee far too well! And besides, sweet, lying lord, your mighty staff has—risen—to the moment! It makes havoc not only of your vows, but also of the smooth, flat line of your breeks!" She giggled, a throaty, taunting, seductive sound, and backed away from him.

Full well he knew she spoke the truth, for he was indeed hard with lust for her! His breeks, as she had so wickedly pointed out, were bulging! He cursed her long and at length as he dived toward her and caught her by the wrist, spinning her back against his chest. "Then thus will I 'punish' thee, witch," he gritted, each unsteady breath forced, harsh and labored, from between his tightly clenched lips.

She made a grand display of reluctance as she hammered her fists to escape his steely, ungentle embraces, summoning all her considerable wiry strength to give her protests weight. She clawed at his ruggedly handsome face with her nails, drumming her heels as they fought in the hope that a chance blow would batter his groin. She gnashed her teeth against the tender web of flesh at the angle of his throat and shoulder, yet all her struggles were in vain—to her enormous delight! At length he tossed her scornfully to the bed and quickly dropped down beside her.

"I win, my warrior maid," he muttered in obvious triumph, glaring down into her flushed and lovely face. But he saw how she smiled, like a cat with a plump mouse between its paws, and his triumph faded.

A sparkling merriment filled her naughty eyes. "Do you, Alaric? Or—am I the winner?" she asked sweetly, and gave him an arch flutter with her lashes.

Before he could respond, she knotted her slender fingers in his inky black hair and dragged his head roughly down to hers. Their faces now but a hairbreadth apart, he saw her nostrils flare, the faint quiver of her moist, parted lips, the naked desire for him that glittered in her jewel eyes. "I want you, Alaric," she whispered throatily, heat spreading through her belly. "Kiss me! Kiss me—and more!"

He needed no second urging. With a low, animal growl he covered her lips with his mouth and returned the ardor of her moist and eager mouth with a savagery that left her breathless. His hunger for her was enormous, his desire a savage beast that ruled him utterly. He let it rule.

She writhed beneath him in wanton abandon, pressing and arching her supple curves against his hard lines, little mewling cries breaking against his lips in her frenzy. Her hands moved over him in feverish caresses, as if by touch alone she could weld their flesh together, like steel forged in fire. She stroked the springy dark curls that matted his chest, and gasped in sheer delight as her hand swept downward to explore the flat plateau of his rock-hard belly. And further down her hand found his manhood, a column of burning steel sheathed in velvet, arrogant and ready—and aye, hers for the asking! Her eyes closed in delight as she stroked him, felt the quickening throb of his hot blood as his body responded to her caresses.

He sank back onto the sleeping couch, his fingers still tangled in her hair, sweat bleeding from his brow and springing out upon his chest like amber beads of oil in the rushlight, as she skillfully brought him nearer and still nearer to the brink.

"Oh, sweet Jesu!" he groaned in unrequited lust as she released him in the very nick of time, and leaned up to draw off her kirtle.

Beneath it she was naked, save for the red-gold veil of her hair that streamed down over creamy breasts and shoulders. Where it caught the meager moonlight that streamed through the wind-eye, it shone like faerie filaments of copper and gold. Her long-lashed eyes were lambent sapphire pools as she gazed like a greedy child with a treasured toy upon his magnificent, virile body sprawled before her. His broad torso was lean, not an ounce of spare flesh anywhere. Dark hair lay upon his chest and lightly furred his hard belly like a jealous shadow. His shoulders wore hard curves of sinew that flexed like bowstrings, lashed taut to the bow, as he reached for her.

She evaded his arms with a low, silvery trill of laughter that made the breath catch in his throat. She pressed him down onto his back and leaned seductively over him, no longer a child now, but all that was woman. She was a wicked temptress, a pagan high priestess of passion, offering up her lovely breasts in sacrifice to her god, his eager mouth. The nipples rose tumescently against his lips, hard nubbins of exquisitely sensitive flesh. He nipped at each one, grazed each in turn with sweetly savage teeth, until she uttered little bird cries of passion; then he drew each rosy crest deep into the fiery dark whirlpool of his mouth, there to suffer delicious tortures from his teasing tongue.

"Now, my Bear!" she whispered hoarsely, aquiver with yearning. "Please, now!" She ached to feel him hot and deep inside her . . .

He sat up, grasped her writhing hips and held her still, before turning her over onto her belly. Wordlessly he knelt above her and raised her hips, briefly stroking the rosy, rounded curves of her bottom before arching forward to fill her silken sheath from behind. His hands slipped under her to fondle her breasts and toy maddeningly with the puckered crests, and she writhed and bucked in a frenzy of ecstasy.

Oh, the piercing heat and strength of him! She pressed her flushed face against the coverlet and closed her eyes, drowning in sensation, driven mad with rapture as he took and took and took . . . and she gave. Their gasping breaths filled the darkened bower. With them sounded the creaking protests of the bed as their lusty, energetic mating taxed the ancient wooden slats to the very limit. On he rode her, on and on and on, until the tense knot in her belly grew unbearable, and she begged and implored him for a release he would not grant. In answer to her pleas, he withdrew from her and turned her onto her back, drinking in her beauty, the hectic color of her eyes and cheeks, as if they were wine for which he thirsted.

"Now will I watch your eyes as you give yourself to me," he whispered huskily. "And at the moment when your soul takes flight to bliss, my own will join it!" He parted her thighs and knelt between them, his strong flanks spreading her open and ready for his entry. As he lunged into her, she embraced his hips with her long, slender legs, then sank her teeth into the flesh of his shoulder. Her nails gouged into his smooth back as her passion for him soared.

The throbbing, the pulsing began, wondrously bursting upon her as a tree explodes in a brilliant blast of fire when struck by lightning. Alaric saw the naked rapture in her eyes and felt his own passion gather and build unbearably in his loins. With a hoarse cry, an anguished roar, he spent himself deep in her belly, and her cries and whimpers of joy mingled with the sounds torn from him—and with the sudden clamor of bells.

"Frey be praised!" she gasped weakly. "What—what magic mating is this? I hear bells, my dearest Bear! Bells!"

"Foolish wench," he muttered fondly against her ear, "'tis the church bells that you hear, ringing matins!" He chuckled deep in his throat.

"Oh!" she responded sleepily, and stifled a sated yawn. "Well, I trust they do not waken your Lady Meredyth from her beauty sleep. She needs all she can get, think you not?"

Alaric, his drowsy face buried in a feather-filled pillow to block out the joyous but strident carillon, nodded drowsily, then added—somewhat belatedly—"Lady who?"

"Oh, no one of import," she reassured him wickedly. "Sleep now, my beloved, lusty Bear!"

With a smug little smile on her lips, Freya snuggled into the curve of his hard, massive body and promptly plummeted into an exhausted sleep.

Chapter 20

Sven awoke in his spartan cell at the monastery of Mucking long before dawn lightened the eastern sky, his old heart thudding with the aftermath of a dream.

He rose from his hard cot and staggered to a basin set within a stone alcove, there splashing his face with cold water to thoroughly waken himself. This done, he went stiffly to the narrow wind-eye of his cell and drew aside the coarse covering.

Lightning danced on the distant hillsides, and the dawning sky bore a faintly greenish hue. The air was strangely still, with no hint of a breeze, and the scent of rain and a coming storm came sharp and crackling on the air. Could his vision have been false, he wondered, a product of the storm that threatened and to which his senses had attuned themselves? But, as quickly, he acknowledged that he dare not take the chance that it was, *nej*, dare not!

As he slept, he had seen his little Freya entangled in a dark net—nay, a web!—of evil, trying vainly to escape the folds that closed ever tighter about her. Her face had been wet with tears, her sapphire eyes haunted with grief. Beside her had been Alaric, his wrists and ankles chained, a terrible agony in his eyes. A large mirror had been set across from him, reflecting his tortured image. Even as Sven had looked on in horrified fascination and confusion, the mirror had abruptly shattered, a million glittering shards exploding into the air to land with a tinkling sound that went on and on all about them.

Sven had glanced down at the shards, and had been shocked

and fallen back a pace or two, crossing himself. Each shard, every tiny, crystal splinter, had thrown back the same awful image: that of Alaric's face, the eyes vacant in death, the mouth agape! Blessed Virgin, what did it all mean, what? he wondered fearfully. Though his visions were often so mystical and obscure, he could discern no rhyme nor reason, nay, not to this one, though it filled him with a dread that spread through him like the gripping tentacles of some sea monster. He could not begin to explain it, he realized unhappily. Nonetheless, the danger to his beloved Freya was clear. Moving swiftly despite the morning stiffness of his old wound, he turned to his desk.

Day had broken when he set aside pen and ink and sanded his urgent missive. There. It was done! He had only to see the letter carried on its way to Kenley, and all would be well. There was a gardener who tended the monastery's quadrangles and cloisters—he would see it delivered. Dear Father in Heaven, he prayed, make my little Freya heed its contents!

For the first time since he had entered the monastery, the old Viking convert wished he were free of his holy vows and could carry the letter to Kenley himself, to make certain that this time she did.

"Attend me!" Alaric barked, and hurt and confused by his brusque manner, Freya shrugged and hurried after him.

If their relationship had been strained prior to Alaric's betrothal in London, it was doubly strained now, she thought sadly, despite the lusty coupling they had shared that night, and she had no idea why. He now came rarely to his bower by night, and by day was often absent from his hall. His mood, when she saw him for any length at all, was brooding and irritable. Though she ached to be with him as before, though she missed his lovemaking, she had felt nothing but relief each time he left her alone again, for to be with him now made her brooding and irritable too. What was he about, she wondered?

He led the way through the hall and outside, to the bailey, and she thought as they went that she had never seen his face so harsh, nor so masculinely beautiful, all at once. Apprehension quivered in her belly. Something was deeply wrong, she sensed. His features were so dark, stern, and set, it was as if they were sculpted from stone. She wanted to cry out, to ask what, what she could have done to displease him so! But she feared his answer would be one she would not care to hear, and so she said nothing.

Lady Valonia, her bower woman, and the lady's priest, dressed in a flowing, hooded robe, waited by horses and a little donkey held by grooms, saddled and ready for them, in the bailey . . .

"Do you have all in readiness, my lady aunt?" Alaric demanded.

"Aye," Valonia acknowledged, her disapproval of whatever it was he intended evident in her unusually grim expression. "Here is the pack of provisions, the sword you asked for, the waterskin, the talismans, and the mantle. Give them to Lord Alaric, child," she instructed the bower maid, and the serving girl hurried forward, nigh bowed down with her weighty burdens.

Alaric took the luxurious fox-fur mantle from her and draped it about Freya's shoulders, forcing himself as he did so not to look into her wide, confused sapphire eyes. He did not dare to look! He knew if he once gazed into those shimmering jeweled pools, ready to brim over with crystal tears—if he allowed himself so much as a single glance at her lovely, glowing face, saw her expression of hurt and bewilderment— he would be lost, his purpose set aside in the hopeless yet unquenchable fires of his love for her. So instead he silently handed her her sword, the one with the gem-encrusted hilt and the silvery blade taken from her in the fierce battle the day she had led the attack against Kenley, and indicated with a curt nod that she should mount up.

Filled with dread, Freya clambered astride the dappled gray palfrey she had always ridden, seeing now that a spare horse, a magnificent burnished chestnut, was to accompany them on a leading rein. Spare horses, food packs, weapons—everything indicated they were about to embark upon a journey of some distance. But to where? And for what reason?

The priest scrambled astride his donkey. Alaric swung into the saddle of his massive Lucifer and gave the upraised hand

272

signal to set forth. As the priest followed him toward the gate in the wooden palisades, Valonia picked up her skirts and hurried to Freya's horse, grasping its bridle to stay their departure.

"Though you are not Christian, I will ask my God to watch over thee and see thee kept safe, child!" she cried. There were tears glimmering in her gentle eyes. "And if He is deaf to my prayers, I hope and pray your pagan gods will guard your path. Godspeed and farewell, proud Viking maid!"

Freya had time only to smile her thanks in return and touch the lady's hand gently in parting, before they rode forth from Kenley.

The countryside was drowning in the rare mellow golden sunlight of a perfect late summer afternoon as they rode on in silence, the priest, Alaric, and herself. The beech trees were ablaze with red leaves that heralded autumn's approach; others were decked in radiant gold or flame. Thick grass carpeted their path, so that the horses' hoofbeats were dulled as they rode. The briars were hung heavily with early, glistening blackberries, teardrops of obsidian. The chestnut trees were weighted down with their green prickleballs, and the fruit trees heavily laden with ripe apples and pears. The scents of summer, green and leafy and sweet with nature's bounty, tantalized the nostrils. The fresh and bracing coolness of the breeze teased color into Freya's pale cheeks and sent red-gold curls furling behind her.

They traversed the meadow and quickly rode on through the still, radiant woods, then turned their mounts northeastward, a direction that they had never taken on her and Alaric's many rides. The dull thud of their horses' hooves was the only sound, save for the rare shrill scream of a hunting hawk circling high above. Her unease grew with every fraction of a league they traveled. What had the Lady Valonia meant when she bade her God guard her path and protect her, what? A frisson of foreboding chilled her. Ahead lay the winding Thames; beyond, the vast Danelaw—the land now ruled by her own people, the Danes. Did Alaric mean to ransom her, after all this time? To demand *wergild* in exchange for her life? But from whom? And why? Before their visit to London he had seemed to be growing fond of her, had seemed loath to be parted from her overlong. Had his betrothal changed all of that? Had he now determined to rid himself of her, his defiant slave wench, once and for all?

They rode for over an hour without slackening their pace, across watery marshes dotted with willows and alders and thick with standing osiers and reeds, where noisy waterfowl dabbled tails-up. They continued on through denser woods, fording sparkling brooks that burbled noisily over mossy rocks and coming out of the forests' deep shade at last onto rolling heathlands, made rough with purple heather, where sturdy pagan standing stones rose straight and ominous upon the hillside, etched sharply against the pale sky, and cast their dark mystery over the sunlit turf. They served to remind Christian men of the ancient gods who had once held sway in these lands, of Woden and his followers and their secret, bloody rites beneath the full of the moon.

At last the heaths were left behind and they came to a crossroads. A rough dirt track led two ways and was intersected by one of the great, straight cobbled Roman roads that traversed the isle of Britain. Alaric reined in his horse by a low stone shrine erected at this crossing of the ways to honor the Blessed Virgin. He dismounted and knelt before it briefly, then crossed himself and stood to wait while the priest did likewise. Freya accordingly reined in her own mount and sat it quietly while she watched the two men. When the priest had done with his devotions, Alaric came to her mare and lifted her down to stand beside him. His hands were rough upon her waist as he did so, and he would not meet her eyes.

"Begin!" he commanded the priest curtly, and without further ado the holy man reached into the folds of his flowing dark robes and drew forth a rolled parchment. As Alaric, scowling fiercely, stood with his massive arms crossed over his chest and Freya bit her lip in anxiety and cast nervous side glances at him, Brother Cuthbert began to read:

"On this fourteenth day of the month of August does Alaric, chieftain of Kenley, Ealdorman of Kent, and Viceroy to the bretwalda, Alfred of Wessex, grant freedom to the slave, Freya, his bower woman, taken in battle from the Viking host in the summer of this 878th year of Our Lord. At this crossroads,

symbolizing the right of all free men or women to choose their own paths in life, the woman named Freya is hereby granted freedom to go her own way. May any man who tries to pervert this manumission or take this freed woman again as his slave find disfavor with God and all His holy relics. 'Tis witnessed here this very day by your mark, my lord, and by your cleric, Sigmund, and by myself." He looked up, peering expectantly first at Freya, then at his lord, like a wide-eyed, solemn little owl.

Alaric nodded curtly, his hard features betraying nothing. "Very well. It is done, according to the laws of our lands and in the eyes of our church. Your work here is completed, Brother Cuthbert. You may leave us now."

"As you will, sir." To Freya he added, "May Our Blessed Lord open your eyes and take away the heathen darkness that blinds them, daughter. You are free, by the grace of God and his servant, my lord Alaric. Go safely, and in peace!" With that he handed the rolled parchment to Alaric and scrambled astride his donkey, and he and the beast trotted slowly away, back in the direction they had come.

Freya, stunned by what had taken place and the unexpectedness and swiftness of it all, swayed a little where she stood, but said nothing. It was as if she had been dealt a blow to the head, and was unable to organize her thoughts. Even had she been able to think of fitting words to say, her lips seemed padlocked, her tongue a huge, alien beast in her mouth, her throat parched and dry. She had expected—feared—several possible explanations for their journey, but never this! Never this . . .

"You understood?" Alaric asked, his tone gruff. "You are free now. No longer Alaric of Kenley's slave, but a freed woman."

"*Ja,*" she managed to whisper, wondering why, *why* his words had not brought the joy leaping through her that they should have engendered.

"The horse you are riding is yours, and also the spare mount here with it. There is food in this pack for your journey," he continued, pressing it into her suddenly frozen fingers, "enough for several days. There is also a small pouch containing some gold mancuses—more than enough coin to

275

purchase food and lodgings for you on your journey north." A bleak smile curved his hard mouth, softening it for an instant but never reaching his gray eyes. "The sword is your own. No doubt you know its purpose."

"Why?" The single word came out strangled, overly loud, as if torn from her lips. Her heart fluttered madly like a snared bird against her ribs.

"Why? 'Tis a strange question coming from thee, Freya," he said softly, and reached out to twine one of her errant flame curls about his finger, thought better of it, and dropped his hand to his side.

He remembered with a pang how he had once imagined her cloaked as she was now, in a rich mantle of tawny furs, and saw that the reality far surpassed even his fanciful imaginings. Her hair glowed like flame against the gleaming russet fur, and her eyes were bluer than the costliest of sapphires. Her satin cheeks, pale as the finest cream, had been tinted delicately rose by the wind, and her mouth was the tempting color of wild strawberries. By Blessed Saint Augustine, was there to be no lessening of the agony within him? Would her beauty be forever etched in crystal imagery upon his soul? The ache within him swelled, became a fierce knot of misery lodged in his heart, a wound as searing and deep as any dealt by the thrust of a blade. When he spoke again his tone was harder, harsher than he intended.

"From the first you railed against my mastery over you. From the first you sought escape from my burh. Now that your freedom is granted you, you ask me why?" He laughed, and it was a bitter, twisted sound. "Go, Viking! Hurry north to your bloody kinsmen, and forget that you were ever enslaved!" He thrust the parchment into her hands, turned on his heel, and strode quickly to his horse, mounting it and cruelly turning its head back toward Kenley. He took no last backward glance at her. He did not dare! Instead he gritted his teeth and rode swiftly away.

Fists clenched, Freya remained standing where she was as if frozen to the spot, as if felled by lightning. She did not move, afraid if she did so she would run after him and beg him not to go, to take her with him back to Kenley. The mellow light seemed dimmed now, its gold tarnished and dull. The vivid colors of the countryside all about her seemed suddenly brassy, overly bright, to her tear-filled eyes. How swiftly it had been done! One moment she had been his in every way. And now she was—not his. Free. Ah, *ja*, free! The word had become a curse! What was this freedom he had granted her? A mockery. Words, only words. They did not ease her pain. They did nothing to free her enslaved heart. Forever and for always, it would be his! And whether he had freed her or nay, so would she, she acknowledged dully. She closed her eyes tightly, her fingers clamping about the rolled parchment so that it crackled and creased under her grip.

In her mind's eye she saw Alaric's face, strong and beautiful as only a man's could be: the glossy blue-black commas of his inky hair spilling about his brow and rugged jaw. The smoky eyes that seemed to ignite as he looked into hers and smolder with lambent, silvery blue-gray fires. His firm, sweet mouth. The hard, broad strength of his powerful body, pressed close to hers. The gentle caress of his callused warrior's hands upon her . . .

Blessed Frey, she was not free! she raged silently, her heart swelling with pain. She would never be free—nay, not this way! The time for pride had long since passed. If she let pride rule her now, she would be a slave to misery forever! Better an Alaric shared with the mewling Meredyth than no Alaric at all! Flinging about, she ran to her horse and threw herself astride it, lashing the reins across its dappled rump as she wheeled it about in the direction Alaric had taken. She scarcely remembered to grasp the other horse's lead rein before she kicked the gray into a gallop.

Alaric had always been gentle with his horses, treating them with a firm but careful hand. He did so out of a deep love and respect for beautiful horseflesh rather than for other reasons, such as safeguarding the valuable beasts he owned. But he was neither gentle nor careful this day. He lashed the great black stallion into a thundering gallop, heedless of treacherous rabbit holes or of sudden rocky outcroppings that could easily trap and break a mount's leg and hurl both it and rider to their deaths upon the hard greensward. They splashed through watery marshes, slipping and sliding up the boggy banks, sending clouds of ducks rising from the dully glinting water into the air in a honking, quacking feathered cloud, and causing the basket weavers, gathering their dried withies on the footpaths amongst the marshlands, to gape at them in alarm. On they rode, the dark man on his dark horse, racing the wind across the rolling grasslands where the evening mist now rose in smoky wraiths from the ground, so that Lucifer seemed to gallop upon air.

The stallion's hooves were a black blur, his mane and tail long, ebony pennants streaming behind them in the wind as they flew, yet still his master urged him on with angry shouts and bitter curses and furious heels, until lather flecked his shining black coat and foam flecked his mouth. It was as if a demon straight from Hell rode Alaric, even as he rode Lucifer, goading him with cruelly sharp spurs to risk his life in this suicidal race.

Race? Aye, race it was, for he sought to outrace the pain inside him, to outdistance it and leave it back there where it belonged, at the crossroads, with *her*. It was a race he knew, deep in his heart, he could not hope to win, indeed had already lost; yet still he fought against it, pressing the valiant ebony beast between his brutal thighs to ever-greater speed, until he knew that to press him further was to burst the stallion's stalwart heart. Indeed, had he ridden a less magnificent, weaker horse, it would already be dead! Angered now at himself and his thoughtless using of a guiltless animal to vent his misery, he calmed somewhat, reined Lucifer in, and slipped from his back.

He walked him in circles for some time to cool him, and then rubbed him down with handfuls of long grass before dropping wearily to sprawl at the base of a tree. The tired stallion came to him and blew affectionately against his neck, nuzzling him for hidden treats. But with a distracted pat Alaric thrust him away, his mind too deep in turmoil to consider anything but Freya.

Squirrels chattered and scolded him from the boughs above, yet he heard nothing. A plump buck rabbit inspected him from a warren, found him threatening, and quickly thumped an alarm to its doe. A vixen slinked past, yet the flirting of her red brush amongst the bare trees failed to draw his eye. It was all to the good, for her russet colors could only have reminded him of Freya . . .

Would he ever feel for Meredyth what he had felt for her, he wondered? Would his bride always be measured against the measuring stick of his feelings for Freya, and found wanting? He feared she would, knew she would. Any other woman would pale against the bright and vibrant memories of her that he carried like wounds upon his heart and soul! *Love.* If this agony of soul, this torment of spirit he felt was love, then in truth he wanted none of it, no part! Must his feelings for her wage an endless blood-feud with his conscience? The wench was a Viking. The daughter of his sworn enemy. The daughter of her who had killed his father and older brothers, and driven his mother to madness. Surely this should be enough to harden his heart to her for all time?

Yet none of that seemed to matter any more. Right or wrong, friend or foe, his heart had chosen her. Had Cullen been right? Had freeing her been the only remaining choice he'd had? He cursed and hurled a small rock at a distant tree trunk, savagely satisfied to see it strike its target squarely. Whatever, it was done. No doubt she was a league or more into the Danelaw by now!

But Freya was far from the Danelaw. She caught up with Alaric toward dusk, finding him quite by accident in a pretty copse upon the crest of a hill, when his weary stallion nickered a greeting to her own mount. Tethering her horses to a bush, she went forward on foot to where he sat. His head was bowed in his hands. His shoulders were slumped. He did not sense her approach, but remained as he was, deep in thought and lost in his own private hell as she came toward him between the beeches and the oaks, stepping gracefully, her feet gliding without sound over the fallen leaves. Two tailors' lengths from him, she halted.

"Alaric?"

His great head jerked up, the gray eyes widening in amazement, then tortured fury. "What—what do you here?"

he demanded hoarsely. "Did I not give you leave to go? Be on your way, confound you!"

"Have I ever done your bidding willingly, sir?" she retorted. "Nay, never! Nor do I intend to start now! You will not get rid of me thus, with a few, pitiful words badly scratched upon vellum, my lord," she murmured scornfully, hurling the crumpled parchment across the grass toward him. "I have returned to you, and by your side will I stay!" Her stubborn little chin came up defiantly, her small fists clenched by her sides. "Say what you will. Do what you will. It will make no difference. Even though you have freed me, my heart, my pride, my very will are yet your eager slaves, curse them! They will suffer no master but thee!" Her mouth quivered. She blinked away sudden tears, wondering if he would refuse her, if he would send her away a second time. If he did, she could not bear it, she knew—!

Silence yawned between them for what seemed an eternity.

"Christ's Wounds! Come to me!" he whispered hoarsely, and he stood, his arms held wide, his whole, massive body trembling with emotion as joy flooded his face.

Never would his life be the same henceforth, he acknowledged silently, for in bidding her come to him he had taken an irrevocable step. Nonetheless, he knew he could not let her go, any more than she would abide sharing him with Meredyth. *Bed, wed, or shed her,* Cullen had said, listing his options. Well, there was only one left open to him now; one that was fraught with difficulties and obstacles. There would be fierce opposition to what he planned, both from Ordway and from others who had no love at all and no little hatred for the Vikings. Aye, in bidding her stay he would be irrevocably changing his life. Yet the knowledge that she had sought to stay with him, wanted him as he wanted her, soared through him, outweighing all else. It was as if a blinding light had been kindled within him, blazing forth from his eyes.

She needed no second urging. With a small cry she flew into those waiting arms, her feet scarce touching the mist-soaked grass. He held her fiercely, cupping her glowing face in his hands as his lips covered hers, his kiss as hungry as her own. Feverish hands caressed her, yet her own trembling hands were little less feverish as they returned each touch, each hungry, yearning caress, measure for sweet measure.

"Hold me, my dearest Bear!" she cried against his rough cheek. "Hold me closely!" And his great arms enveloped her in a fierce embrace in which she felt safe, protected, loved beyond reason and thought, as she had never been loved before, for all time present or yet to come.

She was as bright and warming as a slender, glowing flame in his arms. Desire for her filled him. Love for her dizzied and dazzled him. Tenderly he lifted her up and bore her to the first autumn leaves that lay heaped beneath the tree. There he lay beside her and traced the curve of her cheeks and chin with his finger, stroked the silken red-gold spill of her hair where it tumbled across the leaves, far outshining them in vividness and beauty. Never to hold her, touch her, kiss her again? He had been mad to think he could live thus, without her!

She closed her eyes, a small thrill running through her at his gentle touch, and thrilled again as his lips brushed her eyelids, then her soft mouth, then the warm hollows of her throat. Drawing her closer until her rounded body was pressed against his length, he delighted at the way her tawny head seemed fashioned to fit perfectly into the hollow of his neck, as if made for no other. "My bright and dearest flame," he breathed, inhaling the sweet, elusive sun-fragrance of her. "Where now the icy lips that once disdained mine? Where now the cold, Nordic blood that could not be warmed by the summer fires of my desire? Where now my Freya of the Frozen Heart, my fierce Valkyrie maiden from the north?"

"Tamed, my dearest Bear!" she whispered ardently in return. "Tamed by you. Your summer fires have melted the wintry frost that encased my heart, and now I burn as brightly as do thee!" She laughed, and the silvery sound was filled with joy. "Take me, make me burn anew—sear me with your touch, brand me with your lips—again and yet again—!"

"Aye," he breathed. "Aye!"

He drew the fox-fur mantle down, unfastening with ease the jeweled brooches that held it at her shoulders. The saffron kirtle followed. He groaned in wonderment as she at last lay bared before him on the fur, her creamy flesh outlined by its luxurious russet glow. Surely the pagan goddess of the moon was never half so lovely as she! he thought reverently. Dipping his head, he covered a coral nipple with his lips and worshipped it eagerly, hungrily, with mouth and tongue, a pilgrim worshipping at the sacred shrine of her lovely body.

She moaned deep in her throat at the feel of his warm lips moving over her flesh, and drew his ebony head down to her other breast, bidding him with whispered words to make haste, make haste! Her body cried out like a wanton to seal their reunion in the joining of their bodies, a joining denied her for so many, many days. Alaric was no less impatient. Soon he eased his great weight upon her, yet he did so with such tenderness and such obvious care for her pleasure and comfort that she opened deeply, joyously to take him, and make her possession of him as full as his of her in the giving of her body.

He thrust deep within her silken sheath and found that she was already prepared for his entry. Her sweet, honeyed warmth enclosed him, held him fast, drawing him deeper, ever deeper into her, until it seemed he was drowning—but he cared not!

Her shapely legs embraced his lean, muscled flanks. Her long fingers twined in the thick, glossy blackness of his hair and savored its springy texture. Her soft breasts and belly were crushed sweetly under the rough expanses of his broad chest and hard, flat belly. Cradling her tenderly in his arms, he thrust again and again deeply into her, sending her own desire rocketing skyward. Her body arched eagerly upward like a bow to meet his, to move in unison with him, and a low purr of pleasure broke from her parted lips as they danced the ancient dance of male and female, him and her.

The moon rose as they loved, sprinkling her silvery light between the trees and dappling the leaf-strewn bridle paths and briar-rose bowers of the copse. The ritual love dance went on, their cries of pleasure building in the deepening twilight, their motions growing swifter now as he moved more strongly upon her, drawing her after him ever higher—and still higher—to that pleasure-star above which they would be one, not only in body but also in soul.

The shadow of owl wings brushed their pale bodies in the dusk. Small creatures leaving their holes to hunt rustled in the leaves, were startled by the gasps and cries of the woman and the low groans of the man beneath the tree, and quickly padded away. The wind moaned softly amongst the woods and gently plucked the leaves from the trees. Her bard's song was a lilting ballad of love, sung only for them, and the scents of late summer were the perfume wafted to the lovers on her current. The stars that twinkled in Mother Night's sky cloak and lit their woodland bower were magical lights, reflected by the faerie moon off a million sparkling gemstones caught in its velvet folds.

He awoke first to the deepening chill of evening, wondering in his sleepy, satisfied state if he had imagined their joyous reunion. But no, she was there, real and warm, curled deeply asleep under the furry mantle beside him. For a moment or two he watched her, drinking in her loveliness in the dappled shadows and the silvery arrows of the moon's pale light. A breeze whispered through the copse, chilling him, and he knew he must wake her, that they must be on their way back to Kenley before it was full dark. He roused her with tender, teasing kisses, and saw the love dawn on her face as she wakened. Quickly they dressed, their deft movements belying the lazy expressions of content and peace upon their faces. Alaric went to fetch the horses, glancing down the hillside to the field below as he went. Suddenly he halted. "Come, come quickly, sweeting!" he whispered, awed, beckoning to her.

She came to his side and looked below, where he bade her look, her eyes widening in amazement as she did so.

Below, in the cornfield, a family of hares danced by the light of the full moon, strange, long-eared celebrants of some ancient pagan rite of harvest. He glanced at Freya's face and saw that her expression was rapt, as fascinated as he had been that first time, long ago; still was, even now.

"'Tis rare to see the Hares' Dance," he murmured. "In all my years, this is but the second time I have witnessed it. The first, I was but a young lad of fourteen winters. I recall it was the eve before I left Kenley for Aethelred's camp."

"What does it mean?" she asked, still gazing down at the moon-drenched field below and at the creatures who leaped and bounded there amongst the corn.

283

"I know not," he admitted softly. "But 'tis said by the Old Ones who remember the ancient gods—Woden, Tiw, Frig, and others—that to see the dance by the light of the full harvest moon is an omen of good fortune." He smiled. "I would never doubt it, sweeting. Not now!"

They stood upon the crest of the hill and sealed the magical moment with a lingering kiss. When they stood apart again he stroked her hair and murmured, "You will be my bride, Freya. We will be joined in the eyes of my church, and according to the laws of my people. I will have it no other way. I know now that I honor thee too greatly to keep thee as my leman, or take thee as my handfast wife in the old way. You will be the mother of my sons, and my own beloved lady for as long as we both shall live."

She said nothing in response, and he saw the doubt, the uncertainty in her face, mingled with the joy.

"Fear not," he reassured her. "My betrothal with the Lady Meredyth will be broken, whatever the cost. If you will accept baptism into the Christian faith, I am certain my king would approve our union, as would my church. I will journey to Winchester very soon and speak with my liege and his bishops and advisors on this matter. I warrant Alfred would not be displeased to see a bond forged between the Danes and the people of Wessex by our marriage. For all that he is a great leader, he deplores bloodshed and would rather see peace brought about by means other than battle, wherever possible."

"I will trust to your judgment, dearest Bear," she agreed shyly. "And I shall don the cloth of chrisom and accept baptism if I must do so to become your bride, for in truth I love thee so!" Nonetheless, she wrinkled her nose in distaste.

He laughed. "If you must?" The smile he wore deepened, making the furrows that ran alongside his mouth still more darkly etched in the shadows. "You love me, it would seem, and will bend to my will in many things. Yet in other ways you are yet the most stubborn, defiant wench I have ever met!"

"Would you have me change, my lord?" she demanded pertly, her eyes sparkling with impudence as she gazed up at him, head cocked to one side.

"Never!" he breathed with great fervor, and lifted her up

onto her horse.

As they rode away, Freya knew she would never forget this eve when they had confessed their love for each other, nor the sight of the Hares' Dance amid the corn under the full moon. A portent of good fortune, Alaric had said it was.

Let it be so, blessed Frey, she prayed silently, defiantly calling upon her pagan gods for blessing. *Let it be so!*

Yet even now, all unknown to Freya, the web her uncle had seen in his vision was tightening around her.

The monastery gardener, whom Sven had entrusted to carry his warning to Kenley, even as Freya spoke her silent prayer, was reeling drunkenly from a wayside tavern to his waiting nag. Several times he attempted to mount it, and several times he failed and landed on his backside in the dung, until at last a stableboy came out and laughingly tossed him up into his saddle.

All unnoticed to the gardener, the pouch in which he carried the rolled letter had come unfastened in the process.

As he kicked his heels into the nag's side and it ambled upon its lazy way toward Kenley, the parchment fell from the pouch and into a ditch by the roadside where dock and nettles grew.

Soon the rain that dawn had given promise of began to fall, obliterating ink and message—and warning—in its downpour . . .

Chapter 21

Once Alaric had decided upon a course, he quickly carried it out with the decisiveness and brilliance that had brought him honor in the service of Alfred's army. It was no little wonder then, that since he had determined to make Freya his bride, he should act upon his decision the very next day.

Cupping her face in his hands, he told her with obvious regret, "I must leave thee for a few days, my sweeting. It is a four days' ride to Winchester. I shall need a day or two to speak with Alfred, but then I will return to thee and make thee my bride."

"Ten days? It will seem an eternity!" she vowed, pouting. Before, she had wanted only to be rid of her Saxon master, but now—now an hour apart from him seemed an eternity of loneliness!

"Ten days of a lifetime. Is it too great a price to pay for our happiness?" he chided, his tone gently teasing.

"Nay, I suppose not," she agreed, ashamed of her childishness. "But hurry back, my lord! Even now, I fancy I hear the faint echoes of Meredyth's whining voice in my ears." Her sapphire eyes gleamed with a malicious light.

He grinned. "'Twould seem I have chosen a jealous vixen to be my bride."

"There are none more jealous than she!" she agreed fervently, pursing her lips in pretend irritation. "Shall I speak of our plans to the Lady Valonia?" She bowed her head, suddenly shy. "I—I do believe she has been hoping for just this very thing, if the mysterious glances she has given me of late are aught to go by!"

"She will be the first to learn of it, my love," Alaric promised. "But wait on my return. We will tell her—and my uncle—together." He grimaced. "I wager Ordway will not greet the news as gladly as will she."

"Nay, he assuredly will not," Freya agreed, and there was sadness in her expression.

He took her in his arms and kissed her fond farewell, dispersing melancholy with his ardent lips. "Every night we're apart will be a lifetime," he murmured against her ear, "but I will think of the years to come. They will warm me until I return to thee!" Then with a lingering glance, he strode away from her across the hall.

He had been gone only a moment or two before Cullen hurried into the hall from another door.

"Alaric—have you seen him?" he demanded, short of breath, his face ruddy with high color.

"Aye, sir! He left but a moment ago." She pointed. "If you make haste, you may overtake him yet, by the stables."

Cullen nodded and sped away. After a few moments Freya followed him, though more slowly, wondering what could have caused his obvious agitation.

Outside in the bailey Alaric was already mounted. To Freya's surprise, she saw that Cullen was also. Ordway stood by the head of Alaric's stallion, and fragments of their earnest conversation carried to where she stood watching.

"—the sea cave. There is danger, should the tide turn," she heard Ordway mutter, concern evident in his harried expression.

"Fear not, uncle. I will find her."

Alaric saw her standing there then, and so did Ordway. Alaric opened his mouth to say something, but with an angry glance at his nephew the older man silenced him. He bade his uncle farewell and kneed his horse across the bailey toward her.

Looking down at her from his stallion's back, he told her regretfully, "An errand of some urgency must delay my departure, sweeting. All going well, I shall yet be able to leave for Winchester later this day."

"Is something awry?" she queried, frowning, and saw Alaric's expression grow guarded. He glanced across at Ordway, who was mounting his own horse.

"Naught to concern your pretty head," he hedged evasively, and blew her a kiss. "Fare thee well, my heart!"

"And thee, my lord!" she returned, yet as he rode away she found herself still wondering what could be going on that he would not want her to know about?

Whatever curiosity remained after he had gone dwindled over the next few hours. The happy secret she and Alaric shared was like a warm glow in her heart, and she hugged it jealously to her. Coupled with this was another secret that even Alaric knew naught of as yet: since their return from London, she had cause to suspect she was carrying his child. It was still only a suspicion, for her flux was but a few days tardy in arriving, yet she hoped with all her heart it was so! She could think of no better gift for her future husband than to bear him an heir in the spring.

She was deep in thoughts of babes when Edythe came up behind her in the kitchens, her loud curses jolting Freya half out of her skin.

"That bitch!" Edythe cried indignantly, her plump face red and angry with the livid imprints of someone's fingers. "Why she had to come back, I know not. Better she should stay forever in Winchester than come back here and take out her foul temper on us!"

"Who is 'she'?" Freya demanded. "Calm yourself, do, Edythe, and tell me!"

"'She' is the Lady Kendra, that's who! Boxed my ears, she did, an' all because she fancied the curtsey I gave her when I made my greeting lacked proper respect. Respect—for her what's been tumbled by half t'garrison? Pah! Still," Edythe continued, brightening, "there'll be juicy gossip in the kitchens come this even, and I for one intend t'relish every tidbit of it, aye, and send it on its way!"

"What gossip is this?" Freya asked idly. Gossip was ever rife amongst the serving wenches, but Edythe seemed to have developed a knack for learning the meatiest rumors ahead of all the others.

"Why, of *her!*" Edythe hissed in a conspiratorial whisper, and in a tone that implied she could not believe Freya had to ask. "I was after talkin' t'Walther, the groom, an' he said as how Lady Kendra's bower woman told 'im that she were—"

"Who? The bower woman or Lady Kendra?"

"Lady Kendra, dullard!—were surprised right in the very act of adultery with one o'King Alfred's men-at-arms, no less, and that she were surprised by none other than our royal lady the queen herself! Think on it, the *queen*, Freya! They say she fled Winchester for Kenley before her lord learned of it, in terrible fear of what Farant may do when he catches her. There's talk of convents and high walls for that noble bitch-woman, aye, and I for one am not a whit saddened to hear it! The higher the walls, the better, I says! She should be whipped, she should, cuckolding a fine and gentle husband such as Farant, bless him . . ."

By afternoon the hall of Kenley was buzzing with rumor and speculation, which Kendra's waspish behavior since her return did nothing to disprove. Servants had had their ears boxed, their rumps kicked, their noses tweaked, and their ears pulled as a consequence of her foul temper.

It was with relief that everyone learned the news from Edythe, who had learned it from her bower woman, that the lady had announced she was feeling somewhat out of sorts since her lengthy journey, and would take supper in her bower. All breathed a little easier then—until another whisper made the rounds as swiftly as the first: Farant had returned! Her husband had come after her! The whisper rustled through the hall and the outbuildings, through the entire settlement within the wooden palisades and the earthen ramparts of Kenley Hall, like the widening ripples of a still pond! Everyone moved about henceforth on tiptoe and with bated breath, certain that a furious argument would soon erupt, and reluctant to be the unlucky maid—or fellow—upon whom fell the task to carry the Lady Kendra her supper, and risk her fury!

Freya was no less reluctant than they, and prayed to every one of her Norse gods that she would escape Kendra's notice. She was relieved to receive a summons to Valonia's bower to assist her in dressing her hair for supper that evening, since it would put her out of reach of any summons from the black-haired virago.

She combed Valonia's long, fair hair and braided it, winding the ropes of plaited gold about the crown of her head in the Danish fashion and fastening it with pretty combs of elkhorn studded with gems.

"There, mistress!" she declared when she was done, well satisfied with her accomplishments. "You are as lovely and every bit regal as Queen Ealhswith herself, I would not wonder!"

Valonia smiled a little sadly and touched Freya's cheek. "Dear child! You can ever find the right words to soothe me when my spirits are at their lowest ebb! In truth, I confess, I have a plaguesome throbbing in my head, and had feared to look my worst at supper." She sighed. "First Wilone—now Kendra, aye, and in a fine spate of temper, too—! There'll be a third disturbance, no doubt, since such things always come in threes. Ah well, be off to find your own supper, my dear, and your lady will find her own. A goodnight to you!"

Freya left Valonia's bower and started back toward the hall. She had gone only a few steps across the bailey when she saw none other than Alaric in the doorway of Kendra's bower, his expression murderous. He beat upon the door with clenched fists, and after a few seconds, it was flung open to admit him.

"My dearest lord!" she heard Kendra nervously cry out, yet her tone oozed honey. "I did not expect thee so soon!" Alaric entered, and the door closed in his wake.

Freya felt as if she had been shot through with an arrow, impaled where she stood. What business had Alaric with Kendra, and in the woman's own bower, no less? She realized suddenly that she was trembling, shaking all over, and was not certain if she did so from jealousy or hurt or a mixture of both.

Somehow she forced her legs to carry her onward, to the great hall and to the kitchens, but they moved as stiffly as if carved from wood. Was Kendra the reason Alaric's departure had been delayed, she wondered? Had he learned she was to return to Kenley that very day, and had he ridden out to meet her? A thousand unanswered questions teemed inside her head, but the only answers she could supply did nothing to rid her of a deadness that seemed to steal through her body. Try as she might to give Alaric the benefit of the doubt, she could not cast aside a certain memory, a memory from the very first day she had been at Kenley and had overheard Alaric vow he loved the Lady Kendra, and beg her to love him in return. Did Alaric hope to take the Lady Kendra for his own, now that it seemed probable her husband would divorce her, or at the very least send her away? Did the Saxons permit divorce, as did the Danes? She had no idea! She knew only that where before she had been filled with a warm glow of happiness, she was now cold as ice and utterly numbed.

She was still in the grip of a sort of daze sometime later, when she heard Edythe calling her as if from a great distance. The voice grew louder. She looked down at the loaf of bread she had been carving into crusty chunks as if she had no idea how it came into her hands, then at Edythe.

"Freya! Have you been struck deaf, then? 'Tis her! She wants refreshment, and insists ye be the one t'take it to her."

"She? What? Who?" Freya asked, finally realizing that Edythe was beside her and telling her something.

"The Lady Kendra!" Edythe sighed and shook her head. "What's wrong with ye today, eh love? Now stir yerself, and fetch the tray. Oatcakes and mead is what she's after askin' fer."

"Nay, Edythe, I cannot take it! You do it, please, just this once?"

"I would, lovie, but she asked for you. I daren't go against her, in the spate she's in. Come on, now. Get it over with— then come back an' tell me all about it!"

A feeling of foreboding uncoiled in Freya's belly and reared its serpent's head as she set about loading a tray with the oatcakes and flagon.

She paused at the doorway to Kendra's and Farant's bower, the unease she had felt upon being given the woman's summons deepening at the sound of Kendra's shrill voice raised in anger within. Hesitantly she knocked, yet there was no answer. Her heart giving a painful twist in her breast, she wondered if Kendra had mayhap wooed Alaric to her bed, and if from lusty coupling they had progressed since to a love spat? By Loki, the woman risked much, to be caught in adultery with one man, then straightway take another to her bed!

Clearly, she thought bitterly, the promises Alaric had made her were empty, hollow ones. Perhaps he had even laughed silently as he made them? Anger blistered through her, and she held onto the feeling, for it was far easier, far less painful to bear than the agony of being betrayed. What manner of weakling must her lord's brother Farant be, to allow his wife to betray and cuckold him so openly with his own brother? And what manner of man must Alaric be at heart to do so? One lacking all honor, it seemed . . .

Heartsick, she knocked again, and this time receiving a summons to enter, she pushed the door inward and stepped inside, juggling the heavy tray as she went.

The scene that met her eyes was not at all that which she had expected. No amorous couple wanting oatcakes and mead to refresh themselves after a lusty hour or so spent in pleasurable coupling. Blessed Odin, if only it were! Her eyes widened as she took in the tableau before her.

Lady Kendra knelt on the rushes. At her feet sprawled a body, a man's body, *Alaric's* body. No movement came from him, nor any indication that he yet lived. A slim, jeweled dagger was clenched in Kendra's fist, slick with blood, and she was smiling with catlike pleasure as she looked up to see Freya standing there. A dark slit gaped like a wide, ugly mouth in Alaric's broad chest, bright crimson blood welling freely from it. More blood had splattered across the fine white linen of Kendra's night garment; still more tiny droplets showed like a ghastly pox upon her smooth, golden hands—spattered her cheeks—the rushes—! There was blood, blood everywhere!

The angry color drained from Freya's own face, leaving it waxen with shock and blank with disbelief. Her mouth worked frantically, silently. A scream of denial was torn upward from her heart and then stillborn on her lips. Her mind whirled in horror and confusion. The platter of oatcakes and the flagon of mead toppled unnoticed from her suddenly numbed fingers, spilling to the rushes with a loud crash that was never heard by her—

"What have you done to him!" she screamed, flinging herself

forward across the bower to Alaric and dropping on her knees at his side. She lifted and turned his beloved face to hers, cradling his ebony head against her heaving bosom, heedless of the blood that gushed from the chest wound onto the white of her tunic as she gathered him up into her arms.

His cinder-dark eyes were wide open, vacant and staring, reflecting the tiny flames of the rushlights in their glassy depths; his Christian soul, his life force, had already fled him, she sensed sickly, and it was as if her heart was suddenly imprisoned in ice. *Dead. Dead. Dead!* The word echoed through her mind like the loud, insistent thrumming of a tambour on hangman's day. A keening cry rose from her as if her own soul took flight, a cry laden with grief, and deep and utter despair.

"Murderer!" she screamed hoarsely. "Murderer! You have killed him! Killed my only love! Curse thee!" she hissed, "Curse thee to the gates of Hell! You must pay, bitch-woman!"

With another shrieking wail, like one gone mad, she gently released Alaric's limp body and flung herself across him toward Kendra, clawing like a wildcat for the dagger in the other woman's fist. With little difficulty she tore it from her grasp, wrested it free of the long, slender fingers that had wielded it with such murderous purpose, and turned the blade on the other woman.

Kendra rose and backed away, a triumphant smirk baring her teeth. "Aye, he's dead at last, praise be!" she crowed. "And 'tis too late for you, slut, or anyone else to do aught to bring him back! Too long I've chafed to be free of him, and now he is no more!"

Freya lunged at the woman, who picked up her trailing skirts and fled around the bed, her mocking laughter ringing in Freya's ears. "Come at me, slave! Do what you will! There's a price you will yet pay for worming your way into my lord's heart, aye, indeed!"

"Explain! You speak in riddles, bitch-woman!" Freya seethed, advancing slowly toward her with the gleaming dagger extended in one hand, her other arm outstretched for balance. Rushlight glinted off the silvery blade. "Explain— then die!" Hectic color rose in her formerly pale cheeks, contrasting sharply with the giddy brilliance of her eyes and the bright splash of her hair.

"Explain? Nay, my *lady* Freya! You will understand soon enough!" So saying, Kendra suddenly hooked her hand in the neckline of her night shift and wrenched, rending the finely embroidered linen cloth. Another jerky, excited gesture, and she had torn the narrow golden circlet from her brow and hurled it across the room, sending a rainbow shower of loosened amethysts and garnets to the rushes. Simultaneously, she began shrieking as if taken by a fit:

"Guards! Oh, Blessed Jesu, hasten! The Viking wench has killed him! She's murdered my lord! Help me! *Guards!*" Her golden eyes glittered like the shining yellow eyes of a she-demon as understanding dawned in Freya's. She threw back her ebony curls and rocked with silent laughter, far from lovely now in her unholy glee.

In that moment Freya knew why it was Kendra had summoned her, knew she had played into her hands as innocently as a lamb is led to the slaughter! Alarm pierced through her like splinters of ice: her grief for Alaric was, in that instant, and of necessity, swiftly put aside. Escape! She must escape for her very life, she realized, looking wildly about her. Kendra's screams for help had redoubled, and even now she could hear the swift, heavy tread of the guards coming this way, the barked commands of the sergeant-at-arms as he deployed his men.

With lightning speed she decided and acted, her warrior's training now standing her in good stead, enabling her to think, to plan, with a cool detachment she did not feel. Two swift paces, and she had reached Kendra. The woman flung up her arms, stunned by her unexpected actions. In that second Freya had her about the neck, the bloody dagger gripped in her other hand, its shining blade resting across Kendra's throat.

"You have made me your scapegoat, bitch," she hissed. "So 'tis only fitting *you* should be my hostage!"

"Never!" Kendra rasped, struggling, but the blade nicked her slender throat, stinging her smooth flesh, and she felt the trickle of her own blood and grew suddenly still and silent.

At that moment guards exploded into the bower, bringing up short at sight of their lord's dead body sprawled upon the rushes, and their lady Kendra held at knifepoint by Lord

Alaric's slave.

"She killed him!" Kendra whimpered piteously. "And now—now she will kill me!"

"*Ja!*" Freya acknowledged bitterly. "Let me pass unhampered, or I'll slit her cursed throat."

"You'll not leave Kenley alive, wench," the sergeant-at-arms growled. "Let the Lady Kendra go, and mayhap it will go easier on you."

"I'll not," Freya refused. "Stand aside, and bid your men do likewise. One rash step, one false and foolhardy move on your part, and I will slice her from ear to ear and offer her worthless life to Frey, I swear it on my pagan gods!"

"The wench means it, lads," the sergeant muttered under his breath. "Let her pass! There'll be time enough to take her later, when our lady is safe."

"You there!" Freya spat, jerking her head at one tall lad. "Go to the stables and see a horse readied for me, a mantle, water, and victuals—meat, cheese, bread, and the like, enough for several days. Have them left waiting outside the watchtower. And be warned, my brave fellow, I am no stranger to blood—nor a squeamish Saxon cow who quails at thought of taking another's life. I will kill, if pressed!" Her deadly tone froze all notions of denial on their lips.

"Aye!" the lad agreed hurriedly, and sped from the bower.

"We outnumber her seven to one, sir," whispered one man under his breath to their leader. "Rush her, and she will—"

"—take more of you with her into your Christian paradise than you'd care to count!" Freya cut in, her sapphire eyes as cold and glassy as a frozen fjord in winter. Stepping backward, Kendra forced by the razor edge of the blade at her throat to back away with her, Freya edged to the door. "If you value her life, you will not attempt to follow us!" Freya hissed, and jerked her hostage from the bower and out into the bailey.

"You have but added weight to your crimes with this," Kendra gasped out as they went. "No one will ever believe now that you did not kill your lord!"

"No one would have believed me anyway, and you knew it, Saxon bitch!" Freya retorted, her tone heavily laced with bitterness. "Of what worth is the word of a lowly Viking slave?"

295

The night air was cool in the deserted bailey without the hall. Above, a billion stars pulsed brightly, like tiny diamond chips sewn upon a cloak of purple velvet. The translucent moon floated on high, a medallion of beaten silver, cast for the moon goddess herself.

But Freya saw none of the heavens' peerless beauty. Shuffling and shoving her hostage roughly ahead of her, she made her way between the clustered wattle and daub dwellings to the earthen ramparts and wooden palisade that encircled Kenley and its outbuildings, and thence to the timber watchtower and the wide wooden gate set within them. The guard—the young lad she had sent ahead—was there, waiting.

"The horse and victuals are outside the gate, as you requested," he muttered, shifty-eyed, licking his lips nervously.

Curtly, she nodded, jerking Kendra past the astonished sentries and through the gate. It was as the lad had said. A horse stood ready, a mantle, a leather pouch of provisions, and a wineskin strapped to its saddle. But Freya intended to take no chances. She would not release her sly hostage until she was safely mounted on the steed! Dragging Kendra with no little roughness backward by her long hair, she hurried to the horse.

Suddenly Kendra kicked backward, slamming her slippered heel into Freya's shins. She gasped with pain and abruptly released her hold upon the woman. Kendra took advantage of her momentary lapse to twist sideways from her grip. She jerked free and rolled away before Freya could stop her.

"I'm free! She's yours, guards! Take her! Quickly, you fools!" Kendra screamed.

Her cries galvanized the stunned sentries on the walls into action. With the swiftness of experienced archers they hurriedly drew arrows and nocked them against bowstrings, even as Freya hoisted her skirts and vaulted astride the startled horse. Lashing it across the rump with the trailing end of the reins, she kicked the beast into a frenzied bolt and careened down the rolling hill, away from Kenley. A shower of arrows and the guards' and Kendra's livid curses floated after her on the cool night air.

*   *   *

The ancient mare was lathered and half spent long before Freya dared halt to rest the poor beast several hours later. Kendra would have sent men after her, she knew, and she dare not risk halting, nay, not for any cause!

The stars had almost faded from the night sky, the velvety deep purple of night already being nudged aside by the ashy charcoal of dawn and a subtle brightening in the east, when the ancient mare's heart gave out. The poor creature dropped dead in her tracks beneath Freya's knees, slamming her heavily to the dew-soaked grass. Stunned, she sprawled face down where she had landed, quite motionless, waiting for the bright lights that the jarring fall had torched in her skull to fade; for the sickening, winded feeling to pass.

After several moments she crawled to her knees, then to her feet, looking with longing back over her shoulder to where the valiant mare lay dead before turning resolutely to face north, where a single morning star shone out its pale beacon. A great tear slipped down her cheek. More salty tears followed its course as the dam inside her burst at last, as the tight, aching knot of misery and grief to which she had held fast for so many desperate leagues loosened. Yet just as rapidly she wiped the tears away and set her jaw. She wanted nothing so dearly at that moment as to curl up in the woods like a wounded animal and howl and howl until the crushing agony in her breast was eased—if it ever could be eased. Yet the luxury of mourning her dead beloved was to be denied her for the time being, she acknowledged, closing her ears to the death knell that throbbed throughout her being in time to the dull, heavy beat of her heart. *Alaric. Alaric. Alaric!* She must move quickly on, and cross the winding Thames that marked the borders between the kingdoms of Wessex and the Danelaw before her pursuers outdistanced her. As the Lady Wilone had once done many years ago, she must give thought first and foremost to protecting the new life perhaps even now unfolding in her belly, not her own grief, overwhelming though it was.

Somewhere—many leagues ahead in the direction of the fragile glimmer of the north star—lay Jorvic, the Northumbrian Viking stronghold. And sanctuary.

Chapter 22

By mid-morning of the next day the Thames lay far behind her. She had swum across the river at a narrow point, rather than waste precious time in finding a ferryman to pole her across, afraid that if she did he would remember her disheveled appearance, her bloodstained kirtle, and be able to give directions of her route to those who might even now be in pursuit.

Shortly after dawn, by virtue of the luck granted by the gods, she had stumbled upon the great, cobbled road, built by the Roman legions centuries before and still in good repair, that led straight as an arrow northward across Mercia and into the very heart of Northumbria. It would lead her directly to Jorvic! Yet many, many long leagues—over fifty, she estimated— through wooded countryside and rolling downs, across desolate heathered moors and hamlets, fens and marshes, lay ahead of her. Gritting her teeth and shouldering her pack, she doggedly trudged onward, too numbed by the grief inside her to feel the painful blisters that rose hugely, then burst, then be- came oozing, bloody sores on her feet as the leagues fell away behind her.

Three days she continued on, sleeping in sheltered ditches or grassy hollows, eating sparingly from the victuals in the pack, which were poor scraps barely suitable for a begging hound. She smiled grimly. Saxon offal! They had granted her demands in return for Kendra's worthless life, but in the granting had taken every step they could to see her escape from

298

them was not made easy. A worn-out, aging horse. Food that was scarce worthy of the name. Water that had had a distinctly stale taste to it. Still, would she have done less, had their positions been reversed? Never! She had wanted to cut some flesh from the carcass of her horse to provide meat for a few days, but had not dared waste precious time in doing so, she recalled, shaking her head in regret.

On the fourth day she spied a hamlet up ahead, and passed many travelers journeying toward it from all directions. By the vast array of livestock and goods they herded or carried with them in baskets, or upon carts or in panniers lashed to donkeys, she knew that a large market must be in progress there.

Sure enough, the mouth-watering aroma of roasting meats wafted to her nose and set her belly growling hungrily. Saliva gushed into her mouth. In truth, she thought in disgust, she was close to drooling like a hungry hound! Surely she had gone far enough across the border and into the Danelaw to risk halting her journey for the remainder of the day, and filling her belly? Food and a good night's sleep would do much for her flagging strength, and the leagues that lay ahead would be more swiftly traveled on a full stomach. But—how was she to purchase food, or anything else for that matter, without coin or something of value to barter for it? She grinned suddenly, remembering how she and Olaf, as children, had stolen treats from the kitchens of Danehof. It had become a great rivalry between them to see who could snatch the most without Fat Hilda, the enormously large woman in charge of the kitchen thralls, catching them in the act! They had done it so many times—and with such stealth and skill—that superstitious Hilda, at a loss for other explanations, had declared her kitchens plagued by mischievous, hungry elves! *Ja*, she could turn thief if forced to it, she decided.

She found a brook bubbling up from between some mossy rocks and scrubbed her dusty face and hands in the cool water. After she had soaked her sore feet in its soothing flow, she stripped off her kirtle and attempted to wash the bloodstains from it. They had turned an ugly dark rust color now. *Alaric's life-blood.* Her hands shook. Tears blinded her, salty and

299

stinging. A sob welled up in her throat, but she gamely swallowed it. If for naught else but the sake of the new life she suspected was even now growing inside her—Alaric's son, she was certain!—she would be strong, would not give way to tears. Survival must be paramount in her mind. All else, even the luxury of tears and grieving, must fall second. Sniffing noisily and rubbing her damp eyes on her knuckles, she forced all thoughts of Alaric from her mind.

The kirtle soon dried in the playful breeze, and she slipped it on. Her shoes, of soft leather, were now useless, she realized ruefully. She tossed the worn and tattered scraps that remained of her footwear into a nearby bush, startling the sparrows and the merlins gathered there, raked her hair through with her fingers in an effort to neaten it a little, braided it, and feeling much improved, headed toward the thatched roofs of the hamlet that showed between the trees.

Close to fifty cottages huddled about the narrow dirt streets, and there was, as she had guessed, a market in the village. People were everywhere, decked out in their best, squabbling good-naturedly for the bargains offered by the stall holders, whose awnings were rolled up to show that they were open and eager for business. Grubby children, dogs, and rooting pigs mingled with the marketgoers. She slipped in amongst the crowds and wandered from stall to stall, thankful to see her appearance was not so unlike the others as to be out of place.

What a quantity of goods there was! Though this market fell far short of the teeming trading center of Hedeby favored by Viking merchants, it was nonetheless doing a brisk trade. Horses and cows were herded together in a meadow to one side and were the subject of heated bartering and argument as to quality and breeding, quantities of coin changing hands by the minute. Great wheels of yellow cheese and pats of butter were displayed, golden and tempting, on one stall, eggs and fresh produce on another. Valuable salt was much in evidence, as were blooms of iron, and lead. A fish stall offered heaped, glassy-eyed herring, some salmon, eels brought from the fens, and lampreys. None of them, to Freya's astute nose, could be considered overly fresh, but they were selling well nonetheless, for seafood was a treat here, inland. Rare imported wines from the Mediterranean, leather bottles of oil, and casks of mead vied with the butchers' stalls that offered red meat and swarms of shiny blue flies, the bakers' coarse and tasty dark barley bread, the soapmaker's stall, and the cobbler's. Behind his stall Freya noticed a heap of small leather pieces, thrown away from each shoe or boot he'd made in accordance with the superstition amongst men of his craft that the magical "wee folk" fashioned shoes for themselves from such leavings, and would bless the cobbler who provided the scraps with good fortune. She eyed the shoes and boots longingly, her sore feet, bare now, throbbing. Oh, for a pair of those finely crafted boots to carry her over the leagues she had yet to travel!

"How much?" she asked the stall-keeper, nodding at a pair of fine kid boots.

"Two silver pennies, wench—aye, and a bargain at twice the price, though I says so meself!" The rotund little cobbler eyed her up and down, knowing immediately that she could not afford his wares. She was a house *karl* for some lord, he judged by her poor garments, or a slave given a free day to attend the market. Her pretty face had dropped in disappointment when he'd named the price. If she had two silver pennies to rub together, he'd eat a pair of his sturdy clogs, aye, that he would! Still, she was full-breasted and comely, seemed fairly clean, and her hair had a rare fire to it that he found pleasing, and barter was barter, was it not, whatever the goods exchanged might be? "Or, if ye have no coin, wench, give me a tumble in back o'my stall. 'Twill earn ye a pair o'fine clogs!" he suggested in a wheedling tone, rubbing his palms together and jerking his head toward the rear of his stall. He winked. "It'll not be the first thing ye've earned on your back, I'd wager, eh, a pretty lass like ye?"

With difficulty she swallowed an angry retort. Freya of Danehof had earned nothing on her back like a common whore; the insolence of that porky lout even to suggest such a thing! Her jewel eyes flashed, and hectic color filled her cheeks. "I'd sooner walk barefoot a hundred leagues than go on my back for the likes of you!" she stormed, and turned quickly away from the stall, grateful to be swallowed up by the jostling crowd, for more than one onlooker had caught the cobbler's lecherous offer and her heated response, and their coarse laughter followed her.

Off to one side of the marketplace were huge spits laden with sides of beef and succulent pork, whole chickens, and quarters of venison. They were being turned over pits of glowing coals by two strong, flaxen-haired youths, who chattered as they worked. She was not immune to the appreciative glances and eye-rollings that passed between them as she made her way to a nearby tree, but ignored them and sat down beneath it to consider what she would do next, idly peeling the bark from a twig as she did so.

Her hopes that she could steal what she needed had dwindled rapidly. The stall-keepers here seemed a shrewd, watchful bunch, and had kept a guarded eye on their wares. The boots she so coveted seemed as distant as the moon! She sighed. Her belly growled loudly to remind her it was empty, and she slapped it irritably to silence its petulant mutterings. To sit here, within a stone's throw of dark slabs of roasted beef and crackling pork, running with juices and blood, to be able to savor their aroma but not their flavor, was a torture beyond imagining for one as hungry as she! She swallowed a gush of saliva and stared at the slowly rotating spits and their succulent burdens as if by sheer dint of will power she could draw them to her.

"Stupid slut!"

A shriek and the sound of a blow jerked her attention away from the food and to her right. She saw a man, carrying a heavy pack upon his back, beating an equally heavily laden young girl with a short, hefty stick. The girl cringed and whimpered under his hefty blows, then finally crumpled to the grass. At once the fellow drew back his foot to kick her as she lay. His cruelty was more than Freya, hungry as she was, could bear.

"Stop it!" she cried, and was up and running toward him, had taken his elbow and spun him around, before the gravity of what her interference might mean had ever crossed her mind. "You've punished her enough, sir, don't you think? Let her get to her feet, pray!"

Her outburst ended, she looked up into his face and stifled a gasp. His eyes were pale, pale silver, almost completely without

302

color, yet it was their shape rather than this that caused her to gasp in alarm, for though the irises were round, the pupils were elongated black discs, like the eyes of a goat! His nose was large and misshapen, his mouth a thin-lipped gash with a vicious curl. The hair that showed beneath his soft cap was brown, dirty, and lank. Hair rose on her hackles, and she took an involuntary step backward as he scowled at her.

"What's it to you how I treat my slaves, wench? I paid good coin for her yesterday, and already the slut's giving me trouble! I should slit her cursed throat, aye, that's the way!" He raised his stick once again. "Get up, you worthless sow!"

The girl was struggling to rise and Freya, furious at her master's cruelty, quickly went to help her. "Come on, get up," she urged. "Show him you can do it!"

The girl peered mutely at Freya from between tangles of dirty, matted flaxen hair, the expression in her deep gray eyes that of a half-wit, dazed and uncomprehending. Freya grasped her under the shoulders and heaved her to standing. The girl stood there, swaying drunkenly. Livid bruises showed dark under the grime of her face and on her arms and legs below the short kirtle she wore. From the first her master had not dealt with her kindly, Freya realized grimly, if his comment that he had bought her just the day before were to be believed.

"If you want your slaves to serve you well, you must treat them well, as you would a fine horse or a falcon or hound, good sir," she told the man firmly, her tone that of a woman well accustomed to having her orders obeyed.

"I must, must I?" the man sneered, and she saw a glimmer of scornful amusement in his strangely shaped pale eyes, coupled with frank suspicion—and something more. Her flesh crawled as he insolently looked her over, and it was as if he wore his lust like a ribbon pinned to his sleeve, so effortlessly could she read his thoughts. The cobbler's brother, she wondered wryly, then turned to leave the oddly matched pair and lose herself amongst the crowds in the market.

"Hold!" the fellow cried after her. Reluctantly she turned about to face him.

"Aye?"

"Where's your own master, wench?" he demanded, his

expression cunning.

She drew herself up proudly, summoning all the outraged dignity she could muster as she tossed her fiery braids. "I have no master," she snapped. "I am a freed woman."

"I'll see your papers, then," he said calmly, holding out his hand for them.

She shook her head, tapping the leather pouch slung over her shoulder that contained the remnants of her food. "You'll not, sir. They're safe in here, and here they'll stay." Her expression dared him to question it, and was far more brazen than her belly, which turned over in apprehension, curse it.

Many curious onlookers had gathered to witness the exchange. Some recognized her from the cobbler's stall, and were keenly interested in the comely wench who stood with fists aggressively planted on her hips, glaring at the other stranger in a most unwomanly, hostile fashion.

His eyes seemed to bore into hers, to strip away the pretense, to peel back the layers like an onion and know she lied! Heart thudding, she returned his piercing stare eye for eye for what seemed an eternity, until he looked away first.

"So be it," he said softly, and inclined his head to her. Giving the poor slave girl a vicious poke with his stick, the pair moved on.

Freya watched them go, pity in her heart for the poor young woman. What lay ahead for her? Nothing but repeated rape at her master's hands and endless toil, until finally her heart and spirit would give out, and merciful death claimed her. Her cruel master did not appear to be one who would consider granting her her freedom at any time in the future! Go with Frey, she prayed silently, and turned away.

"Hungry, are you?" asked a young voice. She saw the two youths who turned the spits behind her. Their expressions seemed different now, more admiring than lecherous, perhaps a little conspiratorial?

"Hungry isn't the half of it," she confessed, grimacing, "Starving's closer!"

"Here, then, have a slice or two of this," one offered and held out a trencher heaped with portions of succulent beef. "Take all of it, if you want."

"Why?" she asked warily. "Why would you give food to me, a stranger here in your village?" If there was a price she was expected to pay in return, she intended to know what it was before she accepted their offer!

"For what you did for Ilse just now," the other young man volunteered quickly.

"Ilse?"

"Aye—the slave girl. She's—she's our little sister, y' see?"

"Your sister! Then why didn't you try to help her, two strong lads such as yourselves?" Freya demanded indignantly.

"Because we're slaves just like her," the taller of the two supplied, "though our master is kinder than most. Our father, Sigmund, was a *churl*, y' see. He has a small farm some four leagues from here, nearer to London. Last month he killed another Viking nobleman who tried to force himself on Ilse, but he had no silver to pay *wergild* to the man's family for the life he'd taken. He was forced to sell the three of us instead, so he could feed our younger brothers."

"He sold his own children?" Freya's eyes were nigh round with horror.

They both nodded.

"Aye. Ilse was the only daughter—and the one it hurt him the most to give up, after our older brother. She was Father's pride and joy, his pet since our mother—a woman of Angle—died last winter. He'll never be the same again, not after this. But we plan to work hard, perhaps buy our freedom, so we can go back to Angle and help him on the farm." The lad shrugged. "Until then we run the risk of being killed by our master, if we try to free Ilse." He shrugged ruefully. "For all that he's kinder than most, he's still our master, and we're still slaves, with few rights. What other choice do we have?"

"Go on, eat," the other lad urged. "'Tis our own share, so there'll be no harm in you taking it."

"We've bread, too, if you're still hungry. It's yours for the asking."

"And what of you? What will the pair of you eat?"

"There'll be enough for us, never fear. We're not hungry. We'll eat this evening, and never miss it."

Her worries stilled, Freya warmly thanked them both and

took the trencher. The meat and the bread they brought to go with it tasted like food fit for the tables of Asgard after the meager fare she'd had the past few days. She ate with gusto, tucked the leftovers in her pouch, and washed the meal down with greedy swigs from a horn of weak beer that the older lad, Elden, offered her, before bidding them farewell and quitting the market. It was no place for one so easily roused by injustice as was she. Nor for one who seemed so abundantly cursed by the unwanted attentions of men!

The food served its purpose. New vigor flowed through her veins, and despite her sore feet she made good time the remainder of that day. Shortly before dusk she began casting about her for a place to make camp for the night, looking for a sheltered spot a short distance off the main track she followed, with water nearby. She found one, and a pretty spot it was too. There was a small grassy hollow carved out beneath a pair of spreading oaks, alders, and a few weeping willows. A stream fringed with wild purple hyacinths and irises burbled over rocks just beyond it. Well satisfied, she tossed her pack to the grass and began gathering fallen branches for a fire.

A bundle of kindling under her arm, she stiffened suddenly at the sounds of a woman sobbing somewhere close by. They were pitiful cries, torn from a heart that had long since reached its limits and knew the depths of utter despair. The cries struck chords of recognition in her own heart. Frowning, Freya tossed the firewood alongside her pack, brushed off her hands, and went to investigate.

Brushing aside bushes and briars, she saw the girl, Ilse, whom she had seen in the marketplace earlier, sprawled on the grass. Her skirts were thrust up, exposing her pale lower body, which was mottled by livid bruises, blood, and dirt. She was still sobbing, but not so loudly now. All her tears had been wept. Her master loomed over her, and Freya saw with disgust that he was fastening the laces of his breeches' closing, a smug expression on his hateful face. She had arrived too late to help poor Ilse this time.

For a second Freya was minded to turn away, to slink back

306

to her bundle and leave, find another camp for the night. Did she not have problems enough of her own, without courting the girl's misfortune? 'Twould be easier to do nothing. Her shoulders sagged. She sighed. Nay. Troubles she had aplenty, but she could not ignore this, could not go on and pretend she had seen nothing. It was not in her nature to turn away from another in distress. Besides, it had struck her how easily Ilse's sorry plight might have been her own, had Alaric been less than the man he was. True, he had taken her against her will at the first, but never with such bestial brutality as that with which this lout had all too obviously used his slave. She frowned. How was she to help the girl? It would not do to anger the fellow, she reasoned, since that would only cause him to take his anger out on the girl. A different approach was needed.

She thrust her way between the bushes, brought up short, and feigned a startled expression. "Oh! Forgive me! I meant no intrusion. I—I was looking for firewood, and thought myself alone in these parts . . ."

"So it's you again, is it?" the man growled, yet his sly, pleased smile belied his words. "Ah well, no doubt a 'freed woman' such as yerself can go where she pleases, eh, lass?" The silver eyes gleamed maliciously.

"She can indeed," Freya agreed. "And so I'll be on my way—"

She turned as if to go back the way she had come.

"Nay, nay, there's no need for ye to leave," he coaxed. "I was about to build a fire myself, and I've victuals for the cooking. What say you we forget what happened back there," he jerked his head in the direction of the hamlet, "and share the fire fer the night, since it seems we're sharing the same road."

"Nay, I cannot," Freya said firmly, darting a meaningful glance at poor Ilse, who still huddled where she was, apparently too dazed or weakened even to tend to covering herself.

The man shuffled his feet and looked down, as if ashamed. "Ah. Aye. The wench." He shrugged. "Well, happen I have been a mite hard on the girl, I'll give ye that." The silver eyes came up, bored into hers. "Tell ye what, lass. You stay and see t'Ilse here, and I'll give ye my word to do better by her from here on. She's not much for talking, and I wouldn't say no to a bit o'company. Bargain?"

Company! Freya thought, silently fuming. She knew full well what manner of companionship *he* was after! Nonetheless she forced herself to smile. "Bargain it is, then. It's a long, empty road for a woman such as me, traveling alone. You see to that fire, sir, and I'll see to your servant."

He nodded, trying unsuccessfully to hide a cunning grin. "Aye, that's the way. My name's Toki, lass, and I hail from Mercia. And you—?"

"Freya," she supplied curtly, "bound for Jorvic," and stepped across the grass toward the girl.

She had torn the hem from her kirtle, soaked it in the stream, and bathed the blood and dirt from the girl's body before Ilse volunteered to speak.

"My thanks to you, mistress," she whispered, her split lip and puffy, blackening jaw making speech difficult.

Freya rocked back on her heels and surveyed Ilse with pity in her eyes. At first she'd taken the girl's vacant, dazed expression for that of a half-wit, but now she suspected it was nothing of the sort. She'd seen men wear that same look after a battle, the result of witnessing too much blood and carnage. Ilse had suffered a similar shock, thanks to her master, and her bewilderment and stupor were the result. Curse Toki! With her long flaxen hair and wide, gentle gray eyes, Ilse must have been a comely young woman indeed, before he laid hands on her. It was hard to see that now, however, with so many bruises marring her complexion, and the wounded, withdrawn look that pinched her face and haunted her eyes.

"Don't thank me, Ilse. I've done very little. I—I only wish I could do more for you," Freya whispered, casting a watchful eye in Toki's direction. He was striking a flint to light a fire, but she knew that beneath that lank hair he would be straining his ears to hear their conversation.

"They—they made me do terrible things—ugly, shameful things," Ilse whispered, and her lower lip quivered like a hurt child's. "He—last night—he and some others—men that he said he knew—they—they—hurt me so! They said a lass

308

with—with Viking blood deserved no better." She hung her head in shame, her mouth working uncontrollably. Tears rolled down her cheeks. "I—was a good girl—I'd saved myself—but now—!"

"I can imagine," Freya said grimly, squeezing the girl's cold hands to comfort her, her sapphire eyes hardening. "But don't be ashamed, don't! They were wrong, not you. You were Toki's victim, don't you see? The blame is on him, not you, poor little Ilse, who was innocent. Men like him are animals! They deserve to be treated like animals. You owe him nothing at all. Run away from him, Ilse! That's why I'm here. I came to help you escape him. We'll go north together, to Jorvic."

"Jorvic? But—that's a Viking stronghold! Are you—?"

"Aye, I'm a Viking woman!" Freya admitted. "But you'll be safe there, Viking or nay, I promise you!" Ilse shook her head.

"Nay, it's not that. My mother was an Angle woman, but my father's a Dane, too. That's why Toki loathes me—he loathes the Vikings for taking his farm, his livestock, everything. Nay, I dare not run away! If I escape Toki, he'll go back to my father and demand the return of the gold he paid him for me. Without that gold, our lord will hang my father for murder! I have to stay with him, don't you see? I have no choice, none at all!"

Freya tried to talk to her, to reason with her, until she was nigh blue in the face, but it was all to no avail. It seemed Ilse's love for her father outweighed even the shame and abuse she had suffered at Toki's hands. Despite disagreeing with her, Freya could not help admiring the girl's fierce loyalty and courage.

Later, as the three sat in the deep shadows about the crackling fire that Toki had built and ate oatcakes and dried fish that he produced from his pack, he glanced across the flames at Freya and grinned.

"Tell the truth, now, wench, seeing as how we're friends now. You're a runaway slave, are ye not? And don't think t'lie to old Toki, 'cos Toki can tell by yer eyes if ye lie!"

"Then gaze deep and true, Master Toki, while I tell you again. I am as free as a bird—freer than the very winds!" she said calmly, meeting his searching gaze with a level one of her own.

309

He chuckled. "I like your spirit, lass, aye and more besides! So tell me, if ye're free, how is it that ye be travelin' alone? Where are ye headed?"

"I'm headed north, to Jorvic. My lord and I were separated in a skirmish with Wessex men along the Thames. He and his men fell back and retreated, and I was cut off from them," she lied smoothly.

"So your lord's one o'our bloodthirsty Norse landlords, is he now?" Toki said thoughtfully, and Freya fancied she saw a glitter of something akin to hatred uncoil in his eyes.

"Aye—and a bloodier Dane you'd never want to meet!" she declared, warming to her tale. If she intended to brazen this out, the lie had best be the biggest and best one she could make it! "Vengeance is his watchword, Master Toki. I pity the poor fellow who next takes it upon himself to sport with me, his woman! The last died with the blood-eagle flapping its wings upon his back . . ."

"Did he now?" Toki commented mildly. "Did he indeed? Happen the fellow were a fool, then, not to silence you when he were done."

Freya gulped. His veiled threats frightened her. "Aye," she agreed softly. "But now he's a dead fool—and dead fools get no second chance. Nor will the next man get a first!"

He nodded sagely, and his strange silver eyes gleamed at her across the fire like the eyes of a crazed wolf.

Sleep was the thing furthest from her mind that night. She lay staring up at the stars through the lacy black filigree of the boughs above, wondering, waiting for the moment when Toki would make his move. *Ja*, she was certain he would make one! His friendly manner, she knew, was naught but a facade intended to conceal his lust. And the war of words they had waged about the fire had not deceived him into fearing her one whit! Perhaps the dagger she held clasped at her side would . . .

Sure enough, a slight rustling sound froze her into a state of muscle-tensed alertness soon after moonrise. Even though she had expected it at any moment, the brush of his foul, questing hand against the curve of her breast, the sudden bulk of his stinking body beside her on the grass sent every nerve and

310

tendon in her body screaming in alarm. At once the dagger came up in her fist, slashing down across his invading hand. She felt the warm splash of his blood on her own hand and heard him curse foully.

"You've drawn blood, witch!" he gasped.

"Aye! Did I not give you fair warning?" she hissed, rolling away and springing to her feet, red-gold hair lit from above by the pale moon's radiance. "I am no meek Ilse, to suffer your touch without protest, Master Toki!"

He bound his hand in the corner of his mantle, and to her surprise he chuckled. "Aye, so it seems. You're a plucky one, 'tis clear. A true daughter of our goddess, the Lady Frig. Perhaps even a fitting bride for my lord Woden?" he added softly, so softly that she failed to catch most of his words.

"I'll be bride to no man, least of all to any lord of yours!" she hissed. "At first light I go my own way, Master Toki!"

"And leave that sorry slut you've befriended to defend herself against the likes o'me? Nay, you'll not go, lass! You're too soft-hearted to leave her!" he jeered, sure of himself.

"That's where you're wrong," Freya said firmly. If Ilse had determined not to escape her master, then she must stay with him and bear the consequences. But Freya had no intent of doing likewise—not with the chance that Alaric's babe was growing inside her. The child and its welfare and safety came first.

Chapter 23

Another day dawned fair and bright, the morning sky as pink and rosy as a maiden's blushing cheeks.

Freya rose groggily from her mantle to wash her face in yet another bubbling spring and ready herself for yet another long day's traveling, without even a hound or a horse for companionship. She felt, she thought as she swung her leather pack up onto her back, as if she had been alone forever, though only a week had passed since she bade a hasty—and eager— farewell to Master Toki and his slave woman. She would have enjoyed the companionship of sweet, timid Ilse, if not for her foul master, and was deeply concerned for the girl's safety with him. There had been times along the lonely road when she almost wished she had decided to journey on with them as he'd asked, although she had not liked the man at all, nor the way he had tried to force himself upon her, nor the way he'd looked at her, as if stripping the garments from her body with his strange eyes. Nay, it was better she had forgone their companionship. To stay had boded her ill at his hands, and she had determined to take no rash risks until she was certain if she was with child or nay. Poor, frightened Ilse! What had she done to displease the gods so, to have such a cruel man for master?

The sun was high in the sky and over four leagues had wound away behind her when she halted at midday to rest. Her kirtle clung damply to her spine and her hair was sodden at the nape and temples. She took out a loaf of coarse dark bread and tore a piece from it, munching hungrily, for she had not lingered to break her fast that morning. The bread and the cheese, dried fish, and strips of tough but tasty salted beef that followed had all been received in return for the kindling she'd chopped for an old woman, who lived in a tumbledown cottage by the wayside. She thirstily washed them down with fresh, sparkling water cupped in her hands from yet another stream, from which she also filled her leather bottle, and sighed in contentment. How good even the simplest of foods tasted, eaten out in the fresh air with the furry bumblebees busily droning in the tall, flowered grasses and the air sweet and hot and filled with the dreamy sunshine scents of late summer!

Today reminded her of endless summer days like this one when she and Olaf had lain in the tall mountain grasses by the Shielings, and he had told her tales of the gods and how they had fought to create the world, while she had listened entranced and lazily woven wild flowers in her hair. The scarlet poppies, with their sultry black eyes, and the vivid bluebells that Olaf had said matched the hue of her own eyes had been her favorites among them all, she remembered fondly. Afterward they had slipped off their clothes and swum in the cool mountain pools, both naked, both deliriously glad to be alive and be friends throughout those long, hot summers. Ah yes, the closest of friends—and both touchingly innocent . . .

On impulse, she stripped and waded into the stream to bathe herself and wash her kirtle, hating the fusty salt-sweat odor and grime that clung to her clothes and person after days without garments to change into. She had time, all the time in the world to do as she wished, for the first time since her capture, she realized. The knowledge pleased her as little else had done since she had fled Kenley. Freedom was more precious than silver, more costly than gold! She had no responsibilities save those to herself, and nor was there any need for haste. Her pursuers—if any—would no doubt have fallen back after the Thames river, which marked the boundaries of Wessex. If they *had* been foolhardy enough to follow her into the Danelaw, she doubted they would venture as deep into its Viking heart as was she now!

Humming, she scrubbed the hated undyed white kirtle upon the rocks and rinsed it out, then spread it over some low,

313

thorny branches to dry in the sun. Naked as nature's own, she frolicked for a while longer in the cooling stream, then lay down on her back on a soft, grassy spot, arms cradling her head, to soak up the sun. Birds sang. Bees hummed. The sunshine's warmth felt delightful upon her bare skin, and made red and yellow sunbursts against her closed eyelids. She wriggled to get comfortable, then lay quite still, her body loose, her eyes closed, letting her thoughts drift lazily back over the years to her childhood yet again . . .

She must have drifted from pleasant daydreaming into sleep, she realized some while later, hurriedly sitting up. As she did so she heard the clear, mellow woodwind notes of a flute played somewhere close at hand, and stiffened. Someone was coming! She was up and on her feet and had run halfway across the grass to the bush where her kirtle lay drying, when she saw the piper.

He sat cross-legged upon a bed of curling green ferns, not far from where she had lain. His eyes were closed. His expression was rapt. His long fingers were deft as he changed easily from silvery note to silvery note. She muttered a curse and snatched up her kirtle, pulling it on hurriedly to cover herself. How long had he been there watching her? she wondered, furious. Tossing her hair from her eyes as she leaned down to retrieve her belt from where it lay alongside her food pouch and dagger, she saw that the stranger had ceased his playing and was now watching her. Fortunately, it appeared her meager belongings were still intact! She silently but fervently thanked the gods as she swung about to face him, striking an aggressive pose to hide her apprehension.

"Ah!" he murmured before she could speak, a merry grin curving his lips. "I have erred, it would appear! You are not, as I at first fancifully imagined—on spying you there in all your naked beauty—some wood sprite. Alas, not *wuduelfen* after all, but humble mortal, as am I!"

He stood, and she saw that he was quite tall, and lean as a willow wand. His face was as lively as his words, and far more elfin, to her mind, than her own. Black eyes—or eyes so dark brown that they appeared black—twinkled under a pair of sooty brows so narrow and arched, they gave him a permanent expression of elfish amazement. A snub, freckled nose and a wide, merry mouth added to his puckish appearance. He was strangely dressed, his tunic parti-colored, the left side red, the other deep saffron. The strange garment was belted with a chain of curiously wrought silver links, etched with what appeared to be Saxon runes. A jaunty soft woodsman's cap, also dyed the same rare scarlet, topped his cropped, curling black hair, and a pair of black and white osprey feathers, pinned with a costly round brooch, danced rakishly in the air over the brim. He spread his arms wide and turned about in a full circle.

"Look all you might wish, *aelfsciene,* lovely elf! 'Tis only fair and fitting, since I have already taken the advantage and admired *your* fair beauty!" He winked broadly and chuckled. "Aye, every delightful inch!"

"Impudent, spying cur!" Freya snapped, feeling heat rush to her cheeks as she snatched up her pack. She made to stride off, on her way, but the fellow called after her, "Wait! Don't go! I did not mean to anger thee, fairest of the fair! I beg thee, come back . . . !"

She pursed her lips and ignored him, marching purposefully away between the trees and back up the grassy incline toward the road proper. When she risked a glance back over her shoulder, he had gone. And a good riddance to him too, insolent wretch, she thought, relief washing over her, and turned back to her path.

All at once she pulled up short, gasping open-mouthed in surprise. The strange fellow stood *before* her now, blocking her path! He was juggling a number of painted wooden balls in the air, yet his black eyes were still shining with laughter and he was looking at her, not at the balls. A bulging pack had been set at his feet, from which poked all manner of wondrous things.

"How—how did you do that?" she demanded, the question bursting from her of its own volition.

"Juggle?" He shrugged, while continuing to toss and catch the colored balls without dropping a one, or even breaking his fluid rhythm. "'Tis nothing. An old art, learned in boyhood."

315

"Not that!" she retorted scathingly. She'd seen jugglers aplenty before. "How—how did you get ahead of me so quickly?"

He winked again, caught the balls, and tossed them carelessly to the grass at her feet. Fists on hips, he cocked his head to one side and answered, "How does the wind blow? How does the sun shine? In knowing the answers, such marvels lose their magic, fairest of the fair. So must my magic remain a mystery!"

"Magic! Pah! Step aside, and let me go on my way!"

He sighed and swept his feathered cap from his head, doffing it and making her an extravagant bow. "Your wish is my command, elfin beauty!" So saying, he stepped aside and gestured that she might continue.

With a glare at him, she made to hurry past. Yet as she did so, he swiftly reached out and seemed to snatch something from her hair. She whirled about and saw that between his long fingers he now held a shining silver ball.

"A rare but cunning place to hide such a bauble from robbers, fair one!" he declared. "Do I spy another—?" He reached out, and a second silver ball appeared like magic from her ear. As she stood there, stunned, he plucked out two more, one from her other ear, the fourth—or so it appeared—from her very lips! He tossed them into the air, and to her amazement they disappeared!

"Who are you?" she demanded suspiciously, wondering if she had chanced upon a wizard, for in truth he seemed one.

"I am called Robin—when I am called anything at all that is fit for a lady's tender ears!" He inclined his head. "And you?"

"My name need not concern you," she snapped with a flash of her sapphire eyes and a haughty toss of her red-gold braids.

"Tut," he offered with a disapproving frown. "If you will not trade names with me fairly, then I must guess yours! Would it be Ellyn, perhaps—or Gwynn? Aethelfreda? Berta? Nay, nay!" he argued with himself, and his black eyes met hers in a long and level stare. "Such rare and vivid beauty demands a beauteous name! Ah! Ha! I have it! Is it perchance—Freya? Aye, that's it! Freya—the Viking goddess of love and beauty, of seduction and its many arts. Tell me, lovely goddess, where is your chariot—the brace of cunning cats that draw it? In truth, my feet are weary since my horse was stolen, and I would rather ride!"

She gasped, then paled, suddenly afraid of the merry fellow. "Freya is not my name!" she lied hotly. "And even—even if it were, 'tis none of your business, sir! The day wears on. I am expected up yonder. I must be on the road!" She skittered away from him like a frightened fawn.

In one loose stride he had drawn level with her and taken her firmly but gently by the elbow. "Fear not, Viking maid! Your identity is safe with me—as is that dark and sorrowful secret from which you flee." He saw the confusion and fear that filled her eyes and spread through her, and smiled reassuringly. "'Tis no wizardry, believe me. The knowledge was there, in your mind. I but plucked it out! 'Tis a talent I have, like the juggling, and one that has served me well in many a scrape," he grinned ruefully, "though often men's unspoken opinions of me have been rude and scarce worthy of the plucking! On my word, I mean you no harm. I am but a traveler, as are you, headed for Mercia, and 'tis a lonely road. I had hoped to share a few leagues with you—"

"—aye, and a tumble or two, no doubt!" she flared hotly, for she had seen the bright sparking of desire in his eyes, mingled with the merriment. "In truth, Master Robin—*if* that is indeed your name!—*I* am able to pluck such thoughts as yours from a man's mind, as easily as you!"

He bowed in deference to her accuracy. "Aye, I confess I had such fond hopes! Though you believe me a wizard—aye, admit it, you do!—I am yet just a man, with a man's needs, and you're the fairest maid I have seen in many a league! I would have to be a saint not to yearn for thee—and I am no saint! But think on this, Freya. Were a tumble my only intent, could I not have taken thee by the stream back there, as easily as winking?"

"A—aye," she agreed reluctantly.

"And since I didn't, does it not also follow that I will make no move to do so anon—unless, of course, you should yourself . . . entreat . . . me?" He winked.

Despite herself and her initial fears, Freya wanted to smile.

He was such a droll fellow, and his words had put her at ease, though she would never admit as much to him. She shrugged. "I suppose so."

"Ah, then all is well! You believe me. And I am honored that you find me droll!" Robin said with laughter in his voice, eyes twinkling as he caught the sudden flare of anger and incredulity in her eyes. "Come! Come, fair one! Let's be on our way. The day wears on, as you so prettily said!" He hefted up the voluminous pack that she now saw he had at his feet, took up her own, and gallantly offered her his arm.

And so, side by side, together they took to the north road.

Her misgivings at allowing Robin to accompany her soon relaxed, for in truth he was the most lively and entertaining traveling companion, and not at all frightening. She likened his talent of thought reading to the strange gift of the "sight" that Uncle Sven possessed, and soon grew used to his answering her thoughts seconds before she voiced them. He kept up a steady stream of conversation that, with his keen mind and ready wit, was far from dull, and her own merry laughter at his outrageous tales and amusing anecdotes soon rang out over the rolling meadows and through the deep woods that bordered their road.

Talk was interspersed with mystifying sleights of hand on Robin's part. Golden hoops, silken kerchiefs or rainbow colors, ribands, and silver balls appeared and disappeared in dazzling succession. He tumbled and turned cartwheels across the greensward, agile and seemingly boneless, springing upright and landing before her with a bunch of wild flowers brandished in his fist, which he offered her with a deep and courtly bow. The afternoon flew past on quicksilver wings, to become a foxglove twilight. They took shelter in a derelict hut shortly before moonrise and shared their provisions over a crackling fire. Later, her belly full, her body pleasantly tired, she rested her chin upon her fist and gazed into the golden flames, lost in melancholy thoughts as, with nightfall, her grief returned to her full force, as it had in the dark of each and every night of her journey. For once, the teasing laughter fled Robin's face.

318

"You were wronged, unjustly accused, and all is awry," he said softly. "Forgive me for my careless manner this morn. 'Twas wrong of me, with you so heavy of heart."

"'Tis already forgiven, think naught of it, good Robin," she murmured, no longer surprised that he had read her tumultous thoughts with such ease. "You made me forget for a little while, and for that I thank thee. The talent to make people laugh is a rare gift, which too few are given." She flashed him a warm smile across the fire.

"Will you not tell me all?" he urged, deeply moved by the sadness that shadowed her lovely face. Her sapphire eyes were dark, and he thought that once he caught the shimmer of tears in their depths as she gazed into the fire. "A burden shared is one lightened, is it not? And though I could, if pressed, learn all myself by simply reading your thoughts," and he grinned at the boast, "I fancy you have need of the purge of telling it yourself."

She shrugged. "So it is said. Oh, very well! In truth you are a wizard, sir, for I find myself drawn to tell my tale to you, as I have told no other that I've met along the road."

And so in faltering, husky tones she told him of Alaric, and his murder at the Lady Kendra's hands; of her taking the woman hostage and fleeing Kenley; her intent to journey to Jorvic. When she was done she found she felt a little eased, as he had promised.

He nodded sagely. "Fleeing was your only course, with your lord and beloved slain," he agreed. "But you will be safe now— or at least safe from this wicked Kendra and her wiles."

"There are other dangers?"

"For a woman traveling alone through these lands, whether Viking or Saxon, the dangers are many," he said solemnly. "You could be set upon by robbers."

"But I have nothing of value—!" she began, then looked away and blushed in the firelight as she realized his meaning. "Oh!"

"Then again, there are other forces at work hereabouts— dark, evil forces! Many of the folk in these isolated northern lands have paid only lip service to Christianity, you see. They are ignorant and unenlightened, and cling to their dark fears

319

and superstitions in these hard times. They yet worship the old ones, the savage gods of the times before remembering, and practice their secret rites where Christian eyes cannot see them, nor Christian hearts persecute them. Beneath the full of the moon they make sacrifice to Tiw, god of the sword, or to mighty Woden, Lord of Death and of the Spear, and ask them to grant them victory against their enemies. Their Viking enemies!''

"My people also offer human sacrifice to placate our gods," she said stiffly, "though more rarely now than in the past. Is not this Woden simply Odin by another name? So it is said."

"I think not," Robin disagreed. "For their Lord of the Spear is darker, more ancient and steeped in blood and evil than even your fierce Norse gods, and his priests little more than slaves to his every desire—and, of course, to their own, which are ofttimes more sinister," he added soberly.

"And—and what are his desires?" Freya asked, feeling suddenly chilled.

"The life-blood of innocents, offered up on his altar. From this blood 'tis said he draws his strength and magic. In return he grants his followers victory in battle," Robin murmured, and wished she had not asked him, or that he, fool that he was, had given her some other answer.

She laughed shakily. "Then I am quite safe, Robin! You need not fear, for I am of a certainty no longer innocent, and therefore quite useless to these followers of Woden!" She yawned. "It grows late. In truth, I must sleep! My eyes will scarce stay open. And a long road stretches ahead of me yet again on the morrow."

"Aye, and before myself. We'll travel part of the way together, before I turn to the west road and you continue on north."

"Where are you bound?"

"To the court of Ceolwulf, caretaker king of Mercia—he that lost the kingdom for Burhred, Alfred's own brother-in-law and rightful king—with his fool's promises!" Robin mocked. "The people of Mercia are fond of magicians and bards, and I flatter myself that I am both! They'll weigh my cap down with Welsh gold for a tune that they can raise their voices to in harmony!"

She smiled, suddenly shy. "Would—would you play your flute for me now?"

He nodded. "Aye, and be happy to do so! A lullaby for an elfin maid, who will not let me comfort her!" He shook his curly head in mock sorrow.

"'Tis too soon for another man's comforting," Freya murmured, wrapping her mantle about her and stretching out beside the fire. "But were I to seek comfort from any man, I promise it would be from you, gentle Robin. You—you are a kind fellow, I fancy, for all your mischievous ways!"

He grinned. "Alas! Your gentle words do nothing to quench the fire in a man's loins, heartless wench! Yet—I am perversely pleased by them! Sleep now, and may only the sweetest of Queen Mab's fairy dreams fill your slumber!" He drew the carved flute from his pack and began to play.

And Freya, soothed by the hypnotic little tune he piped and further lulled by the warmth of their fire, slept deeply.

"Alaric!"

"Aye, vixen?"

"But—I thought you dead! Kendra—she stabbed thee, my heart!"

He came toward her, his gray eyes filled with tenderness, a smile curving his mouth. "Nay, sweeting, fear not! 'Twas but a dream, my love, a frightening dream which I will scatter like leaves before the winds . . ."

His arms enfolded her and she melted against him, all the grief and despair slipping from her like ice in the spring thaw. Her arms reached up, curled about his throat, laced themselves in the tangle of thick, ebony curls at his nape that she loved so.

"Alaric, oh my Alaric!" she whispered, tasting salt tears on her lips. Tenderly he kissed them away, parting her mouth beneath the sweet-fire heat of his, then he lifted her and bore her away to where a couch spread with sable and marten pelts beckoned invitingly from beneath a leafy tree. A bed in the forest? How can that be? she wondered dreamily, stirring as he lowered her to the luxurious softness of the pelts.

Her hair floated about them as he lay upon her, caressing her body, and dimly she realized that their garments had

321

disappeared, vanished! Bare flesh met bare flesh as he lowered himself upon her, and the sensation as their bodies joined was as jolting as the jagged fire-arrows that the god Thor hurled from the storm skies to the earth below.

"Aaah!" She cried out as he entered her and arched her head back, moist coral lips parted, eyes closed. Her red-gold tresses flowed over the pelts and onto the greensward like a tumbling sea, alive with vivid color. Her fingers clamped fast into the muscled flesh of his wiry arms as he began to move powerfully between her thighs, and her nails gouged tiny crescents from the hard, tanned flesh as she yielded joyfully to the swelling fullness of him, to the sweet and fiery hardness of his man-shaft that penetrated to the very center of her being and filled her with trembling pleasure.

"Oh sweet love, how I have waited—longed—for thee!" she cried, feeling the quiver spread throughout her to every part, to become a taut, pulsing knot of expectancy deep within her quivering womanhood that only he could ease.

But then, even as her arms enfolded him, even as the moment breathed fulfillment in her ear, he was withdrawing, dwindling, receding. The ebony helm of his hair, the massive darkness of his body were spinning and retreating until only a bright light—like a candle's flame seen at a distance—remained.

Sobbing, she sprang from the bed and ran toward it, twisting and turning in the sudden pitch-darkness to avoid the branches and vines that reached for her like eager, grasping talons. All about breathed Evil, a panting black dog that drooled at her scent and reached with dripping, foaming jaws to rend her body. Heart leaping painfully against her ribs, she fled onward, blindly, desperately, toward that steady golden point of light wherein was love and hope and truth.

The flame was before her now, bright-shining, steadily luminescent. A tongue of fire! Oh the heat, the heat that emanated from it! It nigh scorched her face with its warmth! Yet—'twas him, 'twas Alaric, alive, burning with the life force, bursting with vigor, and she would—she must!—touch that flame, hold it fast . . . must save him from *her!* Aye . . . must . . . save . . . Alaric . . . must . . .

She reached out and closed her fingers about the flame. She felt a sudden draught, as if a door had been opened to let in the night wind, and then it was extinguished, vanished—! The sudden pitch-blackness squeezed close about her.

"*Nay!*" she screamed, the cry torn from her very depths. Alone. Only the panting hound of Evil's breath wafted against her cheek. Foul. Rank.

"Fool!" came a mocking voice. "Did you think to have him back? Nay, Viking, he is mine, mine forever—!"

Her fingers closed on air, only air. And Kendra's cruel laughter sounded on the gloom and on the tomb-dank darkness . . . in which she was now utterly alone . . . alone . . .

"Waken! Freya, wake up!"

"*Ja?* What is it?"

"'Tis morn. After daybreak," Robin answered, his expression concerned. She had tossed and turned restlessly all night, crying and whimpering in the serpent coils of a deep sleep from which he could not awaken her. He tenderly brushed the sweat-dampened hair from her temples. "The dream was a frightening one, was it not, fair one?"

She nodded. "It was. It brought back memories of my Alaric, sweet, sweet memories, and then cruelly wrest him from me yet again. Oh cruelest of dreams, why do you torture me so!" She shuddered and covered her face with her hands.

Not today, Robin thought, drawing her close to comfort her. *I'll not take my leave of her today.*

They parted at a fork in the road soon after midday of the following day, Robin taking the rough road west toward the misty blue mountains, Freya continuing on down the great Roman road toward Jorvic. It was a strangely difficult leave-taking, although they had known each other for so brief a spell, for the closeness they felt for each other seemed to transcend time.

"Fare thee well," Robin murmured, placing a brotherly

323

hand upon her shoulder. "May your gods guard your path!"

"And your own the path you journey," Freya added sadly, wishing they did not have to part. "You made the leagues seem quickly covered. In truth, Robin, I shall miss your company and your friendship."

"As will I your own, fairest of the fair. I hope our paths will cross again some day, in better times. In times of peace between my people and yours."

She nodded, and he gave her a gentle kiss upon the brow, roguishly doffed his hat in courtly salute, and set out at a loose, easy stride, his bulging pack carried effortlessly upon his back.

He turned atop the crest of the next hill and looked back over his shoulder to see her still standing there, a forlorn, slender figure whose red-gold hair made a bright splash of color against the rough heathery purple of the moor. He waved his feathered cap, then kissed and flourished his hand in a last, regretful farewell before he disappeared over the rise.

With a heavy sigh, Freya turned to her own road, set her shoulders resolutely, and trudged on.

Chapter 24

The wan, milky moon was up, but as yet there was no sign of even a single star. More likely than not there would be no stars, not this night, for the sharp, earthy scent of coming rain mingled with the cool balm of the night dew. The shredded raincloud-veils hid the stars from view of those abroad this night, Freya thought as she tended her fire, hugging the mantle tightly about her for warmth.

She had missed Robin sorely since they parted ways, and had longed more times than she cared to number in the succeeding days for yet another glimpse of his merry smile, another sample of his teasing wit, but to no avail. Robin was no doubt halfway on his road to Mercia, she thought gloomily, and she here on the bleak and rolling moors of Northumbria, where every shadow held an unseen danger—perhaps a gibbering ghost or a gurgling demon or a naughty spirit come to torment her, for such were abroad by cover of darkness, she knew. The days spent alone she could bear, but oh, the empty, frightening nights!

The low hoot of a hunting owl rang out across the silent moors, and she glanced up sharply in time to catch the drifting white of its wings in the second before it vanished. She shivered, loneliness washing over her like a soaking, bone-chilling wave. It was not only a physical loneliness, but a crushing agony of spirit. Alaric had been dead for only three weeks, and yet already her memory of his face was beginning to blur. She did not welcome the kind forgetfulness of the grieving mind that fades such painful images to a bearable remembrance, the edges fuzzy and indistinct. Nay! She wanted to guard her memories jealously, to hug them to her breast as carefully as a miser hugs his purse of gold or silver. To take each one out from time to time and polish it to shining brightness with the fond remembrances of love; to recall every line of his face in painful, crystalline clarity, every nuance of his voice, every word and touch he'd ever spoken or given her!

But—already his face had taken on a look in her mind that was him, and yet not him. An Alaric who was as serene and as still as a stone carving on a reliquary or an effigy on a Christian tomb. The fire, the sheer energy force of him, wås dulled. She feared that with the passing of time it would become extinguished, until she clung to a memory that was shadowy and feebly lacking in substance, that bore no resemblance whatsoever to the real Alaric, the fiercely passionate, powerful, virile man he had been in life.

She hunched over and rested her cheek on her arm, willing the huge knot in her breast to unravel, dissolve and become healing tears. But it did not. Though the ache swelled to an unbearable, choking pain, her eyes remained quite dry, burning. From agonized wakefulness she slipped uneasily into fitful sleep, tossing and turning on the heaped furze that was her bed as she wrestled with dream monsters . . .

A sound that was beyond the spectrum of normal night sounds—to which even in slumber her ears had long since grown accustomed—brought her sharply from deep sleep to full wakefulness some while later. She sat bolt upright, her heart thudding frantically against her ribs, leaping and bounding like a frightened doe fleeing the hunt.

Woooodennnn! Woooodennnn!

Was it but the low moan of the lonely night wind searching the desolate moors? Or was it something more—some low, preternaturally malignant chorus that was not of this earth, but of the Otherworld and its shades?

She snatched up her dagger and held it before her, the blade turned outward. All was dark about her camp, dark as the kingdom of Hel, for the moon still hid her revealing light under cloud. "Hallooo! Who goes there?" she cried. Even to her ears her voice sounded thin as a reed, and as lacking in spine.

A trill of low, mocking laughter from the deep shadows sent frissons of terror rising down her arms and jerked the hackles upright on the back of her neck.

"Show yourself!" she commanded, and heard the quaver in her voice as she stood, letting her mantle fall unnoticed off her shoulders to the turf.

"Bride of the Spear-Lord!" intoned the eerie chorus now. *"Maid of the Spear-Lord, come! Come to us-s-s!"*

The last sibilance echoed over and over, like the rustle of the wind in the trees. But—there were no trees on these empty, windswept moors of gorse and turf and heather . . . !

"Who are you? Where are you? What—what do you want with me?" She hurriedly bent down and took up a slender branch from her heap of kindling. Fingers trembling, she lit it in the dying embers of the fire. The branch caught and a narrow tongue of smoking amber flame crackled and leaped up, fanned by the night wind, to illumine her lovely, frightened face in all its stark pallor. Holding her flaming torch aloft in one hand, the dagger in the other, she stepped away from the fire and waited, breath bated.

"You are the Chosen One!" came the disembodied chant. *"Woman of Fire, Bride of the Spear-Lord, we have come for thee!"*

Her belly gave a sickening lurch. Her knees threatened to buckle. She strained her eyes, trying to plumb the black moors all about, trying vainly to see who the speakers might be. Though she could not see them, she sensed them there, very near: a great mass of bodies whose life force crackled on the dew-dampened air, their rank, excited musk as sharp and pungent as that of wild beasts. She shivered. Supernatural they were not, she was certain now, but frightening—*ja*, they were frightening, nonetheless!

The wind rose, and her hair lifted, swirling about her head. The wind also shredded away the cloudy veils that dimmed the moon, sent them scattering like gray sheep before the ravening wolf. The pale radiance suddenly revealed the throng that ringed her simple camp, catching the cunning glitter of an eye, a pale, rapacious face, a moistened lip here and there amongst the looming dark-robed forms. One shadow detached itself and

327

stepped forward from the mass. A male, she knew from the masculine gait with which he moved and from his height. Their leader, she shrewdly judged from his stance.

"Behold, daughter of Frig! You are chosen!" he cried. "Bind her! Carry her to the high mountain!" He gestured to those behind him, and the huddled mass churned forward as one man, their excited mutterings like the rumble of distant thunder, their arms reaching out for her like the choking arms of a horrible dream!

The time for reasoning was no more, had never been, Freya realized belatedly, wetting her lips, for those foul shadows were not to be reasoned with. The crowd-madness ruled them—and the lust that scented the wind. Nor was there sense in trying to fight them. They were too many! Hurling the fiery brand into their midst and sending sparks showering, she turned and fled for her very life.

A hundred paces, no more, and a spear sang over her head and thudded into the turf before her, the shaft shuddering and ringing with the impact. Blessed Frey, protect me! she screamed silently, and forced her legs to greater speed, flying like a madwoman across the springy turf, onward, onward to . . . nowhere!

"After her!" came that strangely familiar voice again, "Bind the Chosen One! Bind the maiden spear-marked for our lord!"

Her breath rasping painfully, she ran on, into the night, over the rough, uneven turf that conspired with her pursuers to trip her, fling her headlong to the ground, a sacrifice to their dark will and their darker lord.

How long could she hope to outrun them? Where could she flee? She was alone, armed with naught but a single useless dagger against a horde that numbered a score or more! And yet the will to live was strong, oh so very strong! Sobs choked her. Her heart swelled, threatened to burst. The crest of the hill loomed ahead. Beyond it the sky yawned, an ashy backdrop to the single standing stone at its very crest that rose upward to the watery moon like an ominously pointing dark finger. Or the head of a massive spear—

"Aaaghgh!" The cry exploded from her as she fell, wrenching her ankle in a rabbit hole. She thudded to the

328

ground, pain knifing through her. Yet even as she landed she was up again, onto her knees, crawling, scrabbling, clawing to escape the howling pack at her back, growing closer, closer with every second. Limping, every breath a sob or a curse or a prayer, she yet strove to escape them, their seething, bloodthirsty mass at her back the goad that urged her painfully onward, ever onward.

Too late, she saw how she had played into their hands! Too late, she realized the folly of running upward, up the hill toward the offering place at its crest! In a last attempt she swerved violently aside, headed back and down, and then the turf slipped from under her in a sickening rush and the black world whirled and wheeled and ran together and the sickly stars collided with the sickly moon and all was pain and terror and darkness and despair.

Dimly she heard the pack close in, smelled their stinking sweat, felt the rough cloth of their dark robes rubbed coarse against her cheek. Dimly she felt the eager grasping of many strong hands as they bound her, gagged her, lifted her and bore her away. Dimly she heard high-pitched, wailing screams, someone calling desperately for "Robin, Robin! Robinnnn!" and knew—on some faraway level of consciousness still clung to desperately by a single, fragile thread—that they were her own screams, her own cries, before all feeling, all hearing, all sight grew suddenly dimmed, then were snuffed out like a candle flame . . .

She came to, whimpering at the agony in her shoulders and thighs. She tried to move to ease the wrenching pain, but could not. Spread-eagled until it seemed her limbs must surely be torn from their sockets, she had been bound to something cold and hard, something stone. Her eyes flickered open. Above her, the wheeling night sky. The clouds racing with the night wind were edged with the hazy silver glimmer of the summer moon's light. There were stars now, tiny pricks of brightness pulsing far above. To her right rose the standing stone, a carved black wand, a phallic form that seemed to throb with evil power. The breath came rasping from between her lips as her eyes were drawn to it, held fast in the grip of an awful fascination upon that looming blackness.

". . . *Lord of Death and of the Spear, accept the sacrifice we offer thee, and in return grant us Woden's victory in battle against the Northmen!*" came a chant, and she turned her head to see nightmarish dark-robed figures ringed about her, swaying slowly to and fro as they chanted their foul litany. Eyes glittered. Mouths moved. Men, all men, not a woman among them! The wind riffled across her body, and with a sweeping chill far greater than its current she realized she had been stripped before they bound her here, upon their altar. Some sort of bluish clay had been daubed and smeared across her breasts in a pagan symbol of magical power. The symbol of Woden! She closed her eyes, yet no tears trickled from under the clamped lids and shone on her cheeks in the moonlight. Even now, she was as devoid of tears for her own impending doom as she had been following Alaric's death.

So this was the moment. This was the point in time to which her entire life had been moving irrevocably from the moment fate had given her birth. Here, on this desolate, windswept hill top in Northumbria—this was where she would die! In this friendless place her mortal body would be offered up as sacrifice to Woden, the dark, pagan Lord of Death and the Spear, in return for victory in battle . . .

The high priest—for such he must be—came to her side then, and looming over her drew back the cowled hood of his flowing dark robe. Staring up at him with a curious detachment, she stared into his face. His cheeks and forehead were frighteningly daubed with more of the sacred clay, and his pale, strangely shaped silver eyes were uncannily goatlike with their oval pupils: eyes she knew!

"Toki!" She tried to cry out, to scream, but the foul sackcloth gag that clamped her tongue allowed only a strangled croak to sound from her.

Toki smiled, a peculiarly hypnotic, evil smile, and let the robe fall from his shoulders. Two of the others took it from him with great reverence, bowing low as they shuffled backward, away from him. Toki was naked beneath it. His pale, wiry body seemed carved from morse ivory in the light and shadows.

He raised his arms to the darkened sky, and she saw that in one hand he brandished aloft a spear, the long, sharp point a-glitter in the moonlight; in the other dangled a length of cord. The host gathered all about him fell to their knees as one man, their heads bowed.

" 'Tis time! Our lady moon is at her zenith! Let us now consecrate the chosen maid! Let us fill her with our life force, my warrior brothers! Let us make her the Bride of the Spear-Lord!" he cried.

She heard the murmur that rippled amongst them, smelled the scent of their lust, rank and hot upon the night air. Her teeth would have chattered, were it not for the foul linen gag between them! She strained her head to watch in horror as Toki stepped away from her. He knelt before the spear-shaped standing stone and placed both spear and garrot reverently at its base, consecrating them. Chills swept up and down her spine as he intoned a prayer in an ancient Celtic tongue she did not know, and pressed his lips to its base.

When he again stood and turned toward her, he seemed to have grown in breadth and stature in some magical way. Up and up he grew, until he towered above them all. An evil smile curled his thin lips, and the fierce glitter of his silver eyes seemed lit by some unholy fire that burned bright in his dark and pagan soul. At his groin, his manhood rose hugely from its bed of dark hair, and she knew full well in what manner she would be wed to their lord Woden. And when Toki and his followers had done with her . . . Her eyes were drawn in horrified fascination to the glint of silver where the spear lay in the turf at the base of the standing stone, and the snakelike coil of the cord beside it. Death would be dealt her as it was dealt by those given to Odin, by spear and strangulation together—!

No escape. No way out. No chance to fight. No hope for rescue. The knowledge froze her. Dare she hope that long before it was over, her life force would flee her body? Could she hope for that . . . ?

Never a coward in her life before this, she was numbed, drunk on terror.

Chapter 25

Time hung suspended. The wind stilled. The very night held its dew-laden breath as Toki strode slowly toward the stone altar.

Torches hissed and flared up, roaring dragon-like as the pitch in which they had been dipped caught and burst into flames. It was a scene from a nightmare, there on the crest of the hill, real and yet unreal: the robed figures pressing forward all about the altar; the torches dancing and wavering and casting shifting flares of light over the dark turf, the shadows beyond their ruddy light made blacker by contrast. And above it all towered the Spear Stone, tall, ominous, and curiously alive, as if therein dwelt the god Woden himself.

"Now will Toki, High Master of Our Lord, claim the woman for Woden!" cried a voice.

"*Claim her! Claim her!*" they clamored, and a ripple of excitement ignited in their midst and leaped from man to man like wind-blown flame. The acrid scent of burning pitch, the mist-dampened turf—and the rank scent of lust, unbridled—rode the cool night air.

Freya strained against the viciously knotted cords that held her fast as Toki loomed over her, yet they held. Sweat rolled in great beads off her brow and upper lip and ran down her throat, making furrows in the blue woad that painted her breasts. A scream was born deep in her throat, but suffered stillbirth on the foul gag that clamped her tongue.

And then Toki's hands were at her waist, her breasts, cold as if dipped in an icy flow. She shivered away from his touch, shrank from him as far as the bonds would allow. His cold caresses were the slimy caresses of a serpent, coiling over her flesh. His hypnotic voice flowed over her, the words foreign, an ancient tongue she knew not, yet in the reeling torrent of her mind she sensed he uttered a prayer, some plea for blessing on her, the sacrifice he would offer to his god. Her eyes fluttered open, met his. Oh, the cold, cold comfort in their depths; the cruel, relentless purpose; the driving lust! She tried to turn from him, to look away and blot him out—but could not. The pale silvery orbs held her fast, her own dilated, terror-filled eyes riveted to the silver-shining, evil slits of his.

"'Tis time," he breathed, and leaned over her, his lank hair damp with his sweat. "Time for the mating, for the taking of the Bride, Woman of Fire!" He ran his foul hand down the length of her body, his lips peeling back from his teeth in a wolfish grin. "You are worthy, Viking, aye, worthy of my Lord!" His breath fanned her cheek. The gorge rose hot and acid in her throat, for his breath was as fetid and cold as the breath of death itself.

"'Tis time, my brothers!" he proclaimed, arms uplifted to the heavens. "The lady moon is at her zenith. 'Tis time!"

All about the altar the chant grew and grew, until it blurred into an hypnotic humming without words; without beginning, without end.

Freya fought for control, fighting the vomit that rose up her throat, knowing that to spill her gorge, gagged as she was, meant certain death. *I don't want to die—not here, not now, not this way!* she sobbed silently. If only she could break free, defend herself in some way. To die helpless like this, like a bound sacrificial lamb, when all her life had been directed toward honing her fighting skills, filled her with a helpless rage that was far worse than the threat of death itself. *Blessed Frey, protector of women, save me!*

She felt Toki's swollen member prod roughly between her spread thighs, and arched her body upward like a bow to prevent his entry.

"Nay!" she screamed, but only a strangled groan escaped the gag.

"Claim her! Claim her!" clamored the eager watchers.

His cold hardness pierced her tender core, growing, expanding, icy as the thrust of a frozen blade.

"Hail Ooodinnn!"

A voice rang out, a fiery blast upon the cool night air. The sudden, ringing cry froze Toki rigid upon her. His member shriveled, hung limp. His head jerked up, the silver eyes widening. Half-stunned with terror, Freya turned her head and followed his gaze.

A loud explosion followed in the wake of the cry, a sound like that of a single crack of thunder on the night. Bluish smoke poured up from the turf at their backs and billowed about a low, craggy tor. The throng about the altar fell back a pace or two, gasping as one man. The smoke was wafting away like misty veils, but from its depths rose a towering giant, spiraling upward, upward, to loom above them all!

Its hair seemed long and shaggy, grayish locks furling from beneath the dull bronze glint of a war helm, gloriously winged. A ragged beard flowed over its broad mailed chest. A flowing mantle was draped over its shoulders, and it fluttered in the night wind. Yet it was not this, but the eye that impaled them where they stood; a single demon eye that glowed red like a banked coal, while where the second should have been was only a black and empty socket.

"And the god, Odin, plucked out his eye, that he might be given the gift of wisdom from Mimir . . ." So had the *skalds* sung, Freya recalled dimly in her terror.

The apparition raised its arms and the throng fell back a second time, for upon each mighty fist there perched a raven: the omen bird, harbinger of death, messenger of the gods. The pair sat still as stone, yet their blue-black plumage and their cruel, unblinking eyes glittered in the torchlight and the light of the moon.

"'Tis Lord Woden Himself!" cried one man hoarsely, and took to his heels, his robe flapping behind him as he fled.

"Aye, and his ravens!" cried another, and also fled. Other robed figures followed them, tripping and stumbling as they went.

"Nay, not Woden!" Toki spat, his expression livid. "'Tis but a trick! Come back, you fools!"

"Trick, think you, Worm?" bellowed the apparition in a voice like the rumble of thunder. "If not Woden, Odin then.

By either name, I am yet your lord, miserable little man! See this, and mark it well, Toki, Worm of Mercia!"

So saying, the apparition flung one of the ravens high into the air. All eyes followed its course, saw it vanish against the darkened sky. All gasped anew as a shower of golden coins rained down upon the turf in its place. The apparition tossed the second raven skyward, and all at once it was likewise transformed, became a mighty blood-axe winking silver fire from its twin blades as it wheeled earthward, to lodge firmly in the apparition's fist.

A dozen more of Toki's number fled him.

Toki circled the altar, Freya forgotten. He wetted his lips, apprehension in his suddenly furtive eyes. There was a film of sweat upon his brow.

"What do you want with us?" he demanded, his voice cracked. "We do only honor to you here, my lord! A sacrifice in your name! A Viking woman was—"

"—defiled! Defiled by thee, Toki of Mercia!" the voice thundered. "You have defiled a Viking bride of Odin with your own foul, mortal body. For this you must pay!"

He brandished his mighty axe toward the brooding standing stone. At once a further crack sounded. More bluish smoke belched from the turf at the stone's base. The dark pillar tottered, rocked on its foundations, poised for an endless moment, then fell in fragments to the earth!

Another frantic exodus of Toki's faint-hearted followers. He stood with only a handful behind him now, and even they seemed poised for flight, only their terror riveting them in place.

"The Spear Stone is no more!" the voice rang out. "Come, my daughter! Now is the moment!"

Toki's jaw fell slack. He babbled like a lunatic as, slowly over the misty turf, a white horse came a-galloping, a ghostly glimmer against the dark, heathery moors. On its bare back rode a Valkyrie maid, one of Odin's daughters. Her tumbling flaxen hair streamed like spun moonbeams down over breastplate and armor that winked dull silver in the meager light. Her horse's wings were as gossamer veils in the moonlight as she drew the steed to a halt. It pawed the turf and snorted, tossing its silky mane.

"Choose, my daughter," the apparition demanded. "Mark him you have chosen for death!"

Toki paled as the Valkyrie raised a slender bare arm, wavered, then pointed straight at him.

"Nay!" he screamed, and made to run. A step. Then two. No more!

None remaining saw the two-headed blood-axe fly from the apparition's fist. Yet all saw it thud home, cleaving Toki half through where he stood. Gouts of blood splashed in a ruby cascade to the turf, staining the man's pale flesh. Then his corpse tottered and fell like an empty sack.

"Who next?" came the roar again, and with that the remainder fled, all but crawling over each other to be first away, down the hill.

Silent, unmoving, Freya waited with bated breath, with eyes tightly closed, for what was yet to come . . .

Dragging footsteps sounded to one side, coming closer, closer. Her bowels churned, became water. *Now! Be done with it now!* she screamed silently. *I can withstand no more!*

"And nor shall you, fairest of the fair," declared a gentle voice from close by, plucking her very thoughts from her mind.

And with those words Freya slipped effortlessly down into blackness.

She came to, to find herself clothed again, and swaddled in warm mantles. A cheerful fire was crackling heartily nearby, and Ilse, of all people, was at her side, chafing her hands to restore feeling to them. Above all, a sensation of safety and relief cocooned her. A sob of relief escaped her lips. Her limbs trembled in reaction to her narrow escape.

Robin—for who else but he could have orchestrated such a display of "magic"?—came and crouched at her side. He held a drinking horn in his hand, which he pressed to her lips. "Drain it," he ordered her softly.

"But how—"

"Drink first. There is time enough for questions later." He threw back his head and laughed merrily. "I'd wager a purse of gold mancuses those Woden-worshipping worms will not return

336

to these parts tonight—or any time in the near future!"

Obediently she drained the horn, spluttering at the unfamiliar, sharp taste of strong wine and bitter herbs. New strength coursed through her veins as the wine worked its own spell and revived her. She struggled up onto her elbows, brimful of questions.

"How?" she demanded. "How did you do it? How did you find me?" She did not need to ask how he had known of her plight. His strange talents she already knew of!

He pressed a finger to her lips, a smile crinkling the corners of eyes that, in the firelight, were dark as sloes and bright as pennies.

"Did I not warn thee that in the telling, magic is no more?" he teased. Then, seeing the determined look in her eyes, he added, "but since you will not be satisfied with less than an explanation, I will tell you. Mark this, curious wench!"

He drew forth a horrid thing, a tall, strange thing from which she shrank. It had long grizzled hair and beard—or rather, what *looked* like hair but more closely resembled trailing moss—and a body that was nothing more than a tall crosspiece of sticks lashed together, a dark mantle thrown over the "shoulders." Robin grinned at her aghast expression and tugged the "hair" away, and beneath Freya saw that the head was in reality just a pumpkin, one "eye" charred black, the other hollowed out. In the cavity a stub of candle had been set, but was now extinguished.

"One-eyed Odin?" she sputtered incredulously, brows arched. Laughter sparkled in her eyes in the firelight. None but Robin could have conceived such an outrageous plot—and none but he would have had the audacity and courage to see it through successfully.

"None other, fairest of the fair!" Robin confessed with a roguish grin. "I held this mighty 'god' aloft upon my shoulders, hence his great and terrifying height!"

"But what of the ravens—the axe—the golden coins?"

"All mere illusions, nothing more. Illusions aided by the moonlight—and the dark fears that lurk in the hearts of all men. As for the ravens, the men saw what they expected to see, Odin and his 'messengers'! In their superstitious minds, the dead chickens I had bartered for my humble supper this noonday became ravens! The gold coins were but a sampling of my sleight of hand—though the blood-axe was real enough, as Toki learned," he finished grimly. "Worm that he was! Never was a man more deserving of his end than he! Would I could have taken his cursed life before he laid hands on thee." The black eyes were cold now, the laughter fled their depths. Then, in his mercurial fashion, the gloom and anger were dispelled once more and he smiled. "Hungry?"

To her surprise, she realized she was ravenous. She nodded eagerly, and he reached behind her ear and drew forth an oatcake. "Then eat!"

While she munched hungrily on the oatcake, Ilse came with a bowl of savory stew and an eating knife. Freya thanked her with a knowing grin. "'Raven' stew, I wager?"

"Raven stew it is indeed!" Ilse acknowledged with a shy but happy smile. "And served ye by no less than a 'daughter of Odin' herself, mistress!"

"Aye," Robin joined in, "and a comely Valkyrie Mistress Ilse made too, upon her white winged steed!" He winked, and pretty Ilse blushed.

They all laughed then, as much from their shared relief that Freya was safe as from anything else. Freya looked at their smiling faces and thought how dear they had become in the short space of time they had known each other. Friends, *ja*, friends in the truest meaning of the word! They had stood by her without thought for their own safety or gain of any kind. "*Takke*," she murmured, looking from Robin to Ilse. "Thank you, from the bottom of my heart! You saved my life, and I can never repay you."

"We ask for no payment," Robin said firmly. "There's enough bloodshed in this world, aye, and greed aplenty. 'Twas well we could help you for friendship's sake alone. That you are here, safe, is thanks enough."

"I should be thanking you, mistress," Ilse volunteered. "Toki had tied me as he did you, and left me in the gorse." She shuddered. "I think after they were done with you, he intended that I should be offered next to Woden! Master Robin here found me," she finished, flashing him a grateful smile, "and told me of his plan to free you, and my part in it. It was the very least I could do. You were kind to me, Mistress Freya,

338

trying to stop Toki from hurting me. How could I refuse?"

Freya reached out and squeezed her hand. "I know how frightened you must have been, Ilse. It took courage, great courage, to do what you did. There were so many of them! It—it could as easily have gone against us!"

Robin nodded. "And were it not for the Goose Fair at Snotingaham—a league or so ahead—I would have gone on my way, and been unable to retrace the road in time to help thee. You have a hungry belly and a greedy eye to thank for your rescue, fairest of the fair, for without them I would have been long gone, leagues hence to the west! I had bartered for the horse and the chickens, and was about to go on my way and seek a camp for the night when I—heard—your call."

"Heard?" Ilse asked, her confusion obvious.

"Aye." He chucked her beneath the chin. "'Tis a talent I have, sweet Ilse—to pluck the thoughts from another's mind."

Ilse pinkened. "Oh!" she said in a small, alarmed voice, and her color deepened.

Robin laughed. "Fear not, thou of the flaxen tresses, 'tis only compliments for me that I see there." He inclined his head. "My heartfelt thanks!"

Freya hid a smile as Ilse squirmed in obvious embarrassment. "So, Ilse, will you return to your father's farm now?" she asked.

"I dare not," Ilse confessed sadly, shaking her head. "His lord might learn of Toki's death, and lay blame for his murder at my father's door. 'Tis better I should disappear for some time. I—I was hoping—?" She broke off, suddenly shy.

"To come with me to Jorvic?" Freya finished for her. "*Ja!* It would please me well, Ilse."

"I would serve you gladly, mistress," Ilse promised solemnly.

"Then it is agreed. But," Robin added gravely, "I will escort the two of you to Jorvic myself. The way is far too hazardous for two comely maids traveling alone, without men to defend them."

"We'll welcome your escort, good Robin," Freya accepted, and they fell to talking companionably until sleep overcame them in the wee hours before dawn.

Chapter 26

Jorvic, Freya and Ilse soon saw a city that teemed with people. Many of them were "Black Vikings," as the Anglo-Saxons had termed them to distinguish them from their blonder Norwegian cousins, or Danes; such was Freya, and also Ilse in part, for her father, Sigmund, had taken an Angle woman as his wife.

Formerly a ruined Roman fortress town named Eburacum, the Danes had all but rebuilt the new city of Jorvic from the fallen and crumbling ruins of the old, repairing its sturdy city walls of stone and numerous huge gates, setting out streets in cross-grids and erecting new dwellings; numerous cottages of wattle and daub thatched with straw, as well as other grander, bigger halls built almost entirely of timber, and still others that were combinations of both, mixed with stone taken from the ancient ruins.

Some of the cottages were shops, and had their awnings rolled up to let in the watery autumn sunshine and display their wares: articles of carved wood such as combs and distaffs, basins and bowls, beds and carved bedposts, benches and stools, all bearing such legends as "Snarri made this," or leather goods boldly declaring their proud craftsman's name; jewelers offering brooches and pins of lead and copper, bronze and precious silver, neckbands and wristbands set with cloisons of amber beads, or amethysts and garnets. There were workers in horn and bone, and coopers fashioning barrels and sturdy water buckets. Over all the everyday smells of dung and beasts and the sweat of the crowds lay the pervading stench of the tannery.

Traders and merchants rubbed shoulders with artisans and laborers, farmers, sailors and soldiers, the center of all activity being on or about the busy wharves of the twin rivers, the Foss and the Ouse, which ran through or around the center of the city. Three-wheeled carts rumbled by, drawn by sturdy horses or oxen. They hauled barrels of herring or Rhenish wine pots, bolts of fine imported Byzantium silk and luxurious furs from the Baltic, up from the wharves to the open market. Falcons—many of which were the prized Greenland falcons the Vikings favored to take a-hawking—perched sullenly in reed cages stacked upon the quayside, along with coops of chickens and ducks, all clucking and quacking noisily. Many *knarrs*, the slower, heavier merchant ships built expressly for the purpose of carrying cargoes and following the trade routes about the Mediterranean, were docked with their striped sails reefed, and were being unloaded to the rhythm of work songs sung by the crews, while merchants haggled noisily and heatedly with captains for their purchase, and yarn-spinning sailors gutted fish and darned nets.

People, there were people everywhere, Freya thought—more people than she had ever seen gathered in any one place in her entire life. Even Saxon London had not been so crowded! Ilse, accustomed to her own small hamlet and the rural solitude of her father's farm, echoed her feelings. Freya did not hear her. She was listening to the Viking tongue being spoken all around her as if it were music to her ears—which, after so many long months of Saxon, it was.

The throng, loud and bustling, jostling them this way and that like flotsam tossed hither and thither by the tide, made them feel peculiarly small and insignificant, and no little disoriented. Wherever they turned there was someone—here a flaxen-haired goosegirl leading her noisy gaggle to the river; there a swineherd chivvying his snuffling hogs along to root for acorns and grubs on the grassy common lands outside the city walls; further on, a lady of the Viking nobility languishing in a splendid curtained litter, speedily carried through the streets by four stalwart Angle slaves; or an herbalist with a pack of herbs strapped to his back, flying to aid some sick fellow, his mantle streaming out behind him in his haste.

Outside the doorways of many of the cottages women sat in the sunshine and spun, or wove their skeins of brightly dyed yarn into serviceable and colorful cloth, distaff or shuttle moving in swift, practiced time to their singing, all the while keeping a watchful eye upon their ragged youngsters, who shrieked with laughter and played "tag" between the cottages like children anywhere. Hounds nosed the refuse dumps and middens for bones or scraps or unwary prowling cats, or half-heartedly harassed the cackling chickens and quacking ducks that strutted everywhere underfoot, pecking at spilled grain.

How on earth was she to find Guthrum's hall in this sprawling place, amidst all this clamor, Freya wondered doubtfully? Hands on hips, she turned about, trying to decide which way to go. Up Copper Gate, through Lund Gate alley? Or would she be better trying North Gate—or Mickelgate—or—

"Oh!" She gasped as a burly oaf of a man slammed into her, knocking her to the dirt. Indignantly she scrambled to her feet, dusting off her smarting derrière. "Look where you're going, friend!" she flung after his rapidly retreating back, ignoring Ilse's urgent pleas for discretion.

He pulled up short and swung about; disbelief on his face as he strode back toward her. Scant feet away, he stopped and towered over her. He was not a handsome fellow, nor even a homely one, nay, not by far! she saw. An old wound had scarred his cheek, dragging down one eye so that the red rim beneath showed grotesquely. His nose appeared to have been broken at some time, and had set and healed badly, the tip veering in an opposite direction to the rest of it. Dirty, straggly brown hair fell to his shoulders, and both it and his unkempt beard were matted with spilled food.

"What did ye say, lass?" he growled harshly, his expression ugly—no difficult feat for him!

"I said, look where you're going!" Freya repeated crossly, her manner queenly and aloof. "You nigh brained me, knocking me down so rudely!"

"And who be you, t'tell me what to do?" His bleary pale brown eyes traveled over her, taking in the simple kirtle of natural off-white wool she wore, quite without kerchief, mantle, brooches, or any adornment whatsoever. "A common house thrall!" He spat, disgust in his tone. "Run back to your master or mistress, slut, before I'm minded to teach you a lesson in manners you won't forget!"

She bridled at his insulting tone, color filling her fresh complexion as she shrugged away Ilse's restraining hand. "*You* teach *me?* Ha! Do not make me laugh, my ugly friend! I am the daughter of Thorfast, *jarl* of Danehof—and I was born with more manners in my little finger than you have in your entire body—or are ever likely to have, come to that!" She raised her very small finger to demonstrate her point.

"Why, you—!" He lunged at her, stubby hands reaching for her waist. Ilse let out a scream as Freya nimbly sidestepped him and he hurtled past her, her scornful laughter ringing in his ears in the fleeting second before he barreled head first into the steaming midden at her back! Horse and cow dung was clinging to his hair and beard when he extricated himself and flung about, and fury blazed in his eyes as the crowd—gathered now to watch the spectacle of a slender thrall wench daring to challenge the one known far and wide, and with good reason, as Harald the Foul—surged forward. He came at her again, roaring and charging like an enraged bull, his great weight carrying him forward with such momentum he failed to notice in time the slender bare foot she extended to trip him. He went down like a speared bull walrus, bellowing in outrage. The crowd roared its merriment and approval, and favored Freya with amused and encouraging grins. True, the comely wench might well be only a thrall, but she had fire and courage aplenty, and being Vikings, they admired both. Besides, Harald was a disgusting, bullying fellow, little better than the pigs that roamed free in the streets, and they were secretly delighted to see him get his comeuppance for once, *ja*, and at the hands of such a slender slip of a girl too!

"Come on, Harald, old fellow—you aren't going to let a wench best you, are ye?"

"Up, great Harald, up on your feet like a man! Mayhap you'll be fast enough next time!"

"By Thor's Hammer, you move slower than an Angle virgin, Harald! Hurry now, before it gets too dark to fight!"

Their jeers enraged him further. He lumbered up, his hairy jerkin caked with street mud and dung, the knees of his cross-gaitered leggings sporting damp patches of it, and yet another

343

streak was smeared across his nose. Chest heaving, he glowered at his slender opponent, his great simian brow knotted in consternation.

"Silence, my friends," Freya said impishly, "whilst Harald thinks. 'Tis a difficult task for him, poor fellow, lacking much to think with!"

Her goad served. Again he rushed blindly forward. Freya feinted a run to left, and darted right even as he lumbered leftward. He spun about, trotted right, and she hitched up her skirts and skittered left. Playing to the crowd now, she followed him before he could turn, briskly tapping him on the shoulder. When he swung about in astonishment, she smartly kicked him in the shins, first one, then the other, so that he howled in pain, clutched one leg, and did a comical dance in small circles like a lumbering fairground bear.

"Enough, mistress!" Ilse squeaked, and was relieved to see Freya nod reluctant agreement.

"Bravo, Harald!" she teased. "You dance quite well. I only wish that I could tarry to enjoy the rest of your performance, but alas, we must be gone! Farewell!" So saying, she took Ilse's hand and the two of them dived between the crowd, receiving pats on their backs and pinches on their buttocks as they went, and made good their getaway.

First, Freya decided ruefully, she must get rid of her thrall's tunic, and also find more suitable attire for Ilse. Guthrum would never grant them an audience attired as lowly slaves, she knew, but dressed passably and with her "serving woman" in tow, there was a good chance he might be persuaded to speak with them. How to find garments for the two of them, that was the problem, with neither gold nor silver, nor tradegoods with which to barter for them? Buying food had long since used up the small store of silver pennies that Robin had generously pressed upon them when they parted ways. A small smile tugged at the corners of her lips, and the dimples in her rosy cheeks deepened. If she could not come by them honestly, then what other recourse did she have . . . ?

"Come along, Ilse," she said determinedly. "What we need is a bath and a change of clothes."

Ilse nodded agreement, and they set off, following a narrow *gate,* or street, through the outskirts of Jorvic and beyond the

344

city walls, into the countryside once more, following the banks of the Ouse. Not many paces from the city walls, Freya heard what she was listening for—the laughter of women. Peering between two bushes, she saw them in the river, bathing or washing cloth lengths or garments on the rocks, or sitting crosslegged on the grassy banks, carding fleeces with carding combs as they gossiped. Now, where had they hung their clothing to dry? A careful perusal of the area showed her several damp tunics spread over the leafless bushes in the sunshine. Smiling, she ducked around the women, keeping to the bushes for cover, until she reached them. Ilse followed her.

All were simple sturdy tunics of coarsely woven linen, differing little in design and all dyed with the easily rendered pale dyes used by the common folk. Not one, however, was white, since white was the color worn only by thralls. She hurriedly selected one of a pale blue shade, and tossed a yellow one to Ilse. Together, they fled a way upstream, out of sight of the women.

Later, shivering a little in the cool afternoon air, yet freshly bathed and clad in their stolen garments, they hoisted up their skirts and ran back toward the town before any of the women could discover the theft. Once at a safe distance, they stopped and combed their hair with their fingers, then braided it tidily. Assured that their appearance was far more presentable now, Freya led the way back through the city gates, greeting the guards there with a cheerful good afternoon as she went. They returned her greetings, eyeing her and modest, flaxen-haired Ilse appreciatively. Noting this, she determined to use it to her advantage,

"If it please you, sirs, I'm new here in Jorvic. Might you be able to tell me where to find Lord Guthrum's hall?" she wheedled.

"Indeed, lass," one man agreed willingly, and winked slyly. "I'll tell ye—if ye'll promise to meet me here when I get off duty?"

She simpered and lowered her lashes modestly, detesting her coquettish role but playing along. "Oh sir, you make a maid blush so, that you do, you handsome rascal! Meet you, indeed! Whatever would my lord father say?"

"I'll not tell him if you won't, lovie," promised one,

grinning as he chucked her beneath the chin.

She giggled. "I'd wager you wouldn't, you rogue, you!" She sighed, pretending great reluctance. "Oh well, then I suppose I'll just have to meet you, won't I, then? In the spinney over there, at moonrise," she coyly suggested, pointing. "And I'll even bring my sister here for your handsome friend," she offered, "if you'll tell me where Lord Guthrum is?"

"Your sister is nigh as comely as you, lass."

"Why, I'm not comely at all compared t'her, sir," Freya disclaimed, nudging Ilse in the ribs, her deep blue eyes all modest innocence. "'Tis said our Dana would make the goddess Freya curl up with jealousy at her loveliness!" Ilse bared her teeth in a grin.

Eagerly the two guards nodded, exchanging glances. "Guthrum's hall is clear across the city, hard by the south bridge over the Ouse. 'Tis half Roman ruin, and half timber. Ye can't miss it, my lovie," one told her, "for the edges of the eaves are heavy with carving, like in the old country, and very grand."

"I understand. Thank ye kindly, young sirs. Until this even, then, *ja?*" She smiled, gave a flutter of her tawny lashes, nudged Ilse in the ribs a second time to make her do the same, then darted them a look that promised all the delights of the world would be theirs, come that evening.

They both grinned foolishly at the two young women, looking for all their height and fiercely worn armor and weapons like callow, bashful lads. "Until this even," they agreed, their voices hearty, and with anticipation in their eyes watched her trim figure sidle through the gateway and on up the rutted, steep street.

"She's mine," one muttered. "Ye can have her sister, *ja?*"

"Nay, my friend," denied the other. "Ye can have the sister, and I'll have that one. Eymundr prefers his women bold and lively, not all sweet shyness and maidenly airs!" He winked and slapped his companion heartily across the back.

"We'll dice for her," the other suggested, drawing walrus-ivory gaming pieces from a pouch at his belt. "Agreed?"

"Agreed," Eymundr acknowledged with a heavy sigh, and squatted down beside his companion with a glum expression on his face. All knew that Gerhard was a lucky fellow when it came to dicing. Curse him, he was as good as stuck with the shy, modest sister. She, more than likely, was guarding her maidenhead against marriage and wouldn't let him so much as lay a hand upon her teats, unlike the bold-eyed one with the vixen-colored hair! Still, the fair one was comely, none could deny that . . .

Guthrum's hall, once one knew in which general direction it lay, was easily found. A massive building reconstructed, it appeared, from an old Roman villa and given a Norse flair by the addition of a turf roof and ornate carvings to the eaves, it was set on a slight incline above the southern banks of the river. Outbuildings housing cattle and horses and thralls clustered about the main building.

It was so reminiscent of Danehof in appearance that Freya had the giddy feeling, just for an instant, that her father's hall had been transported there by some magical means. She stood stock still and stared, her eyes growing misty with memories, longing tugging at the strings of her heart. If only she could go back in time, back to when Uncle Sven had seemed like a god, with the answers to all of life's questions, and when Nissa's loving arms had been all the reassurance she needed to go on! But they were no more. She was her own mistress now, and must deal with her sorrows and burdens herself.

Unbidden, Alaric's dark face swam into her vision, imprinted upon the tears that had suddenly filled her eyes as if imprisoned in beads of polished amber. She fancied she could almost feel his strong, hairy arms clasped about her, his great, bearlike presence surrounding her with love, and his warm, manly scent in her nostrils. *Truly, I loved thee, my Bear! Enemy or ally, right or wrong, I loved thee!* She sniffed, rubbed her eyes on her knuckles, and tossed back her braids, willing the heart pangs to disperse as she marched into Guthrum's great hall with her bright head held high and determination in her heart. Her love for Alaric, that fateful raid on Kenley, they were all in the past now. She was *jarl* of Danehof; the *Althing* had made it so. She must return to Jutland to lead her people, and Guthrum and his power alone could help her to do so.

The hall was gloomy, little of the mellow afternoon light fingering its way through the narrow wind-eyes, yet there were several people about, mostly men who appeared, by their girth and attire, to be warriors of Guthrum's *here*, and who eyed her and Ilse with the sudden keen interest of hounds scenting game. They let the frowsy camp followers and whores that were draped about their necks fall unnoticed to the soiled rushes, strewn over costly marble floors like discarded bones.

"Ah, lads, fresh meat!" one roared as they crossed the hall, and his fellows echoed his delighted bellow. "Your name, pretty wenches? Tell me, and I will straightway carve them upon my chest!"

The two young women, cheeks flaming, studiously ignored them. Freya continued to look about her, trying to decide whom to risk approaching without fear of being casually tumbled to the rushes, the victim of the men's lusty sport, when a man came toward her out of the smoke and gloom, his massive silhouette framed blackly against the shadows beyond him. Her eyes were still adjusting from the sparkling daylight outside to the relative darkness within, so that at first she did not recognize him. But he recognized her.

"Freya? Freya Jorgensen? Is it you, then?"

"Olaf?" she cried, incredulity in her tone.

"Olaf, *ja!*"

"Olaf!"

All at once he swept her into a mighty bear hug that was so forceful, her feet left the ground as he twirled her about! She laughed with delight and begged to be released before he crushed the breath from her, or cracked her ribs.

The watching men grimaced and turned back to their drinking horns, their sulky-lipped whores and the lively song of heroes and giants, of fierce dragons vanquished and distant worlds won, that the harpist was plucking.

"Forgive me, little Freya!" Olaf apologized ruefully, setting her safely back down upon the rushes as if she were wrought of fragile, costly glass. His ruddy cheeks were even ruddier now with embarrassment than was usual. "It is only that—I cannot believe you are free once more, and here in Guthrum's hall, you understand? I had feared never to see thee again!"

She nodded, her delighted smile at finding him swiftly fleeing her face. "'Tis a long story, my dear friend. I will tell you everything in time, but first you must meet Ilse here, who is not only my dearest friend, as are you, but has sworn to serve me . . ."

The introductions exchanged, in faltering tones she told him everything that had happened to her since the day Alaric had sent Olaf hence from Kenley. Well, almost everything. She left out only the painful choice her heart had made by choosing Alaric as her love . . . And Olaf, in his turn, told her of his determination to reach Jorvic after he was sent away from Kenley, and of his intent to persuade Guthrum to send a longship down the eastern coast of Britain, to raid the burh, do battle with Alaric, and set her free.

"But I learned when I reached Jorvic that Guthrum had sailed for Francia, and all the dragon-ships of his fleet were gone with him," Olaf finished. "So instead I've been rallying together all the Vikings here in Jorvic who were willing to take horse and go overland to Kenley and fight to free you. I already have a large following. On the next Thor's day, we'd intended to set out. But now—now we'll wait until you are well rested before we return to Kenley to take our revenge!"

"*Nej*, Olaf, as *jarl* of Danehof, I forbid it!" Freya said sharply, effortlessly slipping back into her position as leader without thought. "We will waste no time in reprisals upon Kenley. We must instead return straightway to Danehof. 'Twill be winter soon, after all, and we have lost many of our men to the Saxon sword—men who were badly needed for the harvesting—not to mention losing precious time. If the crops are not soon gathered in, there will be more deaths from starvation in our clan before the next Cuckoo month."

The sky-blue eyes she had known so well and for so long would not meet hers when Olaf again spoke. He drew her aside into a quiet, shadowed corner, motioning Ilse to follow them, then took a deep, painful breath. He managed at last, but only with the greatest difficulty, to look her in the eye, yet even so it seemed he looked through her rather than at her.

She was reminded of how he had looked when they were yet children and he had had unpleasant news to break—perhaps a pup she was fond of dying, or one of her kittens harmed—and had wanted to spare her hurt and known he could not. Foreboding filled her.

349

"No, Freya. You—you are no longer *jarl* of Danehof," he told her bluntly, his deep voice unsteady with emotion. "Do you remember Ulf the Stammerer?" Seeing her nod, he continued, "I met him here in Jorvic, just a few days hence. He told me that after you and I left Jutland and went a-Viking in the Lambs' Folding, Karl Ivarson's brother, Thorvald Ivarson, put into motion what the two of them had secretly plotted from the first—to take over your father's hall! When you were approved by the Althing as *jarl* to succeed Thorfast as leader of our clan, they were too cowardly to speak against you, and so they waited until you left Jutland. Then Thorvald overthrew Ulf and took control of Danehof! He gave your lord father a choice: leave Jutland forever and end his days elsewhere, or submit to death—a fitting warrior's death, with a dagger plunged clean into his heart. Dreams of Valhalla were all that Thorfast had left to him, Freya. He was old, blind, enfeebled. And so he chose death!

"Thorvald is *jarl* there now, and he has taken your father's young wife, Dagmar, as his woman. You would of a certainty not be welcomed back there, unless you were to agree to become Thorvald's second wife, for he has vowed you will return to your position at Danehof only as his bride! All this Ulf told me. You see, he and others like him who have no fondness for Thorvald sailed from Jutland along with their families. They are now here, in Jorvic. They plan to settle lands in Britain, to the southeast, in the kingdom that once belonged to the East Angles, and farm them. They look to me to lead them now."

"My father—dead? Thorvald *jarl* now?" She shook her head slowly from side to side in disbelief, her mouth working without forming words. Her face had paled alarmingly. *"Nej!* I don't believe you—I can't! It cannot be so, no!" she cried.

Olaf took her firmly by the upper arms and shook her gently. "Nevertheless, it is true, my Freya. I would never lie to you, you know that," he repeated gently but firmly, and was cut to the quick by the wailing cry his confirmation caused. Curious heads turned sharply in their direction.

"Was there word for—for me—from him, before he died?" she asked in a strangled whisper choked with tears, a lifetime's hope in her eyes.

"None," he muttered, hating having to tell her, belatedly wishing he had thought to lie.

"Then to the very last, I meant nothing to him . . ." she began bitterly, and then could not go on, her voice breaking with the depths of her hurt. "If you knew, Olaf—if you had any inkling—of how badly I wanted him to be proud of me! But not once, not *once* did he ever say—no matter how I tried—! Oh hold me, friend Olaf, hold me tightly, or I fear I will surely break in two—!"

In her sorrow she buried her face against his broad chest and clung to him, her arms curled fiercely about his powerful neck, her tears dampening his mantle.

And Olaf, holding her, recalled how, on that long-ago morn upon the decks of the *Wild Bird of the Wind,* he had once wished that she would yield and nestle in his arms in just this close fashion, needing him as desperately as any woman needs her man and his strength in times of heartache. From the moment when she had changed from slim-hipped girl to rounded woman, he had desired her, ached for her to need him, and at last here she was!

Yet why did he feel no triumph, no joy? Had her grief communicated itself to him, for all that he had long despised and hated Thorfast for his treatment of his little daughter? Or—was it because her voice had been filled with such tender, poignant longing when she spoke of the Saxon, Alaric, he pondered jealously, twining her shining braids about his fingers. Aye, he suspected that he was naught but a convenient, friendly shoulder to cry on. Her deep blue eyes had grown as misty as the distant horizon when she'd said *his* name. Pain knifed deep into Olaf's heart, for he knew he could not hope to compete with her memories of a dead man: a man whom he knew, as surely as he knew the lines upon his own hand, as surely as if she'd told him herself, his Freya had once loved, enemy or nay . . .

He met Ilse's grave gray eyes over the crown of Freya's head, and saw the understanding, the pity in their depths. By their expression, he knew that he was right.

Chapter 27

Summer became autumn. Those next two months passed like a painful dream for Freya, one that was but dimly remembered with the morning. She went through the motions of living, yet felt numbed, drained of all emotion.

During her travels and the adventures she had experienced, it had been no hard task to set aside her grief. But here in Jorvic, the everyday life she now resumed left ample time for remembering and grief, and her loss was for the first time bitterly brought home to her. She saw other couples in love and loving, and it was salt rubbed into a raw wound that was her heart.

She and Ilse stayed at Guthrum's hall, finding their beds amongst those of the bawdy camp followers for the first few nights, after which Olaf was able to find them better lodgings with a wealthy silver merchant and his family with whom he had become friends. It was while she was yet in this dazed and uncaring state that Olaf, even while knowing he took unfair advantage of her grief, asked her to become his woman. And Freya, remembering the childhood affection they'd shared and knowing how deeply Olaf cared for her, accepted.

Why should she refuse? Olaf offered her his heart and promised her his deep and enduring love. He told her of the empty years he had spent loving her, ever since she was a little girl, and of the agony of waiting for her to grow to womanhood. He spoke of his fears that his love would never be returned, and of the hall he would build them, where she would reign as its queen. He talked of the children they would have, fine sons of peerless courage, daughters of matchless beauty, and how the years ahead would no longer be empty for him with her as his woman, but filled with joy and meaning. And little by little, she weakened.

Olaf offered her a second chance, the hope of building a new life with him, a chance to live again, *feel* again, when it seemed a vital part of her must have died with Alaric at Kenley, and she could never trust herself to care for anyone again. What did it matter if she could never come to think of him in any way other than as a cherished brother, when it was clear that he loved her so; indeed, had loved her for many years? Many couples were joined with far less affection between them than she and Olaf shared. And besides, what did her own happiness matter now, with Alaric gone? On a bright morning in October, amidst mellow sunshine more reminiscent of midsummer than autumn, she became Olaf's woman.

She twined her red-gold hair in intricate braided loops for the exchange of vows. Ilse threaded the loops through with silver ribbons sewn with sparkling blue glass chips and placed a narrow circlet of delicately chased silver about her brow. Then Freya donned her bridal gown, a kirtle of deepest blue silk from Byzantium embroidered with silver orphreys and cuffs, and fastened a belt of silver links etched with scrolls and flowers and gripping beasts about her slender waist. The embroidered hem of her kirtle allowed a fleeting glimpse of the finely bleached and lavishly embroidered linen of her underskirt beneath it. A violet-blue mantle of indigo lamb's wool, trimmed with furry bands of snowy ermine, was draped over her shoulders and clasped there by a brace of costly silver brooches, all wedding gifts of the silver merchant's lady, Dana.

Olaf too was finely robed in dark blue, his leggings made bright with scarlet cross-gaiters, a jeweled dress sword strapped in a leather scabbard at his thigh, a jeweled dagger at his waist. The purple mantle he wore slung over his left shoulder was fastened at his right by a disk of solid silver, upon which was carved the talisman of the thunder god Thor, the mighty hammer Mjolnir. The latter was a bridal gift from the men of Jutland who had left Danehof and now elected to follow Olaf as

353

their new lord in this new and fertile land.

They made a handsome couple, she solemn and beautiful, he eager and nervous, as they stood before Guthrum's *godi*, priest, and the hospitable silver merchant and his household, and exchanged their vows to remain loyal to each other as man and woman and to uphold each other's honor as sacred as their own.

When the animal sacrifices had been made to the god Frey to ensure their union would be blessed with children, Freya received from her bridegroom the marriage gifts he had chosen for her, a heavy gold torc that encircled her throat and a wide golden finger ring set with a huge, blood-red cabochon garnet that had once been his lady mother's. It would henceforth become the symbol of Olaf Olafson's household, he said, slipping it upon her finger.

Freya had nothing to offer him in return, save her promise to be all that a wife should be to her lord. She vowed him this in shy, faltering tones he had never heard from her before, she who had ever been bold and lacking in womanly shyness!

"I could ask no more of thee, my Freya!" he declared in a voice grown deeper and huskier than normal with emotion. "Your vow is worth more than gold, is more precious to me than a thousand jeweled baubles!" He captured her in a fierce bear hug, and heedless of the watching eyes and the broad grins of the company, he kissed her long and hard before all until her feet left the ground with his ardor.

The rafters rang with the cheers of Olaf's followers. Mead and ale flowed like the waters of the Ouse and Fosse, and their hostess, the merchant's wife Lady Dana, clapped her hands and sent her servants and slaves flying hither and thither to set heaped platters of food before the guests, while she herself hurried to fill drinking horns with sweet wines and mead for her lord husband and his companions. Venison and goose, eel and shellfish steamed from the platters. Fresh-baked barley loaves and fruit tartlets and oatcakes smeared with honey disappeared into grasping hands and greedy mouths. Roasted chickens and succulent duck vanished as if by magic!

The *skalds* tuned their harps and sang songs of bygone heroes and their lady loves. By the light of the fires that crackled upon the central hearths and in the flare of the flaming torches, there was dancing and singing, drinking and feasting and bawdy jesting that lasted far into the night, only to continue again the next morn and the next, when the revelers, refreshed by sleep, rose to begin their merrymaking yet again.

Freya was escorted to her bridal bed in the merchant and his lady's own bower, generously loaned them by the older couple for the celebration of their wedding night, where the maids of the household delighted in teasing the blushing bride and in assisting Ilse, her bower woman, with disrobing and readying her for her bridal bed. There was no time to so much as unloosen her hair before a great roar sounded from beyond the curtain that separated the bower from the main hall, and the bridegroom, a little the worse for wear from an overabundance of mead, was borne in, carried aloft on the shoulders of his men. Biting her lip, Freya dismissed Ilse and her maids.

Ilse paused at the door, happy tears glistening in her eyes. "Joy to you both, mistress!" she murmured. "On this your wedding night, and all the nights yet to come!"

Freya nodded and tried in vain to smile her thanks as Ilse slipped away. Though no untried and terrified virgin, she felt considerable anxiety. Had she made a grave mistake, she wondered for the hundredth time that day? Was it honorable to have wed Olaf while knowing in her heart she still loved Alaric, would always love him, dead or nay, and that there was every chance she was carrying his child? Should she have told Olaf of her fears before agreeing to become his woman? Could she keep her vow to be a good wife to him? And if she did, would she mayhap lose the precious gift of his friendship in the keeping? Her thoughts were chaotic as the tide of merrymakers receded and the two of them were left alone in the bower at last.

Yet when Olaf, all ruddy locks and brawn and golden-tanned flesh in the glow of a single rushlight, came to her—when she saw the love that shone like a beacon from his sky-blue eyes— her misgivings were stilled. What price her own happiness, when compared to his obvious joy? This way, at least one of them had found the contentment he sought, one life had been spared heartache.

His large hands were surprisingly tender as he drew the

coverings from her body, and a groan of longing broke from his lips as he saw that beneath them she was quite bare save for his handfasting gifts, the barbaric golden torc that encircled her slender throat and the savagely glittering blood-red garnet at her fingers.

Even unrobed, she was as proud and regally beautiful as a Viking queen! Her lovely head bloomed like a golden summer rose on the slender stem of her neck, and her shoulders were a smooth petal-pale pink that invited a man's lips to sample their supple curves. Her small yet firm breasts pouted provocatively, tipped with budlike nipples of a deep and tempting coral hue that begged his kisses. Beneath a slender waist, her hips were almost boyishly slim, the taut globes of her buttocks pure poetry of form.

With clumsy hands that shook with the sheer emotion of this long-awaited moment, Olaf unbound her hair from its braids, spilling the circlet and sparkling ribbons to the rushes as he combed the red-gold cascade between his fingers. Desire surged through him. He groaned aloud in his need as he grasped her by the hair and dragged her hungrily against his length, all the years of waiting and wanting, unfulfilled, coming together in that moment of desire. His massive, heavily muscled body burned like a brand as he molded her slenderness to his rugged maleness.

"Too long have I waited for you, my little bird! Too long . . . !" he groaned. "Your Olaf will make you forget what you suffered at the Saxon's hands, *ja*, I swear it!" And then his mouth took hers again and again in fiery kisses that seemed to last forever. And that left her quite unmoved.

He caressed her tenderly, his hands and his mouth encompassing and learning every inch of her flesh in a slow and enflaming fashion that she knew must cost him dear, for his manhood throbbed and burned like a fiery spearhead against her thigh, impatient for release. She knew by the restraint, the knowing gentleness of his touch, that he was skilled in the love arts, and she tried desperately to match his pleasure, to become aroused herself, striving to become joined with him in spirit, as they would soon become one in body. Yet it was as if she stood apart from herself and heard her own sighs and gasps and murmured love words, as if watching another there on the pelts and linen coverings, with Olaf. His lovemaking was most pleasant, sweet and skilled, but oh, how she longed for the tingling rapture of Alaric's ardent kisses, the touch of his hands upon her most secret places; caresses that had sent her soaring to the heights of desire!

If she but closed her eyes, she could make believe it was Alaric's broad chest that crushed the softness of her breasts beneath its weight, his inky, rough curls that sprang so vigorously against her fingertips! And so she played the woman's game, the cheating game played by women everywhere to placate the male pride of their husbands and lovers: the game of feigned passion, the game of sighs and cries that owed more to a woman's mummer's talent than cries of passion torn from a heart that burned with desire. But even as she did so, she hated herself for it. She disliked what she felt was cheating Olaf, for pretending even for one fleeting moment that she lay with another. Yet Olaf suspected nothing. He was like a man who, after years of searching, has found the treasure he sought, and at the last he spent himself deeply within her with a savage cry that seemed torn from his very soul.

After, while he slept with his great, shaggy russet head pillowed upon her breasts, one massive, hairy arm clasped tightly about her waist as though even now he feared she might escape him, she lay awake, gazing up at the shifting shadows, watching the play of firelight upon the smoke-blackened walls.

The sounds of the feast carried but dimly now, from time to time a burst of muffled laughter or a roar over some bawdy jest reaching her ears, or the muted chords of a harp. She idly caressed Olaf's still head, as a mother caresses a sleeping child, and thought: You deserve far better than me, my dear friend! You deserve a woman who loves you with a heart filled to o'erflowing—one who can offer you more than my pitiful remnants of sisterly love, which are all I have left to give thee!

It was with such melancholy and guilt-ridden thoughts that on this her wedding night, a night intended only for joy, she drifted into fitful slumber. The rushlight gleamed on the silent tears that flowed down her cheeks.

The next days were filled with preparations for the

departure of Olaf, his lady wife, and their household.

Olaf had determined to travel south to find lands for farming, lands where he and his people might prosper and grow strong. Possessed of a strong back and a willing heart, Olaf found ample work amongst the people of Jorvic, and by shrewd barter and exchange of goods for coins earned he was able to gather together what he needed to set up his new household. Sturdy horses, a breeding bull and several fine cows, a ram and a dozen ewes, chickens, ducks, and several sows, soon to farrow, were herded together in the growing camp that Olaf and his followers erected outside the city walls.

Freya, under Ilse's eagle-eyed instruction, helped to cut the lengths of cloth Olaf had bartered for in the marketplace, and together with some of the other women they sewed Olaf, themselves, and the growing household badly needed garments that, though simple and largely devoid of adornment, were at least warm and serviceable as the season demanded. There was a chill nip in the air now, a hint of frost on the wind, a suggestion of mist in the early evening that cloaked the purple hills like a gauzy mantle. Winter beckoned.

"It's done. All's in readiness. We leave at dawn on the morrow," Olaf announced as he ducked under the loose flap of their tent. He rubbed his large hands together by the glowing brazier to warm them.

"On the morrow? So soon?" Freya exclaimed. "Why, I thought to have another week at the very least to see everything made ready!"

"Winter threatens to come early this year," Olaf observed, taking the trencher of stew she offered him. "If we wait, the first snows will be here before we know it. Long before then I mean to see a roof over your head, woman, and have a hearth for you to warm your pretty toes beside!"

He winked and chucked her fondly beneath the chin, and she smiled back at him. When they were together like this, it was easy to pretend that everything was well, and that they were no more than dear, dear friends, for their easy camaraderie of years together had returned. Yet even after a month as Olaf's bride, she still found scant pleasure in his bed. It seemed always as if Alaric was there between them, somehow, watching them, and she could not lose herself in Olaf's passionate arms.

"Eat!" Olaf urged, seeing the distant expression in her sapphire eyes. "You seem pale of late, my Freya. Is—is there something ailing you?" There was a guarded eagerness to his tone that Freya understood.

"'Tis nothing," she denied, inwardly quailing before the sudden, giddy light that filled his eyes. Blessed Frey, why was she such a coward, why? How could she deny it, when she was now certain she carried Alaric's child? In too short a time her belly would start to swell, and he would know she had lied to him! Of a sudden, the savory smell of the chicken stew made her belly heave. The gorge rose acidly in her throat. With a strangled moan, she clapped one hand over her mouth, beat a hurried exit from the tent, and reached the outhouse with scant seconds to spare before she was violently sick, once, then a second time.

Olaf was well into his second platter of victuals when she staggered, weak-kneed, back into the tent. He eyed her adoringly as she sank to the skins spread on the grass for covering.

"Are you with child, my woman?" he asked gently.

What made her deny it, she never knew. But before she had given the matter conscious thought, she had already shaken her head.

"*Nej*, Olaf, 'tis nothing." She shrugged. "Just an autumn ague, or something spoiled that I ate, that is all. I'm—I'm sorry."

His face, so bright and eager minutes before, dropped in disappointment. Yet he swiftly recovered. He reached across and hugged her fondly. "No matter," he said in a cheerful tone that she knew was forced, but was intended to make her feel better. "The little ones will come when blessed Frey chooses to honor us, never fear. The sons of Olaf and his Freya will be many!"

In truth, Frey will honor us sooner than you know, she thought dismally, but in answer she only murmured agreement and busied herself in filling his drinking horn from the crock of mead.

No more mention of children was made that evening, nor the next morn, when all of Olaf's attention was spent on seeing his breeding stock, their belongings, his craftsmen and their families set on their way in an orderly fashion. They would travel back the way Freya and Ilse had come for the first several leagues, the Roman road of Watling Street being the easiest road to travel for so large a company. At the Viking stronghold of Snotingaham they would then turn southeastward into the heart of East Angle. There was good land aplenty to be had for any Viking willing to work it in the area of Saffron Waldon, Guthrum's seneschal had promised. The Angle people themselves had grown tolerant of their foreign lords over the years, he added, and intermarriage was now commonplace between the two peoples. Indeed, many of the Angle people seemed to welcome having strong Viking lords to protect them and their families, and to ensure there was food for their tables. He was of the opinion that they would put up little protest should Olaf build himself a hall and set some of his own people to farming the lands about it, alongside Angle laborers—free men who were eager to work in return for their board.

And so it was an eager and optimistic Olaf, astride a shaggy-maned chestnut stallion on which Freya rode before him, who led his people southward the next morning to begin a new life in a new land.

Chapter 28

The countryside about Saffron Waldon was as fair as the rest of Angle, and Olaf took his time to select the all-important site where his hall would be built. He chose a grassy hillside that commanded a view of the rolling meadows on two sides, and where woods would form a windbreak against the winter winds from the north and off the sea on the other two.

That first night they camped about the chosen spot in simple tents of skins. At first light on the following morning the digging of the foundation for the new hall of Olaf was begun, and in two days it was swiftly completed by the willing men of Olaf's band. For all that Olaf was his father's second son, and back in Jutland would have been forced to seek his own fortune in life by raiding, here the men looked up to him as their lord and had sworn him fealty in all things. Their eager obedience to his every command filled Olaf with pride and affection for them all.

The hall was to be built on a grassy slope between two low-lying green hills that would embrace it like a lover's arms. Beech and aspens, their leaves turning to fire and copper with the season, would offer cool green shade in summer months. A sparkling well-spring burbled nearby, and below it was a still, green pool, ensuring a ready supply of fresh water for the household of Olaf Olafson. The meadows all about promised lush grazing for the herds that were yet to come, and the woods would yield flowers, berries, nuts, and herbs for bright dyes and medicines aplenty. Truly, Freya thought, there could not be a place more blessed by the gods! It would be like Uppsala, a glittering golden temple she had heard rumours that the Vikings of Sweden had built, and of which the *skalds* in Guthrum's hall had recited fabulous tales. Yet there would be no human sacrifices offered up in her hall, as were offered in Uppsala; no slaughter of nine creatures of every species to pacify the gods, the corpses left hanging like some awful gallows fruit from every tree. Foul Toki's attempt to sacrifice her to his lord Woden had forever turned her against the taking of innocent lives to appease the gods. Olaf's hall would be known only as a place of good hospitality, of life and light, of laughter and good cheer, where all men were free to worship as they chose, be their gods the ancient Norse gods or the gentle White Christ.

A priest was summoned from a nearby Viking hamlet, and a dog was ritually sacrificed at the *godi*'s instruction, its body buried beneath the foundations in the fertile dark earth of East Angle, to ensure the blessing of the gods upon the new household. Work went forward quickly after that, the scent of fresh-hewn wood and the measured, thwacking sound of axe against timber filling the misty autumn air as the house posts were shaped and firmly lodged in their foundations.

Meanwhile, Freya, Ilse, Ulf's wife Ericka, and the other women gathered wattle and supple wands and reeds of alder and willow, and collected buckets of wet clay for weaving. The walls of wattle and daub and the turf roof with its ornately carved eaves grew in easy succession under the watchful eye of Olaf's new carpenter, a burly man named Thorkel, who had recently joined his followers.

The hall was finished long before the twelve high-feasting days of Yule, and was a dwelling to be proud of. Clustered about the main building were snug little huts, also of wattle and daub, where Olaf's men might pursue their various crafts of armorer, fletcher, smithy, cobbler, and so on, or sleeping bowers for the new lord and his lady. Other, larger buildings, also set apart from the main hall, would serve as byres to house the prize bulls and rams, cocks and drakes, cows and ewes, hens and ducks that would form the nucleus of their herds and flocks in the next breeding season. A sturdy wooden palisade atop a deep ring of earthworks protected the community within.

The vast communal main hall boasted two hearths, and so two Yule logs were dragged home from the forest to burn brightly upon them through the festive tide. The women of Olaf's Hall cut cloth and sewed and made bright, feather-filled pillows to soften the fixed hard wooden benches used for sitting and sleeping that lined both long walls of the hall. After their pagan fashion, Freya and Ilse and the other women also ventured into the woods to gather pine boughs, mistletoe bunches and holly, symbols of fertility and good fortune, to garland the new hall, and the men went a-hunting and triumphantly brought home an enormous-tusked wild black boar to be roasted for the celebrations, amidst rousing cheers and much laughter.

The women donned their finest kirtles and threaded their brightest jewels and ribbons through their hair and about their throats and arms, ankles and wrists. The men, not to be outdone, strutted like peacocks and trimmed their beards and shaggy locks and combed them tidily, before fitting themselves out in their finest tunics, mantles, and colored cross-gaiters. The *skald,* young Ulrik, tuned his harp and practiced upon his *lur.* The slaves and house servants plucked and butchered and cooked and filled horn after horn with mead or ale or the favored Saxon beer, as all readied themselves in their various ways, and according to their stations, for the feasting. A Yule lord was chosen, a tow-headed rapscallion named Knud who was one of Ulf's numerous offspring, and he and other young lads, wearing masks of ram's and horse's heads, caused merry havoc with their tricks and antics throughout Knud's reign of misrule.

On Twelfth Night Olaf returned from overseeing his men to the *jarl's* bower that adjoined the new hall and that he and Freya shared, to find his lady wife at her bath. Ilse attended her, and as always the buxom young girl blushed when the Viking lord entered, her fingers growing suddenly unwieldy. She dropped the phial of rose-scented oil that she had been soothingly massaging into Freya's shoulders, and mumbled an apology as she hurriedly retrieved it from the rushes.

Freya smiled. To any who had eyes to see, it was obvious pretty Ilse had a great affection for Olaf. She shook her head slightly as she cupped handfuls of warm water and rinsed her body. What an unfair world it is we live in, she thought sadly. Ilse loves Olaf, and yet he is my husband. And I—I love a man who is only a memory now. Did the gods look down from Asgard and laugh at the havoc they wrought? Did they chuckle to see the entanglements brought about by mortal hearts who would not love where they were bid, but foolishly loved where they would? She shook off her pensive mood, though only with greatest difficulty. The festive season was no time to dwell on the past, she told herself firmly. She must look only forward now, to the future. She gestured to Ilse to hand her a linen cloth with which to dry herself, and rose to standing in the brass-banded wooden tub.

"Thank you, Ilse. You may go back to the merrymaking now. I can finish quite well for myself, *takke.*"

"Aye, my lady," Ilse muttered, side-eyeing Olaf, dropped her a hasty curtsey, and fled the chamber.

Freya was about to wrap the cloth about her body and step from the water when Olaf gestured to her to forgo the modest towel.

"Would you deny me the pleasure of seeing my lady wife in all her beauty?" he asked huskily, his eyes roving her supple body, rosy, damp, and glistening in the rushlights. The play of firelight over her was like a lover's caress, touching now the downy curve of her cheek, then burnishing the red-gold glory of her hair, then catching the jewel sheen of her sapphire eyes.

"Of course I would deny you nothing that would give you pleasure, husband," she murmured, suddenly shy despite her words. It was still so hard to think of Olaf as lover and husband, after they had been friends and battle companions for so many years! Nonetheless, she obediently let the linen cloth fall at her feet.

A smile hovered about Olaf's lips as his gaze traveled over her face, flushed from the water's heat and from embarrassment, and lingered on the damp, curling tendrils of burnished hair that framed her face. Her eyes shone like bright, dark jewels set above high, curving cheekbones that lent her features a proud, aristocratic cast. Her mouth twitched with merriment as he continued to gaze upon her with unabashed longing, the coral lips parting, the corners tilting upwards, the dimples in her cheeks deepening with embarrassment under his careful, loving scrutiny.

"Enough, Olaf, please!" she begged. "I feel like a slave wench in the marketplace when you gaze at me so!"

"Silence, woman," he teased, tugging thoughtfully at his red beard, "while I ponder the wisdom of buying such a slave. Well. You are comely and seem strong enough, but I wonder—?"

He strode across the room and caught her in an embrace, his great arms going about her shoulders and waist and sweeping her off her feet. While she shrieked in mock terror and loudly protested that she was yet wet from her bath, he bore her to their bed and tossed her casually onto the sable furs strewn there. "I will sample the goods first, and after decide if I wish to buy!" he declared, and winked wolfishly.

"Roguish merchant!" she declared, and lay there, watching as he peeled the wolfskin jerkin he wore from his brawny shoulders, the tunic beneath quickly following. She waited for him to join her with a pleasant sense of anticipation, for he was gentle in his lovemaking and sought always to give her pleasure, and of late she had found she was able to feel desire for him as a man. But—there were times when sudden, helpless longing for the breathless rapture she had known with Alaric would sweep through her, moving her to tears with remembrances of its savage beauty. In its wake a deep resentfulness remained, an unwillingness to accept less than that utter rapture with Olaf, even while knowing that with him there could be no rapture for her, only a pleasant diversion of body and mind, a brief respite from the grief she still carried. *Ja.* Only Alaric had known how to make her body vibrate like the shuddering strings of a harp. Only he had known how to make the blood sing and bubble in her veins like the tangy, sparkling wines of Francia, how to set her heart soaring like a captive skylark given flight . . .

Clad in only his leggings and short breeches, Olaf sprawled on the bed beside her, the firelight glancing off his shoulders, one large hand going at once to the long, slender length of her thighs and idly caressing the satiny columns. Her fragrance filled his nostrils, warm and tantalizing, damp as a dew-drenched rose and doubly sweet, he thought fondly. As he caressed her he lowered his ruddy head to hers and teased her lips with his tongue tip, outlining her mouth. His silky beard tickled, and she giggled.

"Shall I tell thee once again how I love thee, woman?" he asked huskily, gazing deep into her eyes.

Pain gripped her heart, yet she managed to smile up at him. "*Nej*," she whispered softly. "Don't. There's—no need for words between us. Just—hold me, Olaf. Hold me."

His arms went about her, one large hand enfolding and fondling the soft weightiness of her breast, rubbing the nipple between his fingertips until the vulnerable flesh ruched under his caress. His kisses grew more ardent, his caresses more fevered, and she gasped as he kissed her throat, nuzzling the tiny, throbbing hollows at its base, then moved his shaggy head down to press his lips to the valley between her breasts. His hand drifted over her rib cage, lingering there momentarily before it swept on to stroke the hard, gently rounded curve of her belly. His hand faltered, then pressed flat against her stomach and was still. She sensed the sudden coldness in his touch long before she heard the quick gasping intake of his breath. The moment was shattered as utterly as a glass goblet when hurled to the rushes.

His fingers grew still and he drew away from her, the expression on his face now that of a man betrayed, his eyes dark with the wounding. He growled an oath and stood, moving with stiff strides away from the sleeping couch and from her. When he swung about to look down at her, she saw that his sandy brows were creased in a furious scowl, and that the sky-blue eyes, so tender and filled with love and desire just moments before, were now hard and cold and filled with both bitter anguish and fury as they rested on her hardening belly. So must he appear to his enemies in the seconds before death took them, she thought, and wet her lips.

"How long? How long have you known, woman?" he demanded harshly, his fists clamping over the back of the dragon-carved chair across the chamber with such force that his knuckles showed white.

So. He had guessed. She should have known she could not hope to keep such a thing a secret forever. She should have told him long before this!

"Not very long," she whispered, shame in her heart that he should have learned this way, rather than from her own lips.

"Before I made you my woman?" he asked, his voice hoarse with rage.

Oh, those tortured eyes! She made no answer. Her tongue seemed tied in knots, her throat dry.

"You will speak, Freya!" he roared. "Did you know this then?"

"I suspected, *ja*. But—I could not be certain."

"And suspecting, you still said nothing to me?"

"*Nej.*"

"Why not, confound you! I took you as my woman, honored you as my lady, for all that the Saxon cur took your maidenhead! Did I have no right to know you carried another man's bastard in your belly? Or did you hope to foist the child upon your stupid, trusting Olaf as his own seed?"

"Nay, I swear it! I was not certain. And—and I was afraid!" Her jaw came up defiantly even now as she sat up.

His shoulders, so broad, so unbowed beneath even the greatest burden, sagged now. "Afraid? You? Ha! I know you too well to believe you feared me!"

"Not you, dear Olaf. Never you!" she confessed huskily, blinking rapidly.

"Then what, if not me?"

She shrugged. "I did not fear your anger—but aye, I feared *losing* you. I feared being alone again. Everyone I have ever loved has been taken from me. You know that. I never knew my mother's love, or my father's. I lost Uncle Sven to the White Christ and His church, and then—then—" She stopped, and an unguarded expression came over her face that cut him to the quick.

"Well, woman?" he bellowed, his deep voice reverberating loudly about the bower. "Go on!"

"That—that is all," she insisted lamely, the words spilling

from her too swiftly, too easily for truth.

He strode across to her, loomed massively over her. The rushlights gleamed in the russet of his curling beard and his long hair until they seemed afire with copper and red, and put her in mind of an angry Thor, about to hurl thunderbolts across the heavens. His sky-blue eyes crackled with a fierce, lightning-blue glitter that made her want to wither up, shrivel away, in their raging heat. His fist came out, the fingers—hard and cruel now—clamping about her chin. He jerked her head up, the better to look into her face. "Liar!" he spat, jealousy bubbling like venom through his veins, and shook her. "Liar! Finish what you started, my lovely Freya! Add your Saxon lord to your list of lost loves!"

"Nay!" she denied. "I did not love him! I did not!"

In hurt and fury he lashed out like a cornered animal, dashing his clenched fist against her cheek with a force that jerked her head sideways, and brought tears of pain to her eyes. "Whore!" he cursed. "Confess!"

She was peculiarly glad that Olaf had struck her, welcomed the ringing pain in her cheek, for her guilt was enormous. The denial of her love for Alaric had almost singed her lips in the telling. With an overwhelming sadness she looked into Olaf's eyes and saw the inner bruising in their depths, the unseen wound she had dealt his spirit, which would not heal as readily with time as would the trifling bruise upon her cheek. Her heart went out to him. That she could hurt him so, when in truth she loved him—but as a brother!

"*Ja,*" she whispered. "*Ja!* I loved Alaric!" How could she have ever thought to lie to Olaf, after all they had been to each other? More than anyone he knew her, better than anyone in the world. But she had lost him now, she sensed, and felt betrayed. In becoming lovers, in being joined as man and woman, she had lost a dear and treasured friend.

His chest heaved as he fought to gain mastery over the violent emotions that warred within him.

"I have loved you so long," he said heavily at length, "that I can no longer recall when loving thee was not a part of my life! If you had told me that the Saxon had got you with child—that his rape of you had yielded bitter fruit—that I could have

368

understood, and would have placed no blame for it at your feet. But—that you could have loved him, your sworn enemy! He captured you, Freya—used you to slake his man-lust as he would have used the lowliest of his Saxon whores—and in return you gave him not curses and defiance, but the priceless gift of your love!" He shook his great, ruddy head slowly from side to side in disbelief.

She went to him, winding the linen cloth about her to cover herself as she went.

"Nay, it was not as you say, Olaf!" she denied, tentatively laying a hand on each of his massive upper arms. "At the first I fought him, fought him with every ounce of strength in my body. But—his strength was the greater, and I had only a woman's strength, for all my training. *Ja*, he took me—and still I hated him! I swore I would flee him somehow, and return to cut him—and all his kind—down, like stalks of wheat. But then—something—something happened between us—or at least, I believed it did. *Ja*, Olaf, I came to—to love him. And he—he swore that he returned my love. Though I fought against it, my heart chose him, right or wrong, friend or foe— even as your heart chose me! I could not help loving him any more than you could help loving me. But don't you see, all that is in the past now? It is finished. You—you have no rival for my love now, not any more," she told him huskily, her voice breaking. "Alaric is dead, gone. Everything that I am or ever will be from this day forth, I give to you!" She bowed her head and would have rested it against his broad chest had he not thrust her forcibly away.

"You offer me the Saxon's leavings, like scraps flung a cur from the lord's table! Nay! I will not content myself with scraps! And you are wrong, Freya! He may be dead—but he is far from gone!" Olaf seethed. "I had wondered at the faraway light in your eyes—the tenderness in your face when you thought I looked elsewhere, for you have never looked at me that way. I know now that you still dream of him. You say a dead man is no rival for your heart? I say you lie, my lady! Alaric of Kenley is as real, as living and breathing in this bower as am I. 'Tis as if he stood between us, for he lives on in your heart, in your mind! And yet—I cannot fight him for the woman I love. I cannot sink my blade into his heart and claim you as my own, for he is no more!" He laughed harshly, a bitter, twisted mockery of a laugh. "Now there's a riddle for the *skalds*, eh, wife? 'What is it that is, and yet is not?' A memory! A curse on memories—and a curse on the Saxon, may his Christian soul burn in its Christian hell!"

With that, he snatched up his jerkin and tunic and strode from the bower, leaving Freya, her head still bowed, alone.

In the great hall the feasting continued. Smoke from the hearth wreathed about the rafters. The savory aroma of roasting meats and warm bread was everywhere. The laughter and music were loud and merry. Olaf saw none of it, heard none of it. He felt as if he had been dealt a death blow. His breathing pained him, seeming squeezed from between lungs too narrowed to permit air, and his heart was a knot of agony. For a moment he leaned against the walls of his new hall, unable to find the strength to move, to curse, to pick a fight, to kill in bloody rage—do any of the things the pain inside him demanded he should do to ease it. He looked up at a gentle touch upon his shoulder, to see Ilse standing before him. She made him a sketchy curtsey, her cheeks rosy, her golden hair tumbling loose and lovely about her shoulders. It was as if he saw her as a woman for the first time. Her gentle gray eyes were tender with concern as they read the pain in his face.

"My lord, will you take a horn of mead? Or could I fetch you a draught of Saxon beer?"

He shook his head. It would take more than mead and beer to make him numb this night. Far more.

"Then is there anything—anything at all—I can do for ye, sir?" she asked, and her feelings for him were reflected in the longing look she gave him as if reflected in a rectangle of polished tin.

Slowly he nodded. Their eyes met in understanding. Without further words she took him gently by the hand and led him from the hall. Like one struck down in battle and too shocked, too deeply wounded to protest, Olaf followed her.

*   *   *

Freya awoke from a troubled sleep much later, to find Olaf standing beside her bed, looking down at her. The pale fingers of an autumn dawn stroked his ruddy head. The odor of strong drink and another woman's perfume clung to him. Ilse, she sensed. She looked into his eyes, and saw that the blind fury had passed. There was still pain in their depths, but with it there was now acceptance, some measure of calm. He had come to terms with his feelings, it seemed. So, she thought, they have found each other, he and pretty Ilse, who loves him so; found comfort and release from their pain in each other's arms. She felt no jealousy, no hurt, but instead was deeply glad.

"Freya?" he called softly. "Are you awake?"

"Aye, my lord husband," she answered softly.

"You will forgive me—? My words—I spoke in anger last night—and struck thee—yet—!"

"Nay," she whispered, "it does not matter. I am unhurt."

She held out her arms, and he came into them. She held him fiercely, stroking his shaggy head, caressing his broad shoulders, crooning to him as if he were a child rather than a great, brawny man.

"Hush," she whispered as he spoke anew, asking her forgiveness. "There is nothing to forgive, my dearest friend and husband, nothing at all! It is I who should ask forgiveness of thee, for deceiving you these past weeks. It was wrong of me, I know."

"Nay," he murmured. "You were frightened of what I would do, and rightly so. I—I understand now. Your heart chose where it would, as did mine. There will be no more blame, no more accusations on my part, little Freya. All that is in the past. I cannot force you to love me, I know that. But I still love thee, woman! I will always love thee! Nothing can change that. If you will remain my woman, if you meant it when you said that henceforth all that you have to give is mine, then I will ask no more of you. It is enough. And perhaps—perhaps in time you will grow to love me too."

"I meant it, *ja*, with all my heart and soul!" she cried fervently. "And believe me, Olaf, my dearest husband, that in many, many ways my love for you is as deep as yours for me—" She broke off and bit her lip in sudden misgiving. "But—the

371

child that I carry. What—what will become of my child?"

He held her at arm's length, brushed red-gold tendrils of hair away from her face, and drew a deep breath. "I will accept your child as my own. I will raise it as my own flesh and blood. Have no fear for your babe."

"You—you would do that for me?" she asked, her tone hushed, her mouth aquiver. Tears filled her eyes. Another man, a man less noble than her dear Olaf, would have insisted the child be slain, or left to the elements' mercy.

He nodded. "*Ja*. On my honor and upon my sword, Death Bringer, I swear it!" His tone was strong, resolute.

"I do not deserve such a good man as you, Olaf," she whispered, and drew him down to lie beside her, his head pillowed on her breasts.

Encircled by his strong arms, his warm breath fanning her bosom, she slept at last, her breathing sweet and easy now.

For some time Olaf lay awake, wondering belatedly if he could keep the impulsive, lovesick vow he had made—and that had been born, if the truth were known, as much from guilt that he had lain with Ilse as from anything else! He must keep it, he realized bleakly, for if not, he would lose Freya forever. This sober truth acknowledged, he followed her down into the healing depths of sleep.

Chapter 29

From that night, their lives settled into a comfortable, if somewhat unexciting, routine. Aye, to the restless Freya's mind, what they shared seemed dull, lacking in the exciting sparks that sometimes flared between two people destined to love, and made each day a challenge to be met. Nay, there were no sparks between them, or at least none struck from her. She felt landlocked as Olaf's woman, like a dragon-ship beached upon the sands, or a wild seabird imprisoned in a confining hen house. It was not so much a physical stagnation as a thing of the spirit. Nonetheless, Olaf seemed content, more content than she had ever seen him. If he ever yearned as she did for the fresh, brine tang of the wind against his cheeks, the cold spray of the spindrift off the sea, for the heady thrill of freedom enjoyed when braced in the rearing prow of a dragon-ship as it rode west over the wild waves, he did not show it, here in this inland place. But Freya felt it, and keenly. It was as if she were waiting, always waiting for something, without truly knowing what that something might be. Was this what grief did to one? Would the sensation of something left unfinished never lessen?

Her belly seemed to grow larger now with every passing day, and as it swelled and hardened Freya found her thoughts turning inward more and more often, to the new life within her. Her moods changed too. Sometimes she felt almost deliriously happy, eager to hold the child in her arms, almost unbearably impatient for its birth. At other times it seemed as if all the gloom and doom of the world lay heavily upon her shoulders.

At such times she worried that the child would be born unhealthy, or even dead. She feared Olaf would change after the babe was born, become a jealous ogre she knew not and treat the babe ill, or worse, reject it and order it abandoned. She had no true basis for such fears. He was as gentle, considerate, and loving toward her as ever, though she knew that more than once when she had pleaded weariness and refused him her bed, he had sought solace in Ilse's arms. She could not find it in her heart to blame him, or to feel any jealousy toward poor, guilt-ridden Ilse, for there is no jealousy in a heart without love. Her quick-flaring temper and moodiness would have driven away any man, she knew. *Ja*, at such times she scarce knew herself—and liked herself even less. Her patience was short, and she snapped at and upbraided anyone in her presence, only to suffer an agony of guilt the following day, when her mood swung in the opposite direction and she realized how shrewish and unpleasant she had been.

In the cold and dark of the winter months, when the hall became a large and lavish cell, the foul weather a relentless gaoler, she chafed for the springtime, for the freedom of warmer weather, and the freedom of herself that the babe's birth would bring. Now she felt cocooned, imprisoned by her unwieldy flesh. She wanted to ride on horseback across the snow, feel the crisp and invigorating air flowing through her hair, whipping color into her cheeks. She wanted to don carved bone skates like the other young people at the hall and soar like a bird across the silvery frozen pond in the dell. But her treacherous body had grown clumsy with the growing child, and betrayed her more and more often. Her balance was awry with the extra weight and girth, and she tired easily, and so both Olaf and Ilse—now like a mother hen fussing over her favorite chick—forbade her to take such risks.

Other odd moments of that seemingly endless dark winter she spent deep in thought, staring dreamily into the amber flames that danced upon the hearth, her hands busy at some piece of needlework or other for the coming babe. At such times her face was radiant, her sapphire eyes distant and dreaming, her rich hair falling in a soft and shining veil about her glowing face. Needlework! Who would ever have thought she would find pleasure in such a monotonous task? But nonetheless, she had found unexpected satisfaction and enjoyment in creating the store of tiny garments filling the prettily crafted chest that Olaf had caused his carpenter to build for that purpose. So too had the carpenter spent many a night when the snow lay sparkling over the meadows, carving a cradle for the babe. It now waited expectantly in a corner of her and Olaf's bower, and many was the time she found herself drawn to sit beside it and rock it gently to and fro, humming the Norse lullabies she had learned as a child at Danehof:

> "Sleep deeply now, *min yndling*,
> The sea winds sing your song.
> The tides will be your cradle,
> And will rock you all night long.
> The shells will whisper secrets
> Of the treasures of the sea,
> Your ship of dreams will find them,
> And a hero you will be!
> Sleep sweetly now, *min yndling*
> While mother sings to thee . . ."

Sometimes the babe moved as if in response to her sweet singing, and she cradled her belly and thrilled to the flutter of a tiny hand or foot against her palm. Alaric's child—his son, she was certain, though why she did not know—no longer a faint and unrealized hope but moving and alive, growing strong in the haven of her womb. Such was immortality, she believed. The mortal body passed away, but the life force of man lived on in his sons and daughters, as Alaric would live on within the child she carried. The knowledge eased in part the wellspring of grief she had buried deep inside her. The twisting pain had lost some of its keenness now. She could remember Alaric and the moments they had spent together without giving way to tears, and she knew that she had transferred much of her unrequited love for him to their babe.

By the time the last snows had melted and the first buds were

375

bursting into blossom on the trees, her slender, supple body was a thing of the distant past, never to return—or so it seemed to Freya. She no longer walked with a lithe, exuberant grace, but, she decided, now waddled like an ungainly duck. Her breasts were fuller, marbled with faint blue veins, the nipples darker and large as strawberries—much to Olaf's undisguised pleasure. Her ankles swelled like sausages wanting to burst from their skins at the least exertion on her part, and there were times when she was certain her belly must surely explode, so enormous had it grown. Even Ilse, who considered herself something of an authority where babes were concerned, was amazed.

"The child will surely be a male," she remarked, "and a great, lusty one at that! Are you certain you counted properly from the day of your last flux?"

"*Ja,* I am," Freya said firmly but wearily, dropping to a pillowed bench in the hall and rubbing her aching back. She sighed, filled with a rare self-pity. "By Loki, Ilse, I look like a dairy cow ready to calve, all belly and udders, do I not?"

"*Ja,* my lady mistress—but bigger!" Ilse teased, and had a pillow hurled at her head for her trouble.

Freya's restlessness increased along with the size of her belly. Olaf, knowing her well, realized that her enforced, lengthy period of inactivity might sooner or later pressure her into doing something foolish, like a keg of fermented cider exploding. He all but held his breath when he rode in from the fields each evening, half fearing to hear she had saddled a mount and gone galloping like a wild thing across the countryside, or had challenged one of his men to practice her swordplay and done herself some harm.

The Cuckoo month came again, that glad month when birds built their nests in the tree tops and the hedgerows, and ewes dropped their lambs in the fields. In another month the child would be born. Could she contain herself that much longer, Olaf wondered? He doubted it! It was with feelings of relief that he heard of the death of old Queen Disa east of his hall, not because the queen had done him harm in any way, but because he welcomed the diversion her funeral feast—and Viking funerals had been known to last for weeks!—could bring his

376

Freya. He told her that night that they must show their respect by attending the funeral, and was gratified and relieved by the blaze of excitement that lit up her sapphire eyes.

"Really? When must we leave? Will there be room on the horses for a casket with fresh garments? How long will we be away?" The questions tumbled from her mouth like gamboling pups, tripping over themselves.

He grinned, warmed by her pleasure, and swept her up into his arms and twirled her around, kissing her soundly before he set her down.

"We leave on the morrow—if you can ready yourself by then. *Ja,* there will be room, but do not pack too much. We'll be gone for close to a month. There! Have I answered your questions, woman?" he growled in mock irritation, but she was already gone from him, headed for their bower with a speedy waddle that made him want to laugh in fond—but well-concealed—amusement, to select the kirtles and jewels and finery she would take with her.

True to his word, they set off the following morning, traveling slowly to allow Freya frequent rests. The journey took two days, and by the time Olaf and Freya reached the meadow beyond the hamlet where Queen Disa had ruled, many of the preparations for the queen's final journey had been completed. In a grassy meadow a longship had been dragged into an upright position and held erect by wooden braces, its carved dragon-prow pointing seaward. In a chamber at its heart, next to the tall mainmast, the dead queen—Disa, of eastern Jutland—had been placed upon a magnificent bed that boasted finely carved dragon posts at each corner and was draped with costly cloth from Byzantium.

Freya had but a glimpse of the grand old queen, robed in her finest garments with silver brooches encrusted with garnets and amethysts pinning her fine blue mantle, before a tent was erected over her, concealing the body. Still more rich gems were set in cloisons all over the gold-bound jewel boxes placed at her sides, along with her distaff and scissors, chatelaine's box, bone needles, and other sewing implements that she

377

would require in the next life with the god Frey, for Viking women did not travel to Asgard and the warriors' hall of Valhalla after death, as did their men who fell in battle.

Her two favorite slave women, both young girls, had wished to serve her in death and had been given vast quantities of fermented wine in readiness for the ceremony. When they were numb to all pain—or belated thought of survival—they were ritually strangled by an old woman who customarily performed this task, and their bodies placed beside their lady's. Fine horses—four in all—and a brace of hounds had been sacrificed to accompany their mistress and placed beside her in the gloriously painted *karfi*, along with her carved carriage, many beautiful pottery and bronze platters, bowls and urns filled with grain and fruits, and flagons of mead and wine for her final journey. Sealskins, costly sables, and marten furs were heaped beside her, as were bolts of cloth.

All being ready, a *godi*, or priest, took up a flaming brand. He intoned the sacred saga of farewell that had been composed by the queen's favorite *skald* for her funeral, and listed Disa's many kindnesses and good deeds. Then with his back to the ship, facing the expectant throng of people and not once looking upon the vessel, he lit the funeral pyre. One by one after him the people took up brands and in similar fashion added theirs to the blazing longship. The flames curled around the ship, then grew to roaring great columns of fire that quickly hid the longship pyre and its contents from view.

Freya and Olaf likewise paid their respects to the dead queen, tossing brands into the inferno as the others had done, then fought their way through the throng of feasters and drinkers to a quiet place beneath a tree. There they took out the last of the food and drink they had brought with them on the journey: a few oatcakes and some dried meats and fish, along with a leather flask of mead. They ate by the light of the writhing flames that danced over the shadowed grass. The pyre could be seen for many miles in the darkness as the queen rose to her Viking paradise, borne on the wind-carried smoke and fire.

"How do you feel, woman?" Olaf inquired, slipping his arm about her shoulders. Concern was evident in his eyes. To him

378

she appeared pale and drawn in the flickering light.

"A little tired," she confessed. "'Tis to be expected, I suppose, with my belly so swollen and heavy."

"This feasting will go on for several days," Olaf told her. "We'll find a place for you to rest this night, little mother. Tomorrow will be soon enough to seek out old friends."

She smiled at his choice of endearment. Mother she might well soon be, but of a certainty she was not little! Reaching out, she stroked his fair, bearded face, thinking anew how dear and kind he was. She did not deserve such a gentle husband who loved her so well, when she could feel only affection for him.

"*Ja*," she confessed. "I am very weary—more weary than I would ever have believed I could be after such a short journey!"

Accordingly, Olaf reluctantly left her alone for a little while and went in search of a local *jarl*, a towering, big-bellied Dane formerly from Jutland, who willingly granted them an invitation to pass the night in his hall.

"Who has not heard of Olaf Olafson, the Oaken One, and his bravery, which rivals my own heroics in the *skalds'* sagas, eh?" Snorri the Boastful roared. "Bring your woman and join us in my lavish hall!"

Olaf grinned at his modesty. Snorri, it appeared, was well named! He decided to indulge in a little boasting himself. "Perhaps you have heard also of my woman? She is the daughter of Thorfast the Cunning, the former *jarl* of Danehof—and was once a fierce warrior maid we called Freya of the Frozen Heart!" he told him proudly.

"Heard of her? By Odin's Ravens, I have indeed!" roared Snorri. "'Tis said that few men could match the beautiful Freya in courage and spirit when she went a-Viking! Tell me, friend," he winked slyly and nudged Olaf, "is she as fiery in your bed as she is reputed to be in battle—or is she indeed possessed of a frozen heart where men are concerned?"

"More fiery than even Thor's own thunderbolts!" Olaf lied, forcing a grin and wishing it were so.

"Then you are indeed a lucky man, favored by the gods, friend Olaf," Snorri added enviously. "Your sons will be mighty warriors, and your daughters the mothers of heroes!

Go, my friend, and bring your woman here, to Snorri's hall. I would be honored to shelter you both for as long as you wish to stay, and you will find that Snorri offers a groaning table and is the most generous of hosts!"

When Olaf had seen Freyja settled comfortably on a pallet of straw strewn with furs at the kitchen end of the hall—for there were many, many guests in Snorri's long-house for the funeral of Queen Disa, which had attracted loyal Vikings for leagues about Thetford—he bade her sleep well, kissed her brow, and joined Snorri and the other men about the blazing central hearth.

Accepting a horn of mead and bread and a tender hunk of juicy venison from a thrall, he listened with enjoyment first to the vivid sagas recited by Snorri's clever *skald*, Horik, then to the fine playing and singing of a talented harpist, and finally to the conversation of Snorri and his men as they drank and feasted.

"So, Lothi, my friend," he overheard great Snorri ask one of his companions, "what do you think of our chances of adding Wessex to the Danelaw this year?"

The one named Lothi shrugged. "Not good, my friend. As long as Alfred is High King of Wessex, 'tis my belief the lands to south and west of here will remain his. He is a shrewd man, and one blessed with great courage. His loyal armies will follow him anywhere, to a man, as he proved when he returned from Athelney like one risen from the dead, and regrouped his forces about him to vanquish our own Guthrum."

Snorri nodded sagely, quaffing a draft from his drinking horn and smacking his lips in satisfaction. "*Ja*. And it is said Alaric, Bear of Kent, is yet his friend and one of his most powerful ealdorman. 'Tis rumored he has several hundred men in his garrison who will add their numbers to Alfred's *fyrd* whenever needed. With the two of them joined forces, I warrant Wessex will not be ours till after Alfred lies moldering in his Christian grave!" He grinned and raised the brimming horn in his fist, slopping foaming Saxon beer upon the heads of the company gathered about him. "To the worms, who will conquer Alfred and the Bear at last—even if we mighty Vikings cannot!" he roared.

The men howled with laughter and joined in the toast, raising their own drinking horns high. All, that is, save for Olaf. He waited until their merry laughter had drained away.

"Alaric of Kenley yet lives?" he demanded hoarsely, a tight knot of foreboding unraveling in his belly. His ruddy face had paled in the gloom, though none remarked upon it.

"*Ja*, of a certainty he does," Lothi confirmed.

"But—I had heard that he was slain, by—by a member of his own household?"

"Not he," Lothi corrected, "though 'tis said his brother, Farant of Kenley, was indeed mortally stabbed by a Viking slave girl before she escaped from his hall. By all accounts this Farant and his cursed twin, Alaric, were as alike as twin pups! Mayhap that is the cause of the false rumor you heard, Olaf, my friend, eh?" He raised his horn. "Another toast, my worthy companions! To that brave Viking wench, Slayer of Saxons!"

"Aye, to the brave wench, whose courage is that of a she-dragon!" Snorri roared. "And to the lucky fellow that beds such a firebrand!" He shook his head. "Ah, they breed few women of her ilk these days. Olaf here has himself one of the last, brave women of our time—do you not, Olaf the Oaken?" He clapped the suddenly withdrawn and silent Olaf across the back.

"*Ja*," Olaf distantly agreed, his mind in turmoil.

"Then let's now drink to the beauteous Lady Freya, Olaf's woman, lads!"

"Lady Freya!" they all echoed, drinking, and with still more draughts of heady mead or beer or ale, they continued their discussion of Alfred and Wessex and the progress of their own people in conquering the Frankish lands across the Channel, while in a corner of the hall the bard strummed softly upon his harp, his music and storytelling forgotten in the ever-popular talk of war.

Olaf heard none of this. He could scarcely believe what he'd been told, Alaric lived! And Freya—his Freya—believed him dead . . . ! Should he share with her what he'd learned? *Nej!* He had noticed—with painful frequency—the faraway look that still filled her deep blue eyes when she thought him looking elsewhere. At those times he knew the wistful yearning on her lovely face was not for him, but for the man she had believed dead all these months. Alaric, the Bear of Kent! A twofold curse on him! Why had he not died, why? Olaf's belly churned. He shook his ruddy head. To learn this, just when Freya was growing to love him as a woman should love her mate! The new affection and tenderness in her tone, the little pats and caresses she now gave him were outward indications of her growing love for him, he was certain. If he told her that her accursed Alaric lived, she would once again grow stiff and unyielding in his arms as she had been when first they lay together. She would draw further and further into herself and away from him! Nay, he would never tell her—he, Olaf the Oaken, mighty sea-wolf, dare not. He feared losing her!

By the time he left the company gathered about the hearth pit, he was too drunk and reeling to stand. He staggered to an empty corner and dropped like a stone to the rushes, snoring loudly.

The kitchens to the rear of Snorri's hall lay in darkness. Freya tossed and turned on her pallet in a deep but restless sleep, in which she dreamed she was drowning and no one could save her.

She wakened abruptly and sat up, her heart hammering. Blessed Frey, what was wrong? The pallet beneath her was sodden, and there was a nagging ache in her back. The waters, she realized rapidly, the waters had broken. The babe was ready to be born.

"Nay, not ready, not yet!" she muttered. A full cycle of the moon remained until the time of her delivery, Ilse had said. Fearful, she stood and dragged the wet straw-filled pallet from the sleeping couch, instead spreading her mantle over the hard wooden slats. Her movements to change her wet garments roused one of Snorri's female thralls.

"What is it, my lady?" the girl asked sleepily, stifling a yawn as she shuffled across the rushes to Freya's side.

"My child—I fear it is ready to be born," Freya whispered, the gnawing ache in her back refusing to go away despite her kneading fist, the fear becoming reality with her words spoken aloud.

Wide awake now, the girl hurried across to her, taking up a rushlight as she came. "Sit ye down, mistress, and I'll run to fetch my lady and her midwife, and fresh coverings. Here, let me take the pallet to be burned." She started away, then turned back. "Is this your first, mistress?" Seeing Freya nod, she added, "Don't be afraid, my lady! My mistress has given our lord five healthy young ones, two daughters and three sons, all delivered by the same midwife. All will be well, you'll see!" she said confidently.

Stiff and chill with apprehension, Freya sank down, only too willing to let the capable girl take charge.

Snorri's lady, a buxom, dark-haired Angle woman with a kind, motherly face, arrived with the midwife soon after. She was robed richly, her flowing blue kirtle's overskirts of dark saffron pinned at the breast with ornate brooches of silver, both over a hand's span from tip to tip. Still more rich brooches fastened a mantle of saffron wool, trimmed with sable, at her shoulders, and were linked by a chain of gold. A broad belt jeweled with garnets and amber glass set in silver, after the cloisonné fashion, encompassed her waist. Hanging from a chain about her neck was the gold-bound metal box with knife and ring attached that signified her rank as lady of the household. Her bare arms were adorned with snake bracelets of silver, cunningly coiled about her plump flesh, their green-glass eyes gleaming wickedly in the firelight.

"Greetings, Lady Freya," she told her. "Welcome to the hall of Snorri the Boastful. I am the Lady Mathilda, his woman."

"Greetings! Forgive me for causing you to leave your bed at such an hour, my lady," Freya murmured. "'Tis poor thanks for your generous hospitality."

"Nonsense!" Mathilda disclaimed, chiding her gently. "I could not seek my bed when my lord husband still has guests who must be served meats and drinks, could I now? Pray give no further thought to such matters, my dear girl. I have brought my midwife, Una, to tend you. My servant tells me that your child is coming?"

"*Ja*. But it is not yet time! 'Twas not expected until the next

383

full moon!" Freya gasped as pain knifed through her lower back, taking her breath away.

"Lie down, mistress," Una commanded gently. "Let me see."

After several minutes of Una's knowing hands moving over her belly, the midwife told Freya, "Aye, 'tis time, as you thought, mistress. The babe will come with the dawning, or soon thereafter. If it is as you say, it will indeed be early. But your belly is large and the infant will no doubt also be large and vigorous. 'Tis my feeling you need have little concern. Perhaps you have counted the moon's cycles wrongly?"

Unwilling to protest that there was no possible way she could have counted wrongly, since she knew full well when she had last lain with Alaric, she lay back upon the heaped woolen blankets and let them fuss over her, accepting a bowl of warmed wine with soothing herbs added to it, and thankful for the young thrall's gentle hands kneading her lower back and shoulders when the pains grew more severe, as night inched with agonizing slowness toward dawn.

"Where is my lord husband?" she asked between the unrelenting pangs of labor.

"Asleep," the Lady Mathilda answered with a smile, not adding that to all appearances the poor man was not only asleep, but heavily in his cups! "We will let him be. He can do nothing here save get in our way, as do all men! This is women's work, is it not?"

Freya nodded, but secretly she wished Olaf were at her side, or at least nearby, to offer her a word of encouragement and love. He had sworn he would accept and father Alaric's child as if it were of his own seed—but would he, would he *truly*, when it came to it? Her fretfulness showed in her face and in the tenseness of her body.

"You must relax, lady," Una cautioned sternly, seeing the frown that knitted the laboring woman's brow. "If you are taut as a bowstring, then how shall the child thrust its way easily into this world? Calm yourself, little mother. Draw strength from sleep."

Her soothing, crooning voice and the drugged wine combined worked their magic, and she fell into a deep sleep, waking to see the pearl-gray of early morning and a feeble sun through the narrow wind-eye. Dawn had come and gone, she realized. She clutched at her belly, suddenly afraid, relieved to find she was still hugely swollen there. The great mound suddenly surged under her fingertips, drawing upward as if with a will of its own. "Blessed Frey, giver of all life, help me!" she cried aloud as a pain swept over her. Sweat sprang out upon her brow and upper lip.

At once Una, who had been dozing beside the bread-baking stones, wakened and hurried to her side. "The birthing pains have been coming hard and close for some time now, lady. 'Twas exhausted you were indeed, not to have wakened to them earlier. Girl, fetch me some lengths of rope!" she ordered the thrall while she counseled Freya, "'Twill not be long now, mistress. Let's see you made ready."

Gentle hands drew her damp garments from her, sponged her clean, and helped her onto a bed of fresh straw heaped upon the floor. The same hands covered her upper body with a warm mantle and slipped a long-bladed knife beneath the pallet to "cut" the pain of childbirth, after their pagan customs. The sealskin thongs the midwife had asked for were brought and looped about two wooden house posts on either side of Freya's body.

"Hold hard to these when the pain comes, mistress," Una ordered, "and when I give ye the word, bear down!"

The pains doubled, tripled in strength, coming ever closer together as the morning wore on, yet still the babe's head did not crown the birth canal. Freya's face and bare body were slick with sweat. Her strength seemed to be ebbing with each violent contraction. How much longer could she withstand this, she wondered, fearful, before she was torn in two?

"Stand," Una urged. "Walk a pace or two, and then squat down, as do the female thralls in the fields when their time is come. 'Tis often easier that way, even for a noble lady such as yourself."

The pain was like none Freya had ever experienced before. For all her warrior's rigid discipline, she feared she would cry out. Biting down upon her lower lip until the blood ran from it, she squatted upon the straw as Una had said, her hands wound tightly in the sealskin ropes, grunting through clenched jaws and clamped teeth and straining to deliver her babe like the lowliest thrall in her labor, for childbirth paid no heed to wealth nor station.

A burning pain swept through her, centered between her thighs, and with a feeling of such pressure she feared she would explode. She had to bear down—had to! The sensation to push was overwhelming—

"Push, my lady. Push!" Una commanded. "I see the crown!"

"Aaagh!" Involuntarily Freya moaned, then screamed, and the babe's head slipped wetly from her, followed quickly by the shoulders and remainder of the body, sliding safely into Una's capable, waiting hands.

"A fine son, if a mite smaller than I'd expected!" Una crowed, and Freya heard her own delighted cry mingled with the sudden indignant wails of a newborn babe as she weakly fell back to the pallet of straw.

Joy swept through her. A son! A male child, thanks be to Frey! She closed her eyes and offered up a heartfelt prayer of thanks for her son's safe entry into the world. The burning, crushing pain was quite gone now, the memory of it fast receding as she waited expectantly to hold her babe for the first time. "Is my son perfect, Una?" she asked, a new mother's anxiety filling her. "Is he whole in every part of him?"

"Aye, mistress, indeed he is! Ten hand-twigs, ten foot-twigs, and all perfect between them, Frey bless him!" she declared, in her excitement waxing poetic after the Norse fashion. "Ah, and what a pretty babe, besides! Why, 'tis almost a sin for him to be so bonny, and male!"

Laughing, Una tied the birth cord with narrow strips of sealskin rope, cut it, then placed the squalling, bloody infant upon his eager mother's breasts.

He was not overly large, as Una had said, but appeared vigorous nonetheless. To Freya's delighted eyes he was more beautiful than even Odin's son, Balder, renowned for his comeliness, could possibly have been! His perfect little head was capped with damp curls, clinging like wet ink-black commas to his brow, and other similarities to his sire were already hinted at in his baby face—the suggestion of a stubborn chin; eyes so deep a murky baby blue they would surely turn the wood-smoke gray she loved so well ere long. *Alaric's son, in truth*, she thought, stroking the damp black curls and pressing her lips to the little head. The pain of her grief surged through her anew. It cut like a blade into her heart, turning the joy bittersweet. Tears welled in her eyes.

Lost in her fierce mother's love for her son, and in sadness that his sire would never know him, the further pain that knifed through her took her completely unawares. She sharply cried out and Una, fearing some complication with the birth, frowned and hurried to take the infant from her and hand him to the waiting thrall to be swaddled in lamb's wool coverings, before turning swiftly back to the mother.

"So soon?" the midwife muttered under her breath.

"What is it?" Freya asked, alarmed.

"Naught but the afterbirth, little mother, fear not!" Una reassured her.

Yet it was not the afterbirth. Scant minutes after the birth of her son Freya in her pain dragged herself up onto the straw, again squatted, then bore down and delivered a *second* child, this one a baby girl, the image of the first save for the deep dimples in her little cheeks that were wholly her mother's.

"Well, I'll be!" exclaimed Una, beaming as she lifted the infant girl and handed her to a smiling Lady Mathilda. "A brace of babes—aye, and the first twins I've delivered in many a year!"

"A comely pair indeed, my dear," Mathilda agreed, laughing. "And healthy! Look at them! Your Olaf will strut like a rooster when he learns of this, I'll warrant, and shower you with birthing gifts! Shall I take them to him for his acceptance and naming, while you rest and recover?"

"*Ja*, my lady, I—I suppose you must," Freya agreed, suddenly reluctant that the babes should be parted from her. What if Olaf, now that the moment was at last here, spurned the babes, refused to accept them as his own and ordered them thrown into the river, or left out on some barren place to die, as her father had once ordered old Kolina, the midwife, to do at her own birth—? "Please, be careful of them." she begged, love for her children flooding through her, and with it the agonizing fear of losing them.

"I shall," Mathilda promised solemnly, and bore them away, one cradled in the crook of each arm, cooing to them as she went.

Freya watched them go, following them with anxious eyes and an aching heart.

Olaf was awake and in the main hall, Mathilda found, sitting upon a wooden bench with his bursting head cradled in his massive hands. He was groaning. Smiling broadly, Snorri's lady set the babes upon the rushes before him, after the ancient customs of her husband's people.

"My lord Olaf Olafson, your children!" she exclaimed. "A fine son—*and* a comely daughter!"

Olaf gaped at the babes, his befuddlement clear on his face, then looked up at the lady before him. "Two?" he asked in wonderment.

"Two indeed," she confirmed, wanting to laugh at his confusion.

The previous night's conversation about the hearth flooded back to Olaf. With it, renewed anger and resentment surged through his veins—and fear reared its ugly, unwanted head. He was suddenly tempted to reject the two red-faced, black-haired infants bawling in unison upon the rushes; to cruelly order them left to the elements and fate, as was his choice. But then he saw with his mind's eye his beloved Freya's lovely face swollen with tears, her mouth working soundlessly with grief at their death and his cruelty, and his hatred abated in the full force of his love for her. She would never forgive him if he harmed them, nay, never! He knew that she would mother, protect, and defend the two before him as fiercely as she had once waged battle. She was not capable of half measures in anything. 'Twas all or nothing, for his lady. If he accepted these babes, though they were not sired from his own loins, surely her love for him must increase?

And so with a heavy sigh he rose and bent down, clumsily lifting first one babe, then the other, into his huge arms. Mathilda hovered anxiously at his elbow to ensure he did not drop them, having little faith in the dexterity of men where babes were concerned.

"Water?" he asked, and she gestured to the waiting thrall who came forward bearing water in a silver goblet. "Which one is the male child?" he asked, and Mathilda showed him. "My son," he murmured, the words almost sticking in his craw, "I name thee Beorn, for truly you seem to me a bear cub." Dipping his fingers in the water, he touched them to the babe's brow. Turning to the second, he said, "And you, my little maid, blessed with my Freya's dimples, I name thee Edana, for you will certainly be as fiery as your lady mother one day." With that he quickly handed the infants over into the care of Mathilda and her serving girl, as if eager to rid himself of their charge.

"They are well named, sir," Mathilda told him, her brown eyes sparkling. "My good wishes to you, their happy father, on whom the gods have smiled! Tell me, how is it the little ones are both so dark, and you and your lady so fair? Your sire was dark-haired, mayhap?" She meant nothing by the question. It was merely the result of idle observation and curiosity on her part, and she was startled by the darkling look Olaf Olafson shot back at her.

"The dark coloring runs in my mother's family, my lady," he growled. "Where is my woman?"

Taken aback by his sudden abruptness, Mathilda gestured toward the rear of the vast, smoky hall. "You will find her back there, sir, by the warmth of the cooking fires."

With a curt nod, Olaf shouldered his massive way between Snorri's men in the direction she had pointed.

His anger and misgivings dwindled somewhat when he saw Freya. She appeared pale and exhausted. Her sparkling eyes were dulled and full of fear as he strode across the rushes toward her. Weakly, she tried to rise onto her elbows to greet him.

"Be still," he commanded her gently, and knelt at her side, embracing her. He felt a shudder of relief run through her momentarily, and then she tensed anew in his arms. He could feel the unasked questions, the fear in her tense frame even before she voiced them.

"My—the babes? You have seen them, my lord?" she asked

hesitantly, her mouth quivering faintly.

He drew back, took both her chill hands in his own large ones, and looked her full in the eyes, nodding once. "*Ja*, I have seen them. And named them both. They are to be called Beorn and Edana. I am well pleased with you, my lady wife. You have given me a fine son and a comely daughter. My heartfelt thanks to you."

A thrill ran through her. Gratitude to him, her dear Olaf— he who had loved and protected her in childhood and now sought to love and protect her as his wife—swept over her. His words of acceptance, spoken at enormous cost to him she knew, had banished forever the aching doubt in her breast. In truth, she was not worthy of such great love! Impulsively she grasped his great, hairy hand and bore it to her lips, kissing it as tears flowed down her cheeks onto his callused skin. "Nay, nay, do not say so," she whispered fervently. "All thanks are due to you, my dear, dear husband! Henceforth I will try to be a better wife to you, to be all that you could ever want in a woman. By Frey, I swear it!"

The deep gratitude in her eyes, her calling him "husband" so tenderly, more than made up for the resentment and jealous anger he'd swallowed with such difficulty moments before. His lips now sealed for all time against what he had learned the night before in Snorri's hall, his red-bearded, ruggedly handsome face filled with love that was inseparable from the pain he also felt, he nodded.

Chapter 30

The babes thrived, and so did their mother. She recovered quickly from their birth, and true to her word, from the first she attempted to make up to Olaf for all the months she had been his wife and resented it. In this she succeeded. Each day it grew a little easier for her to be the affectionate woman he'd always wanted. If he could have wished her a little more passionate in his bed, that was her only fault, for she was always willing and eager and gave him great pleasure. For him, that was enough. In truth, it was more than he had ever dared to hope for between them!

To Freya's surprise, what was begun as a tender charade on her part in time became true love, of a sort. Oh yes, her new-found love for Olaf lacked the almost painful intensity of the love she had felt for Alaric, but nevertheless her feelings were deep and genuine and had their roots in the long, close friendship she and Olaf had always shared. It was a good foundation on which to build the rest of their lives together, she decided; indeed, more than was given to many men and women, for most marriages in these times were made to cement new alliances between clans, or to heal old enmities or blood feuds, and divorce was all too common.

As for Olaf, he fell in love with his now lively, tempestuous Freya all over again, and sought out Ilse's bed less and less often as the long hot summer became fruitful autumn. Freya saw how longingly Ilse looked at Olaf, and her heart went out to the sweet, gentle girl who had become her friend. But she

391

could do nothing to ease her pain. Ilse would have to endure it alone, and either find a new love or learn to live with the ache of the old. And so it goes on, the wheel of life, Freya thought, around and around. Birth and death, love and hate, peace and war, good and evil, in an everlasting circle. However hard one might seek to hold back the wheel as it spun, the cycle remained unbroken.

The babes, tiny at their birthing, filled out beautifully. Beorn, her little bear, was the bigger of the two, all sturdy fists and dimpled knees, with a lusty appetite to match! Her fairy child Edana's dainty beauty seemed fragile by comparison, as if a strong gust of wind could blow the baby away. Freya loved them both with a mother's fierce pride and possessiveness, and determined to show no preference for her son, as did some mothers. She knew full well the torment a child suffered from feeling like an outcast, unloved and unwanted, and vowed her Edana would never have cause to suffer as she had suffered, or feel she was second-best to her brother or anyone else.

On warm days she'd place the babes side by side, like a brace of kittens, in a broad, flat basket lined with rabbit skins, and carry them up onto the flowered hillside. There, upon a blanket spread on the grass beneath a shady tree, she would unwrap the swaddling that bound them and let them lie naked and unhampered in the patches of golden sunshine that fell between the treetops. Beorn spent his moments of freedom vigorously attempting to roll over onto his little belly, furious and red-faced when he failed, or in trying to trap his mother's long red-gold hair, while the more tranquil Edana was content to lie gazing up at the changing pattern the dancing, leafy boughs made above her against the blue sky, cooing and gurgling in delight.

Sometimes Olaf came with them on their little picnics, and on these occasions Freya knew more contentment than she had ever felt in her life before, to see her brawny warrior gently rocking one of the babes in his muscled arms, or cradling them tenderly to his broad and powerful chest. Could this same man wield a hefty blood-axe mercilessly in battle, and cleave his foe in two without so much as flinching? *Ja*, he could indeed! She had seen him. But he could also be the most gentle of men with those he cared for.

One day he looked up at her as they sat under the trees by the still green pond and gave her a sheepish smile. "I admit I wanted no part of the Saxon's whelps when first you gave them birth, my Freya. They were yours, and I their father in name alone. But now—!"

He shrugged, and she smiled and nodded her understanding. He did not need to continue. She knew what he had intended to say. Now he loved the babes as if they were his own flesh and blood. Indeed, he could not have loved them more if they had been. It was in his voice, in the careful touch of his powerful hands upon the little pair, gestures more eloquent than words.

That summer seemed idyllic, halcyon days followed by warm, scented nights. Autumn promised to be little less perfect. Their first crops had flourished, and the yield of barley and corn from their fields outweighed even their wildest expectations. They harvested in the Corncutting month, everyone from the hall and many Angles from the surrounding countryside gathering to help with the cutting and threshing and winnowing. Their livestock had also multiplied, and there would be enough beasts to slaughter and provide meat for the long winter. Indeed, they had reason to celebrate with a lavish feast, and feast they did, the merrymaking lasting for days on end.

On autumn nights when the golden harvest moon was full, she and Olaf sometimes stood arm in arm under the stars and watched skeins of snow-white geese flying southward for the winter months, the moonlight touching their wingspans with a magical, bluish luster. But on one such night when they left the noisy harvest feasting in their long-house shortly after moonrise, to walk and talk alone in the brisk night air as had become their nightly custom, they surprised not a breath-taking arrowhead of snowy white geese, but a family of hares, dancing and leaping amongst the moonwashed stubble of a cornfield.

Freya stood stock-still, rekindled memories of another eve when she had seen the Dance of the Hares lancing through her. The past months were shattered like a goblet of crystal, as if they had never been. In that instant Freya knew—with a swift

393

and sudden pain that pierced like daggers in her heart—that all her efforts these past months had been in vain. No matter how hard she might try to deny it, smother it, she still loved him, her Alaric! She would always love him . . .

With a keening cry she flung about and fled back to the hall, leaving Olaf standing there, staring after her. His shoulders had slumped then like an old man, a man utterly defeated. What it was that had made his Freya remember her Saxon lord, he knew not, yet think of him she had. He was as certain of it as he was of his own name. Anger and sorrow mingled in his breast. That night, for the first night in many months, he lay with Ilse again.

The wheel of life spun on. Peace had lain across the land like a gentle wing since the Battle of Edington and the Treaty of Chippenham between a victorious Alfred and a sorely besieged Guthrum. Now came the turn of the ravening wolf of war.

Rumor spread throughout Angle that Guthrum had returned from battling the Franks, and now intended to renew his vow to conquer Wessex once and for all time. Messengers rode far and wide across the Danelaw, summoning the Norsemen to unite and wage battle under his command. The city of London was to be their target, Alfred and his ealdormen and their vast *fyrds* the quarry, the kingdom of Wessex the prize! The Viking leader, Guthrum, planned to attack by land and by water simultaneously, trapping the Wessex *fyrd* in a cunning pincer strategy that he was certain could not fail. And then all the isle of Britain would lie under Viking rule.

The men of Olaf's hall talked of nothing but war in those days, often staying up and drinking about the hearth until dawn flushed the sky with gold and scarlet, reliving past bloody battles or boasting, after their Viking fashion, of the great feats of valor they would perform if called upon to fight.

The women thought of nothing else either, though for different reasons, and though they smiled and behaved as usual, Freya knew the fears that plagued them, for they were her own fears. Though she had broken at the sight of the Hares' Dance that crisp autumn evening, bringing back as it did such powerful emotions and memories of Alaric, in many ways she loved Olaf too, and was afraid for him. Unlike the other women of the hall, she had witnessed the horrors of war firsthand.

She clung to the thin hope that if she only prayed to their gods hard enough, Olaf would forget all notions of going off to war, and remain at their hall. But then one morning a large company of Viking soldiers arrived in their secluded little valley and pitched camp on the frosty meadow below the long-house, and she knew her wishes and hopes had all come to naught. The leader of the men was Snorri the Boastful, lord of the hall at Thetford where she had birthed the twins. Olaf admired the big-bellied old rogue and would follow him eagerly to London, she felt certain. She was right.

Winter came early that year. The first snow fell the morning Olaf and the men of his hall were to march with Snorri and his followers for London, there to join Guthrum's forces. The horses had been readied, and were saddled and stamping impatiently in the frosty air.

She fussed over Olaf, inspecting his chainmail, his bronze helm, the weapons she had polished countless times the eve before, checking and rechecking to make certain he had everything he could possibly need: warm blankets and clothing, extra boots and leggings—a hundred and one little things to fuss over that served to keep her mind from her burning desire to go with him, and her greatest fear, his final departure.

When it was time to go at last she clung to him, filled with the sudden foreboding that she would never see him again. When in a moment of utterly foolish, feminine weakness she voiced her fears aloud, he laughed them away.

"You'll not get rid of your Olaf so easily, woman," he teased, chucking her beneath the chin. He looked down at her, wondering despite his brave vow if this *was* the last time he would ever see her. By Loki, she was so lovely, with her red-gold hair falling loose and silky about her shoulders and her jewel eyes shining with tears—tears for him. He added softly, "I'll be back, my lovely, and with Wessex in my helmet as a gift for thee! Nothing could keep me away!"

He clasped her to him, enfolding her in a fierce hug that lifted her clear off the ground, remembering other times when they had fought side by side as equals, she and he. He had had no one waiting for him in the past when he left Danehof to go a-Viking each spring. The knowledge that this time she would be there at their hall when he returned, that she cared and would fret about his safety, filled him with joy. Perhaps the strange, brooding moods she had fallen prey to in the autumn were now a thing of the past. Their lips touched gently, and he tasted the salt of her tears as he kissed her in fond farewell. "I love thee, woman!" he murmured fervently one last time, and his sky-blue eyes glowed with that love.

Too soon the moment was gone forever. The men formed ranks, spears in hand, the *jarls'* horses in the van snorting and prancing nervously, the winter sunlight winking off the shield bosses and conical helmets of the men. The raven standards streamed proudly in the bitter wind. All was ready.

The order to march rang out. Freya felt the women huddled all about her give a collective soft cry of despair. Nonetheless, each one lifted her children to watch their father leave, and bade the little ones wave a brave farewell. Each one embraced her man and wished him a safe return and a victory gained with honor. And each one died a little inside as they mouthed the empty words, for men were men, and as long as men lived there would be wars. If they lived to return, this would not be the last time they bade them farewell with silent tears in their hearts.

Yet when the men looked back over their shoulders to salute one last time, they saw only the brave, encouraging smiles of their Viking womenfolk and their wide-eyed little children, and a forest of frantically waving bright kerchiefs.

It was as if the sun had gone behind a cloud in Olaf's hall after the men left. The women went about their everyday tasks, for life had to go on. They spun and they wove. They sewed and they baked. They swept and did all the ordinary little chores they had to do every day, but the gladness with which they had done them before was gone. No more did laughter and the sounds of women chattering or singing at their looms ring out through the long-house. There was a furtiveness about them now, a distant quality, owing to the fears each one carried in her breast. When they spoke at all their voices were flat and without cadence, or else sharp and scolding, and the children wondered where the harping shrews—who had of a sudden taken their sweet mothers' places—had come from.

Freya felt tied in a knot of dread too, though as their mistress she gamely tried to hide it, finding the bereft women extra duties to perform to take their minds away from the war and their menfolk, and keep them occupied. But Beorn and Edana were not so easily diverted. They sensed her tension and fussed when she nursed them, and Beorn screamed in a hungry rage each time she pulled him from her sore and empty breasts. She knew her breast milk had dwindled from worry, and forced herself to eat and drink well for their sake, though the food tasted like sawdust on her tongue. She retired to her bed early each night, hoping that rest would replenish her milk supply, and when after a few miserable days it did, she made an offering to Frey in gratitude.

Her worries for her babes temporarily stilled, she could now devote her attention to poor Ilse, who moved about the hall like one of the walking dead, shying at shadows, her eyes red and swollen from weeping. Ilse seemed to be avoiding her, and the withdrawal of her friendship and companionship combined with her fears for Olaf was more than Freya could bear. After several days of trying to corner Ilse unsuccessfully in the hope that they could unburden themselves on each others' shoulders, she finally found the girl alone, quite by accident. She had left the smoky, stuffy long-house to take her nightly walk outside in the snow and enjoy the bracing cold air and solitude, and was alerted by the sounds of Ilse's sobbing when she passed one of the byres.

It was difficult to see in the gloom of the barn, pungent with the scent of horseflesh, cows, and dung, but at last she found Ilse curled on the straw in a corner, hugging an old mantle of Olaf's to her breasts. So distraught was she that she did not notice Freya until the latter placed a gentle hand on her shoulders to comfort her.

"There, there, Ilse," Freya soothed, drawing the girl into her arms and stroking her disheveled hair. "Do not cry, for I cannot bear to have you suffer so. Will you not tell me what it is you weep for?" She believed she knew, but would do Ilse the courtesy of asking nonetheless.

"I cannot tell thee, mistress," Ilse managed between great hiccuping sobs. "Do not ask me! 'Tis too shameful to share!"

Freya cupped the girl's flushed damp face in her hands and

gazed deep into her tear-filled eyes. "'Tis Olaf you weep for, is it not?" she pressed her gently.

Ilse wailed and turned her face away, cheeks burning with color. "*Ja*, mistress, *ja!*" she whispered. "How—how did you—?"

"How did I know?" Freya smiled and reached out and caressed Ilse's hair. "I have known you loved my husband for many months. And—that he has come to you when he needed solace and I could give him none."

"Oh, nay! You knew of it? Oh mistress, forgive me, I could not help it, I—"

"Hush, hush, calm yourself now, I beg you, Ilse. You will sicken with all this weeping, and in truth I need your friendship more now than I have ever done! Aye, I knew of you and Olaf, and I thought no less of you or him for it. I cannot love Olaf as he deserves to be loved, you see, though the gods know that I have tried, and have only hurt him in the trying. But you love him, Ilse, do you not? And he needs you. *Ja*, I believe he needs you more than he knows! Dry your eyes, my dear friend. I blame no one for this but the fates. It is they who haphazardly determine where our hearts will love, not you or I." Ilse, Freya saw, was waging a valiant struggle to compose herself now, and her heart went out to her. "Is—is it only our lord Olaf's departure that has saddened you, Ilse, or is there something more?" she asked intuitively, suddenly convinced Ilse was keeping something from her still.

The girl hung her head and nodded as the tears rolled anew down her cheeks. When she was finally able to speak, she said in a voice so low Freya had to strain to catch her words, "I—I am carrying his child!"

"Oh Ilse! My poor, poor little Ilse!" Freya cried, blinking back the tears that sprang into her own eyes now. Her arms went around the girl, and with a cry Ilse flung herself against Freya and clung to her like a mother.

"I fear he'll d-d-die in battle," she stammered between sobs, "He'll be k-killed, I know it, and his child will have no father. I l-love him so, mistress!"

"Don't think of that, don't," Freya insisted sharply, acutely aware as she did so that she dreaded the same thing. "He is a warrior, brave and agile—'twill take a rare Saxon to best our Viking lord!" she added in an attempt to cheer the girl. "I know, for I fought alongside him many times."

Ilse blinked. "Fought?"

Freya smiled. "*Ja!* Your lady mistress once led the brave men of her father's hall a-Viking, and Olaf was her second in command! And though I would not wish to seem boastful, I was a warrior maid to contend with in my time!"

Ilse managed a little smile through her tears. "I think I believe you!"

"As well you should," Freya laughingly scolded, "for it is the truth! We sailed west over the sea to Francia, and fought the Franks for their lands along the Seine. I bade farewell to several men of Danehof who settled there when we left." Her eyes glowed like sapphires in the gloom as she reminisced. "And then the next summer we made that last, fateful voyage to Britain, and I was taken captive by the Saxons at Kenley, as I told you—but that is enough of my adventures for now," she finished hurriedly, realizing that Ilse would draw no comfort from hearing of her capture, fearing as she did for Olaf. "Just remember, Ilse, that Olaf is a true Viking, fierce in battle, unmatched in courage. He'll return, for he has both of us who love him to live for, does he not?"

"I should have told him of the child before he left," Ilse said sadly, yet her eyes were dry now.

"Perhaps. But think instead how pleased he will be to hear of it when he returns," Freya coaxed.

"I suppose so. Mistress, does—does it anger you that I am carrying your lord's babe?"

After a momentary pause, Freya shook her head. "Nay, Ilse. Perhaps it should, but it does not. If I loved Olaf as you do, then I suppose my jealousy would make me far less understanding. Now if it were Alaric's child you carried, I would have torn you limb from limb, and scratched out your eyes," she confessed ruefully, "for I learned once that I am an utter madwoman when faced by a rival for my beloved's heart!" Meredyth of Powys had flashed into her mind, and she smiled. "But, I am sad to say, that is not how I feel toward Olaf. I love him, *ja,* but as you might love your brothers, not as a husband. Therein lies the difference."

She stood and drew her fur mantle snugly about her

shoulders. Compared to the hall with its roaring fires and closely covered narrow wind-eyes, the byre was cold. "Come, let's go inside before we catch our deaths. 'Tis freezing out here! We can talk anon, over a bowl of hot broth," Freya promised briskly.

She nudged Ilse to her feet, and arm in arm they dashed through the swirling snowflakes that had begun to fall, back to the hall.

Olaf and the men had been gone for over a week when Freya had the dream. Or was it a dream?

She thought she had wakened in the wee hours, feeling chilled despite the mound of luxurious furs that covered her. Had the skin covering that curtained the wind-eye somehow come loose, she wondered sleepily? Or had the door been left ajar, admitting the night air? Whatever its origin, there was a definite draft in her bower.

Teeth chattering, shivering in her thin linen night-kirtle, she tossed back the coverings and padded barefoot across the darkened chamber, to where the babes slept. Tenderly she reached out to draw the furry blankets more snugly up about their dark little heads.

Her hand froze in midair as she did so, and a chill wormed its way down her spine. The hackles at her nape rose and tingled— for the heavy, carved cradle rocked to and fro, to and fro, as if a ghostly hand had just seconds before gently touched it, though the babes were fast asleep and quite still in its cosy depths.

Gooseflesh rose on her arms. Suddenly she knew instinctively that she was not alone with her children in the bower. Some *thing*—or someone—else was there also! She sensed the presence through her very flesh, every pore alerted and open to the eerie sensation. She turned slowly about, her mouth dropping at what she saw.

There, in the darkest corner of the chamber, was a pale, phosphorescent glimmer of light. As she watched, transfixed, the ethereal glimmer grew and grew, until it reached from the rushes almost to the rafters. Her eyes all but starting from her head in her fright, she saw that now the light had taken on form and substance. A lovely woman stood there within its gentle white radiance, robed in palest blue. Silver chains were crisscrossed between her breasts, and a girdle of silver links clasped her waist. Her long golden hair was braided in twin shining ropes that swept over her bosom to fall to her waist. Her lovely, serene face was pale and stained with glistening tears, her eyes darkened with sorrow.

"Daughter!" the woman whispered. "My own dearest daughter, hear me!"

Her voice was low and sweet and strangely mournful, yet her every murmured word carried clearly to Freya.

"Who are you? What are you?" Freya managed at last to choke the words out, feeling her knees give way. She sank down to the rushes, kneeling upon them, yet her eyes never once strayed from the vision in the corner.

"I was once your mother, the Lady Verdandi, wife to Thorfast of Danehof," came the melancholy voice. "Now my soul is of the Disir. I have come to warn thee, my Freya!"

"Warn me? But—of what?" Freya cried, her hands flying to her breast to still the sudden threshing of her heart.

"Olaf, your lord husband, has been chosen, little Freya. Odin's fair daughters have marked him for Valhalla. Go to him, daughter. Go to him with all haste, or you will be too late . . . !"

With these ominous weeping words, the vision began to fade, seeping slowly away from the corner until all light was gone, and naught but dense shadows remained in its place.

"Wait, I beg you, don't go!" Freya implored. "Tell me, where shall I find him? You must tell me more—!"

A chill wind stirred her hair. The cradle rocked one last time upon the rushes. Then all was quiet, both within and without her, and she knew the presence had gone.

Shivering with reaction and fear now, more than with cold, Freya stumbled back to her bed and pulled the furs up over her head. Imagination, she told herself firmly, 'twas naught but imagination, brought about by her fears for Olaf.

But the next morning, when she tried to remember her dream, there were smudges of dirt upon her night-kirtle, left there when she had sunk to her knees upon the rushes. And the cradle was still.

Chapter 31

She tried to shrug off the disturbing appearance of the Dis in coming days, yet it continued to trouble her deeply.

Had it been only a bad dream, she wondered, or had she indeed been warned of impending tragedy? The sisters of the Disir were the souls of dead mothers, chosen to be guardian spirits to those still tied to the mortal world by life, she knew. Was her own mother's soul one of them? And had Olaf truly been chosen for a warrior's death by the fair daughters of Odin, the Valkyries, as the vision of Verdandi had foretold?

Her unease grew with every hour that passed. If the warning was real, then she must go to him, somehow find Olaf, wherever he might be! Perhaps she could avert the dark threat that hung over him like a pall. She could not simply ignore what had happened and do nothing. If she did, and Olaf was slain in battle, she would never be able to forgive herself for not acting sooner!

Freya said nothing to Ilse of what had occurred that night. Nothing could be gained from frightening the young girl, who was already heartsick with Olaf's departure. She mentioned only that she was concerned for Olaf's safety, and wished they might be closer to London and any possible news of the battle. The seed, once planted in Ilse's mind, quickly took root.

"Mistress, I've been thinking. If you truly wished to do so, we could be closer to London and the battle," Ilse volunteered.

"How so?" Freya queried, stilling the sudden eagerness that leaped into her breast.

"We could take a cart, and journey to my father's farm," she said excitedly. "'Tis only a league or two distant from there to the River Thames and London."

"But—are you not afraid to go back there? What of your father?"

"Oh, few people travel by our farm in the winter months! 'Tis too desolate. And besides, Master Toki has been dead almost a year, thanks to Master Robin. If anyone questions us, you must tell them that you took me in after my master was slain by—by robbers, and that you are now my mistress."

"*Ja,* you are right," Freya agreed almost too readily. "We'll go! See some victuals prepared for us, Ilse, and warm clothing—as many blankets as can be spared, and furs, of course. You know what we'll need."

Freya frowned after Ilse had sped away to carry out her instructions. Everything was working perfectly, yet she wished she need not take the babes with her and expose them to the cold. Still, she had little choice but to take them, if she was to continue to nurse them. There were no women at the hall with infants yet at their breasts who could serve as wet-nurses in her absence. They would not come to any harm, surely, tucked warmly in their basket amongst the rabbit- and lambskins, her warm breast milk to keep their little bellies full and content? Her worries stilled, she began her own preparations.

They set out early the next morning for Ilse's father's farm, which lay to the southwest of Olaf's hall, riding in a three-wheeled wooden cart over deeply rutted tracks lightly sprinkled with snow. Since the men had gone to war, there was no one to escort them on their travels, so Freya donned leggings and tunic once more, and strapped a sharp dagger to the belt at her waist under her fur-lined mantle. To casual eyes, it appeared a young fellow and his wife and babes traveled the wintry roads, and Freya was glad that it seemed so. Her greatest fear was that they would be set upon by robber bands such as Black Nevin's, brigands in search of easy pickings and food, but her fears quickly subsided. They met few other travelers braving the bitter cold, let alone robbers.

The first two days they covered several leagues in good time. The horse was sturdy and young, and pulled the cart and the two women at a spanking pace between the barren fields and through the leafless woods. At such a speedy pace, Ilse guessed they would reach her father's farm in two more days, and her excitement to see her family again after so long grew with every league they traversed.

But on the third day the snow began to fall in earnest, and several inches of powdery white hampered their horse's hooves and the wooden cartwheels. The bitter wind had turned against them too, piling heavy blizzard-drifts against hedge-rows until the valiant horse could no longer breast them, strong as he was. Icicles feathered his shaggy hooves and mane, and his breath came in white vapor clouds upon the frosty air. His great head was bowed with the effort they asked of him. Sick with dread, Freya realized they would have to unharness the horse and leave the unwieldy cart and many of their possessions behind, to continue on horseback. This they did, taking turns to ride or walk.

"Do not worry, mistress," Ilse said cheerfully, seeing Freya's woebegone expression, "'tis not far now. By dusk this even we'll be snug in my father's cottage, I promise you!"

Ilse's estimate was not far wrong. That day, as gray dusk was gathering over the pristine meadows and gently undulating white hills, they spied a welcome glow of light from a little dwelling nestled in the lap of the next shallow valley.

Before true dark, they had reached the simple cottage, and Freya and the babes were snug and warm, their bellies full and content with milk, hers with helpings of warm bread and savory venison stew, washed down with horns of mulled cider. While Ilse chattered happily with her father, Sigmund, and younger brothers, enjoying a boisterous but warm reunion that continued long after dark, Freya retired with her little ones to the heaping of fresh straw that had been provided for her bed in a corner of the cottage.

Weary as she was from the past four days' grueling journey, sleep did not come easily. Though Ilse had tried to silence her father, Freya had heard the old Viking fellow speak of the bloody battle that was being waged between the men of Wessex and Guthrum's army two leagues to the southwest, had heard Sigmund mutter darkly that Alfred's troops had threatened to spare no man, should the battle go in their favor, and his words had filled her with dread.

Where was her lord husband this night? she wondered, apprehension clawing at her vitals. Did he sleep wrapped in warm furs as did she—or did he lie wounded and shivering in some frozen ditch, his life-blood congealing in the cold air? The thought chilled her own blood. It seemed as if Olaf called to her from afar, beseeching her to find him, and she would not falter. "I am coming, my dearest husband," she whispered to the shadows. "My lifelong friend, I will not fail thee now, as you have never once failed me!"

He needed her in some way, of that much she was now convinced. On the morrow she would leave the babes in Ilse's capable care, and go in search of him.

She steadfastly ignored the pricking, nagging voice inside her head that said she could not hope to alter fate, and tried to sleep.

Her terror deepened the following day as she journeyed southwestward and closer to London, and with good cause.

Wherever she passed were signs of the great battle that had taken place. Farms and cottages had been burned and razed, and the black ruins still smoked in the frosty air. Bodies lay strewn everywhere upon the snow. The dead men's expressions were those of peaceful fellows caught unawares and unarmed in a horror of which they wanted no part. All were broken and twisted in the final undignified and ungraceful poses of death.

The women who had survived fled at the sight of Freya in her man's garb, screaming and clutching their little ones to their breasts, the violation and carnage they had witnessed or experienced themselves mirrored in their huge, terrified eyes. Horses lay where they had been hacked down to provide food for the hungry men of the Danish or Saxon *fyrds,* as did the carcasses of cattle and oxen. Their butchered remains left little but bones for the hungry black ravens and crows who formed croaking, dense clouds over the bodies.

Whether the victory had gone to Alfred and his host or to

Guthrum and his mattered little. The winter would be a bitterly long, hard one for all those who had survived, with many dying of starvation before the Cuckoo month came again, for the stores carefully set aside for that time had been despoiled or ruthlessly, senselessly, destroyed: kegs of salted meat or fish broken open and trampled into the snow and hard earth by the pillagers; precious sacks of flour and seed grain spoiled in the wet snow.

She trudged on amidst snowy drifts piled alongside bare hedgerows and rutted cart tracks, asking of any of the bedraggled fugitives she met fleeing east if they had heard anything, anything at all, of Olaf Olafson or Snorri the Boastful and his followers. All shook their heads, and she despaired of ever finding her husband.

Then, late in the afternoon of the third day, she encountered a ragged fellow with a deep and bloody wound in his thigh, traveling in the opposite direction. He appeared very weak, scarce able to lean upon his makeshift crutch as he hobbled along, yet his eyes lit up when he saw her.

"'Tis the Lady Freya, is it not?" he cried, rheumy eyes focusing upon her with difficulty. Seeing her frown and make to hurry on her way, he called, "'Tis no wonder you do not recognize me, in the state I'm in, but I know thee, Lady Freya! I am Lothi. I drank with your lord Olaf in Snorri's hall, as we feasted the funeral of good Queen Disa. You had recently been brought to childbed, and we drank good health to your brace of little ones, and to yourself."

She went to him eagerly then and bade him rest a while, offering to cleanse his wound and bind it. She gave him sparingly of the foodstuffs in her pouch, asking him eager questions as she deftly tended his wounds. Had he seen her lord? Was he wounded, dead, or, please the gods, unharmed? Who had won the victory, Alfred or Guthrum? When he was revived a little by the food, for he had not eaten in several days, Lothi answered her.

"The victory went to the cursed Saxons, Lady Freya," he said bitterly. "Alfred and his men dug trenches to divert the flow of the Thames, and our proud fleet was left high and dry on the mudflats! The Raven Banner was captured and ground into the muck under Saxon boot heels! There was little else for it but to retreat, which we did. Yet the Saxon *fyrd* hounded us into the countryside even as we fled, sparing no one in their path." The ghost of a smile played about his pale lips. "They have learned our tricks well, these cunning Saxons, and did not give us the chance to feign a retreat, then turn on them and attack, as we ourselves have done many times before."

"But my lord husband—what do you know of him? Have you seen him? Is he safe?"

"I know not," Lothi said regretfully. "The last I saw him he was battling amidst the riverbanks, roaring curses at the men of Wessex and daring them to risk his bloody axe!" His admiration for Olaf's valor faded in his next words, to be replaced by sorrow. "Forgive me, but I do not fancy his chances for escape were good, my lady," he said gently. "He was pinned down by more than three of the ealdorman's soldiers."

"Ealdorman?"

"*Ja!*" Lothi acknowledged, wincing at the pain in his wounded leg. "The one the Wessex men call 'the Bear.' I saw him myself—a great black-haired brute, with a sword arm as strong as any Viking could wish for! He wielded his weapon single-handed, as do we. He sprang down from his black stallion's back and into the battle with a roar and a bloody will that would have shamed even our fiercest *berserkers* with its savagery." Lothi shuddered. "'Twas as if he were a madman, in truth!"

He looked up, and was alarmed by the sudden deathly pallor of the lady's face. Even as he watched, she swayed and seemed close to dropping in a swoon. "Mistress, what is it? You have grown white as a Christian shroud!"

"The Bear, you say?" she echoed faintly, her voice no louder than a rustling whisper. "But—how can this be? Was Alaric of Kent not slain long since, stabbed in the heart by—by a serving wench of his household?"

"*Nej,* not him, more's the cursed pity!" Lothi spat in the snow. "'Twas his twin brother slain, mistress. A learned sort, to all accounting. 'Tis said that since his death, the Bear has been one to reckon with. They say he battles with a reckless valor few can combat and win. They say he's a man who cares little for life anymore, and so fears no man, nor death itself. Without fear, he is invincible!"

Twin? Alaric's *twin* brother, Lothi had said! The words pounded over and over in Freya's mind as truth dawned, and left her breathless with its import. Those times when she had thought Alaric different somehow—those few times when he had seemed to forget words they had exchanged—had she indeed exchanged them with him, or with one who simply bore an uncanny *resemblance* to him? Had she, after all, several times met Farant, her lord's brother, and believed him to be Alaric? And had it truly been her beloved Bear whom the Lady Kendra had slain—or her own husband, the one known always and to everyone as "gentle Farant"? If that were so, then Alaric, her beloved, yet lived—! Her heart hammered against her ribs.

"—lady mistress? What have I said? What is it that ails ye?"

"Fear not, Lothi, I am quite well," she muttered abstractedly, yet her hands shook violently and she felt weak and dizzy beyond belief. "'Tis the cold, that is all. It has chilled me to the marrow. Can you continue on by yourself? I must find my lord, you understand, or I would see you safely back into Angle."

"*Nej*, mistress, don't worry your fair head about Lothi! He has suffered worse than this axing of his leg-branch in the past, and survived to enjoy Odin's mead yet again!" he insisted in the florid speech of the true Viking. "Go swift and true as the fleetest, surest arrow on your way to your lord, and tell him Lothi sends his good fortune with you. Odin willing, I will share the high feasting days of Yule with him at his hall!"

She hastily bade him farewell and continued on, her mind reeling with the tumult of her thoughts. Alaric was alive, alive! The tears turned chill upon her cheeks as they rolled from her eyes, but she brushed them aside as she trudged on beneath the dark pines toward London, her pace faster, more eager now.

All too soon the giddy joy of learning that Alaric was alive became mingled with a crushing guilt, for she had almost forgotten Olaf and her fears for him in the full force of her love for Alaric, long since suppressed, that surged through her, singing through her veins and quickening her pulses like a draught of strong mead. She set her jaw squarely. First she must find her dear friend and husband, must see with her own eyes that he was well and unwounded; she owed him much, much more than she could ever hope to repay in a dozen lifetimes! When she had made certain all was well with him, then and only then, she vowed, would she permit her hopes to dwell on anything—or anyone—else.

Yet it was hard, so hard! Memories of Alaric, of nights spent with him in his bower, assailed her. She imagined he once again held her fast in his embraces, felt again the soft whisper of his warm lips against her cheek, his caresses and the joyous rapture they had shared. Despite her vows, he invaded and conquered her every thought. She saw him angry, eyes smoldering like cinders, dark brows knitted in a fierce scowl, and knew she loved him still. She saw him laughing, his curling blue-black hair glinting in the firelight, his firm mouth curved in a teasing smile, and knew she had never ceased loving him, not even when she believed him dead and beyond her love. And she saw him sleeping, his hard, handsome face as smooth and carefree as a youth's, the dark lashes—impossibly long and thick, for a man—casting shadows of mystery upon the taut, jutting tan of the flesh above his cheekbones, and knew it would ever be so. She loved him, loved him as deeply, as utterly, now as ever! Her body hungered for the strength and warmth of his powerful arms, for the security and lasting joy she had found in loving him and being loved by him, and had never found nor would find elsewhere on this earth.

The dark green pines tossed in the chill wind, and it was his name their creaking needled boughs murmured in her ear: *Alaric. Alaric.* The harsh cawing of the carrion crows wheeling in the pale blue sky above urged her, "Find him! Go to him!"

Yet it was not Alaric she stumbled upon a half league outside the city of London, after touring and inquiring her husband's whereabouts of countless similar small bands. Nay, it was those poor few that remained of Snorri's proud followers.

Only a handful of broken men had survived, lying bleeding, groaning, and dying on ragged mantles in the lee of a sagging cottage. Snorri himself, she learned, had been mortally wounded in the first rush of battle, and her heart filled with sorrow for the Lady Mathilda, who all unknown to herself was a widow now, and would never again share Snorri's vast dragon-bed, nor smile fondly at his brave and outrageous boasts.

"Where is he?" she asked them each in turn. "Is he gone to Valhalla? Tell me, confound thee! Where is my lord Olaf?"

One haggard-faced fellow raised a limp arm and pointed up the hill. "There, mistress! They carried him up there. He said—he said he wished to be in a high place, where he could see the land of Britain spreading away below him to the horizon. He is sorely—"

She needed no further directions, but was off and running up the snowy rise in the direction he had pointed, battling the deep, powdery drifts, her heart pressing painfully against her ribs. Her breath poured in great clouds of vapor on the frigid air as she ran.

Dimly she was aware of the city of London below, of the countless wattle and daub cottages laid waste, razed and smoking, with none of the glory in their numbers that they had had that long-ago day when she and Alaric had visited there. Only the spires and square towers of the many churches, wrought of sturdy stone, still stood, as if to bring home in force to the Viking host that the White Christ had proved victor over paganism yet again, as had the Christian king.

Several once-proud dragon-ships, the pitiful remnants of the Viking fleet—drawn up by Guthrum from all coasts to sail up the Thames and conquer Alfred once and for all time—lay high and dry, firmly wedged in the mudflats. Their stout timbers and tall masts were blackened by fire, their striped *wadmal* sails only smoldering ashes.

In the fields all about the riverbanks milled great herds of captured livestock. Beyond, the tents of Alfred's *fyrd*, encamped in the city, fluttered their proud golden-dragon banners in the wind. Even from here she could catch the faint bursts of victorious merrymaking that carried from the tents, up the hill, on its frigid breath.

She came to an abrupt halt before a sorry lean-to of sticks and furs. It was a pitiful shelter, little more than a windbreak, in truth, and she knew, with a deep, sick twisting in her belly,

410

that Olaf must be gravely wounded. A small fire burned off to one side, but gave off little heat. The drawn gray faces of the loyal brace of men who had stayed with him, perhaps carried him bleeding from the field of battle, said as much as she thrust her way between them.

Olaf lay upon a fence hurdle, heaped with soft young pine branches, which someone had strewn with a mantle. Another mantle covered his body, which to her eyes seemed strangely shrunken. Biting her lip to staunch the cry of anguish that threatened, she unpinned her own warm mantle, drew it from her shoulders, and quickly covered him over with it, even as she sank to her knees at his side.

His face, always so ruddy and filled with color and life, was ashen, drained of blood. His eyes were closed. Fighting tears that threatened to overwhelm her and make speech impossible, she laid her head upon his breast and curled her arms about his massive chest in an embrace.

"My lord! My dearest lord and husband, do you hear me? I am here, beside you. I came to thee! 'Tis I, Freya!"

He moaned and opened eyes that were glazed and unfocusing. "Freya? Is it truly you? Nay, nay, dry your eyes, my little one. Cry . . . no . . . more. Your Olaf will not let them hurt thee again. We fought Eric, did we not, and won, though he is three summers older than us both! So will I fight all who seek to harm thee, and win, little Freya . . ."

She gave a great sob and held him fiercely. Already his mind wandered back, over the past, taking its farewell of mortal life and care. "I know you will. You have always protected me, my dearest friend and lord," she whispered, the tears flowing unchecked down her cheeks. "You were always there, whenever I had need of thee. Not once did you fail me. Not once!"

"Yet—you—you could never love me, as you loved the Saxon," he whispered, and she knew that now his thoughts had returned to the present. "I knew it, and yet I loved you so! I—I wanted you to love me in return. At first—I—I blamed thee. But now I know the blame was not yours. You could not help yourself. Right or wrong, your heart had chosen him—even as mine chose you."

411

"Please, Olaf, don't—!"

"I do not accuse thee, my heart! But—but I would tell you this: he lives, Freya. *Ja*, he lives! I have carried the secret too long, too much in fear of what it would mean to you and me, to tell it. Now I am weary of the burden. Soon I will be gone to Valhalla, and you will be left here alone." He sighed heavily, and blood bubbled in a froth from between his gray lips.

"Nay!"

"Aye, 'tis so. And I have seen how your Saxon lord battles, the rage and grief that blazes from his eyes. He is as a madman! 'Tis grief for thee that drives him, Freya; love for thee he fears lost to him for all time! Take—take the babes, find him when—when I—am—gone. He will see thee cared for, as I would have wished to care for thee myself."

"Hush, hush, I will never leave you, my husband," she denied fiercely. "You'll grow strong again, you'll see, and I—I—will bear you a child, a fine, strapping son to rule our hall when we are old and gray, and can only sit by the hearth and dream of our youth!" She forced herself to laugh gaily, but it was too great an effort. Her voice broke. "You'll see—it will all be as we have imagined, planned together—"

"*Nej*," he said wearily. "*Nej, min yndling*, no more lies—no more pretenses between us, my heart! Now is the time for truth . . ."

He had again drifted into unconsciousness, she saw. With shaking hands she drew back the mantles that covered him, saw the awful wound he'd taken, and was filled with helpless anger and despair. She let the mantles fall to cover him once again, a deep rage filling her. There was nothing she could do. Nothing.

"'Tis no use, Lady Freya," murmured one of his men who stood at her side. "He is too badly wounded. The—the sword spilled his entrails, you see. 'Tis a miracle he yet lives! We asked him if he wished a death blow to ease his agony and hasten his end, but he refused. He said you would come—knew it somehow—and he was right. You came!" There was wonder in the man's tone.

"Who was it that did this to him?" she demanded harshly, ignoring his curious eyes in her fear that his answer would be

412

the one she dreaded. Lothi had said he had last seen Olaf pinned down by Alaric's men! "Did you see it happen? Did you mark the warrior's standard? Was it—was it Alaric of Kent that ran him through?"

"Nay, my lady! Your lord Olaf sent three of Kent's men to their Christian paradise with ease! 'Twas a soldier of West Mercia, my lady, one who fought under Alfred's kinsmen's banner."

"I see," she acknowledged, trembling and weak with relief, for she knew she could not have gone on living had it been Alaric who had mortally wounded her husband. "Bring me warmed wine to ease my lord's agony," she whispered. "There is little more we—we can do for him now."

The man's face darkened with pain. "Mistress, we have none! Nor food, nor aught else, for that matter."

"Look in my pouch. I have a little food left in it. Share it with your comrade, and thank me not. I am deeply grateful for what you have done for my lord husband. I—I would not have wished his body left behind, to be mutilated in the aftermath of battle."

"'Twas little enough we were able to do, mistress," the man stammered. "Would we could have done more!"

She nodded, knowing he spoke the truth. "Drink from my wineskin, but save a little for him," she said softly, handing it to him.

"We will drink only enough to take the chill from our bones," the man promised, and left them alone.

Her sad vigil continued long into the endless hours of bitterly cold darkness. Then, shortly before the graying of dawn, Olaf stirred.

"Are you there, my lady?" he whispered. "I—I cannot see thee!"

She stroked his cheek, reassuring him with her gentle touch that she had not left him alone. "I am here, my husband. Where else would I be, but by your side?"

"The pain—the pain has gone. I feel only warmth now, stealing through me, tingling in my veins."

She touched his bearded cheek again, his large, square hands, and found them icy to her touch. "'Tis my love that

413

warms thee, my Oak, my strong, true Oak!" she said, her voice light to belie the keening song that had begun in her aching heart.

"I dreamed I was there again, home in Jutland, and we were yet children. We rode our ponies up to the Shielings, and you gathered wild flowers and wove them in your hair. Do you remember?"

"I remember," she acknowledged, shuddering. "*Ja*, I remember it so well."

"Even then I loved thee, even when you were just a little maid! They were happy times . . ."

"Aye," she whispered, her voice breaking. "Every day was summer then—"

"Look! he cried suddenly, and in that moment his voice was as strong and resonant as ever. "Look, there in the sky! Do you see them, Freya?"

"What see you, my love?" she asked as the tears streamed down her face and onto his unfeeling hands, for the sky was yet dark, all ash and charcoal. And empty.

"The Valkyries! Odin's lovely daughters! See how their horses' wings beat upon the blue of the heavens, like a thousand white-winged birds! See how their breastplates and helmets flash silver in the sunlight! Do you see them? They have chosen me, Freya! They are coming for me, to take me to their feasting halls forever!"

He sat straight upright then, as if never wounded. His blue eyes blazed, fixed on some vision she would never see—not in this life.

"*Ja*. Soon—soon you will feast with the heroes, my husband," she sobbed, resting her head upon his broad shoulder for the last time. "This night you will drink Odin's mead, and dine on Odin's meat, and his Valkyrie maids will sing sagas of your valor and victories! Farewell, dearest one! Farewell, friend of my childhood! Fare—"

"*Ooodiiiin!*"

He gave a great, joyous shout, raised his hand skyward in final salute, then fell heavily back upon his pallet of branches and lay still.

For a fleeting second Freya fancied she could hear the whirr

414

of the countless vast wings that he had heard upon the chill dawn air, and perhaps catch the faint clash of steel against steel . . .

Olaf's eyes were fixed and staring up at the charcoal heavens above, where the first, bloody glimmer of dawn showed far to the east. A strange rush of wind stirred her hair about her shoulders, and was as suddenly gone. Where it had come from, she knew not, for the wind had died down hours since. In its wake there was only silence, a long, deep silence, as if Mother World herself held her breath in respect for the passing of Olaf's noble life.

She leaned down and kissed his motionless lips, still warm with life, then his brow, then gently closed his eyes. She bowed her head and offered a silent prayer that he would find grace in Valhalla. Then she drew her cloak from his body and covered his face with his own tattered cloak. In death he yet bore the exultant expression with which he had died, and she fancied the gods had heeded her prayers. Aye, and why should they not? They would find few of her Olaf's greatness at Asgard—nay, not even in the warrior halls of Valhalla, she thought with fierce pride, and stumbled away, blinded by tears.

Much later, grief, exhaustion, and the bitter cold combined to plummet her into a deep, painless sleep from which she wished she need never have to waken. Yet wake she did, rolled in her damp mantle by the fire, to find dawn had long since come and fled. One of Olaf's men stood over her.

"If it please you, mistress, we have readied our lord for his final journey. We—we thought it best to see it done quickly, since we must leave here soon, before Alfred's men find us."

"You did rightly. Take me to him."

There could be no inhumation for her lord. The ground was too hard for the digging of the burial mound, the two men wounded, weakened, and half-starved. Nor would there be feasting in his honor or a proud ship to send him on this, his final voyage. And so, as many of their people before them had done in times of hardship back in the old country, they had washed his body and bound it in his own tattered, blood-stained cloak, then laid him upon a byre of pine branches. At his side were his sword, and a few pitiful morsels of food.

Around the pyre they had placed rocks, to form the rough shape of a longship.

"You have done well, friends," she told them, feeling the tears burn anew behind her eyes. She reached inside her kirtle to draw from about her throat the golden torc that Olaf had given her on their wedding day, and also a talisman of Frey on its leather cord. She would not see him go empty-handed into the Otherworld! She kissed the heavy neck ring and the talisman, then tucked them gently into the mantle, close to his heart.

"May the gods speed you safely on your way, my loyal friend and husband!" she murmured, and stood back to wait in silence while one of the men torched the pile of pine boughs. The flames rose as they caught the pine, and the scent of resin mingled with the scent of wood smoke as Olaf began his final voyage.

So it was that Olaf died, and with him, in part, her guilt. With his last words he had absolved her of it. He had known she loved Alaric, and had accepted that she could never love him in the same way, even while loving her deeply in return. She had been a loyal wife and lady to him, and had given him all the love within her that remained after she had thought Alaric dead. She had nothing to berate herself for, she told herself— but wondered if the emptiness inside her would ever lessen. In her grief it seemed that something of herself—her childhood, perhaps, her youth—had died with Olaf, leaving only a fragile shell too vulnerable, too brittle, to withstand further hurt.

Olaf's men asked her to return to East Angle with them, offering themselves as escort. But she refused, saying, "Come what may, I will never return there! Without my lord at my side, the hall is no longer my home."

"But who will become *jarl* in our lord's stead if not you, lady?" they asked worriedly.

"You must tell the new *Althing* that Olaf's child will be born in the spring, to her of his two women who loved him best, the one named Ilse. It—it was my lord's wish that his son by this woman should take his place as chieftain in our hall when he is grown, and that the lady Ilse be honored as his mother." It was a lie, but she knew Olaf would have wanted it that way, had she been given time to tell him of his child. "Until the babe is grown, you, Harald, who cared for your lord so well at the last, must lead the men in his stead. Take this, your lord's ring, to signify my wishes to the *Althing* in this." She plucked the great gold finger ring, with the enormous cabochon garnet, from her finger and pressed it into Harald's palm. "Go quickly now, good friends, before the Saxons come!"

"But—what of you, my lady?"

"I?" Her sapphire eyes, dark as obsidian in her sorrow, kindled with a faraway, dreaming light. "I must try to step backward into the past, and reclaim it for the future. Both for myself and for my children."

"My lady?" they asked, puzzled by her words.

She smiled. "Do not concern yourselves for me. Travel north, then east. 'Twill prove the safest road. The Saxons have already laid waste to the countryside there. There are many women in need of husbands, and children in need of fathers, you will find. Be kind to them, and fare thee well!"

And with that parting, she turned back the way she had come, to the east, where Ilse and her little ones waited for her return.

Chapter 32

As Freya battled snowy drifts to return to Sigmund's farm, her babes, and Ilse, the soldiers of the Saxon army feasted and made merry in celebration of their victory over Guthrum's *fyrd*. All, that is, save Alaric of Kent.

He paced like a prowling bear, from time to time striking his clenched fist against his palm in his disquiet. Once he paused briefly in his pacing to gaze through the tent flap to the snowy hillside above, where just yesterday the roaring flames of a Viking funeral pyre had lit the sky with orange as it bore one of the enemy horde to his pagan paradise. But all was dark there now, as if the flames had never been, nor the man whose body the fire had consumed. He muttered an oath.

How fragile we are, Alaric thought, taken by yet another of the fits of melancholy and helpless rage that had consumed him this past year. Life was here one minute and gone the next, a taper snuffed out by a careless finger or a chance breath of wind, with no warning nor second chances given. So had Farant's life been extinguished; gentle Farant, who had done no man ill. Since his murder, Alaric had felt as if part of himself, the gentler side, had died with him in some peculiar fashion, leaving only that which was bitter and hate-filled and destructive. He sighed, and ran a restless hand through his unruly ebony hair. There had been times in the past year when he would have welcomed death—aye, had even courted her cold embrace on the field of battle—but such release had been denied him.

The tall, slender dark fellow who lolled upon the campaign stool in the corner sighed as he watched the warrior, and drew from the pack at his feet several brightly colored wooden balls, with which he commenced juggling. It was as good a means as any to pass the time until Alaric of Kent had composed himself and digested all that he'd told him, he decided, tossing the balls high with fluid grace and catching them one after the other with equal ease.

"So. You would have me believe Kendra slew her husband?" Alaric demanded at length, a bitter, disbelieving smile twisting his mouth. "Nay, Robin, I cannot accept these things you tell me! My sister-in-law is many things, and none of them good. But a murderess?" He shook his great head. "Forgive me, but I cannot believe it! Nay, it was Freya who killed my brother. She saw Farant and Kendra embracing, and believing him to be me, she stabbed him in a fit of jealous rage." He scowled, his stern expression daring the other man to contradict him. So had Kendra tearfully told him, time and time again, sobbing anew as she recounted the sad events of that night:

"She came in with—with a tray, Alaric, and on it were the refreshments I had ordered brought for my lord Farant. Oh, her face—when—when she saw us together—I have never seen such—such loathing in anyone's eyes! At first I did not understand that she had mistaken Farant for you, not until afterward. You see, everything happened so quickly! She flung the tray to the rushes, and it was only then that I saw—saw she had a dagger clenched in her fist!" Here Kendra had shuddered delicately. "She screamed that if she could not have thee, then no woman would have thee. Oh my lord, I was so frightened, so terribly frightened! It was as if I were frozen in place. I could not move, my lord! And then—then she sprang at him and thrust her dagger deep into—into Farant's chest and he fell . . . he fell . . . blood everywhere . . . all over him!"

Ordway had readily believed and supported Kendra's story when they returned that day from the convent of Our Lady of the Sea to Kenley, and had learned of Farant's murder. He had reminded Alaric of the slave girl's unconcealed jealousy of the Lady Meredyth, her lack of feminine distaste when it came to bloodshed, her warlike demeanor the day her sea-wolves had overrun Kenley. If anyone could have murdered Farant in cold blood, it was the Viking wench, his uncle had said over and over again, until little by little he had broken down Alaric's resistance. Aye, he had come to believe them finally, had he not? They why, why had the words rung so thin and false when he'd told Robin how it had been that day?

Robin snorted. "Admit it, Alaric, you still doubt the truth of what you were told, do you not, man? Look into your heart. You'll find the truth there! Freya loved thee, as you loved her. She could no sooner have killed you than she could have killed the old *skald* Sven, of whom she is so fond, jealous or nay! You must block your ears to Ordway's words, for they are the words of a man twisted and tainted with the bitterness of what happened to his sister. That bitterness blinds him to the truth. It is this Kendra you must guard against, for she is as dangerous as a viper! If you are ever to find peace within yourself you must find your Freya, and make things right between the two of you."

"You say you met her on the road to Jorvic?"

"Aye. And all that I've told you here today is as she told me then—or what I plucked from her mind. She had no inkling that you and Farant were twins, and grieved bitterly, believing you dead by Kendra's hands. 'Tis clear to me now that Kendra used her ignorance, and sought to rid herself of both her husband and the slave girl, whom you loved and who loved you in return, in one cunning move. Freya feared that no one would believe a slave's protests of innocence, and in this she was proved correct, poor child. 'Twould appear Kendra succeeded in her plot after all, would it not? She thought you gullible, and she was right!" Robin's brows arched in mocking inquiry.

Alaric's jaw came up at this, and his gray eyes flashed. "Not completely gullible, good Robin," he said bitterly, "for becoming my lady wife was the second part of her scheme, and in this she failed utterly." A grim smile thinned his chiseled lips, but was quickly gone. "After Farant had been laid to rest, she soon made her intent clear. The lady was most distressed to learn that, according to the laws of our Church, a widow may

not enter into marriage with her husband's brother! I sent her
forth from Kenley, to the nearby convent of Our Lady of the
Sea. It was my will that she should pass her remaining days
there, in enforced celibacy, solitude, and prayer!" He frowned.
"But if it was indeed she who stabbed Farant, as you say,
then—then the Lady Kendra and I will have a fresh
reckoning—!" His expression was as stern and bleak as a wall
of flint, and there was naked steel in his eyes.

"Forget this Kendra and your vengeance, for the while,"
Robin urged impatiently, "and set your mind instead upon
Freya, that fairest of the fair. She is close by, and needs thee as
she has never needed thee before. Go after her, Alaric, find
her—or run the risk of losing her forever."

"Close by?" Alaric's expression changed, flared with sudden
hope, despite his denials. The battle-weariness and the
weariness of spirit that he carried like a heavy burden dropped
away from him. He went to Robin and grasped him by the
upper arms, heedless of the colored balls that toppled to the
hard ground as he shook him. "Where? Where shall I find her?
Tell me, confound thee, minstrel!"

"Ah!" Robin grinned. "So at last you admit it. You do want
her back!"

"Christ's Wounds, Robin of London, stick to your juggling,
your minstreling, and your spying for King Alfred, and leave
matchmaking well enough alone! Aye, I still want her, curse
her, though I'll be damned for a fool to have set my heart upon
an enemy wench who prefers men's garb to women's, and a
broadsword to a distaff! Aye, I love her still, God help me! But I
am not yet convinced of the truth of what you have told me.
Since I cannot live without her, then for my own peace of mind
I must find her and hear what she has to say for myself."

"Follow the Thames as it winds seaward to your own
Kenley. Freya seeks even now to return to you. Never fear, if
you wish it badly enough, you will find her," Robin supplied
softly, well pleased with the way his meeting with the
ealdorman had been concluded. "Waste no time in going after
her, however, if you would find her unharmed. As I told thee,
she is in danger! And when next you hold her in your arms, you
lucky cur, give her this keepsake, to remind her of him who

would have loved her well, had her heart not foolishly been set on thee!" Grinning broadly, he drew a small silver ball from his pack and handed it to Alaric, who took it from him with a scowl.

"I will," the ealdorman agreed, though with obvious reluctance. "You make an eloquent advocate for the lady, friend Robin. Could it be she bewitched you too?"

Robin gave him a merry grin. "Aye, she did! And from the very moment I first saw her, bare as at the moment of her birth, her spell has lingered. Look for her, my lord—else I will!"

Alaric flung about jealously to ask him to explain himself. But Robin—in the mercurial fashion which had so amazed Freya—had already slipped through the tent flap and was gone.

Freya almost sobbed in relief when she urged the horse from the woods and saw the tumbledown little cottage a short distance ahead. Shelter, at last! Her joy knew no bounds when, on riding forward between the towering pines, she saw the silvery gray ribbon of the river beyond the dwelling. Not only had she found them shelter, but, thank the gods, the way they had lost two days before! The little hut would afford her and her babes scant protection from the harsh snows and the bitter winds, yet she had no choice. Without it they would surely freeze to death long before dusk!

She slithered down from the horse's broad back, lifting after her the basket in which the children slept, pulled aside the sagging plank door, and ducked inside.

It was a simple hut of the kind used by peasants, with a sunken floor of packed earth spread with straw that had long since become moldy and smelled of mildew. The walls were of woven wattle and daub, and badly needed patching. The roof was of sagging thatch. A depression in the center of the floor, ringed by stones, was blackened with soot and ashes, and showed where there had once been a hearth.

She set the basket and its precious contents in a corner of the hut, where the wind did not whistle through the chinks, and stripped off her mantle, tucking the heavy fur over the basket to keep her little ones warm. Shivering now in only her short kirtle and leggings, she went outside to tether the horse in the lee of the hut and throw a piece of sackcloth over its back for warmth. She then trudged back to the woods in search of kindling, gasping at the icy chill of the wind as it swirled snowflakes against her face.

Her fingers were numb and her teeth were chattering violently by the time she staggered back to the hut, stamping her feet to bring the circulation back to them. Her cheeks and lips had turned blue with cold. By comparison, the hut's small confines seemed warm and welcoming now. She dropped the kindling to the floor, and hugging herself about the arms, once again made her way outside. This time she dropped to her knees in the powdery drifts and began pushing great armfuls of snow up against the hut's walls, then firmly packing them down. Snow would serve as well as any other barrier she knew of to keep the cold and the wind from penetrating the small dwelling, and would conserve what warmth there was inside. The labor warmed her somewhat, and her breathing was a little easier when she returned to her children.

Praise Frey, her breasts were full, tingling and beginning to leak a little now as Beorn, always the hungrier of the pair, stirred and bawled to be nursed. Drawing an edge of the fur mantle up over them, she bared a breast and suckled him, rocking him gently as she did so. He paused in his suckling and smiled up into her face, cooing with delight to see her. With a happy squeal that reminded Freya fondly of a small pink piglet, he latched onto her breast again and happily burrowed his face against its fullness, uttering little gurgles of pleasure. When he was full and content, she quickly changed his linen wrapper and tucked him snugly once more into his swaddling. By now he had again drifted off to sleep, and so she drew Edana from the basket, waked her, and suckled her at the other breast, crooning a lullaby as she stroked her daughter's small head. Sweet little Edana, with her dark and fragile loveliness. Vigorous, handsome Beorn. How long would her milk last to feed them, without food in her belly, she wondered bleakly? Somehow she must find game, must eat herself, or her body would soon yield no milk for her little ones, and they would

423

all starve.

Four days had gone by since she had returned to Sigmund's farm and told poor Ilse that her Olaf had been mortally wounded and had gone to Valhalla. It was the hardest thing she had ever done in her life, and her heart had ached to see the hope die in Ilse's eyes and her face crumble as she broke down in her grief, but tell her she had. Afterward they had wept in each other's arms and exchanged memories of all the good and gentle things Olaf had done. When Ilse's tears were spent, Freya gently bade her listen, and in firm tones had explained her intentions.

"I cannot return to Olaf's hall, Ilse," she'd said softly. "I never felt that it was my home, and with Olaf gone it is even less so. Nay, I mean—I mean to return to Kenley. Now that I know Alaric is alive, I must find out if there is a future for me there with him, or nay—for my children's sake as much as my own. Tell me that you understand, dear Ilse, and do not feel that I am deserting you?"

"I do understand, truly," Ilse had reassured her. Though her gray eyes were still shadowed with grief, her tone was calm and resolute. "That is why I have decided to do as you have asked and return to the hall to bear Olaf's child. If I have a son, then he has the right to inherit his father's position as *jarl* there, when he is grown to manhood. My father will take me back in the spring."

Soon after, they had exchanged tearful farewell embraces. Sigmund, Ilse's father, had reluctantly lifted Freya up onto her horse and handed the basket after her. "You are certain you wish no escort?" he had asked.

"None," she'd replied. "My thanks for your hospitality, good Sigmund. Watch over your daughter, pray. She has been a good friend to me."

"And you to her, my lady. I will see her well taken care of, never fear. Fare thee well!"

Freya had ridden from the little farmhouse then, Ilse waving goodbye until she crested the hill.

It had been a clear, brisk morning, without any sign of further snow to come, and she had been confident that in a short while the silver ice-ribbon of the Thames would lead her to Kenley, hard against the coast. The journey, she had estimated, would take two, possibly three, days, and Sigmund had seen her pouch filled with sufficient provisions for that length of time. Then yesterday, the third day, a howling blizzard had come out of nowhere, and somehow in its blinding white blast she had lost the course of the frozen river. Her food supply had been exhausted by evening, and she was still no closer to finding her path. They'd spent the long, freezing night huddled under a fence hurdle, propped against a bank of earth to form a small windbreak, over which she had pulled her fur mantle, listening to the blizzard's shriek. Then today, the fourth day, she had spied the little hut, and gladly hastened to it.

Her breasts emptied, she returned Edana to the basket, replaced the fur over the infants, and set about building the fire. It was a painful task. With her fingers so numbed, the strike-a-light and the tinder kept slipping to the floor, but after what seemed an eternity the twigs caught and a fire was begun, smoke billowing out into the hut and making her choke, before she reached up and cleared the blocked smoke hole between the sagging thatch and rotted rafters. There, that was better! If only their little pile of kindling were not so pitiful . . . ! Surely there would not be near enough to last them until the next morning, however sparingly she might use it. Deny it she might, but their situation was desperate, albeit she had found the river. Without food, she had no strength to make the journey to Kenley. Bleakly she rocked back on her heels, staring at the tiny flames that curled up from the small heap, hugging her shivering body, and wondering how she could improve their chances for survival.

Dusk fell soon after, darkness mantling the furred pines and the low hills beyond the hut. Hungry wolves howled in the nearby forest. Roused from a fitful sleep by their howling and the eerie moan of the wind, Freya leaned up and carefully fed the last of the kindling to the hungry fire. With luck, if the wolves smelled their presence and ringed the hut, she could at least frighten them away with a flaming brand drawn from that precious fire. Her belly growling with hunger, her feet quite without feeling, so cold was she, she drew the babes closer to the meager warmth of her body, pulled the fur mantle snugly up about them all, and tried again to sleep.

Morning came. The light, though feeble and gray, and the bitter cold of the air wakened her. She stretched stiffly, then with a start drew back the mantle to look at the little ones. Thank the gods! Her babes were unharmed, she saw with relief that moved her almost to tears. Beorn's thumb was tucked greedily into his little mouth, his bright eyes shining like two new copper pennies as she peeked in at him. He gave a delighted baby gurgle at seeing her, and drew his thumb free to try to trap her hair. Edana's long, curling black lashes were fluttering against her cheeks as she slept on, her little chest rising and falling shallowly. Was it but a mother's anxiety for her children, or did the infant girl seem smaller this morn, less active and more anxious to sleep? She drew her daughter from the basket first to suckle, and was alarmed to find that Edana seemed to have little interest in waking, let alone nursing, for all that she had ample milk as yet! There was a rosy flush to her cheeks that boded ill, and Freya was certain she detected a slight whistling, wheezing sound when the infant breathed.

"Come, *min yndling*, my precious pet, drink for mother!" she crooned, pressing the overflowing nipple to the babe's mouth so that drops of the bluish milk trickled between the rosebud lips. With a feeble little whimper of protest, Edana sucked half-heartedly and quickly fell asleep again, wakening only when her mother jiggled her and gently pressured her to nurse.

Chills of foreboding swept through Freya as she returned Edana to the basket and bared her other breast for Beorn. He nursed as greedily as ever, quickly emptying both that breast and the still half-full breast his sister had failed to drain. His lusty appetite only served to underline Edana's dispirited nursing, and the dread in Freya's belly grew. Her little daughter was sickening, she was certain now, but whether of the cold itself or of some ague, she knew not. She knew full well how quickly such a tiny babe could fall ill and die, having seen many babes die swiftly in the harsh winters of her native Jutland . . .

She scrabbled across the floor and forced the door open

against the snowdrift that the wind had piled against it during the night. It was not snowing now, though the pregnant whiteness of the sky promised further snow to come soon. If she was to find more kindling and—with great good fortune granted by the gods—game, she must venture outside now! Making certain that the babes were as warm and snug and safe as they could be in their basket by the fire, she kissed their cheeks, pulled the fur mantle warmly over them, and ducked out of the hut's low entrance, forcing the door shut in her wake.

The entire landscape around the hut was covered in a blinding white shroud unmarred by even a single foot or hoofprint. Against that whiteness, the pines stood like silent dark green sentinels to mark her passage. The still, icy river gleamed dully like a silver-gray ribbon beneath the wan sun. The powdery drifts that had fallen during the night reached the top of her knee-high boots. Some found its way inside, melting there, and made her feet cold and wet. With great difficulty, she tramped across the little clearing toward the skeletal woods.

The hush seemed alive. The cracking of branches, breaking with the cold, was like thunderclaps on that silence, and more than once she whirled about, breath condensing in great clouds on the frosty air, numbed fingers clamped over the icy metal hilt of her dagger, expecting ambush—only to see a branch, heavy with new snow, plummet to earth. It was as if she and her babes were the only living creatures in this wintry white world, and the sensation was frightening. Gods of the Norsemen, protect me, she prayed silently, and wondered doubtfully if they could hear her prayers here, so far from the lands they watched over. Perhaps the Christian White Christ was lord here, and He and He alone would decide her fate, and that of her children. Should she, unbaptized as she was, and a heathen in the eyes of His followers in Britain, ask Him to protect her? Nay! Better not! He might be roused to ire by the prayers of one not of His faith, and bring destruction down upon her head!

She lost track of time as she roamed between the trees, spying not a solitary bird, nor a rabbit, nor hare nor deer as she went, though the stripped trunks of many trees told her that deer had sought to stave off their own hunger here by peeling the bark from them not many days ago. Her pile of kindling was considerable by now, yet of what use was it to stay warm, when her belly remained empty? She needed both food and warmth if she and her babes were to live!

Then, when she was about to return to the hut, defeated and empty-handed, a flash of color between the trees caught her eye. She froze in her tracks, swallowing her gasp of surprise. Dropping the kindling at her feet, she drew her dagger in one swift move. There was no sense in running or trying to hide from whoever it was. The skeleton trees, stripped of their leaves since autumn, offered no concealment. She must stand her ground or flee—and it was already too late for flight.

As she watched, her breath labored and steaming on the frigid air, the man she had glimpsed walked slowly from between the trees toward her. She saw that a brace of rabbits dangled from his fist, and that something—a hunting ferret, perhaps, that he had sent down their warren to flush out the game?—wriggled in a sack dangling from the other. He was tall and appeared little older than she. His weathered face was bearded. His brown eyes held a crafty glint in their depths that sent an alarm racing down her spine. He was dressed warmly but poorly, a heavy yet ragged mantle of mismatched furs pinned at his left shoulder above a coarse woolen tunic and skin leggings gaitered with rawhide strips. A heavy club was slung across one shoulder. Spying her, he dropped the rabbits and tossed down the sack.

"I thought myself alone in these woods, wench. What do you here? And who might you be?" he demanded.

"I might ask the same of you, sir!" she retorted boldly in his own broad Saxon tongue.

"Aye, you might," he agreed easily, his brown eyes appraising her curiously, flickering from the full curve of her breasts down past the womanly flare of hips and flanks to her slender limbs, encased in leggings. "Then again, I might not tell ye!" He grinned, yet it was a far from pleasant or reassuring grin, and the unease grew in Freya's belly.

"A saucy fellow you are, 'tis clear, good sir," Freya quipped

428

back. "And a lucky hunter too, by the looks of it! Would—would you be willing to share my fire and the warmth of my hut, in return for one of your long-eared friends?" she asked in a rush, forcing a warm, inviting smile. Better she should try to strike some bargain with the fellow, before he realized her vulnerability and decided to take advantage of it!

"Better a warm and willing woman than a fire to keep the cold from a man's bones," he pointed out slyly. "Have ye no man to hunt for ye, wench?"

"Of course," she answered quickly. "But—but he has taken our other horse and gone north to hunt. He left yesterday morn, but said he'd certainly return by dusk today, and with a fine deer. I'm—I'm expecting him back soon. But meanwhile I'm very hungry, sir, and would strike a bargain with you, if you're willing. What say you? A warm at my fire, and I will cook us the best rabbit stew you are ever likely to taste before you continue on your way!" Her words rang thin and false, even to her ears. Would he see through her lies?

Whether he did or nay, she could not discern, for his eyes were hooded now, their expression quite blank. "Your man's due back soon, ye say?"

"Aye," she whispered, nodding.

"Well, he's not back yet, is he, wench? There's time enough before he comes riding home for ye to—warm—this traveling man." He bent and lifted one of the rabbits by its ears. "This," he gestured, "in return for you, wench. 'Tis the only bargain I'll strike. Take it—or go hungry till your 'husband' returns," he jeered, and she knew he had believed nothing she'd said.

His words chilled her as even the wintry wind and the snow had not. That she should agree to sell herself to him like a harlot in return for food, that was what he wanted her to do! Her heart pounded. Her belly churned. "Nay, sir, I'll not agree to that. A warm at my fire is all the offer I'll make ye," she said firmly.

She watched through eyes blinded by tears as the hunter retrieved the game from the snow and made to turn back the way he had come, intent on going on his way. It took all of her forbearance not to run after him and beg him to halt. She swayed, dizzy with dread. Dear Beorn, her little bear. Sweet, dimpled Edana, even now sick . . . What choice did she have, in truth, she thought bitterly, heartsick? Their precious, fragile lives, in return for a few moments use of her body for the hunter's pleasure, that was all he asked. 'Twas a small price to pay in return for the lives of her sweet babes, was it not—?

"Wait!" she cried, her voice husky with unshed tears. "Don't go! I—I've thought it over, and—and mayhap later, if I find I've taken a liking to ye, sir, I'll do what it is you wish."

The stranger turned and nodded. "I had an inkling you might change your mind, wench," he said with a sly grin, his knowing eyes roaming her body lecherously. "Lead on to your hut!"

Gathering up the firewood, she led the way back to the cottage, her feet dragging like heavy wooden weights over the snow as they neared it.

Once inside, she added fresh fuel to the fire, which had died down since she left, not daring so much as a glance at the basket beside it, covered over with her mantle. *Don't cry, my dear ones! Don't make a sound!* she silently willed the sleeping infants within its confines. Better the stranger should think her alone than find her helpless babes and use their vulnerability against her!

Chapter 33

The hunter ducked into the hut in her wake, carelessly tossing the rabbits and the sack to one side. His eyes quickly scanned the narrow confines, and his grin broadened. "Not so much as a stool nor a sturdy pot for cooking do I see. How then are ye to prepare us a fine rabbit stew, lass?"

Flustered, she looked wildly about her. "Oh! Forgive me. I quite forgot—the pot cracked, and was thrown away. If—if you'll permit me, I'll skin the rabbits and roast them for ye over the fire."

He shook his head, dropping to his knees across the small hearth from her.

"Nay, wench. I'm no fool! First I'll see your part of the bargain kept, and then—and only then—will ye lay hands on these rabbits! You promised me a fine stew, and yet ye can provide me none. I'll make sure of your other promises before I keep my part of the bargain! On your back, wench," he ordered, and reached for the fastenings to his breeches, fumbling with the lacings.

Trembling all over, Freya moved as far away as she could from the basket across the cottage and sank down to the earthen floor, quivering uncontrollably in every part of her. "Nay! Not yet—not when my belly growls for want of food! When we've eaten, then—then—we'll see—!"

But the stranger threw himself down alongside her, grasping her chin in his fierce grip and prying her lips apart with his foul, eager tongue. She bore his hateful, wet kisses in silence and his rough fondlings without protest, telling herself she must not resist him, not when her babes' very lives depended upon her compliance. He thrust up her tunic clear to her shoulders to bare her full breasts for his clumsy squeezings. His fingers bit cruelly into her breasts as he kneaded them, pinching the nipples painfully until of their own accord they swelled as he wished them to do, throbbing with pain. He chuckled deep in his throat and whispered hoarsely, "Yer teats know who's the master here, girl. See how they stand upright and full at my bidding? Ah, 'tis a hot-blooded little bitch ye are, after all, are ye not? Eh? Pantin' fer it, aren't ye, girl?" before he renewed his sickening fondling of her body. It took all of her forbearance to keep from crying out, to lie still and submissive under him while he took his foul pleasure of her. But when he again reached for the laces of his breeches, she took advantage of his shift in attention and rolled away from him, hurriedly jumping to her feet and smoothing down her skirts.

"'Tis no use!" she told him desperately. "I cannot pleasure you as you—you deserve to be pleasured, not on an empty belly! What say you we sup first?" She was close to swooning with disgust and trembling in every limb as she awaited his reply. After a few seconds, he stood up and closed his breeches again, without turning away from her to do so, an animal grunt of agreement breaking from between his lips.

"Aye. Good enough, lass," he muttered, leering wolfishly at her, eyes agleam. "Aye, good enough. That comely body will keep a while longer, I dare say!" He chuckled. "Skin yerself a rabbit, and wake me when it's well roasted." With that, he crossed the cottage and to her horror stretched out alongside the basket and its precious contents to sleep, retrieving his mantle and pulling it up over him.

"Let me move that basket out of your way, sir," she offered, panic rising through her as swiftly as the nausea had risen moments before. Getting shakily to her feet, his hateful gropings nigh forgotten with the fresh danger he now represented to her little ones, she hurriedly started toward him and the basket. To her horror he waved her irritably away, all but striking the basket as he did so.

"'Tis of no matter," he growled, leering up at her crudely.

"Cook the rabbit, woman, and leave the basket be! And when we're both well fed, I'll have ye on yer back, lass, with yer skirts tossed up, and see that pretty furrow well ploughed and sown, aye, that I will!" He licked his lips salaciously and winked. "Ye can tell yer 'husband' when he returns that I took good care o'all yer needs while he were gone—aye, and a few o'my own as well!"

Freya forced an eager smile to match his own, yet it was no more than a mask. The second his eyes closed, the smile slipped from her, replaced by an expression of abject terror. Blessed Loki, Loki the Stealthy, Loki the Cunning, help me now! she prayed silently. How was she to remove her babes without wakening him? How was she to avoid his ravishment?

She turned away and snatched up one of the rabbits, taking its limp body to the doorway and drawing her knife from her belt as she went. She looked at the shining blade long and hard before resolutely slitting the rabbit's belly from head to scut and quickly skinning it, wishing—as she saw the dark blood spill forth and splatter the pristine white snow beneath with crimson drops—that it was the hunter's body beneath her blade, his life's blood spilling to the snow! Could she kill him, if it should come to that? Could she take a life in cold blood? She had felt no such misgivings in the heat of a battle when her own life was in jeopardy, but this—this was quite a different proposition. Or was it?

When she returned to the hut, the small animal imprisoned in the hunter's sack squealed frantically on catching the coppery scent of the rabbit's fresh blood and struggled to escape, scrabbling at the sacking.

She ignored it and cooked the rabbit, hefty chunks spitted on her knife over the fire, which was crackling noisily now and spilling its warmth through the little hut along with the mouth-watering aroma of plump, roasting rabbit.

When the first of the rabbit was cooked, she hungrily ate her fill, chewing slowly to savor every tasty, greasy morsel of meat. She had gone so long without food, it tasted delicious beyond imagining. Let the cursed hunter wait! After all, he'd already had a sampling of his share of their bargain, had he not?

A tingling in her breasts signaled that it was almost time for

433

the babes to be suckled again. She stiffened as she felt her breasts engorge with milk, knowing the infants would not be long in wakening now. Sure enough, Beorn stirred and gave a half-hearted sleepy whimper from the basket. Freya froze where she was, neither moving nor saying a word. The sound of her voice, should she try to hush him, might be enough to start his lusty bawling in earnest, which was the very last thing she wanted! But after a little whimpering with no reaction from his mother, Beorn apparently dropped off to sleep again, and Freya drew her first deep breath in several long minutes.

The silence couldn't last forever. What would she do then? Could she hope to turn the hunter out of the cottage into the cold, to see him sent on his way before the babes wakened fully? Her shoulders slumped. Nay, he'd never move on, she knew—or at least not willingly—not so long as there was the promise of a warm female body at his disposal; not so long as the threat of snow continued; not so long as he remained unconvinced that any man would be returning to her—!

The remainder of the rabbit cooked, she washed the knife blade with handfuls of snow and was about to return it to her belt when she thought better of it. Who knew if the moment would come when she needed her weapon? Better the hunter should believe her unarmed. There was every chance that, with slaking his lust uppermost in his mind, he had not noticed it earlier tucked into her belt.

She glanced around the hut, her eyes traveling from the basket to the bundled form of the hunter and on past the fire to the wattle and daub walls of the cottage. There was a small niche close to the earthen floor in one of them, where the daub had broken and fallen out. It was the perfect nook in which to hide the knife, readily accessible should she have need of it in a hurry, yet unobtrusive meanwhile! Edging carefully across the hut on her knees, her gaze never once straying from the sleeping hunter, she secreted the knife there and returned to her place by the fire.

Beorn stirred again, crying fitfully, and the hunter snorted and rolled over in his sleep. Freya's belly churned with dread, yet the man remained asleep. More whimperings, louder and more urgent this time. It was no use, Freya thought desperately, somehow she must take Beorn from the basket and nurse him, or his crying would soon wake the man.

She edged across to the basket on her hands and knees, scarce daring to breathe, darting a furtive glance at the man's face from time to time to see if he was still asleep. He was. Carefully she slipped the latch free and raised the basket's wicker lid. Beorn was wide awake, his eyes lighting up when he saw her, his little arms and legs flailing in joyful expectation of his mother picking him up. Soft baby cooing sounds, sounds that in her frantic state seemed overly loud, rose from the basket. Beside her brother Edana slept on, her tiny face appearing pinched and drawn and pale to Freya's anxious eyes.

"Hush, *min yndling,* hush, now," Freya whispered, sliding her hands down into the basket and underneath her son. Beorn crowed and chuckled in delight to see her, and Freya could have wept with frustration in that moment. She raised him up, one inch, then two, and darted a glance over her shoulder toward the hunter, just in time to see him stretch and roll over to face her. She released Beorn abruptly, withdrew her hands from the basket, and let the wicker lid fall shut, in the same moment moving away from her precious secret.

"Ah! 'Twas a good sleep," the hunter muttered, scratching his armpit and yawning as he struggled up to sitting. "Where's the rabbit ye promised me, lass?" He rubbed his beard and eyed her expectantly.

Forcing a smile, Freya went across to where the remaining joints of roasted rabbit were heaped on one of the hearth stones, praying her expression betrayed nothing. "Here—here it is. Keeping nice and warm for ye."

The hunter grinned. "I see ye've supped yer fill already, eh, ye greedy bitch?"

She shrugged. "I was hungry, and you were asleep. It seemed foolish t'waken you."

"Aye. I suppose it was, at that," he agreed, helping himself to a piece of the rabbit and tearing into it with gusto. "Toss me the sack, wench. I dare say my hunting companion would welcome a bite o'this, seeing as how it was her what done all o'the work!"

Gingerly she picked up the wriggling sack and handed it to the man. He loosened the drawstring that held the neck of the sack closed, and up-ended it. As Freya had expected, a long, slender dun-colored ferret slipped out, bright eyes as cunning and feral as those of her master. He tossed a rabbit bone to the dirt and at once the creature pounced upon it and began eating greedily, long whiskers quivering as she devoured the meat scraps that clung to the bone, shredding the flesh with razor-sharp teeth.

"Good team we are, me and my clever Queenie! I blocks off all the back doorways to good Master Rabbit's warren, save the last one. Then I picks up my Queenie, like so, and drops her in the warren like quicksilver, and sits back on my heels t'wait. Soon out pops Master Long-Ears, fleeing from my Queenie like a mad dog, and with him, mayhap, his plump doe, and an uncle, or even a small one or two. Up go I with my club, and down I crack it across their little skulls with a mighty *thwack!*"

So loud and with such bloodthirsty relish did he pronounce the last word that Freya, listening to him in horrified fascination, jumped in shock, her hands flying nervously to her heart, a small, mewling cry breaking unbidden from her lips. The hunter threw back his head and roared with jeering laughter.

"A mite skittish, are ye not, wench? Calm yeself. It's only rabbits me and Queenie are after—not comely vixens such as yerself. Eh? Is that not so, Queenie, my lovie?" He fondly scratched the ferret beneath the chin.

The weasel-like creature made a number of small, shrill squeaking sounds and writhed from her master's grip. He let her go, and at once the slender ferret began sniffing about the hut, nose twitching, dark eyes bright and malevolent as she scurried busily to and fro. Freya tensed, watching the ferret's explorations with bated breath as it drew closer and closer to the precious basket, willing the horrid little beast to move on.

"Ah, lass, ye'll find no rabbits over there," the hunter murmured, taking another portion of rabbit and chewing.

Suddenly Beorn let out a low, fretful cry, which Freya instantly drowned with a nervous, "Well! It looks like the snow is done with for the while, does it not? You'll be able to go on your way soon, won't ye?" she finished, her tone hopeful.

The hunter licked his fingers noisily and eyed her up and down. "Why would I want to be on my way, wench, when you've given me such a warm welcome here? I'd not find a cosier hut—nor one with such a comely goodwife as yourself to warm my pallet—for many a league. If ever! Only a fool would journey on so soon—and Waite, the hunter, is of a certainty no fool!"

"But what of my husb—husband?" Freya whispered. "When he returns, he'll—"

"You've no man coming back to ye, lass, and we both know it," he barked angrily. "Enough of your lies! I see no sickle, no boots, no mantle—nothing here to show a man's presence— nor over many of your own goods, come to that. Admit it, wench, you're a Danish camp follower, a fugitive from the battle last week, are ye not? An' ye're stranded here in this hut by the snow." He winked. "I guessed as much the minute I set eyes on ye, and knew it fer certain when ye spoke! That's no Saxon wench, I says t'meself, that's a Viking wench! An' I were right, at that! Let's hope the bitter weather lasts a long, long time, eh, girl?"

Just then Queenie started a shrill, excited trilling sound. Freya's head jerked around as if tugged by a string. She saw the slender ferret nosing excitedly at the basket, snuffling and uttering tiny yelps. Milk! The babes smelled of milk, and ferrets counted warm milk a rare treat—!

"Now, my little lady, what is it you're after in there?" the hunter asked good-naturedly, starting toward the basket.

"Just—just the rabbit skins!" Freya cried, too loudly, too eagerly, thrusting the rabbit skins behind her back, out of sight. "The little beast must smell the blood on them."

The hunter, Waite, frowned suspiciously. "Nay, lass, 'tis something else, t'make her so excited. What else have ye in there?" he demanded, and bent to open the basket.

"Nothing!" Freya cried. "There's nothing in there but— but a worn mantle. Come back to the fire, Master Waite. If—if you've your strength back, I thought mayhap we might—?" She let the offer hang unfinished, yet for all that Waite read the invitation in her tone well enough. He turned slowly away

437

from the basket, grinning broadly, his sly brown eyes kindling as he strode across the cottage toward her.

"Aye, I knew it, my girl! I knew you for a lusty one the moment I set eyes on ye! Cannot wait fer it inside ye, can ye, lovie? Ah, ye'll not be disappointed, wench, not with young Waite the hunter. Ploughs a strong, straight furrow—aye, and a good deep one, that he does!" he promised, his voice thick and unsteady with lust.

He caught her about the waist in one long, wiry arm and pulled her to him, his mouth fastening upon hers, his beard scratching her tender flesh. His other hand reached to grasp a swollen, tender breast, the stubby fingers kneading, squeezing, as his hot, wet mouth, tasting of rabbit and grease, smeared over hers.

Revulsion rose in her. Nay, she denied silently, please, nay! Yet there seemed no way out, none whatsoever. Still kissing her heatedly, his mouth moving over her face, then across her throat as he wrenched the neck of the kirtle down to bare her shoulders, the hunter thrust her down on her back to the earthen floor and crouched at her side like a wild animal about to spring.

"Let ole Waite see the fire in ye, eh, wench?" he panted, wiping his lips on the back of his fist as he looked greedily down at her body sprawled beneath him. "The last time I touched ye, ye were as cold as a—"

The loud, unmistakable, indignant bellow of a hungry babe sounded from across the hut, and the hunter stiffened. He whirled about and saw at once that the wicker basket had overturned, and that Queenie was snuffling eagerly about the lid.

"What—!" the hunter cried, and quickly turned away from Freya and jumped to his feet.

"Nay!" Freya screamed, scrabbling to standing, flinging herself across the hut, and clawing at his back. Angrily the hunter shoved her away, knocking her to the dirt floor.

"Get away with ye, slut," he growled. "There's something in here ye haven't told me about, is there not?" So saying, he righted the basket and lifted the lid, his brows rising as he saw what lay inside. He swung about to face her, grinning evilly.

"Ah! So ye've a brace o'babes, have ye? Well, that changes things summat, think ye not?" He chuckled nastily. "There's not much difference between a brace o'helpless babes and a brace o'frightened wee bunnies, now is there, Queenie, my girl?" He chucked the ferret under its chin. "The one is as helpless as t'other. A 'thwack' with my trusty club across their little skulls, and—hsst! No more babes!"

"You—you would not!" Freya whispered hoarsely, her heart suddenly slowing, slowing, until each throb had the measured meter of a slow-beating drum. "I beg you—please, please don't hurt them! I—I'll do anything, anything at all ye ask of me, if you'll only swear you won't hurt them. They're just hungry. Let—let me feed them, and they'll go back to sleep, as quiet and good as you could ever wish for. Please. *Please!*" she implored him, grasping his cross-gaitered leggings as he towered over her.

He rubbed his bearded chin, grinning, savoring his power over her. "Good enough," he agreed. "You give me a lusty tumble, lass, show me all them little Danish tricks ole Waite ain't never seen—and in return I'll let yer whelps be. Refuse me aught, and—!" He made a gesture, as if swinging his club, and her heart leaped in terror in her breast.

Her shoulders slumped. "Just—just let me put them to nurse, and we'll—I'll see to your needs."

He nodded, scratched his groin, and hunkered down across the fire from her. Then in one swift motion he reached out, scooped up the slinky ferret, and slipped it back into the sack, quick as a wink, his eyes never once leaving Freya's pale face. "Aye. Good enough," he agreed thickly. "Suckle the brats, and make haste about it. I'll not take kindly to them squalling while I'm after my bit o'pleasure with their mother." He leered at her, his gaze roving her body, lingering on the full thrust of her breasts against the rough cloth of her kirtle.

She edged across the hut and snatched up the precious basket, returning with it to her side of the hut. Hands trembling, she drew Beorn out, her touch rougher than usual in her nervousness. Darting a nervous glance at the hunter, she drew down her kirtle and bared her full breast, putting the babe hurriedly to the leaking nipple. He latched onto it hungrily. Freya winced with pain as his gums clamped over the tender flesh and he began to suck, greedy as ever. The hunter sprawled back and leaned on one elbow. He watched her nursing the babe through slitted eyes, whistling tunelessly through his teeth in a manner that set her already shredded nerves still further on edge.

Beorn was soon filled, the milk dribbling from one corner of his little mouth and down across his plump, flushed cheek. She bubbled him hurriedly and replaced him in the basket, drawing Edana gently forth, mindful as she did so of the increasing impatience of the man watching them, signaled by the tapping of his kid boot against the hearthstones. Edana was fretful and disinclined to suckle. She whimpered when her mother tried to press the nipple into her mouth, yet to Freya's ears her cries seemed weak and lacking vigor. "Please, little one, please," she urged softly, tapping Edana gently upon the cheek to encourage her to open her mouth and nurse. She sucked at last, but without much interest, and soon drifted back to sleep. Freya felt the infant's brow. It was dry and fevered. The sickness she had so feared was reality!

"My babe is sickening," she said hesitantly. "She must be sponged, to lower the fever."

"Nay," the hunter rejoined sourly, "I've waited on ye long enough. Put the brats away, and come here to me."

Something snapped inside her. All tension flowed away, to be replaced by a curious calm as at the crisis in a battle, a calm in which each word and each action were crystal-clear to her. She knew now what she must do. And she would do it. "As ye will," she heard herself say serenely. "But a moment longer, till I see the little ones made snug, and I'll be at your bidding."

"Good enough," he muttered. "Aye, good enough."

"*Ja,*" she murmured softly as she turned away from him. "More than good enough for the likes of you, Master Waite!"

Chapter 34

She kissed Beorn's brow, then Edana's, praying silently it would not be the last time she ever kissed their dear baby faces. And then, with the curious calm and detachment still encompassing her, she stepped away from her little ones across the hut to where the hunter loomed, waiting for her. He was breathing heavily, and the lust in his eyes ignited as she came toward him.

At once he caught her roughly about the waist with one wiry arm and dragged her against his length. The other hand covered her breast and squeezed. His shaggy head lowered to her throat and he burrowed his wet mouth against her tender flesh. His foul lips smeared her throat, her face, her ears everywhere, even as his hands yet groped the soft mounds of her body. Her skin crawled with revulsion.

"Thought t'cheat me, did ye not, girl, eh?" he panted unsteadily, jerking her off her feet and forcing her of a sudden down to the moldy straw, jolting the breath from her in a startled whoosh as he pinioned her body there by the heavy weight of his own. "Well, you'll not cheat ole Waite, lovie, not now—!"

His lips covered hers, and the sweat stench of his unwashed body made the gorge rise acidly up her throat. Gulping, she wormed one hand free of his weight, fingers scrabbling stealthily across the moldy straw, inch by inch, toward the niche where she had hidden her dagger hours before.

"Please, no!" she mumbled, tossing her head, hoping to

441

keep his attention from what her hands were about. She need not have worried. He had thrust up her tunic now and with greedy, coarse fingers was busily exploring her bared breasts, tweaking and rolling the sensitive nipples between them. "Please—don't!" she murmured again, and with a surge of savage joy, at last felt the icy hilt of the dagger firm under her grip. Her fingers closed around it and tightened. She brought her hand up slowly, agonizingly slowly, even as Waite thrust her thighs apart and hunkered down between them. His rasping breathing came unsteady and labored now on the silence. His eyes had a glazed look about them. Lightning could have struck the hut at that moment, and he would not have remarked on it, so lost in his lust was he! She tightened her grip on the dagger hilt and shifted her weight slightly to raise it, to plunge the blade into his back with all her strength.

"'Tis lovely, lovely teats ye have, lass," he rasped, then slobbered between noisy suckings as he feasted greedily upon her breasts.

She gulped, close to vomiting. She could feel the bulge of his member beneath the rough homespun of his clothing as he thrust his hips against her. He shifted his weight, reaching to unfasten his breeches. *Now! Now!* screamed a voice inside her head.

She plunged her arm downward with all her strength!

In that instant the plank door of the hut flew open. With a curse, Waite rolled off her. The dagger, but a hairbreadth from its target, was dashed from her grip by his body. The hunter snatched up his club and whirled to defend himself.

Through a curtain of tumbled hair, Freya saw a man standing there in the doorway, his massive height, his breadth silhouetted black against the white of the snow and the pallor of the sky beyond. She did not need to discern his features to know him, nay, never! She would have known that tall silhouette anywhere—

"Alaric!" she screamed. "Alaric! Look out!"

Waite lunged at him, cudgel brandished aloft. Quick as lightning, Alaric's arm came up. His fingers fastened about the club, and with a wrench he twisted it from Waite's grip and followed the move with a ringing punch to Waite's nose. Blood

442

sprayed in scarlet ribbons from the misshapen mass, and infuriated with pain and anger, Waite cursed foully and swung at him barefisted. Alaric's head snapped up. He fell backward through the door and out onto the snow. He recovered quickly as Waite threw himself on him and brought his own boot up solidly under the hunter's chin as the lout leaped at his throat. The impetus hurtled the man backward as if rammed by an oak trunk, to lie still on the floor of the hut once more.

"Aye, 'tis Alaric," Alaric growled as if the scuffle had never been. He ducked under the low doorway and came into the hut once more, flexing his bleeding knuckles. There was no welcome, no greeting, no joy to see her in his gray eyes. Only a dark contempt, an icy scorn that froze her glad cry upon her lips and chilled her to the marrow. A thin smile parted his lips. "I would have known thee anywhere, vixen, with that dagger clenched in your fist! 'Twould appear you're still up to your murdering tricks!" he snarled.

"Nay, 'tis not so, nay," she whispered, shaking her head, struggling up to a sitting position. With trembling hands she swept the red-gold cascade of tangled hair from her eyes and smoothed down her rucked-up clothing. "I—we were headed for Kenley but—but lost our way in the—the blizzard."

"We?" Alaric said coldly, glancing from her and then to the hunter, who yet sprawled silently in one corner. "Pray introduce me to your companion, wench. I do not think we have had the pleasure—?"

"His name is Waite, and he is of a certainty no companion of mine!" Freya hissed.

"Really?" Alaric smiled mockingly, his lip curling in scorn. "On the contrary, it appeared when I interrupted the two of you that you were on most—*intimate*—terms!"

"Things are not—not always as they seem!" Freya protested hotly. She snatched up the dagger. "He meant to—to rape me! You see this? Had you arrived but a second later, I would have plunged it into his foul back!" Her eyes flashed as she looked across at Waite, who had come around and was sitting there, rubbing his jaw. He appeared frightened now, his eyes darting nervously first to Alaric, and then back to Freya.

"Please, my lord—!" he began, wetting his lips. "I—I

thought as how she were but a—a camp follower! The lass seemed eager enough, and I—"

"Liar!" Freya seethed, "Foul-mouthed, stinking liar!" But a glance from Alaric silenced her.

"I know how she seemed, oaf," Alaric spat. "Aye, I know full well how the pretty wench can *seem!* Be gone with you, before I run you through!" To add weight to his threat he clamped his fingers over the hilt of the broadsword at his hip.

Waite needed no second urging. Wiping his mouth on the back of his hand, he snatched up his sack and his club and plunged out of the hut, leaving them alone.

"You should have run him through for what he intended!" Freya spat, glowering at Alaric.

"Were I to slay everyone for their intents where you are concerned, vixen, half of Britain would lie dead and bleeding!"

For endless moments, an uncomfortable silence yawned between them.

Freya bowed her head, too shaken and disillusioned for words. For so many miserable miles she had imagined this first meeting with Alaric, had played it through in her mind, over and over, in different ways! But in none of her imaginings had he been so filled with fury, so cold and unrelenting. In her fond mind he had greeted her with joy, with a tender smile so filled with love and delight to see her it had brought tears to her eyes just to think of it. Was this the welcome she had cheated death at Toki's hands for? Was this the man she had grieved for until she feared to lose her mind? Was this—this arrogant, unfeeling Saxon brute the man she had caused her dear Olaf such heartbreak over? He was not worth so much pain! She clenched her fists upon the straw and felt enormous tears well up and begin flowing down her cheeks in hot, salty rivulets, a long, lonely year of misery in her silent weeping. By Frey, it had been easier believing him dead!

Alaric shifted uncomfortably, darting an uneasy glance across to where she was curled, her head bowed, her shoulders trembling. She wept, and he felt peculiarly guilty because of it. Nonetheless, the conflicting emotions inside him—anger, confusion, and love commingled—would not free him to go to her side and comfort her. Tears! Had he once seen her cry before, however desperate her plight had seemed? He thought not. If he had, it was certainly not with such silent hopelessness as she wept now!

"Cease your weeping," he commanded her cruelly. "Your false tears will not soften me—any more than they will erase your sins!"

Her head came up. "Sins?" she managed in a husky, indignant voice. *"Sins?"*

"Aye, sins," he repeated, his tone cold and controlled. "Or do you not consider the senseless murder of my brother a sin?" Anger blazed anew in his wood-smoke eyes. Her thin lips curled in contempt.

"Ja, it was a sin—but not my sin, for it was not I who killed him!" she cried fervently. "'Twas all part of—of Kendra's plot—that she would kill Farant and lay the blame for it upon me. But that night I knew not that Farant and you were twins and—and I—I thought he was you, Alaric. I thought she had killed you!"

"If you were innocent, why then did you flee?" he countered harshly. "Was that the action of an innocent?"

"Nay, sir," she spat, too furious for composure. "It was the action of a slave, a terrified slave who had been falsely accused of murder—and knew not a soul at Kenley would believe her innocence, not with you dead!"

"And so you made no attempt to clear yourself, but instead fled my burh for the Danelaw!" He shook his great dark head, and the chiseled lips she had once loved to kiss grew thin and hard.

"Pah!" she stormed, and there was fire in her jewel eyes once again now. "Clear myself? Surely you jest, my lord! Did you believe the truth when Kendra destroyed the scrivening I had done, and put the blame on me? Nay! You know you did not! You took the part of Lady Kendra, and forced me to redo the work! And when the brigands ambushed Valonia and me, were you not only too ready to believe Ordway's word against mine that I had no part in their attack? If you, who had *professed* to love me, had not believed me then, what hope had I that Ordway would believe me, hating me as he does, with you lying dead and Kendra screaming that it was I who had slain you!"

He frowned, his broad forehead knitting in puzzlement. "Scrivening? Destroyed work? I know of the brigands, but naught of that, Freya, I swear it."

"Huh! Why should I believe you? You have never believed in me, not once!" She flung about, her back to him, and crossed her arms across her breasts, scowling fiercely.

"It must have been Farant," he murmured softly. "He would have taken Kendra's word, even should a holy bishop himself have sworn she lied! But you are wrong about me. I have believed in you, even when others did not."

"When? Name one!"

"When you stood accused of witchcraft. Did I not see Kendra's accusations withdrawn, and yourself freed?"

"*Ja,*" she agreed with obvious reluctance. "I admit it, you believed in me then. But if that were so, then how *could* you have believed I would seek to slay you? I loved thee, Alaric! I had hoped to be-become your bride!"

She saw a look akin to shame pass fleetingly across his hard, handsome features. "Kendra was very convincing, and my uncle—he was certain she spoke the truth. She said that you had struck Farant down, believing he was me, because you—you were enraged with jealousy."

"And you believed that—that blatant falsehood?" Her eyes widened in disbelief. "You accepted the word of a twisted, embittered old man—whom you knew full well loathed me, as he loathed and hated all Vikings—and the lies of a jealous, conniving bitch-woman, against what you knew of me, whom you said you loved? Ha! You think much of yourself, my lord, if you thought I could ever slay another because of you! 'Tis fortunate I was indeed, to have been spared marriage to one who has so little faith in me!" She tossed her head haughtily.

His jaw tightened in annoyance. "You seemed capable of it that night in London. Deny it, and be damned for a liar!"

"The whey-faced Lady Meredyth?" To his surprise, she laughed bitterly. "*Ja,* I fancy I could have killed *her* in cold blood, so jealous was I that night! But slay thee, my lord, who were my life, my heart, my beloved lord? Never!" she finished, her tone husky with emotion. "Never, never . . . !"

He took a step toward her, arms outstretched. "Freya—!"

She skittered away from him, shaking her head. "Nay, my lord, touch me not! I see now it was wrong of me to try to come back to Kenley, to hope that all could be mended between us. Without trust there can be no love, and of a certainty there is no trust—nor love—between us now! I came to you from the sea, and when the spring comes I will return to the sea."

"You'll go back to Denmark?"

"*Ja,*" she said softly. "For there is nowhere else for me to go, not with my husband dead." She saw his head come up at this, and nodded. "Aye. I was Olaf's woman this past year! We were wed last autumn, but he was slain in the battle at London a week ago. My father is dead too. A man named Thorvald has overrun his hall—*my* hall—of Danehof. He swore he would never permit Freya of the Frozen Heart to return to her place there, save as his bride. I will become that bride, Alaric, and perhaps one day, if the gods are kind, I shall retake the hall of Danehof, as is my right," she vowed. "Aye! I will make a place for myself there—and forget you, Saxon, and the shallow thing you call love!"

"You cannot leave Britain! I will not permit it! You forget— you are still my slave!" he thundered, feeling an odd sense of desperation twist in his gut like the twist of a blade.

"Nay, my lord! You freed me, do you recall? You have no claims upon me now. I am no man's slave!" She made to stalk past him, but he reached out and grasped her arm, spinning her about to face him. "Nay," he breathed, "you'll go nowhere!" He glowered at her, meeting her proud expression with a stony one of his own. The haughty angle of her slender white throat, upon which the elegant tilt of her red-gold head was like a fiery summer rose upon a graceful willow stalk, was one he remembered only too well. The vibrant colors of her complexion, her jewel eyes, the vivid beauty that could not be dimmed even here, in the gloom of the hut, were all unchanged. If anything she had grown even more beautiful, with the appeal of a woman now, rather than a young girl's touching loveliness. In his heart he knew that he believed her, that he had always known she was innocent, despite his uncle's—and Kendra's—protests, as Robin had said. Nay, he could never, never let her go, not again! Could not face the years ahead without her, courting death as a welcome friend on the field of battle—! With an anguished growl he dragged her against him and forced her mouth beneath his, his lips brutal in his hunger for her, his fingers steel manacles about her.

"Perhaps you are no longer my slave, vixen. But of a certainty I have become yours, curse thee!" he said huskily, the words wrung from him as he thrust her away. "Aye, Freya, I confess I was wrong! Forgive me! In truth, not a moment has passed in the year since last I laid eyes upon you when I have not longed for you with a need that consumed me, heart and soul! Aye, I fought against it, even as I fought against those other truths, but I can no longer deny *this* truth—I love thee, Freya!" With tormented eyes he looked down at her.

"And what of your bride—do you love her too?" Freya demanded, voice aquaver, trying to harden herself, to deny the softening, the kindling that stole treacherously through her with his words. Her tone was laced with bitterness and jealousy.

"I have no bride," he denied, "and I will have none but thee, my Freya, my Viking bride! The betrothal with Meredyth was broken long ago, my love, much to my uncle's displeasure. Return to Kenley with me!"

"Nay, I cannot, for if you are lying to me, Saxon, I would in truth slay thee," she whispered, "for a heart can withstand but so much pain!" She edged away from him, unwilling to stand close to him, for the effect of his nearness upon her was too dangerous, too potent, for her to think clearly.

"'Tis no lie," he swore, and strode after her across the shadowed hut, grasping her by the upper arms. She trembled beneath his fingers. "Never was a vow more truthfully given, my heart!" He looked down at her, and as their eyes met there was, in the gloom between them, the same compelling magic they had felt that day of the storm, long, long ago, as they stood upon the damp shore. It was simply there, sudden and sweet, in the air.

"Alaric . . . oh, Alaric . . . hold me!"

"Freya, my love, my heart! How I have longed for thee!" And then she was clasped fiercely in his arms, his strong,

448

encompassing arms, and his lips were feverish as they moved on hers, tasting the salt of her tears as they clung together, clung as if they would never be parted, ever again. His lean fingers cupped her lovely face, and as he lowered his lips to hers he murmured, "I love thee!"

"As I love thee, my Bear!"

Their mouths came together. Their bodies melted one against the other. They both shuddered as the pent-up grieving and loving of endless months surged between them like a storm, rocking them with its electric hunger, its crackling ardor.

She laced her fingers through the snow-dampened ebony curls that molded to his neck and gave him her lips, her mouth and her kisses, with a glad joy and a will that drove him to a delicious sort of madness. His questing fingers hungrily traced the slender curve of her spine, clasped her buttocks, and pressed her still closer and closer against him until her breasts were crushed against his broad chest and it seemed they must surely meld into one.

"I love thee and desire thee above all women!" he breathed, nuzzling her silky hair, "Aye, and I want you as never before, my lovely vixen!"

She tilted her glowing face up to his and slowly shook her head. There was laughter in her sapphire eyes. "As I long for thee. But—we cannot, not yet, my dearest Bear!"

He scowled, the scowl of a small boy who has just been told a prized treat will not be forthcoming. "And why not?" he demanded, the timbre of his voice husky and heated with desire.

"The children, my lord. 'Twould not be seemly. We must not, not in front of the—the children!"

She moved away from him still holding his hand, drawing him after her across the hut, and kneeling down beside the willow basket. Glancing at his face, which still appeared deeply puzzled, she drew aside the lid.

There slept Beorn on his belly as usual, his little bottom in the air, his thumb tucked into his mouth. Beside him lay Edana, so still and flushed, her dark lashes quivering tremulously on her rosy cheeks. She heard him suck in an

449

unsteady breath, a gasp of disbelief.

"Your son, Beorn, my lord Alaric. And your little daughter, Edana," she told him. "She has a slight ague, my lord, and I would see her cared for as soon as possible."

"Christ's Blessed Wounds!" he uttered softly, and his expression was so stunned, so filled with amazement and, *ja*, delight, that she could not help but smile. "Aye, of course—at once! My little daughter must be cared for. My daughter! My son!" he echoed softly.

He sounded—and looked, she thought fondly—as if he were simple, or somehow touched, as he knelt there, dazedly repeating her words.

At length he flicked his head, as if to clear it. "'Tis no more than an hour's ride from here to Kenley. Valonia will know what to do for our little daughter. Will you come home with me, my love?" There was uncertainty in his eyes, and she knew that, should she accept, he would never again take her love for granted.

"*Ja*," she agreed softly, slipping her hand inside his large one and feeling like a voyager returning to safe harbor after a long and perilous journey. "We'll go home!"

Chapter 35

Home from the sea came the longships,
Proud o'er the wild, raging sea.
And bright was the treasure they carried:
They carried my loved one to me!

Aye, a treasure they brought me from Britain—
More costly this treasure by far
Than all the bright jewels found in Britain;
Her beauty outshone every star.

Her eyes were as blue as twin sapphires,
Her lips were pink coral so rare,
And bright as the costliest gold from the East
Was her radiant curtain of hair.

Her throat was a column of ivory,
Her breasts were as pearls from the deep,
Her waist was as narrow as birds' wings.
With tears wrought of crystal she'd weep:

"Oh, cry not for me, dearest mother,
Oh, shed not another sad tear!
For I'm gone to the lands of the Norsemen,
To the arms of the lord I hold dear."

Light was my heart as they landed,

The love in her eyes did I see,
And I wept as she came softly to me—
My beautiful jewel from the sea!

The last sweet note of the lute trembled on the hush that followed Freya's singing, and for a moment Alaric was too filled with emotion to speak.

She sat upon a low stool by the heavy wooden cradle in which their little ones slept, lulled by their mother's lullaby. Her hair fell loose and silky about her slender shoulders, vying for luxuriousness with the sable trim of her deep rose gown— "a radiant curtain" indeed, he thought tenderly. She raised her sapphire eyes to his, and he saw that the thick fringing of tawny lashes was spiked with teardrops. They clung there like sparkling topazes in the flickering firelight and gave a sheen to eyes already made brilliant with the radiant luster of love. He reached out a hand, and there was an invitation in his darkly smoldering wood-smoke eyes.

"Come here to me, Marissa, my jewel of the sea!" he murmured.

She set aside the lute she had been playing and moved swiftly, gracefully, gladly across the bower to his side. Perching beside him upon the bed, she leaned over him so that her silky hair swept his face.

"I am here, my lord and love!" she murmured huskily, and sweetly pressed her lips to his. The kiss was long and infinitely satisfying, and both were reluctant to end it. Alaric gathered her hair in his hands and wound it about his throat as they kissed, tugging her down to lie beside him upon the scented linen sheets. Her perfume rose about him, a musk that was fresh and light and as arousing as a field of wild flowers, as tantalizing as the fragrance of a golden rose of summer.

"A fitting song, my lady, for in truth I have often likened you to a jewel, a lovely treasure carried to me upon the sea. Where did you learn the song?"

"From my Uncle Sven, long, long ago at Danehof. When I was a little girl he used to sing it to me. Perhaps—perhaps even then he had foreknowledge of what the future was to hold for me." She smiled shyly. Marissa, jewel of the sea, was the new name Alfred, Bretwalda of Wessex, had chosen for her, a choice which had delighted his thane, Alaric. So had Sven prophesied she would be called some day, long ago when he yet lay recovering from his wound, she mused, as he had also foretold she would become a Christian. On both points had he been proved correct, though she had scorned and denied his prophecies then! Yet she had indeed been baptised, anointed with baptismal oil, and had worn the chrisom cloth about her head for nine days as he had sworn she would do.

Tenderly she stroked Alaric's cheek, continuing, "It is the song of a princess of Britain who fell in love with a Norse invader. She sailed to Denmark to be joined with him as his bride, against all opposition from her family. Her father and brothers disowned her and threatened her with an agonizing traitor's death if they apprehended her. They would not condone her marrying her family's sworn enemy, you see. Her poor mother's heart was broken with sorrow, yet the princess secretly fled the isle of Britain, to be with the man she loved forever. The song is that sung by her beloved lord, when the dragon-ship that had brought her across the wild sea to him sailed safely into harbor, and he saw his princess again for the first time in many long, lonely months."

"In truth, my lovely Freya, I know how he felt that day!" Alaric said with feeling. "On the morrow will you be my bride, as the princess was his, and my lady and my love for all time to come. Nothing will come between us ever again," he murmured, nuzzling the small expanse of bare flesh exposed by the neckline of her gown. Beneath his fingertips, where they lay lightly against her rib cage, he felt her heartbeat quicken. "Your heart beats madly, sweeting. May I flatter myself 'tis my touch alone that makes it so, or is there aught you fear, and have said nothing of?" He frowned as he looked into her eyes, for he fancied she was troubled, though she concealed it well.

"A woman's fancies, nothing more," she said soothingly, unwilling to do or say anything of her foreboding and mar his present happiness. "So are all brides upon the eve of their wedding day—fraught with strange fantasies and fears that have little bearing upon fact."

"Were you so when you were joined with your Olaf?" he

could not help asking, nor could he hide the taint of jealousy in his tone.

She nodded candidly. "*Ja,* I was! My thoughts were filled with memories of my Saxon lord, whom I believed dead and thought would never again hold me in his arms! My heart was filled with the pain of his death, with grief so deep that it was my desire to join him there. Life seemed a bitter draught without the one I loved, all joy lost to me forever. It was a draught I could not bear to swallow alone."

Her sincere, soft-spoken words filled him with shame.

"Ah, Freya, my heart, forgive me," he murmured. "But the thought of you with another—any other—fills me with a jealous rage I can scarce control."

She laughed softly, poking him in the ribs. "And what of you, sir? Were you as celibate as a Christian monk this long year past?"

"Nay, I was not, as well you know, vixen," he confessed ruefully. "Yet the whores and the easy wenches I spent my lust upon never eased the pain within me. A moment's forgetfulness, an instant's respite from my pain, was the best they could offer."

"Aye, and knowing you and your lusty nature, my lord, I wager there were many such 'moments,' and countless such 'instants,'" she retorted with a wry grin, and lay back in his arms. "Yet I am a generous wench, and will forgive you them all!" She turned her head and rubbed her cheek against the muscled arm he had curled beneath her head to pillow it, a gesture of kittenish affection that was provocative in the extreme.

With a low growl he kissed her eyelids, her cheeks, and lightly touched her lips with his own. His mouth swept on down to the warm, pulsing hollow that lay in the angle 'twixt her throat and shoulder—so vulnerable, that little hollow, so tempting to a man's lips. As he tasted her warm skin, felt the flutter beneath his lips, his large hand found the intricate loops that fastened her bower robe from throat to knee and deftly unhooked them. The deep rose woolen garment fell away, baring her alabaster loveliness to his caresses, whether by hand or by mouth. Her pulse quickened under his tongue, and for an

454

instant more he lingered there, before following the valley that lay between the creamy mounds of her breasts down to the softly thrusting mounds themselves.

Her breasts were larger than he remembered, a result of the babes she had borne him. He savored each one with gentle ardor, drawing the swollen, ruched pink nipples deep into the flaming heat of his mouth, sucking and swirling his tongue about each one until he felt her body tense and heard the sudden huskiness of her breathing as her desire mounted. Lower he fondled her, his palm grazing the sweeping line of her waist, hip, and flank, to lodge at last against the silken inner length of her thighs and tousle the fleece of gold between.

As she moaned softly, tossing her head from side to side upon the feathered pillow, he parted her thighs and nestled his ebony head against the golden mound of curls at their juncture. Her soft, delighted cries broke upon the shadows like the gentle summer tides against the shore. He caressed the quivering flower of her womanhood with lips and tongue, tasting and savoring the heady essence of her, her unique, sensual, nectared fragrance. Her cries became elated little gasps as her passion crested, and beneath the probing tenderness of his mouth and fingers he felt a pulsing as her body tensed and rapture swept through her like wildfire.

Only when she lay relaxed and still once more did he cover her softly curved body with the heavy weight of his own, enter her velvet sheath and fill her with the hard, throbbing length of his shaft, succumbing now to the fierce desire he had held in check until she found her own, sweet, first release.

With slow, measured thrusts he aroused her from her languor, capturing her mouth and possessing it even as he possessed her body. His fingers twined in the scented mass of her hair, spilling it, winding the silken ropes of it about them as he kissed her, loved her with ever-increasing ardor, hotly murmuring words of passion in her ears as he did so, his words and his warm breath filling her with delicious tingles of pleasure.

The tempo of his powerful, thrusting flanks, the heady wonder of his hardness surging deeper, ever deeper within her incited in her a wild, savage joy. As he gave of himself, she opened deeply to him and gave back the priceless gift of herself with a sweet, fierce gladness in return, with naught held back. Body and heart and soul, she was his, his alone! She cradled his lean flanks against her hips, embracing him with her slender thighs and legs, curling her arms tightly about his neck until they were one, without beginning, without end.

His lips crushed her coral lips, bruising now as his ardor soared. His tongue darted between them like an arrogant tongue of fire to claim her mouth in his savage desire, lancing again and again into the moist recesses. Her breasts were crushed under his rough chest, yet the taut, swollen pink nipples were hard arrowheads of delight against his flesh, tiny spurs that roweled his passion onward like a galloping steed. Her soft belly, all creamy white flesh, was lost under the hard, swarthy darkness of his as he rode her.

Everything she had to give, everything she was now or ever would be, was his—his for the asking, the taking! She sobbed with a sheer, frenzied joy as the pulsating quivers began to spiral through her anew, building, gathering her up in a crackling storm tide of desire. Surely her blood was not blood, but a strong, heady wine; a hot, mulled wine; a deep, rich red wine on which she was wondrously drunk! His breathing rasped louder and still louder in her ear as he neared his release, a hot, moist whirlwind that only served to heighten her pleasure as he drove harder and faster into her velvet sheath.

"Jesu! Sweet Madonna!" he groaned against her hair as the wave broke. His fingers clenched over her arms so tightly, she knew there would be bruises there come morning but cared not, for she felt the glad silvery leap of his seed as he spent deep within her and knew she had given him the same fiercely sweet pleasure he had given her.

Afterward they still lay entwined, side by side, heartbeat to heartbeat, the galloping tattoo gradually ebbing to a more measured, slower tempo as the minutes passed and calm and quiet returned. He opened his eyes, and saw in the firelight and the dancing play of the single rushlight upon her face that she was watching him too, her sapphire eyes large and liquid in the half shadows.

"Until tomorrow, my Viking bride," he murmured softly,

and gently pressed his lips to her brow.

"Tomorrow . . ." she agreed sleepily, and the fans of her lashes fluttered one last time and were finally still upon her flushed cheeks as she drifted into slumber.

Their wedding day dawned fair for a December morning. The sky was a pale wintry blue, but bore no promise of more snow to come. The meadows and gently rolling hills about Kenley were mantled under powdery white. Crystalline icicles hung from the eaves of the vast hall like inverted dagger blades, flashing wintry sunlight. Frost sparkled everywhere, upon bushes and trees, shimmering frigidly as if handfuls of glittering diamonds had been cast earthward by the careless handful. Like paternal lords robed in darkest, somber green, only the pines and the firs formed a solemn tunnel along the roadside that led to the tiny stone chapel of Saint Cuthbert, where Freya and her Alaric would be wed.

Meanwhile the bride fretted and fussed over her bridal gown as maidens about to be married anywhere will fuss and fret on their wedding morn.

"In faith, my dear child, I never thought to see you a-dither in such maidenly fashion!" Valonia declared smiling, arranging the veil of pale green silk about Freya's shoulders to her satisfaction. For the third time she resettled atop the veil the dainty fillet of gold studded with emeralds and sapphires. "In truth I had feared, were you ever to wed, you would sport a broadsword at your hip, and don leggings for the service!" Her tone was teasing, for Freya appeared pale to her eyes and she wished to coax some color into her cheeks.

Freya laughed, albeit a little nervously. By—by the Blessed Virgin, she had not expected to be so—so unsettled at the thought of becoming Alaric's bride, but as Valonia had said, she was all "a-dither"! There were butterflies swooping and hovering in her belly that Valonia's small draught of wine, pressed into her hand, had been unable to still. Was it the result of the whirlwind of activity her return to Kenley had brought, first in seeing little Edana nursed back to health, and then Alaric's announcement that he would take her as his bride, followed by her conversion to his faith? She shivered, recalling the look of fury on Ordway's face when he had heard they were to be wed. Such foul names he had called her, such awful things he had said, denouncing her dearest little ones as some Viking warrior's bastards, and denying they were of Alaric's seed. But Alaric had steadfastly ignored his uncle's protests, and had bade him be silent . . . "None could be as surprised as I, dearest aunt," she admitted, answering Valonia's comment. "Not only to find myself diverted by feminine frills and flounces, but to be marrying Alaric at all!"

"It has been a match overlong in coming," Valonia agreed, "but fated to be, for all that. It was but a matter of time, once he had found thee. Alaric was not himself after you fled Kenley, child. I feared for him, in truth, for he had the stink of defeat about him. No man should go into battle for his life with such a look of wrath and hopelessness and despair upon his face as he wore this past twelvemonth. I confess, child, I nigh wore out my knees in chapel praying for him all this time, aye, and for thee! Believe me, were it not for my lord husband's arguments he would have ridden after thee that day Farant was slain, found thee somehow. But Ordway cursed him for a lovesick fool, told him over and over again his rightful place was here, at Kenley, that he would never recover you once you had reached the Danelaw. He played mercilessly on his loyalty to Wessex and his burh, and in the end Ordway won, after a fashion, for the heart had gone out of Alaric by then." Her disapproving tone seemed to smack of disloyalty to her husband, Valonia thought, but alas, 'twas no more nor less than the truth.

She shook her head as Freya turned about to face her. "Ah, my dear, you are a beauty, in truth. The fairest bride I've ever seen!" She leaned over and kissed the girl's brow fondly, a smile replacing her unhappy, pensive expression of moments before. "I wish great joy to the both of you, as would Farant, had he lived to see this day. He was a good, gentle man, Freya. You would have found much about him to admire, for all that he was no warrior. I fancy he would have approved of his brother taking you to wife. He often said that vengeance profited no one, that it served only to soothe the wounded pride and outraged sense of honor of the living, not the dead who had gone beyond caring. He once bade Alaric use your capture to benefit the living, and so it will. If your marriage to my nephew can help bring peace to our battle-weary land of Britain, it will save many lives."

Freya nodded soberly as Valonia brightened and stood back to admire the picture she made.

"There! You are ready!" the older woman declared.

Freya held out the skirts of her forest green kirtle, relishing this moment of womanly vanity. The color became her as did no other, she knew full well. The long sleeves of the gown were narrow and clung snugly to her slender arms, but were cut very wide at the wrists, where they were trimmed with narrow bands of fox fur. The neckline was square, cut so as to set off the jewels that flashed against the satin of her pale throat. The paler green of her fine linen under-dress fitted closely to her arms and reached to her wrists, the embroidery thus prettily displayed when the wide sleeves fell back. The skirts molded to her slim, graceful hips, and the hems were likewise trimmed with two narrow bands of fox fur. A girdle of gold mesh studded with emeralds flashed green fire at her waist. From it hung her gold scissors, her gold eating spoon and knife, and a drinking cup, also of gold for this special occasion. Across the bed, in readiness, was spread a mantle of fur, a bright vixen-colored mantle with a deep hood that would luxuriously frame her lovely face, a wedding gift from her lord, of course, as was the barbaric choker of sapphires, pearls, and emeralds set in gold that encircled her throat. Since she was no virgin maid, she could not wear her hair loose and flowing for her marriage, and so instead Valonia and her serving maids had swept it up into a high mass upon her crown. Then they had painstakingly braided the rest of the silken red-gold mass in numerous narrow burnished ropes, and pinned them securely with small bone combs so that they fell in elegant loops on either side of her lovely, glowing face, an unusual coiffure that enhanced her elegant, regal beauty. On account of the crisp, wintry weather, she wore knee-high boots of soft green suede beneath her gown, and warm stockings of the finest, whitest wool, held at the knee by narrow embroidered ribands of green.

Sven had come from his brotherhood at Mucking to give her away in her father's place, and knowing her dear Uncle Sven would be there was the crowning touch to her happiness.

"Are you ready, my dear?" Valonia repeated gently, happy tears glistening in her eyes that her hopes for Alaric and the little warrior maid for whom she had felt such kinship for so long were at last being fulfilled.

"*Ja*, my lady. I am ready," Freya said, drawing a deep breath. The hint of hectic color in her pale cheeks now was like the bloom on an exquisitely beautiful rose.

She picked up her small prayerbook and turned to the waiting serving maid, plump Edythe, who had been raised to the position of nurse to the babes since their return to Kenley a month ago. She had Beorn and Edana cradled in her arms and was babbling cheerfully to them and smiling. "You will see the children brought to the chapel in good time, pray?" Beorn and Edana were to be baptized immediately following her and Alaric's nuptials.

"Never fear, my lady," Edythe reassured her, beaming. "I will see the little cherubs readied—and bring the two o'ye t'see your lady mother wed your lord father, never fear, will I not, my lambkins?" She smiled, and Edana crowed with pleasure and grasped a fistful of her nurse's hair and stuffed it into her mouth.

"Then let us be off," Freya said with a smile. "I would not see my lord bridegroom kept waiting!"

That same bridegroom was, at that moment, in a far less congenial mood than his bride. He glowered at his uncle Ordway across the bower.

"I will hear no more on this matter, uncle," he gritted, his normally swarthy face darker than usual with anger. "Enough has already been said. This very morn I will wed the Lady Freya—or Marissa, if you will!—and you will not raise a hand to stop me."

"You ungrateful wretch!" Ordway stormed, his own face a mask of fury. "I have been seneschal to Kenley these many long years, devoting my life to caring for what was yours until

460

you were grown. I have seen this burh brought from smoking ruin to prosperity, have guarded her walls in time of war and nurtured her people in time of peace, and you—in your lust for that Viking bitch—would throw all that away! Keep her as your whore, if you must have the little slut, but there is no need to wed the wench to bed her. Acknowledge her bastards as your own by-blows if you must, but marry another, more fitting maid, a pure Saxon maid worthy of your name, your wealth, and your lands. Mark me well, Alaric, wed the red-haired vixen, and you'll deliver Kenley up like a roasted pigeon upon a platter into the hands of a woman you know full well to be a Viking marauder! God's Blood! Your father would turn in his grave were he to see you this day, aye, and your lady mother would die of shame, should she have her reason about her! You have betrayed us all in this, nephew. Aye, sir, you have brought shame and dishonor to this burh! Better you had been slain than Farant, for he was ever the less foolhardy, the less reckless, of you two!"

"And the more easily governed by thee, eh, uncle?" Alaric rejoined, cold fury dancing in his wood-smoke eyes. "Aye, I see it all now, and wonder that I have been blind to it for so long— as your love of Kenley has blinded you to all else. I had oft wondered that any man could so loyally remain here at Kenley all these years as seneschal in my absence, could so perfectly uphold my interests, advise my charls, administer my justice, and neglect his own estates in the process. The reason should have been clear to me long since, sir. You covet Kenley, do you not?"

Reckless in his fury, Ordway spat his answer. "Aye, lad, I do! But not for myself, never that. I am no greedy man. For your cousin, Cullen! If ever a man was fitted to rule this burh, 'tis he. I have only my small estates at Dover to bequeath him when I am dead and gone. If I cast covetous eyes upon your burh, then 'tis for him I did so!"

"Christ's Wounds! Father—how could you even think such a thing?" Cullen had entered and caught the latter exchange. His handsome, good-natured face paled. Men had been killed for far less than what his father had revealed, and by far more patient men than his cousin. Alaric's face was grim in the

461

extreme. Cullen turned to the ealdorman. "Believe me, Alaric, my lord, no thought of claiming that which is lawfully yours has ever entered my head! 'Tis my father's desire, if anyone's. Of a certainty 'tis not mine! I have never wanted more than to serve thee!" He stared at his father in disgust, as if he had not seen him before this.

"Silence, Cullen, 'tis no more than your due, my son! I will not see Alaric fritter away his inheritance upon some Danish whore, whose very father cost my beloved sister her reason, and slew the two little sons and the husband that were hers. If he will not give up his foreign strumpet, then let him give up Kenley in her place!"

"Damn thee to Hell, Ordway, Kenley is mine by birthright! My wealth and my title were both *earned* by me in Alfred's service. Nay, uncle, I'll not relinquish my burh to thee—nor my Viking bride, who means more to me than life! God's Precious Blood! To think I once listened to your twisted lies— that I believed and died a little when you convinced me 'twas Freya that slew Farant! How blind can a man be, how foolishly can he put his trust in any mortal man? In truth, I should have guessed such impassioned avowals of her guilt were suspect. Can the Devil not cite even the Scriptures for his own purpose? Get thee hence from Kenley, sir, and your belongings with thee. As for your true and virtuous lady wife, the aunt whom I hold most dear, I will permit her to decide if she will go with thee or nay, but *get thee gone!*" he thundered, his fingers clasped over the hilt of his jeweled sword.

"Do it, father," Cullen echoed softly. "I would support you in many things, but never in this treachery! Begone, before there is bloodshed."

"Aye, I'll go," Ordway seethed through clenched teeth. "But you'll rue the day you wed the Danish bitch, aye, you will, Alaric! You'll not have it all!" With that, he strode from Alaric's bower with a flurry of his dark brown mantle, leaving the air crackling in his wake.

"Believe me, cousin, neither his feelings nor his wishes are mine in this," Cullen vowed softly when he was gone. "I swear upon the hilt of my sword, they are not!"

Alaric clamped a heavy hand over his shoulder. "Nay,

Cullen, fear not, I know it. You have ever served me well. There is no one I trust more, nor any other I would rather have at my side in battle—nor on my wedding day." He forced a grin. "Smile, cousin. We'll speak more on this anon, I promise thee. But for now, are you ready to dance at my wedding, man?"

"Aye, ready enough, sir!" Cullen agreed, and arched his brows slyly. "And—to claim at last a kiss from your fair bride, as is our custom and my right!"

"Then be certain you make it a fleeting kiss. Custom or nay, I am a jealous groom!" Alaric cautioned sternly, and they both laughed and left the bower arm in arm, comrades as ever.

Chapter 36

The ceremony was simple and beautiful. In the tiny gray stone church Freya, who now bore the Christian name of Marissa, and Alaric of Kent knelt with heads bowed before the Bishop of London and repeated the vows that would bind them together as man and wife.

Mellow Latin chants floated up from the choir in the chancel, the flawless beauty of their sweet but melancholy harmony sending shivers of emotion through her. Countless tall ivory candles in elaborate golden candlesticks flickered upon the stone altar, which was draped in white silk lavishly embroidered in gold thread. Their slender flames writhed in a draught, and cast shifting light over the gloomy flagstones of the narrow church and shadows upon the rough-hewn walls. The December sunshine gleamed palely through the stained glass windows and dappled the bridal couple's faces with rainbow-colored light of blue, green, red, and amber. The pungent scent of melting wax and the fragrance of incense that had been wafted from bronze censers still lingered from the celebration of the High Mass that had preceded the ceremony. It was an evocative scent she would remember always and associate ever after with the wintry December morn she became Alaric's bride.

The feelings of foreboding that had plagued her earlier as she dressed had dissipated at some point during the service, perhaps at the moment he had slipped the wide golden wedding band upon her finger. Nerves, she decided, it had been only a bout of nerves, brought about by her fears that she would stumble over the unfamiliar words of the Christian ceremony. She had not, however; her voice had rung clear and true through the church, and her feelings of relief were mingled now with a fierce, sweet joy. Alaric loved her; he loved her deeply! The ring she now wore, his taking her in marriage despite the heated disapproval of his uncle and others had proved the depth of his feelings for her even more effectively than the tender love that glowed always in his eyes. When the fat bishop at last pronounced them man and wife and raised his jeweled hand to intone the final blessing, her heart leaped in her breast. It was done. Now, according to the church and the laws of the land of Britain, and in the eyes of all men, she was in truth his bride, Viking or nay!

They stood, and Alaric turned to her and cupped her glowing face in his palms. His wood-smoke eyes were afire with love and pride as he gazed down into her own, a gentle smile curving his chiseled mouth.

"Joy to thee, beloved wife, both on this happy day and on all those yet to come," he murmured softly. His heated gaze lingered on her lovely face in an ardent, hungry manner most unsuitable for such a holy place.

Never had he looked more handsome than he did this morn, she thought proudly as he bowed his dark head and took her gently in his arms to kiss her. His blue-gray tunic was bordered with bands of silver thread. The cloth was the exact color of his sensual eyes, and it was a hue that also accented his height and breadth magnificently. A circlet of silver studded with sapphires bound his broad, tanned brow and tamed the unruly spill of inky locks that framed his handsome face. More jewels flashed from the silver brooches at his wide shoulders, where they fastened his ermine-trimmed black mantle; still more glittered upon the hilt of his long dress broadsword and dagger. He appeared every inch a prince, as royal as the blood of the ancient kings of Kent that flowed through his veins!

Gladly she lifted her face to his and parted her lips for her lord husband's embrace, dreamily closing her eyes as his warm mouth met hers in the sweetest, most tender of kisses, to seal their vows before all.

And then it was done, and he was taking her elbow, still looking down at her with adoration and pride in his eyes as he escorted her down the aisle to the rear of the church, where Valonia and Cullen and her Uncle Sven and other guests were already gathered to congratulate them.

After the babes' baptism at the ornate stone font at the rear of the church, they would all repair to Kenley, where a lavish wedding feast of roasted boar, venison, and swan, and entertainments of musicians and tumblers and magicians awaited to delight them, she thought with anticipation, and where at last, in their bower, Alaric would make love to her for the first time as his bride and lady. Happiness swelled her heart until it seemed it must surely burst. She felt giddy, delirious with joy, as if she had already tasted of the sweet wines of Francia that would fill every drinking horn and goblet to overflowing at the feast.

She received Valonia's and Cullen's fond kisses, then glanced about. So. Ordway had carried out his threat, and had not attended the ceremony. No matter! They would survive very well without *his* dour, soured countenance to cast its gloom upon this happy occasion. Her eyes swept on, searching the crowd that milled about chattering and laughing and spouting good wishes, for Edythe and the babes. Frowning, she realized they had not yet arrived.

She forced a smile as several noblewomen from neighboring halls came to offer their congratulations and their fervent hopes that her and Alaric's marriage would cement the uneasy peace that now existed between the Danelaw and Wessex following Guthrum's ignominious defeat at London. But her mind was not really on their greetings, for all that she smiled prettily and modestly and thanked them with every appearance of warmth. Where could Edythe be? Had she not cautioned the nurse to see the babes dressed in their christening gowns and brought to the church in good time for the baptism? She sighed and shook her head. No doubt Edythe had got wind of some juicy tidbit of gossip and lingered overlong at the hall to pursue it, she decided, a trifle vexed with the garrulous girl, though in truth she was too happy to be truly angered.

She turned to look for Sven instead, and had just spied his

466

dear gray head amongst the throng when she saw that she had been mistaken. Edythe was there, after all, hanging shyly back from the group of chieftains and their ladies and retinues in a small alcove where she would not be remarked. No doubt she was overwhelmed by the cluster of nobles, and as yet unaccustomed to her own elevation in status, had determined to remain unobtrusive, Freya decided. She beckoned to her, and managed to catch her eye above the jeweled headresses and veils of the women, and the feathered soft caps of the men. Edythe's eyes lit up. She smiled and wove her way eagerly between the crowds to Freya's side. She swept Freya a deep curtsey, then clasped her hand with the new wide golden finger ring in her own work-roughened one and kissed it.

"Joy to thee and your lord husband, mistress!" she murmured, and looked up happily.

"My heartfelt thanks, Edythe," Freya responded, returning her smile with a warm one of her own, for she held a great affection for the serving wench who had befriended her during her time as a lowly slave at Kenley. "Now, if you will, where are the children? The bishop will be ready for their baptism as soon as he has changed his robes. Please fetch them to me now, pray."

The smile fled Edythe's plump, beaming face. "The babes? But—but I have them not, my lady! They were bathed and dressed in their christening gowns and caps as you wished—and what a pair of treasures they made too, bless their wee hearts!—when Lord Ordway came and said as how he himself would see the little ones brought t'the church in good time. I thought it a bit odd, in truth, mistress, but what was I, a serving wench, t'say? He smiled at me real kindly, like, and then bade me hurry to the church if I wished to see my lady make her wedding vows. I thought—I thought as how it were kind o'him t'think of me, and so—so I—I left the babes in his care, mistress!" Her lower lip quivered. "Oh, I do hope I've done naught wrong, my lady?"

The feelings of foreboding suddenly reasserted themselves in Freya's belly, a small knot of unfounded dread tightening there. 'Twas foolishness, this apprehension she felt, she told herself, but the feeling lingered nonetheless. She smiled

467

reassuringly, for the young nurse's face was stricken. "Nay, nay, Edythe, I am certain 'tis but a misunderstanding, and will be easily explained. Pray, do not concern yourself. You have done nothing wrong."

She turned to look for Alaric, who was at the center of a group of chieftains, receiving hearty thumps of congratulations across the back and laughingly fielding the men's bawdy comments about his forthcoming wedding night, and the beauty and desirability of his Danish bride.

Freya hovered anxiously on the fringes of the group, waiting for a lull in the conversation to make known her presence and her desire to speak with him. Endless minutes seemed to pass before a portly thane became aware of her.

"Why, Alaric, you fortunate cur, here is thy lovely bride now!" He grinned broadly. "No doubt the Lady Freya is unable to bear being parted from thee for overlong, eh, m'dear?" He winked. "I look forward to claiming a kiss from the bride at the wedding feast! Ah, you've found yourself a beauty, Alaric!"

Alaric grinned and offering his apologies, drew away from the crowd gathered about him. "Indeed I have, Hubert! What is it, my lady wife?" he asked, his dark brows knotting as he saw that her expression was troubled.

"The children, Alaric," she began. "Edythe was to escort them to the church. She is here, but came alone. She tells me your uncle saw fit to take the babes' charge upon himself, and said he would see them brought here for the baptism. Was— was it upon your command he did so, my lord?" she finished, hoping, oh *ja*, hoping desperately, it was so.

"Ordway?" His frown deepened. "At my command? Nay, Freya, it was not." He turned to the gathering, and offered them a curt half bow. "By your leave—?" he muttered, and turned away from them, taking Freya by the elbow and drawing her aside. Edythe joined them. "Tell me what happened, girl?" Alaric demanded, and haltingly Edythe repeated what she had told Freya. His expression of concern had deepened when Edythe, breathless with fright now, ended her tale.

"What is it, cousin? Is something awry?" Cullen inquired,

joining them. Valonia was at his side. They sensed that something was deeply wrong.

"My lady aunt, do you know where my son and daughter might be?" Alaric asked.

"Edythe was to bring them in the litter, was she not?" Valonia murmured, glancing from Freya's worried face and back to Alaric's. "Are they not here yet?"

"Nay, my lady," Alaric said brusquely, and strode away from them toward the church door, Freya dogging his heels.

"Where would Ordway have taken them, Alaric? And—for what reason?" she asked as they came out into the churchyard, which was powdered with snow. Despite the tight control she attempted to exercise on her emotions, there was an edge of fear to her tone.

"I know not," Alaric gritted, heading across the churchyard to where several horse thanes and grooms held restless mounts or lounged alongside litters beneath the towering yews and cypresses, waiting for their masters and mistresses to leave the little church. Freya followed, all but running to keep up with his long, swift strides.

He went from litter to litter, drawing aside the curtains to look within each one. Nothing. Wherever Ordway might have taken his son and daughter, it was not to the church as he had promised, he realized, and apprehension knotted his gut. *You will not have it all*. Ordway's parting words that morning suddenly echoed unbidden in his head, and seemed no longer the thoughtless, irrational words of an angry man, but threatening and ominous. What had his uncle meant?

"Fetch my horse, and hurry!" he snapped to a groom, and the man tore away to do his bidding, impelled by the smoldering fury in his master's eyes.

"What is it? What do you know?" Freya demanded, her sapphire eyes wide with fear as she saw his grim expression.

"Perhaps 'tis naught, but Ordway and I quarreled this morning. He made certain—threats—that I thought naught of at the time, but now—!"

"You fear he—he has taken our children!" she whispered, her mouth suddenly tasting like cotton with fear.

"I do," Alaric confirmed softly, unable to meet her eyes.

469

The groom came at a run then, leading a frisky Lucifer. The black stallion curvetted and snorted, fresh and eager to be off. Alaric took the reins and swung himself into the saddle in one lithe move.

"Have Cullen call out the garrison," he commanded the groom curtly, gathering the reins in his fists. "Tell him I want this burh and the surrounding countryside scoured for Lord Ordway and my children. And bid him instruct his men to take care, should they find them, to take no risks that will endanger the little ones. You understand, man?"

"I do, sir!"

Freya ran to Alaric's stallion, grasping the bridle even as he would have spurred the great, black beast into a gallop. Lucifer's wicked hooves flashed dangerously as he was brought up short by her action. The stallion screamed in thwarted fury. "Wait, my lord! I would go with you!" she cried.

"Nay, Freya. Stay here. I will not have you endangered also. Wait on my return at the hall! Get up, there!" With that, he lashed his reins across Lucifer's rump, and the black stallion exploded into a gallop across the powdery snow, ebony tail and mane streaming in the crisp wind.

"Confound it, I'll not twiddle my thumbs and do nothing, I'll not!" Freya muttered under her breath, and flung about, quickly scanning the waiting horses. She had arrived at the church carried in a servant-borne litter and had no mount here, but a bright chestnut gelding seemed a strong, speedy steed. "Here you, lad, hand me up!" she cried to a stableboy who held its head, and the lad, astonished by her request, did so. No sooner was she secure in the saddle when, as Alaric had done seconds before, she wheeled her horse's head about and kneed him away from the church.

As she rode out, she heard the frantic clamor of the convent bell of Our Lady of the Sea on the wintry air, muffled by distance. Despite her deepening anxiety, her mind dimly registered that the strident clanging sounded an alarm of some sort, before she was forced to devote all her concentration to controlling her headstrong mount and smother her fretting over the abduction of her babes.

*   *   *

Ordway tugged at the scratchy woolen mantle he had donned against the bitter weather, feeling sweat begin a slow trickling down his spine.

For all that snow lay upon the ground all about the convent of Our Lady of the Sea, inside this spartan cell carved from the cliffs themselves the air seemed stifling! Was it so—or was it but the closeness, the oppressive atmosphere that made it seem overly warm?

Candles burned upon every available space; there were candles and luminaries everywhere, set in puddles of melted wax. They were the cheap, three-a-penny candles of the poor, made of smelly mutton tallow. Their heavy, greasy odor made him want to retch. The slitted windows were festooned with fusty sackcloth that kept out both light and air. The rough-hewn walls were graced with threadbare tapestries depicting vile scenes of hell-fire and damnation; sinners' souls suffering in Purgatory throughout eternity, in countless agonizing fashions. Sweat broke out upon his brow and ran down his ruddy face. His palms were wet. Jesu, he needed air, fresh, bracing, cold air—and badly!

He swore under his breath as he looked across the cell to where Kendra knelt before a little statue of the Virgin, her head bowed, her lips moving in silent but fervent prayer. Pious, fanatical bitch! he thought sourly, still astonished at the transformation the past year had wrought in her, since Alaric had sent her away from Kenley.

She wore the rough, simple kirtle of a holy sister now, and a coarse, dark veil upon her head. Her luxuriant black hair, now threaded thickly with silver, had been cropped raggedly short, he had observed when he entered the cell, no doubt as a symbol of her rejection of worldly pride and mortal vanity. A heavy rosary hung from her belt, which was of simple, fraying rope like that of the poorest serf. God's Blood! Though he knew she had not taken holy vows, she might as well have, he thought angrily. There was no trace left in her of the lusty bitch she had been. His hopes that she could be cajoled into doing his bidding were dwindling rapidly. Nevertheless, he had to try!

"Get up off your knees, girl, and heed me!" he demanded angrily, fists planted on his hips. "Will you do it or nay? 'Twill only be for a short while. I—I need a day or so to talk with

Alaric once more, to convince him his marriage with that—that Danish woman must be dissolved, at once. What harm could a few days do?" he coaxed.

Yet Kendra was not so easily swayed. She rose and turned to face Ordway, pious disapproval stamped on her still lush features. Her moist cherry-red lips were yet wide and sensual, her eyes still seductive, golden orbs fringed with sooty black lashes. Both were incongruous against the almost milky pallor of her complexion, which had seen neither air nor sun for many months, and her severe, shapeless garments, which gave no hint of the once-voluptuous figure beneath their folds.

"I told thee once, uncle, but I will tell thee again," she said sharply, "I want no part of your plot! I was once an innocent, helpless babe such as they. But in shame at my bastard's birth, my dear mother, our revered Lady Abbess, deserted me and entered this very convent to hide from her shame. I will bring no such unhappiness as I have known upon the heads of such innocent babes! If you would hide them from Alaric, you must find another to help you."

"Pah! Do you speak so piously, my dear, when you know full well you murdered your own husband in cold blood? Aye, and no doubt old Lona too! You cursed murderess—you hypocrite! My lady wife and I raised thee as our own, loved you as a daughter. Is this the way you repay our generosity?" he ranted.

"Loved me, uncle? Nay, I think not! 'Twas Alaric and Farant you and my dear aunt loved, aye, and Cullen too—never me, never poor little Kendra. A peasant's bastard was not worthy of your love! If I looked for love elsewhere, then 'twas your doing!" she said bitterly, the jealousy of a lifetime in her tone.

"Nonsense," Ordway snapped. "You will put up this pretense and heed me at once, girl!" he thundered.

"'Tis no pretense," Kendra retorted indignantly, tossing her head. "Aye, I have sinned in the past, and broken more than one Commandment. But I seek now to redeem myself in the eyes of God. The foul mortal desires that once plagued my weak and worldly mortal body and threatened my immortal soul—lust, avarice, and so forth—have been purged now,

472

uncle. I have known—aye, and welcomed!—the rigors of the hair shirt, the agony of scourging and self-flagellation, and have accepted all penances for my sins with gladness—aye, gladness, uncle!" Her golden eyes glittered with her fervor. "Nay. I will not do your bidding. Return the children to their mother where they belong, and leave me in peace."

In fury, Ordway lost control. First Alaric, then Cullen, his own son, this morning, and now Kendra. Everyone had turned against him, everyone, after all he had done for them, for Kenley! By God, they *owed* him more than this! His fist came up, and with an obscenity he struck Kendra full in the mouth. She flew backward with a startled cry, scarlet blood spilling from her cherry-red mouth. As she fell, her head slammed hard against the stone floor; her arm flailed out and toppled a small table upon which the candles she kept lit day and night against the terrors of darkness burned brightly. The candles fell, and she screamed once as hot, melted wax splashed onto her face, plucking weakly at her cheeks before she lay ominously still.

A candle flame caught the fringed border of a dusty tapestry, licked at the dry threads, traveled up them and gained volume as they went, the narrow tongue of fire engorging on the cloth and bursting into a bright conflagration. The pillar of fire roared and reached greedy fingers to the next tapestry and the next, building, building all the while, consuming all in its path in a hell-fire more dire than any the tapestries had once depicted.

The sackcloth at the narrow window slits went next, and the smoldering rags crumbled and blackened, the tatters glowing redly, separating. They fell to the narrow cot below, where they quickly devoured the brown woolen blankets and the strawfilled pallet.

With the sackcloth gone from the window slits, fresh air rushed into the cell. The fire leaped up to twice its former size, roaring now as it drew a greedy, life-giving breath. Black smoke belched out into the cell.

Ordway, who had witnessed the start of the fire in frozen, horrified fascination, began to cough, the smoke filling his nostrils and lungs. Tongues of fire and crackling flames were

473

everywhere about him now, doing merry little dances over chair and desk, robed in scarlet and crimson, orange and amber for their hideous revels. The heat caressed his face, scorched it, and singed his eyebrows and hair. The pain jolted him into action. He saw Kendra, still sprawled on the floor of the cell, unconscious from her fall and his blow. Flames were greedily peeling the dark robes from her body and feasting on her hair, stroking the marble pallor of her limbs like an ardent lover; the last paramour she would ever know, he thought absently. 'Tis too late for you now, Kendra. You brought this upon yourself. You should have heeded your uncle, girl, he told her silently as he flung about and pulled open the heavy cell door.

Air billowed into the cell, and the flames rolled forward to welcome it in a crimson-armed embrace, cackling and chuckling their sly greetings. Ordway flung himself through the doorway and out into the narrow corridor beyond, his eyes red-rimmed and streaming from the smoke, coughing as he clawed blindly for fresh air. Threadbare, faded runners of carpeting softened the cold stone floor. The grasping fire saw it and coveted it, and like a jealous child snatched greedily at it, racing after Ordway as it gobbled up the carpeting behind him in a terrifying game of tag. It leaped into the next open doorway, and the next cell and the next and the next, lapping at vestments and robes, at priceless manuscripts and heavy furniture, nothing spared its voracious appetite.

Panic filled Ordway now. Where had he left the basket with the brats? In the infirmary, he thought, but in his panic he could not be certain. His brain seemed dulled, his thoughts confused, his memory vague. No matter! he decided hurriedly. The convent was afire, and his sister Wilone must be taken outside, to safety. Aye, dear Wilone! Her survival came before that of the Viking slut's bastard babes. But—which way was it to Wilone's cell? The smoke was thick now, his surroundings unfamiliar. He stumbled on, still coughing, his lungs raw and nigh bursting with agony.

From afar he could hear terrified female screams and desperate shrieks of "Fire! Fire!" coupled with loud crashes and the breathy roar of the flames themselves that reminded him of the roar of the surf against the shore below. Above it all came the distant, strident clanging of the warning bell that was set in the stone wall by the convent gates.

In his confusion to find his sister, he did not associate the sound with the fire raging about him, but thought only with helpless fury that the cursed Viking sea-wolves were raiding Kenley yet again . . .

Chapter 37

Alaric hauled hard on the reins to halt his horse as the snorting black beast careened up the slight incline that led to the convent. So abrupt was his handling of the reins that the frightened beast reared up on its haunches, hooves pawing the air above the crystal whiteness of the snow drifts beneath, its breath steaming on the frosty air. Foam flecked its mouth.

His master noticed none of his steed's discomfort, for his gray eyes were filled with shocked denial as he saw the nightmare ahead.

Flames leaped up from the gray of the blackened convent walls, crackling as they devoured the remnants of summer vines and leaped to turn the yew trees that bowered the convent into giant, flaming torches. Thick clouds of black smoke billowed up and hung in the pale blue wintry sky like a funeral pall. Small figures were scurrying about like fat beetles in their somber, shapeless robes. He heard the holy sisters' frightened cries carried on the wind, could discern which of them was the buxom Abbess Aethelfreda, Kendra's mother, with her arm imperiously outstretched to add weight to some command or other.

But this was not the worst he saw, for even as he was about to turn in the saddle to look behind, where Freya, mounted on her borrowed chestnut horse, even now galloped toward him, he spied another horse, a showy, black-stockinged bay, being led away from the scene of the fire by one of the nuns—and knew the horse for his uncle's own!

Sweet Christ, nay! The breath seemed to congeal in his lungs and choke him. For a horrible moment he was frozen by dread. Ordway was here, somewhere. Then so too must his babes be here. Please God, let them yet live! The moment's dread passed. He could move, could act again, as he must.

He urged his horse on up the incline, whipping it furiously, knowing only that he had to reach the convent before his lady wife, must *know* before she reached it . . .

The stallion slithered a little on the wet going as he thundered nearer, for the heat from the fire had melted the snow all about the convent walls. Lucifer screamed in terror and shied nervously at the acrid scent of fire on the wind.

Alaric slithered down from his back and was running in the same instant, racing to the front of the convent and the charred convent gates, before which the holy sisters huddled together and shivered in shock and cold or knelt in prayer, or simply watched the fire, quite numbed. He scanned their numbers, his eyes darkening to the color of slate. He saw no smiling sister with his babes cradled safely in her arms. Nor his lady mother, Wilone. Nor even his cursed uncle—

"Nay!" he roared, and hurled himself forward toward the convent.

He had gone only a half dozen paces, had but grasped the wall to climb over it when the blistering heat forced him back, singeing his dark hair. He felt nothing, heard only the throb of his pulse, grown deafening in his ears, as he saw close up the thick, choking black smoke, saw the roaring orange and yellow of the flames that licked and writhed about the convent's charred carcass.

With a sick twisting in his gut he reeled away, staggering like a drunkard in his anguish. No one could possibly have survived, not in that inferno, he acknowledged silently. He felt something wet splash against his cheek, and realized, with a vague sensation of surprise, that he was weeping as he stood there, unmanned for the moment, looking down at his raw, blistered hands and wondering what had befallen them.

Then a woman's wail of grief lanced through his daze. He looked up to see Freya topple from her horse, regain her footing, and begin running, flying over the snowy ground toward the convent, her face the color of ashes, her eyes wild in her terror.

Before he knew it he was up and heading toward her to cut her off, reaching for her wrists and spinning her about to face him. She fought him like a mad thing, like a wild creature crazed with pain.

"Nay! Let me go! Let me go, curse thee!" she screamed hoarsely, clawing and biting to free herself of his grip. "Do you think I know not? Nay! I saw his horse, I *saw* it! He brought them here, damn his soul! Let me go to them!"

He threw his arms about her and used all his strength to hold her fast, drag her back. "'Tis too late, too late, Freya, do you hear me? There is nothing you can do for them now," he shouted as she writhed.

"I can save them," she whimpered. "I know I can! Please, Alaric, oh please! Let me go damn you damn you damn you let me go to my babes oh God, nay, nay, oh God—oh God—!" she screamed as he lifted her from her feet and dragged her back to safety.

He slapped her hard across the cheek, slapped her so hard his knuckles rang with the pain. Her head flew back, the circlet and veils she had worn so proudly that morning wresting free of their pins and spilling to the snow.

"Let me go!" she sobbed more quietly now, shaking her head from side to side. The imprint of his fingers was livid against her pallor. "They need—they need their mother, don't you see, Alaric? They're so little yet, and they need me . . ." Her eyes were blank, glazed with shock and denial. "They'll be hungry very soon. I must—"

"They have perished!" Alaric ground out through clenched teeth, shaking her roughly. Something within him flinched at his brutal callousness, but he knew this once he must be cruel to be kind, both for her sake and his own. He'd lost his children, his mother, and no doubt his uncle too, this day. He could not bear to lose her too, to madness brought about by grief! "Listen to me, Freya, and mark me well, my only love. Beorn and Edana are no more. They are dead, gone!"

A wail of such abject grief came from her that for a second he feared the shock of his words, the brutal truth of them, had killed her. But then he saw the mask into which her features had composed themselves crumple, contort. "My babes?" she whispered, the flower of her mouth bruised and quivering, her sapphire eyes awash with tears. "My babes are dead!" A massive shudder ran through her. "Oh Alaric, oh Blessed God, why, why . . . ?"

She stumbled blindly into his arms, groping for him as if he were a lifeline and she, drowning. She clung to him and buried her face against him, her tears soaking his chest, his own soaking her hair as they clung tightly to each other and wept. He cared not a damn if it was unmanly to weep. The grief in his heart was too great for any pretense at masculine courage.

For some time he simply held her thus, stroking her hair over and over, whispering endearments and offering his strength and comfort to the slender body that shook uncontrollably in his arms. When the worst of her weeping had died away to muffled sobs, he set her gently from him and removed his mantle, draping it warmly about her shoulders. Then he lifted her into his arms and bore her slowly away from the smoking convent, to where the nuns and their lady abbess congregated, offering prayers as they knelt in the snow for the deliverance of the many, and for the souls of those pitiful few who had perished.

When their devotions were completed, the Abbess Aethelfreda drew away from the others and came across the snow to Alaric. Her broad, plump face was pale and solemn, her wimple and robe scorched black in many places, yet her tawny eyes were bright with resolve and her carriage dignified and determined.

"My lord?" she said, touching his shoulder.

"Aye, my lady abbess?" Alaric responded by rote, his words flat and emotionless. "Was Kendra—?"

"Aye, I believe so," she said softly. "Pray, will you not set your lady down here?" She gestured to a spot devoid of snow, in the lee of a great black rock. "'Tis dry, and shielded from the wind. She can rest there in some little comfort. When she is settled I would speak with thee, my lord, if I may?"

Alaric met her eyes, hesitated only briefly, and then nodded. He tenderly set Freya down where she had bidden, and drew the mantle up about her throat. Her eyes fluttered open, the tawny lashes spiked with tears.

"Nay. Don't leave me. Not yet!" she whispered brokenly.

"I'll not. The abbess wishes to speak with me. We can talk here, beside you, never fear." He turned to face Aethelfreda. "My lady?"

"My lord, you must know that my heart goes out to you and your lady in your grief, and that we will all pray for you both to find peace and acceptance of God's will, and for the souls of those you have lost this day."

"My thanks and our sympathies on your own losses," Alaric rejoined tersely, his words curt in his grief.

Aethelfreda nodded, pity in her expression. "Indeed, I thank God that only two of my sisters were trapped. A handful suffered injuries, but none of a grave nature, thanks be. My lord, I—I can scarce find the words to say what I must say, for I fear to offer thee hope when all hope may yet come to naught . . ." She frowned and wrung her hands anxiously together.

"Hope?" It was Alaric's turn to frown now. "Did you say hope?"

"Aye. A small hope, but a hope nonetheless. You will recall, no doubt, how it was with your—your lady mother; that on several occasions she evaded our nursing sisters in the infirmary, and wandered the shore and the headlands? It is unlikely, I know, but since she knew of the passage, I—I but wondered if mayhap—?"

"The passageway? God's Blood, aye! Ordway and my lady mother might well have tried to escape through the passageway!" Alaric breathed, and a light kindled in his eyes.

"What passage is this?" Freya demanded, struggling to sit up. At once Alaric moved to press her back down, but with an angry shrug she cast off his hands. "What passage?" she repeated. "If there is a chance, however fragile, I must know of it. Any chance must be explored!"

"Aye," Alaric agreed, frowning, wondering if she could withstand still another cruel blow if this new thread of hope was unrealized. "After your father raided Kenley and ransacked the convent those many years ago, my lord uncle

Ordway instructed his stone mason to channel a passage from the convent infirmary down through the cliffs to the shore. It was thought the holy sisters could use the passage to flee the Vikings, should our coast ever be raided again. They did so that day you and your followers attacked my burh, and from that time my mother would often seek escape from the confines of the convent and her caretakers, and roam the headlands and the beach alone."

"So!" Freya exclaimed softly. "It *was* she I glimpsed those times—her presence that I sensed once, in the sea cave! 'Tis there the passage ends, is it not, Alaric?" There was a breathless eagerness to her now, a hectic fire in her cheeks that frightened him.

"Aye," he agreed, "it is. We all swore to my uncle that we would never reveal the existence of the tunnel—and especially not to thee, my heart, a Viking woman!" He grimaced, his expression apologetic. "I know thee better now. But do not hope for too much, I beg you. Perhaps my uncle had no chance to use the passage—perhaps the fire cut him off from its entrance. And—and even should he be there, there is still no guarantee that he took the babes with him. You understand?"

"I understand," she agreed readily. "We must go there, at once!"

"By your leave, Lady Freya, you cannot just yet," the abbess disagreed with obvious reluctance. "You see, when the tide turns, the cave and much of the passage fills with sea water. There is no means to learn if anyone escaped the fire until this evening, at dusk, when the tide again goes out and the cave is exposed."

"*If* Ordway is indeed trapped there, and *if* he remembers the dangers of high tide," Alaric corrected grimly. He paused, then added softly, "You're wrong, abbess. There is another way to find out. I intend to take it."

"But how?" exclaimed the abbess.

"I shall swim through the cave and into the passage, and see for myself!" he vowed.

The sea was no longer the deep blue-green of summer and

481

flat as a millpond. It was grayish-green now, tinged with sullen yellow, and the waves were choppy and rimmed with sluggish, dingy froth. As the abbess had said, the tide had come in. Where they had once raced their horses along the sand and shingle was now deep under water. So was the sea-cave filled, until naught could be seen of the entrance save a small, dark hole that remained above the waterline.

They had mounted up and ridden their horses down the narrow, rocky defile that led to the beach after hearing the abbess's words, but could go no farther on account of the tide. Cullen had joined them now, along with some men from the garrison, having heard the warning bell and seen the smoke from afar, as had they. His face was grave, his eyes shadowed by grief as he looked down at the pounding sea below their feet.

"'Tis my feeling you should wait, Alaric," he urged somberly. "It would be foolhardy to attempt to swim it now. Look how the sea rages, sir!"

Alaric's jaw tightened. He pulled his tunic up over his head and cast it aside; his boots and weapons followed. He shivered in the frigid air, his flat nipples puckering amidst the dark furring across his broad chest, his black hair furling in the cold wind. His expression was resolute, his mind made up.

"I must," he said simply, and clambered down the rocky shelf to the sea. A moment more, and he had arched forward and dived into the icy water.

Freyja held her breath until she saw his dark head crest amidst the green-gray waves. He was swimming steadily, strongly, without haste toward the cave mouth, his powerful arms arcing above the surface as he drew ever closer. She pulled the folds of his mantle tighter about her, nuzzling the nubbled weave of it, inhaling his dear, manly scent that clung to it and offering up a prayer for his safety.

"He's there!"

She heard Cullen speak and glanced up sharply. Sure enough, Alaric had reached the cave mouth. Now came the hardest part of all. He must draw breath, and hold it, then dive beneath the water and find the entrance to the tunnel. Of a sudden, she feared for him. She had not once seen him swim before, let alone dive. Could he succeed?

482

She watched intently as he waved to reassure them, and then saw him draw a breath, then another and another, before he ducked quickly below the water.

"He can't do it, he can't!" she whispered, not realizing she had voiced her fears aloud. "Too many, too fast!"

"My lady?" Cullen queried.

"You cannot dive so," she told him quickly, peeling off mantle and headdress as she spoke. "Believe me, sir, I could swim before I walked. I know of what I speak! The children of Denmark all but live in the sea. We learn very young to dive, drawing deep, full breaths. Do you know what happens when one tries to dive after taking short breaths such as those Alaric took?"

"Nay?" Cullen replied, concern in his eyes.

"Everything goes black! The swimmer loses consciousness. Can you swim?" Seeing him nod, she peeled off her kirtle and stood there, shivering in the wind wearing only her thin linen under-kirtle. "Then come on, Cullen. I'll need your help too. We must go after him!"

Cullen nodded.

The water was freezing. As they plunged in, it was as if they had been struck a mortal blow. Nonetheless, they struck out at once for the cave, Freya's arms cleaving strongly through the choppy water, her slender yet wiry body as lithe and at home as any mermaid's. Cullen trailed valiantly after her, more accustomed to the back of a horse than the sea.

They had swum only halfway to the cave when Freya saw Alaric's dark head. He was lolling face down in the water, his limp body tossed hither and thither at will by the waves. Freya reached him first and turned him onto his back, holding his face above the surface as Cullen padded toward her. In seconds he coughed and came to, for the unconsciousness did not last overlong.

"Here, Cullen, swim back with him to the cliffs!" she cried, spitting salt water herself. Her teeth chattered with the cold.

"What about you?" he asked, reaching for Alaric.

"I have to know, I have to!" she told him earnestly. "You understand, *ja?* If—if there is indeed cause for hope, I'll send up a signal—something—and wait until the tide recedes, yes?"

483

"Aye," he yelled back. "Good fortune, my brave lady!"

With a wan smile, she turned and kicked out for the cave, her red-gold head as sleek as an otter's amidst the gray-green swells.

There was the cave mouth, directly ahead. She tread water and let the tide carry her onward, resting a little as she did so, conserving her strength. She ducked her head as the current carried her inside the cave, out of the cold brilliance of the winter's day into pitch-darkness.

She had not thought to ask Alaric where the entrance lay. She would have to find it alone. She relaxed, letting herself go limp, forcing her grief, her worries, to recede as she tried to remember—to remember that day they had loved in this very cave; the first time Alaric had shown her the rapture of their joining. They had lain upon the damp sand, the craggy walls on either side of them. She could recall no opening of any kind, but then she had not explored the darkness at the rear of the cave. That was where the tunnel must lie, she decided. She would try there first. She drew several deep, cleansing breaths, filling her lungs with air, then without urgency or haste she plunged head-first down into the black water, striking out for the direction in which she fancied she would find the opening.

Her fingers touched rocky walls. Fumbling along them, letting the air stream slowly, a little at a time, from her mouth, she searched to her right, following the cave wall with her fingertips. Nothing. She rose slowly to the surface and turned to see where the light was, trying to get her bearings. There. She had it. This time she would dive straight down again, and search to her left. There was no other methodical way of searching that she could think of. More deep breaths, and she disappeared once more.

She was beginning to despair, to believe she would have to resurface for air a third time, when her fingers closed on— nothing! The walls of the cave fell away beneath her touch, disclosing a wide opening big enough for even a fair-sized man to stoop through, had the tide been out. Once again she resurfaced, but when next she dived she swam unerringly down and straight into the tunnel.

As the abbess had warned them, the passageway was

underwater for many feet. Her lungs felt nigh to bursting with lack of air! Could she hold out any longer, could she . . . ?

And then, when she least expected it, her head broke the surface! Blackness was everywhere—her eyes could discern nothing—but she was no longer underwater. She had made it!

She rested a little while, and then hauled herself out, momentarily finding purchase on a rocky ledge before staggering onward, her head bent, her arms outstretched on either side to guide her.

The passage angled steeply upward a little further on, and she stumbled. Groping with her fingers, she felt ledges rising away from her; shallow steps cut from the cliff itself. She went up them, excitement mounting along with her dread. How far had she come? Was she anywhere near the surface? Oh Blessed Virgin, Mary, Mother of Christ, you know more than any woman the agony of losing a child. Let my little ones be alive! she prayed fervently.

And then, from the tunnel ahead, she heard the low humming of a lullaby. The hackles rose on her neck and she froze in place.

"All safe!" crooned a voice she knew when the lullaby ended; the voice of a madwoman that had once haunted her dreams. "All safe!"

A great sob of joy burst upward from her breast as she heard the lullaby answered—by a baby's gurgling crow of delight.

Epilogue

Twelfth Night came, and all the isle of Britain still lay in sparkling winter's thrall.

The winding River Thames shimmered under silvery-gray ice, its flow stilled, its mirrorlike surface reflecting pale skies and ashen clouds. The long-eared brown hares, ancient symbols of fertility and the endless cycles of birth, life, and death, now wore coats of wintry white as they bounded through wood and field, dimpling the powdery snow. They would not dance by moonlight again until spring once more flowered across the land of Kent.

Yet within the hall of Kenley all was merriment and laughter, warmth and light. The wedding feast of the chieftain, Alaric the Bear, and his lady, Marissa, had continued for a full fourteen nights, spilling over into the glad festivities of Yule.

Beside the hearth in the great hall the shaggy hunting hounds dozed and dreamed of lazy summer hunts, while the festive yule log crackled and snapped merrily, showering sparks to the rushes, which were quickly stamped out by the serving maids and lads who congregated about its warmth, skewering chestnuts upon dagger points and eagerly popping the hot, roasted treats into their mouths.

Soldiers of the garrison pursued the giggling kitchen wenches with sprigs of mistletoe brandished aloft, threatening lusty kisses and promising long, cold winter's nights spent warmly cuddled together under heaped furs, while upon a low, carved stool sat the old Viking *skald*, Sven of Danehof, plucking his harp and singing his minstrel songs. When he was done and the vibrating strings' sweet harmony had trembled away to silence, the company implored him to sing another, but the *skald* laughingly declined, insisting his throat was quite parched from so many lengthy sagas, and that he must wet it before continuing.

He made his way to the groaning trestle tables lining the aisled hall, laden with slabs of roasted beef, joints of mutton, venison, quail, and other delicacies, where his Freya was filling her husband's drinking horn with ale and laughing happily up into his smiling face as he teased her about something or other.

Inwardly, Sven sighed with relief and contentment. Despite everything, despite the whims of fate and the greed and foibles of men, they were together at last, their enemies defeated.

Valonia, in her newly widowed state, kept quietly to her bower or spent many hours in the little chapel in solitary prayer, but time would heal her grief. She knew naught of her husband Ordway's duplicity, or that 'twas his actions, born of greed and covetousness, that had almost cost the dear little babes she doted upon their innocent lives. Nor would she ever learn of it, for Freya and Alaric had determined to let the gentle Saxon lady's memories of her husband remain untarnished, and had told her nothing. As far as she and many others at Kenley were concerned, the fire had been but a tragic accident occurring when Ordway had gone to visit his sister at the convent of Our Lady of the Sea.

For Wilone's part, she seemed much improved since the day Freya had found her and the twins unharmed in the sea cave, where she had carried the infants to safety, no doubt remembering—despite her confusion—how she had once protected and hidden her own babes from danger. With the convent in ruins, she had come to live with Alaric and Freya at Kenley. She had proven touchingly gentle with her grandchildren, and seemed calm and serene when she cradled them in her arms and sang them the lullabies she had once sung her own children.

She had not spoken falsely to Thorfast that fateful day long ago, when she had said that children were a man's link with the

487

gods, his claim upon immortality, Sven recalled. Thorfast and Verdandi's proud Danish blood lived on in Freya and Alaric's children, and would continue on in their grandchildren and their grandchildren's children throughout eternity, as would the royal Saxon blood of Aeldred and Wilone herself. *Ja,* so it was the cycle of life went on through the ages, and would till the end of time! He could return to the monastery at Mucking on the next fairweather day without worrying for the future, knowing his Freya—who even now, after twenty long years, still held his heart tightly in her little fist—had found in Alaric a man to love, and be loved by, at last!

He glanced up to see that Freya, robed for the revels in saffron and sporting a little gold mask sewn with topazes, was beckoning to him. He came toward her, smiling fondly.

"Come, uncle, and sit here beside me," she invited him, smiling winningly herself. "We will watch the dancing together."

He accepted her invitation and the horn of mead she poured for him, leaning back comfortably as a troupe of masked players entered the hall and made their bows to the lord and lady. Soon the mellow notes of flutes and the lively, tapping rhythm of a tambour rose above the chattering of the throng. Tables were thrust back to provide more room. Laughing couples, their faces hidden by masks of animals or birds or fantasy creatures, joined hands and ran to form the circles of the dance. All bowed or curtsied to their partners, and then they began.

One of the players set aside his instrument and wove his way between the dancers to stand before Alaric's table. He made a gallant bow to Freya, and proffered his hand.

"Will you honor me with a dance, Lady Marissa?" he asked, the edges of his merry mouth curving in a smile. His eyes were concealed by a ram's-head mask with curling horns, his voice muffled under its hollow confines.

Laughing, Freya accepted. "I will, my lord of Misrule!" she cried, coming eagerly around the table toward him. "Tell me, Cullen, have you enjoyed your naughty reign this festive tide?"

"'Tis not Cullen, I regret, fairest of the fair, but another who sighs over thy radiant beauty!" the man declared. He reached to her braided coronet of red-gold hair, and her eyes widened behind her mask as he plucked a prettily carved comb of pale morse ivory, studded with sapphires, from thin air. "A yuletide favor for thee, mistress," he declared, "with jewels to match thy sparkling eyes hidden beneath that mask!"

"Robin?" She squealed with delight. "Oh Robin, I know full well 'tis thee! Take off that wretched mask, do, and let me see you at once, pray!"

He did as requested, and moments later she was delightedly looking up into the elfin face and twinkling dark eyes she remembered so well. He was unchanged, his unruly mop of dark curls as unruly as ever, his smile the roguish one she loved. He extended his hand and lightly touched her shoulder in greeting.

"Well, sir!" she pouted, merriment twitching the corners of her mouth. "Is that how you greet an old friend such as I? Where is my welcoming kiss?"

He threw back his head and roared with laughter. "In truth, mistress, I would kiss you and show you the full measure of my happiness to see thee—but alas, see how your lord husband glowers at me! In faith, I am no swordsman but a lowly minstrel, and fear his warrior's anger—and his blade!"

"You lie, knave," Freya teased, eyeing Alaric's scowling face. "I know thee too well. There is naught you fear, for all your merry jests! Come, drink with us, eat at our table. But first I would have you meet my lord husband."

"Meet?" He laughed again. "There is no need to introduce us, *aelfsciene*. We are already old friends, veterans of Aethelred's camp many years ago. By your leave?"

He made his way to Alaric, and they clasped hands warmly.

"Festive greetings, my lord," Robin greeted him.

"And to thee, rogue," Alaric rejoined with a grin.

"You appear content, sir. It would seem my advice to thee in London was taken without regrets?" Robin added softly.

"Without a one, knave," the ealdorman agreed, equally softly.

"And was my gift to the lady given?"

"The silver ball?" Alaric shook his head. "Nay—and nor

489

will I ever give it her! A fool I might have been once, but never twice! See how my lady wife's smile yet lingers fondly upon thee, Robin of London? I like it not! I lost her once, but will take no chances of doing so again.''

"You grow wiser with age, my friend!"

"As do we all. Tell me, when must you depart my burh?''

"Depart? God's Blood, I am but newly come here, sir!" Robin exclaimed, aghast.

''Then of course you must stay the night, and we will grieve sorely to bid thee fond farewell on the morrow.''

Robin grimaced. ''The lengthy extent of your hospitality overwhelms me, sir!''

"I thought mayhap it might," Alaric agreed, smiling wickedly.

Freya watched the exchange, wanting to laugh. The two men were like fighting cocks in a pit, circling and angrily ruffling their feathers before flying into a furious fight. It was flattering to think that she was the cause, but she would not have them at each others' throats on any account. They were both too dear to her to become enemies.

"My lord husband!" she called, drawing Alaric's immediate attention. "Will you not dance with your lady?"

He willingly agreed, and offering Robin a smug smile and bidding him help himself to drink and meats, he took her hand and led her onto the rushes.

Freya rested her palm upon Alaric's, her eyes seductive through the slits of the golden mask.

"Are you in truth jealous of Robin, my lord?" she asked curiously as they moved together, then apart, to the lilting strains of the music.

"Green with jealousy, my heart!" Alaric declared, his woodsmoke eyes gleaming.

"There is no cause for it, sir, believe me," she reassured him, a little breathlessly, for the smoldering ardor in his eyes was playing havoc with her breathing. "We are but old friends, nothing more. My—my heart is slave to no man but thee!"

"In truth? Then must you prove it, sweet wife," he challenged her teasingly, turning her about him as they danced and casually brushing his fingers against the full swell of her

490

breast as he did so. Spanning her slender waist, he observed, was the yuletide gift he had given her but days before, a belt of round golden links. Upon each link was etched the image of a bounding hare. They both fondly remembered the long ago eve they had witnessed the Hares' Dance together, for it was the first time they confessed their love to each other. He had had the belt fashioned for her with this in mind.

Desire leaped through her. "Of a certainty I will prove my love for thee anon, my lord!" she assured him, her voice grown husky now.

He nodded. "When the dance is done, we will to bed, agreed?" His gray eyes raked her with the searing intimacy of a caress.

Under his lambent gaze her nipples hardened against the cloth of her gown. Though he had barely touched her, she trembled with the potency of her desire. So it was between them always, she reflected happily, and would be for all time to come.

"Agreed," she whispered in answer to his invitation, and let him lead her on.

But the intricate steps had quite flown from her mind, she found! She moistened her lips with her tongue tip, and they glistened in the rushlights. She gazed up at Alaric seductively, mysterious with the little mask hiding her eyes. Her breasts rose and fell provocatively against her kirtle with her ardor, and her heart was fluttering so madly against her ribs, she was certain he must be able to discern it. Her red-gold hair was burnished and glorious in the light of the torches.

"Sweet Christ, a plague on the cursed dance!" Alaric growled, looking down at her loveliness with undisguised desire and impatience in his smoldering gray eyes. "To bed!"

While the music still played on, he swept her up into his arms and carried her from the hall, and to his bed.

Robin turned back to Sven and took a seat upon the wooden bench as the amorous pair left the hall. He saw that the old *skald* had also observed their departure, and was smiling fondly.

"So, my friend, are two who were once bitter enemies united! As they have found peace, so there is but one solution for all enmities, for the ignorance, the pride, the hatred and prejudice that lurks in the hearts of all men. You know that solution of which I speak, the lack of which breeds evil?"

Sven nodded sagely. "Aye, Master Robin, I know it full well! We will drink to it, *ja?*" He raised his horn high, touching it against Robin's own.

"To Love!" they said together, and drained their vessels to the last drop.

RAPTUROUS ROMANCE
by Phoebe Conn

CAPTIVE HEART   (1569, $3.95)

Celiese, the lovely slave girl, had been secretly sent in her mistress's place to wed the much-feared Mylan. The handsome warrior would teach her the secrets of passion, and forever possess her CAPTIVE HEART.

LOVE'S ELUSIVE FLAME   (1836, $3.95)

Flame was determined to find the man of her dreams, but if Joaquin wanted her completely she would have to be his only woman. He needed her, wanted her, and nothing would stop him once he was touched by LOVE'S ELUSIVE FLAME.

SAVAGE STORM   (1687, $3.95)

As a mail-order bride, Gabrielle was determined to survive the Oregon trail. But she couldn't imagine marrying any man other than the arrogant scout who stole her heart.

ECSTASY'S PARADISE   (1460, $3.75)

While escorting Anna Thorson to a loveless marriage, Phillip wondered how he could deliver her to another man's bed when he wanted her to warm his own. Anna, at first angered, found he was the only man she would ever desire.